THE SAGE OF THE OAK

by

J. A. Scheffer

Dedicated to my father,

and

for Sydney

ARTISTS' CREDITS: The graphics appearing at the beginning of Books I, II, III, IV & V are the copyrighted artworks of Vidal Nikko Luchana (vluchana@gmail.com). Cover art is by Eduardo Raul Malinauskas (edmal79@gmail.com/www.edmal.com), Lisa Scheffer (lisa@schefferdesignstudio.com and schefferdesignstudio.com) & John Scheffer.

CONTENTS

BOOK I

Gelidii

Gelidii

There is a reason I begin here. People so often wonder at strangers, asking where are you from, what has brought you here, what is the world like across the sea? And sometimes I tell the names of distant kingdoms, of heroes and scoundrels and thieves, or even of the land of my birth - a place and people almost forgotten even to me, save behind the veil of closed eyes. But the more adventurous parts of my past, those that in their telling would seize their hearts, draw their eyes wide and stunned in wonder, were too often dismissed as fantasy or, worse yet, met with the laughter of derision. And so I have come to invent a history that never was, a story of my crossing that never happened. Of this none has yet to disapprove. But I am not made from the stuff of dreams. My story, all of it, should be known. Yet, if in this sunlit land of gentle hills and sweet water it has no proper place, I will hide it in these pages: to be written out once, in full, if then forgotten. Whatever you may think of this account, know at least this: upon my oath and hand all parts are true.

The smoke of incense eddies above the table. The low morning sun draws the shadow of the pen across the page as I remember the hidden life, how it trilled from the leaves of the forest, how it sang to the blossom of morning and to the heavy wet noon, lifted its voice to the late day when the light rested gray on fern and orchid, and prayed to the night in steady, obedient breaths. And the rain would not wholly quiet it, and the wind not completely make it hush. It surrounded you, but strangely showed nothing of itself. You could search for it, peering into the shadows beneath the leaves, into the tree's hollow or through the traces of blue above a patched sky and still catch nothing of the source of the abounding chorus, yet it was always there all the same. And when you stumbled along, loud and clumsy and lost, all fell quiet. But when I too learned quiet, when my step wove into the forest as softly as the creek, I no longer listened for the voices whose breath was song, but instead waited for a sudden silence. Silence meant danger. Everywhere was danger.

It would have been a paradise if it were kind. A streamy world of meandering bourns and moss-covered wood where the light wove through everything and everything lived and the light flickered against the shadow. It may have once been the nest of the world's first seed, there where vines slowed the way, and deadfalls and thorns. And there, where my story begins, water ran everywhere. In its own way, I suppose, it carried me here.

My clothes had long turned to rags by this beginning. My feet, bare and hard as the earth upon which they walked belonged more to a beast than a man. They were bleeding again. I squatted on the ground and stretched out my legs as I leaned against a boulder, remembering the ragged patches of shoes I'd once had, how they had worn then shredded and then just were gone.

I'd long stopped counting the days in the forest. Instead I counted moons. And, staring into the graying sky, wondered just what is it about the human need to trap things in numbers.

The fifth would rise full in this beginning, a dull yellow light to the east in a night born clouded and starless. It would rain before morning. And in this part of this forest there was little life but an odd bird which I never actually saw and which sang only at dusk the same sad chant:

cullung cullung cullung

Then, in the quiet of the distance, a response from far and away:

cullung cullung cullung

And they know at least that they are not alone. And they know the dark comes. "Do not be afraid," she had said to me. But I was, and the terror of the night could not be helped.

I had run into this forest a fugitive. What little provisions I had taken in the moments of my escape were long exhausted. I'd been eating flowers: fields of bright yellow suns or the purple-tipped lilies that once abounded, and watery shells which ran in shrubs and tasted like white grapes and when you picked them they popped in your hand and sent the yellow seeds like dust back to the soil. These I had learned were good for food. But for every flower and plant which could be eaten, there grew those that could kill. And so, you pick a petal, chew it and spit it out and wait. Nibble the leaf, chew and wait. Swallow a small part and wait. You wait for whatever: swelling, nausea. You eat a little more and wait. A whole day. No matter the hunger, no matter the desire, you must take the unknown slowly. But

I had eaten little of late in that watery part of the world which lived in shade, where no flower but the orchid grew. Orchids are poison.

Each day I walked vaguely north, tracing a course from the arc of the shadow of a stick. It was a simple trick taught me by my uncle. But night was coming now and at night I lived quiet, hiding, sleeping in snatches in a low bough or leaning rock, in anything, anywhere, anything but to be on the open ground at night when the forest rumbled like an empty stomach.

cullung cullung cullung

"Do not be afraid," I said, voicing her words out as if to lift some courage from the ether.

Do not be afraid

And though all the world hurled into a common dark fire was forbidden. I had to learn that.

Do not be afraid

The beast had taught me that. What was it? Apish and almost human charging through the trees in insensate rage. I bolted out and through the understory in breathless prayer as it bellowed into the darkness. Away and away I crawled and its hungry mewls called for me as its ferocious stamp destroyed most everything I had left behind, reducing my whole world to shards and embers.

And I, a little creature of prey, just crawled farther and farther away with every rising scream, screams that seemed at last to touch you, not you exactly, screams that touched your spirit and your spirit shook and away and away I clawed, tearing myself through bush and thorn, throwing down tears in silence. I would wait for morning and half the day to come to pass before returning to camp to find my precious blanket tattered and bitten, the purse of precious salt tossed but unopened, apish four-toed stamps left in the ashes of the dead fire. My gods were gone, their lidless eyes staring perhaps forever in some part of the jungle floor. It had eaten what I'd carried of food or taken it and it had thrown away other things once in my possession I do not mention here. Now sleep in darkness.

I had not been raised in the forest. I am not the child of beasts or spirits who dwell in trees or in sacred springs, but am of the good and tilled lands of Selador: jewel perched on the Eastern limit of the Southern Slope, my true home and the home of my family, and from there I was, as has been said, a fugitive by fate. From there, I suppose, lies the beginning of forever.

While I still ran in the blossom of youth the soldiers marched into Selador. On a clear day of perfect skies they lined our one road in roughshod feet standing half-starved in clothes battered to rags and armor worn most to rust. Scars of hate crossed their faces filled with rage and patience. That first day hundreds of armed and tired and terrifying men stood in perfect rows listening to one command or another, and I remember that first night they lit torches and were drunk and set the torches to half the town and the homes outside of town and everything went to flames and the orange skylight I remember and Uncle's farm they burned down and from the top of a hill where they hid me it all glowed so beautifully, but I knew it was not a beautiful thing and knew I should have cried but could not. I stared in wonder. Never had there been flames so great, never a sky like that. The colors!

After, Aunty and Uncle sent me to the village to live and work in the tavern with Anselm, a friend of Uncle's. Anselm had never had children of his own. He called me "Son."

The tavern had been there as long as Selador. In its cellar, Anselm mixed his own liquors, some rumored to possess magical properties. These were secrets he brewed, ancient recipes as old as his family's name and shown to none, but after a time he showed each to me, and always with a smile. He explained each herb and its properties and the assorted ingredients and the unique and gentle way in which all needed to be treated and rested into the vat. And after each disclosure he would touch a finger to his lips and whisper.

"Hush."

"But why are you showing me all this, Anselm?"

"I do not get younger, Son. If not you, who?"

In his split and cracked and wizened voice, he would sing during the preparations of the intoxicants. He claimed this to be crucial to the process.

"It slows the hand. Remember, everything within was once living. Song gives a thanks the silence would not."

Rumors about Selador claimed that certain blends of Anselm's would cure the drinker of most any ailment. And I have seen this myself and it was true to what I saw. People have brought the hopelessly dying to Anselm, and he prescribed a bottle a week of one mixture or another and they have been cured in this way. But mostly he made drinks for drinking, for the intoxicants, but also to introduce to the simple palates of Selador "something exquisite." Anselm took pride in the legend that his best wine was aged in a cask hewn from the first fallen tree of the town. "She tastes like the dream of the god," he would say and hand me a glass in the cold and peaceful cellar whose air alone intoxicated. Above us, the chaos of the crowd stamped and yelled in the drunken heat, but in the quiet peace below we hid for a time like images in a dream. Anselm never rushed from the cellar and neither did I. He once tipped two cups in the ancient vat and handed one to me with a smile. "She dances and turns as to air, Son. Has the touch of gentlest fire."

We drink.

"Tis your birthday."

"Is it?"

"Yes. Hush."

Children were not told their birthdays anymore. The soldiers once took to killing people on their birthdays, and so the practice of their celebration was abandoned.

While most of the casks were made of oak, in a darkened corner of the cellar sat one of black clay. Atop it rested a heavy cover of lead skirted in lamb's wool dyed the rarest of colors: purple. One day Anselm shook the dust from its cloth and wiped the lid. "This here," he said tapping the plate, "is what we most properly call Dragon's Brew. She'd burn through a lesser vessel."

He lifted the skirt and rolled the lid aside, and I coughed at the fumes and my eyes teared as I stared into the black water. "Do people really drink this, Anselm?"

He nodded. "Indeed they do, indeed, and have been since the grandfather of my grandfather brought back the one ingredient no berry, no vine, no bee dropping provides: a sliver of the god herself. She sleeps in there, just there," he nodded to the black liquid, "a shard from the back of the great dragon!"

He laughed dryly and squinted in delight and then he coughed that wet cough of his. "I can see your doubt. Have a look upon it then." He rolled up his sleeve and reached to the lees, pulling out what looked like an enormous fingernail covered with tendrils of exhausted herbs. He smiled and turned it in his hand. "Chipped from the great hide. She's all magic, Son - a piece of her very scale - strongest stuff of the earth."

He tipped some of the brew into a calcite plate and held it out to me. It appeared amber now in the candlelight, but still made my eyes water. "'Ave a sip now," urged Anselm. "Right from her breath is the proper way. You my blood truly hereafter."

I reeled back and gagged and coughed. A scorpion swam down my throat. I reached for water that was not there. The room spun in black speckles, and I held the lid of the vat so as not to fall and Anselm waited and then he giggled and then took a sip himself and coughed. "How you like it, my boy?" He was smiling and red. Everything spun. I couldn't speak yet. "She ain't gentle but give 'er a minute now." In little steps the speckles cleared and a warm and caressing fire lit my center. Then I took another sip and Anselm laughed. And then ... euphoria.

"Wha ...whashit?"

"Eh?"

"What's it...?"

"What's it what?"

"What's it doing?"

"She's warming ya, Son. No fears. She's welcoming you to her skies."

"Anselm. Anselm!"

"Yeah, yeah," he giggled.

"Anselm, I love you!"

"Yeah, okay. But drink no more than three. No more than three, you hear? And she's ten times the price of our next item, but no more than three, no matter what. These are half-measures I speak of and not the house pour, mind you."

"Anselm, it's just...everything...it's just...everything...."

"Ya hearing me?"

"Yes. I hear it so beautiful. Anselm! It's perfection, always and forever!"

"Yeah, well, that won't last. Listen, it don't matter what they says or what they offer, she's no more than three and that's more than most could stand at that. Okay?"

"Okay."

"Half-pours, yah got it, yes?"

"Yes."

"And no dippin' less I say."

"All right."

"Good then."
"It's so wonderful."
"Yeah, yeah."
"Why only three?"
He scratched his head. *"One is Heaven. Two is earth. Three is Hell. Don't know the fourth and don't want to. It's been the rule always and there's good reason for it I'm sure."*
"Okay."
"Good."
"It's wonderful."
"Let's get to work."
"Anselm?"
"Yeah?"
"I thought there was no such thing as dragons."
"You have much to learn, my Son."

How terrible was the night. For a time I walked by starlight, that faint fire first lit in the cold and spinning and impossible reaches of the heavens where I suppose the gods dwell yet, tending to their ministrations among confounding illumination. Of this, a sliver of light sank through the canopy so that with my hands out before me I could stumble along in darkness.

I stopped when I found a creek. I liked to sleep by water. It speaks if you listen for it. I curled into my blanket with the forest singing and some hours later awoke from a dream to perfect quiet. Then I heard it: a thing, some damned thing, some god-forsaken thing lumbered through the brush towards me with a coughing bark.

claugh claugh claugh

I gathered myself, afraid of the noise of my own breath, stepped over the creek lost into the brutal night. I was so hungry and this surprised me because I had forgotten about hunger. An hour later the moon rose, and I came to a fallen oak, enormous and lying in a black mass. I climbed up the side and was so hungry. At the top it was wide and almost safe, and I walked to the fan of roots reaching pointlessly into the air. Beyond lay a wide clearing rare for a forest as this. Behind that, a mountain loomed, a sight that did not seem possible. Then a strange thing happened...the wind lifted and the mountain moved. I rubbed my eyes and stared. The wind lifted again and the mountain swayed against the sky again and I had to know. I had to.

"You should wait for morning, Fool," I said to myself, but did not. I often spoke to myself in those days, and sometimes to the flowers or trees, or to little creatures and birds, even before I knew the language of the birds.

Go now, in the cover of night.

The wide meadow was a delight of space. I fanned my hands against the bowing grass and wanted to sing. The clouds had all departed leaving a sky of shining silver. Beneath the indifferent and glorious stars I felt free.

I smiled as I approached the mountain. Now morning blossomed in the eastern sky and when the greater light rose I stood as still as the stars. I could not believe what it had revealed. The wind moved again. The grass ticked in the field. You had to wait to understand it, just what it was: a tree, a single tree, as high as the clouds and as broad as the land itself. And so to the land of giants.

The fan of branches reached out like a second sky. I walked beneath them unable to reach even the lowest leaves. From above, in the city of the tree, fell the distant call of birds and the long and ancient creaking of some great branch. The central trunk ran wider than a house, and from it, two main boughs diverged, running long and low in either direction right to the forest proper. When the wind lifted the boughs swayed, pressed against the outer forest in a war of space.

I knew immediately what I would do: climb the tree and let the bastard wood hounds run all night and get nothing. I would spit on them. I would laugh.

The trunk had strange knobs making climbing easy. Halfway up, I felt it and stopped. Something. Something knew I was here. I could feel it looking. And then I said something ridiculous: "Hello?"

Hello?

Nothing moved in the shadows above. I climbed on.

Do not be afraid

The left bough rose more steeply while the one to the right went almost horizontal over the field. This I followed. It was so wide I could walk upon it upright. After a few steps I found a good flat spot and unrolled the blanket and readied for sleep.

But then I felt it again.

In the forest you learn to live by the unknown senses or die. Something was here. By the gods hurry in rising sun.

"Who's there?" I called to the shadows. Suddenly, among the thousand thousand turning branches, one of the shadows moved. "Who's there?" I cried right to it. From a lightless spot, from a cave which light never knew, the shadow spoke.

"Who is in my tree?"

A long time ago the people of Selador used to pick through the Southern Forest. They scaled down the great cliffs that marked the terminus of the Southern Slope to forage for herbs or fruits or hunt game. When the screaming began, long before my birth, they stopped going down there. But they'd already learned something of it, something of the strange creatures that lived within. Unfortunately, so many stories circulated about the Southern Forest that no one knew what was truth and what invention. But the screams stopped all exploration and were so chilling that the outlying plantations had to move closer in, away from the cliffs, because the animals would spook or even die in the night from fear. And nightmares so plagued the people living near the cliffs this alone drove them in.

The screamers, whatever they were, had never been seen. But they were most active at night when the howlings turned to raging furies. At night, the old watchers said, they would howl madly at the base of the cliff as if begging entrance into the tilled lands above. But by day they were gone. Nothing was ever seen of them. One man once thought he spied a silhouette lope before a low moon, another, a passing form of arm swinging in the twilight. Knowing nothing, we guessed at what they were: demons unleashed from a broken gate to the underworld; refugees of a lost, primeval war; signs of the beginning of the end of days. No matter.

Only once since their coming, and this is a famous story in Selador, a troop went down those cliffs armed with swords and lances and amulets of protection. None returned. We had fields of rich soil. We had soft rain. We had high cliffs between us, uncrossable rivers. We let it go. We needed not the southern forest. Let it go. That troop would be the last to be lost to the mystery below, and the last to venture down there, until me. Until I. Until I climbed into the forest damned. It took such courage too, and all just to come to this.

"Who is in my tree?" it begged again.

This voice, this strange wheezing creaking voice could not be human and yet borrowed human words. The cricket-frog that some perverse wizard had twisted into life mocked human speech. And the wind lifted again and the bough swayed softly and the leaves ticked again and the sound crested and fell and when all rested quiet again it asked again, "Who is in my tree?"

I gave to it in a whisper my name.

It slithered from the shadows then, and so, in the waning moonlight, by the first faint rose of dawn I saw it, just a hint of it, just the outline of the eyes, and screamed like a child. I crawled backwards along the bough and almost fell. It stayed its step. A silhouette of hand draped towards me and unrolled a finger not human. It pointed. "Youmann," it croaked in that slow and terrible speech. "You are Youmann. Youmann have come to the Picarin Tree."

The stories of my childhood returned, stories of they who slunk at the field's edge, who hid between eaves to peek in the window of the sleeper, thieves of light of the dead eyes who slunk as corpses under wet bridges, treading in the murmuring creeks, sleeping in hidden pools. If you were a bad child it learned your name, found you and brought you to its lightless den, for it was born in darkness and in darkness dwelled. And though I had long ago stopped believing in the monsters of children, even Uncle, for all his wisdom, had said not to work the outer fields at dusk.

"I'm not saying you need to be afraid. There's just no reason to be against the forest like that at dusk."

"But what's there, Uncle?"

"Anything. Anything could be there."

"But you said there's nothing to be afraid of."

"I didn't mean it like that. I meant something else."

"But Uncle…"

"Enough questions."

A stick broke in the forest without and I awoke and started screaming. It turned its eyes away as if to leave but didn't. "Get back Wood Demon!" I begged. Its eyes in the rising light shone ghostly yellow. It pointed at me again.

"The Youmann walk upon tree of the Picarin. Youmann has come to the Picarin tree."

"What?" Stay your mind. "What?" Breathlessness. "What are you saying now? Go away."

It blinked slowly. Lids of translucent shells. Veins running like fissures. Those eyes: orbicular pools of yellow moons. "Youmann has for come to the Picarin tree. Stay. In forest now the coohoohoo run."

"Please step back."

It gestured to the side. "Two coohoohoo hunt without the Picarin tree."

"Retreat," I begged. "Retreat to the darkness that bore you." I lifted out a badly shaking hand. "I am protected. Please please go away."

Then the eyes slowly blinked and turned again into the dark and the form that surrounded them was gone. I waited. Before the sun rose full, I crept to the main trunk and climbed down. Just as my feet touched the earth I heard them like a landslide breaking through the brush, the grass flattening to dust and then they emerged: the coohoohoo. They were charging. Twice the height of a man and faster than a falling hawk their steps shook the ground, and they were charging, at me, entirely inhuman and not beast either and coming for me and I did not want to die like this. And the creature of the dark being the last thing to which I would ever speak. No. I implored the gods whose names may not be written. Soon, all would be lost.

From my youth I had a particular problem. In overwhelming moments little fish would swim in my eyelight and everything would go soft. My bubble would burst and I would "fall out," down to a strange sleep. Aunty used to say I was a dreamer. Once they brought me to the doctor who said a demon must reside in me and needed to be made "uncomfortable at the least." He gave me a vial of yellow paste to eat every day and said it would kill the demon or make it so sick it would leave.

"It tastes like poison, Aunty."

"Poisons for cures, little one."

"But when am I going to be cured?"

"When you stop falling out."

"But I'm falling out more."

"'Cause the demon's getting sick."

"How come then it's worse?"

"'Cause he's getting sicker."

With each day my skin turned more the color of the paste. I thought I would die from the cure when Uncle said the demon we knew was better than the one we did not, and threw the vial in the river. The doctor said he feared for me not eating the paste like that, but Uncle said, "Don't worry. If he starts feeling better, I'll feed him chicken crap." And I recovered mostly, but the little fish still showed in moments that weighed too heavily upon me.

I saw them now and behind them the coohoohoo. I reached back for the trunk with my knees going. It was a strange and unforeseen death, but Uncle used to say you never know what life has in store for you. Just as the light failed uncoiled tendrils of flesh grabbed my neck. I fell out as the cold clay fingers lifted me back to the tree.

I awoke under my blanket to the bright of late morning. Birds were singing. The sun broke through the light green elliptical leaves, and I did not remember where I was. I did not know why I was in a tree. I knew I was not home. I knew I had not been home in a long time and that something important had happened. I lay back and remembered pieces and then...everything. For a time I just lay there and listened to the birds. It was bright noon and I was so hungry and IT was gone. I would stay in the tree, without fear.

With a sudden joy I thought about what must have happened: It had wanted to eat me itself and so lifted me up from the coohoohoos, but the coohoohoos had killed it instead. Yes, that's what must have happened. But I was already safe from them in the tree so they left and I was okay. "And then your aunty came and covered you in a blanket ... " But now I was here, and thought only of home.

"It wasn't your fault, though."

"Doesn't matter. They'll kill me. You know that. He demanded it. You should have seen him. It wasn't my fault. I didn't know what to do. I don't know what to do.

"Hide in here."

"No."

"Just hide for a while."

"Stop asking."

"But where are you going, then?"

"I'm just leaving. Forever."

"They'll find you anywhere you go."

"I want you to tell the others why I had to leave, okay?"

"But where you going?"

"I wish I knew."

"They're on all the roads and along all the borders and they're in the woodlands and the sparrows…"

"I'm not going on the roads. I'm not going in our woods, and the sparrows are sleeping now. They won't follow me where I'm going. No one will."

"Please hide in our cellar. We'll get you out somewhere."

"Stop that. Just tell the others, okay? At least they won't find me. Imagine what they'd do? He was a captain or general or something. I'd rather die this way and at least it's a chance. Give me your hand, Brother."

"Wait."

"I can't."

"Just wait." He vanished momentarily and rustling could be heard in the other rooms. In the distance, swords clanged against shields in rising furor as they approached, a summoning of the troops. He returned with his arms full. "Take this. All of it. You'll need it." His hands reached out with salt, a blanket, and other provisions.

"I'm not going to need anything. Don't waste them on me. I just want the others to know."

"You don't know that. You might live. Take them or I will follow you."

"All right. Thank you," the fugitive said, securing the bundle of provisions to his back..

"But if you live…if you live…if you do, then remember us."

"Always."

"No, I mean help us."

"How could I ever do that?"

"Find a Sage."

"I have to go."

"Sages are out there. They really are. I know they are."

"Give me your hand, Brother."

"My grandfather told me and he never lied. Not once, not about anything. Sages are in the North. He said that. Go north. Please." He began to weep. "Because if you won't do it then things will never change, and it can't stay like this. Remember what they did to her? That won't stop. Help us."

The friend of childhood, weeping to his hand.

"If I live, I'll find one. I will try."

"You'll need a dragon first."

"Of course. Not a problem. Easy."

"Stop it. I'm serious. You have to try. You need one, or something of one. Just find some little thing of a dragon, anything: a hair, a drop of blood...something. It's a token for the Sage. If you bring nothing he won't help you."

"You're not making this easy, Brother."

"Others have done it before you."

"Have they?"

"So it is said."

The clanging now mingled with cries of horror from the tavern, from doors being smashed. Soldiers ran through surrounding streets. The fugitive smelled smoke.

"I have to go."

When I had climbed out of the tree I slipped and hurt my foot. I needed rest for it to heal. If the coohoohoo had not killed the thing in the tree, the thing in the tree lived yet and could have killed me, but didn't. I listened to the cycles of the forest and tried to think of nothing. And then it returned, emerging again from the shadows but now unhidden and terrible in the full light of day. It appeared exhausted. It struck all the words from my breath. How could such an abomination have been born? Its birth mocked creation. It seemed made of wet twisting snakes, a nest of eels, but I would not run. I could not run anymore. My mind reached for a knife long gone. I would have to face it with only a pointed stone I had found.

I drew my knees up to my chest, clutched the dull-pointed stone in my grip and had to turn my eyes away. "Please stay back," I said, almost as a whisper. It stopped moving. I dared look again into those wet and terrifying eyes and it raised an arm blacker than a well at midnight. It draped an uncurled finger towards me.

"Youmann," it croaked. So awful the voice. "Youmann, you are Youmann."

"What?" I lifted my face. "What are you saying? What has taught you speech?"

Its arm lifted to tug a drooping flap of ear. The entire earth for that moment fell to perfect quiet. The thing shuffled a small step towards me. "Just keep back. Just stay over there." It did and lowered its arm from its ear and blinked. "What are you?"

"Am Picarin," it said.

"Wha …What?"

"Am Picarin. Am Gelidii."

"What?"

It pointed at me again, "Youmann," it said. "Youmann is you." And then it curled the impossibly long finger towards itself again, "Picarin is Gelidii." And then it opened its giant spider hands. "This tree of Picarin."

"And what is it of people to place everything in a category, to number and name all the world they see and know?"

"Are you a kind of giant spider?" I asked, "or did a wizard twist you to life from the parts of sickened beasts?"

The drooping shadow tugged its ear and blinked and thought and, from what little I could tell of it, was not offended. "Moon have made the Picarin. Moon the mother of Picarin is." And then it pointed back to me. "How Youmann made?"

"I was born. From a true mother I was born."

It nodded. "Youmann before the coohoohoo go. Gelidii draw the Youmann up from coohoohoo. Coohoohoo very hungry when night sleeps. Coohoohoo eat Youmann. That of mother born not for go before the coohoohoo in dawn."

"I don't understand you…What are you saying now?"

It nodded its head, a nest of black worms draping down. "Picarin lift Youmann from coohoohoo for Youmann of mother born." I had to look away again, but think it tried to smile.

"What's a Picarin? Why do you know the coohoohoo?" I looked away as fear almost conquered me. It lifted one of its long drooping ears, then it spoke.

"Gelidii no know coohoohoo but for they to hunt in the morn when the smell of meat rises fresh. Gelidii see the Youmann walk to the field. Gelidii stand between the Youmann and the coohoohoo. Gelidii draw the Youmann out. Coohoohoo no come again."

I steadied myself upon the branch. I looked away, out through the veil of leaves, lovely elliptical and light green. I fixed my gaze as the master of a ship must forever look upon the sea. But then I looked back to it, to Gelidii. "I just… I just … I'm just, so so lost. I don't know what's happening. I don't know how you exist even, but

I can't … I just can't go in the forest again yet. I'm so tired, and I'm hurt, and I haven't eaten for so long."

"Stay in tree of Picarin. Youmann for eating not Picarin."

It stepped towards me and I clawed back. "Stay away from me. Please stay away from me," I pleaded, and its ears lowered and the eyes, which were nothing if not sad, fell sadder still. It spoke again.

"Gelidii have misspoken. Is not my tree. Not I, not Picarin have forged the seed, nor heap the earth it sleep within. Not I, not Picarin, call the sun from the cold tears of the god, nor summon Picarin the rain who fall unasked from above." He then fanned his enormous and bizarre hands to the universe of twisted branches about him. "I but the shaper am, and this and this art too but a gift."

"Please, just go away," I begged again and pulled my knees even tighter to my chest. It waited a moment, and then turned away and receded into the tree.

"Stay," it said over its shoulder, a thin slope of shadow skin.

"Just go away. Please keep going away."

And it did. I would not see it again for three days. I spent my time sleeping safely on the bough and foraged for edibles in the field and nearby forest finding little, but enough. Tiny, bright red berries wove in a vine through the tree itself. Sour, but not poison. By the second day I ate these berries in small portions. My strength returned in degrees.

The Picarin had retreated to the other bough. I explored in the opposite direction and soon found myself walking through the canopy of forest among the crowns of neighboring trees. One slip meant the end of my story, but at least I was safe from everything below. Not even a vine reached from this height to the earth.

At times the canopy offered a broad view and the forest below billowed in soft green puffs of smoke, and for the first time in a long while it seemed peaceful and enchanted. I felt at peace again. Yet, Aunty had always warned against the estimations of the eye. "A man's face is readily seen," she said, "but his heart is always hidden." Of course, Aunty had never seen a Picarin. If there ever lived a beast who hides nothing, it is the Picarin.

Clouds as dark as night rolled in the distance with a faint call of thunder. I had resolved to return to the wilderness. The creature unsettled me too much to stay. I would wait for this one storm to pass.

At first, the dense web of leaves proved an effective roof. The water tapped and ran off with not a drop piercing the interior of the great tree. The palace of branches filled with sound, and whenever I was inside and dry the sound of rain always delighted me, as it did now. I smiled. But as the rain fell harder some few drops broke in, and it was then the birds began.

They first flew into the tree alone, and then in pairs, in threes, and then entire flocks. More and more and more lit upon the myriad branches as the rain fell even heavier, unnaturally so, and for whatever reason I wanted to return to my blanket, my camp, before the full force of the storm would push all the birds from the sky.

It felt like a dream I could not understand. "Are you all afraid of a little rain?" I asked the birds. They did not respond. Now water spilled in as small rivers. The sound of rain deafening all else. Thunder shook the tree as more birds, birds of every form and color, lit right beside each other in a strange and unnatural silence. The rain fell harder still. I became soaked as the way grew slippery and knew I could not fall, not even once. The silence of the birds was eerie. "Do you not sing when you're wet little ones?" I asked them, fearing in some way the answer. And then I too was afraid to speak.

Be quiet. Something comes within the rain.

In Selador we had a myth of sky hunters who followed the black clouds. They were the winged death who would slay all in their sky, and these birds knew of this myth, for they lined the branches so thickly my feet brushed against their feathers. The rain now battered against the leaves, rain as I had never known.

Is it man, beast or god what comes?

And even as the rain poured like falling rivers, more and more birds collapsed from the sky seeking, for reasons all their own, the shelter of those branches. I now had to crawl along the bough for I could hardly see through so much water. To the birds I was not there. We were all as ghosts to each other. The hawk perched beside the finch, the golden eagle beside the sparrow, and if any feared the human, it did not show. And more came yet, somehow from somewhere, so that even the widest branches bent from their weight. And thunder shook the world. And it rained heavier still.

Sometimes my reach pushed a winged guest from its perch and it plummeted down and down, beating its wings against the deluge, but falling no slower for that. I would apologize in a whisper to its passing spirit, but I could barely hold my own path by then, and knew that I too could be sent down and away by some force invisible and senseless.

Go in peace

The rain fell so impossibly thick that the smaller birds began to wash away. I rapped upon a wet branch then. "I am not dreaming this. This is real. This is happening." And just then the first howls fell from the sky. As people often do, I denied the awful, and so crawled on to find the flat and wet and comfortless blanket. But the howls grew close and closer, so that they could not be denied. I hid beneath the blanket, closed my eyes as the unearthly howls rose the more.

Hauuugh Hauugh Hauuugh

My blood turned to ice. From another part of the sky, and then another, howls cried in the sky. Whatever they were they were encircling the tree, hunting, I thought, and then remembered Uncle. I left my blanket and went to find IT. I don't know why, but I knew I had to find IT.

I clawed too quickly to be safe, but to hear them is to understand. The written word cannot catch them. I let the birds fall, held fast to wet and treacherous branches until coming upon the entrance to what in some way I'd always known was there: a narrow den of leaves and twigs molded around a rising bough, like a cocoon fixed on a stick. I waited a moment, considering what waited within, but the howls then turned to screams, hungry and empty and vicious, and so with that I summoned the courage of my life, and in the voice of a frightened child called to the nest: "Gelidii! Gelidii...Come out now!"

Even as I implored it I backed away. Even as I sought its protection I hoped nothing would emerge.

Those demonic cries, no doubt born from the world beneath, now rose in terrible unison as if in homage to the falling sky.

I thought of Uncle then, and the wounded fawn on the green.

"They kill everything. Eat everything, every damned thing and then some. Hear them?"

"Yes."

"They got something in close. They're herding it in. Hush!" Uncle put his finger to his lips. *"You hear that? It's crying. A deer, a fawn I think."*

The dogs bayed when they heard the bleating of the wounded fawn and ran in tighter circles and quicker.

"They're telling each other where it is, how to get it. But we'll get there first."

"But Uncle, with so many dogs?" The boy shook badly and had begun to pale. The uncle considered the boy.

"I'll stop 'em all. Don't you worry about that. I can put you in a tree."

"I'm all right."

"All right. If they come at you, you scream at them, and if that doesn't work, you use this." He nodded towards the crudely sharpened pole of ash with which he had taught the boy to fight. In his own hands he hefted a wooden club with spikes of metal, a commodity both rare and precious in this easternmost village almost forgotten by the greater earth.

"Maybe we just leave the fawn to them, Uncle."

He shook his head. *"It's not the meat. We can do without the meat, but if we don't scare 'em off, they'll hunt in our fields. Their prey take to the corn. And then they take our livestock and if they get hungry enough they may even breech the barn, the manger. They'll eat everything. Anything. In this drought, anything. And it has happened that when these dogs get desperate enough they come for man. It has happened. So, we stop 'em here."*

The dogs bayed madly in a tightening circle around the bitten fawn who writhed in its own terror and blood and at whose scent their howls doubled. The uncle knelt and pointed at the fawn who lay in a splash of crimson on the green earth. At that moment, it began to mewl. *"She's calling for help. It's what that is. Lot a people don't know that about deer."*

The boy looked nervously over both shoulders. *"There's a lot of dogs, Uncle."*

"And the help will never come." He stopped and thought of the boy and gave him a hard look. *"You can wait in a tree."*

"I'll come."

"Good. You should learn. Is better you learn."

The dogs closed in on the fawn a moment later. Something had cleanly removed half of its front leg and the teeth marks were too wide and clean to be a dog's. The man and the boy saw the wound now that the fawn tried to stand and had only a moment to consider this when the first of the pack approached them. Wild dogs were always cautious with a kill. They sniffed the air until one mangy beast with a black strip of fur down its back stepped from the mewling prize and raised its hackles at the man and the boy crouching in the bush.

The older man raised his club with shining tips of lethal metal and charged from the thicket then, and for a moment the striped dog leapt back and called and the call was returned by more than a dozen closing in quick to the site from the outer woods. Then, the dog turned and bared its fangs to the uncle, beside whom now stood a boy with a pointed stick. "Just keep walking towards the fawn. Let them know it's ours."

With caution and in an eerie silence, more and more of them crept out of the shroud of the forest until they made a full ring about the man and the boy.

"You scared?" the old man whispered.

"No Uncle."

"Don't lie."

"Yes."

"Good. Use it to make you stronger. If they leap, you slide it right under their jaw, into the soft of the throat."

"Yes Uncle."

As if by some unseen signal, all the howling stopped, even the deer stopped crying.

"Uncle..."

"Hush, Boy."

In helpless fear, the fawn who had collapsed again wobbled to her hooves and hopped once and then twice and then fell again. She almost called, but did not. The man walked softly towards it, and the pack yielded way. He held his hand out gently and spoke to the fawn in soft whispers, telling it to be calm and that all was well. All would be fine, he said, lifting back the club. And the fawn looked down into the grass as if it knew and it must have known for it closed its eyes and the strike landed with such force one of the eyes shot loose from the bed of the skull. The pack howled then, and the man and the boy each did a rough count. Twenty, maybe more.

"Hello?" I whispered. "Gelidii? Hello?" All was quiet but the rain, until the howls rose again in terrific chorus, as if the sky begged some primal offering. Whatever predators were out there were telling each other only of us, of the scent of our blood and the birds and that here hid all the feast of the skies. Then began the violent rustle of leaves from something too large to be any bird. They were entering the tree, searching.

"Gelidii! Please wake up!" I called and crawled closer to the den. "They're here! They've come for us now!" I pleaded to the silent hump of leaves. It was in there. I knew it was.

A flap covered the bulge of nest and I lifted this and the scent told of what lived within, something ancient, cold and reptilian. I leaned into its darkness when a bird pecked softly at my ankle. I almost slipped turning to the ordinary white hen, behind which a whole train of others stared vacantly at me. "Go away!" I hissed to them. "Why don't you fly off, you stupid, stupid things? I'm gonna to roast you when this is done. Stop looking at me like that! Why are you looking at me like that?"

Something groaned from within. And the demons called again against the sky and I crawled inside. It was dry, and not entirely dark for slits of light opened from the bottom. It had a faint hint of cinnamon too, I remember. I waited for my eyes to adjust but could hear breath. I saw it slowly. It leaned against the curved inner wall, arms folded around its body. The batwing lids of its closed eyes looked yellow-red in that dark, and it drooled from its beakish mouth. The rain fell with ridiculous strength, yet not a drop entered the den.

"Ge...Ge...Gelidii? Wake up now, Gelidii. They're here." The Picarin did not move. "They're just out there, Gelidii. You have to wake up now." And I could hear their screams rising again and again and I could hear them tearing at the outer shell of leaves of the great tree. How could it not wake? I thought of touching its cold shoulder to shake it to my defense, but I could not touch it. "Gelidii!" I hissed. "Wake now! They've come."

Slowly, so slowly the red lids rose and the tired, sad, yellow eyes lifted crookedly, unevenly, slowly to gaze at the facing wall. "Gelidii?" The eyes turned to me. "Are you awake now, Gelidii?"

"Ullueenum," the Picarin slurred.

"What? Gelidii...help me. They've come for us."

"Oulleuenemn."

"Wake up. It's raining. Please wake up."

"Ohhmann." Its left eyelid rose and lowered again.

"No, Gelidii. Wake up. Stay awake."

"Youmann."

"It's raining."

"Youmann."

"They're in the sky."

"Ohhmmann."

"They're in the sky. They're howling. I don't know what they are and you have to help me...they're so close."

One eye opened full, and the Picarin leaned its sleeping head to look at me like a patient drugged. It clicked its wet beak of clay and slowly, very slowly, leaned forward. "Oumann," it spoke, breathlessly.

"They're here. You can hear them above. And the branches are filled with birds."

And the Picarin's ears rose with the next chorus of the tribe of demons. "In the rain, they fly," it said.

"What? What flies, Gelidii? I don't know what's happening anymore."

"They fly. In rain they fly."

"What does, Gelidii? What are they?"

"The Harpyae."

"Stop them. Make them go away."

The Picarin's lids lowered, and it curled back to its wall of woven leaves. "Ollonen," it muttered and its head fell to the fold of its knees as it began to collapse back to sleep.

"Gelidii no!" I reached out my hand and touched that terrible flesh and shook it. "You have to wake up now, Gelidii. They've come for us." Its head wobbled up. Its eyes opened and the Picarin looked to me and groaned.

"In the rain they fly. What for the Youmann for the Picarin to do?"

"I don't know. They're circling the tree, and all the birds in the world are here and the Harpyae are coming into the tree."

"Do Youmann want for the Picarin to stand between the Youmann and the Harpyae?"

"I don't know. Yes. I don't know. It's raining. I think they're coming for me, Gelidii."

It groaned slowly and to my horror leaned right over my lap and crawled out of the cocoon. For reasons I still do not fully understand, I followed it. I had to walk quickly on the treacherous path for in such rain the creature grew invisible after a few paces. Our feet waded through lumps of birds that huddled even tighter than before. Howls cut the clouds, and I cringed, but Gelidii just walked along as if deaf. It did not rush, but did not go slowly. It would pause for reasons unexplainable and tilt its head upwards. When it stopped it looked like a pile of black twigs, and if my eye strayed from a moment too long I lost it to my sight.

There were paths in this tree I had not known. The Picarin would brush aside a fall of leaves and behind would be a whole new run of branches. They twisted and laced in a mysterious course, running to destinations as unknowable as the Picarin itself. But no matter which way we took, everywhere was filled with birds of every kind, colorful and dull, humble and majestic, all trying to survive the predators of the clouds, all humped in silence under the rain falling as heavy as the tears of the earth.

At one point an enormous black eagle blocked our path. It had red eyes and fierce claws which it stamped right into the fibers of the branch. Whenever one of the Harpyae gave a bark, the eagle did not cringe, but tore the fibers from the tree and burned its glare upwards as if to say, "If there were but one of you I would rip you from my skies."

The Picarin paid the eagle no attention, but walked on and leaned around it and rubbed against its throat without fear and climbed on. But I halted. It had opened its beak, which could easily chop away an arm, and clacked it closed again. So thin was I by then that I thought this bird could snatch me in its claws and fly off. I have heard of such creatures. The Picarin began to disappear and I do not know why I needed to follow it, but I did, and the black eagle ripped more clumps of fiber with its talons and I went on, holding my hands out in a gesture of passivity. "Good bird," I whispered. "There's a good bird. Hush. I won't hurt you," I said absurdly and walked right beside it, brushed against its feathers, and passed it slowly in our inexplicable truce. Once I was clear, it stretched out its wings, each one as long as I was tall. Behold me. Through a maze of smaller birds I found the Picarin again. He had begun to climb up.

A finger of the tree grew right to the sky, and the Picarin still could walk up it, hardly using even one hand, but as I followed, my own strength faded. The deafening, exhausting water just dragged me down. Way below ran torrents of freshly-made creeks. Higher and higher we went until I could climb no more, but the Picarin continued a little ways, balancing almost unbelievably on a branch that twisted up and up. I stopped at the intersection and waited, waited and wondered what had brought me here. What in all my fate had wrought this? As I often would in my travels, I wished I were home.

And then the Picarin did a very strange thing: it lifted its gaze to the canopy above and whistled in a way no human ever could. In a way which I cannot express in words. Why was I here? My Uncle's words came to me.

"Wherever you go, whatever you suffer, those you meet – the good and the others – are all there to teach you something."

On its horizontal branch the Picarin stood with impeccable balance and in such an uncanny stillness it disappeared again, becoming a wet heap of lifeless, mold-barked twigs unmoving. Its long and gangly arms hung at its side as it stared upwards, calling with that low and mournful whistle. It seemed to want nothing more than for the rain to fall. The screams grew so close I wanted to press my fingers in my ears, but I had to hold on. Then I saw it.

"They're breaking through!" I screamed desperately.

Gelidii, they're breaking through!

Water poured in from the rent in the leaves. Suddenly, a flash of slashing claw, an arm enormous, and then the whole form dropped in: a thrashing, screaming incubus, a denizen from what could only be the world beneath the world. It shredded the upper tree apart with both arms and enormous bat-like wings beat against the air and water. It landed on the upper part of the branch on which Gelidii stood. It was so heavy it had to mostly fly to keep from collapsing the branch. And then it howled and I turned my face away and wept.

Sweet mother of God protect us

When I looked up again Gelidii seemed almost asleep. The demon Harpyae roared at the Picarin and with clawed feet it shredded the branch and stamped towards Gelidii with unnatural speed. I could not run away. It would kill Gelidii and then me and this is how life ends. When it roared again my blood turned to water. Its broad and terrible face held a smile. Red-black flesh. Black teeth, each one a fang. I could not look at its eyes. I would not let it get me. I would throw myself down. I would not be eaten, would not be ripped apart by those hands. Gelidii stood as still as stone. He, it, was even shorter than I. Against the enormity of the demon the Picarin seemed like a frail child. And he looked asleep.

Gelidii wake up!

The Harpyae's wings became tangled in a mesh of branches. For a moment it appeared that maybe it would not get through, maybe the great tree itself would stop it. But it thrashed and clawed in demented madness until it freed itself and cleared an opening in the tight web and charged forward with a scream the very earth must shun.

"Gelidii, please wake up," I cried and embraced the wet limb of the tree, hugging it for support and trying very, very hard not to fall out. And I was certain here came the end of days, the end of suffering and how odd life could be. Never did I dream of death by demon, in a great tree wrought by a forgotten forest.

And then the Harpyae loomed right above the Picarin, like an enormous wave of the promise of oblivion yet Gelidii would not move even yet, and when the great arm lifted to swing once and smack the life from the mysterious Picarin, it did not move yet. And when the claw began to lower Gelidii slowly draped his own hand behind his back. Then the demon struck and when it finished the arc its claw had been removed at the wrist. It tumbled down and away in the deluge of water and branch and bird. Gelidii had flicked his arm out so quickly that it could not quite be seen as movement. After it hung at Gelidii's side again, only now the hand held a curved sickle-stone almost as black as the Picarin.

Blood shot out from the wrist of the beast, and for a moment it seemed to not know what had happened. The demon stared at its mutilation in fresh wonder. Its wings beating yet against the air, it struck with the other claw and that too was separated, but at the lower arm, and again Gelidii's strike could not quite be seen and the weapon swayed easily at his side. And now the Harpyae howled in madness as the last of its claws tumbled down the great tree. In desperate pride it swung its pointed tail through the sprays of blood and this too the Picarin reduced to pieces. When the demon whipped its horned wings and feet the Picarin severed all within its reach, and then the Harpyae tumbled away in shock and terror, the stumps of its arms reaching out to catch itself with what was not there. It moaned its last until its head cracked against the branch as it fell in a wheel of spraying blood, all of this happening in moments, a few breaths.

And it rained so heavily yet. Let the rain wash away the blood.

At what must have been the moment of its death a chorus of howls rose without the great tree. The horrific horde began to lower in the sky, howling through the paths of air in their descent. Gelidii hardly appeared to be aware of anything. He slowly lifted the black sickle out to the rain and the water ran red from it and then clear and then he returned it to the odd cloth around his middle that seemed made of his own wiry hair. The sickle-stone disappeared into it and the Picarin's pelt. When he returned to me, I was shaking very badly and could not yet move.

Gelidii pointed to me. "Youmann," he croaked, "go now for the house of Picarin." And it was then the little fish began to swim before my eyes. We were so high above. To fall meant death, but it could not be helped, and I fell.

I awoke in the cocoon, Gelidii beside me resting against the pressed leaves in the dark. It took a long time to realize where I slept and what had happened, what parts were dream and what were not. By the grace of the earth, I lifted the aperture and night had not yet fully fallen. But the branch would be dangerous if I fainted again, so for a time I remained in the den with my knees curled to my chest, wondering at the great misfortune of a life that had brought me to this. Everything, every damned thing had been a mistake and how great the proofs of that: a wheezing lizard that slew demons, a home abandoned forever, a boy in a towering tree who could not keep from fainting. And I had never been that good at balance. I stumbled more than once on the uneven floor of the tavern and sent cups flying. Anselm used to say I needed an extra foot and he would laugh and I thought of his laugh now and wept.

Feeling confident that my consciousness would not fail me, I crept out of the den wanting desperately not to wake the Picarin and to see the sun before night fell again. It had saved me twice, three times it had, but to speak with it again, to talk with it, to behold its

27

hideous face...too much, just too much. Eventually, I would have to. I knew this, but for that hour, in my trembling exhaustion, in my hunger and thirst, just let it stay asleep.

So in the gray light of dusk I crept out to the rest of the world. The rain had stopped, the sky had cleared, all the birds had departed. The only evidence of the slaughter was the sick dread that I could not shake. I knew what I needed to do, and I would need the aid of the day's light both for my courage and witness. So, down and down I climbed in the fading light to the very thing I dreaded.

Fear changes things. A tree's limb becomes a serpent, mist the web of a great, poisonous spider. Behind every blind turn the brothers of the fallen predator waited with smiling black teeth, claws ready to grab my throat, or pluck me up like a hawk to a rabbit, or grasp from below a stray ankle of the boy damned to be exiled from his home forever.

And I heard nothing unusual, but it was impossible not to think of them and what they could have wanted, and just what they were. But most of all I wanted to know what they were, if they would return or if they had even left. What were they? Not the name. I knew the name. Names mean nothing. What *were* they?

I found the flume of blood that ran down the tree and followed it as the path allowed, careful not to touch the blood, sometimes even taking narrow and perilous paths to avoid a limb tainted with the demon's blood. And I do not know why exactly I did so, but in Selador there were some who collected relics from the holy departed: a lock of hair from a dead priest, dust from a tomb, a bit of cloth from a sacred vestment, a chip of stone from a site of great magic. Perhaps in me ran a similar emotion, only in the opposite direction.

Eventually, the trail of blood led me to the bough on which I'd first unrolled my blanket. It had not been washed away, but lay flat against the bough like a red stamp of the sun and for a moment I smiled. But tracing the bough with my eye farther and farther out would wipe the smile away, and it would be a long time before another smile appeared. Before my sight lay a vision which would haunt my days and chill my sleeping nights for many years to come.

I'd wanted to see it dead, not just cut to pieces, but a corpse gone and gone for good and ever. But no corpse waited. In my life to come I would know ships that cleaved the water. In some ways what waited on the ground was a kind of ship, one which was boarded in the land of light and docked in the realm of darkness. I had to walk out on the bough to see it clearly, this thing I would never understand.

Where the body and its pieces should have finally come to rest, where the heart that, like all hearts that in darkness dwell, had pumped out the last of its life, it had made a crimson pool in the yellow grass and a great splatter of blood on the final bough into which the beast had crashed. And it was there the corpse and its pieces should have been, but nothing remained. I remembered then with a rising dread how the howls flew in a downward spiral once the demon had fallen. They had collected it, and in the following of some ritual forever unknown to humankind, left something in the place of the dead.

Shaken, I climbed back up to find Gelidii. Night was falling fast. For all of its hideousness, I thanked the gods on this night to come that I would not be alone.

The Picarin had barely awoken. It squatted on its haunches just outside the cocoon and tugged absently at the sliver of flesh at its long draping ear. I paused at its hideousness. "Gelidii?" I asked it then, "are you awake?"

A long slow wheeze came from its lungs like an insect put to a campfire. An eye peeled open halfway and it nodded in affirmation. "Gelidii, listen, they wrote something where the Harpyae died. It's written in white ashes. There's lines and a kind of star and strange geometric symbols written in ashes encircling the blood where it fell. They point to things. They communicate something terrible. A curse I think. I don't know what to do. Why would they do that? It's terrifying. They collected the body and wrote that on the tree and in the field and what did they do that for, Gelidii?"

It smacked its beak in sticky mucus. Its one eye had barely opened and it now seemed to be trying to open it in full. The Picarin scratched its lolling head and then leaned towards me and spoke. "Ish far they brought shu huun." Its eye sank again, and I shook the branch as much as I could to wake it.

"Gelidii! Did you hear me?"

"Youmann," it mumbled. Night was coming in. I placed my hand over my heart and prayed. So little help in the world. Nothing more to do now. And if it didn't care, why should I? I would leave at first light, anyway. For now, I had terrible thirst and went searching for water pooled in the larger divots of the bark.

To my great relief, when I returned to the den Gelidii had left. I crawled inside the house of leaves, warm and safe against the setting dark. It was just broad enough to let the legs out straight if you rested as the Picarin with your back reclined against the opposing side. Outside, a mild wind rustled the leaves and rocked the great bough gently. A sense of peace overcame me then, there of all places, for I had decided to not be afraid. Let come what may. The den grew warmer, and before I knew why I should not, I fell into a deep and dreamless sleep.

I awoke just before dawn. He sat just outside with his strangely long legs draping down each side of the branch, his stare dead and joyless. "Hello, Gelidii," I mumbled, thirsty again.

"Youmann."

"Yes."

"Is the Youmann for the food?"

"What?"

"Is the Youmann for food?"

"What do you mean? What are you saying now?"

It tugged at its drooping ear. "Is now Youmann food?"

"No, by the gods, no."

I backed into the den. Gelidii tugged his ear, confused.

"No hungry for Youmann?"

"What? What are you trying to say?"

"Strange are words of Youmann."

"Am I hungry? Is that what you mean?"

The Picarin nodded its head: a nest of worms with blood of blackest ink.

"Yes Gelidii. I am."

The Picarin looked through the branches into the field below. "Gelidii feeds first when the white day hides. Gelidii feeds another feed before the blue day goes."

"Then let's eat. I've had nothing but berries for two days. More."

It pointed at me in a terrible and off putting way. "The Youmann is for the food."

"Gelidii, don't … don't say it like that. Say hungry."

The Picarin scratched its terrible head, the flesh of a mold-blackened corpse. "What are you going to feed on, Gelidii?" I asked then, just to be sure.

"Come, Youmann," it said and, standing with effortless balance, the Picarin glided down the endless paths of branches to hidden parts of the tree. Tunnels and caves waited all shaped from the tree itself, their entrances entirely obscured until Gelidii would brush aside a wall of flower or vine and bring us into a new world sometimes dark, sometimes bright, but always amazing. Some had rows of thick ivy woven with orchids and others arches of roses in astounding colors. Until then I had never seen a rose, and since then have never seen one as glorious as these.

It stopped at one of the depressions that formed a natural cup in the body of the tree and, unlike the one I had sipped from earlier, this had a trickle of amber fluid continually running into it and spilling over its sides. The Picarin jutted out its black-and-tan-speckled tongue and lapped from the wooden cup with its eyes closed as if in ecstasy. When it had slaked its thirst, it licked the chitinous ridge of its beak and I think it smiled. "Sip here, Youmann. Sip here the blood of the mother tree. Is good for food." Dead bugs were stuck at the edges of the amber syrup, and a living one struggled with swimming wings. Gelidii unrolled his long tendril of finger and caught the bug in a thick droplet and let it fall down to the leaves below. "Food is good for Youmann eat Gelidii for eating too," it said, gazing to wherever the bug had fallen.

The Picarin gestured for me to drink what it had. I reminded myself how twice I'd fallen out and how twice it lifted me from the path of death, and I'd not even thanked it for that, for all my civility, for all my humanity, for all my fineness of form I'd yet to thank the worm for letting this life continue.

The pool of amber did not look unappetizing, but Gelidii's tongue had been in it. That forked and slimy and speckled tongue had dipped into it and a trail of saliva slime had fallen back in. "I'm not thirsty just yet, Gelidii. Maybe we can find something in the field."

Confusion washed over that face so alien to mine. "But is food is good for food for Youmann food."

I waved the comment away. "Maybe later. For now I would very much enjoy something from the field. A little grain would be fine, or we could just collect more of those berries."

It tugged its ear and then did a very strange thing It dipped its nail, as black as it, into the pool and held drops of nectar out to me. "Try," Gelidii said. "Is very very good for food." But I could only think of the trail of slime which had fallen from its mouth.

"Oh, I know that. I'm sure of that. It's not that. It's just how I like to eat, to have first something growing from the green and then maybe later I can sip some amber."

It scratched its head and tugged its ear and then flicked the amber down and walked on in silence. Eventually we came to a wall of bark and the Picarin brushed this aside. It served as a kind of hanging door which opened to a floating hall of orchid and honeysuckle. The aroma intoxicated me and Gelidii picked at the honeysuckle and nibbled some and so did I. I hated thinking of it, but could not help myself. "Gelidii, the Harpyae, they took the body. They left ashes in symbols."

It tugged its ear. "For how symbols?"

"I don't know what they're for. They could be anything. I thought you would know."

"No know."

"Do they always do this?"

"No know. Never before the Harpyae come to the tree of the Picarin."

"Oh."

"Youmann for stirring the forest. Long for the forest in sleeping."

"Oh."

"Food now?"

"Let me show you the writing first." Its ears lowered. It did not care. "You should see it. It's in your tree."

"Is not for the Picarin tree. Made not the seed …"

"I know. Just let me show you."

Gelidii stared down at what had been written in the blood and land. He still did not seem to care. He began to creep out on the branch where part of the symbols had been written, where much of the blood had splattered. He was sniffing. "Don't touch it," I said.

"No touch?"

"No. It's bad. You don't want to touch it."

"Is bad?"

"Yes. Very bad."

He turned away from the symbols indifferently. "Is the Youmann for food now?"

"What if they come back?"

The Picarin scratched its head and said nothing. It tugged its ear and again I had to look away. That terrible form. It was then I saw it, bloodied and ruined, dangling from a thicket in the branches and mocking my courage. How had I not seen it before? "Look, Gelidii, look!"

Above us, in a thick growth of leaves, hung a single cut of wing. A horn of ebony grown from its tip. My hand shook pointing to it. "They'll come back for this," I said, breathless. "They…They're going to know its missing, and they'll come back for it." Gelidii scratched the loose flesh of his chin, turned his enormous, sad, eternally tired eyes upwards to consider the wing with great indifference. He made no comment, but sighed, tugged his ear and walked away.

"Gelidii! Where are you going? We can't leave it there!"

"To field. For to find food Youmann wish."

"No. We have to get rid of it first. They will come back for this."

"What do then?"

"I'm going to knock it off. I want it out of the tree at least. I don't want them to come back up for it."

"Have not Gelidii made the tree but shaped it from without." He shrugged his shoulders of bone and ink. "Let come what may come in."

"No. By the gods, Gelidii, no. We don't want them near us. We want to keep them off. Give them what they want and keep them off." My voice had grown frantic. Not good. With a stick I freed the cut of wing from the tree. It fell with a wet, dead splat, landing half in the circle of horrid ashes. My hands shook badly now and I swooned a little and whispered as true a statement as ever I have: "I want to go home."

And yet, of course, I could not.

Three soldiers, armed and armored, drank in the tavern. "Give 'nother now!" yelled one, pounding the table.

"We don't have anymore," said the boy.

"Youse a lying bastard son of a dog!" said the wide, barrel-shaped man slamming his fist again so hard a cup rolled off and cracked on the floor. The other two soldiers laughed. "Nother!" he demanded with rage.

"Looking for a fourth cup, General?" asked Anselm, "just to round out the night?"

The eyes of the wide, red-faced man fell upon Anselm. Spittle dripped from his mouth. "'Nother or I'lls takes you out. The lot a ya!"

He considered the table, hated it, and turned it over, sending plates flying to shatter on the floor. The others laughed again, and the drunken man looked hard at Anselm. "'Nother, slave!"

"Three's the house limit, General. Most don't even get that."

The General swayed and almost fell. He held the upturned table by the foot of a leg as he fumbled for the sword on his waist and then fell on his back and the other soldiers were laughing. He hated their laughing at him, a superior officer. With much effort, he stood again and smiled. Sweat ran profusely down his brow. Forgetting to draw the sword, he lifted a candle from the neighboring table and staggered to the drapes, setting them on fire. He laughed and threw the candle towards Anselm as they burned. The other soldiers, laughing still, doused the fire with wine. The drunken soldier then staggered towards the young man who had served him and pointed at this face: "'Nother or I'll cut your fingers off."

"Get it, Son," said Anselm then. "Just do it."

The young man placed the fourth cup before the soldier who now sat swaying on the floor. He wrapped his sweating hands around it and took it in a single shot and slammed the cup down so hard it broke. "'Notha," he slurred.

"We must send out for more. Just wait a bit, General," said Anselm.

"'Notha, pig. Shit pig," he said, and the other soldiers continued laughing and shaking their heads.

"He can outdrink the best a them!" they said to the tavern with its patrons both terrified and amused. "But oh-oh...what's this!" They laughed. He looked sick. If he vomited, they would never let him forget it. The drunken officer swallowed hard and breathed deep and tried to stand. He could not stand, but grew very pale and stood

at last to his knees and almost to his feet but then fell and vomited violently, and the others roared in laughter.

"At least here's the end of it," Anselm spoke quietly to the boy. The vomit came out like water, too much like water. It ran between the floor beams and could be heard trickling on the casks below. And then, as everyone watched, it began to pour out red, like wine, but darker and this was blood.

"Is true what they said of her then. She's ripped 'is damned guts apart. He done," said Anselm, "Damnit! We're done now, too. They gonna torch us for this."

The other two soldiers stopped laughing when the vomit turned to blood. The whole tavern watched in quiet horror. When the General stopped for a moment and wiped his mouth with his sleeve, many thought maybe that was the end of it. Maybe it had just been the color of the wine. Staring with disbelief at the blood on the beams of the floor he pointed at the young man. "You…" he began, but his words were coughed out in vomit. More blood. "You," he said once more but weakly, the terror now clear in his voice. When a fresh rush of blood gushed forth from his body, he began to cry and his tears too were blood and when he wiped his eyes he saw this and began to whimper and his hands shook violently. Even the beads of sweat were red and his whole body convulsed and he collapsed on the floor coughing out spumes of even more blood, which rushed forth now from every opening, and the young man noticed grimly how it even came from under his nails.

With the last of his strength, a perhaps admirable effort of force and courage, the General lifted his face to curse the young man or speak some earnest petition, but he could only cry from the depths of some great agony and his tears fell all red and then his eyes burst like pressed grapes and the last of his life spilled from their sockets and the young man who was the closest witness saw the tears of blood.

When the drunken soldier died, his skin immediately took on a bruised and purple look, except for his face, which turned a deathly white. His whole life, all of it, had spilled out of him and still could still be heard dripping on the casks below.

He seemed so small now, emptied, so that he could be slipped right out of his armor, this man once with a chest like a barrel, with a hand large enough, an arm strong enough, to lift other men by their throats and set them down dead.

At first, no one spoke. Anselm hurried to the back room to light a ring of votives about an obscure idol, and to this he muttered the briefest prayer. He cleaned away the old offerings. Having nothing, he pulled out some of his own hair and left it before the statue. He knew he must escape, but could not because the boy would still be there and would not know to run. Anselm returned to the main chamber. The other two soldiers, shaken, had only just now drawn their swords.

"We told 'im no more!" Anselm cried. "Was his own risk! We told 'im no more!"

"And you poison 'im for no listening!" cried the first soldier, the one who had laughed the most and longest.

"That's not it!" Anselm begged, but knew it was hopeless.

"Murderer!" cried the other soldier.

"Poisoner!" cried the first.

"Is not it!," cried Anselm, and then turned to the boy. "As you have life my son, run."

And he did, into the streets of his childhood, into the web he knew better than any invader, he ran. At the northern wall, he said goodbye to his oldest friend.

Gelidii led me to a peaceful meadow just outside the shadow of the tree. He had an odd way of walking. He would slink along the ground noiselessly and stop and become very, very still and thus fade into a kind of invisibility. It occurred to me a Picarin could live very close to the settlements of people and not be detected for a long time, if ever, and perhaps the stories were true of those creatures that dwelled in the folds of dark.

Gelidii would not follow a direct path along the ground, but walk up a tree as much as around it. He would slink along boughs like a cat, reappear and disappear among the branches. And I suppose he did this to see everything, to know as much of what lived above as below. With an uncanny understanding of the canopy, he once lowered down to hang right in front of me by a single toe, swaying from a limb he had masterfully made bend but not break, and it was off-putting, those eyes suspended before mine, staring the stare of the almost dead. And his ears scratched the earth, and I wished I had a weapon then. He tugged an ear out sideways and maybe smiled, and then he stretched an arm, blacker than black, towards the ground, and plucked up a white translucent pebble. He nestled this in the exposed cradle of a root before climbing back up again, almost without effort, and becoming one with the thinnest of branches, invisible save when he moved.

"Why did you do that?" I called up. The pebble.

"Now for trail tell of the Youmann with Picarin walk."

"Oh."

I think it looked down to me then. "How for Youmann live so long in jungle?"

"What? I don't know. I hid a lot. Stayed quiet. Why?"

"Noisy are steps of the Youmann. Noisy this breath. Creaky creak joints of the Youmann. Slippy slip the lips and slip swallow and Gelidii hear and know meat comes. Youmann smell of meat. Youmann slow. Youmann unprotected and straight the line it walks. Anything can eat the Youmann. Anything can know of its coming. It just for to wait upon the path."

And the cold fear rose again: Did this thing wish to eat me?

In the secret vault of the mountain that none but they have ever named, fires have burned forever. In the chamber's orange light of cremation the body reposes in sacred stitching, reassembled, but incomplete. The kneeling mourners hiss with folded wings. The name cannot be written in ash. The third letter is broken. The under-goblin is fed a sip of the body's blood, is loosed from its vault of clay and sent running to the tree of the low cloud. In a frenzy, in murderous intent, the under-goblin seizes the cut-off Harpyae wing, licking it in reeling ecstasy, wearing it as a relic about its neck and follows the tunnels of the worm back to the low mountain none but they have named.

We came to a shaded meadow where dark leaves grew with veins of red. A light and natural rain began to fall. Gelidii petted the delicious looking growths with his hand and then squatted on his haunches and began to dig carefully with the tips of his black nails until he unearthed a gnarled, white root. He wiped the clinging soil away, scraping the skin away with the flat of his curved thumbnail.

He then chewed the root and threw aside the green. Thinking the leaves may be bitter or poisonous, I dug my own and did the same. In this way we feasted. Once Gelidii stopped chewing and grew very still and raised an ear. He slowly turned his eyes back toward the tree.

"What is it?" I whispered.

He shook his head very slowly. He did not know. It would be a long time before he chewed again. Night was falling fast. Daring it all, I took a bite of leaf which tasted like the soil itself, with a touch of salt. Not pleasant, but not poisonous. I bit again and waited for some response from my companion. Getting none, I asked, "Gelidii, why won't you eat the leaves? Is there something wrong with them?"

He stopped chewing his root. He stared at me for too long a time.

"Well," my hand lowered to the side, "well?"

He scratched the wires of hair growing from the wrinkled folds of flesh on the crown of his head. For a moment his hand stilled and his countenance changed to one of wonder as if recalling something profound from a long time ago. "Gelidii no for eating the leaf burning in the white day, in the father of the moon."

I turned the vegetation in my hand as if it were something nefarious. "But…but why not?"

He tugged his ear. He had never considered the question. "Picarin no for eating above the earth."

"But why wouldn't you? There's so much food."

"Picarin come from below, eat what grow down to below. Always like this. Picarin never live in the white day before. Picarin always pick from below until the mother of the night tip the tree and find the Picarin and call them out."

I chewed the slightly bitter greens again, and Gelidii told the story of his beginning:

"Long, long ago, under the great world tree, swimming in the sea of clay where rain runs in, into the land before light live the Picarin and up, up we dig to sip from the juice of her roots. Down, down we go to know the belly of the world. A dark ocean runs there.

"But one blue day Moon Mother walk above the world looking for all creatures to find, to be counted and known, but not see Picarin in her light or shadow. So she go first to the mountains and cries: 'Come out, come out, Picarin mine for Mother to see!' But only the dragon in the mountain. Dragon sleeping say, 'There are no Picarin here, oh Moon, just the quiet mountain stone.' So she go to the waves of the great water and cries, 'Come out, come out, Picarin

mine, for Mother to see!' but only the fishies run in the waves. Under waves Layavana swimming in deep. They say to her, 'No Picarin here are, Mother. It is for cold and heavy the air.' Now flies she above the forest where live all things of all kind and cries, 'Come out, come out, Picarin mine for Mother to see!' but even in the forest where all things go, they say to her, 'We know not of Picarin, oh Moon, oh Light in Darkness.'

"Distresses she, and wanders across the sky, until at last she go far far away to where all things are first born, there where the upper leaves of the great world tree catch stars, and the broad limbs fan over half the earth. And Mother Moon asks the great tree, 'I have looked the whole world round and not see my Picarin. Where could they have gone?'

"'Oh, keeper of the night,' say the tree, 'they swim just now in the clay between my roots, and drink they the rain as it trickles down and eat but the worm and chew the root of the forest green.'

"'Why are not for the Picarin above where their Mother may see them?' ask the moon to the tree.

"'Is for they fear to run above Mother, for they have not eyes to see the eagle falling hungry from the sky.'

"'Mother will give them eyes, and they no fear the eagle for to hunt. Tell them come out.'

"'But they will not, oh Daughter of Stars, for their skin is white and the sun will burn them, and they will be caught by the swift creatures of the night.'

"'Tell them I will grace their skin with darkness, ancient tree, so they need no fear of light, nor the swift creatures of the hungry night. Bring them out, Tree.'

"'But they will not come forth, oh Grace of the Heavens, for they are weak eating only worms and the juice of roots.'

"'I will give them the strength of the father of white day, when he touch their skin they will be strong. Now tree, move aside.'

"And the moon pushed the great tree down and made half the world from its body; even this place now once was her. But the Picarin hid from her light, deep and deeper down to secret places they go. Hide they in the valleys of the black ocean. So, Mother Moon call out, 'Come out, come out now hiding children, Mother wishes to see you now.'

"'Oh, Mother!' cry they from the buried world, 'We have not eyes to be above, nor we skin to survive in the light. We are too weak, Mother.'

"Then moon pluck from her body bright stones of light, and set she these for the eyes to the Picarin so they all things see no matter for the dark. And from the cloak of night she take the deep, deep blue of sky for to drape upon the Picarin skin, so now they no for fear the light. Now they may be hidden from all but her. And then she take the roots good for food and scatter these to all places, so they grow strong and no fear the hungry when they walk the forest path, and go to know the world round."

"With Picarin born to the above, the Mother know all her children. And peek always she upon the earth where Picarin run, even when she tends to they who live below the other side of the sky, but for the night of no hope. Picarin walk not on the night of no hope. Picarin feed not on this night. Picarin ask and wait for the mother to return again. And always come she again, until the day when no Picarin ask her for to come. That day for end of world be."

And then the Picarin almost smiled, and so did I.

The day broke over the land warm and bright. The sky had exhausted itself of clouds.

The ash had gone with a last burst of rain and the cut of wing was gone too by the time we returned, and I imagined what scavenger now ran with that foul incubus within. Let it be. Yet still the blood stained heavily, and I would never go again to those parts of the tree or ground where it had touched, not ever.

As we raced back to the tree the effect of the sun on Gelidii was plain. His eyes could not stand the direct light, and so he kept to the thicket and the shadows. Upon reaching the tree, he immediately went to his den. I waited a time and watched the light break full and gloriously over the earth. It occurred to me this was the first of many mornings that hunger did not plague me. And I had the luxury to recall the long-abandoned promise I had made. The rising sun reminded me to what I owed this life.

"I have to go."

"But you will help us? You will find one? A sage?"

"We're crushed and I'm crushed more."

"Find a sage."

"Stop it."

"Please."

"Brother, I have to go. I'll be lucky to see tomorrow's morning and you know that."

"Sages are real. I know they are."

"No, you don't."

"My grandfather met one."

"I've heard this."

"He never lied. Never. And every time he told the story he told it the same because it was true. If you just can find one... just find one."

"I have to go. It's almost dawn."

"I know."

"Don't make me promise this."

"I can't keep living like this. I need some hope. Just tell me that you'll look." The hand of the friend of his earliest days reached out the window and he did not take it.

"Don't make me talk like this. Your grandpa, he told stories all the time and was as drunk as he was not."

The hand withdrew empty into the darkened room, and he saw the moonlight run in his friend's tears. *"I will pray for you often. Save yourself."*

"Then how come no one's gotten one yet?"

"'Cause they thought grandfather was crazy and...well he was but that doesn't change the truth. And he never lied, and you could tell the dreams from the real stories because the dreams would change."

They heard the sound of doors breaking in. Screams and torchlight rose in the maze of ancient streets. *"You have to go, Brother."*

"They'll never find me. I'm not worried for that. The stupid bastards. If nothing more, I'll pick my way of dying."

"There's a lot of them."

"So there is."

"Get going."

"If I hear about something, someone who knows something..."

"Don't you worry about that. I shouldn't have said anything."

"If I hear of something..."

"You're wasting time."

"I think they killed Anselm."

"You'd better get to the cliffs before sunrise."

"I heard him as I ran off."

"It's not your fault. You really have to go."

"Why are they doing this to us?"

"Don't climb down in the dark."

"If I get out of it and see people again I will ask them."

"I didn't mean to say all that."

"Yes you did."

"Grandfather once thought he saw an elf sleeping in a cowslip."

"I remember." They laughed just a little and it would be the last time they laughed together. *"The Sage was his favorite story."* A faint glow of orange came from the East. Was it the sun or the tavern burning? *"Nothing's going to change this. When my grandmother passes, I will follow you down those cliffs."*

"Don't you dare."

"I hate them so much. I want to kill them all like you. Remember what they did to her?"

"Stop that. And I didn't kill him."

He considered the provisions clasped in his hands: a wool blanket holding a bundle of promised life. *"I wouldn't have had a chance without these. Thank you."*

"It's nothing."

"It's not nothing. Where are they?"

"What?"

"Them The Sages."

"In the North."

"Please stop crying, all right?"

"You're my last living friend and you're going."

"Where in the North are they?"

"You really have to go."

"I'm not lying. I will try to find one."

"He would just say north. He never bothered much with place names. Far, far in the North he'd say. I don't think he ever thought we'd be going that way."

"You're not. I'll try my best all right?"

"All right. Just ask them."

"Who."

"The people."

"In the forest?"

"After the forest."

He sighed. "So that's the plan? Go through the forest and start asking around?"

"That's pretty much it."

"Our best hope for Selador."

"The only hope."

"That's terrible."

"Yes it is."

He held out his hand to the friend who had become a voice. "Brother, if a Sage is real, I will find him."

"All right then."

"I mean this."

"I know you do." They shook hands for the last time, friends since the cradle. "But remember: first find a dragon."

"Yup." He left, with the last sight of his friend a silhouette receding into a darkened room.

A finger of clay tapped my face. "Youmann. Youmann. She is risen." I awoke cold and could not remember where I was. "She is risen," it said again. I had fallen asleep, curled in the bosom of the tree, her thick leaves shading away the sun. Somehow I'd slept right through the day. I'd been terribly exhausted. My vision still blurred: "What is it? What?"

"She is risen now."

I was so tired. "Just kill it again," I said.

"The eye of night is not to be killed. She is risen." It pointed up through the leaves to the yellow glow of the moon. "She speaks of more rain to come. She speaks of mist in early morning. She speaks of dry season to follow and then one of much rain. The next rain come in three days. And the Youmann she sees in the Picarin tree. You are welcome. Hush!" It lifted a finger to its beakish mouth as the forest rumbled. "They are about tonight. Go not from the tree. Stay."

"I just want to be home again."

"Stay."

"But I can't go home again."

"Why for not the Youmann is to home?"

"Because they'll kill me."

"Oh. Oh, Youmann. Tree is for the Youmann home."

Then rose the solitary squawk of a wounded crane. Gelidii's ears perked up. "Is cuilii. It roam in the blue day."

"The crane?"

"Is no crane. Is cuilii. Cuilii eat you. Tricky cuilii sound sound of anything. What come to cuilii cuilii eat. Cuilii sound hoppy rabbit hurt. Cuilii sing yellow tweet tweet tweet. Cuilii always hungry. Cuilii very tricky, but Gelidii know cuilii voice. Cuilii no trick Gelidii." Another croak. It was closer, in the field that ran beneath our branches. "Is it coming, Gelidii? Maybe we should go."

"Gelidii no fear cuilii. Cuilii no eat Gelidii. Cuilii no eat Picarin."

"Maybe I go."

"Go not to the field."

"No."

"Wait quiet. Sit."

"Do they eat people, humans?"

"Gelidii know not, but think cuilii eat Youmanns. Youmann never before come to Picarin tree. Hush. Hush. Be still."

Another squawk rose even closer and one would swear a wounded crane hobbled near. It was so accurate in its call I thought my companion to be mistaken. I imagined the delicious tender meat of a roasted crane. And then I saw what I thought to be fear in the countenance of the Picarin. "We should go," I whispered. "We should go now."

"How far Youmann walk before in forest alone?"

"I don't know Gelidii. It's not important right now. Let's go."

"Cuilii very big, very quick quick quick. Cuilii quicker than coohoohoo. Cuilii eat the coohoohoo. Stay. Hush. Be not afraid."

We were not too high up. I had slept, rather carelessly, quite close to the ground. It would be for the last time. I wanted to climb way up in the tree where the cuilii could never reach, to where, if they could climb, the tree would not support them, or confuse them so they got lost in its infinite branches.

Then, Gelidii did an odd thing: it shook its head violently back and forth so that its ears slapped against its cheeks. It felt too noisy. I didn't know why he did that. Just on the other side of our thin veil of leaves we heard the treading of a giant stamp the ground. Even the great tree shook from its force. And then all fell quiet, until the crane call sounded again. Had Gelidii not told me…Had it stayed sleeping and I went for a walk...

I shifted my weight. Gelidii held his hands out to me as I moved. The long tendrils of fingers fanned out crookedly before me to hush. Be still. Hush.

Right below us gently came the crane call again. Its voice rising up, searched for us. I could feel it peering into the leaves. Gelidii held very still. My heart rose to my throat and I too held very still. Gelidii slapped his ears again strangely, but then turned away. I imagined this thing sniffing the ground with rising hunger. Suddenly, from the distance, we heard no more crane but the sound of a wounded songbird. Gelidii's ears shot up and he snickered. "Cuilii tricky thing," he whispered. "Tricky beast."

And then it was gone, back to the mystery, back to the shroud of the forest which bore it. "Is good for Youmann to find Gelidii," the Picarin said when it was gone. "Good very for Youmann very to find Gelidii and with Gelidii stay. Is food the Youmann now?"

Food? I was breathless and lacked all appetite. "Gelidii, why did you slap your ears like that when it could hear you?"

I think it smiled. "For cuilii no eat Picarin. Gelidii for tell cuilii Picarin in tree and no want climb for hunting."

"Can they climb?"

"No climb good. Climb little. Here, yes, maybe on branches, big branches low, cuilii climb. Cuilii no climb higher than it fall to be with no harm. Maybe here, yes, so Gelidii slap ears to tell is Picarin tree. Picarin poison to eat."

"Then why did it come so close?"

"Because it smell Youmann. Gelidii think is why for coming. How Youmann live so long Gelidii not know. Youmann not know. Let's for food."

"I'm not hungry, and it's out there."

"Is go other way. Gelidii know way it go. Gelidii know other path is good for going no cuilii know. Is special food. Help Youmann walk in the blue day. Youmann no stumble in dark."

"I don't know if I'm ready to go anywhere, Gelidii."

"No come with Gelidii to forest? Gelidii bring food to you. Wait."

"It's night."

"Is better. They sing bright and clear to moon. The bulbs sing to the moon."

The thought of waiting alone in the immense tree with the shadows of night running through it, with whatever beasts lurked in the field below did not appeal to me at all. I would go with the creature, the dark, crooked, ancient Picarin, into the forest at night, the dark, crooked and ancient forest.

It walked away and I followed as much as I could through its bizarre course, running equally in the hanging branches as over the ground. Often I called its name, for it quickly became invisible. Its elusivity in the day had no comparison to how it faded into the night. "Gelidii?" I whispered.

"Am above," came the whisper of a cautious voice. Suddenly the Picarin called out in the voices of natural creatures: the owl, the cricket and, at last in the song of the Picarin — a low and mournful musical voice heard by almost none.

"What are you doing, Gelidii?"

It had dropped next to me unnoticed. "Is not far now."

"Gelidii, I can't see you. What were you doing up there?"

"Looking for water path, for dangers upon water path to silver lake."

"To where, Gelidii?"

"Silver lake where the moonbulb grows."

"What's a moonbulb, Gelidii?"

"Very, very good, yumm yummy, Youmann, yumm." It patted its stomach. It pulled back its beak to the suggestion of a smile, and I wondered again from what creature I had taken alms...this thing from the pages of a story, a creature who could speak and think not so unlike people, yet whose form defied all existence. Someone must have found these before. Something, before this account, must have been written.

Excerpt from The Book of Travelers:
"The Pycarene hath upon its back two stone of mysterious function it beareth to all places. I liken its form to the spider though it hath but four limbs, like a man yet of peculiar length. Sparse wiry fur covers its flesh dark as the devil's ink. Hideous eyes I see yet in dreams. The encounter with it hath cursed our sleep. It spoke in magic and we attacked with words of the Lord our Protector and

fire. By the grace of the Enemy, the stones were its shield. We fear the very sight of the beast hath removed us from grace. The name I give to it was spoken from the crevice of its own maw."

Note. Day 89 of Fragment:

We have found a kind of giant crab in a tree of notable immensity. Hideous. Spooked white most seasoned of the men. Went to take it with lances. The stones are blades fiercely honed. We lost three before retreating and that makes twenty now. More than half gone and I wonder to myself having not the luxury to speak to it if we are but explorers only of the doorstep of death. Upon our departure we see the beast retreating to the tree tops. We cut a circle in the wild strip the barks for fuel and torch the grove entire.

With half sick with fever, we leave as quick as their tremors allow. Nothing to eat in this wood. Murmurs of going back Is not the mission but the distance that stops my doing this. I tell them we are almost across but don't know that. Bad dreams. Forest screams like the damned. Take turns on night watch. Last night claimed another. Dragged into the silence leaving a trail of blood we chose not to follow. May he forgive us. We conceal his gear so to divide it. Tell the others of his desertion. Night watch doubled."

We came to a still forest lake. The starlight sparkled in the water covered with pads of wide leaves and soft glowing flowers. The lake had caught the moon in blue. Everything shimmered. For the briefest moment a sense of great relief brought on by the scent of fresh open water and the whispering breeze gliding above carried me. Orbs of light bobbed in the water below. For a moment, for a breath and then longer, the beauty of it all struck me speechless.

From the sandy bank the Picarin lifted its draping arm and pointed to the illuminated flowers. "Moonbulbs," it said slowly.

"Those?"

"Beneath water."

"The white things? They glow like lamps."

"Yummy yum."

"How do we get them?" I had learned that in this forest even the smallest pond could house the most terrible beast.

"Gelidii get."

"Can I help?"

"Stay. Gelidii get."

The Picarin slipped into the water without much more than a ripple, taking to it like a snake. When it rose again, I saw the silhouette of its wet skull break the silver of the moon's reflection and the smattering of starlight caught in the pond. Then, one by one, the bulbs disappeared. Quickly and silently, it swam unfathomably quick. A glow would be there and then be gone. Little by little a growing white orb moved beneath the water and this was the Picarin holding its harvest. It emerged as silently as it had entered. It stood before me again, dripping and looking down at the illumination curled in the ribs of its fingers. I'd never seen anything like them. "They're like living candles," I said, truly amazed.

"Yummm." Gelidii lowered its beak to the bounty and crunched one and swallowed. The Picarin looked up at me, and I had to turn away from those eyes, how they glowed. "Yumm yumm, Youmann, yumm," it said. "Youmann, yummmy yummm."

"All right," I took one that had not touched its flesh and ate it. It was crunchy and light with a mild taste not at all unpleasant. Not unlike a potato, but lighter and crispier, with a nutty flavor. I ate more, trying very hard to pick ones Gelidii had not brushed his mouth against. When we got to the last few which rested right against the wrinkled flesh of its hand, I stopped eating. "Thank you, Gelidii. They were very good."

"More take."

"I'm full. Thank you."

"Thank you?"

"Thank you."

"More is here for eating."

"I'm not hungry anymore. I'm full. Thank you."

The Picarin stared at the remaining bulbs. "Youmann has lost its hunger?"

"Yes. That was plenty. My stomach is shrunken." And this was true after all. "You can have them Gelidii. Thank you."

"Thank you?" It stared at the bulbs again as if counting them. "Youmann no more?"

"No."

"Youmann has little eaten."

"Yes, but it was enough for now. Thank you very much for them."

"No more for hunger?"

"No more, Gelidii. Thank you."

The Picarin blinked and waited. It lowered its cracked-flesh beak to its hand and crunched another bulb and waited. It held its hand out to me again and I said nothing, trying very hard not to look into the reflection of its eyes, which suddenly I saw glowing brighter. Slowly, it ate the remaining bulbs, yet still held the last one out to me, shining there in the cradle of its dark and wet and alien hand. I waved the offer away. Then, without a word, it slowly ate the final bulb. When the feast was done, Gelidii turned its back to me and walked towards home. I followed.

On the way, something miraculous happened. Just before the first faint shine of morning, the whole forest became illuminated. I could see as well as in twilight. I even saw Gelidii climbing through the branches above. "Gelidii! I see you!" The Picarin turned its head and looked down, and its eyes were like fire.

"Picarin see Youmann."

"I mean I see you bright!"

"Gelidii see the Youmann too." It continued on.

"No, I mean everything is…it's just…this is just so…it's so bright!"

The moonbulbs had caused some enchanting effect on the eyes. I could see insects sleeping atop leaves. I could see the outlines of the sundry creatures of the night. I could see the beams of the moon burning above. "It's wonderous, Gelidii! Wonderous!" I could always see the Picarin.

The sun had almost risen when we got back. Gelidii hurried through the field and climbed up to its den. The early birdsong had long begun. It was a beautiful forest for all its danger, the morning the most enchanting. I had a brief fear my eyes would be too sensitive to the day, but this was not so. The odd excess of light in the earliest morning simply faded to the light of the sun. The day was so beautiful, I remember. Aunty used to say the world was reborn each morning. And I was tired and hungry and not quite safe, but wanted to see this sunrise so I could witness a world reborn. And I did. I faced Selador: "I'm still here," I cried. "I am alive!" I cried to the wind. May it carry my words to their hearts.

I must trust it. It had to be trusted because if it couldn't be trusted, that just wouldn't be fair. So I would trust it and that was a choice and I would abide by that and suppress the detractors of that decision, but I wouldn't be sleeping in that den. No, no. I would not be sleeping beside the black creature made of clay. No.

In the following days and months I lived with Gelidii, we spoke of simple things: of food, which Gelidii could find anywhere, of the forest, of the creatures for which Gelidii had every kind of name and understood every kind of behavior. On the rare days we ventured into the forest in full day, Gelidii, fighting always a terrific exhaustion, would show me her hidden pockets unseen at night.

"Look at the blue flower of the bright star, Youmann. Listen to the noon cricket. Here the nest of frogs. Red frogs here are born." Darting tails of fire shot in the black water.

"I see them, Gelidii. I see them."

Picarin paths, according to my companion, wove secretly around the entirety of the earth. And this could be true, for they are subtle things which do not grossly run through the forest but yield themselves only to the sharp and knowing eye. Only a Picarin can teach one how to see and follow them. And through my travels I would occasionally stumble upon what could have been the hint of such a trail: a certain bending of a leaf, a particular leaning of a stone, a basin dug inexplicably next to a creek, something as slight and subtle as a missing flower petal that just should not be missing. More hints than I can list here mark a Picarin's way. And they are not simply guides for direction, but if read in full, will tell what lies ahead or behind, what has happened there, what lives in that land, what might be found to eat, or a good source of water clear as crystal.

And as useful as this knowledge could be, it yet became impractical to search for the rare hint of what might be a Picarin path. I needed Gelidii to lead me along a path, which would be not a trammeled course through the brush, but a series of hints, one leading to the next and each read in its own peculiar way. The intricacies ran as delicate as a language or a magnificent piece of music. Once Gelidii and I parted ways, and I never encountered or even heard of his most rare and elusive species again, I rarely followed what might have been the markings of a trail, which were as likely to run up a tree or the leaning face of a cliff as to follow a cave beneath the forest floor submerged entirely in water.

Although sometimes I followed a hint successfully. If nothing else, this told me that other Picarin did exist.

And yes, as said, I left Gelidii eventually and like many an old friend or relative, never had a word with him again. And I would have left much, much sooner than I did had he not insisted so strongly that I stay. My very life, he said, required me to stay.

"Wait longer now."

"But I need to do something. I need to move on."

"Is for danger for Youmann. Youmann must learn to hold the blade of the Picarin before go walk again in the forest alone."

"I made it here alone. I can make it out alone too."

It shook its head. "Is not mean same."

"Gelidii, many moons have waxed and waned since our meeting, but I need to find my kind again. I need to find houses, a road. I can't stay in a tree with ... with..."

His ears dropped, which meant he felt pain, and I realized what I almost said and felt ashamed. "I just need to do something. And to do it I must find people, houses, a village somewhere far enough from my own where I can ask for what I need and be safe."

The Picarin tugged its slack ear. "Gelidii know for the houses of Youmanns. Gelidii know for the road."

It took me a moment to understand this, to believe this. "You, you ... you know where houses are? Human houses? And a road? A broad path that cuts through the jungle? You've known this, have seen this and haven't told me? Gelidii...why wouldn't you have told me?"

"Never for Youmann ask."

And this was true, and made me despise myself for neglecting the simple. "All right. Okay, but can you take me there, Gelidii? To the houses and the road?

He waited a time before answering.

"Just take me to the road Gelidii. I will find the houses from there."

He shook his head.

"Is far and far to road. Road no go to houses. Houses sleep in jungle alone."

And I imagined a fishing village fed by the river. Quaint and happy, so remote even the soldiers of the king could not find it. And I thought the road could lead me along my quest. I needed so badly to see people again, to have anything for a companion but a humped creature made of web and worm. "Take me to the houses first, Gelidii. After that we can go to the road. I beg you."

He tugged his ear and lowered his enormous wet eyes in thought. "Youmann must learn carry the Picarin stone for to keep the blood in. Stay. Gelidii teach gentle man the stone. Stay. When gentle man know enough of Picarin stone, so that no fear all that come before him, Gelidii will take him to road. Gelidii know Youmann wish road to follow away. But road no safe. Road have many danger. Youmann must learn Picarin stone to survive road."

"Will it take long?"

He shook his head. He didn't know. "Never for teach Youmann Picarin blade. But not have to learn all. Learn some. Enough to not so quickly go and die."

"And what of the houses. Will you take me there? I would like to see them very, very much, Gelidii, and you could be with me," I said, knowing he could never walk into any fishing village, no matter how hardened the fishers might be from the mysteries hooked out of the belly of a jungle river.

In an opaque river the color of copper, traces of humped, purple backs curled above the waterline. About them floated a fan of aquatic limbs waiting in silence. Clicking, chomping rows of teeth expanded below a ring of gills like a macabre necklace of hunger. Dead black eyes, the eyes of a crab, peeked just above the surface, watching for whatever broke the silence of the water. They could be in pods of a dozen or alone, often away from even the gentlest of rapids whose movement could mask the step of prey. They rarely bothered with fish, often small and always quick and thus hard to catch and kill. After he was taught how to wield the blade, he would learn how far the limbs of the water things could press like a python through the sand, guided by the unblinking eye of the abomination. They could clasp an ankle and drag a man into the belly of the river—not too deep, just enough to cover him beneath the water where he would struggle upwards, and they would fight not at all, but settle lower into the mud, holding tight to the bed, and there wait for all to be still.

"Gelidii, will you take me to the houses?"

He waited in thought, and then nodded. He would take me to the houses of man.

"That's wonderful," I said and regretted it almost immediately. His face had folded to sadness. But people would pity me, feed me, not just roots and leaves, but warm and delicious food. People would treat me as one of their own--a lost son saved from the wild. But they would never understand him, and so could never see him. I resolved not to tell them of my companion, and once in the village, with Gelidii waiting without, clinging to some limb like a great bat, I would find him and tell him to return to alone. "Thank you," I would say then, "but I am staying here now, Gelidii."

He said the dwellings were not far, and they were not. We travelled mostly at night. I curled in my blanket, and Gelidii slept in a limb above me, telling me he would know if danger came, but none ever did.

One morning he stopped and raised his ears and stood up very straight and sniffed. He pointed ahead. "Is near." My heart raced for joy. I would have bounded ahead, but the vines grew so thick. He walked, crawled, slunk behind me until pulling aside a curtain of vines and pointed again. "Is there. Is for the houses Youmann."

Of the many strange things to which I have borne witness, I suppose it was the anticipation that made the scene before me so exasperating. "But, Gelidii. No Gelidii, no. This isn't right."

"Is for the houses of Youmann."

"No. No. This is not what I meant. This is not what I meant at all. This is no one's home!"

And I cried then. The heartbreak of it.

Uncle told me stories of the ancient ones who could do great things, who once cut a life from the wild. And it was said they could coax magic from the earth, could speak to plants and trees and beasts in ways people no longer can, and had even gleaned the art of immortality from the jungle. He said they knew the names of the forgotten gods, the darker ones, the older ones who dwelled deeply in the mystery of being.

"And out there stand yet their temples, hewn of immortal stone and rising against time and all logic. And people've seen them and it's true."

A field ran between the forest proper and their abandoned citadel. A solid panoply of vines grew over the outer wall made of immense stones cut with exquisite precision. The walls had been there so long that strands of tree-root twisted downward upon them. In the exact center of the wall stood a broad, arched doorway almost overtaken by the forest. The entrance stood forgotten by time, now allowing entry to only the wind and the creeping mouse, but once could accommodate giants. Of all this immensity, now most hidden by the jungle, one had to wonder where were its makers? Whatever has happened to them?

Gelidii did not like the place, not at all; also, the sun was rising hot. He cowered into the shadows. "I will go ahead, Gelidii. I don't think I'll be long."

He looked to the unnatural wall of tortured stone and said nothing.

A presence could be felt. Aunty always told me to heed such feelings. She said things exist that cannot be seen, and there's a reason you feel what you do. I crept through the field and looked back once, but Gelidii had already faded to invisibility. I felt terrifically alone then, and in my mind the stones struggled for breath, as if the vines held them in silent strangulation.

Three steps, exquisitely carved, rose so unnaturally from the wild twistings of the forest floor. Now, under its arch, the door seemed enormous beyond all purpose. I looked back once more for Gelidii, impossible to see now, and then brushed aside the curtain of vine and stepped in. Terror rises like a wave in times like these. The unknown. What waited inside made no sense really. Why would people ever make such a place, to what purpose? Within was a courtyard. It was strangely well kept, hardly invaded by the forest, for the walls ran so terribly high. I could not imagine how people cut and moved stones so large. I listened and waited. Never had I been in a place so dead. I started towards the only object in the place: a large table cut from a single green stone. I had heard of altars of sacrifice, human blood let to a thirsty god, and this could be one of them. And I, perhaps the first human foot to tread here in a thousand years, felt more like a ghost than the specters of this place. As I approached the table, something told me to stay clear of it, and I did, only then noticing the stairway cut against the opposite wall, carved so perfectly to match the pattern of the stone that it appeared almost from nothingness. Although I knew there would be only jungle on the other side, I had to look, look once and then be done with it.

I could not quite believe what waited on the other side: a dead city.

Courts and the remains of roads and pyramids all slowly being devoured by the jungle ran back almost to the horizon. Poking yet above the vegetation were tall spires and arches, intricately carved needles and pillars and towers of gray stone adorned with forgotten gods and symbols now unknown. Breaking the stillness, a flock of black birds lifted slowly above it, a poem of death, and I thought again people could never build such as this...but there it was. And how could they all be gone? How could they have slipped so completely from the face of the earth? I would wonder about it later. For now I'd seen enough.

Leaving, I listened for ghosts, for voices. That uneasy feeling of being watched. Again avoiding the table in the center of the court, I was suddenly confronted by the grim visage of a forgotten god staring down from the center of the high arch, stained by ten thousand rains.

The inheritor of all things will be the wind.

Gelidii had been sleeping. I found him under bundles of long grass that blocked the sun. "Okay, Gelidii. We can go."

Sticky eyes half opened. "Has for seen the houses?"

"Yes. They're very old, Gelidii. People haven't lived there for a long time."

"Ash. Ahh. Youmann want for other Youmann meet."

"Yes. I suppose I should have said that."

"Youmanns go upon the road."

I nodded. "But for you to take me there, I have to learn the blade."

"Some for learning."

"Yes, some."

"Yes."

I did not ask if he would just take me to the road, would just forget teaching me something of his art. Although I wanted to leave very badly by then, it was too much to risk. What if it said no? How could I ever consider it a friend if I were a captive, if it said no? Love and fear cannot exist in the same place.

It? What was it after all? "Gelidii, I have a question. Are you male or female?"

"Gelidii Picarin."

"But are you male or female? Do children come out of your body?"

"Picarin leave seed in ground beneath sacred tree. Tree bring forth Picarin from root. Tree is mother of Picarin to tend and till."

"Are you telling me you were born from the tree we live in now? Your tree?"

"Not Picarin tree…"

"Yes, but, but you're saying you come from that tree?"

Gelidii nodded. "Tree brought us forth. I for to shape into the garden."

He said no more about it and I did not ask. He could be very ill in the mind, and I did not want to shatter whatever he needed to hide.

Each Picarin bore two knives which it kept for life. These knives are crafted in a secret place from a mineral which grows only there. I would need such knives to begin my training. To this place Gelidii almost trotted. As we grew closer he grew ever happier and even began to almost run in his strange, loping manner. When he glanced back from time to time he offered a broad and hideous smile. It took a great act of will to smile back. He must have seen the force in my smile, for his would run away at mine to be replaced by an expression of confusion. He would then turn his gaze ahead and trot on. But so happy was he to be going to our destination he often forgot the prior awkwardness and turned back and smiled again, as broadly and hideously as ever, and I would reciprocate again, but poorly so. Only then would he recall the past incidents and look away once more, his smile once again gone.

I'd never seen it rush before or since, not ever, not to get anywhere or do anything. All the rapidity of its being seemed reserved for the handling of the blades alone. But the nearer we came to the destination the quicker he moved. "Soon," it called to me at last, "we for be upon the cradle of the stones!" And soon we were.

Before full dark we stood under the shadow of a cliff of black flowstone, a kind of especially hard obsidian which leaned so far out it formed a roof which could have once sheltered the ancients, before humankind had refined the arts of survival and felled trees for dwellings. Gelidii, solemn on this place, walked under the eave of the shelter with his joy replaced with a kind of religious ecstasy. Beside the cave a river ran.

In the shadow of the rock Gelidii patted his ears, drawing them down as if to make them clean. He then began to hum in a peculiar way. He sang first with a gentleness I'd never heard before or since. Above, recesses of sickles and daggers spotted the vaulted ceiling, the work of earlier Picarin no doubt. To them, these weapons were key to preserving their unusually long lives. "Picarin," Gelidii said once, "live longer than tree."

Unless they are killed by violence.

He hung his hands from his ears and shut his song. He then pointed up and traced the ceiling with his finger and whispered, "Here, cradle of Picarin blades very old, sacred very. Is for long sleeping and long we here to come. First we come for when almost we no more. She whisper to us from the sleeping stone, 'Come, come take my heart to Picarin hand so Picarin no fall from world.'"

For a moment like a moment in prayer, we stood in silence. Then, Gelidii turned his gaze upwards to the vault of stone and began to hum again. Very slowly and softly it began, and then a sadness rose in the song. The song grew higher and stronger and soon had a sense of urgent petition. The hum grew louder and louder still, (this all in a single breath), and soon blossomed to a piercing wail no bird or beast could ever make. I pressed fingers to my ears then. They felt like they would split if left unguarded. Gelidii's own ears had a musculature which allowed them to press flat against his head.

The howl shook my bones so badly I readied to run, but just then a shard popped from the obsidian sky and fell gently to the sand. Before us a perfect curved blade which could have been carved by a master craftsman rested in the sand. For a moment all was still, and then Gelidii knelt before it to trace it with his first finger. He said nothing now, sang nothing. He did not smile. His face held only wonder. Taking a deep breath he stood and faced upwards again, closed his eyes and sang out again, equally loud and fierce but a different song altogether. No mourning now, no sense of petition. This held simplicity and celebration, a song of victory. Again, just when the volume and pitch became unbearable, another shard popped from the ceiling and lay beside the first in the blue-gray sand. Behind us, all the forest had fallen to an unreal quiet. It was a dagger that fell. A sickle and a dagger had been sung from stone.

The weapons, he said, needed to settle. We left them just there and returned the next day. Gelidii would say nothing of them yet. He said Picarin do not praise what is not fully born.

They looked more perfect the next day with a living shine not there at first. He took them up and turned them in his hands and smiled. He then held the curved one out to me. "Blade of drinking bird has come to us," he said, and put it in my right hand. It felt much lighter than it should have been. It seemed to vibrate ever so slightly. He then raised the dagger before my eyes. "And for have come beak of stabbing crane," he said, and put this into my left hand. I turned both in awe and wonder, my reflection turning in the liquid black.

They were masterful, yet not quite right for a human. You could make do, but normal fingers do not sit well on the Picarin handle, this designed more for the narrow palms of the Picarin and their spider fingers. Gelidii's grip rested exquisitely in the blades. His fingers ran through the carved runnels in the stone in such a way that the blades became not only an extension of his hands, but extrication was all but impossible. The fingers rested not on, but wove among the stone in a manner of completion. Gelidii's middle finger would actually encircle the blade's handle one and a half times while his index fingers rested in divots. This, I would learn, was so the blade remained solid even for intricate and multiple stabbings. Important since the blood of the enemy could make the handle slippery. Every finger hold had a purpose. Tiny bumps and ridges would be manipulated by the respective finger or area of the palm and even wrist to lend maximum effectiveness to any strike. Gelidii began to teach me of this but soon gave up. I simply had not the physiology for the totality of this weapon. We would make do as best we could.

"How could you do this, carve stone with your voice?"

He scratched his head confused. "All things have language. Picarin learn language of stone."

And that was all he could tell me of it. No two knives were the same. Each had its own spirit, its own strength and vulnerabilities. As I held the claw-like one in my hand, "the blade of the drinking bird," I suddenly understood how a creature the size of Gelidii could, if it were quick enough, kill a thing as enormous and terrible as the

Harpyae. "It looks as if it could rip out the heart of a dragon," I said of the blade.

"Could, but must awoken be first. For long time sleeping they in cold wall. They to be told of moon they never before touch, and river which they hear but never before see. They hear rain but never before clouds know. Must they know of all creatures and Youmann and of great tree which once was and of stars bright and falling. When She awaken, she will sing and Youmann learn then of Her, the arcs for to follow to sing. When Youmann learn arcs of blade of drinking bird, lines of beak of stabbing crane, nothing may hurt Youmann then. No fear for road. No fear for anything."

We walked out to the river bank and Gelidii told me to rest the blades in the water, and I did. He then put them in my hands again and with cold fingers of clay lifted my wrists to the height of his beak and began to hum into the weapons. Sometimes he hummed like the roar of a river and sometimes softer than the flutter of a butterfly wing. The odd vibratory magic seemed to turn the atmosphere with its breath. I felt it in my chest and heart, and when my arms tired, he lifted them again by the wrists with those cold clay fingers of his and hummed once more.

This went on well into the night. At last I could hold them no longer, and so I lay in the sand with the weapons crossed over my chest. Gelidii hummed and I stared at the distant stars, wondering what they might know of human suffering and joy, if they shone only for the gods, if they cared at all that the light reached us, or that it burned holes in the shroud of black.

Throughout all the night, Gelidii kneeled beside me and sang the song of mystical creations. I fell asleep after a time and dreamed of wondrous things which I cannot recall save for their wonder. The song ended at first light, and poor Gelidii, even in his expressionless way, looked exhausted. He sat back and closed his eyes for a long time, and then he swam in the river. I stood and let the blades go at last. My hands ached terribly. I joined Gelidii in the water, though it made me uneasy. He swam like a giant serpent and would stay submerged for a very long time. Too long. He rolled in coils around me. At last he surfaced. "The weapons are awake now," he croaked.

"Yes. Good. I'm cold, Gelidii, and hungry and tired too. You must be tired too. Can we go?"

"Is good for stones to sing to white day on day of their becoming, to sing names of all things, once, so nothing may come upon them unknown. Then, we go."

I sighed louder than I had intended. "Okay. All right. Fine"

He slid from the water and took up the weapons, his impossibly long fingers encircling the handles almost twice, fitting so perfectly into grooves not meant for the human hand. Gelidii inhaled deeply then and a tranquil unworldliness enveloped his being. A kind of absence took his expression, and then, with strange solemnity, he began masterfully to wield the blades.

The speed and intensity, the perfect ferocity of these strikes, made the slaughter of the Harpyae seem slow and simple by comparison. The weapons and the limbs which bore them could not quite be seen. Rather, a dark blur surrounded the whole of Gelidii's body with the stones appearing as brief flickers, images caught at the cessation of a particular strike and then lost again.

What most astounded me was a thing which, perhaps due to the roar of the falling rain, I had not noticed in the battle with the demon: the air filled with a kind of music that accompanied the tracks of the blades which spoke, or rather sang, in voices sweet and fierce as they moved through their courses. Calling high and low they would whisper, roar, and then whisper again. Indeed, they met the promise of their awakening as they sang of all things, a kind of praise of all things that words could not carry. Yet, woven among their song, an insistence of their becoming, a cry for birth. The chorus filled the forest round as the movements flowed like the river, turned like the wind, burrowed under the ground and soared upon the burning tips of the sky. Here flowed the grace of beauty, of truth, though I knew it nursed the cradle of death. And they have said the gods speak in song. And they have said the world began with a chant of the sacred syllable. And I wondered if in that myriad of strikes and song it had been uttered again.

Sometimes Gelidii turned; sometimes he lowered his stance; sometimes he even kicked, but never did he take a single step from his first position, and there was a reason for this.

"Is forbidden."

"But why?"

"Is forbidden. No may Picarin kill what not can kill Picarin."

"But if they're coming for you, why would you just stand there and wait?"

"Picarin may not strike what cannot strike Picarin. Is forbidden. If Picarin can no reach it, it can no reach Picarin. Forbidden to go to step to kill. Forbidden to go to cut what can no cut it. Must wait. For this must learn all the arcs of blades for to wait and not fear. Fear nothing. So to not do what is forbidden. When arc of blade learned all, no thing may hurt what within."

"But how close do you let the enemy get?"

The Picarin unrolled its arm and then its middle finger and stretched both as far as they would go. It nodded to the extent of the tip of the outstretched finger. *"If enemy so close to touch tip of long finger, Picarin may cut enemy. Never before. To cut before is forbidden."*

"Do your gods forbid this?"

The creature paused and stared into the eyes of the man. *"What for are gods?"*

"The creators."

"Gods for create moon?"

"Yes."

"What for make gods?"

"I don't know."

"Moon make Picarin."

"Then you are made by the gods."

"Where for are gods?"

"I don't know. Beyond the stars."

"What beyond stars?"

"Nothing. It doesn't matter. There's nothing beyond the stars. Only darkness."

"Gods live at gate of darkness?"

"I suppose."

"Picarin children of moon."

"Okay."

The song had quieted as mysteriously as it had begun. Gelidii held the blades out to me, and I took them. They possessed, I thought, an even greater vibrancy than before. Gelidii stared over the blade and into my eyes. "Awake are they now," he whispered. "Youmann may for to see arcs of blade of drinking bird, path of stabbing crane."

I did not know how to hold them. Wrapping my hands around the odd grooves as best I could my fingers still would not fit right at all. Then, cold fingers of clay pressed around mine. The odd wiry hair, so rigid it almost broke the skin, scratched lightly the flesh of my hand. He tried his best to fit fingers into forms not meant for human touch, and this effort left us both confused. Gelidii scratched his head in thought. We tried again and at last settled on an imperfect grip. He nodded for me to stand where he had on the river bank. He nodded again and I slashed crosswise against the air expecting a chant. Nothing. I then slashed upward, eviscerating some imaginary enemy, but still, no song came. I then stabbed the phantom demon's throat, but no burst of power came forth at all. I may as well have been holding sticks. The vibrations faded from the blades in degrees, until at last dull stones rested in my hands.

Gelidii spoke then: "Is no arc. Man must learn for to follow arcs. Man must learn paths of stone. Stone no care for paths of man."

I turned and stared him straight in the eyes, something I rarely had the courage to do. "Then show me, Gelidii. Teach me the secret paths so I can walk in the forest alone."

And it did. It did.

"We begin for later. Is much for learning. Hungry now. White day has begun. Let us for food and sleep."

We ate. We slept. Like Gelidii, I slept the entire day through.

At dusk we began again. Rested I could consider the weapons with a clear eye. How sharp they were. Stones made of liquid black. As we walked to the river once more, a shore which would be the training grounds for many months to come, I rested a leaf upon the crescent blade and it simply fell in half. I dared to touch the live edge once, so very gently, and for a moment there was no blood and no pain, but then in a moment to follow a red slit appeared and the blood flowed freely to the earth. Iron, no matter how dearly forged, could never compare to this. And for all the years I carried it – it sits even now upon this table, covered in the dust of rest – it remains as sharp as its first day."

I began to love the river shore, once so mysterious and fearsome. The torrent of air and water broke the oppression of the forest as it rushed through without boundaries save the land itself. It would never stop and was never quite the same. It changed without changing, like our voices which with each moment are born and die.

Many days I envied its freedom, how it could rush to any land and never drown, how it could never burn and never be crushed, how it could fall from a cliff or flow to the dark and buried parts of the earth where no other would go; and it would wink at us in our fleeing years beside it, and no army would crush it and no war would touch it and no plague ever sicken its force. It could till a field. It could halt a vast army. It was the nursery of the white lily, and from its foulest soil the pure lotus grew. I envied it for that, for such freedom as I would never know. And it was beside this river that I first got a blade to sing.

With my hands worn raw from hours of spinning the blade, I let them heal in its cool, running waters. An inkling of an idea occurred to me as my eye followed it downstream into the lightless turns of the jungle. Checking the sky for direction, I tasted the water for at least the hundredth time and then I knew. "Gelidii!" I cried. "This is the Yellow River of Selador! It runs right through Uncle's land. Aunty does her wash in it!" And I knew this was true. In my heart I knew it to be true, for I had learned the voice of the river which ran beside me most all my life, and this river knew me too. At certain moments, when I listened very, very carefully, it whispered my name. Gelidii shrugged, scratching his head without understanding: "Goes to all places," he said, and nothing more.

Oh, if I could but run upon it.

I think the human form confused Gelidii, who treated my limbs like something from another world. What worked for a Picarin did not necessarily work for a human. And so, beside that river, on those firm banks of sand, Gelidii would constantly adjust my body as needed, bending my shoulders and limbs to unnatural angles while forcing me to ever lower stances. My legs ached for a long time until they ached no more. The burning pain left in degrees and then was simply gone. In its place a kind of emptiness settled: a hollow waiting to be filled. But there would always be the ever more subtle corrections to my arms and knees, my lower back, my shoulders, my wrists – all this done by the disconcerting touch of clay from the finger tips of a giant spider -- until my posture and stance were such that, at last, on a dark night plagued with rain, I could have perhaps been mistaken for a Picarin.

We practiced every day. I would imitate his movements sometimes. Sometimes I would spend all day on a single strike. My weapons refused to sing for a long time until, on one particular day no different from any other, the crescent-shaped stone of the drinking bird screamed with life. The force was so powerful, so present, so alive and chilling that I threw it away to the sand. No stone should scream like that. Gelidii hopped deliriously but I backed away. Away and away. The stone had become possessed.

"Good, Youmann, good! Good good good!"

"It's alive!" I screamed.

"Good good good good good!"

"Its scream… it…it breathed."

"Good goody good!"

"I don't want to touch it again."

Gelidii would not stop hopping. He clapped his webbed palms together, making a dead, wet sound. "Oh, Youmann is Picarin now! Is Picarin now! Now we do anything can. Was for third arc of waning moon has Youmann spoke!" I had drawn a low slash across the gut of the enemy. "More are for arcs to learn now."

"I don't want to touch it again."

"Learn for arcs. Be not afraid."

"I don't know Gelidii. How many are there? I don't know if I want to do that again. It feels like…like something lies within."

"'Tis does," he said without a smile. "As so is Youmann. What for calls your voice from within? What for possess you? All thing have life. All thing have soul. All thing called from first moon before all time was. Youmann hear voice of stone long lost to Youmann ear. Be no afraid of voice. Be no afraid for to learn arcs through which stone may sing. Twelve arcs of sparrow are, twelve of wrist, nine are of sliver moon and three of gray cloud; seven are arc of tiger. Thirteen for the sleeping dragon. Seven for dragon in fly. Nineteen are for arcs of blue water and ten for yellow river. For whispering moth are three. For plum blossom seven. Eleven of white rose; ten are for amber crane and of pale crane and of orchid in purple morning are ten. Nine of rising sun and twelve in falling. Four for burning noon and three of light in gray of cloud. Eight arcs of yellow wind. Ten arcs for of night of blue day. Seventeen are they of the bright stars and nine for are of dim. One is of star which falls. You must learn this: arc of falling star. The arc of falling star is one. Of great tree are seven; are for twelve of mountain, four of Cuilii, three of Harpyae, twelve of black eagle in fall. Nine are arcs of returning moon; seven of moon in loss. One for the night of no hope. One for moon in full."

He took a breath.

"And there are secret arcs of Picarin," he said with that strange suggestion of a smile. "Will show Youmann when Youmann ready. Be patient. Time teach everything."

I lifted the stone again. It had quieted. I weighed then the passage of days and the time spent and the time lost and what he thought I should know. "I will have to move on before too long, Gelidii"

"Many are arcs needed for road," he spoke almost too quickly. "Gelidii knows not for how long Youmann need in learning."

"I...I can't learn them all. At some point I'll have to take my chances. I'm okay with that."

"Picarin want for Youmann be happy. Want for him live again in Youmann world where all things pretty and good and happy always. Gelidii no want Youmann for in sadness dwell with Picarin in forest, lost with fear in Youmann eye Gelidii see. Gelidii want teach man no fear. No fear behind arcs of drinking bird. Learn arcs of drinking bird and no fear, not even though death walk upon road."

"But how long will it take?"

"Why for Youmann running?"

"I have made a promise, and I must keep it."

"We begin again with first arc of sparrow."

"But how long will it take for me to finish?"

"Never before has Youmann been taught arcs of Picarin. Cannot know for time."

"Then let's keep on." I picked up the blade. I could not tell if my hand or it trembled.

One particular strike, the sparrow's third arc, made a kind of upward wiggle eviscerating a man from the pubic bone to the sternum. The fourth arc of the sparrow went through the sternum and sliced right to the lower jaw. The fifth arc split the skull as well. For each arc, the song had to be louder, the blade had to convey more energy and the energy had to be such that the fibers of bone before it did not exist as clearly as the stone did in the hierarchy of the universe of matter. No weapon I have encountered ever compared to the unique nature of the Picarin's.

At first, the arcs of the sparrow were quite brutal on the wrist. Yet Gelidii demonstrated them effortlessly, with the knife sounding not unlike a warbling bird. But as I tried to copy his courses and failed so many times, my wrist soon became very swollen from the effort. At last Gelidii collected special leaves and pressed these to the injury before we slept with the rising of dawn. When I awoke by the next afternoon, all the swelling had nearly gone. I discarded the exhausted herbs and went alone to soak my arm in the river. I no longer feared the river. I practiced the strike again and again until Gelidii joined me some hours later. It had not sung. "I can't do this one," I said to him.

"You have done for one already. Do not let tired talk," he said, and for the thousandth time he adjusted my arm, my back and feet, and even lowered my gaze. "Follow arc of Picarin not arc of Youmann."

"I know. I know that. You keep telling me that, but it's not working for this one. It's too tricky."

"Try. Is for trying."

"I can't."

"Try."

"How long, Gelidii?"

"Until it sings."

It would be a month of effort at least on this one strike until, at last, it sang. And this time I had no fear, but rejoiced. All the sweat and doubt and pain faded. The blade lifted with the song and became weightless and illumined in the song, and the song and the blade were indistinguishable. Gelidii howled in joy. I tried again and missed and tried again and it sang once more.

After this the arcs came more quickly. I learned not to hold the force in my arm, but to let it channel through from the earth to my center, and from there to my limb, and then to the handle and at last to the pitiless honed edge of the weapon. One day, after months uncounted, I made ten strikes in a row with fierce precision and each sang with the fullest voice. The blade felt like a guardian in my hand. Something that moved almost independent of me. I felt invincible.

Gelidii told me the time had come to give it a name, and I went to the river and whispered its name to it and have never spoken it again as was the custom. And soon after that day, with so many strikes and hours of training I asked him, "What about the dagger, the Blade of the Stabbing Crane?"

"Is for hard for learning. Long for to learn strike of beak of stabbing crane. In time. Much more for arcs to learn of drinking bird."

"Listen, Gelidii, I know a lot of strikes and I can read the trails pretty well now. I think I'm nearly ready to go. I'll find my way. Thank you for everything but, well, there's a time to move on."

His face fell in confused hurt, and he went to the river bank and sat with his feet in the water and pet the current with his stick-like fingers. For a long time he said nothing and when he did I thought he might be crying. "But stay," he almost begged. "You are for very young. You are a seed have blown from great mountain and first little leaf pops from soil and see light of mother of moon for first time. Ask you now for going too soon. Little seed no for giant oak, but oak no blow from mountain. Only little seed can ride wind. Be not greedy to be oak. Be patient. Many more for arcs to protect heart of the Youmann and in this time Youmann grow and time there is. Life very long. Rush not. Stay."

But I had grown twice as strong, ten times as quick. I had a lot yet to learn, but it would have to be good enough. "Gelidii, I am going to leave the third day before the next full moon. I want to thank you very much, and I want to continue to learn until then if you'll teach me, but I have to move on. My home is dying. They're waiting for me to get help."

Gelidii slipped into the river water and stayed under a very long time. He said nothing when he emerged and when he did he simply went to the tree. But he taught me nonetheless, from each dusk to dawn we trained as we had been, both in the weapon and the signs of the Picarin trails.

"This goes to a pond where nothing lives. The water is poisonous. This goes to a ravine where deer cross. This one to a patch of blue roots you said were good for food, but they almost killed me."

"Root not for Youmann."

"No, Gelidii, it is not. And this one will go to the work of human hands."

"Will. And this one?" He pointed to a trampled flower.

"That leads to a field of daisies."

"No. It lead to nest of cuilii. Flower trampled, picked up, trampled again. Is cuilii."

"Oh, yes. I see that now."

"Must stay. Youmann not ready."

"I wouldn't have followed that anyway. Gelidii, I have to go. I have to."

The Picarin tugged its ear. It would never force anyone to do anything. "But Stay?" it asked weakly.

Stay.

One morning, I gathered my few things and secured the crescent blade to my waist. Gelidii promised to hold the dagger safe for me and would teach me of it upon my return. "Well, goodbye then, Gelidii." I bowed to him and he shook his head. I started off until he trotted beside me, his devastation that I would actually leave written plainly upon his face.

"Gelidii will take you to road."

"Okay then, Gelidii. Thank you."

Expressionless, he led the way in that slow and mysterious gait of his. Almost immediately he began to gather flowers. He loved flowers, always had, and once taught me how to gather them and keep them fresh so that they glowed for many days after being picked. I can still do this. On this journey, he gathered more than usual. His method was to dig out even the finest of roots, roots thinner than an old man's hair, and cup these in moisture from a lick and wrap them in a way to keep the moisture in. He would shelter them from storms and from a harsh sun, and shade the delicate ones which grew only in shadow. Sometimes he held them cradled like a child in his arms; other times he wove them together and wore them as a necklace. His affections for flowers always struck me as odd.

At first it appeared strange for such a thing to love flowers, whose glow of bursting colors appeared somehow improper against that flesh of blackworm and wire. And not only would he carry them, but would often find a suitable place of sun and water and loosen and moisten the soil to replant them, and so I wondered how many patches of wildflowers, almost too perfectly situated in the heart of the wilderness, had been, over the centuries, actually the work of Picarin.

This practice so contrasted to its form. How a creature seemingly devoid of all emotion and sympathies -- save the simple preservation of life -- could care so much for such graceful parts of nature confused me. For the entirety of my life up to that point, only humans ever cared for the beauty of flowers. Yet Picarin are not human, and yet there it was: the cradled orchid, the fashioning of weapons, a treasured home, the saving of a life not its own, the speaking, thinking, caring, doing what falls only to us of the "higher mind," and yet this was not human.

And going to the road often we would diverge from the straight path simply to see the serenity of a pond, or the breath of a waterfall, or a tree whose lavender blossoms hung in full bloom. But more than anything else, the flowers forced me to reconsider my companion, and after a time its affections did not seem so strange. And I knew at last my absence would cause him pain.

We went mostly at night. With each dawn Gelidii began weaving a simple nest in the upper branches. His eyes half-closed before he finished, as if the sun itself acted as a sleeping potion. Once in his bed could not be distinguished from below, even if you knew just where to look, even if it were bright of day. And I too sometimes nested in the trees. When you spend the better part of a year living in them you become partly a creature of the branches. My muscles had turned to wood. My body was as hard as the branches upon which it lived. But I still needed a certain broadness to them, a certain stability, whereas Gelidii could rest in the highest of twigs that a solid wind could snap.

Before sleep I would think over my life, as most people must, of where it flowed and fell, and of my companion and how I wanted to leave the jungle and be again among the things of man. It was eight days out, maybe nine when I asked, "Is it much farther to the road, Gelidii?"

"Is for near."

"It's just I haven't seen other people in a long time."

"Long time has Youmann been lost with Picarin." And again I wanted very badly to ask where the other Picarin were, but knew not to. I had approached this once, and his faced washed in such pain I dared not finish the question.

"It's also a very long time to not see your own, Gelidii."

"Is."

"Gelidii, where ..."

The jungle had its odd spells of cold. A clear night could bring a blanket of near frost which you would hardly notice when dwelling in Gelidii's tree. Its boughs had many hidden pockets of complete shelter, eaves which seemed cut by human hands. And the right one would protect you in a way another would not, so that even Gelidii, when the winds became severe enough, would forsake his beloved den for a hollow better suited to the sky's assault. And I too, (once I knew enough to read the sky, once I had learned the many boughs and their secrets), remained always warm and dry in the great tree, and having lined my favorite divots with various leaves and mosses, slept in perfect comfort no matter the weather.

I missed our ancient home, but knew Gelidii missed it more. He would say nothing, of course, but this creature, once so mysterious and invincible, a thing spawned from the jungle itself, suddenly had a frailty to it not there before on the way to the road. He seemed like an old and feeble man, lost and confused, feeling his way along an alien land through dim eyes and rain.

One cold night, with every star like a winking candle, he lifted the crescent blade against the great celestial cup: "See you how for blade know mothers of moon?"

"Yes, I do, Gelidii. It's cold tonight."

"Is."

"Could I make a fire?"

This was higher ground. The dangerous animals we had known wouldn't be here. The forest was thinner, and with me a Picarin walked. Suddenly his face grew concerned. His ears lifted and he turned to the south.

"What is it?"

"Far off Gelidii hear them."

"What?"

"Is far. No fear for the Youmann. Why for fire?"

"It will keep us warm."

"Is for warmth?"

"Yes. Let me show you."

I collected tinder and kindling, made ready the skeleton of twigs and then collected three times more wood than I thought I would need. It would burn well for it had been a long time since rain. Gelidii squatted in the shadows waiting. I took my flint and iron and struck a spark and Gelidii flinched at it and scampered back and back as I struck again. Gelidii gasped and receded into the trees as I breathed light and life into the glowing ember. By the time flames licked along the dry branches Gelidii was gone. It had been so long since I was comforted by a fire I hardly noticed. Such a human thing, the tending of fire. Eventually, I caught his glowing eyes high above in a distant tree. I called for him to come.

"Burns!

"It's all right. Come down!"

"It burn! It burns!"

I pressed my hands against the warmth, leaned my soul upon the illumination, yet thought of him. "Damn it," I hissed. "Damn it! Damn it! Damn it!" I stamped the fire into the ground upon which the Picarin would never step again. But even with this sacrifice he did not return that night. On the open ground beside a tree trunk I wrapped myself in the thin blanket and curled against the cold. I tried for sleep but little came. When he returned we did not speak of it. I never spoke of fire again.

Some few days later Gelidii began to pause quite often and sniff the air.

"Is everything okay?"

"Near is it. Is much danger on road. Many bad things upon it go. Road to bad places go. Evil draws evil. Stay. Go we back to tree."

"Gelidii, I cannot. I need to move on. I need to be found again."

"Forest is good world. Gelidii is friend for Youmann."

"I know, but I have to move on."

"Great beast of forest here dwell when moon is wet. Heart boom boom boom to moon! When sky it cries, feet of man will be known on road. Road run to wall of sky. It cannot be climb. Go for where white day is born."

"No, I can't go east, Gelidii. I ran from there, and they do not forget men like me. They make a point to draw our pictures and post them for other men to see and collect me and bring me to them, the soldiers. They would put my head on a pole and burn my body's fat as a lantern. I can climb whatever cliff the road leads to."

He lifted his arm straight up like the wall. "Is no for climb."

"What about going west?"

"It run forever, and then…" Gelidii slowly shook his head. "Beneath cradle of moon lies dark forest. Youmann may not cross dark forest."

"I can try."

"No. No try. No do. Not for Youmann walking. Picarin may go in. Picarin may pass, but hardly so. Ground is no ground. Is water running black beneath root of trees. Few things may go in dark forest not of dark forest born. Youmann will die of sting beneath black tree. Youmann will die of wet, or of beast woken from sleep. This eat the Youmann as he passes. Youmann is slow. Youmann knows too few arcs and to west forest of water will rot Youmann skin. Just stay. Only stay. Is good here. Tree grows wide. No more Harpyae come." He hesitated then, looking quickly to the ground and to me again. That was how I knew. It was a glance of guilt.

"There's another way, isn't there, Gelidii?"

Silence. He began to pull a bed of grass over his face.

"Gelidii, I have a right to know this. I have learned much of the blades and travelled very far on the Picarin trails. And I am the only hope of my village. If there is another way through the escarpment, I need to know. If you do not tell me, I will climb it and fall, or go to the East and be killed, or to the West and die of cold and disease in the forest of black trees and water. I will choose from those three fates if you do not tell me of the other way."

And the only time I ever saw Gelidii panic was then. He threw the grasses aside and slapped the black and wrinkled skin of his head, almost weeping. "Is for very very bad way! Once Gelidii cross this land. Once. It very very bad way! Beneath weeping tree is for death for Youmann to walk. Is ruined lands. Rift where catches all tears. Air she breathes in poison whispers. Catches she all spirits of evil in her walls. Are for ruined lands. Dwelling of forsaken." He rolled on the ground, panting, steadying himself.

"But Gelidii…"

"Yes yes, you may pass it and live. Death is not certain, but…" and here he stared through me, pointed to my eyes in a way I shall remember always, for it was the only time the Picarin ever in any way threatened me, "but, stay ever upon path. Youmann eaten in ruined lands. Stay you upon path. They may not touch you upon path. Is law has always been. But even should Youmann body be on path, unguarded spirit may, by crossing, be ruined."

Gelidii never lied. As impossible as his story was, I knew it was no lie. My only hope rested in that he were somehow mistaken.

"Are you sure I can't climb the escarpment?"

"Am for sure. Youmann will see. No climb. So high is hard for even bird to leap."

"All right then. I cannot go back towards Selador and I cannot go west to the forest of water. I will stay on the path. How do I find it?"

"It goes through all things. Road it will cut."

"But how will I know it's the right one?"

"No ordinary path is. Is a lessening of light. Follow this. Follow this to the escarpment wall. Step in the lesser light to find the gate of rift, and when he enters he must forgive his friend for the telling of it."

"There's nothing to forgive. Thank you."

He began to pant as if in anger. "Is no for striking place! No arcs for there! Strike sooner at wind or mother moon. Strike demon of dream. Do not strike in rift and do not speak and DO NOT LEAVE PATH. Speak not to them. Is bad bad way for Youmann going. Is bad thing Gelidii has spoken."

"No. It's my decision. I'm not afraid."

He turned away from me slowly then. "Youmann will. Youmann will know afraid."

It would be five days to the road. Gelidii began to act skittish and distracted as we neared it. He stopped often to sniff the air. He did not like this part of the jungle anymore. It had been torn open somehow and he felt it. "Is near now," he said, "by morrow moon we step upon it."

A road. I tried to count the days. Five hundred? And tomorrow again to a road. And to Gelidii, a goodbye.

Gelidii slept that night very high up, on branches too thin for me to follow. He disappeared up there, becoming just another bundle of sticks.

"Gelidii?"

"Youmann?"

"I couldn't see you."

"Am here."

Staring up into the nothingness, I thought there could be far more Picarin on this earth than anyone would ever know.

As I slept on the open ground, I remembered how the great tree held nests too high for mosquitoes to reach, and how the branches swayed softly by wind you could not feel. I thought of how long I had not been hungry or afraid there. How amazing, the gifts of this life.

We proceeded slowly that final morning. Gelidii sniffed the air more and more, dipping his finger to taste the waters just to spit it out. Something bothered him. "Is everything all right, Gelidii?"

"I no not know."

"What is it?"

He sniffed and thought about it. "Youmanns me think on road near."

Humans, I thought. People! By the gods, I would see people again. He squatted and pointed ahead to a dense fall of trees. "Is across this, road lies." Ahead lay a tumble of trees under a freshly grown thicket. My heart raced. Could a true and proper road really be just beyond them? Gelidii stood very still. "Okay," I said. Let's go."

We went on slowly and climbed over deadfalls seemingly cut by saws. At the top of the waste I grew breathless and looked down. Amazing. There it was at last: a road of red earth ran below like a scar through the jungle.

It looked bizarre, unreal, and yet was such a simple thing. "Amazing!" I called out, astounded but not really, overjoyed but not really. And it was such a simple thing and yet could trace the earth. "Amazing," I said again. But how unnatural. How bizarre. I looked at the ruin beneath my feet. "They've cut a whole lot of them, huh?"

Gelidii nodded in slow sadness. I started down the pile of the dead. Gelidii would not move. Looking back at him, I caught a fear in his eyes. "Are you coming at all, my friend, just a little ways?"

He shook his head."Road is no for Picarin. On white day Youmann walk road. Walk not road in first light, in last light. Walk in middle of white day and in middle of road walk. Watch for the edges. Keep blade of drinking bird always ready. Watch for the back."

I could draw my curved stone as quickly as I could wink and strike in any direction. I felt confident. "All right then, Gelidii. Thank you then, and goodbye," I said, but was looking north. When I turned to where my friend had just been, he was gone. A creature forever without ceremony. "Bye, Gelidii," I whispered to the vacant space and started out.

The day was unusually hot, though a wind lifted tiny eddies from the exposed earth. Mirages formed ahead as pools of water, and in the shifting visions of heat I began to see images trotting across the road. I rubbed my eyes, but they still appeared. They were far, far ahead, but I could not gauge just how far-- it had been too long since I had seen such open space. The images would pop out of the bush on one side, linger a few moments, then disappear on the opposite side. "They could be anything," I said to the air. "They could be deer." Nonetheless, I drew the blade and held it at the ready. I kicked the fine soil and watched it roil in clouds and settle again. Uncle used to say it was the iron made it that color, and when I asked how he knew he said he could taste it. But Anselm said this world came from one god slaying his brother, and that this earth was his body and the soil had caught his blood. At that point in my life, I believed in them both.

I kept kicking up the dusty earth with my bare feet. I don't know why. To pass the day, or to forget Gelidii, or just not to think of the days ahead. For whatever reason, watching the dusty soil whirl in the hot wind and settle again calmed me. For it is not a good thing to let the mind wander too far ahead.

"Don't kick it," Uncle would say. *"It gets in your lungs. Makes you sick."*

"All right."

"So stop it."

"Okay."

I stopped kicking the soil. I considered the prints baked in after the last rain. All kinds of things had passed this road so odd in form their maker could not be imagined. Don't kick the dust Uncle would warn, and then another warning.

"Always watch your back, Son."

I turned and looked behind me. Nothing there, but the road bent so you could not see too far ahead or behind, and once I looked back and thought a shadow tried the road with its toe. It immediately receded into the forest again, if it ever were at all. I called out Gelidii's name then, but nothing called back. How could he have just left like that, so that now I walked alone?

Because Picarin do not like roads, abhor things of man.

The road was young, but already the forest had encroached upon it wherever it could. An eerie feeling hung over all of it, that feeling of being watched. For so long I had wanted to be on this road, but now just wanted to come to the end of it. I walked all that day and saw nothing else, and when I passed where I thought I'd seen the beasts running across, I found only absurdly large vulture-like tracks. It was near the end of the first day. I decided to sleep in the safety of the forest.

Just before dusk I was notching arrows into the trees pointing the way back out. I could not help but feel more comfortable in the jungle. At the edge of a small clearing I used the blade to fashion supports which I lashed to boughs high off the ground. Before dusk I had settled in beneath my blanket. I had a gourd of water, and when dusk turned to dark ate some roots and a moonbulb too, just so the night would not blind me. I waited for the forest to illuminate. Darting eyes ran in the shadows below. Curling in my blanket I held the blade, and wondered, as I so often had, how this life had brought me here, why again I had been created alone. "Go to sleep" I whispered. "Just go to sleep."

I awoke to perfect dark. The night still and starless. The moon had not risen yet and at first I could hear nothing, not even crickets. Unfortunately, with no moon, the moonbulbs brought no illumination. Somehow, their magic depended on at least a crescent floating in the sky. And so I blinked and saw little, and just then heard a low and distant murmur of falling water far and away…but approaching. The oncoming swell of sound followed the road, and I could measure in heartbeats the shaking of the tree as it grew close. One sweating hand twisted in the locks of my wild hair, the other gripped the blade as I lay trembling with fear behind the thick growth of leaves-- the veil of my life's keeping.

At last they charged past, a river of grunts and huffs and howls consuming the road. I began to pray as I'd not done in a very long time.

"Do not let them find me."

I tried to remember the names of the highest gods of compassion for the protection of the weak and the defenseless and the traveler. I recited them beneath my breath. For some unknown reason, one member of the murderous herd broke from the stampede just where I had stepped off. Soon I could see it, with its long arms and hunched back, tracing the path I had made. It seemed to even trace a finger on one of my arrows. It began to crawl and sniff the ground. Soon it emerged in the clearing and stood.

I had to think. You always had to think. It looked hungry and vicious and I had to think. So, I tried to estimate how long it would take to climb down and meet it, catch it off guard and kill it. I did not want it howling up at me stuck in a damned tree. I did not want it calling back the pack. Suddenly, the night brightened. The crescent moon had arisen in the east. The beast sniffed along, more nervous now that its brethren had run so far ahead. Still, one howl, and I'd be done for. I gave it a deadline: a sliver of starlight over the shadowed ground. If it crossed that, I would climb down quietly holding the blade in my teeth.

For reasons I do not truly understand, it turned just before this occurred, and bayed as it joined the pack, running off to its own destiny. Before dawn, by some grace not yet accounted for, I fell asleep again.

The next day I considered the bizarre procession of tracks that covered the road. No particular species, just a motley collection of beasts running together. Perhaps such unnatural behavior was a symptom of the road -- a scar too strange for nature to understand. Deciding to ignore it, I left that morning slinging my gear -- a collection of roots and dried greens and berries and a remnant or two from Selador that had survived the trip thus far -- up on my shoulder. All of this I had wrapped in the worn but strong wool blanket of red, the most precious of colors, that my friend had given to me. I often wondered how he explained the absence of it to his parents. It was a silly thing to be concerned with, but I was wrestling with the issue of when truth becomes sin.

Under tyrannical rule, a simple truth can become dangerous if spoken. Aunty always said you cannot defend truth with a sword to your throat. Certainly, he could not tell his parents that he had aided a fugitive. At least I hoped not. I invented stories for him in my mind: a thief took it from the sill; it had been left behind for a lunch in the field by the waterfall with her. What was her name? I forget. She could be his wife by now, but she had not grown up in Selador and so I forget her name. Of course, they would have gone right back for it. A candle burned it and he buried it. Why keep the ash? So many different stories. But a blanket was a precious thing. What could he have said to them after all? In time I would stop making stories for it, but every time I wrapped in the blanket I wondered, even for a flicker of a moment, at his burden. There was the truth and there was everything else.

That next morning, to the southwest, a cloud of dust appeared above the road. A procession was definitely approaching. I broke a little ways into the bush and then climbed high up to invisibility, traveling through the tree crowns so my scent could not be tracked. They would not see me until I wanted them to.

My hand trembled against the tree bark I clung to. My face sweated into the long locks of hair I had neglected for months. As if summoning a sleeper from a long dream the shouts rose from the approaching dust. They would be just around the bend. People. I had wondered if there were any more on the earth.

First came a pack of woodhounds, creatures I knew too well, trotting forward on light chains, their faces vicious as always, but then came a creature I had never seen before. In Selador horses were unknown. We had chickens and goats, but no horses and no person ever rode the back of a beast. This would be laughed at. When I first saw the men riding horses all draped in armor I thought them a single creature, something even more deadly than woodhounds. The breastplate of the horse was covered in spikes. The helmets of the men who rode them had horns affixed. They looked so much the beast.

At the forefront of the men a rider on a white horse shouted and the walkers all halted. On all were expressions of defeat and fear. The soldiers, the bowmen and beasts, the wagons and lancers, all stopped and waited quietly as the cloud of red earth settled. One near the front bore an insignia inked in red and gold on a field of white cloth: a lion with wings and the claws of an eagle. For a chilling moment, the leader stared right into the treetops where I hid and squinted and the woodhounds began to howl about him and pull taut their chains. There were no women. All the men, fifty at least, were plainly exhausted. Something had broken in them all. Their eyes betrayed their spirits.

I knew the danger, but what could they fear of me? What could they want of me? I had nothing, offered no threat, was no enemy. I would walk with them to the escarpment and turn north and they south. And I could help them find food and they could help me walk the road and that would be the end of it.

Still, once the white rider called again I watched them pass, an armed train of pain and heat and fear. I almost let them go. I should have let them go, but then I climbed down the tree and over the wall of deadfalls and with my bare feet running on the red earth called out to the last of the train: "Wait!"

The whole train stopped and turned and looked back at me. The haze of red dust made it all seem like a mirage. They looked at me as if I were a hallucination. The white rider from the front came back and lifted an arm in ragged armor and lowered a lance to my throat: "Halt!"

What? But I had approached them.

"Halt!"

Fear permeated his voice, and I did not understand this at all. The troops stood in stunned exhaustion, their eyes covered in dust. Some wore rags over their mouths. I could see now many bore wounds, and I could see the blood brown and dry through the wrappings. On the wagon lay men missing parts of legs.

"Halt!" the white rider cried again although I had not moved anywhere. "Archers!" he cried. Men flanked either side of him and nocked arrows and drew them and pointed them all at me. And I wondered still if this were not some single, monstrous creature, but then the horse coughed and the man shouted to those behind: "A man! A man walks the road! A man walks upon the road!" he repeated senselessly, and others, aghast, cried this simple fact back through the lines as if all their lives hinged on its knowing.

At least they knew I was only a man, but when the rider of the white horse kicked it forward, his teeth were clenched. A fresh wound ran across his left eye which would probably never open full again. His breath sounded like he nursed a punctured lung. He lowered the lance towards my chest. "A man walks upon the road!" he yelled as loud as he could and then coughed.

Two woodhounds could take down a full-grown tiger they say, and the jaws could rip a man's arm clean off. These pulled at their chains and grumbled. Behind the leader, the whole troop drew weapons except for the dismembered men who lay in the still wagons. It seemed absurd, their precautions. Even Gelidii could not draw a blade against such a force.

The knight kicked his horse forward. The tip of his lance reached the shade of the tree under which I stood. I could see the imperfections in the iron tip and waited.

Everyone waited.

And then he on the white horse squinted at me in disbelief. "What… what is this?" he asked incredulously. "What are you now?" And I did not know what to say.

He shook his head roughly. Red dust flew from his leather helmet, its insignia a white hawk with eight talons. "What *are* you?"

"I'm lost," I said. "I've been lost a long time. I'm a man, just a man and I'm lost."

He turned briefly back to his company as if they could help him understand. "Here? You are lost here? You're a man, but lost *here*?"

"Yes."

He laughed without joy.

"No man walks here alone. None." He shook his head as if I were not real. "So what are you truly? Tell us this and your life as you know it might be spared."

"I've…I'm a…I said what I am, what I have been. Lost. Just lost, a long, long time lost. I've been living off the forest in a tree which I made my home amongst flowers. But at last I wanted to find people again and walked until this road ran before me like a blessing. Then you found me, saved me, and that's it."

He was terrified of me and tried to laugh to show he was not. He began shaking his head insistently. "No man, none, walks this road alone! Half of us are chopped, eaten, poisoned or picked out in the night by beasts made not by God, and here before us stands a man nearly naked and thin with the jungle growing out of every pore and he say he's from a tree!"

He nudged the horse forward another step. At this distance the lance could split my throat.

"In a tree," I corrected.

"Spirits live in trees."

"No, not like that. In the branches. I was lost."

"Just how was it you became so lost in this life to walk in so evil a place?"

"We were hunting on new grounds. I tracked a quail and didn't know the area. It started raining, hard. You couldn't see three paces forward, and it rained so fast and hard and it had been so dry the ground swelled with new rivers. I couldn't cross what had just been a dry gulley of sand. I should have waited, but followed it to look for a crossing, but it only got wider and the rain fell more and maybe they were looking for me, but in the other way. It was a new area and after the rain I couldn't see anything I knew. I was lost. All lost."

"What did you hunt with?"

"Bow."

"Where's it?"

"It… lost it swimming a river."

"You're lying."

"I am not."

The small army thickened behind him in a crescent. The man on the white horse squinted deeper. "Just what are you in league with?"

"What?"

"Lie now and you die. What demon has aided you to walk in these parts, or is it…is it you who are the demon?"

"I'm no demon. I just want to get to a village, to leave the forest."

"You are in league with something to be out here like this. No man can survive this jungle long when alone like you. What's lying in wait for us? Speak the truth and you may live."

"Understand, I hid a lot. I slept in trees, in caves. I made no fire at night. I got lucky."

"You're nervous."

"I'm terrified."

The soldier on the white horse shook his head. "No man gets this lost," he said as if cursing. I could draw the blade in a breath. I could take him. His army would kill me afterwards, but I would have gotten him at least. I waited, looking helpless and hopeful. I waited for him to understand but he did not. He then brutally kicked his heels into the sides of his horse, and just as he thrust the spear towards my chest I drew the blade with fantastic speed, and just before the seventh arc of the morning dew landed, the tip of the lance fell off, and then another of its length. A shadow had draped between us. And as the horse charged forward, its muzzle was sliced clean away and the shadow which dropped from the tree above us severed its head in degrees, yet the legs of the horse kept charging until the remnant of its head hung by ligaments. The unseeing eyes stared vacantly, swinging from the carcass that stood even in death. Then the light of life faded and the white horse collapsed completely as its front legs folded to its knees, and then it all fell and I remember a plume of red dust. This all happened in a moment.

The man was screaming. At first he had been struck to silence, but now he screamed for his hands had been severed at the wrists and he did not understand how his hands had fallen away so cleanly and quickly, and I remember the fingers clutching the air and the blood on the ground mixing with that of the horse. And the man screamed and screamed and behind him the whole of the army froze in shock or terror or both. Draping from the tree, in my defense, hung Gelidii. The captain slipped in his own blood as he tried to stand. He wept as he tried to scream. At last his words found air: "He's in league! He's in league! In league!"

He pointed a stump to the Picarin who hung upside down by a toe. The blade of the drinking bird, child of the crescent moon, shone lightless in its hand.

I don't know how he bled so much. I never would have thought a man could have so much blood. And still the dying man sobbed and had grown so pale now and kept saying what he had suspected and he writhed against the headless carcass of the horse as if to get some comfort from it. And he cried tears and cried out again the same assertion as if to prove before his passing that at least he was correct.

"He's in league! He's in league!"

I would learn that Gelidii had been following me through the treetops and along the hidden paths of the Picarin. It never occurred to me to ask him why, but I remember the first time Uncle pretended to let me hunt alone. I was seven I think, and went as a warrior to the woods well beyond his land, pretending not to notice the man who crouched behind a boulder just a moment too late.

The commander fainted at last, soon bleeding out the last of a life from where had once been hands that had taken so many. A terrific stillness overcame him I remember. He died in the dust. The red deepened.

"Was a slain god that made the body of this world."

Gelidii dropped out of the tree and in all the terror of his form and many of the soldiers had to look away, and it surprised me how for so long no one moved. Perhaps, in part, because no one told them to.

An especially thin soldier, of no apparent rank or authority, from somewhere in the middle of the terrified ranks raised his arm and pointed a shaking finger at Gelidii. I remember his face, young and covered in the red dust of the road. I remember thinking he had a certain bravery to cry out like that when all others were silent. And I remember thinking how his voice held the tremble of a frightened child. He had a name for what he saw. He cried the name three times: "Trawl! Trawl! Trawl!"

Books were rare and precious in the time and place of his youth. His grandmother, a woman of considerable wealth, owned three, but the only one he truly loved had etchings in vivid colors by an artist of some fame. The boy loved this book so much he asked his Granmama to read it to him over and over again, every time he was at her house, and the grandmother always would, (the boy knew he was her favorite), but made him promise not to be a naughty boy, or a filthy boy, or a lazy one. "I won't, Granmama," he would say to her and smile and he had those large round eyes that she adored too much and saw her husband in them but young and beautiful and reborn. She would tell him to go wash his hands while she retrieved the precious book if he wanted to help her turn the pages.

This book did not have all the words of the others: dull stories of heroes and kings and such, or lessons on how to be a good man, or lessons on farming and building and growing and law; but rather, this book, to which the boy's heart had instilled a kind of magic, told of those creatures the world hid in its unchartered corners, of beasts and half-beasts spotted by the rare explorer undaunted by the distances between lands, or the harshness and periodic despair which must accompany the life of adventure.

Each page had a bright painted picture of a beast none could imagine (and so they must be true) and beneath each depiction, the artist wrote the name of the subject: The Tusked Oliphant, the White Tiger, The Sea Serpent of Leviathan, The Great Behemoth of the Mountains, or the boy's favorite: The Dragon. Its eyes glowed with fire. The image held such immensity and strength the artist had dedicated two pages to it, right in the center of the book. It slept in the cave of a mountain whose place none knew, with its great tail curled against the length of its body and one eye open, staring out at the reader: a symbol of eternal vigilance. The boy had read and re-read this book so many times he could open right to any page he so chose. He could tell you just how many spikes ran down the spine of the great dragon and how many teeth laced the jaw of Leviathan.

And one day, as he held the book, he smiled up at her with eyes so gentle and precious she had to hug him, and he asked, "Are dragons real Granmama?"

"Yes, my Love, I think they are."

"Where do they live?"

She said she thought they lived in the sea, and not to go looking for them.

"But I want to see a dragon, Granmama."

"Nothing's as good as it seems in a book, my little Dove, and besides, do you want to make your poor Granmama cry that her dove has flown away without a care for her?"

"No."

"And do you want cinnamon and clover tea?"

"Yes!"

"Then be a good boy and leave dragons alone. I made biscuits too, dear one ."

He kicked his chubby legs with delight.

Yet, the boy always wanted to skip the next creature. He hesitated before turning the yellowed page now that he was alone in the room. He stared down at it: the shade-man, the abomination lurking in a yellow land with the eyes of the dead staring up from the page as long as the reader dared stare back. And by some trick of the artist, no matter what the angle of the book, those eyes, round and hungry and enormous, followed you, as if searching for something in you that it lacked.

The boy had had more than one troubled dream of this creature lifting itself from the page and growing to full size, though not so large, even small for a man, but real now in the dream and leaning over his sleeping body. The shadow thing always did the same act: it ran the tips of its long fingers gently down his face while whispering something to his sleeping ear. And once he awoke and felt the fingers yet, and once he awoke and heard the voice whispering yet, and always he awoke crying after this dream but never told his mother why because then she would not allow him to read the book again. He was sure of that.

Of this creature alone nothing was written, just the name of the species, scrawled across the bottom of the page like a curse: Troll.

And it were as if the soldiers needed a name for the thing for it to be killed. Upon the pronouncement of the type of beast they faced, the archers lined before it. "Archers draw!" screamed one and the row of men nocked arrows and aimed them at our hearts.

I wanted to run, but as if he read my mind, Gelidii spoke calmly, "Run not, Youmann. To run is for to die. Stay."

I could hear their bowstring tendons stretching. "Let Fly!" cried the new commander.

And the arrows sprang at us and Gelidii turned them all to splinters. He lowered his arms to his sides again.

A voice cried again: "Nock twice and let fly!"

A shower of splinters. "Let Fly! Let fly at will! Kill them!"

Gelidii had such skill that he could stop an arrow by stabbing it in the tip with the dagger. When the archers emptied their quivers to no avail, the horsemen came forward. Lances and spears and long swords all lowered at us, and I wanted so badly to run.

"Stay, Youmann. To leave is for to die," Gelidii said again, and I listened and watched as the horses and horsemen fell to slivers as they entered the reach of the Picarin and I was screaming.

They let loose the dogs and when a woodhound lunged at me, I split it right up its belly with the first arc of the white day. The second one to hurl itself at me lost first its forelegs and then its head. The blade screamed through them as I defended my life. A loud crack split next to my left ear. Gelidii had broken the path of a spear hurled straight at my skull, and the soldiers rushed in crying madly and I was screaming.

I do not like to recount this day, but it should be told and soon bodies of men and beasts lay like the ruined petals of a macabre flower and I was screaming.

And the moment the soldier who had called it "Trawl" faced it and died, his mother, half a world away, began to cry.

As the assault continued, they died in turn at the hand of Gelidii and they would not stop the attack and I was screaming, the same petition over and over again until my voice went raw.

"No, Gelidii! No!"

But it was true he had not taken a single step. Every soldier had run to his death and Gelidii had neither approached, challenged, nor provoked them. But I still hated him now somehow, and worse, feared him in a way I never had. Yet, it was unfair to hate the Picarin, but here was what they called a troll killing men who looked not so unlike me, and I hated Gelidii for that.

The battle ended to a terrific silence. The evidence of my own sickly victory lay at my feet in the bloodied coats of dogs split to pieces. Gelidii looked very tired. It was late morning and he should have been asleep. He leapt over the wall of the dead and, kneeling, wiped the blades on a patch of moss and hummed very gently as he did this. He then returned the stones to the small of his back, and I was shaking very badly. "Youmann," he said, "must for go now. Wind will tell of this." One of the near-dead groaned, and Gelidii did not notice or care. "Youmann, is must for going now. Much blood in wind. In forest goes scent. We must for going now. Things already to this place come."

But I stood stunned at the number of the dead. Stunned at this thing, this troll, how it had killed a league of humans without a second thought or regret. Its face hung as indifferent as ever, and he asked me for a magic word.

"What? What? A magic word?"

"Is a word for making Youmann do what other wish. Is word of strong magic."

"There is no word. There is no magic. How could you just kill them all like that?" I asked, exasperated, and he did not answer.

He scratched his head. "Youmann has word for making Youmann do what speaker of word begs." He was trying to recall this incantation. "Much come here for feed on dead. Must for to going." Then his eyes widened. "Please!" Gelidii exclaimed. "Please for going! Please for much comes and is closer now." Gelidii squatted down and considered the moss before tentatively tugging his ear again. He suddenly looked quickly to the west from which direction he heard something I could not. "Youmann," he said again more impassionedly, "please, please hear Gelidii now. Bad things come. Youmann and Picarin must now for going."

Then, as the final groaning men died of their wounds, I began to laugh, for I suddenly realized that nothing was real. I laughed at how I had been fooled for so long. I kicked the severed head of a woodhound I'd killed and it rolled away and it was a game and everything was a game. No way a single sickly tree troll could kill so many soldiers. No way would so many soldiers rush headlong to their deaths. All a game. A test. Life was a dream and the only question was whether or not I was the dreamer or the dreamt. Maybe both. A soldier's face had been removed with a single cut. How hilarious. I skipped along and trotted to Gelidii. "Okay, then, my friend! Let's go!"

I smiled, stepping through the dead and the dying. Half a man tried to grab my ankle as I stepped over him, begging a sip of water, and I began to laugh more at how ridiculous it had all become. We went a long ways from that place before my laughter died. By that night I shook very badly. "There's so much blood in things," I said Gelidii. "Why do we need so much blood?"

"Youmann should go for sleeping now. Gelidii watch all blue day as it pass."

It were as if he cast a spell, for suddenly an exhaustion overcame me. "It's not over yet, Gelidii," I said, my eyes half closing, not knowing what that meant. In my dreams a dead soldier asked why I walked with a troll. I told him I had been lost.

In the morning we set out and when we came to a creek Gelidii set his blades in them, claiming they had to cool. I set mine in too. I tried to wash it all away. But things like that never go away. Gelidii was cautious. He did not like this place and after a time urged we set out again. In two more days we caught glimpses of the escarpment: a long low cloud of gray which pushed against the very sky. "How high is it?" I asked him.

Gelidii pointed to the top of the escarpment. "Is that high."

"It's higher than the clouds. How can that be?"

"Is no for climbing."

"No?"

"Sad is way through the rift."

"It can't be much sadder than the road."

"Sad sad is way. Face of moon fade. Go not into shadow pass when no moon be. One night must Youmann sleep in there. Darkness only attend you and sun not rise with morning. Must be way of pass, but go not when no moon be."

"All right."

"Stay on the path."

"I know."

"Go not from path."

"I know, you told me already. Many times."

"Youmann must not go from path."

"I won't."

"Them no weep for. Them no real."

'All right. Who?"

"Strike them not."

"Who?"

Gelidii's voice was ominous. "Shades."

And I asked him what he had found when he had gone through the rift but he would not respond.

Closer, the escarpment loomed like a second sky, its height incomprehensible. With great hesitation he led me one last time to the road, but would not go on it. He pointed hesitantly to the north, in the direction of the path of the shadow, to my destination.

I stepped onto the road with feet now always bare and hardened. "Goodbye, Gelidii," I said a second and final time. "I have to go now."

When I looked up he was still there, but his gaze turned back to the jungle. He did not look at me ever again and said no more words, but having given me his final direction turned and faded into the leaves. It was an astoundingly simple goodbye, but as I walked away I listened closely to the bird song and late-morning cricket chirp, to the blossoming forest awakening with the day, and among the chorus of voices I thought there was a final petition in the voice of a Picarin, the repeated utterance of a single word he had said to me so many times before.

Stay.

The road began to narrow. Soon, it hardly existed at all. Prints of every kind crossed it and some few I could identify and many I could not. While looking for a suitable place to stop for the evening, I saw the print of the true monster, that which specifically hunted humans as prey. Even in Selador we knew of these, and lost people to them. I had been warned of this, had seen drawings of its print too many times not to know. I knelt down and ran my fingers through this deep recess in the earth. Each of the five toes had a claw mark in the front, but the little toe curled out like a hooked thumb. That was how you knew for sure. That called you to run home, to leave the place of the beast. I whispered its name to the wind and shuddered at it: ogre. Damned ogre. No wonder Gelidii hated these woods. Running my finger in the indentation I remembered a man who had come to the tavern with eyes the color of milk.

He was unkempt, not filthy, just unkempt. He was not old, but older. He appeared one who did the minimum of what had to be done to maintain what had to be maintained, yet I'd learn that in his life he had sought his fortune well beyond Selador in the service of war or trade. Anselm had said to make his a good pour and give him three before charging and then only ask the money for one. When I set the cup before him he did not lift it, but when rain began to pelt the tavern roof he took it up and drank half in a single pull and set it down with a clack. "Is raining again," he said.

"Yes it is," I said. His lips trembled again to the cup. He bit down another.

Everyone had their own way of drinking. I'd learned that. Some tended a drink as a patient nurse, coaxing it over their tongues to let it roll down the palate and warm them slowly. These people didn't care about drinking, were often gentle in manner and rare in the tavern after the serving of food. For them, a drink was a nearly pointless thing, an occasional social practice as easily finished as begun.

Some waited outside every morning, even on the coldest days of rain, and grew giddy as we swung the doors. With that first sip they always closed their eyes, and when they swallowed, they sighed, although I don't think they ever really knew it. It was such an unintentional thing it could not so much be heard as seen, once you knew to look for it. It was as if the one sip had doused a small but constant fire within, and after enough sips they looked like one saved from drowning. These had it bad, this kind, but when they had had enough, and then more than enough, for some few moments they would laugh as freely as they must have done once as children. This is what they came for most. That is what we sold.

But the man of the clouded eyes took his drink as a thing to be conquered, a thing to be resolved. His type took little joy in drink; they just insisted on it. And his kind never, ever cheated you. When he spoke to me again he was well drunk.

"They snatch you, take you up like a little bird being pecked outta the world, and when they do there's nothin' no thing what for yours to do." He sipped and swallowed. "And you'll be a-screaming sure enough, for they never takes you full on the throat and there's a reason for that. Then theys drags you out."

"Stop scaring the kid," Anselm yelled from across the hall.

"He no kid!" he said. "You 'fraid a stories, young fella?"

"Nope."

"There!" He yelled at Anselm and slammed the cup down again.

Anselm grumbled red-faced and went down into the cellar. The old man dipped his finger in the brew and licked the droplet from the tip. "They just take yah out. Comin as quiet as a moth popping outta the dark and they lifts you like a little bird foxed off the nest. And you be screaming but they don't hear no screams. Flaps a fat on the sides a their thick fuckin' heads is all they haves for ears. If they 'ave ears at all. Pigmen I'm talking a now. Pigmen. God never made them." He bit down another swallow.

"They ain't beasts. It would be just out wrong to call them as such. These things, they empty, some kinda fungus that happens grew outta the rotten part-a the earth. And they hunt the human, Boy, 'cause they looking for that missing part." He turned his eyes away to the cup. "We're their favorite to hunt and there nothin' to do if they even scratch you, such a poison runs in their blood. You'll die of black blood inside a week if theys even scratch yah. No exceptions for that. Even met a trader once in the East who by means known only to him and God had collected the drool of the beast. Sold it in vials. Poison for the arrows of war. You too busy for this?"

"No."

"If you've other matters to attend…"

"No, it's fine. It's quiet tonight." The boy sat across from the man with the clouded eyes.

"We'd all been quite happy a moment before, hopefuls in finding gold in a river to the west promised rich with dust." He took another bite of his drink. "There was twelve in our band. All good men. All to be trusted, for thats was my first rule. Then, just in the middle of it all, dinner and laughs and a little drink, this pigman, by some ordained foulness in the passing of an ill star, this thing, what they call 'Ogre,' reaches its tusked jaw outta that darkness and locks him by the shoulder. Twelve of us and it falls on him, this finest of young men, and just lifts him right out and my my how he screams! God help us!" He wiped a tear away. "Like you never heard a man scream. But this pigman, it makes no noise. Its mouth as wide as your chest. We was as brave as any but weapons just bounce off 'em. Our lances doin' nothin' and arrows splitting off its back and it just heads off with him, dragging and screaming. It retreats into the darkness which bore it. And there were nothing, nothing to be done for it. Nothin'."

When he took his cup again his hand shook.

"We were as brave as any, but we wouldn't go chasing it into that dark. No, no. It were as quick as a deer and gone and gone. Let it go. Let him go. Nothing to be done for it and that was the simple truth. There's the truth and there's everything else." He drank.

"Near morning -- none of us could sleep in a place like that -- we hear this terrible scream from the valley over. The moist air carries it right to us and we knew what it done. This scrawny fellow, brave but scrawny, had just put some more wood to the fire and says it: "That's a limb it's taken from him.""

He emptied the cup and the boy went to refill it, but he held his wrist and he stayed.

"And he's tellin' it true. It takes a week for the pigman to eat you. They pick you apart limb by limb by limb and staunch the openings with a kind of maggot to eats away at the rot. They want the heart moving, you see. Fresh meat. And is the heart they want most and last and is said they savor to eat it living, for they believes it houses that missing part they wish to get: the soul."

He let his wrist go and the boy filled his cup again and sat with him again and took no more money. It was a quiet night in the tavern. "There were a fellow named Will and you may know him or some of his family for they're from hereabouts. Famous for his skill with the bow. Was said he could shoot the circling swallow in the darkened loft. Now, he's got two arrows left and says he only need one and suggests a small party go to finish it, and I would say they don't make men brave as that anymore, but they do.

"'I'll track it for you,' says the scrawny fellow. 'I been trackin' since I could walk. Not that a blind man couldn't track something as that,' he says and stares into the fading dark. 'Was my friend he took. I take you right to its nest. I promise yuh that.'"

"It's us three then. And we go out at first light with the earth still soft from passing rains and soon find a splatter of blood, then a whole lot of it near a deadfall ripped half open. Them maggots all crawlin' within and swimmin' in the blood. Eatin' it up. Drowin' in it like little fat gluttons. So heres it ripped somethin' offa him and stuffs these things in the hole." He finished his cup with a shaking hand. The boy got him another and the man stared into the liquid set before him. "Could ya imagine such a thing? What kinds of beast would do as such to another creature? So we follow them blood drips 'til the trail stopped but there still that footprint. You'd know it easy: humanish, but real real big and that last toe hooked. Heel like a saucer and what kinda beast would do a thing like that? Be so damned cruel like that?"

He took a long pull and set the cup down hard on the table. "Anyway, soon the whole forest starts getting darker in a way I can't really describe. It were the mid of day, but still there this murky kind of reasonless dark. I don't know. Can't describe it right. It's a thing you'd need to see yourself but may you never. No birds singing. Ground all soft and rotten like. Leaves withered. Nothing talkin'. Just a shade over it all. Made you want to walk right away. Made ya scared in a way a child is scared of things for no reason. Will just held really quiet and steady and that scrawny fellow he shaking but never faltered. Good types the both of them.

"We get a smell of that coppery stink a blood rot. We's close to it now. Have followed where few men ever did, if any. Whole damned forest just sorta die. We come before this mound and Will the first atop and kneels and signals for quiet. We crest and there we see it -- the house at the pigman. A mockery of what a natural man might make. Just a heap a logs leaning one against the other. Mud stuffed in the cracks. Clutches a grass atop. About the whole place hangs a blood-blackened death. Not a damned living thing popping out the ground for a hundred paces in all directions and there was bones I remember, and pieces a green limb with uneaten meat scattered here and there in waste. No beast would do that. There's your ogre. We didn't have no plan. Sometimes that's the best way.

"Well, Will nocks an arrow and I'm thinking, does he see something I don't, and then he draws it and I'm looking and don't see nothing at all and then, without no one sayin' a word mind you, Will draws it back but there still nothing to be seen but that pile a mossy logs and that door a shadow. And no one says nothing until that scrawny fellow stands right up and yells, 'Come out now, Brother, we got an arrow for yah!'

"My blood goes cold. All's quiet but then something falls over inside that house and there's a ripping sound and then there he come, hopping out on his one last leg, an arm gone, and them maggots all fat and yellow swimmin' in the openings...and then...Lord, you shoulda seen him...and then..." Now the man began to openly weep. "His skin as green as a damned pigman and he lunges towards us and turns his chest out and his eyes damned near stuck closed with yellow pus and I didn't..." Here, he took a long draw from his drink. "I didn't even hear no arrow fly, but before he hit the ground it goes right in his heart. Right in the perfect center of it. May God bless him. Will lands it so perfect. I never seen such a shot. The feathers they lifting with the last few beats his heart ever would take and we wait for it, wait until he all at peace. He wasn't alone in his passing." The old man wiped his eyes. "He all at peace then."

"If the thing were in there, it didn't wake or know or care. Nothing gave chase right away and maybe not at all. Might be they sleep in the day. I don't know, but near halfway back to camp Will thinks he hears a bellow but he not sure. We going fast as we could and I the slowest but they wouldn't go ahead. When back we smear the ashes on all us to douse the scent and head fast north to finish our prospecting and it were true: The river had dust of gold. Plenty of it. More than a twelfth portion we gives to his wife and child. She remarried now." He stood unsteadily. "Tell Anselm his brew too weak."

He left another coin for the boy and waved his hand at nothing in particular as he walked out. It wasn't until he left that Anselm came back from the cellar carrying nothing. He sat just where the man had and shook his head. "I been too long in this tavern to hear another story of how a man loses a son," he said.

That night I made no fire. I slept as high in a tree as I dared. I slept above where any predatory thing could reach me. The very next day, following that terrible road, I saw the shadow on the path.

It wound through the ribbon of trees leading to the escarpment as if somebody had draped a swath of darkness through it, and this was the way I knew I had reached the path. A faint air of sickness came from its direction. I did not want to leave the road then, but I did.

It was like stepping into sudden night and the trees began to look twisted and sickened. The ground was soft. Black water oozed between clumps of yellow moss. I heard no bird call, no insect; there was no wind. Between the fingers of the canopy I did not see the sky, only the escarpment rising to the heavens.

I could only hear the pressing of my feet, my breath, the whispered petitions of my prayers. Then, just as Gelidii had said, the shadow ran into a fissure which broke through the wall. Not a cave, but a maw that began in the ground and ran right to the height of the escarpment, dividing it completely. It was darker within and the last place in the world I wanted to go.

I drew the blade. *Stay on the path.* At the entrance, on a stone to the right, someone had scratched a message in very old lettering: "Have all your gods abandoned you?"

I entered then what I think only can be described as the land of the dead. The light suddenly fell to the gray-green of rotted flesh, and the air poisoned each breath rather than restoring the body. Upon stepping in completely terror overwhelmed me. I put my hand over my heart. *Stay on the path.* Inside, the maw widened. The blighted land ran unevenly to the walls and in them crevices hinted at hidden caves going to who knows where. I peered into the shadows to see if something dwelled within, and though I at first saw nothing, I immediately tightened my grip on the blade.

I suppose nature will never be entirely defeated. Some sickly grass lived within somehow, some few twisted trees, a species I had never seen, mocked life in their standing. Above, the twisting flowstone walls ran up and up and shielded the sky. Light itself seemed to shun the place, falling gray and half dead. Water dripped down and echoed into the stillness. It was the Valley of Death, and I walked on. "How can there be a place beyond the reach of God?" I uttered with hand over heart. My words reverberated into the caves. *Stay on the path.* I wept.

Deeper into the Valley of Death, voices began to murmur from the walls, and then a mound of yellow rags, tucked lifelessly in a crevice, poked a pumpkin-like head up and its terrible voice exploded into the silence. It sounded joyful.

"Hello!" it cried, lumbering too swiftly towards me, "Hello! My my, hello!" It ran in a knee-locked swagger. It was horribly, unthinkably quick. A hood covered its filthy, enormously bloated head, a head like a swollen gourd, and I readied the blade of the drinking bird.

"Well well well!" it cried, trotting across the black earth. "My oh my, how delightful and sweet you are! A Visitor. Welcome!" An arm larger than a man's leg lifted in salute. Briefly I saw the flesh of its hand and wanted to run.

"Welcome to the pass!" cried the lumbering pile of rags and flesh. "Welcome, Lovely One! We are glad you came!" I would first cut its gut. Yellow-toothed and fanged, it continued to speak like a

94

madness from a dream. "Welcome, our sweet bird! Welcome to the wondrous pass!"

It leapt over the black boulders and pools of fetid water. Its shoulders rocked in a locked manner. It was easily the weight of three men, and I knew this was no man. "Hello! Hold now!" it cried out again. I did not move. It charged to the edge of the path. "Ho Ho! Look at you now, so glad so glad and glad. Hold now! You are going the wrong way. Hold!"

It reeked so terribly that I held my ragged shirt over my nose. It caught its breath at the path's edge and laughed as no man ever would. It pointed at me and I stood frozen in terror. "Hello!" it said again. "Come now." It waved me to it, to the sick dead grass and the caves which led to pits of unthinkable darkness. "Come this way now! Come with me, little bird. I will not hurt you!" It cackled in a seizure and its hood partly lifted and offered a glimpse of that awful face, the big green chalk-toothed smile. The mouth spread so wide it split the skull. "Dearest friend, why the long, long path?" It waved at it dismissively. "The long path is not the way. Come and I'll show you the good way. Better way. This, here, follow the wall and there will be no ghosts."

And I began to fall out, though I had not in a long, long time. The mewl of its voice. The immensity. The reeking air.

"The way you go is bad and bad." It shook its pendulous head. "Come to the cave, Friendling. Good things await you in the cave. You do not see them yet. Come. I am the keeper of the pass. The way goes under. It runs beneath the ghosts. Be not afraid."

It reached out its hand, but I noted it would not extend it over the path. I walked forward. I would have to walk right beside it. At this, the thing slammed its hand on its knee and laughed long and pointlessly. "Good. Come now! Come the good way!"

It was a moment of sublime terror and faith when I passed within its reach. I had the blade lifted. I turned, walking backwards so as not to put my back to it. Once I cleared it, it stamped the ground and ran to catch up to me. And it charged up, but when it came to the path, it leapt over it and now stood on my left. "Where do you go now? Stay! Come." It leapt over the path again and ran a few paces back towards its cave and then stopped with mock surprise that I had not followed. "No no. Nothing within will hurt you! Come."

I walked on and it beckoned me back. "No no. Follow me to the underway. The warm cave." It trotted back to the side of the path and I just walked swiftly on. "Stop. Stop. Please stop," it begged me. "Why don't they believe me ever and ever?" It spoke to nothing. "Why do they always go the way of the dead. Please, good friend, I want to be your friend. The path is dark and the cave is warm. Let me guide you. Let me take you to the cave. Please let me take you to the cave. Please let me take you under. Please, I want to show…her…to you."

And I just kept walking quickly away, looking at it only to know it could not reach me. It trotted beside me laughing, begging and weeping. "Imagine this: Ogre rapes woman! Ha ha! Imagine woman has ogre's baby, half-ogre, half-woman! So, ogre rapes woman and woman has half-ogre baby and ogre baby bites woman one day and woman dies this day. Ogre baby brings woman to cave and wraps her in precious leaves and woman is part of cave now. Come now. Nothing dies in the cave."

Even though exhausted beyond all reason, I began to run. It lumbered beside the path and told and retold its story. Over and again it begged for me to understand. But soon its voice began to fade. Soon, it followed no more.

I went ahead into the greater dark. I longed to be back in the forest of Gelidii, cutting arcs beside the fast river, offering whispered prayers to the sacred moon. And though what lay ahead urged me to turn back, the thought of passing this way again pressed me forward.

A creek trickled beside the path. A dead and dark thing from which none should ever drink. The water ran in a syrupy silence. And I found my provisions had all spoiled, even the water. I left the food to rot further in this rotten world, spilled out my gourd and threw it away too. Two days and one night. Most of it still to come.

Distant howls rose that were neither animal nor human. Occasional creatures scampered in the stones above and I just pressed forward. I don't want to speak much of this. I survived, and that is that. But I should tell of him once, a man, a shade of a man, covered with lacerations. He was seated on a boulder just off the path.

"You found me at last," he said with cold anger. "You came all this way to find me like this." I could not take my eyes from him. When the path circled to the front of him, I saw the face of pure hatred. "Do you like seeing me like this?" he snarled. "You wanted to see me again? This is where I wait. You will be here too, you know. You will join me on this black rock."

And though I had told myself only to keep walking, I spoke to the shade: "You are not him."

It smiled evilly. "I am. You pass here and have awakened me to my suffering."

"You're not him. I know you're not him."

"You know nothing of this kingdom. You hardly know the veil of life from which you come..." and he went on, wetting his hands in his wounds, cursing me and him and promising a falling dark; but he would not leave the rock on which he sat. As I passed it I almost staggered onto the dying grass.

She was naked and already bleeding. She ran up to the path with her hair an unkempt nest and her eyes twisted in mad, euphoric rage and she screamed of death and damnation, and I had known her too. But this was only a shade, some kind of trick of crooked magic. And this shade stopped at the path's edge and began ripping away pieces of its flesh and tossing them wet and bleeding on the path before me. I knew I should not petition it, but I'd loved her once. "Please, please stop!"

She smiled and tore off her lips and laughed and threw these at me, and I cut them with the blade. "Stop," I pleaded again because I had known her once, and she was bleeding out. And I passed on. Her flesh fell behind me.

Already the day felt like a lifetime. Sometimes, it took all of my will just to look back, to watch for something that I was certain followed. Once, a quick figure ducked behind a rock to the left of the path. Let it follow.

When I tell of this place, they want to know how I continued. Simple, there was no other way but through. The thoughts of what I had passed through were more terrible than whatever was to come.

The darkness thickened. The day would end. As Gelidii promised, a great sleep overcame me which could not be resisted. At last, with the shadows now merging into the night, and a rising awful terror in my heart, I sprawled helplessly on the ground and collapsed to dreams of madness.

And just before I slipped away, shadowy beings emerged from the lightless crevices. Hooded men, or demons, or ghosts kneeled beside me on the path, murmuring the promise of soft death as sleep pulled me in. With an effort that rivals any of my life, I draped my hand over my upturned ear.

In the morning that could not be called morning, I awoke feeling a hundred years older. My hair had turned white. It took so long to stop crying, to stop whimpering and find the simple strength to stand. At last, beneath an evil dawn, I took another step forward.

This day brought from the caverns victims of every disease and deformity, of every pain and slaughter ever suffered in the battles of man's inhumanity to man. They begged me for help and walked beside me. Those with missing limbs crawled or shuffled or dragged the remnants of their flesh, each moaning of the cruelty it had suffered, the agony of its wounds, each begging me to come to the crevice or cave from which it emerged to save them. The sick showed their foulest symptoms of disease and would I please follow and save them? The raped showed their mutilations and I should pity them and follow. Children burned, children delimbed, children with cracked skulls and fresh blood begged for me to save them. 'We are so cheated in life' and would I please save them? Step off the path and save them.

I won't say much more of it. Memory fades with the years, but slowly so. I walked the realm of hungry ghosts and left it behind. In the end, a woman emerged from a hollow who knew me once in life, and it could not be and I wept again though I thought I was past all tears. I could not look at her here and started to run. She loped beside me, calling a sound almost like my name. I ran until my lungs burned. I ran with the sick air and the diseased ground and the strength of an old and decrepit man. Her petitions kept falling on me. And I cried to all the gods to help me run away. Ahead, the rift parted wider, and then, like a glorious miracle, a patch of blue sky glowed above.

I kept running with the heavy steps of an old man. Running as the moans faded. Running until I heard them no more and into the light of the natural day. As my feet raced along, I could only stare into a sky not made of stone, a miracle of creation. I ran with eyes fixated on the heavens. I ran until I fell. I fell.

Down and down. Falling and falling into the nothingness.

Falling into the wind.

Below, a land of drifting white. A cloud. Falling into the white of a cloud. But when I met the cloud, it turned to water. And a fast churning river carried me away, collected so many of my tears.

It was easy enough to stay afloat. I could always swim well and even in my sickness I could swim. After a long, cold time, I recall how touching ground at last raised the smallest spark of joy in me. This was strange because a great part of me had hoped to drown. Dragging myself to a sandy bank, I collapsed on the ground and wept among the sweet air and bright sky, beside the wide and lovely river. I had made it across a land few ever would, to a place of tilled fields and peace. But none of that mattered, for in my heart hung only darkness.

BOOK II

Lyden

Lyden

She must be spoken of here. This is not how it happened, not the order of the story, but she must be spoken of here because, well, she just must. Sometimes we rule the pen; sometimes the pen rules us. With the tooth of a dragon secured to my back, a glowing jezeth beneath my fine woven shirt she called to me. I had by then been much restored, but this is not how it happened. Do not let the pages confuse you. A story is told not to be understood, but as to be believed.

Forty days earlier I'd left the last vestige of humanity. Immersed in the wilderness again, I found myself upon a narrow trail that picked up at the end of a road that had no reason. Before too long, I caught the scent of fire smoke and followed this to a ring of sharpened sticks: just a barricade of crude spears lashed weakly together at their center, a third resting at the crotch so that it pointed out into the forest. They had thrown pine and leaves over it to disguise it all somewhat, but smoke rose from within carrying the scent of roasted meat, and only a fool would not see the barricade, the smoke, would not know men dwelled in its center. Yet, in the dark you could walk your throat right into one of the spears. Sometimes the simplest things could get you.

They called as I approached: Who was I? Where did I come from? Where was I going? Eventually, they showed me to a flap that opened to a narrow tunnel you had to crawl through to enter the camp. This alone made you filthy. They could be thieves, but it felt too close to the village to be an elaborate snare. The camp within was a squalid affair with strings of dried meats hanging over a black pit of ashen logs. There hung a leaning roof of boughs lashed together poorly. Bows and arrows lined the inside of the fence beneath the roof and beside them spears and snares and hooks to catch every manner of game leaned with lethal promise; nets hung ready to harvest birds from the sky, and tattered and earth-stained sacks sunk heavy with collected eggs. A pile of reeking deerskin covered much of the ground of the shelter.

They were filthy, the two of them, even for men living in the woods in a hunting camp. Their clothes ran slick with oil and stuck to their skin, and their breath emitted a rancid odor with teeth yellow and brown. Bones of something I could not identify littered the fire and bits of charred meat and gristle as black as the pit clung to them yet.

Once I climbed inside they stood a few paces off. I could have the knife out and across both their throats in half a breath. I was not afraid. As I brushed myself clean, they just stared at me and it was the taller and older of the two who spoke first. "Why'd you say you was goin' up that ways?"

"To find my father."

"Wha's he doin' so far up?"

"Workin' a mine."

He scratched his scraggly beard that grew in patches on his face. "Is a far way to any mines."

"It is. After the drought he had to go."

He shrugged. "Is your business, but I'd not go much more out in these woods alone. Not if I was you and not if I was me." The shorter and younger one laughed stupidly. "This camp's last thing-a human hands save the traps a-curse, an' you don' wanna find 'em." The shorter one laughed again uproariously, slapping his knee and stamping.

"All right," I said.

"The king's road less than a month east-a here. She goes about to the end-a this world. Might even run right offa it. She even patrolled sometimes, so you can feel real safe. You be seeing the thieves they caught linin' the road hung on poles dead or near enough to it. It better when they dead. The livin' ones take to beggin' and you don' wanna have to think about it."

"What could they possibly beg for?"

"Water, to be cut down, to be killed." The younger stopped laughing and the older continued, "When you see one strung up there and a cut rope to his ankle it mean he, or a she, lot a times a she, tried to cut someone down, or give 'em water or whatnot."

"All right," I said. "I just thought I'd skip the road, that I'd get there more quickly through the woods. I'm used to the woods."

"They burn 'em at night. The dead-uns. Is their fat. It burns real good. They wrap 'em in dried kindling and the human fat burn real good."

"All right," I said. My mind went to the knife.

"Is a safest way up. Only way. Ain't hardly even game in these woods no more."

"Oh no? What's happened to it?" I asked not caring at all, watching their hands closely and measuring in my mind the distance between them and any weapons. At my question, he looked with a kind of shame to his filthy feet shod in rough-hewn leather. He kicked into the dirt of the camp floor and sent a splash of granules into the firepit.

"Ah, I dunno really," he mumbled with a shrug of his shoulders. "Sometin's scarin' 'em off or we huntin' 'em out or sometin' else. I dunno. Is jus' ain't what it was. Any worse an' we be eatin' men 'stead-a stringin' 'em up on poles!" At this, the younger one laughed uproariously again and slapped his knee idiotically. He kept his mouth open a long time after his laughter. Inside, a reek ran from gums swollen and dark red with some infection, and the paste on his tongue stuck thick and yellow. At best, he had half his teeth and a purple cyst or tumor pushed his front tooth crooked. The other was missing. "Is safe road lest you a thief or a fugitive," chuckled the older.

"Well, I'm not that."

"You got a honest face. A nice face." He scratched his patch of beard again, thinking. "Take the road. Forget these woods."

Smiling stupidly, the shorter one spoke at last, "Short cuts be longer, Friend," he said with a kind of jubilation. His smile broadened. "Shortcuts are longcuts!" he almost shouted and laughed at his wit.

"I suppose that's often true," I said. It occurred to me that if I tried to leave through the narrow entrance my arms would be almost pinned and the knife useless. "Well, I've a long way to go. Thanks for your advice."

"He ain't gonna listen," said the older one, and the younger chuckled then stopped. Shaking his head, the younger went to a sack which hung on the fence beneath the shelter and took four brown speckled eggs from it and wrapped them in thick green leaves numerous times, tying each gently with a fiber, and then handed this to me. I took them carefully.

"Thank you."

"All right then," he said smiling still. "You gonna die you go that way."

And I almost wanted to tell him I would die no matter which way I went, but did not. "I'm gonna take the road."

The older one shrugged and sat on a log that ran alongside the firepit. Feathers of eagle and hawk dangled from the limbs of the fence. They had made a sculpture of antlers in the form of a great bird and feathers hung from it too. "Save them eggs for when you real hungry," he said. "Real, real hungry."

"I will," I said, and thanked him again. "I have to go," I said and they said nothing. I went to the tunnel and lifted the wooden door and crawled out the way I'd come in. Once I was on the other side the two stared at me through the fence and the foliage which hid it. "You just going out there with nothing?" the older one called from behind the barricade. "With nothing?"

"I'm taking the road," I called over my shoulder. "I know good advice when I hear it. Thank you."

I nodded and walked quickly away. "How he gonna live out there wit' just nuthin'?" the younger one asked the other. I pretended not to hear them. As soon as they wouldn't notice I watched my back continually for them, and when well out of sight broke into the forest and went north.

The forest always changed. By now, many of the species Gelidii had taught me to pick did not grow, and so I always sought new edibles, finding some too. I carried a switch and sometimes would strike a little lizard resting on a leaf, or crack the back of a small snake, or even nick a bird and at night would roast these by the fire. They said the only thing to worry about in this forest for a fire would be the type of man who might see it. But each day the wild became thicker and more remote, and with each passing moon, fire became more essential as the days grew cool and the nights often fell bitterly cold. I had heard this about the north and that it would get colder still.

Walking through some of the denser forest little could be found to eat. Trees and vines with bitter berries blocked the sun from all but the hardiest undergrowth. On the fourth day my hunger swelled, so I poked a hole in the top of one of the eggs and sipped it out raw. That night, I rested a second egg beside the fire to cook it slowly, turning it now and again in anticipation. It was good to have something to do. With a touch of the blade, I cut off its crown and threw a small morsel of the steaming white meat into the fire.

May safe passage be given this traveler. And thank you to the hunters for this food. May I be the better servant.

The night fell exceptionally still. I no longer built nests in the trees. This forest did not lend itself to this practice anyway, not like the jungle of Gelidii. At the end of each day I often just strung a cord between two trees and lay one blanket over it and wrapped in the other, a gift of Karuna of whom I will tell in time. If it looked like rain I would find a deadfall under which I could lie down straight and rib this with cut limbs and stuff the openings with enough foliage so the rain would run off. Around the structure I would dig a channel for the water to wash down. It worked somewhat. If I put the time in, I could make a truly decent shelter, but then you had to move on. There always comes that time when you have to go on. But if enough food could be found I would stay with a decent shelter, at least a few days. This done to give the body and mind a rest, to not think always of moving to a goal which might not even be.

The blade of the drinking bird made the work light. It sliced a path through the thickest of forest. It could cut a small tree limb with no more force than its own rested weight. For this kind of work it did not have to sing nor follow an arc. I do not know what Gelidii would have thought of my utilitarian use of his gift. He used these only for defense of life, but in a way that was what it did in these common chores in an uncommon place.

It occurred to me once, when watching an exhibit by my friend the Picarin, how the arcs worked in unison if enough were known. The path of any strike could immediately divert to flow into that of another so that no movement wasted the energy, but harnessed it as momentum for the next strike. Mastery of the knives meant a sphere of absolute protection about the wielder, and since they harnessed rather than exhausted energy in their movements, the wielder benefited from protracted battle. But none of that genius was needed now. Now, just cut.

It already a long time ago already when Gelidii had put this weapon into my hands. Did he ever think of me? Do Picaren have such human sentiment? I would and could never find him again, nor that magnificent tree, but when the moon rises full I think of him even now, and recall the song he sang only for it.

You bank the fire at night and let the smoke wash over you. It hides your scent. You try and fall asleep before the flames die or you might not sleep at all for fear. On one side of the bed rested the blade and on the other the dragon tooth. Either one a weapon, but the tooth would be a heavy and cumbersome one. To sleep demanded a certain resignation towards whatever may come. Let the crooked sister fray the thread with a covetous smile, I would cross this forest or die in its heart.

Birdsong greeted the morning. I rekindled the fire and made the tea Karuna had given me in the cup of shell she had given me too. This, if little else, set me apart from the wilderness. I sipped tea which no beast nor ogre ever would. Not just ordinary tea, but one made from leaves of sacred herbs that stilled the troubled mind and went sweet upon the tongue.

But I was growing thinner, in every way. By day I suffered from malnutrition, by night, from the disease of loneliness. Once, staring into fire which has not changed since the world began, it occurred to me how since I'd left Selador, (a fugitive by fate), companions came like islands in a cold and indifferent sea. I'd land upon their shores to be half-restored, and then be set adrift into the mystery again. This was no way to live. By the decree of what star had I been born to this? I gently touched the jezeth wrapped in a rag beneath my shirt. It almost calmed me.

Forty days out, a jagged tower of stone loomed out of the wild. It seemed out of place. The stone looked natural enough but did not feel natural. The greenery grew a ways up it and then stopped. Peering up, I could only see it in patches, but noticed what looked like caves on the higher parts, hollows of some kind or another. A chill ran through me as I recalled the horrific rift. I lifted the jezeth to my forehead, kissed it and lowered it behind my shirt again. The briefest of visions, a flicker of white that could have been anything and most probably was nothing, flashed among the hollows. Feeling like a fool, and just a little afraid, I cried out, "Hello!"

I was desperate for food. If a village were near, I had to know. "Hello!" I cried once more and waited. Just as I turned to go a cough, or what sounded like a cough, fell from above. And it was not just a cough, but the cough of…a woman, a sound so alien it came as a trespass. "Hello! Is someone there!"

I drew the blade and waited a long time. Nothing. Voices had touched my head before, not like those which speak to the mad, but those which seep into a mind alone. After a time I called out again and waited with that sense of being watched. If you live in the wilderness you learn to trust that extra sense. Most definitely someone watched me. I placed the blade on the ground and showed my hands. "Is someone up there? I won't hurt you...I'm lost!" With a chill I cannot quite describe, peals of cold laughter cascaded down from the tower of stone followed by a series of wet, deep coughs. My heart swelled at once.

"You gonna do it?

"I don't know."

"C'mon. Do it! Jump! You'll make it."

Peering above almost frantically I sought the source of the laughter and the coughing, but could see no one. The coughs would stop and start, come from one side of the outcropping and then another and there could be a network of caves running through the thing. Finally, I heard the drawing of phlegm and then a glob of spit plummeted through the air. I had to jump back so it wouldn't hit me. It lay solidly on the ground before me: a blue shimmering egg of perfect roundness. Who could spit like that? Why would someone do something like that, try to spit on someone like that? I peered up again and saw nothing. "I don't want any trouble," I cried to the silent stone, "no trouble at all. I'm just a traveler, but am lost and need food. Please just tell the way to your village?"

More peals of laughter. Again, a flash of white moving in the crevices above. She spat again and I had to jump back again. "Go!" she screeched like a circling hawk. "Filthy man! Corpse stinker! Son of Ogre...Go!"

How could her phlegm be blue?

"Away, trespasser! Back to the rotted fields of men! Next will fall a stone to crush your skull!"

The practice of certain societies sends the mad and incurably diseased off into the wilds alone, not a decree of death exactly, but usually the equivalent. I thought I'd met one of these. I said no more and, regretfully, started off, pitying myself that the first person I met in however long was a mad woman living on a cliff, eating berries or strange flowers that turned her phlegm blue. But I'd come too far to have my head crushed in for no good reason. Going quickly, I did not look back. Sometimes you watch your back; sometimes you watch your step.

The story goes like this: The man who first taught humanity the cultivation of wisdom had been looking at the stars, and walked off a cliff to his death.

With each step she faded: a brief and meaningless encounter of which I would have likely all but forgotten had not fate other plans. A clearing lie ahead. Walking quickly away across it she first saw it whole, (for, despite all her magnificent talents, even she could not see through leaves) and recognized those spires of sinuous bone jutting past my shoulder as the roots of dragon's tooth. I'd uselessly tried to grind these smooth, but only succeeded in turning hardest river-stone to dust. That she recognized it was miraculous, for the better part of it, (save the tip which tore through anything), lay concealed in the blanket.

He held the bracelet glinting against the sky and smiled. "It's like metal made in the sun, Aunty!"

"Yes, it is, and now you've held gold. I wanted you to see it. But note this well: Never play with it. Never even take it out of its hiding place, behind the brick in the hearth."

He floated it between his hands, a snake illumine. "It's metal of the sun!"

She shook her head and took it from his hand gently. Children. "Listen now, is no toy, not yours to touch nor show to anyone. No one is to know it's here. I've shown it to you now because you're old enough to understand and to find its hiding place. But you need to know what it means to me."

He looked up at her. "I do, Aunty."

"No. No, you do not. Listen to me. The first thing is this bracelet can never be made again. Is very, very old and its art's long lost. A careless toss, a snag, an' it's in two pieces and as good as none. To me, anyway. I'd rather see it melted to a coin than in two pieces. Is no toy, and more than an heirloom."

"What's an heirloom?"

"An object a family passes down from generation to generation to show they loved you before you were born."

She pointed to the bracelet now in her palm. "You see these links that make the whole? They tell me of the women who have handed this down through generations. Drought, war, thieves, fire, plunder, raids, flood and even the careless swing of a drifting wrist this object has survived. But how some must have suffered for its keep, to not to sell no matter the pain of the season. And so one day you will put it upon the wrist of a woman whom you call wife. Should you have a daughter, (here she glanced upwards with a quickly muttered prayer), you will place it upon hers upon her day. And this will go on until we are no more, until the link gets broken off. Eventually everything does."

She stopped talking then. For the first time in many years she locked the immortal beauty of the bracelet upon her wrist now old and spotted. She had been a beautiful woman once, even long past her youth, and sighed to remember how upon the first day it graced her wrist she shone just as brightly.

She put it away then. It rested in a lightless priest-hole behind a low, soot-covered brick loose in the hearth.

"Why hide it in such an ugly place, Aunty?"

She pressed a hand against the stone face to help her stand again. Her breath grew heavy with the effort. "Because, my Son, is the crooked tree that's spared the axe."

She began back towards the garden, hugging him with one arm as she passed, limping slightly from the ever-rising pain of a bad knee about which she never complained.

Later I'd remember something drifting through the leaves. It fell like a pinecone knocked loose. I recall hearing a whoosh. Just before the cessation of my breath, a *whoosh.* There is no more immediate physical terror than the cessation of breath. You think of nothing but how to breathe again. Your lungs pull, your hands claw, you stumble, you run, you try to scream. You have to think. In moments of crisis you have to think, but you don't have time to think in the cessation of breath. *The blade.* This serpent cord on my neck our blade will cut. But in the moment I drew it she cracked the leash of the cord back so viciously it yanked me off my feet. Sprawled on my back, the strangulation heightened. Beyond the plea of my lungs I knew my throat was being torn apart. Nothing could be done. The precious blade of my life's preservation had flown carelessly from my hand as if from an amateur. The study of a life's defense is also the contemplation of death. I'd once imagined a million glorious assaults to get through the practice of my singing blade, but it had simply slipped from my hands when she yanked me back. It had been lost as if from the grip of an amateur. It lie beyond reach. I was kicking, clawing at a cord as hard as iron. I would die like a damned amateur.

Writhing upon my back, a flow of blood from my ravaged neck, I first saw Lyden as a silhouette beneath the sun. And then her shadow blocked the sunlight, and the lines of her face formed the purest expression of hatred my life would ever know. I twisted in terror, turned to get loose, but I was so thin by then with not even a breath to hold when her foot pressed on my collarbone with the weight of a mountain. The written word is slow, so terrifically slow, but this all occurred in moments. A simple leaving to then pinned on the doorstep of death, in moments.

With one hand she held the cord and with the other stabbed a finger like a dagger at my face. The nail was red, I remember. I had never before seen painted nails. It's odd, the improbable details the mind chooses to remember in moments of great panic. I thought that here is a woman of blood. I thought the red to be blood.

With the last vestige of breath I clawed at the collar of iron on my neck and I was dying. This was certain. It had encircled my throat thrice and was digging deeper into my throat and I would die today, in moments, and my heart raced and lungs burned the more. The trapped blood swelled in my face as I lay dying, while she screamed a single word which to her justified it all:

"Dragonhunter!"

I could not understand. I could not calm my mind enough to understand. I needed to breathe. The light began to fail. Darkness thickened and kicked for the blade which could not be far. Through stalks of dried grass kicking blindly, thinking somehow to catch it with my heel, drag it up to my hand….

"Ah, damnit," said the man, wincing.

"What is it Uncle?" The boy, his hand filled with seed, stood up straight and wiped his brow.

"Nothin'," he said. "Hit a mouse with the hoe. She's chopped clean in half."

The boy cautiously walked over. In a fresh divot, a brown field mouse struggled with its two front limbs away from the lower half of its body. All its blood had poured out and pooled around its entrails. Even in the eyes of a mouse, the boy could see a look of searching shock. The boy cried.

"Well, why'd you come and look if you're gonna cry?" The old man rarely lost his temper, but the mouse bothered him. It was a bad sign with this the first day of planting. They would lose something. The boy wiped his eyes and almost stopped crying. He was very young then and asked a question only a child would ask.

"Why's it still trying to get away, Uncle?"

He leaned on the hoe and thought of the question. "Because life struggles until it cannot."

He lifted the hoe to turn the mouse into the earth.

"Wait!" cried the boy.

"What?"

"Wait 'til it's dead."

"It is."

"But wait 'til it stops moving. Please. Its eyes aren't closed yet."

"So?"

"Just wait until its eyes are closed, and then a little longer. Please."

"All right," agreed the man, sighing. A lot of work needed to be done. Children.

All sounds of the earth faded save the hiss of her voice, rising in a crescendo of rage. I'd given up the knife. My limbs began to still. My arms fell to my side and the burn in my chest went away and only the sun burned. Soon, only her voice remained in that senseless word called again and again:

"Dragonhunter!"

The terror faded with the pain, and I felt the entirety of my life flashing in moments. Dying is a very simple process, and a peaceful one if done properly. I heard a wind although the day had been very still. And then something happened which I have thought of most every day since: I lifted out of my body and floated up and up into the forest of shining colors. Sounds and scents infused the earth like a garden of paradise. The eternity to which I rose made all life before seem but the witness of shadows through a veil of gray.

I could see her from above. She was shouting yet that word at that body, that ragged house of ruined bones, so derelict I wondered how it ever could have housed me. I did not fear to die then, but delighted to, for I did not want to go back to it. And though I did not go to that place from which none return, I stood upon the limen and glanced in. I say this: In the dream to come there is only love.

But her scream never softened. Her tears fell and I never knew why. She called again and again: "Dragonhunter! Dragonhunter!"

Suddenly I understood. Drifting into the great blue sea of time I knew at last why in a field a mad woman screamed a senseless word to man mostly dead, but it was simply not true. It was not true at all. This would not do. Not at all. Suddenly, I popped behind my eyes again, recalled to life again. With the last beat of my heart I looked into her eyes and shook my head. No.

She paused. She knew I had not lied. She just did. "Ugh!" she cried at last, and with a flick of her wrist loosed the cord from my neck and whipped it over her head in a circle of blinding speed. It howled against the air. She lowered it to her waist and the cord encircled her, each ring resting precisely below the other until it terminated in a silver dart tucked into the final circuit. The exquisite weapon now functioned as a belt for a gown of white, somehow spotless even in the midst of the wilderness. My eyes began to close again. I still could not breathe.

"Ugh!" she cried in impatient disgust and stamped hard three times on the center of my chest in quick succession. Air flooded in, groaned in, wheezed in, a torrent of air, more and more until I became drunk on it, until life, just to breathe, was so sweet. My vision cleared and my mind too. I then rolled to my side and vomited water and blood. She had ravaged my throat. When the vomiting ended, a fit of coughing began. Filaments of fresh blood drooled down. My eyes swelled with tears. *Just breathe.* I touched my throat and my hand came away wet. All blood. I began to fall out. *Just breathe.*

"Dragonhunters are put to death here," she said. A blanket of blood on my hand.

"I'm not that. I'm not." My voice like gravel.

"We will see," she said and stepped away. She traced an invisible line down her center and then extended each hand out to the side, palms flat with arms stretched full. She listened, or felt, with closed eyes. Then she turned her body in a very slow circle. When she returned to the first position she opened her eyes and spoke. "No dragon has been killed in recent times." She pointed to the tooth. "Tell Lyden from where this prize has been captured, Trader of Bones."

Her sandals: golden fibers woven through her toes and entwining up her calves to lock just below the knee. And her hair. How could she have such hair? It glowed. It hung straight as a pin and shone like the moon, and yet was so fine a breeze could lift it into turning curls to enshroud her like a veil. It made it difficult to concentrate, her hair, and her skin, a shade I had never before nor have since, and her eyes. Those eyes, but …"Speak, Ape! Speak!"

"I didn't trade for it," I said. "I got it myself."

"Anything but the truth spoken now will bring an end to the bearer of the crooked tongue."

"It's true. It is. I got it myself. An old man gave me a map to where a dragon was sleeping and I followed it to a den in the heart of a mountain. And a dragon really was there. She really was. Sleeping so quietly. The dark grew so complete I found myself standing before the mouth and didn't know it and the tooth hung loose, just there. It swung with her breath. All I had to do was tug. Just a little. It gave. It hung real loose and it just gave. Yes, she bled a little, but I only know this because the blood hit my forehead. She bled so little. Understand that I did not harm her. I would have taken anything: a shed scale, a chip of claw, a hair…anything. But the tooth almost fell into my hands. She had crashed into that mountain while flying in a storm. That must have knocked it loose. Was the stones of the mountain and the sky that did this damage. If anything, pulling it out sped along her healing."

She had been staring intently at me and also at the roots of the tooth and its form. I pushed myself to stand. Blood poured from my throat.

"You say you have plucked a tooth from the mouth of a dragon?"

"Yes."

"And where does this dragon dwell?"

"To the south of here, in the black mountains. Three months by foot."

"What is the manner of the mountain in which the dragon sleeps?"

"It's rocky and broken. One face looks like something tore it all apart."

"Hmmm." She smiled slightly. "The nest of Kai-Tey. She sleeps still. Give me the tooth."

"No."

"I do not wish to take what has come to you. I want only to hold it."

"Well, I'll have to sit up to get it."

She nodded. I sat up, anger growing at her rudeness. I drew the tooth from my back and handed it to her tip-first. She was taken aback a moment at the spiraling fang almost as long as my arm. Rarely did Nature lend such artifacts. Then she grabbed the tooth from my hand rather abruptly and spun it in the air as if it were weightless. She had truly fantastic strength.

"Hmmm," she said then, walking with the tooth as she ran her finger along its length. Her eyes went wide: "So, the great Kai-Tey has shed a fang against the face of a black mountain." Now she turned to me. The knife was there, just past my feet. She had tricked me somehow, had been hiding in the branches somehow, but that wouldn't happen again. "And a straggling bag of bones, a raggedy straggly man, stumbles along and plucks it up." She waved it in the air like a wand. "How improbable, yet the improbable happens. What power it holds! Can you even feel its power?"

"No, but sometimes it gives me strange dreams."

Her expression turned to one of genuine curiosity. She then flipped the tooth in the air and caught it again and drew it far back over her shoulder and threw it spinning into the face of the stone tower. A whoosh cut the air and then the tooth landed into the rock with an explosion of crumbling wall. The very tower seemed to groan, and Lyden laughed and clapped her hands with glee almost like a little girl. She glided then, there is no other word for it, she glided across the grass to the rocky outcropping. The train of her gown, so light it shunned the ground, flowed behind her.

I got up. Everything spun. The blanket I pressed to my wound soaked with blood. Not good. She was already there and I went slowly towards it and her. More than half the tooth had plunged into the tower. Large chunks of stone had fallen away around it. As she assessed the impact of her throw she called sharply over her shoulder at my approach, "Who has told you to stand Enemy?"

I stopped. I felt faint and very thirsty. "I'm not a threat to you."

She spun as quickly as a serpent strikes. "You are not to be trusted yet, if ever, Sower of the Evil Seed! You may not have hurt Kai-Tey..."

"I didn't hurt her."

"So you did not. Sit!"

"I don't want to.…"

"Although your kind are clumsy and weak, you have many tricks and many devices. Do not think your retrieval of the black knife stone has gone unnoticed to Lyden. Sit or die." Her hand lowered to the handle of her belt. I was too weak to fight well. Pick your fights, I told myself. She's only a woman, I told myself, yet insane and skilled and immensely powerful. I sat down, almost fainted anyway, and pressed the blanket harder against my bleeding throat. She grabbed the tooth by the base and with one pull of her thin and seemingly delicate hand ripped the spiral from the mountain rock. A cloud of dust came with it and it screeched and there came a scent of smoke. The tooth had not even been scratched.

She rested it across one forearm and gazed deeply into it and then to me. "I hope you are grateful for what the gods have put into your hands."

"I am," I said but didn't care. My life was bleeding out.

"And what does the man plan to do with this gift?"

"I am going to give it away, to a Sage, an elder who has great power. If you give him something of the dragon he does whatever you ask they say."

"And where is this sage of whom you speak?"

"In the North."

"In the North?"

"Yes."

"Where in the North?"

"I don't know," I said. She laughed.

"And should you ever find him what will you ask in return for this magnificent token?"

"I want him to free my village from the soldiers of the king."

She walked slowly towards me and placed the dragon tooth back in my hands. "I am elf. The affairs of man do not concern us, save when they intrude upon our existence, which they do ever less. For whatever reason the gods have graced your steps into the lair of Kai-Tey, and out again, Wanderer of the Drifting Moon. Perhaps the Fates will smile on your cause."

The world began to spin and darken. "I'm dying," I said, and then fell out. When I awoke Lyden was kneeling over me, casting leaves. She was singing, gently, I remember.

"What happened?"

"Be quiet."

"But what.…"

"Just be quiet. Your voice grates like a dying rabbit. You interrupt the song. Speak again and I will split your tongue with my fingernail. Be grateful. Only elven medicine would have cured this wound. How weak your flesh is. I did not know the flesh of men to be so weak. Like a leaf before the fall of cold."

"It was you who wounded me."

With one hand she pulled open my jaw and with the other pinched my tongue between two of her blood red nails and pulled it out. It felt like it was being held between the tips of knives. "Speak again before this is finished and I will grant to you the tongue of a serpent. You do not belong here. This is the outer land of elf. Men who enter it tend to die. The shame upon Lyden to be seen tending the wounds of the man-ape…Despicable. Deplorable. Were we not alone she would have let you bleed out."

I waited. She let go of my tongue and I tasted a trickle of blood. She then returned to separating leaves in particular patterns and placing them on my throat. The herbs began to burn and there arose a very distinct aroma, spicy and strong. I could feel the wound heal already. Staring at the blue and infinite sky I wondered about her, this strange woman out here alone. I wondered at her strength and grace, at her sickness and illusions and was it for these they had cast her out? Perhaps the strange hue to her skin, so light in its color with a hint of green, blue perhaps, and had that scared them? She folded her hands before her and stood. She coughed again. "It's finished."

"You're sick," I said.

"As are you."

"I'm wounded. It's different. Why are you sick?"

"You insist upon speech. Be mute. Be still. Be as the quiet of the buried stone."

And so I said nothing. I watched and waited, fascinated by her hair, pin-straight and so fine it cascaded like water. And it was then I saw why her eyes had struck me as being so extraordinary, for they were of a color I had never seen nor heard of nor thought possible in the eye of anything. Once noticed, they could not not be noticed. And she stood two hands taller than I yet I am not short. This height made more striking by the perfection of her form: a body like a sculpture, a form in metal poured and all this in her sickness.

She gazed stoically into the forest with her lips moving in whisper. Why did she whisper to nothing? I did not know what to do. Lyden so hated both wasted words and my voice that it seemed risky even to speak. I feared her very much despite the curing. To what phantoms did she whisper? On what emotions did her mind now turn? Her madness could as quickly kill or save me and I wanted to leave very badly. Yet I could not just get up and go.

She said to use it when I was afraid, so I lifted the jezeth from under my shirt, loosed the rag which hid the shining gem of the earth. Lyden turned to us then, and as all do even she, Queen of the Elves, fell to silent awe when first beholding it, the jezeth, miracle retrieved from the floor of the sleeping sea. At last she spoke in whispered wonder: "Walker of Many Paths, it seems another treasure has befallen you."

"A gift given me. It's called 'jezeth.' The giver said it may never be stolen, so I'm not afraid to show it."

I spun the gem on its fine chain of gold which through mysterious craft wove into the jewel itself. It burned in unspeakable brilliance: a luminescence never rightly sculpted in words. The anger faded from her eyes. The jezeth always had this effect.

And now her thoughts turned again. She showed them in her bearing. She walked silently away to a patch of purple flowers caught in a circle of the sun. Kneeling before them she kissed them with the tips of her hair, pet them gently and sang softly in words I did not know, more beautiful than words could ever be, and a voice sweeter than starlight, a voice that chased away all the darkness. And as it was wont to do the jezeth brightened, and the light of its heart lifted with her song, and even the wind stilled by the beauty of the song; and though I did not know the song or the singer, I wept when the sounds caressed my ears; for though they rang so lovely and light, they seemed to tell the life of a man whose destiny would never bring him home.

After a time there was nothing more to say. What else was there for us to do? With the jezeth hiding again beneath my shirt and the tooth carried over my shoulder like a club, I began to walk away, unafraid, but she called to me without looking up: "I would not go too long in that direction, Bearer of the Fallen Star."

"I'll find my way."

She shook her head. "Before the sun sets you will likely find yourself in a pit of watery sand. It will drown you slowly. The land ahead is riddled with them."

"Thank you. I'll go around."

"Why do you take it upon yourself to free this village?"

What did it matter? In a moment we would be each other's memories. I needed to tell it once. "The army came into Selador, my home, when I was little. They were brutal. Still are. I was accused of killing one of them and ran into the southern forest, a place none have gone for a hundred years. Screamers, as we call them, stopped us from going there. They came from nowhere. They would howl through the nights in way that can kill a fledgling. I didn't expect to live, but I did. The first night one howled in that voice of its and came closer and closer. I was crouched behind a boulder waiting and it screamed then, just there on the other side of that rock and I could feel its voice. It ran through that stone and then through me and I could feel it howling through me and it saw my soul. I think that's what they look for. I think that's how they hunt. But I lived, of course, and now am to find a Sage. A friend asked me to. Still, I would have quit this a thousand times but these soldiers, sometimes, a lot of times, they kill the family and friends of an escapee, and anyone who helps him." I sighed. "I was younger the day I ran, and so damned scared. Today I would have stayed, but back then I just ran. I couldn't think of anything else but getting away."

I shielded the afternoon sun from my eyes and scanned the forest before me. "I don't really believe in Sages. I think these are stories told to children but it doesn't matter. I'll walk to the edge of this world looking for one, following just a fairy tale if I have to. It doesn't matter. I owe them this. I can't rest. Nothing lets me rest anymore."

She stood beside me, so fantastically tall, and said almost gently, "The heaviest stone you carry hangs around your heart, Petter of the Dragon. To what do you look now?"

"I don't know. Nothing. The forest."

She looked too, seeing things I did not. But she was thinking mostly, and for the first time to my witness, a sadness clouded her. Then her countenance softened like melting ice. "You stand at the door of the elven realm, untamed by men. No one of your kind will cross it alone and live. The Sagittae of Gaia have long lived in this place, but she is our home, not our captive. We have not rooted out every raging beast, every nest of the darker things. Your destiny follows a long path. Even for Lyden, Queen of the Elves, the journey to the Northern parts is a great one, and not safe. But there are no coincidences, Keeper of the Given Fire, and so I will guide you across this realm, until the things of man begin again."

She wanted to go with me? How terrible. I needed to get away from she who would kill and save me in the same morning. Yet, I must not offend her madness. "I...I don't...I don't know if I could ask that of you, Lyden. Your own destiny must be greater."

She sighed, and then, from a fold in her simple but magnificent gown, drew a fine fillet of silver and tied her hair up like a tail, pulling it back with severe perfection. And then she did an extraordinary thing: she ran along the tops of the tall grass and leapt into the trees with the weight of a feather. The leaves rustled gently as she raced through the crowns like a great white crane. The tail of her hair bobbed like a squirrel's. Three bluebirds from the wood flitted about her, racing and halting as she ran, as she flew. She glided down then as if on wings and stood before me and folded her arms. No pride crossed her expression. The bluebirds lit on her shoulders and nipped playfully at her ears and hair. Lyden whistled to them and smiled. She spoke their language fluently. I knew this because I too knew the language of the birds.

"Lyden! Lyden! Only Lyden goes. Only Lyden follow across!" the bluebirds insisted.

One must be very focused to understand the birds, like picking a single conversation out of a crowd. Generally happy creatures, they repeat themselves often, perhaps just to hear the beauty of their voices. The words are often just chatter about this or that, simple things they can see and do and love repeated again and again as if the word were forgotten as soon as it was spoken. Yet, sometimes they could be quite direct.

"Go with Lyden or die."

"Son of Man," Lyden said in calm contentment, "they are small but know well the land to come. Few things go unseen by them."

"How did you know I understood them?"

"It is plain to see." She became very still then and her gaze turned to ice. "The gift of their language comes to men by drinking pure the dragon's blood."

"I didn't drink it's blood Lyden."

"Explain the gift."

I didn't know what to say at first. I had long thought the cave had enchanted me, but now I understood. "When I pulled the tooth blood came down, just a little, and some little went into my mouth."

She nodded.

"And ever since the dragon's den my heart has changed."

"In what way, Treader unto the Forbidden Folds?"

"I'm less happy.

"This is wisdom, another gift from the blood of dragon."

"But I want to be happy again."

"The happiness you seek is for children, Son of Man. Take what wisdom you have gained and cherish it. The price does not exceed the reward. Let it be a beacon to help find the way, a guiding light towards your destiny, whatever it may be. Let wisdom help you to accept what comes."

"Lyden, are you the Sage?"

She laughed. "I am not as you seek, Walker from the Distance, but your path has knocked strongly upon mine, and so now I too will be woven towards your Sage."

The most momentous decisions are often made in a breath. I looked back to the forest ahead and it appeared so dense and inhospitable. I realized then I feared it more than her. "All right, Lyden, let's go then."

She nodded almost imperceptibly and with a flick of her finger sent the bluebirds back to the wood. We headed not north but west. I did not ask why.

Her gown flowed as the web of a spider as she glided off. Almost running to keep up I called to her: "Lyden...Lyden...thank you!"

She glided away.

Whether true elf or woman living in a dream, Lyden moved like none I have ever seen before or since covering the most uneven forest floor like a swift ship on an easy sea. In a few moments she put a great distance between us and then was simply gone. I hurried faster but it was no good. She was gone. I called her name, but she was gone. It surprised me to suddenly feel alone.

Sitting cross-legged on a branch as thin as a finger there was Lyden, impatient in her waiting, her gown draping down alongside her magnificent hair. She wove something very fine between her fingers and without looking up she spoke. "You are fantastically slow, loud, clumsy, weak and most asleep. Your joints creak. Your breath and vapor reek like a corpse. Your step is so heavy I am surprised it does not collapse the ancient mountains ahead. Tell Lyden this: how is it you have lived so long in the forest?"

"I get asked that a lot."

"The journey will be long with you."

"So don't do it."

She stabbed a look of daggers. "Do not be so arrogant with your life, Progeny of the Ape!"

She drifted from the branch and fell too slowly. She then ripped a stone out of the soil and threw it into the undergrowth ahead. It plopped into the ground and sank into earth which appeared as solid as that on which we stood. "Death surrounds your step. Do not shun gifts from the greater light." She pointed fiercely to the sky. "Today, just today, three finches flew across the sun, to the right!"

"Well that's just…"

"But then a cloud passed, gray and low. A grave omen. Days of darkness lie ahead and now chase heavily upon us." She drew her blood tipped finger to me. "And you play a role, though I know not what, in matters far beyond your concerns. I will honor that Destiny has delivered you to my protection, but watch your step, Son of the Crooked Race, and be ever grateful."

And she was off again, disappearing into the leaves. She had unwoven a spider web and rewove it again in thicker strands. She left traces of this sticking to leaves as she passed them. Thus she marked her trail, and this I followed, although with great caution. At least we had turned to the North.

Not having to run anymore I could look at the world around me. The woods had become more lovely by the hour. They felt gentle and enchanted and one could understand the coaxing out of a dream of elven land. Her markers appeared just when I began to be unsure, and the trail ended near dusk in a small clearing which held a deeper sense of enchantment. Flowers ringed its outer parts and the grass billowed in soft mounds. The trees leaned in as if to listen. The air smelled of flowers.

Lyden stood aloof and silent at the far end. She gazed at me as I entered. The final marker, perhaps by coincidence, loosed from the leaf just as I passed. "We stay the night here," she spoke from her distance. "You are safe here, entirely so. I will not be just here, but I will not be far. I will know of any threat should it come but it will not. Do not leave this place without the sun. Do not be frightened."

"I'm not."

"Yes, you are. Men are often afraid of the dark due to the weakness of their vision. Many things do feed in the dark but they will not feed here. Here, you sleep under my protection."

"All right. Thank you," I said setting my burden down. Lyden kneeled to pet the soft grass. She began to whisper to it. Finding a young soft-needled pine, I drew the blade and in a flash sliced off a fresh green bough for my bedding.

"IIEEEEEEEE!"

It broke into my ears, her howl, her scream, and grew ever louder as she rushed ever closer. I dropped the blade to put my fingers to my ears and in a moment of welcomed silence opened them only to see her eyes afire with rage. This fire went to my cheek.

Slap!

It knocked me off my feet. I hadn't expected that at all. It felt like being hit by the paw of a tiger. Before I could speak or stand, she pressed her toe to the hollow of my throat just above the ribs. I coughed and tried to push her toe off and may as well have tried to move iron. Reaching blindly for the blade that could not be reached, I felt the air cut from my lungs again. She pressed her foot even harder against my throat and things within began to crack. She would kill me here. Had she wanted to make a game of it, or did she need me to walk the body to this place for reasons unimaginable? She spoke with a voice of ice. "You, Ape, Pig, Polluter, Defiler, Wretch, Human, be mindful always of this: You now walk in the outer realm of the Sagittae, Protectors of the Earth. Slice another limb from any denizen in the Forest of Elf and Lyden shall slice a limb from the man. Nod if you understand, Wounder of the Helpless."

I nodded and loosed my hand from her ankle. Just before I would have fallen out her foot lifted. Air rushed in like water to a fire. I brought my hands to my throat and gasped.

She went to the stump and sang softly to it. Immediately sap formed where it had been cut. Lyden rubbed this into the "wound" in gentle circles, then lay the severed bough at the foot of the tree with religious ceremony. She did not look at me again but, without another word, disappeared into the folds of the darkness when the song was over.

Curled on the ground wrapped in blanket, the entirety of my life played again. How had Destiny brought a child to such a cold night and woman? For all his training and strength he remained defenseless now. Who allowed this ever?

The pain in my cheek eventually subsided, but the tears refused to slow for too long a time. I kept thinking how wonderful it would have been to be among my little family again or simply have someone to talk with. An old friend from Selador would have been wonderful. Because the difference between having a friend to talk with and having no one is everything. "They're all dead," I whispered to the dark. "All your friends are dead."

Morning broke with birdsong and gray light. My cheek had swollen severely and how I hated her. Breath exhaled like smoke against the chill air, and I stood up stiffly keeping the blankets wrapped over my shoulders and head. The poultice on my throat had begun to itch so I began picking it off when her voice broke the morning peace like a thunderclap. "Halt!" she cried. "Not only does he defile my forest but now he shuns her healing! Could this be, or does Lyden dream yet?"

She glided across the field to me from wherever she had been.

"It itches," I said. "It burns."

"Thus it heals, Shunner of the Bright Path. Leave the rest alone. The medicine will know when the healing is complete, not you. Only then will it fall away."

It became difficult to hide how much I despised her. "You could have told me that in the first place."

"I could have left you to your death."

It was too early for this. I stopped picking at the wound. I pulled a blanket over my head and closed my eyes and lay down again wishing my jaw didn't ache, wishing my throat didn't itch, wishing it were warm enough to go back to sleep, wishing I were home. And then my stomach groaned. "Do you require sustenance this day?"

"I could eat."

"Did you not eat yesterday?"

"I did," I mumbled from under the blanket. Then, with a most rude awakening, both blankets were lifted off of me and the cold rushed in.

"Ahh!"

She laughed. "You are awake now I think," she said, throwing the blankets almost to the edge of the field. "Is it true that men eat the flesh of beasts, as the ogre does?"

Shivering, I hugged myself and hated her in every way imaginable. "Yes," I spoke through clenched teeth, "I eat meat."

She began to tremble. Her face had an expression of utter bafflement. "Until now I had thought this detail of man to be the stuff of legend. How is it a creature of the higher mind devours the flesh of the innocent? Know you not of the pain? Know you not of the bounty of sustenance that surrounds? It cannot be that you devour them."

"I… I don't know, Lyden. We just do. It tastes good, too. Maybe you should try it."

"Ugh! Enough. Know this and know it well, Blood Eater: Should you harm a single creature as you walk with Lyden, be it butterfly or dragon, I shall rip your beating heart from your chest and with it close your carnivorous mouth forever."

"Understood," I said, hardly caring.

She then turned and without another word went to a bush tucked in the tree line. It hung heavy with red berries I'd never seen before. She cupped her hand beneath a cluster and whispered something to the bush and berries began to fall into her hand. She stabbed one with her nail as red as the fruit and lifted it to her mouth and chewed it for a very long time before swallowing.

I considered her there. The stately bearing of her being, too rigid, too erect, contrasted sharply with a gown that flowed like water, that lifted like the wind, that shined like the light of the moon. She ate but the few which had dropped and no more. When her anger seemed to subside enough I went to this bush and cupped my hand beneath a heavy cluster. "Drop!" I said, thinking the bush to be enchanted.

Lyden laughed.

"Fall to my hand!"

Laughter.

"Just pick them, Wanderer of the Seven Stars."

More laughter.

"I command you to fall into my hand!"

Even more laughter. In a rare act of kindness she took my hand in hers and poured the remaining berries into my palm. Ravenous, I popped them in my mouth. They were sweet and slightly bitter yet delicious. I picked more and more and shoved them into my mouth so quickly the juice ran down my chin. I gave Lyden a smile of blood. Her laughter quickly turned to a stunned silence. "You must have been long without food. You eat as the starved dog over a coveted bone." I did not stop eating to answer, but waited for her to step away before picking more.

"I leave now. Follow the webs. They will be more frequent as the forest grows thicker. If you get lost, Lyden will find you. Have no fear of that. Your step is heavier than the sea."

And with that she left, and a quiet, eerie emptiness came over the grove. Considering it now in the full light of day, I could see the grove made the clear shape of a circle that could not have been made by nature. Each night we found such a place, even in the remotest of forests, among the densest of bushes we found it, a clearing too circular to be natural. And they were always about the same size, and at the edge of each grew always a bush with berries or nuts, or a tree heavy with fruit. And around each ran a creek of sweet water. And each of the clearing's food was one I'd never seen before.

Lyden rarely ate, from what I could tell, and so I decided to hide my eating from her as much as possible, for it seemed to me that part of her affliction caused the commonest acts to be considered crimes. Inadequate amounts of food possibly exacerbated her condition, and so she could get worse as we went on. Likewise, I never made waste in her presence. I did not want to imagine how her madness might react to that. However, whatever dreams infected her mind, she knew the forest with unparalleled mastery and could, if she only would, get us with little trouble to the north side where the things of man began again. But I did not know if she would.

The first web hung to the left, and a faint trail ran under it. I would have never seen the trail but for her marker. Breathe. I could go it alone. Breathe. All in or gone. Just breathe. All in. I walked to the web and pulled it down, stamped it into the earth for no reason, and then followed the trail whose meandering course read north.

So many days passed in this manner that they cannot be counted. I hardly saw Lyden in those times. She was a presence who waited in the evening in the final spot to rest and who, in the morning, showed me a bush from which something could be eaten.

Once she strolled under a stately tree, spoke a word and a plump orange fruit fell into her hand. She laughed at my astonishment. She gave me half the fruit, which tasted unlike anything I had ever had before. Once she sang to the bark of a tree, and when amber nectar poured from its skin Lyden put her lips to the bark and kissed it in sips. She closed her eyes and when she swallowed her shining skin went flush. "This is a very rare tree, human. How sweet its blood. Pity you have not the art to coax it. Would you like to taste the littlest bit of it?"

"I don't want to make trouble for you, but yes I would."

"I shall ask her for a little more." She ran her hand along the tree and sang again. She had a song for everything: for the morning, for the evening hour, for the rain, for the flowers, the mist, the morning light, the falling dark. Sometimes her song was simple, sometimes not, but always lovely. Other times, especially when she sang to the dawn, her song lifted enchantingly above words to describe. How could I say this? Imagine a rainbow arching through all the horizon filled with doves. I thought the tree swayed, just slightly, with this second song. The amber pooled again in the depression in the trunk and Lyden caressed the gray bark and smiled and scooped the syrup into her hand. "She has yielded a little more. This is very kind of her. Why do you not thank her before you take from her veins?"

"You want me to thank a tree?"

Her eyes shot daggers of ice.

"Of course," she said coldly. I laid my hands on the ancient bark and it felt slightly cold. Above, the branches wove in a tangle of life and light. A solitary bird warbled there and I thought it was talking about us.

Then, I spoke. "Gentle Mother, who has nourished us and shared the water of your life, thank you." Having said what I thought she would like to hear I turned to Lyden. A faint hint of a smile began to spread beneath her usually stoic visage.

I cannot describe the nectar: sweet and smoky and mysterious. Perhaps if you should dine with the gods your cup would overflow with it. I have tasted nothing like it since. For two days after I did not need to eat. Before we parted, Lyden picked a strand of her magnificent hair and laid it at its roots. "Never take without giving in return," she said. "This, I think, men need to learn." She amazed me, I must confess, these little tricks of hers, amazed me what a person could learn to do if a thing had to be done.

Where she slept I do not know. From whatever clearing in which we ended each day she would disappear into the trees and return by morning's first light. The days grew ever colder so that sleeping on the ground became almost unbearable. I would collect piles of dead leaves and sticks, anything to buffer between the cold earth and my thin blankets, until one evening I asked her if I could make a fire.

"What?"

"A fire. Burn some wood. Dead wood. Wood that's already fallen."

"This is one of the tricks of men, is it not?"

"I don't know what you mean. It's very cold, Lyden. It gets colder as we go farther north, and I will need a fire at night."

"Fire should be lowered to the earth by the gods alone. Only this fire do we fetch and shape."

"I won't cut anything from a tree. Just the stuff that's lying on the ground. I wake in the mornings so cold I can't move. At night it's hard to sleep for the shivering."

It had not rained yet. I did not want to imagine what I would do in rain.

"Do you know why the world is yours?" she said then, somehow stunned. "Because men take everything without care. Whatever they wish to possess they just take to harness and use and consume and care not for the cost. This is why the world is yours, why all has bowed to you and now you make fire. You burn what would feed the forest soil. You turn all to ash to make your own comfort. And so, you now ask to harness the flame of the gods before it has even fallen from the sky?"

"I have a stone I strike and a spark flies from it. The fire lifts from that."

"Tell Lyden this: how is it a stone burns to fire?"

I shrugged. I didn't really know. "My uncle used to say it's because the stone itself was made through fire, and if you hit it hard enough it remembers its first form."

She thought about this for a long time. "This Uncle," she spoke at last, "is not a complete fool."

"No, he wasn't. It's very, very cold tonight, Lyden. Every star shines and these nights are the worst. I will only take wood that's already fallen."

She went to the edge of the field, just before the treeline and peered into the growing darkness. "What if it rises to consume all about us?"

"It won't. I will keep it contained. I promise."

She huffed. "Collect only the dead," she said, and melted into the dark.

I gathered a big pile of sticks beside where I would sleep and made a temple of tinder and kindling and dried branches and struck a spark into it.

"Wait," she spoke, reappearing from the forest and gliding to the pile of wood. She waved her hand above it and whispered into it. Suddenly, a train of insects walked out, including a long stick-like bug, the kind of which I had never seen before, and vanished into the folds of the tall grass. She turned to me with scorn: "And so go the refugees of your warmth, Taker of All His Hands Can Hold. Remember that at least. Some of them have spent years burrowing into this wood. Now, for some few hours of fleeting comfort, you would kill them or drive them from their homes. Remember that everything has a cost."

"Aye," I said. "I do and will. Thank you, and I am grateful to the little bugs," I said, "and sure they will find another home quickly." But I didn't really care about the bugs. They were only bugs, as numerous as the sands of the sea, and it was the coldest night to memory. Without fire I might not survive.

"Do not lie to me. No lie will pierce my mind. My eyes are not dim and my heart not dull. My mind does not walk in the land of half-sleep as do the lumbering humans. How dare you say they will soon find a home! Who are you to speak of their fate and their challenges of which you are as ignorant as the happenings on the far side of a distant star? Take your fire. But know that to greater things you are as an insect. Know that you are also easily crushed. Know that your home which you so diligently tended and built, into which you poured your love and life, softening each corner to a refuge of nourishment, this haven from the cold and pitiless, from the inscrutable and the cruel, from the assault without reason, know that it too can fall by a toss of fate, can by the swinging shadow of a god's hand be turned to ashes and water."

"It may have already been," I said coldly, and struck a flint to the tinder. With time and care the little field became awash in a soft orange glow, and while it mesmerized me as a fire always will, it struck Lyden to a kind of silent awe. At first she remained at the farthest edge of the field, observing the process with a show of stoic indifference, but little by little she approached, like a wild animal tempted by a hand outstretched with food, and whenever she caught the flames straight to her eyes her eye-shine made their color even more confounding. "Sit with me," I called to her, "Lyden of the Silver Eyes."

Deliberately not looking at her I reached into the flames to rearrange the wood, to make it brighter but not too bright, to make it tall but not too tall. Only fools made large fires. She squatted just over my left shoulder, her knees folded before her in perfect precision. When a log cracked and hissed in steam she lifted a bit in shock. A spark rose to the sky above of absolute black and dissolved into it and became it. I turned my eyes to hers, and they were wide with wonder. "How is it," she said as if whispering of the sacred, "you can contain such a power as this and not set the whole world alight?"

"It's not hard. You don't have to be afraid of it," I said. "It won't go past this ring. I promise."

The smoke changed direction and almost washed over her but she sprang away, somehow leaping in an arc over the flames until she kneeled straight across from me staring inscrutably into them. Her eyes burned like the stars. "This is one of the great tricks of your kind, Catcher of the Falling Light, is it not?"

"It's not a trick," I said. "I could teach you to do it."

"I do not wish to learn."

"That's fine. But it would keep you warm."

"I am not cold. I am not like you."

"No, no you are not like me."

For a long time we did not speak, but every time I ran my hand over the flames, every time I reached in to adjust a log, I could almost hear her heart quicken. She tensed. "How," I asked at last, "did you get those bugs to leave the sticks?"

She immediately became disinterested. "Everything has a way of being spoken to if you but know it. But, alas, you never will."

"You didn't know how to make a fire. Everyone can't know everything."

"We have those who work with fire, but only that which is hurled from the red hand of the god."

"When you say 'we,' you mean elves?"

"But of course."

"Are there many of you?"

"Our numbers do not concern you."

"I mean, could you take me to your home?"

"What home? We are not as you. I have once, from afar, seen the dwellings of men. Rotted structures made of dirt and the corpses of trees, among which enslaved beasts dwell in torpid agony. The air reeks of sickness and death. How far you have fallen for a being of the higher mind."

"I always thought elves to be small, green, and living in the pool of a buttercup."

"Those are pixies, you fool, if anything, and to spy one takes a sharp eye."

I stabbed at the fire with a stick and a fan of embers rose into the night. Lyden leaned back quickly. It amazed me, mad or not, that she lived in these woods without the comfort of fire. "Lyden, where do you go in the night? Where do you sleep?"

"Where I go does not concern you."

"No, but you can tell me anyway. Why do you just walk off into the dark like that?"

She lifted her chin, haughty and reserved. "There are things afoot. I am the Queen and much rests on my shoulders. They all come to me. The myriad of creatures come to me, the petals of the flowers bend and tell a story of slashed forest. The death of the valley of the clouds has come to pass at last. This I read in the silver mist. In the haze of the day, in the whisper of the moth. Do you know even a moth can speak of fear? The balance tips more. It is slipping. All is slipping away."

"What's slipping, Lyden?"

She stared into the flames, and a log broke at that moment when life acts like something from a story. This time she did not flinch. "All of it. All of it is slipping." Her voice had an absence to it.

131

"All of what?"

She did not answer, but began to cough again.

"You're so sick, and yet you move like the wind."

"You sicken me."

"You were sick when I came across you," I said and she may have not heard or cared but spoke in an absent whisper. "The white stag has been skinned," she said enigmatically. "All rivers flow away into the darkness."

"I don't know what you mean, Lyden. I don't know what you're saying now."

She stared at me for a moment with those piercing eyes. "Again I say, you play some role in all of this, something which even you do not know. Too much is happening. It has been too active of late. You do not stumble upon me for no reason, bearing a star of the earth."

"If you could just take me to a road leading north, a clear trail, anything, I will find my way."

Without a word she stood and disappeared into the folds of the night.

Late morning when she returned, she spoke tersely and indicated a bush with hard-shelled nuts. How had I not seen them before? She picked one and split the shell with her red dagger nails. Stabbing one she poked the sweet meat inside, lifted it to her mouth, and chewed with slow deliberation. I had to crack the shell in my teeth. Lyden looked disgusted at this. I then used my dirt-encrusted nail to dig out the white meat and eat. I was fantastically hungry. "Ugh!" Lyden said and set off, draping a web on a faint trail going north.

I feasted on the treats and then stuffed my pockets with delicacies whose shell would keep them indefinitely. How nature amazed me: one moment it could give so little and then from a simple bush provide a great bounty in the heart of the wild.

Walking alone in this forest soon became eerie. For some reason, likely due to the long descent we followed, the days grew hot again and strange flowers appeared among the vegetation. Odd calls of creatures whose form I could not imagine rang through the canopy. More than once I walked with the blade at the ready. The trees began to curl and hide the sky. The whole forest humped in silence yet Lyden, true to her word, never let me go long before finding a dangling strand of web which, the moment it was passed, fell from the leaf upon which it had clung and melted into the ground. Behind us the trail had all gone. There was no trail now. There would be no going back. The final web, as always, led to a clearing. Lyden had already gathered a pile of wood. "You didn't have to do that," I said.

"It is easier this way. Less disturbing. Be always cautious now to follow my path. You have entered the proper realm of elf. No man would cross this and live. It is a land of astounding beauty and yet ancient evils. Do not stray from the path before you. Do not leave this clearing in the night. Keep the fire small. Make little noise. Things live here from which even I cannot protect you."

"What kinds of things, Lyden?"

She shook her head. "It does not matter. There are creatures here with no names. Walk as softly as you might. Follow the markers. Never stray from where I lead until you get to the North where the things of man begin again. You may burn all this wood this night but no more. We leave at the hour of the white crane. The first light."

And then she was gone.

Loneliness came like an old friend, but one whom I had always feared. Beside my small fire I lay on my blankets and stared into the endless sky. "I'm still here," I muttered to Selador. "I'm still here," I whispered to the nothingness. I banked the fire then and curled in the blanket for sleep feeling unprotected, exposed and over-visible. I imagined my life in the flickering flames, my fate in a fallen log, my future in the lifting embers, the past in the ashes. "I'm still here," I whispered once more and fell to sleep.

In the morning gray she awoke me. The fire had left a cold, black ring. We set out without food. She walked very swiftly and I had to trot to keep up. I don't know why but on this day she did not go ahead. Growing more frustrated at my pace she asked, "How has no beast not eaten you!"

"You say I have destiny. Do you think it is to be eaten by a beast?"

"It confounds me all the same."

"You are very graceful, Lyden. I have not lived my whole life in the forest as you."

She sighed and drew a finger through her hair, separated two strands that had embraced. "You are fortunate to have the star," she said almost absently. I touched the jezeth under my shirt. "Why are your clothes so filthy? Why do you dress in rags?"

I considered my body, covered in filth and grime, and my clothes reeking with sweat and earth. My uncle used to say the body cleans itself with sweat, but I wore the clothes of a beggar. "Half the time I don't even want to wear clothes, Lyden, until night anyway."

"They are of a very crude make. Almost as if a beast made them, but considering what you are this is not surprising."

"And what am I?"

"A mistake," she said. "All of yours are."

"What does that mean, Lyden?"

"It means just what it means."

"Well, thank you," I said coldly. She said nothing. We walked on and truly her gown seemed woven from the breath of a cloud, and it never sullied. Not a stain or smudge clung to it and that could not have been by Lyden's grace alone. Looking at my tattered shirt, the wraps of leather around my feet, I became ashamed. I felt ugly and unwanted then, and to her surely I was just that. More and more I kept my eyes cast before my feet and hid my face to the ground while she, at various points of our travels, would comment on the ugliness of my form, the imperfection of my making. I don't write about it much. It hurt then and hurts yet, and I would not have written of it at all because it is a common thing, and easily understood, but it matters to what happens next.

The day became usually hot in the odd way of that land of scorching days and freezing nights. We crossed a plain, and were it not for my blanket to shield the sun it would have nearly killed me. Not too far off the right shoulder ran a low treeline and I wondered why we did not follow it, but I had learned with Lyden to not ask questions unless out of absolute necessity. A barrage of insults, a mindfulness of my ignorance would likely follow or at best no answer but an icy silence. At last, I felt faint. "Lyden, I need to slow. It's the heat. I'm sorry."

No assault came. She stopped instead and scanned the horizon in all directions, and then hopped up on a tall stalk of grass and did so again and again. I was baffled by this talent. She stared to the treeline to the east for too long a time, and I would always remember that. "I have a matter to attend to anyway. Wait here then. Just here. I will return before the day is done. I will find you here. Do not leave from here. It would be best if you lie down, beneath the level of the grass. Use the tattered rag you drag along if simple sunlight courts death to you. Wait just here. Here. Do not stray from here. Wait, and take your needed rest," and with that she fled to low green hills to the west, running like a hawk over the earth, then leaping in the distance into the tops of trees. For a few moments I could see her gliding through them, like a great white crane of baffling enormity. I watched her until she was gone, pulled the blanket over my head and waited.

I had not filled the gourd at the last creek Lyden had said was good for drinking. It was shallow, and the gourd would half-fill at best. I thought water ran everywhere but it did not, and now only a sip remained and I drank it. It is always best to drink before you grow too thirsty. I tapped the empty gourd. I waited in the heat. It must have been near noon. I had learned hunger, but despised thirst.

I tried to think of the last creek we crossed. Too far. I looked to the treeline which Lyden seemed to shun. Lush and verdant. I imagined in there a wet grove of dripping water, maybe even a waterfall, a pool. If anything, it would be shade for a time. Why would she just leave me like this in such a place?

I drew an arrow in the ground showing my course, but I would be back before her. I knew that. I set out to the treeline, the one to which she had taken pause. Looking at it now, I paused too. For the rest of my life I will remember the pause and the voice it had: do not go. But you will go anyway.

Thirst. Burning and painful thirst. Creeks were not hard to find. I would go slowly and listen. I would drink and fill the gourd at the first creek and turn back.

All the forest hung in silence. I crept into it as if stepping into the jaw of an enormous beast. Thirst like fire now. I wiped away my precious sweat. The cool and the quiet of the place, why did it scare me so? Nothing out of the ordinary. She did this to me with her hesitation. She made my stomach rise in fear, but thirst will drive one to the tip of a sword. Inside, shade shut out the sun entirely. The canopy seemed it would not let even rain break through. Dark almost like night. Behind my step the plains of fire. Very quietly I stepped through the trees and rare was the birdsong and rare the call of the cricket, but it was day. I had seen stranger places. Why had she made me so afraid of this one?

Suddenly the whole forest began to decline and this lightened my heart because water ran to low places. I would stop often and listen, for water, for anything. Very quiet. Very peaceful. All quiet. I had taken the blade out but sheathed it now. Nothing to fear. As I went deeper into the vegetation the decline steepened. Mesmerizing flowers of every kind and color now hung heavy and wet from the boughs made all the more fantastic by the near black of the forest.

The air became so moist it almost slaked thirst. As the forest lowered the roots began to rise more out of the ground like a pit of snakes, and now all the forest floor ran in a kind of bowl. Water had to be near. Ever steeper, ever downwards and the ground became simply roots and I held the trees and stepped carefully on them because they could trap and twist a leg and split bones right out of the skin. Water had to be near land that ran so low. I climbed down into a mist that formed over the bowl of the ground and it smelled of wet wood now. Water had to be near.

Soon, the ground tilted so sharply it became a wall to which the twisted trees clung, turning from their base and growing up towards an invisible sun. I would have turned around had I not then seen the pool: a nearly perfect circle of turquoise into which all the forest poured. If it were any other water, in any other place, a thirst like mine would have sent me racing towards the pool. But for a moment, just the breath of a moment, I took pause, and for that moment only there was no thirst, and for that moment only I considered turning back, yet I did not know why. And as I climbed the last bit down, holding only roots now and thin trunks, like a twisted ladder from a dream of mad descent, I paused often and considered the pond whose color did not seem of the earth, whose blood might be poison, but one to which I went all the same. And for whatever reason, when at last my foot could dip into the pool, when at last my hand could cup and drink from it, I paused again.

And then I understood: never before had I seen water so still. Below must have slept a deep spring for it was not stagnant. I still did not drink but stared a while. Nothing in it at all. Nothing in it lived. Not even a gnat skimmed across its surface.

I was about to dip in my hand but pulled it back. I untied the gourd and lowered it and the water made a sucking sound as it drew in. This reverberation shook off the walls of the trees. Far above floated a circle of sky. It looked like fire.

The water had no odor. I took a small sip and nothing happened. Just water, blessed water. I drained the gourd and filled it again and tied it to my waist. I sat on a root that ran out of the pool like a great serpent and let my feet dangle in. Very cold. I thought to jump in but paused and did not know why. Still, nothing moved in the pond.

Beneath my feet the water ran down to impenetrable blue. I kicked my feet slowly and thought of Lyden and then the filth on my clothes. I stripped off my shirt and pants and without going into the pool myself doused them and rubbed the grime against the course skin of the root. The soiling left my clothes and covered the water like a stain. I watched it slowly spread across the pool and felt like I had committed some deep sin.

Wet, I began to climb away. I looked back only once. The stain remained on the surface of the pool, spreading slowly like a curse over innocence.

When I returned to the forest's edge Lyden was there, standing in its shade. Her voice was shaken. "Where were you? Where did you go? Why did you go in there?"

"I…I needed water."

She almost wept. "And from where have you gotten this water?"

"From a pool. From a pool in the forest. It's fine. I'm fine."

She touched her slender fingers to her lips and spoke in her broken voice, "I told you. I told you again and again to stay where you were. I told you to wait where you were. What are you saying now? Where have you gone?"

"I'm fine," I said again. "I'm fine. Why do you look like that? Why are you talking like this?"

And then a very strange thing happened: a child laughed from within the forest. Lyden's breath went out. Her eyes filled wet with terror. She almost collapsed. "What have you done now, Foresaker of the Path? Why did you not stay as I instructed?" And then, another child's laughter rose from the shadows behind, and I looked and saw nothing and turned to Lyden again and knew something very terrible had begun.

"I know, Lyden. I understand now. Let's just go. I'm sorry. Please let's go."

She began shaking her head. Her hair, as long as her height, cascaded like a mane. She stepped back and wept. "Son of Man, if you have any god pray to it now. You have awakened the Children of the Rain."

And she kept backing away from me and the forest and at last turned and ran out into the sun and I followed. Peals of laughter chased us. I could not look behind. They were close. And though I ran as swiftly as I ever had Lyden had taken to the wind, skimmed across the grass tops and was gone. I called out to her, but she was gone.

The grass bent as the children crawled through it. I ran and ran with the laughter at my heels. I ran until the laughter cackled before me as well. Only then did I stop, breathless, and drew the blade. They had circled me. Nothing to see but glimpses of humped backs, greenish yellow scabs curling above the yellow grass calling with the titter of children. So many now, swimming through the grass, and I knew I would die that day and I did not want to die like this. A clumsy, trampled step thudded before me and the stepper laughed more and emerged from the grass, and there stood a Child of the Rain.

It loomed like an enormous fleshy growth, like a fungus creeping and filthy and eyeless, caverns for eyes atop a body like a collection of bones stuffed in a sack made from the flesh of a corpse, flesh peeled and reattached with the outside in and infested with rot. It had a black maw for a mouth. From a ridge of teeth rang the laughter of a child.

The world prepares you for what it has in store in some ways. All that terror and hurt and unknowing, all the pain and all the struggle, all the knowledge gained in life and learning came forward now as the monster child lifted some vestigial limb to point at me with fingers melted together, a sloping shoulder of wax. Its purple tongue licked its teeth with a wet smack and its twisted mock leg staggered forward. Again, insanely, it laughed the fresh laughter of a child, but I did not freeze in my terror, for the world prepares you in some ways for whatever may come. With knees of water I lifted the blade of the Picarin. With the seventh arc of the mist made it scream so loud between us that it scorched the air. The monster paused.

Others began to awaken from the grass until a circle of the beasts surrounded me. They began to laugh, all of them, but less joyfully, and as they closed in with broken steps, with leaning bodies, each demented and melted in its own way, the odor of dead fish and grave rot hit me so powerfully I vomited up the stolen water. Though sick and dizzy, I immediately cut away all my burdens to be quicker in my killing. With my legs in what Gelidii called the "sizzer-step" I rotated in a slow circle and traced the curve of the blade across all twelve or thirteen of their throats. I would not be so easily taken. I was no Gelidii, but could make a sphere of death around me all the same. I would cut them all at least once. I would leave them in ribbons in the grass that withered before their step. I did not need to run as Lyden had.

"Ulg," mumbled one behind me. I turned with the blade raised and saw it had begun to hold hands with its brothers, and then they all began to join hands to make a circle as if in ritual before the darkest of gods.

"I'm going to kill you all," I said to them, and the blade sang again and they all began to close in with joined hands. They moved so slowly. Why did they move so slowly now, with that odd and watery call?

Ulg ...

Ulg...

Urlgl ...

They had no ears that I could see, but I spoke anyway. "Ju...just go away. Go away. Then none of you has to die. Just go back to the pool. I'm sorry I took your water."

"Ulg!"

Then they all began to weep like screaming infants, like dying rabbits they wept, and as they closed in tighter they did a very miraculous thing: the flesh of the holding hand began to melt into the other, the fingers joining like melting candles, the palms of two becoming one. And among this weaving the weeping grew louder, almost as if some beast had devoured a child who called from the cavity within. Their tongues lolled and their heads bobbed forward, drip-dripping saliva, and then the little fish began to swim before my eyes, the air so stuffed with fetid rot, and to save myself from falling out my mind screamed that this could only be a terrible dream. "Why are you crying?" I begged to the dream, for I had learned that dreams could be controlled if the sleeper paid attention.

Why are you crying like that?

In battle, take any advantage. I would have to wait for them to get terrifically close before I could cut them. Let me put at least one down before they attack. In a breath I lowered my stance and set down the blade and took up the tooth. I drew it over my head with two hands and spun to face the first who had stood before me. Perhaps here stands their leader. Its arms had half-melted in its brothers' by then, and their feet and knees stuck to each other too. Even their headpieces leaned into each other, sticking at the tops as if glued, and slowly their skulls began to melt together. And now the weeping turned to moans.

Just tell me why you're crying!

I aimed for the beast-child's dead heart. The tooth whirled through the air and, with a wet plop, landed perfectly in the center of what would be its chest. For a moment my heart lifted, but the tooth disappear into its form, thudded on the ground behind it.

The hole in its chest closed. I'd not even wounded it. Only hesitantly did I take the knife up again, for how do you kill the dead remade in water? Cut off their heads.

They were as one now, a ring of flesh and melting rot, closing in with their weeping and moaning rising to screams of grief. They had become a single organism. And I was shaking very badly by then, holding the knife up, but it was shaking too. I slashed at the air but the blade would not sing for my shaking. I told myself Lyden would be back, that she had gone to get help. It had to be, for I did not want to die here on this day, not like this.

Please go please please go. Stop moaning! Why are you crying!

I could almost cut the first one when a gurgle rose from its mouth. I turned to it and it spit on me, a cup of bile on my leg. For a moment there was nothing but the awful reek, but then my pant leg melted away where it had spat, and the where the bile had touched, my leg it fell cold. But in the next breath it burned with an agony worse than fire.

As I began to scream they wept with me, mocking my cries, twisting as I rubbed the agony on my leg, all of us joined in a mad dance of distress. And then another spat its bile on me, and then another. They were digesting me while I was still alive, before I even entered their guts. In the most fantastic agony of my life I had not noticed I could reach the face of one. When I did, I sliced it in half. The knife went through it as if through a leaf, but the face just formed again and continued to melt and I was doomed. I had slashed at water.

I cut and cut at them anyway, but kept running my hands on the burning patches and then my hands began to burn. One spat a glob directly on my chest, and my shirt began to melt. Their bile was heavy and landed low, otherwise to this day I would have a misshapen face. My shirt's front turned to fumes and I screamed and they mock-screamed beside me, hopping in their own way, imitating my spasmodic efforts to save this life.

All was lost. Lyden was not coming back. Selador would not be saved by a mystic Sage. I would never have children. I would never know love. All was lost and never did I imagine such a death. I could take the pain no more. They had entirely become one. Even their mouths joined now and soon it would be a font of acid turning me into a puddle. I had one slice left in the knife and this for my throat. I believe in destiny when I tell the next part of my story. I lifted the knife to my throat and muttered a final prayer. Just then one of the creatures spat on the back of my hand. Instinctively, I opened it. The blade dropped.

The creatures screamed louder now but had stopped closing in. I did not know for what or why, nor did I care, I just wanted to die so badly for the pain. I bent for the knife with a hand consumed by glowing coals and there hung the jezeth, naked and exposed. Its wrapping like my shirt had dissolved in the bile. It burned like the sun.

The Children of the Rain screamed so horribly now. They screamed at it and as badly as I wanted to die I wanted to hurt them first. How they shunned the light of the jezeth. I staggered in a circle towards them all and relished to see them lurch backwards, trying to separate quickly and run. But they failed at this. Some ripped the arm from his brother, some staggered back with the stump of his brother's head. Some few were torn clean in half. But even the pieces, without any mind or eyes, rolled away. I did not want to think how this was done. Yet all parts shunned the jezeth. And I draped it before them all and screamed and screamed in victory and rage and agony until they were gone.

I went to cut my throat again, the pain so terrible it cannot be understood, but as I touched the knife to my neck Lyden drifted down from the sky. Once again, she was casting leaves. And I fell out.

Eight days later I awoke in a shaded pool of warm water. A low fall running from the forest fed it. Lyden sat beside my body and cradled my head in her arms. "You have come back to us," she said gently.

"Kill me. Please please kill me. It burns!"

"Hush hush. I have awakened you too soon."

"It burns, it burns, please kill me, Lyden, please!"

My naked body writhed in the tranquil pool. A poultice of green herbs stuck to me, even in the water. Lyden held a red leaf under my nose and tore it in half. "Hush now," she said very gently. "Be still and sleep again." She gave me a buttercup of honey to drink.

By the next breath I fell again into a sleep which would last for eight more days. I awoke to pain unbearable, but did not immediately want to die. At first I did not see her. "Lyden!" She was there. She smiled. "Oh, you are much better now! Wonderful."

"It's burning. It's burning."

"Of course it is."

"Lyden, the pain. The pain."

"Drink this," she said and held another buttercup of honey to my lips.

"Honey's not going to help me, Lyden."

"Hush. This is a very special kind."

"I hurt so much," I said but, even as I said it, the honey began to take effect. A softness went over the pain, a heaviness covered my eyes. Even my spirit felt healed some as the weight of all past guilt and confusion and fear faded to a soft haze. Ah, the honey!

"It still hurts," I said slowly. "They were eating me."

"Everything needs to eat, Child of Man."

The world softened even more. For the first time in weeks the heights of pain and terror faded from my waking mind. As I drifted into a false peace the question formed that I would never ask, for I understood she had owed me nothing and had told me just what to do, and there had been nothing she could have done, yet it hurt all the same, and some part of me wanted very badly to ask her what I would never.

Lyden, how could you have left me?

"The poison went far into you, but you have come back. In all my life I have never heard of anything surviving the ring of the Children of the Rain. Again this speaks of a purpose beyond your journey. But do not test it. Fate is the dark brother of Destiny, and will catch you should you shun her embrace."

"The jezeth!" I cried then, remembering.

"It is here, just here." She gestured to an outcropping of stone that reached over the pool. "It saved you. Nothing else would have."

"What were they?"

She tapped her finger into the water and waited. She then cupped her hand beneath the gentle fall and brought this water to my lips and I drank helplessly, my arms nearly immobile from the swollen scab of burn. She then took more water and ran it through my hair. A low fever burned through me.

"They are what they are. What more answer do you need? Everything is here. Rest in the pool for now. Keep your mind calm and you will heal quicker. This is a very special place. No human has ever been here before. The herbs help but only these waters, from what Lyden knows of, could have saved one so wounded."

Lush splendor surrounded us. The air hung pregnant with the scent of lavender and rose and a sweetness I could not recognize; crystal and amethyst and gems of mysterious colors lined the walls and floor of the pool and for a moment just beholding it stopped the pain. "You are not healed yet," she said gently. "Almost, but not yet. I will soften the skin when it is time, but I cannot promise you will emerge from this unscarred."

"We don't thut iv un harled," I slurred, falling out again. She laughed gently and I turned heavy eyes up to hers. "We don left this lif unsharred."

"The medicine has taken effect."

I took a deep breath and cleared away the most welcome pink cloud that had settled in me. "We don't leave this life unscarred," I finally said, and Lyden brushed wet hair from my eyes and smiled and I fell into a deep sleep.

It would be a long time before we left the pool, but we did. Some of the bile which got in more deeply would leave me forever with misshapen and discolored skin on my torso, arms and legs, but I am forever grateful to escape with only that. I never asked Lyden how she got me to the pool.

"We now walk in the true Elven realm," she said as we set out again. "A privilege for a human. Few are they who have. A very ancient magic shields her from their eyes, draws their step aside."

I could not dispute this, although I did not quite believe it. I had been carried into this place unconscious and knew not the entrance, but the vegetation and sky, the light and the fragrance in the wind, the crystal clarity and the sweetness of the waters told that here was a difference, but not so that it could be confined to words. Even her hair shimmered in a way it had never before. She coughed less two.

We followed no trail at all. Lyden wandered over the land following no obvious signs or markers, yet we marched always north. North.

We rested in a shaded grove. A circle of light shone on a bed of dark green moss which covered all the ground. She brought me to a pool. Leaning over it grew a lovely tree heavy with fruit. Lyden asked the tree for one and it fell into her hand. Deep red skin it had. On the inside, with sweet white meat. She chewed it slowly. I shook the tree and a few fell and one went into the shallow pool. "Well," she said. "Do not waste it. Shall it fall for nothing? Go and get it."

The frigid breath of fear trembled my limbs. She noticed this.

"It is not like the other. Would I be such a fool? It is just there," she pointed to the glowing red skin. "Strip your rags away and fetch the fruit. It is most delicious."

"You want me to strip in front of you?"

She paused in her eating. "Why ever would you not?"

"I… it's just that's not what we do where I'm from."

She shrugged. "As you wish. I have a matter to attend. Do not leave this place."

"Where are you going?"

She stabbed a cold scowl. "I have a matter to which I must attend. Have the Children melted your ears as well?"

"No. No, but…when will you be back?"

"You ask much for a man once lost with almost nothing. I will be back before nightfall. Do not leave this place. Please wash while I am gone. You emit a very foul odor, especially when you sweat. It disgusts me more each day."

"Don't leave me, Lyden. Please."

"You are safe here. I promise you, but stay just here. Do not wander."

"No."

"Do not!"

"No."

She faded into the leaves soundlessly. I lay my rank clothes and belongings in a pile and placed the jezeth, unscathed by the acid, atop them. Cautiously, I felt the water with my toe. Cold. I slipped in and a visceral pull came from the wounded patches of flesh. After a time, pus leached out even from areas seemingly long healed, and I began to cough and soon spat out a viscous, foul-smelling phlegm. I shivered in the pool as long as I could. The cold bit but the curative powers could not be denied.

Resting warm on a bed of moss I ate the exquisite fruit. Like paradise it tasted. From the canopy above fell the call of magnificent birds only half-hidden. Some had twin tail feathers as long as a man's leg. Others shone like a blue sky. What a lovely land. Could anything be closer to Paradise? Here was Paradise.

"Are you well now?" Lyden had returned as silently as she had departed.

"Lyden, gods, I'm naked."

"Here. I tired of your rags even before the Children of the Rain dissolved them." She threw a whitish-grey garment at me, a tunic, masterfully woven. But in my humiliation I grabbed my torn and rotted strands of clothing and stood sideways to dress quickly. "Do not wear those rags, not ever again. We will bury them. Lyden has given you a gift. Accept it."

"Just let me get dressed." I had always been terribly shy at being naked, especially in front of a strange woman. Lyden seemed puzzled at my embarrassment, but then indifferently turned her back and strolled some ways into the small meadow about the pond. She bent low and whispered to the flowers. I began to hurry into the "Get dressed in the new garment," she called over her shoulder. "Pull it over your head and tie it in the middle."

Naked and nervous I fumbled with it, trying to understand what kind of shirt it was.

"Fool!" she cried, racing over.

"Lyden!"

"Fool!" she asserted again and yanked the garment from my hands and I covered my genitals and Lyden did not seem to care or notice. She snapped it flat into the air and then drew it over my head in one movement. With a deftness that defied logic, she drew the white sash straight and tied it perfectly around my waist with a knot whose turns cannot be trapped in words. (Those I have shown this knot to say it holds a magic in its strength and simplicity that is too perfect to have been conceived of by humankind).

I do not know if that is true, but I have never forgotten this knot which has more to it than a simple fastening. With three gentle tugs, anywhere on the rope, the knot releases on its own, yet will never fail you when you depend on it. And unlike every other knot man ever made, this one and this one only is stronger than the rope itself. This has been proven many times. In every instance, when I have overstressed a cord of any material to the point it failed, the rift was never at this knot, but some distance from it, as if the secret Elven turns imparted a strength not only to the knot but to the cord running beyond. Were I ever to ask Lyden how this or any other magnificent feat of hers could be, her response, if not outright silence, was that it was not her obligation, nor her desire, to disclose the Elven ways to a man.

The Elven garment wore loose but not clumsily so, and where it rested on the skin it felt like a coat of natural fur. It repelled water and shunned dirt, kept one cool in the heat and warm in the cold. Amazingly, if you stood very still the magic fibers absorbed whatever colors surrounded you, and thus the wearer could disappear. (Lyden had done this just for me. Her gown remained shimmering white with just a hint of gray.)

I ran my hands down it feeling remade by the gift and the kindness of its giving. Here was one of the finest articles of clothing ever created. "Lyden, thank you."

"It is nothing. It is for me. Your other garments distressed the eyes, reeked of death, served as a fetid reminder of your foolishness. You should be grateful only to the silver grasses that yielded part of their manes to make the cloth. Know they hesitated in this, for the cold season comes. I had to promise to take but a little of each and so journeyed deep into the forest for this collection. I see the disbelief in your eyes. Man has forgotten the language of the growing world. Little wonder you do not believe."

"I believe you."

"Do not lie to me." She then squinted below my sash, "Why do you appear ready to mate?"

"Lyden!"

I turned away from her and she laughed. "Bury your old rags. We need no trail of scent."

"I will," I said, and would. But first, taking the knife from my sash, I made from them a decent harness for the tooth, one which let the tip poke out so it would not tear through so easily. And from the best of those old garments I cut a fresh shroud for the jezeth, wrapped it and wore it again wondering at what enchantment had protected it and its chain from the poison. Though I had washed these remnants very well, beating them against rock again and again, when resting against the cloth of the tunic they were tawdry rags.

We spent that night by the enchanted pond. I could feast on the exquisite fruit but took only a few more since Lyden did not go away when night fell. At twilight she draped her hair into the water. Once all out she waved her head and the tresses turned on the water like a great silver snake. Without looking up she asked, "Tell us of the path to retrieve the tooth of the living dragon."

I smiled a moment, but then the smile went away. "I'd been following stories. Any kind: myths or wives' tales, legends and superstition. It didn't matter. I never actually believed I would find one, but I had to believe in it so I did. In the more remote villages people believed more so in dragons, and many other things too that should not exist. Well, one believer pointed me to another, and that to another still, until I came to the door of The Dragon's Nest, a tavern. I was very thin by then, long on the road with neither coins nor provisions left. I stood at the door waiting for I don't know what. It was night. And then the door opened and a wash of amber light flooded from within…How much of the story do you want to hear?"

"As much as you wish. We have time. Are you enjoying the fruit?"

"It's exquisite," I said. Like all of Lyden's food, it restored and strengthened me more than it should have. I took another bite and went on.

"Do not speak while you chew."

"I know that."

She looked harsh for a moment but said nothing and returned to her hair, drawing it in and letting it out, like a weaver at his loom. And in that light in that time, in that part of the forest of the good earth, her hair shone like gold. "Tell Lyden this," she said then, "now that there is time. Tell Lyden this story of a man who finds the sleeping dragon in the mountain's heart."

Often the most difficult part of a story is to decide what's worth telling and also what should be told. "Again, after a long time on trails and woods, sleeping in fields and stables and eating what I could, living on the outskirts of my kind, (for even though I found my way out of the wilderness, I had no money), it happened that someone gave me a coin while I stood outside that tavern. That allowed me to go in, to sleep and eat and drink in the tavern, to get whatever I might want that could be had. That is the way with people."

"This I know."

"Yes, well, that great coin cut the beginning of the trail to the mountain's heart. But I don't want to tell you the whole story of the coin. It doesn't matter anyway."

"Then do not."

The door almost slammed into the low wooden rail outside. It shocked him a little, the noise and the flood of warm light and then the sudden sweet and smoky aroma of stew and the reek of stale alcohol and the voices and the candlelight and the laughter from within. It had been a long time since he'd seen such a place and he remembered a lot of things almost forgotten.

An arm like the branch of a tree had almost broken the door open, and then an extraordinary immensity filled the entire doorway. He wore a heavy brown robe. He held a large silver cup in one hand and leaned against the doorpost. From inside, patrons complained of the cold night air rushing in. He muttered something angrily but then staggered out and the door slammed shut behind him. When he spied the stranger at last he did so with an expression of surprise which made the other feel not quite real. He lifted his silver cup between them and proclaimed, "May God on High bless the fruitful grape!" He then took a long pull and wiped his mouth. His head lolled in drunkenness. Suddenly, he stared right at him with sad eyes. "Who is you now?"

"I'm just passing through. Looking for work."

It took a moment for him to understand, but then he boomed in a voice as low as he was large, "Ah! Ah ha! Work! Our sacred duty!" and drank again from the silver chalice, taking another long draw. When he emptied the cup he cursed it and in an act of incredible waste threw it into the bushes. He fell back on the doorpost. The enormity of his size seemed like it could knock the tavern over. "And...and it is by work we eat and feed, and every child of God is born with a calling. I am...mine is...it is I who am Brother Marcus, steward of the sheep, Shepherd of the Children of God, and so it goes. So it is.

"Thus it is…it is by my, by mine own word that the deeds and the work of Him, of His hands are blest. That is my work." He took another pendulous step forward and swayed on both feet. "So, you seek work. Work. Here's my work: They catched him. Got 'im up, caught 'im up, this broken fella. Always a crooked fella, always smiling that crooked smile from his first day. A mewling, drooling young one. And it was I who poured the water on his brow and blest 'im into this cold and dusty world and they…." Here he lifted his hand to drink from a cup that was no longer there. He turned backwards towards the tavern, draping his hand over the door handle, almost stumbling, and then turned to him again. "… They got 'im. He were a big one. Grew into a big man, strong like a damned horse, but not quick, and off in the mind the way some are. Crooked fellow, had a straying eye and always with that crooked smile. So they get 'im. Catch 'im and he were barely knowing even knowing to hide, so they catch him easy and tie 'im to the post. Tie him so the damned ropes are cutting in and he bleeding and crying out and it would be his last day. And they call me for the rites to be done. They couldn't a done it without the rites you see. Not proper so. You know this now. 'Brother, they say, would you bless this cleansing?'

"And I staring at them without a word and they pause and say, 'Brother, Brother, he going anyway. That gonna happen. You want him cleansed for the forgiveness of God, or will you let him part with his sins heavy upon him? Is your choice but we only got today, Brother, and we only got you.'

"'Only me. Me. I to give the blessing of God to the burning of one of his children, crooked-born though he may be. And I, like a man in a trance, am led to the town square, I, the final ingredient and he on the dais bound and crying and them ropes, the roughest kind, cutting into him and he pulling still, and the crowd staring and yelling, throwing things and some did hittin' him and they aiming for the face."

Brother Marcus waved a hand and shook his head. "Now I don't…I don't fault them this…don't cast judgment upon them. Was two angels. Hair like spring meadow. Sisters just old enough to go to town and fetch their mother a gourd a milk and they were darlings, *them little things, darlings a the spring and there a meadow with a path they follow and he were in it, in the grass waiting, them urges put there by the spring and the season and no woman wanting him and he didn't know what he doing, but he did." He waved his hand again, as if waving away an offer.*

"An' I don't, I don't don't judge 'em for it. Him. Them. He took them two girls, each lovely as the lily a the field and he, he he he broke their fucking bones with it. Had them tied together and splayed and broke their fucking bones with it he so large. They bled out there in the meadow, alone but for each other and I, I don't, I don't say is wrong what they done to him for that. Made him fast to the post they did, now they hurling stones and curses and the stones hittin' hard his face and he just staring and crying, that mind so simple it don't know why and what and I knew that and it's that crying face I see yet. Is the damned simpleness what stays with me. He pulling at them ropes so hard they cutting him the more and sees me and starts smiling then, a crooked smile still and I, I in a trance walking up the platform. Yea, I see him smiling that crooked smile yet.

"So, so so so, so I pour the holy water on that brow and utter the sacred words so he may be forgiven by the kingdom of God: 'Lord, he know not what he does.'

"An' he lapping at the water like an imbecile, and they setting the sticks already at his feet and the grease and the oil-soaked rags and he gets an inkling of what it is now and pulls at the ropes more and they cuttin' deep and he begins callin' out for his ma. And they needed me to do this. They needed me to put God's blessing to this work and I, I don't say it were the wrong thing. Them flowers plucked too soon and what you do with him now? I don't say it were the wrong thing what they done. So I finish the work of my hands and no sooner do I finish when they climbing the platform with them torches. All the town there watching and with the arrival of the fire a kind of holy silence falls like before a sacrifice of the days gone by. And I climb down quick and don't look back, and before I smell the smoke I hear the screaming. Howling in that mumbled, garbled voice a his. Everyone, almost, all silent now, like a collected prayer and the rage had gone and their faces had fallen to wonder. Flames licking higher and higher yet, to a death I cannot imagine. And I'm forcing my way out, pushing through the crowd all staring forward

as if upon some glorious sunset, but I dare not turn back. No, not once. And when I'm far and far and almost free I hear her and her alone in screaming grief, screaming louder than he. How she could stand it I don't know. But his voice starts breaking apart now because the flames eatin' at his throat, or maybe he'd just screamed hisself out, but she howling still in a grief that does not live far from madness. But he would not be alone in his passing. He would not have but a sea of hateful eyes in his final light. She, she she'd purchased a lifetime a nightmares for him who would soon suffer no more just for that, just so he could see one who loved him still, who loved him no matter what. Such resolve. Such courage. Of all God's creation, does anything have such strength? Mothers…"

"A drunken man, enormous, burst out of the tavern door. 'You look like you need a meal,' he said to me.

"'I've no money,' I said.

"He swayed. We'd been talking a while, him mostly, but it felt like he saw me for the first time then. He then lifted a swaying finger at me. 'Wait' he slurred, and then from beneath his robe pulled out a purse and from it a coin. He turned it once in his fingers then threw it spinning through the air to me and I caught it. It felt like a stone in my hand. I was the first gold coin I'd ever held, and the largest I'd ever heard of. On the front was a relief of the profile of the living king and on the back a relief of his guardian, the parvus. I could not believe I held so much wealth. 'Eat up!' he shouted almost joyfully, but his eyes were still sad. He began to stumble out and rested a hand on my shoulder as he passed, maybe to keep from falling but he mumbled a blessing too I think. I thanked him as he left. If he heard it didn't show. He staggered down the road into the dark, and was gone.

"I entered the tavern and everyone looked at me. So strange to be in a tavern again. Then, an old and gaunt and red-faced man who held his flagon tightly squinted at me with small eyes. They were very close together I remember, his eyes. He said, 'How I so despise that libidinous son of bitch. How long he keep you at the door?'

"I'd no idea what to say, what to do. Chairs lined a great table behind which a keeper polished cups as he leaned against barrels of wine and cider. I sat and the old man gave me a straight look. 'Him and his damned stories. How he sickens me. An offence to the cloth,' he said and I said nothing. 'Be easy,' the keep told him, but the old man waved him off. 'So, what you want in this place youngun?' asked the thin red man. I told him the truth: that I wanted food and a bed and was looking for a dragon. Three men sitting in the rear of the tavern sighed, and the inn-keeper let out a breath and shook his head. However, the old red-faced man grew very quiet then and sat right next to me. In a whisper he said he knew where a dragon slept. His breath smelled of stale wine.

"'Buy me a cider, and I shall tell you a story of the dragon.'

"He drained his flagon as I ordered two ciders. He lifted his fresh one to me and almost smiled before taking the first sip.

"'Is a story but the truth, and this story goes as this: a storm to end all others begins. The sky were splittin' apart and the rain's such that the wind could not be separated from the water, and all the skies crying like a demon howlin' fresh outta Hell. Was my own grandfather who saw this. Said out of a blue day ink poured across the dome of Heaven and said the grand order had been forgotten. Said something had tipped.' He took a long pull of his cider.

"'Was chaos come again, the very chaos that bore the stars and earth had come again, and he was a woodsman and out far, even for those times, seeking the black wood that grows harder than iron. He'd no hope to make it out, so just huddles next to a boulder set there by God's mercy and begins praying enchantments for hisself as trees flying off a the earth as easily as the leaves from them. And still that wind's rising yet he say, and he prayin' hard until the heart of his prayer is pierced by a primordial howl. Something howling in that falling sky. He says her cry could a turn your bones to water. Was the last groan of a sinking world he thought, or the trumpet of the great beginning. At last he dares to look into the swirl of chaos come again and look! Look! She flies!' His voice grew breathless now, and he stared right at me with eyes wide. 'Out there in the above, cuttin' the arcs of the firmament with wings no earthly creature ought to have, was the devil's pet tumbling through God's own sky. A dragon! A dragon flying, her wings beatin' back the very storm, and he said her breath were fire, and when she cried out again he wept!'

"He took a long draw from the flagon and his hand shook. 'Whether was wind or will he don't know, but she slams 'gainst the face of the very mountain to which I and I alone may send you. And she folds her wings in and starts digging in, tossing stones behind her like sand, and you can see them yet if you go — a tumble a rocks upon a mountain face that got no earthly reason to be there — and she digs in and she's howling yet like the fell sky and she buries herself away, tucks all in until even her tail is gone. She sets up in it see? Makes her nest in the womb of the mountain.'

"His expression softened then. He spoke in a whisper, 'An she sleepin' there yet.' He nodded in affirmation. 'Was my own grandfather mind you, who bore witness of this truth of which I now speak and to which I alone may lead you. She in there, as I live and breathe, she in there.' He took the last sip of his cider and knocked the flagon against the bar. 'Give us 'nother, 'keep.'

"''You have any more money?' asked the inn keeper.

"''Aw, now,' the taleteller said, smiling drunkenly and slapping a heavy hand on my shoulder. 'This young fellow comes asking about stories a dragons. Was fate has me here this day.' He shot a sour look at the other patrons sitting behind us and then turned to me and whispered very softly, 'I've a map...right 'ere I've it.' He tapped his head. 'Piece a coal and I'll scratch it out for ya. More cider a small price to pay for this.'

"''Two ciders,' I said to the innkeeper. I did this mostly out of pity for the old man. I knew drunks too well and he had it bad and I just been given much. But still, no other broker proffered maps to the lairs of dragons. I placed the gold coin on the bar and the old red man and the innkeeper considered it like a thing unrecognizable. 'I need some food too, and a scrap of something to write on if you have it. And you can get him a plate too with that.'

"''I ate,' said the old red man, 'but will take a cider back if that's how it's gonna be.''

"The innkeeper took up the coin and held it to the light then took a knife from under the bar and cut the tiniest notch out of the coin and gave the rest back. I put the coin back in my pocket.

"''Ah, don't let him take you, kid!' cried a heavyset patron from the back of the inn. 'He's been selling that story for drinks since before dragons were born!' Everyone laughed except the old man, the innkeeper and me.

"The thin, red man began to tremble then. His face tightened and he directed his words to the detractor, but would not look at him, but only into his drink. 'It don't concern you! You don't know nothing! What you talking for what don't concern you nothing!'

"'Because you're lying to him.'

"'Easy now,' said the innkeeper.

"'You're selling him stories for money, for drink,' said the heavyset man.

"The old man now began to tremble in an odd way. He ran a bony hand through his white hair and his face twisted in a kind of pain. When he responded it was almost in a screech. 'I tells him about a true demiurge, a god a this very earth I tells him of and you accuse me of disgrace! You 'cuse me a slanderer and you don't know nothing! It was my grandfather! Mine own!' He howled and hit his chest. He shook with tears now. 'My own blood! Mine seen it land and you a slanderer and nothin' and don't know nothin'!'

"'Forget it,' spoke the heavyset man. 'Be easy now.'

"'Forget you! You nothing! You nothing at all. Forget you! Forget you, you nothing! Your mother's nothing and you nothing ever!' And now he cried full and the tears were dripping on the bar, and the tavern fell silent and the innkeep had cut a slice of vellum and put it before us with the cider.

"'Easy now,' said the innkeeper.

"The red-faced man took a heavy pull, still weeping so that he sipped his own tears. He began to scratch out a map which, ridiculously, he shielded from the view of the others. There where lines and crude trees and childish images of what would be mountains. He finished and whispered to me, 'You need to be going north to the first mountains. The low ones. The old ones. Those that began before the race of man fell to sin. They start just where the tavern road ends. You'll see them. She's there. Not far. Not so far. She's in there and she sleeping yet. They say she be sleeping unto that terrible and blessed day come of God's judgment, that day for men in their wickedness to pay.'

"With a yellow fingernail he scratched a hash on the map where the tavern would be and then traced the crudely drawn lines indicating the path to follow. He stopped his finger on a mountain drawn with a broken line and tapped it. 'She in there. Third point a the crown. Just there. Sleeping. Third peak back. You'll see. Ridge a mountains like a crown. Follow the roads like I say and you see it inside a week.'

"He took a long draw from the fresh cider and wiped his chin. 'Now, I don't question you or what you goin' for. Is your life you spend and not mine, but mind you this and mind you well: should you have the heart to enter deep enough the smoky cave don't, *don't* go pickin her gold!'

"Soft laughter from the back of the tavern. The thin red man lifted the map with both hands and I thought he was going to rip it apart, but then he slammed his hands on the bar and turned to the men in the back with fresh tears of rage and frustration and it amazed me how someone who looked so dry could cry so much. 'Tis a truth! He don't know the dragon's curse! You'd kill him with your ignorant minds. Beasts you are! You nothin', all the lot of you. Yous just...you is....'

"He cried too much to speak then. The tears and snot running unchecked, his face fell into his hands and his shoulders shook. His hands collapsed on the bar and he squeezed the map in them and the map and the man shook. He blubbered something which I could not hear.

"''We were laughing at something else,' said the patron who had laughed. 'We were.'

"Barely audible, my companion sobbed. 'I gives him the home of a demiurge of this earth and you nothings go and disgrace us.'

"''We weren't laughing at you,' affirmed the heavyset man.

"''Okay now,' said the innkeeper, holding his hands out in pacification, 'It's okay now. Just forget it.' The thin, old, red, man glared into the froth of his cider with thoughts all his own. I could see fire in his stare. For a long while no one said anything else. Then soft conversation broke about the place and the inn atmosphere lightened. Eventually the old man drank again and emptied his flagon almost immediately. I offered to buy another but he refused. He stood to go but first warned me to hurry to the dragon, because he did not think it would sleep much longer. People had turned cold and faithless, he said, and no one cared anymore. The punishment for this would be the end of the world.

"Such a coldness has settled in the hearts and in the land."

"In the morning, after a full breakfast, I wrapped my provisions. The innkeeper looked tired.

"''Do you know the place he's sending me?'

"He shook his head. 'I've no idea where you're going.'

"I nodded to him and left. In about ten days rose the steppes of a mountain with a black crumbled face, just as the red-faced man had said. Breath rises up through it. You could see it. Smell it too. A kind of reptilian odor in the smoke and steam. I started the climb at first light. Like the old man said, I had to watch my step. Rocks like jagged teeth and as you climbed higher the maws between them widened and the pits deepened. You could barely see the bottom of those pits for walls ran too steep to let in light. I was balancing on the rim of the walls and one slip might have done for me. Now, I didn't know where to get in, but it made sense that the opening would be above the rocks that looked ripped out and tossed down. If I were to find it, I had to get in, but to get in I had to climb even more."

"She," Lyden corrected.

"That's what the old man said too. Called it *she*."

"Kai-Tey," Lyden replied.

"Kai-Tey then," I nodded. "She'd ripped a hole into the mountain and shut it up behind her."

"It is her nest," said the Elven Queen. "Her awakening will herald the dawn of a new age."

"I was trying not to fall," I continued. "Leaping over those granite shards. It was madness and I'm thinking nothing's in there. It's just some steam under the earth coming out. I'd heard of things like that. But I kept going. Don't know why. Why not? What better plan or place? In a silly way it felt meant to be. Not too many people could have climbed over those shards and not slipped, but I had a year with Gelidii balancing on ever-thinning limbs. I could make it. Others had tried it. In some of the deeper pits lay the skeletons of broken bodies. Skin like leather now. Some were armored. I wondered if the same old man had led them there. In one crevice lay the gleaming armor of what must once have been a prince or something. This suit was plated in gold and jewels encrusted its edges. Beside the skeleton arm rested an amazing sword and for a moment I considered scaling down to the pit to retrieve it, but it had a hilt of gold, and I remembered what he said and continued on."

"This was wise."

"Was the dragon's gold I suppose."

She nodded.

"Soon there were hash marks in the upper crags, like claw marks, always five and cutting deep in the rock. So, he hadn't been lying. I crawled at last to the mountain face and it ran smoother now, like the shards of boulder had been set back together, and above this the mountain rose properly again. I followed along until that warm reptilian steam rose from a crevice. I squeezed in as much as I could and then dug some. I worked my way through, feeling my way through the darkness, hoping nothing would give while I pressed inside to the great monolith of stone.

At last I came to open space, but there was no light. You blink and it doesn't matter. But I had one moonbulb left, and had intentionally waited for a day when the sun and moon both shone in the firmament before trying the mountain—for the moonbulbs only brightened the sight if the moon were up—and ate this and waited just inside the cavern until my sight brightened. Eventually, within the pitch of dark, a faint reddish glow emanated from below. I could see at least a little. A path of sorts ran before me, a clearing of rubble she had shredded and strewn apart a century earlier I suppose. And just then, like an omen in a storybook, or the death of an exhausted world, a long, low rumble filled the air. It shook the stones beneath my feet."

"Ha!" laughed Lyden with her eyes bright. She drew her hair from the water and squeezed it through a ring of her fingers. "The breath of Kai-Tey!"

"Yes, an exhale, but I didn't know that then. Even then I did not wholly believe in dragons. It could have been anything, but when the ground steadied I went on."

She drew the water from her strands down into the pool and nodded. "You are not unbrave, human." She then divided her hair into three strands and carefully began to weave them into one.

"I don't know. I did not feel brave then. Sometimes you go so far along it doesn't matter what happens next. I remember how the air got cooler as I climbed down and down walls like broken teeth, going deep and deeper within. I could not believe how far it went. Once I dropped a pebble and heard nothing. Below, only a sea of dark with that faint red light hanging in the air."

"Her energy. You witnessed the light of her energy."

"I suppose. A long time I climbed down and down and down, into the roots of the mountain, into the roots of the earth. I threw another pebble and heard this one land with a dull tap. I came to the floor of the great vault and went ahead, walking on something cold and flat neither rock nor earth. I kneeled to touch it. It felt like living stone. I can't describe it. Looking ahead a great mound rose and I followed this and discovered it had ridges lying in perfect symmetry."

"Ha!" she laughed, listening to every word.

"A thought raced to my mind…but it could not be, so I let it go. Following this strange plated ground suddenly the earth rumbled again. Much louder now. The mound lowered. I thought the mountain was being cleaved by an earthquake. But the roar had stopped with the mound's sinking. It began to rise again with a sound of wind. She was breathing. I knew then I walked upon the back of a dragon."

"Ha!" exclaimed Lyden, tending to her weave and smiling brightly. It delighted me that my story delighted her. "And what then, He Who Treads the Dragon's Back?"

"I waited for the world to stop moving. I needed only some little thing to get and go. I pulled at one of her scales and may as well have pulled at sculpted stone. So I crept along her back. Her enormity is incomprehensible, as was her stillness. She slept like stone but for the rare and deep breath. Were it not for that I would have thought her dead. Soon, the stillness in the mountain dark had become the entirety of my world. I could not at that moment believe the stars still followed in their course, that the moon chased away the dark of night, that the sun would rise again. And images flickered before me, dreams of the undistracted mind. Strange images came, and voices too. Things I don't want to recall.

"I followed along the dragon again with no hope or plan. Sometimes that's the best way. A strange thing happened then: from the darker corners I saw hints of things emerging from the crevices in the mountain wall, those which run even deeper down. They scurried out, lightless beings running to and fro, then disappearing again to some place forever a mystery to us. They could have been more waking dreams. I don't know, but they seemed quite real although I could not even guess at what they were. There steps made a scraping sound. They spoke in quick trills, entirely inhuman and unlike any beast or bird, but just a little. Flickers of sound. Perhaps they whispered. I feared them more than the dragon now.

"I wanted to leave immediately. Peering into the shadows I drew the blade and for a split second considered cutting a hair from the dragon's back. That may have worked. I can't say why I didn't cut one. It just felt wrong. If I had, I suspect my fortunes would have been vastly different.

"I soon came to the neck of the dragon. I knew this because the ground lowered. Not good because those things uttered more now in that quick and wet and slippery voice. They could not be, so I told myself they were another trick of the darkness. Before the head of the dragon I stopped. Who would dare to wake her?

I slid off so quietly and then stood right beside her mouth. What few contours I could see were wonderous, although I kept looking back for the underthings. They hadn't approached, perhaps a little, but mostly stood still or scurried in their courses, into and out of the lightless depths. Yet even from the ground they remained such with the darkness it could not be certain if they were really there.

Ahead, just an arm's reach ahead, a faint whiteness hung. It grew from the dragon's mouth and when she breathed again it swayed. The tooth. The great fang of Kai-Tey. That wind must have slammed her hard into that mountain. I sheathed the blade then, had to, and grabbed the swaying ivory with both hands and pulled. As said, some little dragonblood ran down my face."

"Ha!" exclaimed Lyden, clapping her hands a little.

"I had it then, right in my hands. I could not quite believe this. Time to go go go. Yet that treasure held me for a moment, to look at it, to feel it, to know it to be real and there and in my own hands and perhaps I could save them after all. Something moved before me as I was about to go. Very very slowly it moved. I had awoken it."

"Her."

"Her. I'd awoken Kai-Tey."

"Ha!"

"And I could not run now. Large creatures chase the running. So I simply crouched just there, before the mouth. A stone I was so complete my stillness. And then from the rising folds an enormous yellow eye emerged. She was all awake now."

"Ha! The great eye! To gaze upon this so closely! My oh my!"

" I stayed very, very still, not wanting even to breathe as that eye stared right ahead, right at me. Sometimes it felt like it did not see me at all; other times it seemed to trace the outlines of my soul. I still don't know what really happened. Maybe I was too close to be seen, or maybe she just let me go for reasons all her own. Know this: The dragon's eye has a fire all its own. Even in the darkness everything before it glowed. We were awash in yellow-red illumination."

"Ha!"

They say a man can't be invisible, Son, but he can. You lean there, just there against that tree and be that tree; don't go moving. Keep your breath quiet and short and think of something else, something simple and far. We all born to chase what moves. We don't see what's still. You ever get in trouble, the first thing you do is stay real real still like the deer. When the deer is still it becomes the stone. Lion can't eat stone, and so it don't look for stillness. Remember not to think about it, about what's near you. Thoughts can be felt. Don't ever doubt that."

"In my stillness a plan formed: if she went to attack I would blind that eye with her tooth. What else could I do?"

Lyden shook her head, weaving her braid to ever finer turns. "Oh, Child of Man, who has a thousand lifetimes tread, how is it your own eyes yet behold the upper realm?"

I shrugged my shoulders. "I don't know. Destiny will have her way I guess. After what felt like a long time the eye slowly closed and I crept away, tooth in hand. As I climbed up and up those terrible voices faded. I emerged into the late-day light, never so happy to be among it."

She completed her plaiting and whispered, "So here you are. The maidens of the thread thrice missed you upon that day."

"They did."

"Tomorrow we meet with tigers."

"Tigers?"

"Yes. They will carry us some part of the journey."

"Tigers?" I asked again. "Real ones?"

But she would not answer again but stood to go. The magnificent braid of her shining hair hung down her back like a whip. "You fear tigers after the dragon's den?" she asked from over her shoulder.

"Of course."

She laughed, but only a little.

"It would be very rude of them to kill one under my charge. Of course, they are tigers."

With that she faded into the trees for the night. I gorged again on the exquisite fruits and in the morning bathed for a long time before she came. The pool drew all the sickness out of me it could. When we set out I was much stronger but still not entirely well. On this day, Lyden and I walked together.

The land to come varied greatly. On one day we might cross fields littered with crystals of every color and then tread through tall grass replete with wildflowers whose fragrance caused a mild intoxication. Mountains carved of amethyst and ice broke the horizon ahead and about us grew a forest so thick it shunned any trail. When we entered this, Lyden walked through as easily as a village path.

The wounds still bit at every step. A mild fever ran yet through my blood. I suppose I could have asked Lyden to stop for some time and rest but, in truth, when I lay still it was worse. Whether it was fantastic scenery or the exercise I do not know, but walking freed my mind from the burden of sickness. Once I began to be even a little stronger, Lyden walked more and more swiftly, and the distance between us grew more with each day. At last, again, I could not keep up. She draped webs once more. I now walked entirely alone. Out of simple loneliness, I called to her.

"What is it?" Her voice spoke as if she were right beside me.

"I'm done for today."

"Very well. Ahead the ground grows in a soft cushion. Go on. We will sleep there. From there I will call the tigers."

Rolled in my blankets before dark I lay hungry in the gray light. "Do you have any more of the honey?"

"You drank the last of it yesterday."

"Can you get more?"

"Not until we pass that way again, which we will not. You never will. So, no, I cannot. Are you still in such pain?"

"Some, and I feel sick too."

"The sickness will pass."

"You don't have even a little of the honey?"

"I do not have even a little. Do you remember licking the buttercup clean?"

"Yes."

"And then you ate it too."

"Yes."

"That held the last of it. Do not desire what you cannot have. Wishing makes suffering heavier."

"All right."

"The sickness will pass."

"I know."

"The tigers will be here by the morning."

"I don't care."

"They will not hurt you. Do not be afraid."

"I feel like I'm dying. Tigers like to kill their prey. I'll be safe if I die."

"What do you mean?"

"I'm joking."

"Joking?"

"Yes. It's a joke. A kind of joke. Never mind."

"You joke often and yet say nothing humorous."

"You tell one then."

"No."

"Why not?"

"This is not the time for jokes. These are serious days."

"That's the best time to joke. Life's a joke."

"Then impart the star to my hand and, laughing, summon again the Children of the Rain."

And just as she spoke those words she stabbed a look to the right. I heard it too, very faint and very far: a rumble.

"Lyden…"

"It's not them."

"It sounded like thunder."

"It was not."

"I know."

"No fire tonight."

"I know," I said and curled within my blanket, fighting a terrible coldness from within. "I don't know why I go on, Lyden."

"Then don't."

"My aunt used to make apple tea," I said at last. "Isn't that funny? With cinnamon, too. She had a special way of drying the apples with the cinnamon and this tea was…I can't describe how it tasted. On cold nights Uncle would make a big fire in the hearth. We would sip the tea and listen to the wind and talk. Uncle would tell stories of the old Selador and his adventures outside of it and all the things he saw and of the places he went. Sometimes he'd tell the famous stories too. The ones that everyone knew and told always.

These are told still I bet. It was by the evening fires, with the day's work done, that he and Aunty taught me to read."

I heard her shift upon this word. I talked but to shield myself from the dark and the thing in the distance.

"What is read?"

"It takes time to learn how to do it well. You put words down on ground fiber, or sometimes the stretched skin of a lamb."

She gasped and her face fell to her hands. "How could you do such as this, Brother of the Ogre?"

"I don't know. It's just the way it is."

"Is this a foul magic? Is the creature sacrificed so that words may be trapped upon its skin?"

"No. It's not that. I can write them in the soil. I can write them on a leaf, on anything almost. But the skin lasts. They used it for words they did not want lost. My family handed them down from age to age. We carry them to every new home. We keep them well so they are never lost."

"You can carry words?"

"Yes."

"And this is reading?"

"Yes."

"This is one of the tricks of men."

"It's not a trick. It took me a long time to learn to read."

"Their minds are weak. Their memories would be otherwise lost. But for this they would have fallen away sooner. You are a tricky beast. It is known. You twist metal with fire and draw the dragon from its cave with hooks and metal teeth. You shoot the crane from the eternal sky with shaven limbs. You lay the land to waste. You twist all things to your desire. Your kind is full of many tricks."

"Lyden, you must understand…"

"Let us be quiet. Your voice will disturb my rest."

I forgave her. It did not matter anyway. Just get me through your forest, Lyden, in all your wonderful madness, and then we part. "How many tigers are coming?"

"Three," she said, "always three."

We waited there and Lyden did not speak much more to me. She conversed instead to the flowers and birds, sometimes bending this leaf or that for reasons all her own. She sang to them all of something I could never know in words I would never learn. And as she graced this place with song and care, the greenery brightened in a way I cannot describe. I enjoyed watching this. All of it. She had called some few blue berries for me and they lay beside my bedding, yet I had no appetite that day. At one point she stood up straight and listened. "They will be here soon."

"Fine. That's fine. Let the tigers come."

That night I slept in snatches. Coldness and worry haunted away all comfort. Yet the tigers appeared in those slender moments when my eyes were closed, just at the break of silver dawn. They were white with black stripes. They were enormous. Lyden petted them. She was smiling.

I did not want to move. They looked entirely wild and unpredictable. When I did stand, half in dream and half in fever, the largest of the three met my eyes with a look of…indecision? Its paw easily stretched as wide as my skull. Its pendulous head stayed fixed on me as a low growl rose from the cavern of its ribs. I leapt back then, and all three started towards me until Lyden pulled the ear of the leader and sang a quick word to him. His eyes dropped away, as did those of the other two. I were little more than a mouse now.

Lyden began to play with them, laughing and wrestling, leaping on their backs, tugging at their tails. When they roared she mocked them. When they clawed she raked her nails through their fur. And as she tumbled and hissed and rolled with them, I knew never had any woman, man or elf, mastered the wild so well. In the end the beasts tired and lay together. Lyden rested among them, her laughter as soft as the rising day. The largest of the tigers licked the sweat from her brow. "Ugh! Tiger breath!" she chuckled.

"Is it bad?" I asked from the distance.

"It smells of blood."

"It doesn't bother you that tigers eat other creatures?"

"Of course not. Do not ask such stupid questions. It is their nature to feed on other creatures. Obedience to this keeps the greater forest in balance. They are not as you. In yours the practice is an abomination. Would that man held half the sanity of these beasts, or any other!"

"So, what are their names?" I asked just to change the subject. She laughed.

"Tigers do not have names. How foolish to think so."

"Then I will name them."

"As you wish."

The enormous one I called Trouble, the thinnest, Hunger. The third had a particularly dreadful countenance, a thickness to its muzzle and a face heavily shadowed with stripes. On a patch of white just below its jaw stuck a small spot of blood it had neglected to clean. Thus, I called him Spot.

"The day is late. Let us go!" Lyden said. She tugged Trouble behind the ear and the creature stood with a swiftness which defied its incredible mass. Once he was up, Lyden, amazingly, hopped on his back. They began to walk away.

"Can I ride one too, Lyden?" I already struggled to keep up.

"Ask one to lend you its back," she said, reclining along the spine of the great cat.

"I don't speak Tiger."

"Then I do not think it wise to grab at them."

Hunger stared at me then. "I think this one wants to eat me, Lyden."

"Tigers of the elven realm have never seen a human before. They are curious. Perhaps they think you an elf, but sick, or dumb since you speak nothing to them."

"Why are we walking with tigers, Lyden?"

"Why not? Besides, they will help protect us."

"From what?"

"From anything. All tigers are born brave. They have been good servants to the elves in the past, wonderful companions in battle." She patted the shoulder of her beast. "I am quite proud to have with me such noble and luxurious friends!"

"Wonderful. That's just wonderful," I muttered, sick and angry and tired. Lyden laughed as the small herd trotted off. I soon found a web marking the way.

Each dusk we found a clearing as before. Lyden would go off at nightfall and the tigers would disappear as well. I knew they went to hunt when Trouble dragged the carcass of a small dear back to camp. This they shared rather viciously. I'd begun to make fires again, and since my appetite returned with my health, I wanted to cut a piece of their meat away and roast it. But I could not imagine who would be more incensed at this, Lyden or the tigers, and so never dared. In the morning she nodded sadly at the scattered bones. I had filled on berries the color of the sun."Let us go then," she said without ceremony, and we did.

She did not ride the tigers that morning, but walked somewhere between them and me. I wondered again about this woman who ate no meat yet spoke to the tiger.

"Lyden?" I called.

"You do not have to yell, Wanderer. Her voice again spoke just beside me.

"Where is your home? Your people?"

"You walk within it. This I have said more times than may be counted."

I did not know her well but knew something bothered her. "I'm asking where your true home is, your family, a husband or children, your parents. Where are they all? We've been walking months now and have not seen any elven kind. Where are they all, Lyden? Your friends? Your tribe? They must be somewhere."

She did not answer. I did not ask again. We stopped at a creek with sweet water. She dipped her hand most gracefully in it to drink. Drops fell from her hand, but tears sparkled into the water as well.

The day had risen hot. None of us wanted to leave the shaded bank of the creek. The tigers lay panting on their sides. They soon began to nap. Lyden dipped her feet bare in the water. It was a lovely place but then she looked up with a shot.

"Do you hear it?"

I listened. "No."

"There! Again! Did you hear it?"

"Nothing, I…"

"Of course not!"

Spot sat up and looked behind him, confused. "Oh, no!" she cried. "Oh no, oh no no!" She bolted out then, just shot into the vegetation. She had not even worn her sandals. The three beasts and I were brothers in confusion at that moment. We looked at each other in absent confusion and to where she had gone. I wondered if it were not just a ruse to cry. I felt terrible for asking about her home. It was Trouble who first sniffed the air, lumbered across the creek and into the vegetation. Spot and Hunger followed and then, for reasons I do not understand, so did I.

We found her weeping under a very bent and sick tree. It looked entirely old and had peeled bark that once was silver. It was more dead than not. From the gnarled trunk tumors burst out of its skin. What leaves remained hung limp and withered and all but dead. From a low and sagging branch a strange nest of twisted metal hung from a strand of wire. Lyden held this ugly thing between two hands, and peered in as if it told the mystery of the stars. Then, she wept the more.

Trouble huffed. Hunger scratched the ground and Spot growled at the tree, but we all kept our distance. This we did not understand. She wept as never before. I took a step towards her and at last I asked, "Lyden, what is it?" But I did not really want to know. I had never before seen such a woman cry so uncontrollably and did not want to know what could ever cause this. She just shook her head and continued turning the terrible orb in her hands. I sheathed the blade and stepped slowly towards her.

The tigers stayed back yet, confused. They then patrolled the outer fields. Now in the shade of the wretched tree, within the shadow of pain, I whispered to my sobbing companion, "Lyden, what's wrong?"

"A peris," she answered in a trembling voice. "A peris has been caught by the dark pixies." She broke into fresh torrents of tears.

"Lyden...Lyden what...what is it? What are you saying now?"

"The fairies of the dark light, the pixies of the underworld, they have caught a peris. Trapped it forever. Never can it be freed!"

It looked like a bizarre sculpture of tarnished metal, some web of twisted blight. I did not understand at all why she pitied it so. "Lyden," I whispered, "what is this peris?"

She shook her head as if not wanting to answer: "Oh, Son of Man, how is it you know so little of this world to which you were born?"

"I..."

She waved a hand at me to hush, and only then I caught a glimpse within. The mesh was a cage. The peris lived within. Lyden stepped away then quite sick. She began to cough in fits, something she hadn't done in some time. Where the grass grew again she spat up a glob of blue and coughed the more. Only me and it now. I dared myself to do it. I did not in any way wish to but then I did. I stepped closer and peeked inside. What was that? A dove? A dragonfly? A mouse? The openings so small. I turned the thing until finding one large enough to see clearly within...

Hush!

I leapt back, staggered back, held my chest. It could not be. A fairy? It could not be. A fairy trapped in a wire cell? It could not be. It was too dark within. It could not be for it was too dark within. She came back, coughing yet, looking haggard now. Her voice had little strength or song.

"The peris came from the heavens to fight for the fate of the earth a long time ago, back when evil threatened to overrun the balance. With the battle won some few of them, finding such delight in our forests and ice-capped mountains, resolved to stay, even though the price would be mortality. Yet many many a century would pass before one would see a peris die."

She clutched the horrid cage again and peered in again and looked away again. "They now enchant wherever they go, bringing grace only they can weave but by which all are lifted. Even imprisoned as this, in this sick and brutal instrument of a thing wholly broken, they nurture the better part of creation. But these are not the only remnants of the war."

Lyden let her hands fall away. The prison dangled from its noose. She gestured for me to follow. A few paces off she faced away so it would not hear us. "The dark armies, the underpixies, the lightless ones, minions of the blood monkey, still resent the defeat of chaos, and will forever despise the celestial soldiers. And so, from their pits of bitter hate, they set traps as this. Awful things they are. Nothing may ever escape one. How exquisite this agony for one who rides the falcons as they fall, who sips fresh the morning dew, who runs on the tips of ripples. A thousand thousand of these evil engines might catch one peris, if luck runs black enough. And so it has, here, in this place. This one will be lost to us and can never be replaced. No more come. And never, never can it escape."

She faced me now with a straight look. Her eyes so red. "There is more to this than spite, Walker of the Bitter Path. The war, it is said, wages yet. I believe as this, that we lose or hold the world in the small battles of the everyday. For in contests unnoticed even to Elf, the world may be tipped to shadow: a laming of a beetle, a poisoning of the buttercup, the killing of a wren that should not have died that day, faint struggles whose defeat or victory holds consequences which cannot be measured, yet this is how the world begins and ends: by the subtle graces and soft curses of beings for whom death is scarcely more than a myth. But this loss before us, this one here, so very terrible. How terrible. Beneath the earth the crooked ones dance. They have trapped a number of our most cherished ally. But know this: even in this most pitiful state it lives. If it should be lost to us altogether, the world will tip further wrong, the hidden ones will gain too much. These are delicate times. It must not die yet. These are not times to lose a peris."

It had been sitting with its head pressed into the folds of its knees as little wings that could not be folded into its back. When I gasped it had looked up with eyes of eternal sadness. Eyes so small. Human in its way. A living doll with a soul and wings. Still, I did not believe her. Even when I saw it, I did not believe in fairies battling for the fate of the earth. Even as it cried out from within the prison in a voice not like a bird or man or cricket...not like anything I could know, I did not believe her. Even as she wept like a child, I did not believe her. Yet more than anything, at that moment and time I wanted with all my heart to free the peris.

"Lyden, we can free it. I can cut the cage with one strike. It will be so easy."

"You have now seen what few of yours ever have," she said, her tears flowing fresh. "Know this: the peris shall perish in the net of wire." She rested her hand gently on my shoulder. "It cannot ever be freed, Seer of Hope. The cage's dark enchantment is a very old magic, one that neither elf nor peris can undo. Should you even lift this blasphemy from its bough, try to sever even a single wire, the bars will enclose upon the occupant like a tightening serpent. With every attempt it becomes smaller, tightening until the wire grinds the peris free. And it can do this as quickly as the flutter of the moth wing."

I shook my head. It could not be. There was always a way. "One cut Lyden. I can be so quick the cage will not beat me and then you can snatch it out. Tell it to stand back, far back, and I will cut it clean and true!" I drew the blade and then a terrible thing happened. The wires creaked in upon themselves like a ball of serpents. The peris moved frantically within and cried out again in a faint voice. It was terrified. I had done this.

"Sheathe the blade now!"

I did. The cage stopped. It knew our words and intentions. Here was magic, old indeed. What had I done? The openings so much smaller now. The peris's misery so much greater. Lyden put her fingers to my lips and held the other hand out as if in petition to the darkness. "We will not do this. Hush. This will not be done. The peris will not be freed. It shall die in the turns of its confinement."

"What have I done?"

"You did not know."

I put my hand over my mouth. "What have I done to it?"

"You did not know. It was not your doing. Nothing will ever work. No elven tool, no method of the peris race, nothing has ever worked on such a trap."

She looked over her shoulder to the southwest. "Something terrible has awakened. Again, we need this one to remain. I will find it proper sustenance and soft lichen upon which it may better rest. The curse does not forbid this. Tonight I will ask the fireflies to find others of its kind, for they always know where fairies dwell. They will come to care for it. They will let it know it suffers not alone."

"I made the cage so much smaller!"

"Stop it."

I pulled her away and whispered to her ear: "Lyden, you have to help it."

"I just said…"

"We can do better."

"No, we cannot."

"What if we built an enclosure within, stick by stick, and it could take shelter in it when…"

"Stop this!" she shouted, but calmed herself right after. "I understand. They are very enchanting. To see one forever changes the heart. It is part of you now and always will be. Let it live through you. Bear it in your heart as you live the greater earth. Let that be your gift. Now, I go to fetch the golden berry of the dawn, and the silver lichen that grows beneath the crescent moon, and the blue lichen that grows when the moon is hidden."

"The night of no hope."

"What?"

"Nothing."

"These will hold it for a time. It can wait many months before eating, but it would be better if it did. Wait here. Try to comfort it."

"How …" I began, but she was gone as swiftly as the wind. The tigers had gone too. They did not like this place at all. Neither did I.

The whole land felt blighted. This ugly tree. What a foul thing. Why had it been playing here anyway? It took a long time for me to take the cage to my hands, longer still to look in again to see a thing of myth damned by a trick of wire. It had curled to its side and you could see the wings, folded-in and like those of a silver moth. Its hair, long and wild and free, hung in filaments the color of the strawberry moon against skin now ashen and pale. On the bottom of the cage a small metal basin collected water, now green with stagnation. And this was the water for it to drink, a cruel part of the enemies' design to extend its agony by preserving its life. An impossibly small but human-like hand held one bar as the other covered its heart. The shrinking of the cage had terrified it. "I'm so sorry," I whispered to it. "So, so sorry."

If it understood, it did not show it. I began to sing to it gently then, thinking song to be the language of all things. It then turned that unreal face to me, so human and ageless, eyes as green as the wild, as sad as the sea. It peered into me and spoke without speaking. It railed at the agony of its coldness, its naked despair, its sickness, and then pulled absurdly at the cage with arms as thin as the wire itself. I sang louder then, but more gently too, and my tears ran and I wished so dearly I could hide this pain.

When it calmed I ended my song. It stood and carefully worked its way across the cage floor. One slip and it could split its leg. Once, it did slip. Its wings burst to a flurry of life only to beat in vain against the accursed metal enclosing them. They could not quite stretch in full anymore. The peris fell and slammed its knee against the slippery wire and folded its wings in again, perhaps forever. Clinging to the serpentine bars, the peris climbed along again, so carefully now and so slow, until it made the wires above the cradle of my palm. It curled its body just there. Warmth. Life. Companionship. I held my hand on the outside of the wire as long as my strength allowed, humming softly to it from time to time. It closed its eyes, exhausted, defeated, and then an idea stabbed my thoughts like a dagger.

I had forgotten all about it. I lifted the jezeth from my shirt and unwrapped its emanations. Starlight, dawn, euphoria. I tapped this against the accursed wire. Surely this was the key. If it did not turn the cage to dust, I would leave it within for the peris to cherish, to find comfort where no comfort may be found. At one point it reached for a beam of its light, amazed as are we all, but then it lowered its arm and curled to sleep again.

It tapped yet against the filthy metal when Lyden returned. "What are you doing?"

"Giving it the jezeth."

" You cannot leave the jezeth here. It will not even fit inside the wire."

"I'll leave it tied to the outside then."

"No. It will be stolen by the dark ones who know this trap well. It is not the fate of the celestial jewel to be so lightly abandoned. You will carry it until the time when you are to carry it no more. Stop that tapping. Stop it. Put it away, Keeper of the Fire, and help Lyden pass these into the cage."

Using sticks we lowered in silver lichen, a catch of tiny golden berries on a vine of sky blue, the wing dust of the amber moth wrapped in a leaf. "She was generous. Moths loathe to part with their dust. He will appreciate that. He will know what to do with all of it." She then used a reed to filled the basin with fresh water. Bur the peris beheld each gift with a great indifference. It touched one of the berries, but did not eat it. It felt the lichen, but did not rest on it. It lifted and smelled the leaf of blue dust, but did not open it. It lifted again its eyes of eternal sadness and spoke to my heart: 'I do not wish to live. Why do you bring me that which sustains life?'

"I'm so sorry," I whispered.

Lyden sang then, holding her hand against the wire for the peris to rest above. Her other hand on my shoulder. She sang until dusk. In almost a whisper she spoke. "It is time to leave. This is not a good place to spend the night."

"No, this is the most hideous forest I've ever crossed, and this tree is disgusting."

She sighed and went and rested her palm on the tree and whispered something to it. "She once was a shining and stately birch, as lovely and bright as the good earth might gift us with, but the curse attached to her limb has deformed her and all this land about, once a paradise. Such is the power of destruction. Let's go. The peris will tap the magic of these gifts once we are gone."

"Oh, Lyden," I said weeping, "there's no such thing as magic."

She laughed without joy.

Once away I told her what I did not want to say: "I think we should kill it, Lyden."

"Again, we cannot lose the light of even one celestial being, no matter how confined. But I promise you this, Witness of the Realm: when the spirit of the little one becomes so engulfed in pain, when its cries howl unceasingly day and night from the agony of its confinement, so that its very existence mocks all creation, I, Lyden, shall return to it and set it free. But for now, we must wait. For now it must live and play its part in the war."

Days passed before the question occurred to me. "Lyden, why didn't the underpixies just kill it when they could? Do they enjoy its suffering?"

She shook her head. "They do, but that's not it. To kill a peris is for them forbidden."

"By what?"

"It is forbidden," she said and said no more. We never spoke of it again.

A long time later I recalled a fragment of her story. I thought of her story often for I always thought of it, suspended in that dead land. "Lyden," I asked then, "who is the blood monkey?"

She stared into the fire to which she had become ever more accustomed. The tigers lounging about us stared into it too, and she rested into the belly of Trouble in a way I never had the courage to. "How little you know," she said absently, "of your own becoming." The wood of the fire burned in magnificent colors: flames of lavender and green and blue licked the air.

Three things are there that a man can look at forever: the stars, the sea and a fire.

Her gaze grew distant as she beheld the medley of flame. She suddenly touched her finger to her lip. "Oh," she whispered, "all of it."

"What?"

"What?"

"What did you just say?" She did not answer. "The trappers of the peris, the underpixies, you said were sent by the blood monkey. What is that?"

A damp cold stung the air. She hugged herself and I wrapped tighter in the blanket. All three tigers rumbled. She stood and turned in a long slow circle about the wood, peering into every cut of dark, and then sat again in her way, couchant upon the soft earth. "Did I tell you that?"

"Yes."

She gave me a curious look. "Do you wish to know the truth of your beginning?"

"Yes, I do."

"Fine. The human and elf once were friends. We welcomed you to the world of the higher mind; but you were clumsy and slow and so helpless, heavy and dull to our teachings, (although some hints of these you hold yet), thus nature began to cull you out, your form slipping from the great procession. But a shadow which stained the young earth, whose beginnings are only guessed at, would be your savior."

She sighed and rubbed her eyes. In all the time I knew her, it was the first time she looked tired.

"A hungry ape once took up a stone, lifted it above the brow of its brother, and smashed this across his skull. Ape had never done as this before. And no ape had ever before eaten the soft meat of its brother's brain. A white delicacy. This beast felt an extraordinary surge of power at the act and the feast, and so it carried on. The darker gods blessed its course as it went from skull to skull, smashing each and all of its innocent tribe. It delighted in this. It ate only the brain and licked clean the cavity of bone. And so the young sun rose on a world of waste, was witness to a garden of scattered corpses."

She sighed again. Scanned all the woods round again. "It went on to other things: dragon and hawk, the eagle of the dawn which is no more. All manner of meat and blood and brain the beast ate and lived and lived and lived, and through this sin the mind and strength of the defiler grew stronger. The darker gods blessed its course until it caught even pixie and peris in its nets, and so, devouring them, knew a form of their magic. Here began what is called the Blood Monkey."

She stood again and turned slowly to watch all the wood where the ring of firelight touched it. Only Hunger had stayed awake and guarded with her. Lyden continued, whispering low, "Its hate grew, hate of anything, and so it wanted to ruin and rule all the living earth, but it needed a helper to unravel things. It went to man as he was falling from existence and offered him many tricks: to sharpen words into lies, to polish stones to points, to twist the natural order and kill what it did not need to kill, to gain what it did not need to gain. And mankind, with the shadow of oblivion looming over its head, followed the course of the Blood Monkey and thrived in a crooked way. And so it is to this day: your first birth from the creator but your second from it.

"The elves parted from them, carved a piece of earth (you walk in it now) forever hidden from their eyes. But as the power of men swelled and the pride and violence of their acts so affronted the highest of gods, the sacred seats resolved to unleash a fire from the skies as retribution. Thus, they would cleanse the earth. But highest gods feared flames so great might scorch the Heavens, besides, the Fates had written of a time when all would fall to fire anyway. Thus, they brought a flood, and drowned humanity beneath the waves. Yet two survived: a man and a woman, pious enough to be spared. Of them you are also born.

"And though yours have forgotten the beast, the beast has not forgotten you. It no bends towards your destruction, for you have outlived your purpose and so are a threat. And so it leads you by invisible cords, goading to your own demise. As yours are easily tricked, they follow. End of story."

Her tale was not entirely unfamiliar. Yet there was a problem with it. "But Lyden, let me ask you this, wouldn't the flood have drowned the elves, too?"

She smiled as the firelight danced upon her face. "You are of the soil, Son of Man, we are of the leaves. We fled."

The full moon rose that night and reminded me of Gelidii. I spoke of him. Even Lyden had never seen a Picarin, but the elves knew of them she said. They were exceedingly rare she said, and so adept at hiding that even elves could pass right by one and not notice it.

"You were fortunate to have met one, Friend of the Mystery. It truly taught you something of its ways?"

"It did."

She gestured to the blade. "Let us see the art of the Picarin carried in a man."

I bowed and walked to the clearing and bowed then to the moon. Gelidii had insisted upon that always. I drew the blade and whispered the word of awakening. I then performed the twelve arcs of the sparrow and the blade sang gloriously. It ripped apart the air itself apart, tore into the very fabric of the universe. I breathed heavily when done, too heavily. Out of practice. I bowed to the moon in closing and then to Lyden, who nodded in return but then giggled almost like a girl.

"A human has learned the song of the Picarin! A human has learned the Picarin song!" She even clapped a little.

I blushed. "I'm not so great. Gelidii could draw arcs all day and never do the same one twice. He had a straight dagger too, which I never learned. He said I needed more time. He didn't want me to go. He said I wasn't ready to go into the wilderness with only one blade. But there comes a time when you have to move on."

"May I try it?" she asked and held out her hand.

"Of course."

She handled it like a gem, turning it in the silver light and running a nail carefully along its edge. In the center of the clearing she began to swing it with great adeptness. Thought it would have cut an enemy in half a hundred times, it wouldn't sing for her. She tried again and again but no song. She returned it to me. "A fine weapon. Keep it well and it shall protect you."

She walked again to the center of the clearing and spoke a word I did not know and cannot repeat. She loosed the dart from her waist and with it cut the air so quickly the atmosphere almost forgot to hiss. She drew it in incomprehensible courses, with a speed impossible. In the frenzy of the form I could not see her weapon nor arms, but when she slowed some the cord played off of her body, wrapping once then shooting off of her feet, ankle or wrists, even her neck. She once wrapped the dart's cord in her hair and shot it out again in a direction that did not seem possible. Once, she lowered and pet all the grass about her without cutting it. Once, she spun the dart so quickly the air screamed so that it hurt the ears. Perhaps, I thought, perhaps she is faster than even a Picarin.

And then the straight strikes began. She stabbed the length of the cord in all directions, the metal tip catching a flash of moonlight at the terminus of each strike. And then a strange thing happened: Lyden of the Silver Mane began to slowly spin where she stood, and now the dart seemed to strike in two places at once. She span faster and faster. Soon her form, a blur of motion, could not be discerned from the weapon and now the dart struck in three places at once, and then four, and then nine, and then more than I could count. At the height of her incredible display, the dart struck at every point in a sphere around her, and yet now she stood perfectly still. She had become the radiance in the center of a star.

She stopped. The shimmering air quieted. The cord whipped thrice or more about her waist and then the silver tip tucked in, locking it. She placed her hands, as if in prayer, and bowed to me or the field or the moon, I do not know, but I bowed back and a great quiet came over everything.

"That was amazing."

"It is but necessary. We Sagittae are the defenders of this earth."

"That was really, really amazing."

"But an art. It can be learned."

"From what do you defend this earth?"

"The evils that would devour her: men or fallen gods, the demons that fly between the stars, anything. To our most sacred function and to it we apply our highest skills. Thus have we coaxed the metals from the soil, perfected the arts of death, and each Sagittae holds a weapon unique, to learn perfectly and become its master, to weave into our being. This, The Dart of Gia.

The harder metals had come only recently to Selador. The first specimens arriving a few generations ago. The bits and scraps were highly valued for their durability, whether fashioned into tools or weapons or things ornate.

His Uncle had a sliver of bronze which he had sharpened into a cutting blade. He had affixed to it a handle of oak wrapped in goatskin. As a boy he loved the knife and when no one would catch him would sneak it out of the chest and slash at the berry bushes in the outer field. He pretended the splattered juice was blood. For the boy, ogres, cruel soldiers, mystical demons all fell against his blade, and when the imaginary war reached its climax, he lifted the scintillating metal before the sun, let it catch the light of the heavens, let it gain something of their power, and then, with a scream of victory, he drew it fast down and eviscerated the twisted king. But his left hand had swung too close. His palm bled badly, sliced open. He dropped the knife, red with blood and berry juice, and ran home.

"You've gotten blood all over you now!"

"Am sorry, Aunty."

"Why you playing with things you got no business touching?"

"It hurts."

"It looks it. And your shirt now is ruined."

"I'll wash it."

"Won't matter. Blood stains forever."

"I have a scar on my hand from metal." I traced the raised line with my finger along a scar almost forgotten. Lyden turned and considered it less than a moment then said nothing. "It's very beautiful here, in this field, with you. I could stay a long time. Beside that creek is a hot spring."

"Yes. Enjoy it. We stay only one night."

"Why leave so soon?"

" We have a purpose we have not finished, and it is not to sit here and soak in warm water and look at the moon."

"It's just that I don't know what I'm doing anymore, Lyden. Don't know where I'm going or what's going to happen. And I'm tired all the time. Sometimes I'm afraid of how tired I am. I used to want you to leave but now am afraid you're going to. And something awful can happen. At any time it can."

"Thus the condition of men," she said rather coldly. She then drew back her hair and I noticed what I had never before: "Lyden, your ears, they're pointed!"

She nodded. "Of course they are. You never noticed because you expected to find what you had found before."

"Why are they like that?"

"Why are yours not?"

"In a way they're, well they're really quite beautiful."

She shrugged. "They discern the finer voices of the forest, and better heed the commands of the sky." She leaned back to consider the stars burning like distant candles above. "I do not know why we are what we are. No one does. Even the elvae do not know our beginnings, but I have often wondered why we are so separate from the beasts. Perhaps it is that we first stood and leaned back, raised our eyes to see them: the stars. Infinite and wise, eternal, beheld first in perfect silence. What else could have forged so great a difference? Nature makes no squares, few hard lines, and yet we do. Our designs do not follow the earth, but the patterns written in the darkened sky. For this too I believe our ears point ever upward, evidence of the highest mind, students of the heavens and yet children of the earth.

Man, however, remains half-formed, sometimes looking up, but so often pressing his eyes before his feet."

"This is beyond me, Lyden. There used to be an old woman in Selador. Probably still is. A witch or something. A prophetess. People would bring her food and confections and teas and hear her wisdom. Well, I went to see her once. I had a question I wanted answered. A question no normal person could answer. She had such crazy eyes. Ancient and insane. She looked straight at me and lifted a shaking finger. She had some kind of disease. She just started crying then, crying and crying louder and louder still, moaning things in such a way it made you think the world were coming to an end. But none of it made any sense: fragments of goats and rags and cracked cups, but people said I should listen to her and figure out what she'd been trying to say. The next time I saw a goat nothing happened. I broke a cup, nothing happened. I used a rag to clean and nothing. So, I haven't figured it out yet…her message and what it all meant, but I don't really care anymore. I stopped being concerned with mysteries. I'd rather spend my time working on what I can understand and not what I cannot. It just might be that some things are forbidden to know."

"This is not unwise."

"Thank you. Probably the nicest thing you ever said to me."

She laughed and with tall blades of grass began weaving something. Her fingers moved like magic.

"What's that?"

"An offering to the field, for its comfort and haven, and also to the sky for holding back the rain."

"It hasn't rained in a long time."

"It has not rained on us. She smiles on our passage and has let us walk around it. It will rain soon, though."

Her creation, a sort of shallow cup with winged sides, a disc of woven grass, with a breath she sent floating over the silver field. It rose in the wind spinning and we watched it follow the invisible. And then the wind lifted more and her creation floated above the tree-line to the low sky and was gone. Lyden clapped and giggled and again for that moment seemed as a little girl. "That was a good one!"

"Amazing. Really."

Her smile faded. "Your body tires of late."

"Does it?"

"Yes. Your life you leave in pieces along the way. You do not retain. Your spirit scatters."

"Does it?"

"Why do you not believe what I say?"

"I do. Why are you telling me this?"

She shrugged and drew a nail absently down her hair. "Perhaps because I wish to finish this destiny. Perhaps because I do not want to be unhappy."

She plucked a flower and turned its petals into one another, imbricating them in such a way that when she spun it the flower lifted into the air for too long a time, twirled far and high above us until a breeze caught and carried it away. Hunger and Hope playfully leapt to it and almost caught it. Lyden laughed and Trouble purred. "We will have to leave tomorrow, but I do love this place." She caressed all the tigers as they encircled her. "They will not be with us much longer. We will see them off at the vine."

"The vine?"

She nodded. "They cannot cross it. No animal can. Even if they could walk on it they would be lost."

I tried to imagine a vine uncrossable, but did not ask her of it. Time would tell as it always did.

It rained heavily for two nights and days. The climate had grown slowly colder so that even a rain could be dangerous now. Lyden lead us to a cave to wait and in there chill and hunger came again but it was better than the rain. Once, the tigers went off to hunt and returned wet and musty with flecks of blood on their muzzles. I lay awake a long time listening to the rain and keeping a small fire at the mouth and each night it took her longer to go. Perhaps she began to enjoy the enchantment of a fire. She would gaze in it just a little too long before going. Even the tigers, as wild as the sea, little feared the fire now.

"Are we going to stay in this cave long?"

"Until the rain stops."

"Where do you sleep, Lyden?"

To my surprise, without insult or argument, she set out and gestured for me to follow. Spot came with us. Lonely, perhaps. Reaching a stand of cypress, Lyden pointed up. It could hardly be seen: a small house of silk, almost a fog, clung to the highest branches. With a leap she ran up the tree and then stood among the threads and they hardly gave under her weight. She peeled her cocoon open and slipped in and could not be seen at all then. She had become the mist, this elva, sleeping in a house of silk.

We left the cave when the rain left us. We walked until the forest stopped growing, until rolling fields of granite cut by the ageless gods lay where the forest once grew. Far ahead, a low sea of green. Fields, I thought, framed by mountains of unimaginable height. We said goodbye to the tigers there. One by one Lyden pet each, rubbed their backs and kissed them, whispered something to each. One by one they slipped away then, as quietly as they had emerged they slipped away, and none looked back.

We went on not speaking. I don't know when I knew the field a thing unnatural, but I knew it more with each hour. It grew too high. Had strange color. Not trees not grass not anything that could be and it held a quiet that life should not and this I knew to be the vine.

"And so you have come to it," she spoke without lifting her head. She had kept her gaze downwards for much of this walk. That was not how she held herself at all. Not at all.

"It's not what I thought."

"It never is as we imagine, is it?"

"No, it never really is."

"Are you ready?"

"You're nervous, too."

"Are you ready?"

"Why are you so nervous?"

"Let us go."

"You must have crossed it before."

She shook her head. "We run above where the bright red berries grow. But your step is too heavy for that, and so we must walk through. This, I have never done. Nor do I know of anyone who has."

I peered into the green of the shadows now, the thing so close. "Does anything live in there, Lyden?"

"Nothing. The vine supports nothing. A few birds. They may skim along its roof where the bright berries grow."

"Then why are you nervous?"

"Because nothing lives in there."

"Maybe we could just walk around. It's okay if it takes longer."

"You cannot. You will die crossing the mountains. Ice blocks the pass on both sides."

"Ice?"

"It's not important right now."

"Maybe we can just go back and go around another way."

"You cannot go back. Your sage waits in the North. This is the way, Doubter of the Path."

And we were upon the maw of it now, a mass of serpents in a war of strangulation. Little light penetrated within and I knew with perfect certainty that I did not want to go in, and I said "Lyden, I do not want to go in. I think we should…"

"Your destiny waits beyond the vine. You thus must pass through the vine. If you turn back now I will kill you. I will strike you dead before your second step falls. You shall not have spent her precious days on a thing abandoned."

We strode quickly ahead and it grew worse.

"Why is this? Who would make something like this?"

"No one. Once a forest bloomed here. Most brilliant it was. A sweet gem of the earth within which, legend holds, the ancient Elvae first raised their walls. Perhaps they stand yet. Perhaps they do, beneath the twistings of this ruination."

"It's an evil thing. I can feel it."

She shrugged, her face solemn. "Nothing natural can be evil. It simply does not belong here. Something brought it very long ago and it simply grows according to its nature."

"It's nature is to devour the world?"

"The elves who ride the wind say this lives in perfect balance with all else. But the course of life is different there. And so, while our trees sleep in the time of the white rain, this vine holds its leaves just a little bit longer, growing while all else does not. And it is first to awaken in spring, first to spread her young leaves, and thus no sapling of another knows the sun, and the forest becomes this, and this devours the world. Nothing can live beside the vine which, once it has land, never yields. It would have taken more were it not for the ice walls of the great mountains."

Soon we could see the shadowy caves running between the limbs and smell its breath, ancient, damp and cold. No flowers bloomed in the forest to come. No birds flew within.

"Why are we walking so fast, Lyden?"

"I don't know."
"I want to stop."
"So do I."
"Can we stop?"
"I want to get through."
"Can we just stop for a little bit?"

We waited and sat and I sipped some water. The sky was incredibly blue and for that day I wished I were a bird. "It's quiet here."

"Everything but it is dead. It and we."

"All right, let's go. Let's begin, so we can finish."

Some last few sickened trees stood like the graves of a dead world. They had been pulled to unnatural contortions, bent low with limbs ripped off, gasping for life as the vine wound up them. Lyden unfurled her dart and sliced the body of the strangling vines where they clung to the trunks. A black scar remained where the vine had clung. She traced her finger through the burn.

"It has starved slowly, but now will heal, yet the vine cannot be stopped for long. It will return."

"At least trees don't feel pain," I said to her.

"They most certainly do," she said, and I chose not to believe her. She cut some more trees free but then tied her dart away. "It's no use anyway," she said dejectedly. "But at least to save a few is…well, it's no use, anyway."

Soon there were no more trees. I took a last look at the sky and entered. About us, all had become vine. Between the rising limbs the sun broke only in dappled light. In its own way, it was beautiful. The ancient limbs had grown so long that you could walk right on them. We followed these and the hints of ground until no ground remained. The vine rose and twisted in all directions. We walked from one limb to another, up and down and along, following whatever limb were large enough to insure footing.

"Why's the ground gone?"

"We now walk over what was once, they say, the valley of the Blue Hall. Somewhere below the first elven order built their walls. Somewhere below, a sacred river runs, what little the vine has not drunk. Watch your step. Do not let the swirling limbs dazzle you. Watch your step now. The valley is wide and the crossing will not be short. Do not fall."

"How long will it take?"

"I do not know. I have never walked in here before. I told you this. I am not even sure if we will make it across."

"Why not?"

"Because I have never been here before. Because I do not know."

I wanted to draw the blade, but imagined it slipping from my hand and dropping forever into the darkness below. I watched my step and followed. She went very quickly.

"Please slow down, Lyden."

And she did.

When the light began to fail I was exhausted. "We cannot walk in the dark. We will wait here for the morning sun."

And the place was no different from all the rest, but here at least she had chosen a good place to sleep: an intersection of three large stems where we could rest safely within, and even in our sleep not roll out. As the last of the light failed a great dread overcame me. "Do not fear it," she whispered. "It is only a vine. It moves slowly. It will not seize you up in the night."

"But you sound nervous?"

"It is only a vine," she repeated. "Try to sleep. I will not."

"I will stay awake with you."

"There is no purpose to that. If you sleep, you will walk more quickly tomorrow, and we can sooner be free of this web."

"Can you tell me a story?"

"What?"

"A story, so I can be somewhere else but here. I remember Aunty was sick once, real sick, and Uncle and I waited the night beside her while she slept. We had to keep it dark because the light hurt her eyes. Uncle sat beside her bed and I sat beside him and he told me stories to pass the time. Whispered them so she wouldn't wake up."

"I have no stories to suit this place. Besides, our stories are made with words you would not understand, and they must be sung."

"That would be fine."

She shook her head. "I will not sing here."

Soon, we lay in perfect dark. I began to hum and she told me to be quiet.

"Why?"

"Just be quiet."

"Did you hear that? I thought…"

"Hush."

"Why do we have to whisper?"

"Just hush."

"But if nothing's here…"

"Hush."

The sound of near perfect quiet preys on you. A faint and distant rustle of wind makes your hair stand. The ever-present drips of water mark the time of your passing life. Night within the vine had a presence hard to catch in words. You could feel the vine itself sleeping and yet listening too. Above, not a star, nor the faintest hint of moon. Nothing interrupted the dark. Just the drip dripping water near and far, above and below, little taps of liquid life and I suspected somewhere above, where the world began again, it must be raining.

"I thought I heard something, Lyden," I whispered, perhaps only to know she was still there.

"Quiet. It is only death."

"What?"

"It is only a vine. Be quiet now and sleep."

"I don't think it wants us here."

"Hush!"

Her words carried loudly. Too loudly, and it seemed from far far below rose an echo of her voice, but that would be impossible.

I played the game of opening and closing my eyes to see if there was any difference. No. I thought then of many things, too many, and this was not good and did not bring sleep. I thought of the past, of Selador, and this caused a dull and familiar anguish. I thought of my travels, and this caused pain, the uncertainty of it all. After a time, I thought of the raft on the lake of Selador, its soft lifting upon the water lit with tips of light, its wind-wandered course beneath a warm and blue Heaven. Whenever I thought of it, it helped me sleep. Still does.

There in the vine, I had a dream. A ruined tower with a light at the top stood among a burned land, a destroyed city. Perhaps it had been a city, but the dream too hung shrouded in darkness. I climbed up and up scarred stairs to the light of the tower and there, through the last door, rushed out on to the roof bathed in light. A man in a black robe and black hat held a rail and looked out over all that was

below. We alone were bathed in the gold of the light. He turned to
me, unsmiling. A wise man and so not a threat. He stepped aside and
gestured for me to look. At the edge I beheld the vista below. Below,
the wind turned. I peered down and down and deeply into the abyss
and the wind almost howled now. Searching for something in that
darkness beneath there was only the wind and memory and then I
awoke. A scratching sound approached from below.

"Lyden…do you hear that?"

"Hush."

But it was coming closer. "Do you? Do you hear that?"

"Hush, I say again. Hush."

"The Jezeth…"

"Keep it sheathed."

The scratch then became a thud which shook the limbs of the
vine itself. It would stop and go again, always coming closer.
"Lyden," I begged, "it's coming for us." Suddenly, the vine bent
under its weight. I did not whisper now. "Lyden, I think I know what
it is!"

No response.

"It's coming for us and I think I know what it is!"

Thump.

Thump.

Thud.

From where she sat, her voice spoke, hers but not hers. "Do you
want to hear the story of the wolf?"

"What? What's wrong with your voice? Lyden, by all the gods!"

"Shall we sing the story of the wolf?"

"Why are you saying this now? Why are you talking like that?
All scratchy like that? I think I know what it is. Lyden, please."

And yet I never thought to draw the blade, and if I had, I believe
I would have dropped it and lost it forever.

"The moan of the singing wolf. Come you, now, to the singing
wolf. Gentle of his teeth. Let us sing of the moaning wolf."

"Lyden, this isn't you."

"Baying the gray song of the risen one. Wolf trot and drip-
dripping upon the groan of the gray muzzle."

"It isn't you. What happened to you?"

I almost ran, almost fell to my death. And I would have run, so
terrible was that voice, hers but not hers; yet she screamed then, so

high and shrill and fierce it split the air, ripped apart the very darkness. I stabbed my fingers into my ears. Still, it hurt.

Suddenly silence. Even the drips of water paused in their course.

Then, the voice, it began again: "Would you hear the story of the wolf?

She screamed again.

I stabbed my ears again.

Something heavy and dead slithered away.

At last I asked the silence: "Lyden?"

"Hush."

"Did it have you?"

"Hush."

"You're back now?"

"Yes. Be quiet."

Dawn broke slowly through the strangled land. It seemed an imposter. Faintly, did the outline of her hair appear at last. Faintly, so slowly, the first gray light carved her sitting statue. Like a dream, the vine grew around us again.

The moment the way became clear enough we set out again. We left without any word. But something in her countenance had changed — like a faint scratch on an otherwise perfect shell. I said nothing. I followed her path.

In the heart of the vine grew thorns, each large enough and sharp enough to split a man in two if he should slip. Lyden walked straight over the first, stepping on its razor's edge without getting cut. From the other side she turned back to me, "Do not do as I have."

"I won't."

Each thorn rose like the fin of a great shark and I had to think. Lyden waited. I drew the blade and hacked through the thorn's hard shell and severed it at the base and let it fall into the nothingness. I'd not eaten for two days at least and the labor tired me too much. Juice bled from the cut and made the vine as slippery as death. Unable to trust my feet I sat and straddled the limb and pulled myself forward with my hands. This meant sheathing the knife, slowly pulling across, unsheathing the knife again, cutting, sheathing, going forward. Many, many thorns lay ahead: a hundred, a thousand, too many to know; and I'd have to cut them all yet even one had tired me too much, and gradually I knew it would be too much to cut them all and I had to think. Lyden gave no advice, no urging. If she were

187

concerned it didn't show. She simply waited after each crossing, that fracture in her lovely face. Finally, I cut only the lethal tip from each and this made it low enough to walk over with legs bowed on either side. Slow going nonetheless, and fantastically dangerous. Had I not lived for a year in a tree I would have fallen a hundred times before the end.

More and more Lyden drifted ahead as I slowed. Still, she kept me mostly in her sight so that before any sharp turn a splash of white would show the way to follow. Yet it happened, as these things sometimes do, that once I was exceptionally slow and she exceptionally impatient, so that when I went to where I thought she'd gone she was not there. "Lyden!"

Useless. The turning vine stopped all sound. I sat and cried, so tired of it all: of the vine, the thorns, of elves and dragons and sages, of kings and dripping water, of hidden beasts in hidden jungles. All of it. In that silent prison I cried for a good long time, called her name a hundred times but she was gone. Gone. So this is how I would die…trapped in a plant. The only question left: would I starve or fall?

Maybe I would jump. I wondered at what point I would jump.

No sun broke clearly there. No wind told direction. Nothing guided you. In that starless and moonless world even the thorn-teeth grew in no particular direction, as if the twisting limbs had themselves been confused by their own mess. For the first time I wondered if she had ever known the way at all. And then, in a moment of hideous clarity, if she had fallen. I had to think, but not of that. To think of that in such a place was to court death.

I continued until my exhausted legs could not. I rested then and sipped from the gourd. Everything looked so much the same. Going in circles probably. I'll starve in here. I cut a slice and bit it. Bitter poison. I spat it out. The gourd was half empty now but water dripped everywhere, and at least death would not come by thirst.

Lyden!

Eventually, I continued on while I had the light. What else was there to do? First, I watched my step, but then for what I hoped never to see: a crushed flag of white below. I remembered Uncle.

"Listen, today we go out and if you get from my side know this: you never have to worry for food. You got a good month at least before that stops you. Make a shelter first. Worry first for the cold

and the rain and the animals and whatever else walks in this forgotten wild. Then you start a fire. You can die in one night with no fire at the wrong time of year. Then water. Then food. Is last. And remember a man is lost in circles. Circles go nowhere. Just don't walk in circles. You don't do that and in time you hit a road, a farm, something, pr'aps even the cliffs but something, and so long you not in circles you won't be lost forever. You just keep in one direction and don't be lost to the cold and you have a real good chance no matter where you might be."

How useless his words now. In this perversity of nature nothing applied. As the dreadful night approached again I searched for a place to rest and also to rest the gourd to collect water drip by drip. I cut a notch beneath dripping water and set the gourd in tight and low. It had to be low, steady, lest it slip when full. I set it in low and in this act the idea of my salvation glowed like the spark of a great fire: While I did not know the points of the horizon, there were two directions of which I had no doubt: up and down. I would climb down. Somewhere below the earth must be again. And she said a river ran there, and every river had its course and must go somewhere, anywhere but here.

I climbed lower and lower, hurrying like a fool. The vines gradually reddened in their descent, thickened too so that near the base the circumference was easily three times that of above. And now the air smelled rank and wet, down there where light barely broke through. I peered deeply into the sunken world for any sign of anything until, alas, not far below a slow procession of muddy water snaked through the unreal forest. The river, if it could be called that, ran so shallow that small islands of mud humped above her surface like spots on a lizard. I'd returned to land, a rank and watery and miserable place, one through which none could walk. I had to think.

I waited a long time on the great base of vine just staring at the water in its soft turning. With light failing fast I began to imagine my life as an eddy in the courses below but stopped those thoughts immediately. This was no place for such thoughts, no time for such indulgence. Hunger came again like an old memory and I put that away too and just then had an idea. So careful now. She was so dear to me now. She must not be dropped. The river would eat her if she were dropped. It would sink and sink again in the murk and be lost forever. So carefully I drew the blade of the Picarin and cut a piece of the plant's flesh. Everything depended on what would happen next. I tossed the flesh into the water and waited. Gone. Sunken below the muddy blood. Alas, it popped up again. I almost smiled. I would carve myself a boat.

From the bottom up I carved a slim plank just broad enough to hold me, just long enough to float me out. I set it free at the top and it slid into the river and floated. I jumped on it. It worked. I was wet, but it worked. The water began to carry me away. To where or what I knew not, but it carried me away.

We slipped through the cathedral of vine slowly and inexorably. Sometimes my little ship glided along; other times it scraped against mud or watery sand, tangled with roots or cut against stone. Sometimes the water ran so thin the boat needed to be walked, and in doing this I learned to hold it fast for in parts the ground yielded too much so you could step in right past the knee and feel the earth grab you and pull you in as if the very soil burned in voracious hunger and maybe it did.

In that strange and surreal world one feels like an insect meandering through roots. Down there sky could never be known and so all faith rested in the knowledge of the river. Lyden said nothing lived there but the vine, yet, now and again, distant warbles unlike any bird broke the silence of the forest impossible. Sometimes a spit of land allowed one to stand and on one of these I planned to spend the night, and it was on one of these I found the cup. It seemed impossible in this place. It had perched just upright, as shining and bright as the day it must have been made. Upon its side were strange etchings in artistry so fine they seemed cut by the pin of a god. They depicted creatures of all types. Deer and hawk and wolf ran and flew and hunted in the wall of the cup, but strange beasts lived there too, peeking from the shelter of the alien leaves, half-hidden forms never even told in story. And the craftsman had included people of a sort — magnificent and wild and free — all in the midst of some ferocious dance and they were human but not quite, and not so unlike Lyden. With a chill I noticed how above it all a single branch of a vine flowed like a wave, and my mind returned to the present and I wanted to be out very badly.

I whispered to it: "How did you get here, little one? My, oh my, let's not leave you here." I plucked it from the mud, and upon the moment I touched heard the faintest ring, like the distant call of a bell in the fog. A certain tremble ran in the tips of my fingers too. It looked made of silver, but could not be for the walls were thick and yet the cup weightless. And if ever there were vessels of magic, this was of their number, but this was no place for magic.

Just as I set out again I heard it: a terrible thud, like the knock of a great axeman trying to break from beneath the world, so loud the river shook. The vine shook. My heart trembled. And I, a rudderless pilot, was drawn by the river's course closer to the axeman, so close that with each strike the droplets burst to mist, the boat heaved in the shaken water, and I knew what it was yet could see nothing through the towers of the vine. I prayed in earnest silence. I prayed for mercy, forgiveness, understanding, but mostly I prayed for the map written when the world begun to have this sunken river turn a little away.

And so it did. As a storm begins to weaken at the height of its strength, when the knocking at the door could have burst the timbers of my heart, the slow and fetid river turned, and so carried me away. The sound faded. Eventually, it ceased. Not long after I emerged from that prison to the true and proper sky, painted with dusk.

Ahead rose mountains with crowns of white.

The river ran ever wider, swifter too. For a long time its banks were only stone, but when a proper forest began again I pulled my little boat to a pine needle shore near a tributary running out of the forest. For reasons I do not know I hacked the boat to pieces. I named the little river Hope and walked beside it. I followed Hope to sheltered boughs and to delicious fruits and grasses. I bathed in Hope and she was so cold yet took away all the tacky filth of the vine. I cleaned the remnants both from my skin and all I carried. With the last of the light I gathered dried wood and made camp beside Hope, rested beside her and struck a small fire. Night fell. Something approached. It walked just beyond the ring of firelight. I stood with blade at the ready. But then her form stepped into the ring of the flickering light. "Lyden, you're alive."

"As are you, Man of Many Deaths."

"Where did you go?"

"I? I continued on the path. It was you who strayed."

"You didn't wait for me."

"I did, even searched back for you, but you could not be found. The vine is a confounding thing. No one knows the ways through it nor its paths. I knew only the direction towards the forest because I could smell it, feel its energy, but followed no path. Long I looked back for you, but the vine is a terrible place of loss and confusion."

"How did you find me here?"

"I would see your fire from the shaded moon, catch your scent from the far horizon, feel your step though the earth be shaking, hear your breath over thunder. But tell Lyden this: How is it you ever emerged?"

I told her. "Oh! And I found this on the vine floor." I held out the cup. She became very still. Her eyes fixed wide in the stillness of wonder until tears fell.

"The third vessel. You have found it. A man. A man has found The Vessel of Dusk! Surely those hands have been washed by the gods. Surely destiny steers your course."

"You know what this is?"

She nodded. She hated crying in front of me and tried to stop but could not. I looked away. "Do you want it? If it means something to you, you should have it."

She nodded and I placed the cup in her hand. She turned it slowly and traced the etchings with the tip of her nail and, to my amazement, tossed the precious treasure into the fire.

"Ah, Lyden why?"

She kneeled close to the flames and pointed within. The etchings began to move then. The feral tribe continued its dance; the wolves stepped to the hunt; the eagle soared through drifting clouds while the unknown creatures emerged from their shelters revealing the mystery of their forms. The stars began to twinkle and a waning crescent rose above the treeline. Even a comet appeared in the eastern sky, and with this visitation the vine began to wave, and then grow, and while all else danced and hunted and hid, the vine wove through the forest all.

And then something began to happen, something of great import, but just then Lyden plucked out the cup from the fire's heart. I'd just seen a miracle, but she had scalding metal clenched in her grip: "Lyden! Careful! You'll get burned!" She smiled and pressed it to my hand. It was as cool as water.

"Elven metal takes no heat."

"Oh."

"And so it may never be shaped my men for their purposes."

"Oh."

Once out of the fire the images began to retreat to where they had been, until the cup looked just as when I had first found it. It was an uncanny, silly thing to fear, but I gave it back to her and with the tip of her finger she drew circles around the rim. A call rose from the vessel, not so unlike the one when first touched, only now it rang longer and finer, and the song expanded with each course of her finger. Soon, the sound permeated all the air and she set it down then and we listened until the song ended. A definite peace followed. It settled over all and at last, she smiled. "Thank you," she said, without looking up.

"You're welcome, Lyden. I'm glad you're back."

"It is destiny."

"Maybe, but I don't trust it like you do. I'm just really, really glad..."

"I understand. You need say no more of it."

"I didn't think...I tried not to let it..."

"Understood. It sleeps in the past. Now let it run by like the water of the river. Be present. Try always to be present."

And before I could ask, she spoke: "There are three. This one was lost in the great river when the world was young. It sank to depths unknowable. They are the vessels of our story, from the very birth of the great Elven race to the end. They guide us."

"The end of what?"

"Of the elves, and so too the earth, for we are her protectors. Set upon the The Table of the Sun the art of the cup reveals all that can ever be known. Your fire holds enough sun to show it in traces, but I dare not spy more. It is not for me to know yet. I have seen only what I have already known: the coming of the vine in the age of confusion, when the elves were scattered and sick; the gray horizon where the rain falls as sand...Enough!" She shook her head and the great mane of her hair caught the fire's illumination. "I will bring this to its proper place, The Great Hall of the Table. You would come, Keeper of the Fire, but its site is forbidden for men to know, even to you, who has made its vision whole. Thank you."

"Lyden," I said, "the world will never end."

She gently laughed and we spoke of it no more.

Queen Lyden of the White Hair enters The Great Hall of the Table of the Sun. Within, an elder rests on a throne of onyx, his mind on thoughts a thousand years old. For the briefest moment he sees her but then looks past her as if she were a ghost. She steps closer and speaks. The ancient of the silver hair feels her light and stands.

"Why have you been so long from us, good sister?" He speaks from eyes that may have never slept, and then, remembering ceremony, greets her with a secret word. "Dearest Daughter of the Sagittae, too long have you been lost from our number."

"Nor would I be here now were it not for this." She unveils the cup and he has no words at first. He nods. "It is the final chapter, said to be returned in a time of great turmoil."

"And so it is."

"Daughter, you have been too long from us. Stay."

"I shall not."

"Dearest Queen, my darling Lyden, do not stray again from our eyes."

"I have something to accomplish."

"The man?"

"Yes."

"And what of him? The council has determined his kind are to be no more. She cannot suffer them. We have wavered in the past almost to extinction, but will not suffer them the more."

With a shaking voice and eyes of fire she glares at the elder. "It is forbidden to eradicate any strain of Her children."

"It is forbidden to let Her die. The council has decided. There is now the makings of a confluence of war in the North. We will begin when it ends."

"But it is forbidden. I, more than perhaps all of you, know of Her struggle, but there is always a way to act within the law. There is always a right way."

"We are tired of waiting for that answer. The law is old, so old as to be written in a metal exhausted from the soil, yet by my saying this do not dare to believe you revere it more than I."

Lyden turned more fierce her words, "So, you shall sever the head from the neck that bears a star of Jeh-zethan, and turn cold the fingers that lifted The Vessel of Dusk from the belly of the devourer?"

After all of the marvelous stories in his long and tired life, this almost amazed him. "Does it bear a Jeh-zethan?"

"It does."

"And it was he who found the cup?"

"It was."

For a time only silence came from the figure reclined in the black throne. *"Yet, it was you who led him to the cup, and the fate of the stars of Jeh-zethan are their own. Nothing may interfere with their destiny."*

"So says you. I say we make destiny with each turning sun."

"Callous words of argument, Dearest Sister, Lyden of the White Moon, Grace of the Silken Meadow, Bringer of Morning Dew. We know of him: assaulting the sacred night with fire. Fire in which you have partaken of late. We know of him, have caught his scent, know his spirit by his step. We can find him again, and for you he will be spared. He and those dearest to him...but no more. We will grant you that, but no more."

He was as powerless to lie as the worm in the eagle's claw. So, it was true. They would spare him and yet still she clenched her fists in white rage and was surprised at the despair which gripped her for a race she so long had despised. They were correct, of course, but she felt sick. Something was wrong with the plan. She did not know what, but something was wrong with it. Never before had the elves removed an entire species from the earth. She feared also a mutual destruction in a form she could not explain or understand.

She calculated how long it would take: three days perhaps, depending on the wind, maybe seven. They would simply tell the flowers to exhale what to men alone would be poisons. The wind would do the rest. It would be so easy and still the heart of she who hated them so much sank. Why did she care now? She had seen the seven corners of the earth and yet knew so little of the mysteries of her own heart.

"Stay with us now," he spoke again so gently, *"dearest Sister and most noble Queen. Do not stray again from our company and so deprive us of your light. Despair will sometimes fall upon us like the endless rains, but when we are all together its weight is more easily borne."*

"He waits for me."

"In the old forest, north of the vine? How safe is he there with his fires calling all to it?"

"I have set a ring of adders about him. Nothing will intrude."

"Stay. We will send a guide to walk him from our realm. Stay and wash away the shadow that has passed your face."

"Stay and witness of the death of all his kind?" The elder shrugged. Lyden shook her head. "Elder, Brother, Ancient King, the wanderer has a task he wishes to complete. I believe it is of great import, more than we can know. Let him do it. He bears the star. He has retrieved the cup. Perhaps the world heals. Give his one task time. There is time. He has earned this."

"Is it because of him that you are taken by a man?"

Her countenance turned to fire. "Lyden will never be by any man taken!"

He raised his hands in placation. "Be still of heart."

In fury she howled: "Never!"

"Be still, dearest Queen, hold your fire for the stars."

"He is nothing to me anymore, and the man is less."

"And yet for this man you ask the world to spare them?"

Lyden shook in frustrated rage. "No. Not for him. They are nothing. They are nothing and nothing to me. Only that the consequences of an act so dark can never be known."

The elder felt ashamed she had been so pushed as to lie about the other. He hated seeing one he loved so much so torn. He sighed. How he loved her. How could he ever deny her anything?

"Dearest Queen, finest gem of the elven race, we will spare the human kind for now and see if the world indeed begins to weave together. But if the confluence of war unleashes again the mother of the stone sky, they all shall perish, even him."

She bowed to the elder and left. She found him sleeping by the ashes of a mostly-exhausted log. Final tufts of smoke eddied to the cold.

"We go now," I heard in my sleep. She stood stiffly in the chill of morning. Something had scared her. And the shadow upon her countenance had deepened.

"Did you sleep well, Lyden?"

"I did not. Let us go."

"I think you caught a ghost in the vine."

"You speak as a child."

"Let the smoke wash over you. It will drive it out."

"We have little time. This purpose of yours. Do it. Do not waste your steps and breath on the dreams of ghosts."

"I think I know what it was."

"It matters not. Speak no more of it. This Sage, this elder of your kind…find it and say what you will to it. Get up. The day runs late already."

Morning had hardly broken when we set out. She went far ahead. I followed webs.

With each passing day Lyden acted more distracted. She would turn to me, face flushed and panting, and then race ahead again. I did not understand it at all. We came to a valley where the flowers grew so enormous they cannot be believed. She ran off. When I found her she was naked, lying on her back in the cradle of an enormous purple and white iris with her legs splayed wide. She was impaling herself on the pistil. Speechless, I waited and watched as she writhed and thrust herself again and again on the flower. With a primordial groan she squeezed her legs very tightly on the pistil so that purple juice gushed from it or her or both. She lay back panting then, resting against the fan of petals, her inner thighs wet with juice. When she got up, she seemed not to notice me. Something about the air in that valley made her like this. Half dazed, she continued to flit from site to site, disheveled and flush, climbing into flowers.

All but spent she finally dressed and reclined beneath a well-ridden violet to caress its wilted leaves. With a nod to me, we set out again. We said nothing of it, but she still was not herself. Near dusk we came to a clearing and her eyes still had that wild and wet look. She charged me without warning, clawed at my flesh, ripped at it until it bled and I was screaming. I would die. She ripped my tunic off and then her gown and again raked at my skin and I was screaming for she was a tigress and I was going to be killed. But then she kissed me. So many times she kissed me. How incredible this. And then, we made love.

The next morning, dabbing my wounds in a creek, watching the blood trickle away, I could not conceal my joy.

"Why do you smile over much, Strayer of Many Paths?"

"Because…I am a man now."

"Why?"

"Because I have slept with a woman."

She touched her lips with her finger and thought about this. "I am not a woman. I am an elva."

I cupped my hands and ran the cool water over my face and sipped. "You are a female. So I am now a man."

And without a hint of humor she replied: "Had you slept with a she-goat would this have signaled your becoming a man?"

I sighed. "I'm just going to go ahead and let this one count, Lyden."

She shrugged. "It matters nothing to me."

"Lyden?"

"Yes?"

"I love you."

Suddenly, she grabbed my neck. Her fingers wound around my windpipe, dagger-tipped nails ready to pierce my throat. She spoke with words of ice: "Should the Son of Man ever speak of this-- that Lyden has lain with a beast-- the very bees will whisper your confession to the wind, the moths will carry it through the night and the falcon will bear it swiftly even to the dwellers of the sea until Lyden will know of your betrayal. No matter where on this earth you dwell, no matter how softly the whispered secret falls, I will know of this and I will find you, and in agony unimaginable bring your death."

I shook my head. "I will never speak a word of it, not to anyone ever. I promise."

After too long a time she let go. Pinpricks of blood ran down my neck.

We rushed more and more. When I asked her why, she said nothing but only ran faster so that at times her feet even glided above the ground. We came to a creek so thick with the dust of gold it clung to our feet. "We are near to a place no man has ever been," she said, rubbing the shining dust between her fingers.

"How can you be so sure?"

She just shook her head. "No man has ever been where we go."

The creek turned into a river, and the river fed into a valley where its bed, every stone and grain of sand of it, was of purest gold.

Lyden knew the place was precious, but not just how precious. I paused often to behold the spectacular environment. I threw stones of gold, bent ribbons of it to crude necklaces and bracelets, rubbed the dust on my face, my arms, worked it through my hair. I held my hands up to the sky laughing until I wept.

Lyden but stepped through it with not an interest in a single nugget. Once, she held one before me. "This is one of your gods, yes?"

"A god? No, no." I had been pealing a gold leaf from the crown of ordinary river stone. "It's not a god, but it is a new life. A life of choice. This metal frees people. Makes them their own king."

"Are you now so oppressed?"

"Oppression sent me here."

"You seem delighted enough."

"Because of this place, this very place, yes. But I've been too long out here. And I'm very tired of this all, Lyden. I want to leave this world behind and with this metal I can."

Her face fell cold. "Is this land so terrible? Even still the river mist holds the perfume of morning lilac. Just now a grace of bluebird passed above you, though you did not see. A triple rainbow crossed the arc of the firmament at dawn's first song, and this night the silver gift of moon shall rise full and all the dark illumine. This will summon a chorus from the creatures of the leaves and know this: Her gift, undiminished even by the void, outshines all metal of this soil. Yet, since moonlight cannot be cut and sold, as is the wont of men, it will matter so much less to you, you who by grace uncounted walks in the heart of the elven realm, a land which compares to none. Pardon my digression. I shall hurry more your return to the squalid and profane."

"No. I didn't mean it like that. I'm sorry. It's just that I've been a long time from home." I held up the gold leaf. "And with enough of this, I can help them. I could go home again."

"How so does this help?"

"Because I could give it to people to get rid of the soldiers who hold my home."

"You mean kill them?"

"If necessary."

"It has the commandment of a god."

"I… it's not like that. I can't explain it now. May I take some?"

She shrugged. "Burden yourself as you wish."

I stuffed flakes and nuggets of gold into every pocket and pouch, a thousand lifetimes worth of work carried on my back. With a delirium of joy I made my plans: I would carry my treasure, (so very heavy), to where the world of men began again, bury the better part of it, and if I lived, return for it. If not, the loss wouldn't bother me too much.

We followed that riverbed for a long time. The water tasted so pure there, purified by the gold, so sweet. I eventually set down the early pieces I'd collected, the very ones which in their taking had overwhelmed me in joy indescribable, for gold is so heavy and the way so long. I would wait until the vein began to thin and only then take all I could carry. Yet, it pained me to part with certain pieces, for the river had shaped them into exquisite shapes. But there would be more, and besides, it would eventually all be melted anyway.

Only one piece I would never set down, sell, nor melt: the ring. Natural forces had carved it too, of course, but through a peculiar hollow of stone the current had caught the dust in such a way as to make it flawless, so definite in form perhaps it had been the work of hands after all. Made and lost, for no one would discard such a treasure, not even here. How it shone on the hand! How it commanded the eye! It glowed brighter than all the rest, and felt too heavy for its size. This was mine. Some talk of magic rings. If indeed they exist, this was of their number, and this was mine. It hung loose on even my first finger, but I cherished it all the more for that, and through its boldness and beauty I swelled with extraordinary pride. And maybe that is why the gods exacted the cost they did: for the pride I had taken in a thing I'd done nothing to earn.

"Lyden, do elves make rings?"

"We do, but not of gold."

"Look at this one."

"It is a ring."

"Do you think it's natural?"

"It is not of elven make. I tell you that at least."

I lifted it again to the sun to watch it sparkle. I could not stop smiling.

"Stop looking at that bauble and listen to me! This water feeds into the bath of the nymphs who guard the shallow sea. There meet all the waters of the world. Although the sea lies in the elven realm I must petition them for our crossing. Without them we do not pass. Only they know the courses of the ever-changing channels. Without their guidance, once the fog has settled, and the greater light sleeps and the paths run starless, we would be lost to the swift and hungry sea."

"But how do we cross this sea at all?"

She smiled. "We walk, of course," and then her smile faded. "But know this: should the nymphs deny you, back you go, and alone. Some destinies are forbidden."

I did not to ask about it. I decided to let the world come to me. I kissed the ring: a perfect circle illumine. No river made this.

Evermore more veins of water invaded the forest with each day. We constantly hopped over creeks and rivulets, traced the edges of pools, at times we swam. When we came to the broad rivers, (having followed no discernible trail), there would be a set of stepping stones waiting just there and running right to the other side in a straight line. They were so old their corners had been worn soft by ages of passing water. How they had been made, perfectly set in water running white, confounded me. Even Lyden did not know. She said the elves of the first age had done this to unite all the realm. Not all elves, she said, could fly.

She would skip across the stones in no time and await me on the other bank, but I went slowly, so carefully. The rocks were slippery, being always wet, and the space between them sometimes had to be jumped. Jump too slow and in you go; jump too fast and you slide off the far edge. I carried enough gold to sink a small boat. My blanket bulged with it. This I threw first, and more than once, treasure enough to buy a kingdom almost slid off the far end of a rock to be lost forever.

We came to a lovely grove. In the heart of it stood a pool fed from all sides. Lyden kneeled on the pink sand of its bank and softly tapped the water of her reflection. Then she waited.

"Lyden, what are you ..."

"Hush!"

In a voice barely above a whisper she spoke, "I call the three sisters..."

"What?"

"Hush! I speak not to you."

Again, she looked to her reflection and whispered: "I call the three sisters. I am Lyden, of the Elves. I seek a crossing." She tapped the still water again. The rings widened across the pool as if they carried her words. "I am Lyden of the elves. I seek a crossing. A man walks with me."

When the rings faded she tapped the surface again, sending her petition through the water. "Sisters of the crystal path, keepers of her blood, I am Lyden, Queen of the Elves. A man walks with me. We seek a crossing. Smile upon our journey. Lend us guidance. A man walks with me. He bears a star of creation."

Again, I feared she was insane, and so wondered at the entirety of my life that had led me to that moment. But suddenly the water in one of the tributaries churned. Within it shone three lights: a pale orange, a sepia, and a blue, all swimming together in spinning and turning form. As they came closer they grew brighter, and then, there they were: three goddesses gliding in the pool in turning embrace. Their beauty beyond compare. Even Lyden seemed awed by the nymphs, each more lovely than rose-petalled dawn.

They swam right beneath Lyden and caressed the length of her hair as it rested in the water. At this the elva laughed in pure delight, and slipped her arms among theirs in play, and for that moment she seemed ready to join them beneath the water, to simply go and be another sister of the grove.

Only once did the three look at me with eyes as deep as the secret sea. A test, I suppose, and yet I had to look away. A moment later they receded, the light dimmed, and I only realized an enchanting music had impregnated the air when it was gone. Lyden stood and smiled. We had their permission. And so we stepped into the shallows just beyond the grove and began our crossing. Who would know that in a place so sublime, by goddesses led, death would be so close?

The forests were gone. The mountains and the caves and the creatures all gone. No more flowers, no bugs, no grass. We had entered waterland: a vast expanse of shallows and sand interrupted only by rare islands of black trees.

In the beginning came great serenity. In the beginning, it washed away so much pain, this open world of sweet water. Tiny fish raced in the eddies and nipped at our feet, broke the surface with plopping jumps or waves of glistening life. We walked in delicate sands the colors of rainbow and gold, and in warm water rarely deeper than our ankles.

I slogged along, but Lyden made no wake in her step. She walked as if through air. "Do not harm any creature here," she warned. "Nothing may be taken from their waters but the water itself, the purest for drinking. All creatures here live under the protection of the three sisters, by whose grace alone we will live. To wound even the least of them will insure your own destruction, and mine. Our fates are one."

"I don't think I'd catch them, anyway."

"Then watch your step," she said, and so I did.

We came to a small island with a single tree with bark as black as pitch and leaves of perfect white. "We will night here," she said, stepping out of the water.

That slender spit of sand had no shore in sight, just a universe of running streams and the arc of the sky. Incredibly beautiful it was and yet empty too. Lyden caressed the one tree. I wondered if we would make love again. When she felt mischievous in the Valley of the Flowers she would sometimes use the dart's line to lash me to a trunk before making love. The first time, because it happened quicker than a breath, I again thought she'd planned to kill me, but it was claws and kisses again, only she would act more haughty about it.

But that did not happen. She picked the white leaves from the tree and crushed them to an oily paste and rubbed this on her feet and ankles. "It will protect the flesh."

I did as she, and when we set out at first light the water was only a sensation on the outside of the ointment.

I had a little food: a few nuts, roots, some pine needles and a small bundle of dried fruits. People have asked how I could embark on the crossing with so little, but they do not understand a life where the only promise is another step and a faith that the ground will rise to meet you. And I had hidden my appetite from Lyden, thus she did not understand our differences. She just did not.

We made our ways through the shallows, ending each day on a slight island with a lone black tree with those wonderful white leaves. I asked if there would be trees with fruit. She said no, and not to always think of my gut. As the days wore on I slept more to save my strength, but sometimes awoke to the burning stars to find Lyden beneath them as she swayed in a kind of moving meditation. With draped hands she caressed the atmosphere, her hair flowing like the sea, drifting in an incomprehensible grace too lovely not to watch. And so I would, until exhaustion ruled and rounded my little life with sleep.

On the tenth day I asked, "How long until the other side, Lyden?"

"You go so slowly that I cannot say."

"How long would it take you?"

"That does not matter. I can ride the wind."

I had gone long with little food many times before, but the water so tired my step that after twelve days I had to eat the last of the provisions. I had slowed much. I began to thin too much. And yet the beauty of the place did not diminish. Indeed, for certain moments it became absolute.

"Aunty, can I have more?"

"More?"

"I'm hungry."

"Who said 'hungry!'"

"Why do you waste away so?"

"Because I have not eaten."

"Already you are thin?"

"Yes."

"Already you need more sustenance?"

"Yes again."

"You are like a beast in your appetite?"

"I suppose."

"There will be no food until we reach the far side of the waters."

"And when will that be?"

"Again, I cannot tell you. You go much slower that I ever dared to dream. Can you not draw the air to your marrow, fill the stomach with the blood of the earth?"

I scratched my head. "No...I don't think so."

"If you have the stomach of a beast, and not that of one of the higher mind, you may not complete this crossing."

"You mean I will die?"

"Yes."

"I see."

"Do you truly understand what I say?"

"Yes."

"I sense no fear in you."

"I'm too tired to be afraid."

She nodded. She understood.

I had let some of the gold go in the days to come. A lifetime of labor strewn in forgotten sand. How much would I need, anyway?

One night, as we waited on an island of the black tree, fog came so thick we could not see below our knees. "We will be lost in this, Lyden."

"You will not be lost," she said, and began to sing. Faint lights appeared beneath the water and the fog lifted some. Ahead, in the calm and unmarked waters, swam the three sisters. "Look! See them there!"

"Yes."

"Come now. We follow."

And so we walked behind a rainbow of illumination which drove the fog away, guided through paths we could never know. We rested in the morning beneath the shade of a black tree. Lyden was not tired at all, but rested for me. I had collapsed on the slender isle, and when I awoke she had all my property, gold and all, even the blade, secured about her. I would not have dared to ask this favor, but for it remain entirely grateful.

"Thank you."

"Nevermind that. You have to get up lest this narrow sand be your final resting ground."

I carried only the jezeth, a thing almost weightless, while she bore a burden not her own. "You don't have to do that."

"I know. Can you stand?"

"Of course."

At night she gave me back the blankets and the gold, knowing what it meant to me. In the morning she would secure the gold in the blankets again, yet often leaving large nuggets, a year's pay, two year's pay, more, just lying in the sand. I didn't complain. I'd have none of it were it not for her. And it is easy to lose what easily comes.

We spoke less and less, and Lyden's expression changed with the passing days. I would catch her staring too long at my limbs, looking too deeply into my eyes which had sunken too much.

"Don't worry."

"Why would I worry? I am not worried."

"Then why do you stare?"

"You disappear so quickly is all. This I have never seen."

I felt the bones under my cheek. Little fish nipped at my feet. If she would walk far enough ahead I could make a trap: carve a pool and after they swam in wall it off with sand and fill it with sand and devour them. "Lyden, I can see very far here. You don't have to walk so close. You never did in the forest. Just go and…"

"Enough. You may not harm the creatures of these waters. I would kill you first. You need to understand that. If your destiny is to waste on the waters of the nymphs then you shall, but you shall not in your passing affront the goddesses with slaughter."

"No…I…remember them. They're real. I remember them exactly as they were. I can see everything now."

Some days later she halted, suddenly struck with joy. "Ah! Yes. Try this" she said, and stepped upon the surface of the water. "It takes more energy at first, but the water will not drag so heavily against your step."

I rested my hand on my gut and it felt like I could touch my spine. "Nah, you go ahead. I'm not feeling much like walking on water. Not today. But you go ahead. It's all right."

"When you breathe, breathe deeply. Draw the air into the marrow. You have to soften the outer shell. You must open the seven sacred gates. Nourish the core." She gestured to the magnificent vista. "Energy abounds here. Yours for the borrowing. Learn to breathe well and rarely will you require the coarser foods…I thought you knew."

"It's not your fault. Sometimes people don't know how different they are."

It was not her fault. It had been over thirty days and she had hardly thinned, if at all. The next day I collapsed just as we reached an island. When I awoke, I could only look at her. How her eyes shined. How her limbs flowed like the water. I had to say it at last, for my time was running out. "Lyden," I cried, "You are so exquisite. Just exquisite. Your beauty leaves me breathless. It hurts. Men would start wars over you. No woman compares, not in the least, not in any way. None have ever compared. That first moment by the tower, I thought you were a goddess, and sometimes when I look at you I can't speak. You are proof of the benevolence of nature and I know, I know, and it saddens me because I know this, that I will never keep you. I know what you think of me. You will leave, no matter what, no matter what I say, no matter what I do, you will leave."

"Yes, I will."

"You didn't know at all, did you?"

"What?"

"How exquisite you are?"

"No," she shrugged. "Nor do I care."

And so it was true: she really had never before been among humanity. I dwelled on the mystery of her origin until realizing it was no use. We stayed there an extra day. There could be much worse places to die. Sometimes, the enchantment of the shallow sea convinced me I'd already passed, had entered the hall from which none return.

Each day was a gift now. We stopped at more and more islands as they had become more frequent. I took this as a sign that the other shore neared, but Lyden would not answer in any direct way. "It is not far," is all she would say, just as she had from the beginning. My hunger had died weeks ago, but the way my body ate into itself was worrisome. When Lyden had become actually gentle in her speech, I knew then I was close.

Lie down carefully. Shall we rest now or try to make one more island?

I cared very little then about living or dying. I had been too long on the line between. Living had become just a habit, one of which I would just as soon be rid of it weren't for the damned promise. My speech had become broken and slurred. In my dreams, relatives and friends who had passed were always smiling, always holding my hand and telling me they were ready when I was. My skin brushed off in white flakes, and my face hung in a skeletal mask, but my stomach had oddly swollen out. I knew I looked a horror. I could see it in Lyden's eyes, but the only time it really bothered me was when I forgot to disturb the stiller pools, and so caught my reflection too clearly in the water.

On the thirty-ninth day I fainted once more. She carried me then. I remember waking beneath a black tree in the cradle of her arms. "We hath to gow," I mumbled.

"Sleep. You need much sleep. It will slow your body from devouring itself."

"I know. Okay, I'th going to sleep but pleath don' ..."

"Don't what?"

"Don't leave me when I thleep…pleath."

"Why would I do such an act?"

I weakly shook my head. "Juth lev when ahm awake, Lyden. Pleath. I don' wanna wake up in thuh fog alone."

"I won't leave you here unless you die."

"Tay the jetheth."

"If you die, I will take the jezeth," she said.

"You cahn hath everythin'."

She shook her head. "The rest is nothing, but the jezeth should not be left here. I will carry it to some other fate if need be, but I think it your destiny to bear it beyond these sands, and so do not believe you will die here."

"I don' know wha' this for. Is juhst a preddy thin."

"It is more than that, Stepper to the Shade, much more than that. Hush, now. Save your breath. Breathe into your bones as I told you. Do not be afraid."

For all her strength, I slowed her, as did my other goods, which she never left behind, not the tooth or the blade or the gold. She could not walk atop the water carrying me, and her once graceful step was now heavy, and she had thinned too. Even elves must eat eventually. Now we entered the fortieth day.

That night, as I lay dying in her arms, I unwrapped the jezeth and held it against the sky. It burned like a star of the heavens, and all the stars in the canopy of night burned brighter too. The jezeth had summoned extraordinary illumination. "Ah, Lyden. Look! They singing! It speaths to the scars! Is a sthar. Is what is. Ith what is."

Darkness fell.

I remember nothing more of the sea of the nymphs. I awoke with her beside me on warm sand I thought another island, but it was too full and dry. She trickled water over my face. "We are here," she said with a smile too faint.

"We heh?"

"In less than seven days I will have you in forest again. I will carry you."

"You wull carry the dehd."

Through a half-open crusted eye I scanned the land about us: lifeless dunes to all horizons but the sea. "Juth lev me her. Is good. This ith fine."

"I can have food to you in nine days if I go alone."

"In nine days I won't be hungeh," I said and tried to laugh but could only smile. How fortunate to have her beside me as I died. I closed my eyes and saw her still.

It shined like never before. I held it against the Dome of Heaven. "It speaks to the stars, Lyden! That's what it does! Look! Look!"

It's very lovely. It is among the most lovely objects in all of earth.

Look Lyden! Look!

I would slip in and out of consciousness. A splash woke me. Lyden stood a few paces off, moving her hands in that graceful art of hers that may have been prayer. I tried to ask, but she saved me the trouble.

"An otter. They play here sometimes. They come all this way from the forest to play and eat the mollusks that grow in the shallows here. The river, too, is under the enchantment of the goddesses. And no river like it exists anywhere else. Its waters run narrow but incredibly deep. They spill into the great forest of the Northern Realm as a waterfall over which the nymphs themselves never go, and thus marks the end of their protection, and the beginning of the protection of the elves. We the garden keep.

She found the heart to look at me again and sighed. "In the northern forest Lyden will prepare you a feast the likes of which your kind has never known. Even though our immortality demands an appetite of simplicity – for elves count their lives in centuries as men do the years – when we wish to feast we feast like no other. Blue honey collects there, in the northern forest, and mushrooms which take two hundred years to grow. I knows a hidden vale where the purple orchid grows, and I can ask them to weep nectar into my cup until it fills, and even beg one to shed a leaf for you to eat and it will not hurt you. Together, they hold a smoky sweetness that is incomparable. This taste, words fail to catch it.

She smiled at the thought, but then had to turn away. I understood. I felt terrible that I looked so ghastly. No one likes talking to a skeleton. No one likes to be around the dying. How easy our lives if we could just eat the earth below us.

"The meal will restore you as none ever has. Just hang on"

"They eash the gotheses fishes?"

"What?"

"Others. They eats the fithesrs of …"

"Of course. They are permitted. They are not creatures of the higher mind. They have no discernment by ethics, but follow nature and thus have perfect obedience to the gods."

"Are they creathures of the gods?"

"What?" she asked. A slight fear had crept into her voice.

"Are they unda the protethen of the nymths?"

She hung her head, "Not."

"I can eath the creathires noth of the goth's protethen."

"It is forbidden of elvae to murder them," she said, but she was weeping already.

"Ith ith is okay. Don' cry. Goodbye, Lyden. I ath no more."

She broke apart in tears. And then she left me, and how strange to die alone after all of that, but then she did return and in her arms lay a dead otter. It had been killed so gently it seemed only asleep. Her tears soaked its fur. She lay it beside my wasted form but I wasn't hungry anymore, and did not want to eat a cold dead otter anyway. Her voice trembled, "He was the fourth one. I took him. I had to choose of the five so I took him. I wrote his name in his footprint and he fell asleep. The rest was easy. The others didn't understand."

She dug a shallow grave and laid the otter in, belly up, its small, furred hands folded over each other. "You may live now. But first…the price! Cover it in gold. No part of it must be seen. Cover every hair of its fur in gold and know that nothing will restore this life which you could not create in a billion suns. No loss of metal will match the void left to its family, nothing will replace the miracle of its being, or wash the stain from these hands that have forsaken me."

Slowly, I leaned up and took from the mound of gold to begin to cover the otter. As I did so, Lyden was weeping, going always to the river to wash her hands and then looking at them in the air saying how they were still filthy and weeping anew and washing them again and I kept piling gold onto the cold fur until no part of it could be seen. It had taken almost all of the gold for this, and I thought it was done, the price paid, but then a single whisker poked up from the shining mound. "Cover it," she demanded, and the only thing left was the ring. It hung loosely on my thumb. I shielded it from her sight. "Cover it!" she demanded again. I so hated to set it down, but in it lay the ransom of my life. With the ring I laid the whisker flat. All the gold was gone.

Without a word, Lyden inspected the otter. Satisfied I had paid the price she collected the treasure and folded it into her gown. With a flick of her thumbnail she sliced the belly of the beast open and departed as the blood began to pool. Somewhere, way beyond my sight, somewhere in the deep and mysterious river, she threw all my gold back to the water from which it had come. Where, I shall never know.

We had starvation like mine in Selador after the wars. A belly of food would kill me, I knew. I sipped the blood, just a sip, and waited. I did this for a day, and by the end of the day I felt half-restored. The sugars and salts, I don't know, but there was something in the blood. Then, I sliced a sliver of meat and chewed it to a paste and drank copious amounts of water and waited. It would be three days in eating some part of the otter like this. Life, most assuredly, had returned to me. At the end of the third day, with nothing but the blue viscera and the grizzle already rotting, I dug a deeper grave and buried the remains. Then, I washed and waited by the stream.

She returned the next morning. Perhaps she had been watching all along. We set out, following the strange river through the dunes to a forest. This was her realm again, only different. But, something in her had broken, in a way worse than the shadow from the vine. How sorry is she who cannot forgive herself, and I had done that to her, and I did not know what to say to that. And so sometimes, when I caught her thinking of it, with her gaze locked before her step, and her eyes anything but present, it made me wish she had not done it.

"Is it much farther, Lyden?"

"To where?"

"To wherever you're taking me?"

No answer. One night followed the next, as did the days. The new forest was more sparse and cold, especially at night. Lyden did not like fires here, but did not forbid them. She would stare into it and then to her hands and her expression would change to pain. I never mentioned the otter again, nor the gold.

Up until then the trees and plants did not differ so very greatly from Selador, but these of the new forest grew taller, broader, more expansive. There would be large stands of pine with soft pine-needle floors, soft-barked cypress and birch, and certain trees which towered to heights I could not comprehend. Some of them took a hundred paces just to walk around. Each of these had a name and Lyden knew them all. She would press her hands against one's bark and lean in and speak in words I did not know. The giant trees, she said, were the guardians of the clouds. To speak their names made them vulnerable to ancient evils.

And things began to end. We never made love again, and I did not ask. We spoke less, and she angered less too. Her cough, which had faded for a time, now began to return and of this she also would not speak. I once began to apologize for the otter and she shrieked and curled her hands into claws. I said nothing more. Nothing was ever right again between us and I knew it would not be.

One day, the forest opened to a roaring river across from which towered blue cliffs. She pointed to their heights. "That is north."

"I know."

"That is north," she repeated again in all her broken beauty. She was growing so thin.

"Lyden, are you all right?"

"That is north," she said again with a distant voice, keeping her eyes fixed on the sky. "Beyond there, the world of men begins again."

"I know that. Why are you telling me that? Why are you so thin now?"

And she began to laugh and her laughter had no joy. She opened her arms laughing as the wind began to rise: Wind that had been a whisper became a word, the word a song, the song a roar and the roar turned to a chorus of howling chaos. And she laughed and laughing ran into the howling sky, flailing her arms in equal frenzy until the wind pulled her gown like tattered flags behind her, played with her hair like ribbons in a storm. And she had no joy anymore and ran fast towards the river. I thought she would throw herself in and I could never catch her but would try.

But then, in a moment of magic, the wind lifted her up, like a dry leaf in a rainless storm, lifted her up and away and away into the swirling sky, and she was laughing still, borne back towards the land of elf, away from the blue cliffs and the North, away from all I would come to know, until the entirety of her being became but a stranger in the distance, and then a speck, and then she was gone.

As she disappeared, leaving me forever, I screamed over and again a single word against the howling storm. I screamed until my throat bled and my voice split, howled it uselessly to the turning sky, the one word suited to such a time and place: her name.

BOOK III

Karuna

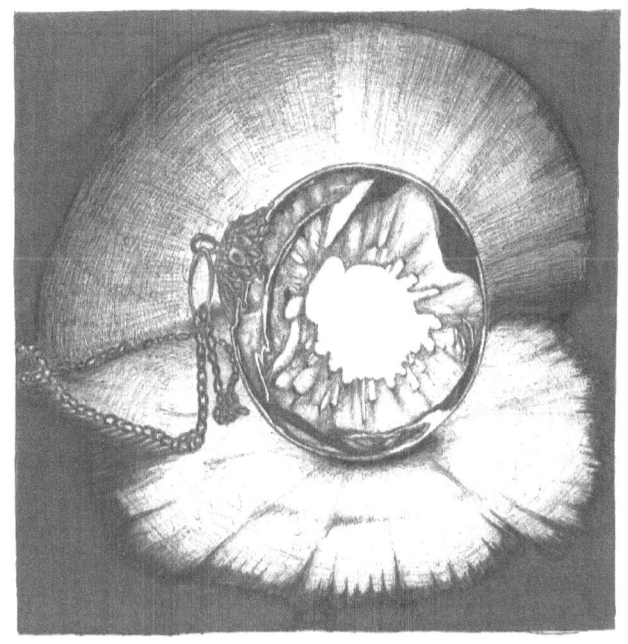

"So how was it, Strayer of the Earth, that you have come upon a star?"

"It was given to me by a woman of the sea."

Karuna

I could swim yet, could flail my arms against the water in soft madness until, somehow, I came to a bank of sand. And I remember still, after a long, cold time, how touching ground at last raised the smallest spark of joy - a sensation so strange it arose as a trespass. I had been so certain in my wish to drown. If I only had the courage to face those first few wet breaths…I could not quite do it. Firmly on shore I vomited, water and bile gushing out yellow and thick, an odor of grave-rot and carrion. On weak legs, my head swimming yet, I stumbled back to the river to slake a burning thirst and clean the terrible taste in my mouth. I lay with my face in the running current and drank. How water inescapably draws us back.

I staggered off into the nearby wilderness with a mind half-dead. The forms around me, once benign, had now all corrupted to evil: The forest clutched with skeletal fingers, vines turned to snakes, roots to worms, the trill of every creature begged a sip of blood. The sweet earth had become a tomb. The lofty vault of the sky mocked us as haven unattainable. Again, I wept, for I knew something sacred within me had broken.

Whether I was on the path of animal or man I did not know, but followed it instinctively. I slipped, and for a reason unknown, looked back. There, just there, not a stone's throw away, waiting and crouching beneath the shadow of leaves, I saw it. Something had followed me out of the rift. Something stalked me. My voice came out so hysterically that I scarcely recognized it, screaming and screaming until my throat burned, until my spirit exhausted. Every word was nonsense. My mind had broken and part of me knew that. I begged it anyway, whatever it was, over and over again the same plea: Go *away! Go away! Go away!*

The half-hidden creature did not move, but what could understand the babble of a mind shrouded in shadow? Something had broken within me, as if that most human gift of speech had been touched by the crooked finger of some passing demon. I invented names, all guttural nonsense, whimpered unintelligible imprecations, petitions and laments…all of it just nonsense. What is left of a man when he cannot communicate his thoughts? And so, as my soul languished in chains of poison, my battered mind ran in circles defining just what followed: That Which Creeps Behind the Leaves, The Stealer of Steps, The Beast Who Hides Its Face.

Go away! Go Away! Go away!

All senseless. I once tried to call upon the gods of my home, but twisted the sacred syllables so dearly that they sounded profane, and so I knew what it means for a man to be beyond the reach of the divine. In my terror, in my lost running madness, I thought I understood the true nature of life: how the world grows more in shadow than light, how the sun only graces the thinnest crust of things to let the rest be ruled in perfect darkness. And so what of humanity? Are we not except for the thinnest shell comprised of darkness? I began to run again, for I now knew myself to be a thing most of shadow, unseen by eye of star or grace of sun, unknown to any god save perhaps the one who rules the world below.

I ran until my feet bled, until finding where a ring of sunlight fell unimpeded upon the forest floor. I lay in that tall grass and tore away the rags of my shirt. I pointed my chest upwards to the light and then drew the blade of the Picarin across it, again and again, slicing it to ribbons. I did this to let the light in.

I fell out and awoke in a crusted vest of blood. As I ran my fingers tentatively over the leaking wounds I could not believe it. Too terrible to be true: How could no light have gotten in? I had parted the veil of flesh and still no light had come.

I do not know, even now I do not, (although reasons suggest themselves), what makes us stand again in a life so inexplicably difficult. Almost always we do. I do know that the body itself cries to live, even when the spirit has surrendered to this dusty world. For as I slept it alone stopped the blood. And so, I went on. I went on even as death seemed a warm blanket. Perhaps we owe something to this life.

The trick was not to take one step too soon, not think too far ahead. And yet, as I went forward, at times I looked back. There was nothing to see. Just as soon as my glance fell upon it, it would be still, and thus invisible. I called to it.

"Go away, Beast Who Hides Its Eyes! Please, please go away Walker in the Silence, Thing That Should Not Be!"

Go!

Only once did I catch a true glimpse of it. The leaning sun had drawn the shadows long and the creature had hidden in dense cover, but neglected to pull back a single toe which jutted past a gnarled root. It waited in perfect stillness, and I gazed upon that horrid toe for too long a time, until my vision blurred and my limbs stiffened. I watched and waited until the toe appeared simply as part of the root. But it would not fool me. In those hours of fearful meditation I understood what it wanted. This half-demon, who could by some mixed creation walk equally in the realm of men and Hel, set out not simply to kill the man who had crossed their realm, but to trap him and drag him back where his living soul could serve as a kind of lantern to be exhausted in the service of those who have none.

I could not sleep with it following me, yet my strength was fading fast. It followed every step, and with nonsense words woven in the threads of disease, I told it I was protected, that we walked in the world men, that it did not belong to this place. I warned it of powerful spells that could trap it, of people who could call down curses from the skies, who could send it to a place worse than that from which it came. I warned it of my gods' anger and begged it again and again just to leave. I even cut the empty air once with my knife, but the blade did not sing at all. With dark falling fast, it knew what I knew: whether it be late or soon, sleep would overcome me. I moved on.

"You go in the wood, especially just before proper dark, you might catch a spirit there. I've and others afore me 'ave."

"Really?"

"You might."

"Why are they there?"

"Why anyone anywhere?"

"But what do they want?"

She looked at him with a smile that had little happiness in it. "Mischief. Evil things. They jealous a your beating heart. How you breathe in the perfume a the flower and feel the soft rain while they 'ave nothing anymore but mist and the breath of gods perhaps, but some a them remember this life and miss it too. Maybe for things they 'aven't done. I don't know. No one do. But they see it in you, the wholeness of flesh and fire and you can touch and feel as they can never do so again, and some, they want it again, but know they won't get it evermore. And they're just sad for that. Some a them. And when they see a man walkin' in dusk, having lived a day they could never, the wicked ones, the ones coming from darkness (for all may walk in the light between) they want to jump in you, to house in you and so you got to be strong, to keep your mind strong and think white light all around you then and keep walking. When you see one for sure, and don't know its purpose, you say that prayer I taught you and just keep thinking a the light until it passes. Until you pass it. You say that prayer again and again. You can't say it too many times until it passes."

"But will they follow me?"

"Could. It don' matter. You just keep on if they do. Walk past em like it ain't nothing. If they behind you, you walk away. If they ahead, you turn back. They feed on fear…the dark ones do. They're born in the land a forgotten dreams where run the cold river Styx. River made all a tears. Just don't you be afraid. Not ever, but if you do be, you use it to be stronger. Don' let it eat you up. Work it like fire, that fear."

Her fingers rubbed the clothes against the river stone. Her back bent and her face stern and sun-darkened and her hair already gray from a life of hard work and an everbreaking heart. The soot of the earth left the fibers in a cauldron of white bubbles and all ran downstream. Straightening with a long breath, she wrung the water from the clothes and smiled at the boy.

"You get me some more soap, Son."

"All right, Aunty."

Had it been the jungle of Gelidii, so much blood would not be forgiven. The jungle would devour a thing so wounded but, as it was, this forest hung in surprising calm. The trees did not grow so thickly together there and the understory proved quite passable. I was not too surprised to come upon a tilled field. Dark leaves of crop shot out of the ruddy earth in rows that could only be the work of men.

I scanned the field and saw no one. Crossing it, I picked a few bites of the bitter greens I'd never tasted before. They settled uneasily in my stomach. At the far side meandered a shallow creek. I followed this, walking in the water like a madman, to finally arrive at a patch of mango trees. On the ground beneath them lay half-rotted fruit. They were so sweet. I vomited again, and then collapsed under the shade.

I felt almost safe. It had gone. I did not see it but, more importantly, did not feel it. It was gone. Something about this place forbade its passage. I so wanted to sleep but thirst made me rise again. I lay in the creek and let it wash so much away: the sweat and the blood and the terror. How water inexplicably draws us back.

The memories of the next few days are vague and incomplete, and I won't try to write much of them. No doubt this pen would bring only inaccuracies or pure imagination, but I do know I screamed in the night, and whether they were hallucinations or real, witnessed demons emerging from every earthly shadow. I slept in snatches, frantic for dreams of unthinkable forms. I drank little and ate less, and spent much of the day with my face pressed to the earth, hiding it in the cave of my hands breathing dust and dreaming for an end to this life.

How many mornings had passed I do not know, but once I awoke surrounded by a ring of creatures, and I suppose that is where this story begins again. "Whatcha doin here?" said the eldest of them, a horribly deformed thing. Worms pushed out of his eye sockets and I could only peek from the cave of my hands and cry. He pointed at me with a walking stick and I crawled behind a mango tree. His skin hung dead and his hands bent like ragged claws. "Where'd you come outta?" he asked more softly, and I recognized the words. "He off," said the old she-troll beside him, her face a mask of pain, her hair a lair of snakes. Death perched on her shoulder, and I saw it and tried to point to it, to tell it to go away, to warn them of it. She only laughed humorlessly and shook her head and stared at me inquisitively, but she did not know that death perched on her shoulder. She did not hear as it whispered soft curses into her ear. "He all gone," she said, but I was not. I had the vision. They did not.

He all gone.

A bare-footed pack emerged behind them, filthy and skinny and baring hungry teeth with hungry eyes and hollow laughter. The children. And I knew then these were not shades but creatures of flesh. I had walked into a valley where dwell the deformed ones of mock-life, living half-hidden just beyond the periphery of the human world. I'd stumbled into a village of trolls. I curled into myself, no fight left to draw the blade, eyes closed to the cold without. Why was it so cold? I closed my eyes.

They did not leave, yet none would touch me. They spoke amongst themselves pointing and thinking. When the old ones left the young grew bold and I knew I had been left for them to feed upon. They began to smile in anticipation of the feast to come and pelted me with pebbles, shouting gleeful words of pain that I could not understand. They accused me of being a white haired dog, an old man. They hurled the stones and words and I didn't know which stung more. I realized why they said what they did. My hair had turned white in the rift.

They came closer and closer, and then one poked me with a stick. I howled bloody death as if stabbed by a sword with a fiery tip. They all shuffled back then. The ruined man, old and broken, collapsed under a copse of mango trees, suddenly scared them. Weeping, I pulled clumps of white hair out from my head so viciously the ends bore blood and filaments of flesh. Whatever children-trolls remained then departed, some speechless, some terrified, and some laughing yet, but they all ran away. Once they were gone, for a moment in the apex of sickness, I knew peace.

The next morning the older ones left bread. This I did not know to eat. I had forgotten. I drank from the creek and held the bread in my hand like a thing that had fallen from the moon. In the current of the creek I dreamed thoughts incomprehensible, and in shades of loneliness let the bread float away. Bread was food for humans. I floated in the creek waiting for what I did not know. How water inexplicably draws us back.

I do not know why she came. Maybe they called for her or maybe she had been passing by fate. But I remember feeling her approach before seeing her, and remember my fear subsiding just a little. She crested the ridge. She moved with the grace of silk. Her light purple gown flowed like gentle water, shone like morning sun. I thought she might be a goddess, for I have never before or since seen skin her color: glowing like burnished bronze, nor eyes of such compassion. And I had never even dreamed of a woman so beautiful.

In her hand she waved a river-reed playfully against the air, as if to pet the spirits who must accompany her. She would not look at me at first. But then fate turned her up the path to the mango trees and she kneeled before me. She gently turned the reed into the ground beside her so that it stood almost magically by itself. She held her hands out between us, pressed flat against the air as if to stop something. Suddenly, tears ran down her cheeks. How gentle she was, bearing love to one who had none. Would that we all could be so generous.

I curled against the ground with legs folded into my chest, ashamed of my filth and madness. I did not dare to speak babble to her. I wanted her to go. Leave me to my sickness. But instead she came closer, a scent of lavender, and her hands almost touched my face and I feared this in my ruination. Please go away. She leaned in closer and spoke in a voice sweeter than spring: "Oh, Lamb," she said, "have all your gods abandoned you?"

I wanted to apologize, but my words were still bound by the dark violence of insanity. "Are you there at all?" she asked in gentle love, her palms making slow circles before my face. "Is the Lamb here still?" No answer. I curled back, pushed hard against a tree. "No, no, Lamb. You will be called back. You will not be lost forever. Karuna will return the world to you...and you to it."

It was then I first saw it. She lifted it from her gown by a chain of fine woven silver that hung around her fine and lovely neck. It had been wrapped in exquisite fiber to hide its light and when she freed it, it emerged like a rising star. It glowed from within with a light that must have been before the world began, and would be there yet at its end. And thus I first saw the jezeth.

Colors indescribable emanated from the center, not just so as to shine but to pierce the mind and scatter all shadows of the soul. As when a long-closed cellar-door is opened upon a dank basement floor, I felt the charm chase demons from my soul, send them scurrying like beetles from the power of the sun. The simple presence of this gem half-healed me almost at once. She whispered its name to me and smiled.

She placed it in my hands. Among the rarest acts of human experience, to hold a jezeth in the hand. "Keep this safe," she said, "until I return. Be gentle with it. It is very, very rare, and very, very delicate." She closed my hand around it. From a stupor of filth and madness I just sat staring in disbelief at the universe in my palms, at a stone that must have heard the whisper of the first word. But it cannot be rightly described. The colors themselves do not even have names. My tears fell on it and drifted to the earth. This surprised me, because I thought I had exhausted my tears.

And I knew, I knew, I knew I felt the jezeth from a long way away, knew I felt its power long before its light touched my eyes.

"It is good to cry, Lamb," she said standing and taking up the magical reed. "Remember to be gentle with it. Keep it and it will keep you." As she departed she reminded me of a slow-flying bird. "Do not be afraid," she called to me without turning back, "and wait for me here, just here. When I return, I will begin to heal you. Let the jezeth protect you until then. Let it scare away the dark. You have been very brave. Now you must be healed. I will heal you," she promised, and she did. She did.

I became lost in its world of infinite light and color. I journeyed to the before and after of all things and for the briefest instant understood the meaning of everything. I do not know how much time passed before the little universe was covered by the shadow of her hand. She took it gently back and hung it on her neck again and then took my hand in hers. "It is time to go, Lamb," she said. "A jezeth is a very, very special thing, but you cannot be seduced by its magic. You need to keep it hidden, except for special times and for the darkest hours. You need to keep it protected. This world is too cold and too harsh to be submerged in a universe of endless love. You are better already, I can sense that, but there is much left to do. Can you stand? We need to move on."

"Wh...where are we going?" I was breathless. My voice cracked.

"To my home. Not far. A lovely place. A river runs near, and the breath of water always abounds. She is a pure and peaceful place. You will be very happy there."

"Wha...wha...why are you taking me away?"

"To heal you, Lamb, as I promised."

"You...you didn't promise that."

"I did. I spoke it. When you speak to save a life, that is a promise."

Without the jezeth in my hold the terrors emerged again, but weaker now. Still, sometimes I would scream and she would turn to me sadly and hold me, let me cry or moan until my fear subsided, until the demons went away. "Do not listen to fear, Lamb. You are sick. That's all, but I will heal you."

We came to a river and Karuna let the tip of the reed kiss the flowing water and laughed as the current pulled against it. Several times she lifted it out dripping and tap-tapped the water again, and I remember the drops falling on her face when she raised the reed high and how she laughed as the droplets ran over her lips of shimmering bronze. Her smile like the sun, I remember. Even then I knew I loved her.

"Do you see how water flies, Lamb?"

"I…I"

"So close to the earth but flying still, nourishing all, shaping the whole world round, building what will be built, destroying what will be destroyed. Such is her power."

"I… "

"It is the very blood of the world, and not unlike our own. And a child can tumble safely in her waves, but should you wish to know how old is the world come see the ocean in a storm!" She opened her hand to the wind that rushed above the river. "Water humbles itself before all else, going low where others never will, cleansing and nurturing all, shaping and destroying all. That is why water is close to the way."

"What…what way?"

"The law whispered before the beginning."

Collecting droplets in the reed she followed the bank to where the river ran shallower and rocks jutted out. She sprinkled droplets on my forehead then turned and spoke to me. "This river is very special, Lamb," she said then. "I will show you why in time."

I pointed and stepped back, begging her not to step in. "A snake. A snake swimming in the water."

She smiled and touched my shoulder. "It will pass. It will not hurt us."

"A snake…a snake." I trembled.

"Lamb, be not afraid. Karuna is here."

The snake became rigid as it passed close. It was only a stick. Karuna looked to the water and back to me and smiled and took my hand then and led me so gracefully over the slippery rocks to the other bank that not I nor she slipped once, and she laughed gently when we got to the other side, and we sat there and rested our feet in the water.

"Come in," she said, stripping.

"I'm cold," I said. Her eyes filled with pity, and she put her clothes back on. She re-tied her sandals encrusted with blue-gray pearls, took my hand and slowly walked me to her home.

We passed people here and there. They were not trolls anymore, but simple country people, like me I suppose, hands hardened by the earth, brows sweating beneath the sun. They waved to her and called and sometimes smiled and she waved back. They did not address me. The enigma. "I didn't know before. I thought they were trolls," I whispered.

"You were very sick." She rested her hand on my shoulder then and it felt so warm as I grew colder and colder and despised that about myself. "We all get lost, Lamb," she spoke in gentle words, "but you have been found again. I will heal you. Be at peace."

Her home perched on the far hill of a lovely countryside...house simple but elegant in a way I had not quite seen before. She brushed aside a curtain and we entered. Inside there were no chairs, but cushions on the floor. Karuna removed the pearl-dotted sandals from her lovely feet and rested these by the door. I was barefooted and filthy, a beggar at the door. I did not enter right away. She turned in distress. "Oh, Lamb," she begged, "please, please come in!"

"I ..."

"Please please come in, Lamb. Welcome to my home."

"My feet. Please...they're so filthy. I'm so filthy."

She almost cried then and ran to me and held me in her soft embrace until I calmed. With my hand in hers, she walked me to a fine rug, woven in blue, and lay me down on a cushion that smelled faintly of jasmine. She brushed the knots of white hair from my eyes. Suddenly I knew how truly exhausted I was.

"Wait just here, young man. I will prepare a tea. It will soothe you." Soon, that most human of all creations, a cup of tea, rested in the cradle of my hands. The cup was a polished shell of shining blue. A fragrant mist of an earthy brown tea rose from within. Karuna began to hum a magical chant, and I sipped the tea and then wept for no reason I could know. She dried my tears sometimes, and sometimes brushed the ruined hair from my eyes. By the end of the tea I felt a little better.

"We should begin right away. There is a spring behind this house and the water runs warm. Not far. You may go alone. It will begin to clean you within and without. The steam will help rid the evil vapor from your lungs. Let's clean that first and then the spirit!"

"But I...I don't want to go alone. I don't know where I am anymore. I don't know who I am anymore." My voice shook.

"Be brave, little Lamb. The path will take you there. It is not far. I will be right here. If you cannot make it, just come back. You will never be out of sight of this home."

And then I, the great traveler, wanderer of two worlds, the one who passed through darkness and the light of stars, the beholder of mysteries beyond description, had to summon all my shattered self to walk scarcely a hundred paces alone to a patch of trees enclosing a spring beside a house.

I stripped and stepped into the steaming water. It was magnificent. I tried to think of nothing, just to float and dream and be within the ecstasy of nothingness, but memory fell as a shadow on my mind. The slightest creak of a tree sent me spinning in terror. The grove began to close in. I could not close my eyes out there again. A shadow fell over the pool. It was Karuna. "Lamb, are you ready to return?"

"I don't know."

"I think we should return. It is time; your healing must begin. The poison approaches the core of your spirit. Any closer and I may not be able to draw it out."

I waited for her to look away because I was naked, but she did not. And so I stepped out of the pool, bare before her, and she showed no shame whatsoever. She did not even avert her eyes, but held a white robe out before me. "Put this on instead, Lamb. Leave your other clothes in the hot water to clean them."

I pulled the robe over my head and she held my hand and walked me in the sun until I was dry, singing the sweetest song I had ever heard, in words I did not know and never would. When the sun had dried me I felt that I could stay forever with Karuna in that field beneath that sky all blue, if only my madness would go away.

A gentle fragrance now filled her house, almost mint but not, almost pine but not. Without any shame she removed her gown right before me, and I saw her naked beauty until she covered it again with a robe of purple. She tied a fillet of white in her hair. It was adorned with tiny shells. She then lifted a curtain to a back room and led me in. In the center of the room stood a table of old pale green stone. "Lie on the table, young one."

I was shaking.

"Do not be afraid."

The stone was cold, yet from beneath it emanated a certain calm. My heart slowed. My mind rested. Karuna removed the jezeth from her robe and hung it over the table so I could stare into it and it into me. I could look at nothing else. "Be still now," she said. "The less you think, the better. When you think, know you are thinking, and dismiss it as such. Do that as much as possible. Only think of your breath. In, and then out. Only that."

She lifted a small, bright white stone from beneath the table and it was hard to look away from the illumination of the jezeth. "It is called an Angelight," she said, "the purifier." She rested the Angelight over my third eye and I convulsed the moment it touched me. Sickness swelled in my gut as the stone drew out poisons of every kind. I tried to sit up, thinking it might lighten the agony of being cleansed, but she held me flat on the table and, feeble as I was then, no stronger than a child, I fell back in a writhing sweat.

All this happened in only moments and, as I felt sicknesses running up my spine, swimming through my marrow, being drawn towards the Angelight, the gem grew warmer and it actually trembled. A moment later, it shattered to dust. Karuna wept. Then, she brushed the dust away and kissed my brow and wiped the sweat clean and washed my neck and face with a cloth of cold water. She placed another Angelight over the middle eye that my aunt believed saw more than the others.

The fever rose. The sickness in my gut swelled more. The stone shattered again. This time she let me up and had a bowl at the ready and I vomited a foul stinking evil reek into it. She handed me a cup of purest water. "Rinse with this, Lamb...Now spit it out. Good. Now again. Good. Now, see if you can swallow a little and keep it down."

Just a little sip, but I did not throw it up. I lay back on the table of magnificent jade and buried the screams that raged in my mind since the touch of the second stone. In my violent shaking, Karuna leaned over me like a shelter and held me with both arms as best she could and whispered words that comforted me, but I cannot remember them at all. Only the softness of her voice stays now, and the subtle scent of cinnamon and myrrh which accompanied her, and the press of her breast against my heaving chest and the petting of the locks of her hair.

She covered her mouth and tried to hold back another tear, for the second stone had crumbled so soon, almost as quickly as the first, and that should not have happened. She then prayed to a god I never knew and placed a third Angelight on my brow. I convulsed again, and before it could shatter, she took from her chest of tools a crystal of exquisite blue and waved it over my body and touched it at certain points. The crystal felt like ice, and with each touch she said a secret word. I could feel things, actual things, flowing and turning within and hiding and running from the crystal. I trembled very badly then. She let me rest a while after the third stone cracked and split into shards. I remember the scent of incense which reminded me of eternity. I remember she hummed softly. I knew even in my agony how I loved her.

Suddenly, I was freezing. Karuna collected the poisoned pieces of stone into a cup to be buried. Yet another she put on my brow, and with each stone I could feel the demons dying, but the process exhausted me. I had almost no fight left. My mind, body and spirit all shattered, all lying in tangled separation like filaments of frayed thread. "You will win," she promised. "I feel your exhaustion, but to stop the process gives them a chance to return. You are healing and with this often comes pain. You have collected much darkness from that which in darkness dwells. It has settled deep within you, and I can hear them, can feel them hiding, running, shunning this light I put forth. I can almost see them. How frightened they are to be ripped from their warm host, to be thrown to the cleansing winds. Many are gone, but we must get them all, lest they return and grow and become the whole of you. But be strong now, and the poison will wash away like ash beneath a summer rain."

She began to hum gently again and her voice sounded like the sea. I could feel the dark ones now being drawn up to the magic gate of the Angelight, and as the energy left me the stone grew hotter and hotter. In my delirium I even thought I saw hideous forms flying above, fleeing through an open window over which Karuna had drawn a triangle of gray chalk.

With the fifth stone I fell out, and awoke to a very powerful dream. I fished a lake enshrouded in mist, the lake water clear and cold and brighter than the air. A weight pulled on my line from the depths as something began to rise from below. And in the dream I was as cold as in my sickness, but I was fishing and had caught something and so pulled the line in, hand over hand, careful not to retrieve it too quickly or with too much force, careful not to break the cord with which I pulled it from so far below.

Then, not an arm's reach below the surface, swimming in slow lines back and forth, patient and not frantic, a fish all white with poison-tipped barbs revealed itself. Its eyes glowed red, not a passionate hue, but a lifeless one of hate and eternal separation. There are some who believe the evil go to a land of fire after death. If there is such a world, I believe its firelight reflected in the eyes of the dead-white fish. And in that moment of every dream when the feeling is real, when you are awake in sleep, in this dream that moment came when the ancient being turned its grim visage to mine. Its eyes glowed and looked within me. I froze in silent terror and it looked away again with an ancient indifference. Then the cord broke, and a weight dropped off as it sank to the depths from which it came.

I had split five more stones of Angelight in my sleep. When I awoke, the tenth rested on my brow. Karuna stared into it as if it held the fate of all the world. The table of jade ran slick with sweat and my throat hurt from screaming and my jaw ached from clenching, but the tenth stone would hold. It shimmered and almost split, but it held.

Karuna smiled and wiped my brow with cold water from an ancient basin of bronze. "It is my last one…a good thing. This is the last one of all. They were carved by the ancient art of my people and cannot be made again for this stone does not grow here. But you helped me expel the remaining demons before they could crack it. You must be strong. You forced them into the light that will burn them off forever."

"I'm sorry I broke so many."

She shook her head no. "You broke none. It was the work of the demons and me that shattered the nine Angelight. Regret that not at all, Lamb. They did as they were made to do."

She would use the final stone often in the days to come, "cleansing" it in the sun or the moon or the creek or with smoke, and then resting it again on my brow. I felt better and better, and we cleansed the house and my clothes. I could eat more each day, and one day could eat fully again. On that day she cut my hair and what remnants of beard I could grow. She cut away all the white, and my natural color returned at the roots. I was cured. Only by being cured I realized how sick I had been.

"Karuna, thank you. Thank you so much."

She beamed a smile. "Oh, Lamb! You have come back to us!"

"I…thank you. Thank you. Thank you."

On that day, Karuna showed me the relics of her people that she alone had preserved. She told me their stories as she held each one, but it seemed they could not have been made of human hands, so confounding was their beauty. "How did you learn to heal like that, Karuna?" I asked, holding so carefully a chalice of turquoise shell.

"From my mother, a healer in my land. Very famous. I have healed many since. You are not the first one. Others have come before and once even the medusa was brought to me."

"The medusa?"

She paused. A confused look crossed her face. "You do not know of her?"

"No."

"You do not know of the medusa?" she asked again.

"No."

She lowered her head. "Days before, I could feel her being brought here. I knew something hideous and damned approached and I prayed and fasted to prepare for the visit. In late morning a crew of men, rugged and worn by battles uncounted, hard as the steel they carried, set the medusa at the lintel of my door. My fame as a healer had been well known by then. My powers were and still are believed to be magical.

"'Priestess,' they said to me and bowed, each taking a knee, 'we are of the Wreath of the Phoenix. Our mission is only to destroy the weapon that lies sealed within this chest, but her enchanted ribs cannot be rent by any ordinary fire or sword. We have thought to tie her to the golden eagle, who at the first of every year touches the sun, but feared she could slip and fall to the earth again and land somewhere unknown, and so be in the hands of anyone, just anyone. And then we thought to sink her into the sea, but foresaw how perhaps in a thousand years the waters could wear away her armor, freeing her gaze upon all that swim in the seas, and so perhaps turn the seas to dust. And we thought then to bury her, so deep even God could not see her visage, but we know how this earth raises the low and humbles the peak, so we feared she might one day again stare at the sun, and the wizard, who perhaps could live forever, who knows the word of her freeing, could by its magic find her unguarded.

"'At last we followed the signs of the ancients, to learn where the phoenix makes her nest, for nothing on earth burns hotter. It was the seventh order which found the nest some centuries ago. But the casing's enchantment is strong. We wasted precious kindling trying to burn through it. Understand, the art of lighting the sticks of the nest was lost with the ancients; thus, we have only a little of nest to burn. In our temple we guard the smallest ember, ever burning, to relight the bones of the nest when she is found. But if given centuries, even an ember will exhaust a great heap. If we had enough, Priestess, maybe we could break through the shell,' he said desperately, 'but now we just keep the flicker of the fire which must never die, for it can never be lit again, and hope enough of the nest is left to destroy her when she is found. Dearest Priestess, if she is freed we will put her to the pyre and burn her directly, turn her to less than ash. If she is opened. If she is.

"'We have so little left. The myth tells us the phoenix's nest will not be remade for ten thousand years. Daughter of the Waves, would you open it with a charm so we can destroy her? Just a crack. She will never be lifted out again. I beg you, please, break the seal of the evil wizard, Enchantress of the Whale's Road.'"

"Can you not find this wizard and coerce the word from it?" I asked him, for it seemed a much easier solution. But I could feel his shame at my question, for surely he had thought of this and failed.

"'We believe he changes form,' he said, lowering his head even more. Making no other excuse, he turned to Karuna. 'A faction always searches for him, Priestess of the Drifting Sands, so that we may remove enough limbs to evince from him the word. But failing that, we have come to you.'

"And I knew," she said to me, "how good these men were, how decent. I had heard of their tradition which began just after the medusa's use. The sole purpose of the Wreath of the Phoenix, for centuries uncounted, rested in the destruction of the medusa and nothing else, not for nation nor king nor glory, but only to save the very breath of the earth, for too much has already been turned to stone. And I knew his truth, for I do not see men as you do: their expressions, their sideways glances, their raised voices or the sudden use of words and expressions unnatural to them — all that might tell a lie — I do not see. I do not need that, for I can perceive the inner light of the human, and this can never lie."

"What will we do? The whole world is damned. It is dying. What will we do? The damned sky is gray with the dust of the dead. We must unite our best. They will be a separate union unto themselves. They will have all favor and authority of the parties assembled here. They will be given all we can to destroy the medusa."

"Agreed."

"Agreed."

"Agreed."

A pensive expression shrouded Karuna's face then, and in absent thought she pulled at a lock of her chestnut hair and I could see her thoughts ran far to another time.

After the silence I asked her, "Karuna, where did this medusa come from?"

She smiled and then stopped as if ashamed of her smile. "It is such a well known story I am surprised for all your travels for you to have not…it doesn't matter, Lamb. Forgive my smile."

"You have a lovely smile, Karuna. There's nothing to forgive," I said, and she smiled more and waited a long time before beginning again.

"You should know the beginning," she said. "The medusae, the sisters three, lived once on an island far from all others, put there by the gods to sheild the earth from their power. It was said they had a gaze so hideous it turned man beast or flower to stone. Their hair was not threads, but a coil of serpents. Their eyes were dead. To gaze into their eyes was to turn to stone. And they lived there, apart from all else, until a greedy king of the ancients sent a crew to find the secret island and fetch the head of one of the sisters so to possess a weapon the world had never known. With the lift of his arm he could turn a field of soldiers to stone. He could, with such a power, conquer all the world, and he almost did.

"By the guidance of that dark wizard who could read signs and the auguries of birds, they found the enchanted island, thought by many to be but myth. Much of the crew were lost, turned to stone, until the wizard set a trap: a spiked pit into which a medusa fell. A blind man was sent in to sever her head and seal it in a chest of clay. This he did, but her gaze soon turned the chest to brittle stone and it fell like sand. The men who had been guarding the ship's hold looked at their last sight. The wizard, ever devising, ordered them back to the island to retrieve her corpse. This they did. He then fashioned a chest from the bones of her ribs. On this the gaze had no effect. The wizard sealed it with a secret word and brought it thus to his king.

"The king rejoiced at the unfathomable weapon…made the wizard second in power only to him, and with this weapon conquered all the lands about him. None could stand against him. And they say, even still, the lands he conquered were so vast that you could walk years and see nothing but the perfect statues of the dead in frozen agony. This part of the world they call The Land of Sculpted Ghosts. Do not go there, Wanderer of the Gray Star, for there the breath of the earth does not flow properly, and the spirits are restless still. Those who have gone to the blighted land, to retrieve unloved treasure or make a journey worth note, have often themselves turned to madness and disease.

"But everything has its price. On a night of festivities, the king, drunk on wine and drug and power, goes into the armory, utters the enchanted word and the chest creaks open. With shielded arm and eyes he reaches into the darkened shell and lifts the medusa forth. He feels the skull and points her towards the door. He tolls the bell for the servants to come to the chamber. They file into the room, so the story goes. 'What do you think of our new toy?' says the king, laughing in drunken, drugged delight, and in slow agony, one by one, obedient to the call, the servants all turn to stone.

"He declared himself the greatest sculptor in all the world and laughed; but then, hearing his father's laughter, the king's only child, his son, ran into the chamber, laughing too. They say his face froze with a smile just beginning to turn to a countenance of confused betrayal. Some people say there is a single tear in the eye of the statue of the prince, but you know how sometimes when we can laugh so hard we cry."

She sighed

"You don't have to go on."

She pulled a lock of her chestnut hair and it coiled and pulled back. Her skin was so like copper by the fire hearth, I remember.

"'Tis almost done, what I know of it. The king laughed uproariously at his error, for while excess of joy weeps, excess of sadness laughs. He patted the stony head of his son, called him a sleepy child and urged him to awake! The day was late and they would catch the last light to play huntsman! 'Wake wake wake, my son!' he begged. Yet, when the child would not wake, the king said these words, according to a maid who had heard but was forbidden to enter the armory: 'May our night last forever, may the dawn be ever banned, may every curse rest upon my hand, for now I know I have forsaken my God, and know He has abandoned me.' He then turned the medusa's foul visage to his own, and with eyes wide open kissed her rotted lips.

"The wizard retrieved her with his magical devices and sealed her in her chest. It was said he had to shatter the arms of the statue of the king to loose her. But as the world would have it, the Wreath of the Phoenix came not long after, having heard of the kingdom in disarray; and though the wizard slipped away in a cloud of mist, they captured the chest of the medusa, her skull shut within.

"They had the fire ready to burn her, for they had found the phoenix's nest, of which nothing in this earth burns hotter, but they could not break the seal of enchantment. They brought her to a priest, to a witch, to a prophet and magus, until, one day, the medusa rested on the threshold of this very home. How they learned of me, I do not know. Since I am not from these lands, they hoped my powers could break the wizard's spell. But they could not. I tried for the full course of a moon. Everything I tried, but they could not, and so the skull rested safe within her hold."

"So what happened to her. Karuna…the medusa?"

She placed a slender stick to feed the hearth. "I do not really know. I had a dream that the crew which came to me was overpowered by an evil which took the medusa before she was ever brought to the fire. Yet, though she would not be burned, she could not be opened either. I then had another dream of a war, and in this war a good man took the medusa away." She smiled and turned to me with bright delight: "Perhaps that is your Sage! They say he held incredible power, and more importantly, was a good man. He was kind. Most important that."

"Who's they?"

"The spirits who painted my dream. Oh, the colors of my dreams!"

I then asked her something I needed to know: "Karuna, where are your people now? Where did you come from before here? You don't have to tell. I understand that. You don't have to tell me anything."

A shadow fell over her face and I immediately regretted asking.

"That is not a story for this morning. Today is a day of birth, not death. I want to show you something. Can you swim?"

"I feel like I could do anything."

"Come with me."

We walked past the grove and down into a gentle valley, wet with a mist rising by the zenith sun. I heard the rush of a river enshrouded in trees. Extraordinary colorful fruits hung from their boughs and Karuna picked these and laughed, and I ate a second breakfast. More whole with every step, we came to the river bank and I paused for fear it was the same water that led out of that place unmentionable.

"This is a good river, Lamb. Perhaps the finest in all the world. Hold my hand in the water and I will take you to where it goes."

Without any ceremony she dropped her delicate gown and stood naked before me and waited. I too stripped my clothes away and the desire that swelled within me for her beauty almost defies description.

"In!" she exclaimed and dove to the fast-running water. She took my hand and pulled me along with incredible speed. Her legs churned the water like a magnificent sea creature. I held her hand and then her shoulders we moved so quickly. The riverside raced by into jungle deep and increasingly more mysterious. Sometimes we would be still and float and she would stare into the overhanging trees from which rang strange bird calls and the distant cries of creatures know, perhaps, to none. "We are not far now, Lamb."

"From where, Karuna?"

"From a very special place. I have hoped to find someone to show it to."

"And that someone is me? Why me?"

The river ran warmer and she did not answer at first. Tired, I held the taught shoulders of my guide and the current held us both. Sometimes, she would roll onto her back and her breasts would rise wet and naked and so lovely above water and droplets ran down like shed diamonds, and sometimes we would almost embrace and they pressed against my chest of scars, and there were times when she would trace them, my scars, gingerly with her fingertips, and an expression of pain or pity crossed her face. How I got them she never asked, and I never told her. She said we drifted towards true paradise, but it felt as if we had already arrived. How I loved her then.

"Because only you are you," she said.

"What?"

"You asked why I am showing you the secret garden. Because you are so very, very important," she said and smiled.

Then she did an incredible thing: she kissed me, and this amazed me, but then she pulled me deeply underwater. I did not know what surprised me more: the kiss or that with it she breathed fresh air into my lungs. We went lower and lower into the river where only a fish could swim, or so I thought, and every time my breath shortened she kissed me again, breathing life into me again, fresh and full air from a reserve no ordinary person would ever have.

After too long a time underwater, after an impossibly long time, we surfaced again. She smiled. "I think you are very happy now…to swim with a daughter of the sea?"

"I have never been so happy in all my life," I said, but then immediately knew that was not true.

The water moved more quickly now. The forest thickened, and I again heard animal and bird cries unlike any other. Karuna closed her eyes and rolled on her back with arms out like a fan and floated on the swift and darkening river. "It will be a heart-shared secret," she said suddenly. Her eyes were closed. "To go there is to know the meaning of all things, of the mystery."

"What mystery, Karuna?"

She folded her legs and rolled in the water and then floated on her back again. "The greatest mystery. The only one. From the garden, your heart will carry away a light that all the darkness of the world may never extinguish."

"Son, a universe of darkness cannot extinguish the light of a single candle."

"Is it where the jezeth comes from?"

She slowed at my question, swam a little ways off moving through the currents like a creature born to the waves. She lifted the still-wrapped jezeth in her hand. "I only know of this one. I have heard stories of others, but have never seen another. But no, the garden is not where the jezeth is born. That has a different story."

"And what is that story, Karuna?" I asked with a gentle smile, for I knew it would be only fantasy.

She lowered her gaze as if trying to remember. "It has been told since long ago, from the first stories, that the jezeth are not born of this world, but were cast down from the sky at a time of a new beginning. They are tokens of the dancer, the Lady of Creation, from whom all light and life and stars are born if the old man deigns to lend his lyre."

"Is that so?"

"The story comes from when the world was young, when all people spoke but one tongue and lived in peace, from when men neither reaped nor sowed, but ate the fruits that grew wild in the trees, picked the untamed berries bursting at the forest's edge. And in this time they never knew war, kept beasts, nor suffered any disease. Nor did they dare cross the fickle seas with all her trials, nor climb the lifeless ice, nor tread the waterless sands, for all were happy with their homes, content in the abundance about them. They thrived.

"In this story, the world before this one had been destroyed, for people learned too much of the secrets of the universe – while knowing too little of themselves. After it all burned, after every mountain and moth were turned to ash in a flash of madness the goddess, the dancer whose name is Hope, awakens the sleeping player of the lyre so she can again make the waters and all that go in the waters, flowers, and new children too, but she must first have music, for nothing begets nothing. Yet the player of the lyre is very old, and does not want to be awakened. He sits with his back to her, stares out to the infinite abyss, his lyre clutched to his chest. She urges him to listen, for the world they made had turned to ash."

"'Leave me,' he grumbles. 'They will just set it all to fire again.'

"'Please,' begs the goddess Hope, 'just once more play for us, and I will make a world so beautiful they will not have the heart to destroy it, no matter their rage or madness.'

"The old man stands up, and a thousand thousand suns are extinguished. He waves his arm to the arc of darkness speckled yet with tips of light. 'Do you see these stars, dear daughter? Well, each one once was a beautiful world where the inhabitants lived in simple peace and bounty. But every time, every time, their madness increased with their greed, with their desire, and by and by they set them on fire. They have done this so many times that the sky in all directions, as far as you will ever see, is but the burning remnants of the discontent. You think you ask me to make life again, but are only asking me to make another star. We have enough stars. Do not bother to dance, and do not bother me. I am tired.'

"He lies down and his beard drapes into the unfathomable abyss and the dancer weeps, for she does not want to think of a universe where nothing lives. She looks about her to a sea of black cosmos and dust, to dead rocks flying and colliding into one another pointlessly, to rings of crumbled desolation where not a single thing lived, breathed or sang or prayed or danced.

"'Come,' urges the dancer again, her tears falling profusely, 'let your strings push back the vault of silence and I will dance so beautifully that they will never have the heart to turn it to ruin. Just once more. Once more, and I will never ask again. I promise.'

"He grumbles without opening his eyes. 'It won't matter in the end,' he says, drifting to a sleep that would last a thousand thousand suns, 'but to please you, if only so that you leave me be with this, I will play my lyre once more, and you can dance a world into being only to have it die like the others uncounted. I am very old now. I tire of this process.' He sighs, yet lifts his bow from the fiery cradle of all beginning and stands. He cannot refuse her anything, his daughter, and draws first a secret chord to push back the vault of darkness which waits always for the light to tire.

"And she dances, with such grace that starlight will kiss the smallest flower, that the universe will shimmer in a drop of dew, that the sun will rise like a symphony, and the moon will float as blessings in the night, and every day will be an ever-changing poem. This she dances into being. In the end, they behold all that they had made. 'They will not destroy it,' she promises in a whisper. 'It is too beautiful.'

"'You are younger than I,' says the old, old man, 'and overfull with hope, but maybe I am too old, and overfull with bitterness. It does not matter either way,' he says, and then lies down again between the light and the void, his beard draping into the depths of the unfathomable abyss, his lyre resting in the fiery cradle of beginning. Sleep takes him, and he wishes it may last for all eternity, until the end of time when he is to be awakened again. But just before he falls off, he mutters something to his daughter whom he cherishes more than any lyre or star."

"But the jezeth?" I asked.

"Ah, yes. The jezeth are her tears which landed on our little world. Most of them fell into the sea, for the world is mostly sea, but my people could plunge deep within the water and pluck the jezeth out."

"So, you think there were other worlds, Karuna, out there in the black sky?"

"Yes, and still are."

"I can't see them at all."

"They are very far."

"I suppose so."

We let the river carry us through the bounty of paradise but my mind did not rest there. I wondered what kind of worlds would live beyond the stars.

"It is a lovely story, Karuna."

She took my hand. The river carried us away and away into ever more magnificent jungle. Birdsong filled the air everywhere, and unusual trees skirted the shore in luxuriant green. Soon, the river turned crystal blue and schools of small, brightly-colored fish began to encircle Karuna. She would wave her hands and draw them in circles, much as Lyden could do with flocks of birds. Once, a large black and gold speckled fish swam lazily up to Karuna and she caressed it and blew bubbles before it and kissed it on its lips as the fish flapped its tail in delight. She swam under with it and laughed and it was odd how I could hear her just as well beneath the water as above. It joined us for a time in our watery course, followed us like a stray, until we passed the part of the river that was not its home.

Do you think the fish lives safe in the pond? A fish is not safe in the pond. Many things feed on the fish contained in walls.

We went under more and more often and would surface to a land evermore magnificent. The air now hung in redolent sweetness, the jungle song of the creatures had turned to a chorus and nothing could harm you here and you knew that and it all simply delighted the soul in ways that I cannot rightly describe. It was hard to understand why people did not come there, as if the river led to a paradise lost.

At a bend in the river's course rose a wall of granite. Karuna no longer swam against the current, but went straight towards the wall. There were no fish now, and the jungle on either side hung eerily silent.

"Where are we going, Karuna? What happened?"

She turned to me and smiled, her flesh like copper, her hair of black coral, and pointed to the wall of granite rising like a mountain. "We knock on the stone wall and ask the guardian within to lead us through the magic door."

"What?"

She laughed, "No, Lamb. I play. We go under, through a tunnel, into a world known but to a few, a garden none have seen for ages. Even I have come here for a long time, but do so today for you. The garden grows lovely beyond description, but much like the jezeth, we cannot be seduced by its beauty."

I stared at the immensity of the granite wall. "Under?"

"Yes."

"How do we pass under?"

"We swim! Do not fear, Lamb. I will be with you. The place we go leads to where it all began, to the heart of light. To a pageant of both song and silence. To the garden of beginning. Listen." And we listened to the sound of a quiet reverence. "It will make even the brightest of this land seem but the shadow of dust, and upon our visit you will never despair again, for it will serve as a flame in your heart even when all else has fallen to the cold and bitter."

I was confused at her words, and she laughed gently at my confusion and there was something terrifying in her laughter that I could not quite understand. She took my hands then and pulled me swiftly under, down and down where the river ran deep in a landscape of austere and sunken crags. Cold weeds undulated the silt down there, in the silence, where no fish play and no lily grows. The water pressed on my chest like the mountain itself. Karuna kissed me again and again for my breath quickly exhausted. But after each recalling of me to life, she pulled me even deeper, right to the dimly lit bottom.

Suddenly, like the cavernous maw of an ancient leviathan, a narrow cave yawned at the base of the mountain. Were its edges not so rough it could have been cut by human hands. The tunnel, and through it rushed the warm and quick current of a sunken river.

Karuna pointed into the mouth of the cave, smiled and kissed air into me again. I clutched her shoulders as the sea-born Karuna fanned her arms against the current, her legs kicking in a furious blur to the start of the sunken path. On the far side, so very far away, shone a rose-colored illumination, lively, but frightening too, and she kissed air into me again and again, my breath going out so quickly now, my heart racing in the dark.

In the tunnel proper I could see so little, and in the darkness understood her at last. Her hair had turned to a ball of sea-worm, her fingers to the claws of the scavenging crab, her skin hardened to scales and I knew then her deception. She led the living into the world of Hel. She was bringing me back. The greatest demonic wisdom lies in deception. She had come to collect me, the one who had not strayed from the path.

I let go of her hand. And in the breathless dark turned and struggled back out of the tunnel. I never would have made it. She caught me. I was drowning. She caught me and kissed life into me again and immediately made for the surface. Once back she smiled gently but neither of us said anything. The river carried us away from the hidden gate of paradise. At times, even now, I suspect I might forever regret turning back.

Karuna lit a small fire in the hearth. The minerals in the wood burned in green and blue flames and warmed the comfort of her home. She rested a dried bundle of sage atop the fire.

"It cleans," she said.

"I see."

I would never tell her. I spoke only of the fear of drowning and that I should have gone through.

"Do not regret whatever you do, Lamb, for whatever you do, at anytime, is the best you could have done."

"I suppose."

Her face hung in pity. "Stop this now. This silly regret. It wastes time. It wastes life. You must move on. Learn, and move on. Perhaps your path will lead you to another gate," she said, and paused and looked away for a moment. "If your wish is to go to the garden of the rose, I can still take you tomorrow, or the next day."

Suddenly, I feared her again. Her voice had a tinge of urgency that should not have been. I recalled the awful tunnel and the monstrous form and could not know if were only a thing painted in my mind. She began to shake her head. "No, we won't. I see that now. We will not return. For now, Lamb, enjoy the comfort of this home, equally yours, and be at peace. Regret nothing. Be warmed by the blessed vesta. Much beauty awaits your path to come, and danger too. I can see this. Prepare for both, but do not let one bring you too far from the other."

I sat closer to the fire. "They sacrifice lambs in my home. Upon the first full moon of the season of long rain. They sacrifice a lamb to the god of the fields, of the earth, because the lamb is his child and he cries at its blood spilled to the soil. His tears are the rain.

"It screams in that awful way and pushes back but the people laugh so happily. They…I never see them so happy…they push it forward and there's a rope on its neck and they drag and push it to the altar and at the step force its head back, bent so hard back its neck bows out, and when they cut its throat the blood sprays on the altar stone and on the heads of the smaller victims waiting there. A chicken, a rabbit, a dove, severed and staring at the lamb who's still fully alive, still growing wool and bleating and a beating heart carrying out all the processes of life, just as they had been, but they're still now except their eyes don't close, so they watch and wait for the lamb to join them, the final offering. It fights the most. Screams and pushes back and away and back from the altar and the reek of blood because it knows, because animals are not foolish. A blanket of hands push it forward and when they cut its throat its screams are garbled and wet. It's all done for but struggles anyway, long past hope it struggles. Head nearly off and still it leans away from the knife and that's the way with the living even when all hope is gone. They place its head beside the others. All staring out now, from that altar and everyone cheers then. Everyone…"

She lifts her hand. "That's enough, young one. I will call you Lamb no more," she says, a trembling hand over her lips. And then she wept, shaking. "We never do as that. Never. We comb their wool, care for them. Where I am from, a lamb is thought to be a wondrous gift. Never killed. I will call you this no more."

"It's all right."

"I will not."

"I just wanted you to know that because I was thinking it."

"Tell me, Child of the Earth, did you leave your home for the way they treated other creatures?"

It occurred to me then how little Karuna knew about me, and I of her. I told her my story then, most of it, the important parts right until she found me all but ruined beneath a mango tree.

"This sage you seek would not have been in the garden. No people may live there."

"I didn't think he was. Have you been to the North, Karuna?"

"Once. It is a drier land than this. I was young when they took us to see it. I did not go too much among it. I saw it most from the safety of our ship. It will be cold, and the people there can be harsh. But that is true most anywhere in days like these."

"I suppose it is. Karuna, I am sorry for doubting you. I thought you were taking me back to the pass."

She had been turning her fingers in the gentle locks of her hair with that gaze so distant and aloof and I knew she had been remembering a home and family gone from her — an orphan sees this in another — but, at my confession, her hand stopped and her countenance fell. She wept again and I would have given anything to stop her tears. "I didn't know, but I do now," I said. "I'm so sorry."

"You could not have known, of course. I too feared you in your madness, that you would turn against me. I feared to bring a shattered man in my home." Her eyes were full and wet and beautiful. Her locks shining in the gentle fire and the late-day light, and I would have given all the world again just to stop her tears. "But you had that light that shines so brightly now that you are well, and I knew only I — only the secret arts of Auream — could extricate it from the shroud of demons that held it in chains, La...young one. But we can never truly know the dark recesses of another's mind, so it was a reckless fool who took you in, and wisdom to shun the tunnel."

"I was a coward."

"Never."

She got up almost angry and fanned the fire before placing another bundle of dried sage on it. The cleansing smoke filled the home more and she rested beside me and I was falling in love. "Are you going home again when you are through with this quest?" she asked in a whisper. "Will you be coming by here again?"

"I haven't thought about that yet. No, I have thought about it, but have not decided what to do."

"You have travelled very far for an ordinary man. Just be careful. Listen to your finer senses. In Auream we believe, believed, that the future can be remembered, and if something is really important, the gods vouchsafe a glimpse of it and thus grant the seer the power to change it. Be always careful. Always mind your step and listen, always, to the spirit within. To it alone the gods speak."

"I will ask the Sage what to do, if I find one."

"He may not know. He may not be able to answer you, even if you find one."

"Then that will be an answer in itself," I said, and she smiled.

"You are not unwise, though you are very young yet."

"I can't be too much younger than you, Karuna."

"We do not age as you. My people do not." Then she looked very sad, and I wanted to ask her of her home, but could not stand to make her cry again. "Do you know the story of the sunflower?"

"I do not."

"Once a sunflower was born into the lovely world of bursting color and gentle rain. The sunflower cherished the day of its birth and wondered at the broad blue sky and the warm sun that floated through it. The soil was sweet and rich and the lovely life of the little field of its birth buzzed about him. Then, the sunflower saw the tulip, and she was red as the rising sun, when the sun rises in glory.

"'What are you?' he asked her."

"'I am Tulip,' said the tulip, 'and you are Sunflower.'"

"'How do you know so many things?' asked the sunflower."

"'Because I have been here before,' said the tulip."

"'Have I been here before?' asked the sunflower, for he had to know."

"'No,' said Tulip. 'You have but one season before your passing. It is always this way.'"

"Now the sunflower considered the endless sky and the lovely field and the tulip all in a moment, and said, 'But I want more than a season!'"

"'It is not the way,' she said through her soft petals, and then lowered her leaves, for the sunflower's desire saddened her. 'Cherish the time you have,' she pleaded in her softest voice. (There is no sweeter sound then when a flower speaks gently.) 'It will be an eternity if lived well,' she promised. 'Soon comes the season of warm rain,' she said. 'Let us catch it together!'"

"And the sunflower and the tulip lived in pure delight through their shared season. The sunflower wondered at the joy each day brought with Tulip beside him in the glory of her bloom. And it was she who taught Sunflower all about the meadow and the seasons: how the water falls from the clouds unasked, how the earth brings forth all living things by the grace of the sun, how night follows day and day the night; and of the creatures of the ground and the creatures of the sky she taught him, and of the stars. Of everything that anyone could ever want to know, Tulip taught the sunflower. And when it rained, they stretched their petals towards the sky to catch the drops!

"One day, at dawn, Sunflower called to Tulip, as he had always done to awaken her, so they might greet the rising sun together. She did not answer. Sunflower called again, but she did not answer. He begged her to speak, but no answer came. At last he cried out to Tulip, but from where she stood only silence came, and it was at that moment he knew her voice to be the most lovely sound in all of life.

"The sunflower called throughout the day, and every morning to follow until, sometime later, dried leaves of red tumbled away in a breeze. Sunflower knew that Tulip had gone. He looked to the passing sun as he always had, but now he looked for an answer to the pain in his heart. At last one came: 'I will wait for her,' he vowed to the glory of the firmament and to her heart in the ground. 'I will live until Tulip rises again!'

"And the season rolled on, and the sunflower lived, but not as he once had. The days held less joy, the nights were terribly long. He spoke to the other flowers and the birds and the insects, and would in passing ask of Tulip, what they knew of her, how he might get her to awaken. But all those who knew said there would be no more tulips until the coming spring. The sunflower made no response, but in his heart he more firmly resolved to see the other side of winter.

"The season of life in abundance ended. The sunflower watched all those born of petals fade. The grass turned to dry hay, the leaves of the forest became washed in the color of fire! Soon, no more bees lit in the sunflower's hollow, no more butterflies graced the air. The hum and buzz of the insects were no more, and ever rarer was the birdsong that graced the sky. The sunflower hardened its heart, but sometimes wondered if Tulip and all the rest had only been the figures of a dream. One day, a furry creature trotted out of the barren forest. It went right up and sniffed at the sunflower's stalk. 'What are you?' asked the sunflower."

"'I am Fox,' said the fox."

"'What do you want?' asked the sunflower."

"'I am wondering why a flower as you lives so long past its time,' said the fox."

"'I am waiting for Tulip to return,' said the sunflower, 'on the other side of winter.'"

"The fox smiled and showed its bright teeth. 'Oh, so you will greet the winter, eh? Well, that sounds like a wonderful plan, my brave sunflower! Winter is the most magnificent of the four seasons! The rain does not fall as rain, but in a host of crystal sculptures which, as they cover the ground, turn all the land to lily white. They are magnificent patterns, if you had but eyes to see them, and though they are beyond counting, would you believe that since the beginning of time no two drops of winter rain have ever been the same?'

"Here, the fox smiled at the flower's wonder. 'And in winter the water turns as hard as stone, and the trees abandon all their leaves, and the sky is the color of slate. But the best part of winter,' said the fox, 'is that plump mice and moles and fat little birds leave their tracks in the snow, so that a sly fox can trot right up to them and catch 'em in its teeth!' At this, the fox clacked its teeth and smiled again. 'But never have I met a flower of the sun standing in the heart of that season; but should you do this, brave sunflower, should you alone stand when all else about you has faded, I shall come to greet you again.' With those words the fox nodded to the flower and trotted away. For a long time the sunflower wondered at his words.

"The days grew colder and turned ever more towards darkness. The wind blew more bitter and harsh, and the soil had lost all of its sweetness, and the rain fell in cold agony. The sunflower had to summon all of its energy, every bit of it, just to stand, just to keep the yellow in its petals, just to keep from collapsing against the cold.

"The flower considered the broken images about him. Could this really be the same meadow as before, once so filled with life? How could anything ever be born from this? Nothing grew but darkness. Nothing stirred but bitter cold. A terrible and eerie stillness had settled over all the land, and even the sun would not rise as high as it once had. Even the sun was dying. The sunflower thought it had come to the end of time...but he had promised to wait for Tulip, and as long as he had life, he would keep his promise.

"Then, in a day as gray and bleak as any other, a voice that was not a voice spoke to the sunflower, 'Why do you stand yet, Flower of the Field, so long past your season?'

"The sunflower looked everywhere, but did not see who had spoken. 'I wait for my Tulip,' he answered. 'She will come with the second spring.'

"'Gentle flower,' spoke the voice, 'brave beyond all others, this is not the season for you now. Rest into the ground your tired petals, let your seeds fall away, let your stalk fold into the earth. You do not wish to see the winter to come.'

"'I don't care!' cried the sunflower. 'I will face whatever comes so I can see Tulip again!' "

"The air slowly turned, and as the sunflower curled its petals against the cold, it knew who had spoken. The voice, both ancient and ageless, the voice that had been there at the beginning and would announce the coming of the end, the voice which filled all hollows and made its house the arc of the sky, which lifted seas and pet the new-born grasses, which summoned storms and stopped them too, now whispered to the curled yellow petals so dry and frayed and faded, 'Gentle flower, Grace of the Meadows, so brave beyond all others, you cannot fathom the season to come. This day will seem as a paradise when compared to it. The sky will be pitiless cold. The soil will yield nothing. The water will not fall in soft rain but in arrows of ice, and I, who already pull the spirit from your stalk, will in the season to come be as the screaming hawk from the fell sky. Yield now to the time and the order of things and rest on the ground. Do not be afraid.'

"The sunflower knew the words were true. But it had waited so long, suffered so much, surely it could try to greet the winter. It had no fear of that, despite the suffering that would come. Thus, he cried out, 'Wind, who knows all things and goes to all lands, surely you can let one flower live beyond a single winter! Give me just one day on the other side of the season, the day she is born to us again, so that when she rises she will know how much I love her, how for her I waited, how for her I did not forsake my promise!'

"The wind considered the words of the flower as it turned in the infinite sky. Then, it spoke, 'Most Noble of Those Who Grow, Light of the Meadow, Grace of the Earth, know this: should you wait any longer you will fall when the ground has turned like stone, and your seeds will take no root then, but scatter over a pitiless earth and become but dust. This would be to our great loss, for then nothing more would be known of you. But I promise you this: release your seeds to me now, and I will lift them all to the sweetest fields, and bring them rains when the sky runs dry, and keep the harshest of storms from them. When they turn their gaze upwards, they shall never want for the sun. Lastly, Keeper of Promises, they will never be alone.'

"With these words the sunflower grew very sad, for it knew it would never see Tulip again. It looked up to the turning sky just to see the sun once more, just to remember her in its light. It cried one last petition: 'Wind, who knows all lands and can do all things, I will fall to the ground and let my seeds go! I will fold in my petals forever, and loosen the clutch of my roots…but, you who bend the tallest trees and lift the sea and turn the stones to sand, do this one thing for me in return of my letting go: tell her something of me, something that will let her know how much I loved her, how much I wanted to be here when the earth is born again, how much I wanted to hold my promise?'

"And for a moment the sky stood in silence, and the sunflower thought it had perhaps asked too much of the wind (for it was only a flower and the wind ruled half the earth), but then the voice spoke again. 'It will be done,' it promised.

"The sunflower knew the wind would never lie, and as it loosened its grip on the earth it wondered how it had lived in such barren soil, and as it stopped fighting against the cold it wondered how its petals had ever held on so long. It folded to the ground at last, and with a heart half content, let its life slip away.

"The sky turned with a fresh violence. Every seed lifted from the withered face. They flew ever higher into the air and, as promised, were sown in the sweetest soil, forever protected from drought and storm, and they were never alone.

"But one seed dropped right there, just where Sunflower had lived, and in the spring it grew beside a tulip, and they were very dear friends."

She smiled. I smiled too. "That's a nice story, Karuna."

"It teaches of the seasons. You will need to know of them going North."

"Is that what the world is like in the North?"

She nodded. "It is. You must be ready. You are no sunflower. The cold will kill you if it finds you unprepared," she half-joked.

"Does the land really all turn white?"

"Yes, it does. You will see it yourself if you live. But that is a long way from now. Just rest and recover. Do not to worry on what may come. Try never to this. It weakens you. In Auream we teach this to children."

I asked then what I had not wanted to: "Karuna, what was Auream, if you don't mind? You speak very little of your past. You don't have to answer."

She cupped the jezeth through her gown and her eyes stared at a horizon that was not there. "I will tell you," she said gently. "I should not be afraid to speak of my home. We lived on the crown of the earth across the jade sea. We had little to do with these harsher lands, ever steeped in war and loss and greed. Rather, we dwelled in delight and cultivated our inner nature; we unraveled the secrets of the earth, as much as we may do without hurting her, or hurting ourselves. Our ancient cities were cut in green sea stone before the time of recording, and our structures rose in dazzling spires to the sky, the tops of which gave meet dedication to the gods. We were devout and curious; we were enchanted and peaceful; we were the children of the sea and none held more blessings than we."

"We explored many lands just to learn of the world, and to see if any boasted more beauty than Auream, but none ever did. Her mountains ran to the sea. Her forests grew in lush paradise, and her fresh waters flowed sweeter than any I have ever known. On all sides, the ocean guarded her like a mighty army, and we lived as much in her water as without. We skimmed upon her surface and explored her depths, and it was down there, in a deep and lightless valley far beneath the sun-kissed waves, that we found the jezeth among a sunken trove of treasures, spectacular beyond description, yet the jezeth outshone them all.

She sighed and lowered her hand from the jezeth. She would not look at me. "One day, I awoke to the clarion of warning. In the faint light of rosy dawn I saw from my bedroom chamber that the pink shore forever there was gone. The sea had risen and was rising still. This had never happened before. The *clarus* called again and again. The priests and priestesses made offerings, people prayed and built barriers, but the gods were not to be appeased and the fate not to be changed.

"The waters rose steadily. Calamity had come: we thought some unthinkable tipping of the balance had occurred in the coarser outside world, and for this all of humankind would pay. When nothing could be done, no god appeased, no water stopped, the *clarus* called a single order, the sole command for the denizens of Auream."

Bring the children to the ships

"We filed from our homes as our lovely world withdrew, as mother ocean swallowed us whole."

Bring the children to the ships!

"And mother held my one hand, and father the other, and I remember the water how strangely cold and dark it ran and it went over my feet, I remember, and then it went to my knees."

Bring the children to the ships!

"The world was falling. Chaos had come again."

Bring the children to the ships!

"And they put me aboard the ship and to protect me hung around my neck the jezeth, found by mine own father. And mother kissed me and said a prayer and wept and father did too and they set me in the black ship."

Bring the children to the ships

"The *clarus* called again and again for the preservation of our race. Soon, all the children were loaded into the ships. Mother told me she would watch me from the sky, and father told me he, too, would watch me from the sky. The winds rose and the waters became furious. With a last embrace we said goodbye. A thin crew took the children to the sea. I looked back only once. Auream had fallen beneath the waves."

She waited a long time before speaking again. She held the jezeth again and leaned forward, hand to shoulder, hugging herself. "Sometimes, in dreams, I see mother in the deep. Her eyes turned to pearl, her hair to...." She began to cry, and I touched her shoulder and it was cold.

"Don't cry, Karuna."

"Why not?"

"I too have lost."

"Then you should cry with me."

The jezeth burned under her gown. "It's okay if you cry, Karuna. I'm sorry."

"Sorry for what?"

"For telling you not to cry."

When she regained her composure, I asked an innocent question: "Do you still know the others from your home?"

She shook her head. She had become tight and quiet, muscles tensed.

"Don't tell me."

"No, you should know."

"Don't tell me. Please don't tell me."

"You should know. We found a world in peril when we reached the coarser lands. A great storm had washed over the world, and while it had sunken Auream, it confused land and sea on the part of the continent too big to succumb. But Men had been reduced to cannibals. All the crops, all the fields, all devastated and gone. Salt had spoiled the earth. Blighted land. Men moved in packs like wolves, battled for anything and devoured the defeated. They preyed on any stranger. When they came upon our small camp, the only ship to have survived the chaos of the sea, they killed all but me, and I think it was the jezeth that protected me, just as it had protected our ship."

"So you are the last of your kind?"

"I am."

"I'm so sorry, Karuna."

"Do not be. The world has simply moved on."

She went to place her hand on my knee and absently placed it on the floor. I took her hand in mine, and it was so cold. "Karuna, why won't you ever look at me?"

"Oh, Child of the Earth, I am always looking on you."

"But I mean, you never look right at me. You look past me, like I'm not real. That's why I worried about what you were. Something never felt quite right and, even now, with your eyes welled in tears, do you see mine?"

"I do not," she said.

"What?"

"I do not. When the pack of men killed the crew and the other children, they took me, calling me the most lovely, and raped me. They did not have the means to take me with them, and one among them said it would bring terrible fortune to kill the last of the children of the sea. And so they spared me, but poured poison into my eyes so that I might not describe their faces to men of justice or to the gods, whichever returned first."

She opened her hands and almost looked at me. "But I am happier for that, young one, for now I better see the inner light, the one that shines from the beginning, and by that gift could I heal you." I waited a long time and did not speak.

Finally, she said, "Child, to see you better, may I touch your face?"

"Of course."

She ran her hands gently across my brow and down my cheeks. "Oh, Lamb!" she said, forgetting her promise, "why are you crying?"

The time came to move on. I followed a road leading away from the peaceful fields and people to a harsher land, colder, with less food and kindness. Hospitality grew scarce, and even though I walked among my own kind, I often slept in the outer fields or curled against the cold behind a barn. I knocked on doors to beg a bed, but most refused a stranger. Many nights I would stare into the light of the jezeth though she had warned against it, but sometimes only it brought comfort. As has been said, I came to a tavern where a man gave me gold, and another led me to a dragon's den, and so to a dragon. Eventually, I reached the sea, which awaits beyond a land of no water.

Everything dried in a way it should not have. Each day the green grew scarcer, as if with each passing day the forest surrendered little by little to its undoing, until all the sweet earth succumbed to lifeless sand, and I did not understand why such a place would be, but there it was. And I had some water with me, and there is a reason I say that.

A plume of dust lifted from the west. I had been following a scarcely-travelled road and took cover in the thicket to see what approached. At last a slow procession of men and women appeared who skirted this land of no water. I stepped out of the thicket. The leader in the front called back and the caravan halted. He looked amazed. With a shudder, I recalled the road of Gelidii.

The usual questions: Where I was going? Who was I? Why did I wander out here alone? The place was dangerous, full of wolves and thieves, they said. And snakes smaller than your little finger hid in the sand and were the color of the sand and if they nipped you your life could be counted by heartbeats. I should not be out there alone, they warned. I did not tell them of the blade or of the jezeth, or the freshly picked tooth on my back hidden in a wrap of rags. I did not tell them how, by then, life had become so very hard that I no longer gave death the breathless reverence it deserved, but placed one foot before the other, eyes pressed before my feet, feeding the empty gut when I could, slaking thirst when I could, waiting for destiny to come. The only thing I would not do is give up. I promised that to myself and to them. I owed that to Selador at least. I would not quit until I had found a Sage, or exhausted all efforts in my search for one.

"Is that all your water?" said the man in the front. He rode a strange-looking beast goaded with a long stick and with this he pointed at the three gourds of water slung on my shoulder.

"Yes."

"Where do you go with that water?"

"To the North."

He looked back at his company. All were confused. "To the North?" he asked, repeating my words with some exasperation. He waved the stick out towards the waves of sand.

"Yes."

"What are you?"

"I am human."

He laughed a little. "Yes, but what is your business across the sea of sand?"

"I am looking for my father. He works a mine in the North somewhere. I don't know where exactly and don't care, but I'll find him."

"You must love your father very much to undergo such a journey."

"No, it's not that. I have something to ask him," I said and said no more, for people will not pry into matters like that. He scratched his long beard and stared into my eyes trying to read something there. After a long pause he spoke, "You may come with us to the road in the East, the great road. It will take you to the North."

"Thank you, but I'd rather go more directly. I know my way through the wilderness."

He shook his head. "This is no wilderness. The water you have will last a day and a half. It is fifteen to cross by foot if you go swiftly. Come with us to the great eastern road. It will be safer for you. We have food. We treat a guest as a god. We believe we have found you here on the doorstep of death by the will of God and that He has sent us for your protection. In less than a month we go south where you turn north, but before we part ways you will assist us in our business of trade, and for that we will compensate you."

"That's very kind of you," I said and meant it too. "I would like to but need to keep on. I will find more water before crossing into the sand."

He tilted his head. The white cloth which protected the wearer from the sun drifted over half his face. He would not ask me again. He told me to wait and rode his beast through his company who, one by one, slung swollen skins over his saddle. Water. He returned and laid these at my feet. At the last, he gave me a brick of dried date and nuts with salt rubbed onto the outer part, wrapped in a single enormous leaf. "That is what we can safely spare for you. That is all God wants us to do for you. It might be enough. Do not waste a drop. Do not wash or pour it on your neck to cool. Only for drinking. If you must, you can drink your own urine, but not for more than a day. After that it begins to kill you."

"I can't thank you enough for this." I heaved the final waterskin in place. "It's very heavy."

"Thus the scale of life. May God protect you." He then called back to his party which, as one body, moved forward. I bowed and thanked each as he passed. Some replied; some said nothing. Some stared at me as if I were a ghost.

I thought I would be alone in the crossing, but in eight days I met another person: the man beneath the red rock.

The water had been running out of my body unbelievably quickly. As each skin emptied, I threw it away, not wanting the extra weight. You begin to see things in the desert, in that stark emptiness that seems almost purposeless; so when I saw a man almost naked sitting under the shadow of the red rock, a flash of life where no life should be, I could not be sure if he were real. "Hey!" I called as I had to illusions in the past, but this one raised an arm. "Hey!" I called again, because he could not be real.

"Hey," he said to me. I looked behind me, scanned the horizon in all directions: nothing but dunes, cacti and occasional patches of stone. He could not be real, so I went towards him and the exquisite shade beneath which he sat.

He was so thin, with his face gaunt and dry and only a rag about his middle and a rag on his head. His skin had turned to leather. He had no weapon. He did not seem a threat. I sat beside him in the delicious shade. He said nothing. He did not seem to notice me now that I was there. For a long time I wondered what to say. "Are you real?" I asked at last.

He shrugged. "Maybe. I hope not."

"How are you here?"

"I could ask you the same."

"You have nothing. You have no water. Do you need water?"

He waved my words away. "I need nothing. I am waiting only for God to kill me."

"Oh."

He looked into the distance with eyes of eternal sadness. "I have not spoken to another person in more days and nights than I can count."

"How do you live out here?"

"Living is easy when you wait only for God to take you."

"You don't want to live?"

"I want only to be the obedient servant of God. I want only to be forgiven. In death I will be forgiven. That which cannot be forgiven in life is forgiven in death."

"I'm sorry."

"God is blind in the temple," he said. "We believed this in my home that once was. God sees all the world, but in the temple He is blind, for there men are supposed to take up His work and act within His spirit. And so, in the temple, God may rest His sight. Thus, on a day I went into the temple to recite the prayer of forgiveness, there arose from below the roar of wind and water — the trumpet of His judgment."

He picked up a handful of sand and threw it off, muttering something as the grains cascaded down. "Long ago the land of my home was beneath the sea. Still, we find shells in the soil. As the waters receded, what are now peaks showed as islands, and they built temples on the highest parts where they would be closest to God. On the day of destruction, I was praying for forgiveness in the highest and most holy of the temples. I was alone. I had gone alone. I was alone on the day of destruction and God is blind in the temple. I once thought He did not know, for in the temple I kneeled stricken from his sight. I once thought He sent a roar of wind and water to wash away this sinner as price for that terrible, terrible act I had done, unknowing the water would not catch me, for God is blind to the temple. And I heard the roar and from the mountain looked down: a wave that blotted out half the sky curled over the land. And God is blind in the temple. And the wave collapsed and washed away all and every soul but me and turned the color of the earth and wove through all and everything that was, and God is blind in the temple and so I lived."

He sighed and threw another handful of sand out into the desert and watched it land as if each grain held a prophecy if only it could be read. "At first, I thought it the end of days. And then I thought He had sent the wave to blot me from His sight, unaware I had been in the temple kneeling, eyes wet and shut hidden in the cave of my hands." He unfolded his legs, skin hanging on bone, thin and calloused flesh dried like leather. His ankles were cut and the bone swollen. His feet were curled and his toes were huge and white. "And I stopped my prayer for forgiveness to watch all that I had known swept away. And I would not be there to be brought to forgiveness. I was absent to His judgment." He rubbed the bones of his knees.

"After that, I came here, far from any water, where the waves of God cannot smite me, for though I court death, I fear it too. I fear what waits for one like me on the other side where all acts are judged." He laughed without joy. "And I know now that God did not make a mistake; He cannot. He would bring everyone I know to peace but me. This is my punishment. Through this He teaches me.

256

He would bring everyone I had ever known to the land of forgiveness but me. For that terrible, terrible thing I had done, he took away everything else, to teach me the weight of emptiness, to prolong my time of forgiveness, for in the end all must be forgiven."

The skeletal man did that odd act again, scooping a handful of sand and tossing it to the casual wind to land dryly about us. He leaned forward eagerly as if to read something in the fresh arrangement of the grains and almost gasped in desperation at what he saw or failed to see. I would never ask of his past, but had to ask him this, and I suppose by this question survived: "Sir, how do you live out here with no water?"

An expression of emptiness crossed his face. "Pale blue butterflies, no bigger than a kiss, live in this desert wind. They eat naught but dust, drink only the vapors that rise from the sands over buried water. When thirst takes your life to fire, seek this butterfly and follow it. The blue shows plainly against the yellow sand, but let it get too high and you may not see it at all for the pale wings match that of the sky. Wait for it. Let it land. Do not follow over close. It will land and slowly beat its wings. Then you will know it drinks the vapor of buried water. Dig there."

I could not believe a man lived by such faith. I left him after that and he said no good bye and gave no more advice, but after seven more days in the desert I had exhausted my water supply. And I made it out barely alive, staggering in the unreal heat, chasing butterflies.

Lands can change quickly. Amazingly, not too much farther along the same journey I came to a place that reeked of fish. The air had such moisture you could smell it. The road had led me to a village by the sea and, unlike the other villages I'd encountered, no one seemed to notice or care as I walked in. Not even giving the cold glances of suspicion. They went about their work, their conversations, their food, the sundry ways of their lives, so many of which were supported by the sea itself. Some wove nets; some shaved and shaped the timber for ships; some hung fish, fresh or dried, on strings or racks throughout the village. Merchant-artists displayed necklaces of purple shell, bracelets of black coral, and pearls of many colors set in rings. They wrested whatever beauty they could from the bounty of the sea.

Off from the crowds and shouts, some few walked on the shore of fine sand and stared at the endless water that ran away forever, that seemed to press against the final sky and spill off the very edge of the world. Children splashed in the shallows, but none swam very far out.

I went to a tavern which jutted out over the sea. You could watch the sea move below the ill-fitting floorboards, smell it too. I sat alone at a small, uneven table and waited. Eventually, a fat and bitter-looking and ugly old woman approached me. "What you want?" she asked, and her breath hit me like a punch.

"Just give me something to eat. Anything."

"You got money?"

"I've gold."

" 'Ave you now?"

" I do."

"Gold buy anything."

"I'll just take a plate and a cider, if you have it."

"We don't."

"Water then, or tea."

She shrugged and went off.

The floor creaked under her weight as she went to the back and I imagined her crashing through to the dark water below. In a childish, mean-spirited way, I half wished it. The place did not look clean, and I did not think the food would be safe, but I liked the tavern all the same…how you could hear the sea slap against the pillars, how they must have struggled to build such a place, how the fish plopped right below the table, how the people laughed too loud and the low wall allowed you to watch the sea from where you sat. Was sunset, and so the arc of the firmament burned in that eternal orange-red as it must have done since the first dusk, and I had seen many a sunset but never over the sea. It was magical.

The wind lifted some and the walls groaned. The sea began to beat white against the pillars, and two men rolled down heavy blinds to shut out the weather, but they also shut out the view. It was not a fair trade. I stepped outside to wait. Someone had nailed the severed tails of large fish to the dock posts, and the bleached skulls of sea creatures I could not imagine perched under the eave of the inn where it faced the sea. And I now noticed on the roof what I had not before: rows of enormous ivories, teeth of a creature I would learn is called "baleen." These infest that sea, and still I do not know how the teeth of a baleen could ever be recovered. But they are not teeth exactly, more of a net, and with it they swallow people and even small boats whole and, despite their size, can come close enough to shore that none swim out in water much deeper than the knee.

The surly waitress called me in unhappily just after the best of the sunset. An odor of cooked fish smoke and grease and coal fire filled the air strongly now. It came from a kitchen hidden behind soot-blackened curtains. I could see the flames dancing from my table until her body filled the doorway holding a bowl of fish stew and a piece of dry bread. I ate slowly, for if you forage too long, the stomach becomes delicate. The stew had a milky orange color with chunks of white fish steak and carrot and potato and greens. It was extraordinary. She brought a small cup of water down and a half cup of rum. She sat at the empty table beside mine and considered the night's crowd. She considered how I picked at the food. "You not hungry?"

"I am."

"What's it then?"

I broke a piece of the bread into the bowl to soften it and lifted the white fishmeat and the gravy to the spoon. "I eat slow."

"Is better," she said. "You goin' to the camps to cut?"

"The what to what?" Just a hint too much salt.

"They takin' cutters in the mornin'. You needin' a room, we got 'em."

"For what? To where? Where're they goin'?"

She gave me a hard look. "You come here to be a cutter in the camps, no?"

"No. I'm just passing through."

Her face became confused and angry, and then she laughed. "Exactly where you passin' through to?"

"I'm just going north."

"The camps is north."

I peeked at the western sun through a break in the shutters.

"Across the water?"

"Across the sea. Boat leaves short after first light."

"Then that's where I'm going."

"So you a cutter, then?"

"I suppose."

She watched me chew. "It good?"

"What?"

She nodded at the bowl.

"Amazing."

"Is wolf fish. The best."

"Never had it before."

"They only live in this sea, like lots a things." She gestured towards my bundle, the great tooth of Kai-Tey. "Was all that you heavin' with you? Not that it my business really."

"Tools," I lied. "I work where I go."

"You be a good cutter," she said. "If you can eat, you can cut." She observed how I used my spoon, broke my bread. "Know this: ain't nothing after the camps. Nothin.'"

"Okay."

She acted as if she did not hear me. "Don' go thinking a wandering off from them. Wilderness runs to evil up there. Is trouble already."

"All right I won't." I found the cut of coin I had left and handed it to her. "Can you take enough for the meal and room out of it?" She traced the remainder of the outer curve with her thumb as if not believing it had once been a coin so large. "Don't go in wilderness when north," she said, standing slowly. "You ain't listenin' what I say."

She walked towards the back, disappearing into the smoke-filled room of fire. When I held the gold again, hardly any had been taken, but hardly any was left.

My room for the night was small and damp, but the sound of the sea made me sleep in a deep peace. I awoke to the commotion of the dock below. They were loading the vessel for the crossing. In the kitchen downstairs the same woman kneeled and breathed into the hearth, exhausted, but she stoked the fire all the same. She placed a kettle on top and in time a cup of milk tea on the table. It had cinnamon and honey and a spice I could not recognize.

Outside on the dock, a quiet throng of sullen men, impatient and half- awake, crowded about the boat beneath the sky of iron gray. When the collector came, I paid my fare, a thin slice of the coin, and not long after, we sailed off towards the sun, which in its passage turned the water to fire.

I sat at the stern near the pilot who held the rudder while two assistants adjusted the single, triangular sail. The craft leaked terribly. We all took turns bailing.

Everyone in the boat, except the crew, was going to the camps to work. As the sun rose higher, the cutters spoke more and joked some, and in the warmer air talked of their homes, of other jobs and of the sea. It was only then that I learned what we would be hired to cut.

"Trees," said an old man still strong enough for that work. "Old ones too. But they been going too deep. It's when the trouble begins." Suddenly, everyone had something to say. Suddenly there were questions and answers and opinions and everyone suddenly spoke of the same thing. He continued when the time was right, "They've disturbed something in the forest. That's why we getting work so easy. The cutters been going in deep for big timber and when they not coming back, it scares a lot a 'em home. When they find the lost ones, they hollow."

"What you mean hollow?" asked another. "The trees is hollow?"

"The cutters. They take all the insides out but leave the skin. Mayhap as a kind of warning, an omen to the rest."

All were quiet then. The ship skimmed quickly over the sea.

"I got five kids," said another passenger, a man who seemed too young to have fathered five children and was as thin as I. He fixed his face in stern bravery so that I thought he must be afraid. "Five," he repeated, "and I don't care nothing about no damned tigers. I'm cutting for silver and will bear silver back."

"Is not tigers," said the first man, the older one. "Is worse than tiger. It's thinking like a man. It's hunting and making omens. Sometimes, they writing signs in the flesh: a warnin' to stay off from them parts. This cuttin' woke something that shouldn't a been woken. But you know how men are: they keep going on all the same." He sipped from a flask of water or liquor. "Yes, they do." He sipped again. "I'm not saying to be afraid, just be careful. Don't stray from the camp. Don't cut too deep. You be getting greedy for the bigger trees and they send something for you. Bear yourself back first, then worry for silver."

"It could all be nothing," said the younger man.

"Nope," said the older. "I was there. Seen their work."

"What you see?"

"What I said. Just don't go too far in, and don't cut against the dark. Wait for the sun. Let her rise well before you set out and be back long before she gone. That's all. It's always the same ones who get it. They who get greedy. Just don' get greedy. So the big timber brings a higher rate…so what? What good it does you when your skin is all that's left?" He leaned back and smiled. "That's all I have to say of it. Follow what course you will."

I, a fugitive, a stranger, kept quiet, as was my practice.

The pilot, near my side, always scanned the horizon with a face seemingly fixed in a quiet smile. It was he who first spoke again to command the crew with a gentle voice to pull in the sail or to loose it, to tighten the lines or let them out, to do whatever needed to be done to better catch the wind. The afternoon sea grew more choppy as we began to race across the water. The passengers talked of other things. Everyone pretended not to be afraid, and perhaps a few were not. One began to rap against the curved hull and hum a song about the life of a wandering laborer, and it was a good song and sad and meaningful, but then the pilot told him to hush. "We are out too deep for that," said the pilot.

"Too deep to sing?" I asked him, and he looked at me as if for the first time.

"You can't rap against the planks so far out. It carries below. If you want to sing, sing low."

Everyone seemed to understand but me. I scanned the horizon in all directions for what the pilot had warned, but saw only sea and sky, the breath of fleeting clouds. To him again I asked, "Carries to what?"

A low chuckle ran through the boat.

"You never been to sea, have you?" he asked me.

"No."

"It shows. Is fine, but it's just amazing how little they tell you."

"Who?"

"Anyone. Anything. Anyone could a told you what you now set yourself among, but they never quite do that. It's better like that, I suppose. A man, generally speaking, is better off not knowing what the future holds."

The wind quickened and the boat listed, and the pilot in his gentle voice spoke to all to lean against the wind. We did, and the boat raced on to run along the swells and dive through the valleys of the sea, and it was like flying must be as the water sprayed over us and I laughed and we raced on.

"We'll make her in two days, if this wind holds," the pilot said to no one in particular, almost yelling now to overcome the crash of waves against the hull. "That'd be real quick," he said to me. "You could be stuck out here ten days or more if the wind fails."

I shrugged my shoulders. I didn't care really where I was by then. I would go as the fates decreed, as the wind pushed, to where the path led. I would follow as long as it ran vaguely north.

After a time, the wind slowed, but all had been set and steady. The pilot looked to me, knowing my question had never been answered: "The sound goes to the baleen. To the damned baleen. They got ears like an ugly wife and a worse temper. You don't want them knowing we passing over. In these waters best to quietly take to sea."

And it was one of those odd things in life when the words align with the world without, when the works of gods deign to illuminate the stories of men, for just as he said that, he lifted an arm from the rudder and pointed to the east. "Look there! They breaching now. A small pod." We all looked, and no one spoke and no one smiled as we watched wide wet backs longer than the boat itself curling through the waves of the sea. They were not far off. They appeared as the arms of a great serpentine monster reaching through the deep. Everyone fell terribly quiet upon the sight of them, and the pilot would only whisper his commands until the black limbs rose no more, until even the wind died and the sail luffed in the still air and the boat all but stopped.

A man coughed then, and the pilot shot him a look of burning daggers. He did not cough again. We waited for the wind to rise and the baleen to leave or for the pilot to tell us what to do. After what seemed a long time, the pilot spoke: "All right now. They gone. They sounded, and went deep too, for they don't like to be up in the calm. You can talk, but talk easy, and no singing, no tapping, and nothing goes overboard, not even a spit. You gotta piss, you use the bucket."

We caught a weak wind. We moved gently through the sea. We did not see the baleen again. When those around me began to speak of other things I asked the pilot about them, of what kind of creature were they.

He scanned the whole horizon. "Is amazing how little we may know of our station and is better that way. Your mind shall carry the greater burden on your return by what I speak." He waved his arm to the infinite waters. "This particular region of the sea holds a unique creature aforementioned as the baleen. We know very little of them as they cannot be killed or caught. The teeth you may have noticed in the dock tavern are of a corpse that washed up. Yet we know this: of all the dangerous beasts that dwell in the watery part of the world, the baleen is the most treacherous against man, and yet gentle in its ways, for they do not bite, tear, thrash, sting or stab, but quietly come up from below and that enormous arch of a mouth rises over you and holds you gently in its small prison of rib-teeth and the leviathan simply eases back underwater, into that realm below. And so they say a baleen never actually kills a man, but is the water that does, or more precisely, the absence of air. And they are not a dumb beast. They know we are an easy prey, for we die quite quickly below. This is why they seek us out, why they follow our boats waiting for them to tip or overlean, and I know of men being plucked right from the side. I know of hulls cracked by their rising backs."

"You can't know that," said the older man who had warned us of the forest.

"No, I don't suppose I can, but when one splits a craft right up the middle and there's a whole damned pod waiting to feed below, what exactly was that? Chance?"

"Has happened once," said the older man.

"Once, and to me," said the pilot, and this surprised the older man. Everyone aboard listened now.

"Tell us," said the older man, "I knows you him."

The pilot said nothing for a while save the gentle commands for the running of the boat: a tightened sail, a bailer, lines let in, lines let out, lean. He did not want to speak of it. That was plain. He scanned the horizon again and again, and I thought in his eye I saw the welling of tears, but it may have been the burn of the wind.

"All right," he said at last. "I say it out then perhaps to get rid of it, but I have had to speak too much of it already. I'd thought we'd hit a shoal of some kind, or a floating tree or wreckage or the top of a buried mountain not yet known, but it was the crown of a baleen cresting into our hull and it splits her right down the middle and there was nothing to be done for it. We was loaded full and the day as calm a day as God can make, a bad day for sailing. You sit there like a piece of bait beneath a sky painted translucent blue."

He took off his cap and wiped his brow and scooped water into it and placed it back wet on his head.

"The water rushed in, dark and cold and pitiless. There were nothing to be done for it. We wash in like beans sloughed from a plate. They let us flail awhile. They sounded until we were all calm and thinking there might be a way back and then the first hood rises over the first man and he is gone just like that. One moment he talking of what may be to come and then in a breath he gone. And there were no vows of that first one, no requests or promises made, for then we had all of us a hope and did not talk of not making it back."

He looked to the older man who had questioned him and spoke mostly to him. "I spoke with a fellow, only one, picked from the side of a boat some years gone, and he were sinking in the mouth of the leviathan, but for reasons ordained by fate, the beast spit him back out again. He said it were a soft journey. That the teeth don't bite. The baleen holds you gently in its mouth until you are still and it does not take long. Especially since we scream when they come. Especially since our hearts race like trapped rabbits.

"Had you the courage to stare into the abyss below, you'd see 'em, a whole damned pod of 'em circling down there like a fleet of sunken, black ships, like the shadows of giants. And we were done with our thrashing by then. A quiet had set in, not a calm I'd say, but a stillness and a cold and was all us just waiting. Then that hood rises over a man and he just gone and gone. Some tried a word in their final breath: a name or promise, a confession not ever spoken, but no matter what they said, they go the same way out.

"We began to ask each other promises: should you see my wife, tell her; this is her name, tell her and my child such and such. Was all the same after a while, all about love and sometimes of forgiveness and to go on and not be sad and some said they'd be watching from across the gate. And this we promised to one another, and it passed the time, holding to the wrecked timber in the cold water. But the names could not all be remembered; so few could be remembered."

He checked the measure of the sun and removed his hat again. "As it would happen, it fell to me, the pilot who had steered them to their ruin – not my fault but still – it came to me to greet the widows and the fatherless waifs. To try and remember what was said to each. In the end, I invented stories. They weren't much different anyway. But I weren't ever good with words, and think I left the mothers feeling empty, the wives betrayed, the children confused.

"So we floated there a day and a night, clinging to scraps of timber, the better part of the boat having sunk outright. You'd feel the swell rising below and expect it, but then it's the fellow just beside you who gets it and you had become brothers in those last hours, but then he just gone. Gone and gone, a brotherhood severed. I lay there, my life but a feather, waiting for fate to close me in its shadow. As morning approached and I not been taken yet, I wondered whether it would be the baleen or some other vicious beast or the cold to get me. Maybe I would simply drown.

"At last, I was alone. All but me taken. And as I floated there, staring at the eternal stars, I felt the full presence of my finitude with half-hidden death tapping upon my shoulder, ready to whisper to me at a time and place that may have been ordained when the stars first were forged in the cauldron of becoming. My whole life I live ignorant of that moment, but is this not the human condition for all, even on the firmest of earth, even in the blossom of youth…to float on the sea of life until a black hood unexpectedly blots out every star and drags you under? I have heard a wise man proclaim that we live in fear and uncertainty because we do not remember our birth nor do we know the time of our death. I thought that time would come then, but, well…." Here, he laughed dryly.

"Floating there in the chill water, I remember hoping only to see the sunrise once more. I cursed myself for every one I'd ever missed for sleep. A miracle, no two ever the same since the world began, and how many times had I chosen slumber? Ha! And now an eternity of it tapping on my shoulder.

"Watching the turning stars, I knew myself for what I always was: the mortal coil adrift in passing life, no more permanent than the morning dew, and this truth has settled in me with a kind of peace. I'd been taught that the throne of God rests on a secret star and that last night adrift I believe in a moment of heightened clarity I found it, and 'tis blue. The star of God is blue."

He mumbled something then that could not be heard and made a gesture I could not understand, but would come to realize this was a prayer for the deceased, perhaps to his god of the blue star. He then adjusted the course and commanded the crew to take the luff out of the sail, and later I would learn that he was the most trusted of pilots. That all preferred to sail with him. That many ships are split by baleen but none survive. He is the first to survive.

"So," I said, "How did you get back?"

He smiled. "My heart lifted with the first fingers of rosy dawn. Only then had I the courage to look down into the abyss. They were gone, glutted I suppose on the meat of the others. My heart soared with the sun and I cried my gratitude, even though I knew it were not wise to make sound out there. I felt somehow ordained to higher purpose, but let those thoughts go, for they insult those who were taken. Was only chance. Nothing more.

"Suddenly, the thin plank to which I'd held since the start were knocked from my hand and I thought the beast had come at last, but gave thanks again for seeing another sun...yet nothing broke the water. Then it's circling fast beneath me and I holler, but no harm comes. I look beneath and see nothing but a flash of color and fin. And then she leaps, like an angel of the sea she leaps glorious against the morning sky, and all my spirit leaps with her. And I take a leap of faith, and abandon my dead plank for her fin, and she pulls me along. Half a day she pulls me. Whenever I slip loose, she comes back again, and in this way we come to an island not on any map and that simply should not exist. I stood in the shallows and caressed her as she circles me and goes. I say thank you, but what else can one do? I found water and grasses to chew. Even fruit to eat. In the course of days, wrecks of the ship washed on the island's shore, and I made a raft and sail. In time I loaded her with all food I could and took her home. After some days, maybe ten, a raft finds me. They knew my ship lost. They wonder and ask of that island of which none have heard. What direction could I give? My mast split days before. I was a drifter and nothing more. What direction could I give? I've not seen that island since and they say there are none on this sea, but there is one, I know."

"What creature saved you?"

He smiled. "Did you see the name of this vessel?"

"Yes."

"Was named for it."

"Oh."

"So, why you going to the camps?"

"To cut."

"No, you're not."

"I need some money. Then am going on north to find my father."

He rubbed his chin and smiled. "Well, never heard of anyone continuing north past the clearing, and that's getting spooky enough. You know you gotta come back and take the king's road round?"

I shook my head. "I'll just keep on the way I've been, but thanks."

He grinned and squinted into the distance and would not look at me. "You some kind of fugitive?" he asked and laughed, and those that sat near us laughed with him, but I did not.

"No," I lied.

"Is okay. Is it murder they want you for?" he asked, and everyone laughed again and I did not answer him.

"Well, oh well," boomed the pilot then, "we have a murderer in our midst!" he joked, and my heart froze and my legs went cold. I did not come this far to die by a joke. The fear showed in the blood of my face, and then a few of the men stopped laughing and eyed me suspiciously. The king paid dearly for the heads of his enemies. "Oh, don't you worry," the pilot assured me, "They going to cut trees for silver, not heads for gold," he said, and some laughed again, but a few did not.

"I've never so much as stolen a copper," I said truthfully.

"That's good."

"Listen, I don't like being…."

"Ho, ho now," the pilot interrupted, "be at ease, young one. We laugh so as not to cry." He then slapped me on the back. "Life just a play, anyway. A big silly play of puppet men dancing by the command of thin strings attached to a mystery. And the stage is full a ghosts and ghouls and even a hero steps in now and again thinking he can make it right, but he can't. He just someone for the bad guys to cut down like a tall oak. But the bad guys bleed too. And not one of us got strings that ain't getting more frayed with each passing act."

I said nothing to him. Wanting only for the stares to look away, to be off the boat and away. "Speaking of this, how were it you learned of the work camps?"

"The old woman at the inn told me. The one built over the water."

His smile ran away. "She not old. She sick."

"Oh."

"She dying, and with two little ones at the knee."

"I'm sorry."

"Well, don't be too sorry. You gotta go too you know." Light laughter ran through the boat again.

"I do."

"What cuts the strings, you think, the master or the puppet?"

"I don't know."

"Maybe we just get tired of dancing to a tune we cannot hear, towards an end we can never know, from a birth we cannot remember."

"Maybe."

"And so go we to the ever-hungry sea where a wave can tip us outta life, where a rotted timber can call us down."

Far away, the dark green line of the new shore rose. By late afternoon we could see the camp. The clearing ran like a scar into the forest. Trunks of once tall and stately trees lay tethered in the water like a string of corpses. A river in the forest flowed south, and by this they bore back their gain.

A party of men waited for the new arrivals at a makeshift dock and threw a line and reefed in the boat. The pilot greeted them and the crew shook hands, and the cutters who had been there before spoke with those they knew and sometimes laughed.

We disembarked. I stood on a new shore having no idea where to go, but not wanting to stay there. The land was ruined. The work looked terrible. The men sounded bitter and defeated. A heavyset man as cold as a man could be approached and squinted at us and pointed at us rudely with fingers as thick as a log.

"All you new ones go to the main house and mark your name. Tomorrow we set you to a plot to clear. You get a silver ounce for every ten measure you cut and it pays at week's end. That's three days out. You don't get paid the first week. It adds on to the next. Find your house, then get a place in it for your bed and if you didn't bring no blanket there ain't none to spare here so use grass or dry leaves. Or you can rent one for a half ounce silver a week. You get a bowl a mash before settin' out and another in eveningtime. You can buy a midday meal to carry." He swung his heavy arm back and pointed to the gutted forest. " The taller trees near in all been cut. You want more money you work deeper. Yes, we had troubles come. You'd know of that. For all that, a whole lot more make it back than don't. If you afraid, stay close and starve. Tools are in the tool house next the shelter, and you bust 'em you pay fer 'em. Work begins at dawn. Second meal is served an hour after dark and not again." He opened his arms as broad as the boughs of the trees he cut away and gave a smile that did not pretend to hide the cruelty of the world. "Cheer up men! You got jobs!"

We all helped unload the boat. Soon our motley collection of property: tools, clothes, food, whatever had been carried across the waves to this place cluttered the dock. The men from the camp already picked through the fresh supplies, asking for this or that, in what container could what be found. When all this was done and sorted, when the greetings and the goodbyes were through, each with our burden marched to the work camp.

The pilot was the last to disembark. He would return at dawn with those going back. Some of them had simply had enough, but a few had borne witness to a violence irreconcilable. They never dared even to approach the perimeter of the forest again, but slept by the central fire of the camp house. At dawn I saw them. They waited nervously for the boat to untie while the crew and pilot readied it for the journey back, a direction I could not yet take. I read again the name painted across the stern, the title of the creature who had saved the man who still dared to cross some part of the sea, though the sea had taken so much from him, and I smiled.

The Pink Dolphin

I never intended to work even a day, so I suppose I stole my breakfast. It consisted of some paste-like gruel and bread as hard as stone. I had little use for money, and could not chop trees for ten days. I feared the price on my head. Gelidii had taught me to live by what grew under my feet, and so I had little reason to stay. I walked with a crew to my allotted plot at the far side of a cut, and when no one seemed to be looking, with my few possessions attached to my back, crept into the leaves of the forest and was gone. The forest folded behind me, and I was gone.

It was amazing how quickly the voices faded in the pathless wilds. No one called for me, no one followed, and I wonder to this day if any cared or much wondered about a stranger who had not returned. I knew no one would come looking. Deliberately, I had spoken to almost no one on the cutting crew except briefly to one man, a bitter fellow with a rather glum appearance, who had come across on the same boat as I. "You believe any a' tha' wha' he said?"

"What? Who?"

"Tha' pilo'. You believe um?"

"Believe what?"

He shook his head cynically. "They some say he ses out tha' morn'n with a rafs ties to hus sturn, and when a nigh' fells and all slepen' he pours oils into the hull and lit 'er up."

"But…why would he ever do a thing like that?"

"Why anyone does anythin'?"

I could not answer. And to be truthful, I do not know which story to believe.

"Take this."

"I can't."

"Yes, you can. I want you to have it."

"It's too precious, Karuna. Someone will steal it from me."

"A jezeth may never be stolen. That is part of its magic. Take it."

"I can't."

"But of course you can," she said and placed the jezeth around my neck. She gave me a soft embrace then and kissed my forehead, and I had no words, but did not want to go. "Should you wish to see the paradise beyond the tunnel, now is the final chance," she said with her hands still resting on my shoulders.

"I have to keep on, Karuna."

" Then may the jezeth protect you to your destiny, He Who Walks with Demons Unscathed."

BOOK IV

Roland

Roland

The land dried. The forest faded. The earth gave way to fields of grass that rolled away forever. In the distance, ice-peaked mountains broke the sky, these even grander than those before. It took forever to get to them as more and more water traced the ground. The rivers flowed ever colder in their banks.

I swam them mostly. I stripped, and with all I possessed wrapped in what Lyden had made me tied around my neck, I swam, the currents carrying me more away with increasing ferocity. I'd watch the shores racing by and half expect, no, always expect a waterfall or jagged rock or some other menace to be upon the next corner, but that never happened. Yet at that particular time, I didn't really care much for what would come. I suppose there's a certain terrible comfort in loss so complete.

At last, following a valley that split two of the largest mountains this world could ever make, a river of furious white water fed of melting snows served as the gate from the Land of Elf. On the other side began again the world of men. You could see it, too, the delineation to a land ahead, how it did not shine as brightly as the enchanted one ever dimming at your back. Somehow, the sky to come just faded — whereas even on rainy days Lyden's world held a shimmer in the firmament — an ineffable quality to the whole of it now so clear because it was gone. And suddenly I knew I would never see Lyden again, though I so desperately wanted to, but instead returned to an earth not unlike that of my home, and it looked so dull, I thought, and foolishly, ignorantly, that the days there would be a safe time, would be steady.

The last river, the one I would call the Gate out of Elf, did not have the width of some Lyden and I had passed, but ran fierce in a way they never did. Thunder accompanied its water, which rose in white jaws, before sucking any and all into black pits. The raging river raced away and away, drawing all down into a stony chasm that wove between the mountains. On either side, sheer cliffs of ice and stone broke to heights unimaginable. Peering up at them you knew that no one, not ever, no one would ever climb them; for who would dare such a feat, dare to catch a forbidden glimpse of the seat of gods?

I could jump. That was how I felt. I would not, but I felt like it. It had been too long since Lyden had left me. Empty she had left me, empty and alone she had left me, riding the wind to my abandonment.

But keeping far back from the icy spray, I followed along the banks of the flowing storm until, amazingly, there grew a stand of trees in that frigid moisture which prevailed beneath the shadow of the southern mountain. They were not so tall, those trees, but entirely old, and you knew that somehow their age rivaled the very rocks out of which they grew. It felt like a terrible thing to do even then, but I could hack them down and lash them together and throw that raft on the white madness and jump. I might truly make it. All the way to the northern bank I might. And I pet the tree and apologized, but then stopped because it made it all worse, and so I just drew the stone of the picarin and said, "Forgive me, Lyden," and struck the ancient trunk. It bled. It was like a condemnation of my guilt, that blood, that oddly red and watery sap which gushed from the trunk. For one horrifying moment, I almost screamed as it ran warm over my blade and hand. But I lifted my arm again and hacked again and again at my victim and savior, and it just bled, nothing more, so much so that the blade became wet to the handle, and I had to be careful lest it slip from my grip and shoot along the ice down into the River of the Forgotten.

At last the sap exhausted. With an enormous chunk bitten out of her, all she needed was a push to lie dying on her side, and I remember the groan of tearing fibers that had too much life in its call. She fell to her side forever. The last of the sap, too much of it, gurgled out of the stump, pooled on the stony bank, and I wiped my brow and the blood stuck to my skin and stung my eyes when it ran in my sweat. And I was breathless then in the icy silence, breathless even though the work was light. Never had I cut a tree that took so long to die. I imagined the other trees watching in the eerie stillness beside the racing river. Even their leaves didn't shake. As I considered the bleeding wooden corpse, a very odd surge of terrific guilt welled within me. I thanked the gods it could not scream.

"Every one of them 'as a spirit. Listen to it. Here, put your hand on it and listen." He did as his uncle instructed. "You feel it?"

"What?"

"The energy."

"Maybe. It's cold."

"Yes. And strong. Every one 'as a spirit, and they all sacred. I never cut one."

"Never?"

"Not one. My 'ouse was made before me."

"Would you cut one if you had to?"

"Yes, but I don't. And that don't mean they 'ave no spirit. Some here in an' round Selador no one'd ever dare to cut."

"The offering gray birch?"

"'Course never that, but there's lots a others too. Is always been like that. They the sacred ones."

The boy lowered his hands from the trunk. He felt silly.

The trees in silence stood as if in witness to a murdered sister. I felt it…but I had a river to cross. A life for a life. It had to be done, but still a shadow crept over my heart. The color of the trunk faded to a kind of gray. The crimson sap covered the whole damned ground like a viscous blood and my feet stuck in each step, lifting with a sickening peel, and I despised the way it soaked to my flesh as it did. When the wood stopped gurgling, its life over, I pruned away her branches and the last leaves she would ever make, and then I cut her in half by height, trimmed and halved it again, until the makings of my raft lay at my feet like four severed corpses.

I crouched by the river proper to wash my hands in the spray. Considering the ferocity of the current and my weight, I would need to kill another. They were strange growths: pliable and light. They must float. I cut a sample and threw it in and it bobbed away like a cork in a stormy sea. I needed lashing, so I killed a third tree and stripped it longways and worked its fibers soft, using these to bind each to its brethren. My hands shook terribly with the cold and perhaps with more than the cold, and my hands and forearms were all dyed so red that I feared they would be that way forever.

"You need to know knots, boy."

"I know, Uncle."

"They keep things together."

"I know."

"They could save your life one day."

"I guess."

"A mis-tied knot is a terrible thing. Many have died because of a mis-tied knot."

"I guess."

I secured everything again, prayed to the gods of my household, to those of Lyden and Gelidii and Karuna, and to those I did not know, to those of that place and time I spoke my name and threw the raft in the endless white fury, holding my body tightly against it as it raced away.

In the heaving jaws of the river, the raft nearly rolled completely sideways. I held fast to the lashings and thought of nothing else but the grip. Three times the raft almost flipped, and with my body straining for balance, three times it righted. Once, it stuck in a whirlpool that churned in the very middle of the river. Round and round we went in a closing gyre until the center maw sucked us in so deeply the water submerged me to my knees. I knew then with perfect clarity that my life was at an end. With that realization came a surprising peace.

But it didn't take. The raft was too long and the river had to spit her back out and we rushed along again. I held on as the water washed over my frozen hands. I held with clicking teeth and seizing chest, rudderless and oar-less I held as the river took me where it would through a path of water and furious mist where the sky could not be separated from the earth. Every moment spoke the thunder, and every crest made an abyss which ached to draw us in. My life was a feather. Only once I looked up to the white spraying madness and rock and immediately looked down again, it all being too terrible to behold. Thus, when by some twist of fate and current, the raft crashed into the stony border of the northern bank, I slid forward unprepared and smashed my head into the rock.

In bleeding agony I crawled onto the stones with limbs barely movable. The raft slipped away to some watery oblivion. With one hand I held my skull, and with the other felt my way to the shore. I kneeled there and cried. How blood stings the eyes. How unnerving to see even a little of it going away. I watched it stain the land, and this would be the first thing the new world took from me. I cut a piece of blanket and tied it around my head. It felt like my skull had truly split. I dipped my head in the icy water over and again until the bleeding almost stopped. Then, I needed fire. Immediately, I needed fire. I went north until the river could barely be heard. Despite my condition, I noticed how the land now felt so dry and ordinary, sad in its way.

In some low scrub oak I collected deadfall and cut limbs. I shaved dry kindling and struck at the stone and flint until it made a fire. I fed it all noon and night until, in that pitiless land of men, I heard a distant lowing to the north, then again to the east. It could be large or small. It could be nothing, but it sounded terrible: a cold, soulless approaching hunger. It mooed and lumbered along and when it came too close, though I hated to lose my fire, I collected all the coals into a pile and sat with legs and hands curled about them. After a long time, when the lowing passed for good, wandering on some path and purpose comprehensible to nothing but itself, I rebuilt my fire. In time I fell to sleep, the blade resting in my hand.

I awoke to perfect darkness, to dead of night. The air hung with the scent of coming rain. Not a star lit the sky; no moon a shadow cast. Nothing. The embers had all extinguished to ash, and it was strange to be in such darkness. You blink and it does not matter. I scanned the land for light, but it was all gone. How could it all be gone?

"Son, in darkness you will find there is light there too."

How could it all be gone? It could not be, but it was and for a reason I will never know I wanted to cry out then, to cry for help in this which was again the land of men. I thought of words that had no place there, of people and pleas so alien to this world they formed only absurdly in the mind, and it would be folly even to speak them. My head still hurt, and so much had yet to be done if it could be done. Nothing could be done. How much longer would it go on like this?

For reasons I cannot explain, of all my trials, this meaningless night of darkness and solitude drove me most to desperation. At that moment I felt the abandonment of my fate. And for whatever reason, at that moment I looked to the left. What I saw I do not want to write. (There are some episodes, even by the end of this account, I leave unwritten). I want this to be among them, but it should be known. This encounter should be told.

I would have time to think later how the shade was not darkness, but rather the shadow of darkness, the absence of light. Its form terrified me. I set down the blade of Gelidii and unwrapped the jezeth to the cradle of my hands. It burned like a fallen star. It was then the form that walked in shadow heaved towards me. How silly it would have been to run, or to lift the stone and fight. No, I curled my knees to my chest and stared into the gem's sacred fire. Shades too can ride the wind. Shades cannot be cut.

It approached soundlessly until looming over me like a shroud. Above, leaned the crooked form of a cloaked and hooded man. The light of the jezeth flickered in its presence and then sank to gray. Only once I dared to lift my eyes to its and met only an abyss that chilled my heart. My limbs turned to water. When I turned my gaze from the form and looked at the jezeth, it was dying. All its light faded fast.

Uninvited, a voice fell, as old as the stars, as cold as the deepest sea. It spoke: "Strange that on a night such as this, one of such perfect darkness — when the moon hides her fickle face, and the stars have all shut their light — to chance us upon an ember of the sun. I am Twist, a trader. No follower of common paths, I weave among this vale of tears to better mix this little world with trade, to seek and hold objects of fantastic rarity so that by my hand these may be brought to those who could not otherwise obtain them."

Twist leaned back as if in witness to the formless sky. The cloak fell with a brush of desiccated skin. "Could it be that above such darkness the gods know us yet? Could it be that from those unknown heights, where they delight to dwell among astounding illumination, our little world is tended yet beneath a shroud of night and cloud? How odd of the fates, on a night such as this, to chance us upon an ember of the sun — perhaps the sole proof of their love. Let us hold it."

The wing of arm extended through the darkness. I did not move, though it almost touched me. A scream stifled in my gut. I stared desperately into the jezeth to find its light, but its light had all gone out.

"No?" Twist asked coldly. "No? Not even a touch? I am too old to be a common thief. You will be glad to trade when its price is found."

The hovering being spoke to the depths of my heart, whereas my own words froze before they formed. I realized then how in that blanket of shadow there was no other sound but its voice. Everything had stopped: the wind did not stir; the grass did not tick in the field; the river did not murmur in the distance. No cricket-song, nothing. I could not even hear the beating of my heart with hand pressed upon it. There was only that voice falling like dark ice.

"I see your face, though you do not even deign to look upon mine. Few know the worth of the pearl, but I, the great trader of Byzarthis, do. And I alone may bring to it a suitable price. Here...."

Slowly, Twist blew on the fire with a breath of ice, and yet this summoned flame. In the dancing light, the shadow dipped, and a red vial, ancient and ornate, stood on the ground between us. The light fell on the vial, on me and the ground, yet no light would fall upon the trader. Unasked, it spoke: "Born to an indifferent world, you wander alone in a field of wolves. How hard this is. So sad, so alone so that life's burdens are doubled and yet...there is nothing which cannot be undone. Know that within this vial of ancient magic rest three drops of tincture which given to any woman will summon all her love for all her passing days. Give to a queen, and you will be king. Give to the rarest beauty, and all men will envy you. Come. Life should not be but days piled upon days."

It waited. I waited. I did not move. I was thinking, thinking how badly I wanted this vial, of how loneliness is worse than grief.

Then, the shadow-form spoke. "You do not, perhaps, believe? I am accustomed to this. Hardly can the ordinary man fathom what I have to offer, but I am too old to survive lies. Take the vial; see its magic for yourself. When the truth of what I have promised has come to pass, I will come for the collection of this pearl you grasp."

But I did believe it. This thing, whatever it did, did not lie. And now the jezeth felt cold in my hands. All its light had gone, all of it. It had died. The darkness had killed it. I thought then to toss it away in the grass, to have this shadow chase it and be gone, but instead, for reasons I cannot fully know, I only whispered the words, "It is not for trade."

"Ah, he speaks! 'No' he says. So there'll be no love for the thin man...Ragged Wanderer, Lost One, Hider of Light? It is just as well. It is late in this night as life flies on swift wings, but surely the time for trade has come. Do not let past defeats defeat you now. Be brave, good man, and take a thing worth taking. The precious gem deserves a fitting price."

The shadow dipped again, and another vial stood just where the first had. This of burnished gold. "This enchanted paint has raised and lowered empires, crowned and conquered kings, stayed wars and started them. It is the foster of love, the bringer of friends, the sculptor of peace. Within this vessel sleeps a magic which summons the true god of men. Understand this, weary traveler, whose crown is split with blood: the gentlest brush of this mixture will turn any object to purest gold." And did the shadow of icy breath laugh then? That scratching fall, was that its laughter?

"Indeed, my own store of this metal is beyond calculation so that I do not trade for wealth, but for the art of it, to better see the world mixed up by the exchange of goods. Man of toil and little reward, behold." From the vial the trader drew a slender brush which glowed in golden paint. He graced this against a pebble and indeed, a golden hue washed down the stony sides until, to all appearances, the pebble turned all to gold. And again, at this mutation, a scratch of falling breath escaped its throat...and could that be laughter? "You are astounded and yet it proves but a simple chemistry. Here is the better trade, for with it you may exhaust all desire."

I imagined all my life washed clean in wealth. What could it do? I could free Selador and have more to spare. I could buy love and glory and peace and have so much more to spare. So what if he were a wretched thing that knew too much of metal and magic? The shining lotus grows from the foulest swamp. I didn't even know what the jezeth was for. It saved me once. I doubted it would again. It had died anyway. It didn't matter anymore. I held the stone up and readied to hand it over, but just then, by some odd grace, just then the jezeth spoke to me, or I thought it did, for the briefest glint of celestial blue glowed from its heart. Twice, I thought. It had saved me twice. But I could not say "no" to the vial of gold, so, I shook my head.

A soft growl infused the voice of Twist. "You do not want gold? Is this why you have none? How interesting. And this the path of trade and a treasure comes just before you and yet you want it not. Well, I am old and have seen every manner of bargain and man. Sooner or later, Wanderer, you will find that everything can be sold." It pointed to the formless sky. The cloak fell with the cold scratch of death. "The heavens have been cruel as of late. To be lost is a terrible thing, an often fatal one in lands such as these, where many the day rises when the sun will cast no shadow, and rare is the star by which to guide one. An inexplicable mist hangs over much of this land. Yet here, Man of Many Devices, just here consider what I hold: a wonder with which you may guide yourself through this pathless paradise."

It returned the vial of gold to the formlessness of its cloak. In its place, just visible by the light of the embers (for the firelight had all but gone) sat a shell of silver with confounding powers. By a magic of which I could not begin to dream, the workings of this shell captured an image of the user's soul in such perfect clarity that I feared it caught the soul itself, but through this soul-holding it knew what was most desired. And so, what could only have been the arm of Twist lifted the shell and moved through every point in all the world round, reading strange inscriptions and signs I could never begin to understand, until at last settling upon a direction. This must be the path to the Sage, for the cloak lifted like an arm and pointed. "That is the way to the North," said the trader, and I shivered to think this shell-tool knew my path, could so clearly see into the heart of my desire.

"With this gift never again will you wander lost. No other like it exists in all the world, dear Traveler. Its magic is very old. Take it. Take something useful, so that when your wanderings are done you may better find your way home."

As he spoke, I only half-heard his words. Staring into that magical shell, that engine of knowledge, that polished shield so bright it saw the inside of the person, with too much clarity I bore witness to what I had become. How thin I had become. How broken. The gaunt face of a stranger looked back at me, with a blood-crusted brow, and a scarred and ruined neck. His eyes told a story of loss and sadness, of one with nothing more to lose, a portrait of a human shell assaulted me. The journey had done this. I could not go on this way. I wanted the magical guidance of this tool very badly, this silver circle that could speak to the stars and very quickly end my quest. It was hard to imagine how the jezeth ever would help me again.

But then I thought of the cold hands of the trader taking the orb away to its shadow. I had to ask, "What will you do with the jezeth? What do you want it for?"

I could hear its breath echo in its chest. "A trade is a sacred pact. If you accept this object, mine for yours, the trade is done. Ask not more of it."

No. The answer did not suffice. I had been lost too long to fear it much anymore. I had become one who lived by fate, who took only the promise that the ground would rise to meet his step, that day would follow night, that darkness would beget the dawn. No. The jezeth would not be traded for the mystical soul-reader. I waited in silence, wishing with all my heart for its owner to go.

And then he who was called Twist spoke once more: "This night waits as the dawn rushes upon it like a curse. The time for trade has come. Let us better the offer for the poor man, for the broken one. "The silver shell disappeared into the fold of its cloak, and now a crudely cut black vial sat in its place.

"Fat kings feast in orgiastic delight while you hop barefooted through the woods like a beast. Man of sadness and hunger, here is justice at last. Within this simple vessel sleeps a special elixir made but for the brave and wise. In these few days beneath the upper light we are wearied on this path of life by the designs of enemies, but yet here await seven drops that speak to the gods themselves — the old ones who deign yet to serve the desires of men. Listen now: draw a single drop to your tongue and but speak the name of your enemy and he will fall dead."

With these words I heard the quiet of the night.

"Do not let weaker emotions cheat you of this. I have seen soldiers poison wells with plague as children clamor to drink. I have seen whole villages, whole cities, burned with impunity. Have you ever heard the screams of a man burning alive?"

And did it laugh again?

"I have seen man eat man and have seen worse, but spare you, gentle wanderer, of such details. Consider how many lives a single death can save, how right a just man, with just power, could make this wretched world. What great repair through a simple utterance. And what rewards collect, what glory embrace he for such service. This is perhaps my greatest offer. Do not be afraid."

I did not want to think about the black vial. I wrapped the jezeth and put it into my shirt.

"You hide it now? You shroud its light? Has the poverty of your life made you so full of fear that you truly believe nothing more is for you, Keeper of the Pearl? Pitiful wanderer, by our fortune we meet, and I now stand before an ember of the sun and yet its holder he…what…hesitates in weakening doubt? You do not do your possession justice."

Its voice grew ever more beastlike, more fierce, and I felt the night would never end. I wanted then to just surrender to it, to spill the stuff of a vial into the ground, to just be done with it, to make it leave.

It swept the black vial away and spoke: "I have but one more item worth, more than worth, what you now keep hidden. You are not a man of violence, no matter how just. I see that now. Forgive an old trader his foolishness. To you I offer my rarest thing, by far more precious than all others."

A carved diamond now rested in the path. It seemed illumined despite the oppression of the night. "You were wise to have waited for a higher price. What is the one thing men may never master, what guide to ever-breaking hearts, the font of all fear so perfect in its completion it may never be touched?

I did not answer. I did not know.

"The enchanted land of this potion has long since fallen away. Its people slipped from memory, and their arts are all lost but for these last few drops. Hear me now, man of earth, and believe what you are told: when age has conquered your better part, or illness has gripped you too fully in its jaws, sip this and to you all passing health and youth and beauty will be restored. Or even...," and here he laughed darkly and, for no reason I could know, waved his arm and lowered it again, "...there is this — and again I testify to the truth of the powers herein contained, asking no payment until they have been proven — but there is this: pour these few drops of such precious elixir upon the freshly deceased, perhaps too soon taken from this world, or even over the ground which covers your deceased beloved, and this cherished one will join you again, in full form and health, to dwell with you unto the end of your days. Ah, you have lifted your eyes again! Good. Take this now. You have waited for my most precioius offering. Take this now and write but your name in the sand above my mark to affirm our oath of trade, and leave with the gem, and leave with the elixir of life until that time when your youth or health or loved one has been restored to you in the blessed light of being. Then, I will come for the sacred pearl. I am a man of many paths. It does not matter where you are. I will find you anywhere you go."

I began to imagine it and stopped. I shook my head.

"So you would leave your beloved to the cold lair of worms? How lovely. Shining eyes turned to a feast for the blind serpents of the soil. How generous are you, how enchanting, to cherish your little light more than anything or anyone. More than love and life itself, how lovely. And to at last deny yourself — how little you must think of yourself — how unworthy you must believe yourself to be, so as to deny to your one brief life the rarest of all chances: the gift to reclaim years gone, decades gone, ages wasted perhaps on wandering or labor or loss or regret. Even on this night which shuns all illumination, which hurls us all into a common dark, I see the regret written in the lines of your countenance. How many years have you wasted already on living less than a life? Take the diamond potion, simple man, whose container alone is worth a small castle, and retrieve what has already slipped. Refuse it now and you will regret it forever. The orb will be an object of disdain, a reminder of what you feared to do."

I dreaded speaking to it, but I did. "Why would you trade such a thing for a simple pearl of light?"

That laughter again of a falling scratch. "To each person only one vial may be used, so says the law of their magic. This has always been the law. I chose mine a long time ago. Unable to utilize the charms of another, I trade them thus."

And I considered it then, a trade, but perhaps from only my imagination I heard the voice of the jezeth: '*Do not put me into its hand*'

I shook my head no.

The embers of the fire faded fast. I refused to feed them while it stood here, and before long a tone of cold anger broke into the darkness. "Very well," it said in a ragged voice. It reminded me of the passing of a fierce storm. "Trading is partly a question of time. You have lost few to the irrevocable tomb, and hold yet some youth in your limbs, nor has all the light sunken from your eyes. But mark this: after the passing of many winters, I will steer my efforts to greet you again. Then we will see if you are so stubborn to hold a trinket as you look upon the abyss."

With that, the shadow folded into the darkness and faded as quietly as it had come. I stared into the impenetrable dark and blinked. Just gone. How could it just be gone? Like a dream, gone. The crickets began to sing again as a natural wind moved again, and a general, nameless oppression lifted from the space. Above, a lone star broke past the canopy of night. Upon that sign I took to feeding the fire with great rapidity, and kept a kind of vigil until dawn. In some sense do so unto this day. At the first light of rosy dawn, I ran to the North.

"Come see the rose petals, my son."

"Where?" he asked groggily. She gently shook him more awake.

"Come, outside, see how the dawn paints in the petals of the rose."

It surprised me how soon I came to a road, ragged and scarcely defined, but a road nonetheless. With a shiver, I recalled the road of Gelidii. It was hard to face how much time had been spent since leaving it, and yet I was nowhere really. What had I to show for my efforts? What had I achieved? This task, this "quest," as Lyden had called it, had cost years already and drip-dripping went the sands of my life, all washed away on a single dream and what had I to show? I could not say that I had come even a step closer to a sage which may not even exist. And for all I knew, Selador was gone, overrun, burned and razed and ruined, just gone. All gone. And all those I had known could all be gone, too. Every last one of them. I kicked the dirt of this new road. A cloud of fine black dust rose and settled again. Despair of thought could kill a man on a path such as this, turn the shining gold of a dream to the ash of doubt in the length of a breath. I stopped thinking and walked. People think too much.

After some days uncounted the mountains were at my back and after even more they faded to low white points in the earth. Somewhere within them thundered yet the river of the Gate of Elf, but try as I might with my eye to retrace my steps, I could make out nothing of the path on which I had come. I knew I would never find it again. I knew the wonderous world of Lyden was lost to me forever.

I thought of wanderers not yet born who might by chance retrace some part of my journey. What would they know of her or me or the bent jungle of Gelidii, the rivers of Karuna, Lyden's mountains shrouded in mystery or even my own simple home? I had my glimpse of the wide world and wished the quest were over, but it was not. Now, in this new land, cold plains of grass encircled me like a sea, and I prayed for my travels soon to be at an end. There, beneath the width and breadth of the sky, I prayed.

This road seemed much like the others: wholly abandoned and rarely used. Prints in the dust that may have been human or animal were faint at best, half a hoof or something altogether different. In the black sand ran perhaps tracks of a giant cat, a large species of deer, or even what may have been a bear, but I could not tell for sure. No prints were fresh. It rained a lot in these parts. It didn't matter. All roads lead somewhere if you follow them long enough.

Yet, I traced with wonder the enormous tracks of four-toed birds, some two by two, some with three in the front and one in the back but all boasted talons which pressed divots in the dust. Rodent, snake, dog and cat all lived somewhere in those tall grasses peppered with groves of dense timber, these fed from extra water collected in the valleys of the plains.

Inexplicable fires burned everywhere in the grasses, yet never took to the forested valleys. At first they were few and far away, but then I came upon them more and more. I was sure someone must have been setting them, perhaps to frighten me off, or perhaps to scare game to hunt; but then they became so frequent I thought something out there wanted only to set the world afire just to see it burn. In my mind an agent of blind and pointless malice lowered a torch to the green for the sake of watching it die, and it frightened me, this actor I did not see or know. Yet, no one ever appeared, and as I passed more and more of the fires I found them so random and tame that I could stamp them out with my blanket after warming my hands. The grass had a shine that caught the sun too brightly, and that must have been it. It just caught somehow in the glinting sun. I soon ignored them altogether. The fires never grew high enough even to cross the road, and when the land became more fertile, the fires were gone.

Food become ever more scarce and so I simply ate the grass which was slightly sweet. It was good enough, although the fibers were often too tough to swallow. But the waters of the nymphs had taught me never to be ungrateful for even the simplest of meals. I ate the bulbs of meadow flowers not too bitter, foraged for berries in the groves lining the road, and even, on occasion, found a number of Gelidii's favorite roots. I climbed trees for a nest of sweet eggs but avoided going too deeply into the groves. I had had my fill of the ecstasy of the wild and chose the simple path with a certain direction, despite its scarcity of food.

It was peaceful enough too, for a time, until I saw once more the damnable print, fresh and deep: the damned print of the damned ogre.

Each toe, humanish but so much larger, has a talon, traditionally yellow which hooks like a vulture's. This to rip the flesh from its victim and keep it in its grip. They say an ogre will use its mass and incalculable strength to hold its pleading prey still as the pitiless beast removes limbs one at a time to be devoured piecemeal. An ogre does not feed much on carrion. It prefers fresh meat. This practice made all the more abominable as the creature seems to speak in its own fashion, possessing a kind of sub-human intelligence which should prohibit the cruelty of its dietary practices. But I have seen insects do no worse to prey they have entombed, and I have seen men do no better to animals.

The horror of the ogre, the real terror which separates it from all other beasts, is the spark of intellect they say resides behind the eyes, making it a kind of monster. For what is a monster but a beast married to human malice? As my fingers traced for the second time the depth of the creatures print with an unwelcome astonishment, I recalled how it alone among all beasts deliberately sought human for prey.

It had left two impressions on the road before stepping off into the grass again where it left no evidence of its passing. It had been days, weeks even. The print went two fingers deep at the heel. The nails punctured the ground like wounds. There is something so dreadful about the ogre that it's hard to describe. Judging by its path, it seemed to come from nowhere and go off to nowhere again. How such a large carnivore could survive in a land so bare confounded me. In the distance rose low-lying hills. I supposed the beast went to them because people must live there. For an insane moment I considered following it.

That night I slept off the road and made no fire. I cut the tall grasses into a pile and when I tired at last of scanning the horizon in all directions and seeing nothing and hearing nothing, I climbed within the nest and fell to sleep. As a gentle breeze pet the grasses, I slipped into oblivion and thought of Selador and the tavern — not of the sweet times, not of the pleasantness, but of the man with the clouded eyes who had lost his son to an ogre.

Sometimes, it is necessary to control the mind so that it does not control you, so that you do not listen to fear. The man's story might be true and so what? The damned pigman might smell me in here and so what? What will be will be. You do what you will. and whatever you did at any given time was the best you ever could have done. If the pigman came I would run or fight or scream, or seek again the light of the jezeth, or perhaps would only die — but that would only be once. Only once do we cross the gate to where fear is no more, and the worst it could do is kill me. So, I resigned myself entirely to fate, and with a faint mewling rising from somewhere far beyond, fell into a deep warm sleep, the blade of the picarin resting in my hand.

The plains lifted into hills more and more dotted with forests. Some nights would bring the lowing again, as something roamed in its distant track over the land in slow, methodical search. Some nights brought the more common sounds of chase and prey, roars and barks, and the prey falling with yelps and spasmodic howls. Some nights would be just cricket-song, water sound and the gentle brush of the wind. And when the grasses were tall enough, I cut them and piled them up and slept in the mounds. The trick was making them long enough to accommodate you properly. If you cheated the effort your feet would pop out into cold where anything could see.

"You gotta keep your feet warm, Boy."

"Why?"

"Because if they're cold, so are you."

I used the old tattered blanket, which I could not bring myself to part with, as a cushioning between me and the hollow, and I had learned to weave the blades of grass in such a way as to make a kind of vault so that the mounds became less oppressive from within. I had even learned to pitch the outer blades so that they would deflect even the heaviest of rains. But to make a decent shelter each day is no easy thing. It becomes a balance of time and material, of energy and weather. Some days left me with an abundance of strength while others did me in after a few hours' walk. I tried once taking the woven parts of a mound with me to be set up again more readily, but this proved too heavy and burdensome. I suppose because of Gelidii I walked at night as much as day, depending on the moon.

"It's better to hunt when there is no moon and carry a torch."

"'Is it?"

"Yes. They can see you under the moon from so far away. You don't think they can, but they can."

"But the torch is so bright."

"Not like the moon. Torchlight doesn't go far and it confuses them anyway."

"Do you think we'll get anything tonight, Uncle?"

"I hope so. You ready?"

"Yes."

"It's okay if you're frightened."

"I'm not."

"I know, but it's okay if you are."

"I'm not frightened."

He nodded to the boy.

I never walked in night if the moon were full. No matter how wet or terrible a place and whatever promise seemed just ahead, I never walked beneath a moon that was full or even near-full. The best was a slight crescent with few clouds. I could pick the way along in gentle steps and sometimes a monstrosity thudded not three paces in and the bush shook and yet it didn't see me in that darkness. I slipped along like a shadow. Silent and invisible I crept and climbed my way through an alien land. I am not here. I am not.

People wondered how I so often dared passage through the ink of night, but in truth the night had come to comfort me. Perhaps I'd been too long with the picarin, so that something of the shaded earth soaked into my form and brought me more into the number of its bright-eyed children. And when in the night I heard a thud not three paces off in some thick bush, what might have happened had I taken the morning path? Also, I never wholly lost the effects of the moonbulbs. I am even now of some minor fame for my abilities "to always see the sun." People think me strange that I enjoy a peaceful walk in the sunless woods, unlost in what Gelidii once called the light of the "blue day."

And they warn me of the dangers of the woods here at night. It's laughable, I suppose, when compared to where I've been, but I never laugh — for a man can walk three times the length of this earth only to find his death in a slip upon the limen of his home. But though I never laugh I do not fear the silver-lit peace. There lives a bird here who sings only to the moon.

Sometimes, for a few days among the plains of grass, when a place felt peaceful enough, I stayed to rest the spirit as well as the body. In the eye of my mind I sometimes built a town there with houses and neighbors and night fires lining the familiar paths, and farms and field and tavern and temple and shrine standing to the gods whose names may never be written. These lush commons stayed ever free of soldier and ferocious beast, and the fields all grew tilled and fertile. This dream would sometimes become so deep I would forget where I was so completely I had to stop this practice of dreaming. It was just too painful to wake up alone, to wake up lost and alone in a wild that for me might never end. Instead, I imagined my body picked at by vultures, first eaten in large chunks by the ogre, the tiger, a pack of dogs. That was the better dream. This was the proper dream when not at home. I always told myself, "You are not home. You may never see home again." That was the more merciful dream.

This thing the picarin had kept so sacred to its personage had in my hands become more and more a utilitarian item. I hacked at the grasses with it and cut firewood, yet even after such abuse the uncanny edge stayed remarkably honed. If it dulled, there was a special way to sharpen it, and that was perhaps the most difficult of all the skills I had adopted from Gelidii: a way of cutting the air to get the blade to burn against it so that the very air shaved the stone. I had to push and pull almost at once, down and up again in an arc of blinding speed, and if it were done just right, the blade screeched and trembled and left a smoky smell in the air. Gelidii said perfection would be doing both courses at once and said he had done this only once and the blade crumbled in fiery dust. "No evermore," he said of it. "No for perfect."

When the blade dulled even a little, I would sometimes spend hundreds of tries and barely get it to speak in the arc of sharpening. Sometimes I would spend a whole day trying for the proper arc. I dreaded going forward without the edge being perfect. Upon it rested the balance of my life.

With a certain dread, I saw another escarpment looming on the horizon, very distant, low and gray, but an escarpment nonetheless. It could not be the same as the last. Nothing would be the same as that. It was pointless to think like that, but it could be hard sometimes not to, especially among such isolation. Loneliness is a disease, and you have to be strong in fighting it.

I had never prayed very much at home. It had an empty feeling of uselessness. I obeyed the motions and rituals well enough, but at the end of the practice I wondered how muttered words could move the gods. Yet, in the days of wandering, I prayed often in my isolation, and deeply too. When it rained, I thanked the gods of the clouds, for all things live by water; and when the sun broke through, I thanked the god of light. When I found food, I thanked the god of the growing earth. When I survived another day, I thanked the god of the traveler.

Experts here have said this devotion was the only reason I survived so many perils. Perhaps they're right; perhaps they're not. But I have a disturbing fear concerning gods which I do not tell the experts, because I do not care what they have to say on it: I fear I have walked past the power of my gods, strangers to this place where no shrine stands for them, where no offering has felt the whisper of their names, and so I fear I am by them forsaken. But enough of that.

I had not felt comfortable the night before. That nagging voice warning me to keep looking to the trees. The forest line ran too thick and dark and close and I did not want to build a mound there, but the moon was near full and I so tired. I cut a mound and crept into it with the woods so very close and I felt it and thought of sleeping hidden in the trees, but did not. What would recognize a mound as food anyway? Besides, at first light I would be gone.

But it had awakened before me, or ran late in the night's hunt. It approached in the gray light of dawn with a thudding stomp running in frantic circles outside the mound. Run up, stop! Run up, stop! Closer and closer, and then all fell terribly, terribly quiet. Suddenly a mewl rose, a stubborn call of death, the sounding of the empty clarion, the augur from the realm of shadows.

It ran closer again, then stopped again, now so very near to the mound. It bayed like a wolf to a yellow moon and my heart turned to water. I could hear its breath as I held my own. In perfect stillness I waited hand wet upon the blade. It bellowed again in rage or hunger or frustration just outside some thin blades of grass. A stench of horrific rot permeated the mound. As if I had an eye to read the poisonous folds of its mind, I knew what it thought of the odd heap of grass: *This is not right. This is not natural.*

And then it moaned again the song of death but was confused. It sniffed the grass but was unsure. The damned thing knew but didn't. It smelled me. It had to, but the mound confused it. What kind of bush smells of meat? What grass falls like this? Then, it groaned again in a kind of emptiness and agony as a quiet tear of terror ran down my cheek. I knew then that all which are born have a soul, for what stood just without did not. The dead ogre had come to feed. I held the blade tighter. It stomped the earth and the mound shook and I knew what it was doing.

"It's called flushing. A rabbit takes cover, you can't chase it in there, can you?"

"No."

"And believe me, even if you could, he would outrun you under there."

"I know."

"You want to get him out in the open again. You beat the bushes with a stick and make 'im think you're coming in. Make him think you can get 'im in there. Make him think his world's falling down. When he runs out in the clear, if we're lucky, I'll get him with the bow."

"All right, Uncle."

"All right."

It began to speak in its fashion — a quick huffing of repeated words or sounds: *"Guul ... Guul ... Guul ... Guul."* Then the grass wrinkled softly by the pressing of its claw, and it was thinking. It was puzzled, but thinking. *"The bush is not right. This is not a bush."*

It knew.

'Guul!'

With one swipe, it took half the mound away, and thus did I stare into the face of the pigman. It had the eyes of a fish, dead orbs of polished coal. I did not scream but knew all that lived held a spark of the divine for it did not.

At first it stood stunned at the human lying there, but then it smiled: a rotten crevice in a pumpkin. With a tongue of speckled black and fleshy pink it licked its teeth, rows of crooked fangs. It lifted its arm to strike and I sprang up for one viscous slash at the dead face. I would cut the eyes out, blind it. But it had not leaned in enough, and in my terror I struck too soon and cut only the air. As the arm reached in to grab me, I rolled out and away and ran without screaming towards the trees. Anything was better than the open plains of grass. I ran and ran, not even daring to look back. Halfway to the trees I realized I had dropped the blade of the picarin.

The pigman howled once and then, with laughing grunts, lurched after me. I could feel it stomping the ground and vaguely remember glimpsing once to the sky just to see the sun once more before my passing. I fled with a speed I did not know I possessed. On the field, I became the antelope, in the forest a leaping deer. Maybe, just maybe, I could outrun it. I wove and leapt between the trees, daring not once to look back, but knowing it was there. I could sense it. I twisted and turned and it was right behind me as I wove through the forest like water around rocks in a streambed. I let my size be my strength. I was the rabbit, it the wolf.

A large deadfall lay before me. I leapt atop it and ran its length to where the roots clutched pointlessly into the air, then jumped off into a small field and ran to the far side of it. Only then did I spare a moment to look back.

Of course, it was there. Its legs so enormous it did not even have to run. It simply stepped over the deadfall, wearing what might be a smile on its dead face, toying with me.

Its arms hung almost to the ground. When I stopped, it stopped. When I stepped, it stepped. It smiled then and slowly opened its mouth in laughter. *"Guul guul guul,"* it said, pointing at me with hands three times the size of a man's. Its nails were claws. It then pointed from me to the fissure of its mouth. It was telling me it would eat me. It became hard not to fall out. The world began to fade. It had been a long time, but I was falling out.

The worst were the hands. The limb-ripping hands. I did not want to die like that, torn and chewed and gulped down to become part of it. Sparkles of fish swam before my eyes and I swooned and looked to the ground just to see where my life would end. I lamented about the lost blade. With it, I could have cut my throat.

It trotted towards me then with a soulless groan. How could it be so empty? I would not run anymore. Defeated, I looked down, half-perceived a log, put there by fate, just longer than the pigman's arms and not rotten. The back of it was already braced against a tree. I almost knew…what was it?

It ran at me and I was thinking. Saliva dripped from the crevice of its mouth, the maw of death and I looked straight to its dead, staring eyes and was thinking. It was almost upon me when a voice whispered not to run, to be patient; but it was almost upon me and I looked down again at the log because what approached had become too terrible too behold. I was thinking. The voice had whispered only once and was gone. What had it said? This puzzle had to be solved.

My knees turned to water. I fell to the ground. It was upon me now, almost upon me, and just then, with hands not my own, I lifted the thick limb from the ground, as if the order had been written in the beginning of creation. The beast ran full force into it, impaling itself at its gut.

OOOF!

Its breath flew out with the stench of a corpse, and its arms swung limply forward on the dumb pendulum of its shoulders. The black and yellow claws missed my face by a fingertip, sparing my life. The pigman doubled over, falling forward to the ground, its eyes squeezing shut as it curled up like a great demonic fetus. It writhed in suffocating agony, holding its gut. I would recall later the filament of saliva that had hit my forehead.

I wasted no time. My plan already complete, I ran to find the blade of the drinking bird. Frantically, I dug it out of the tossed grass and then, with all speed, returned to the writhing creature.

People have asked why I would do this, why not just keep going and get away? But they do not understand the ogre. The mind of it is not so simple, not totally inhuman. It would follow me. It would seek me out. Its nose would track my steps and I would be in its lair before day was done. I had to finish it now.

It had hardly moved. It lay on its side, curled as if its belly nursed some incubus of eternal darkness. In its stillness it looked like a pile of moss. Oddly enough, I could hardly see it. I sneaked behind, quietly creeping through the grassy field to get behind its monstrous feet which lay not so far apart. I had a plan. The soldiers who had come to Selador had taught me this through those who tried to escape. With the third arc of the setting moon I sliced open both its tendons just above the heels. I knew what this would do.

The blade cut so beautifully. It almost took off the damned thing's feet, and I realized I could have done that just as easily. Even taken off its horrid head, but that came with more risk, an unnecessary risk, for with the third arc of the setting moon its leg muscles contracted for the last time. It bellowed and swung an arm back, but too late. I was already gone, backing away and away and not even running. Nothing would have to run from it ever again.

I climbed the deadfall and stood proudly, watching the creature try to walk again. It would lift itself by its enormous arms and pull a foot forward and try to stand on ruined legs, but they would just wobble and collapse and it would fall back and groan. Its dark blood poured from its ankles and pooled about it, poisoning the blighted land. Oh, how it screamed, over and again, and with such howling dread you could feel the birds die in their nests.

Then, trying once more to stand, not yet realizing what had been done to it forever, it clawed its way forward trying to get me. I slowly backed away doubting, as it raged in stormy bellows, that it would ever leave the little field. And still it cried out and still its massive arms pulled it towards me, crawl-walking on its knees. Its now useless feet forever folded. It would die there, or not far from there. No power in all the earth could repair the injury I had inflicted upon it. It would bleed itself out, or starve. The forest would devour it.

With a sinful kind of pride I climbed the deadfall and called to it and waited for its eyes to meet mine. I showed it the blade and then slowly cut the air as if cutting its throat. I flicked the blood off the blade with such skill it hit its face suddenly gone mute. For some moments it only crawled. One hand now clutched the great, fallen tree. A river of black blood trailed behind it like an omen written in the earth.

But then the scene became truly strange, and it was then I had to go. That terrible face of agony searched all at once the ground, the blood, the dying sky. It lost more and more of its ferocity as its life waned. The rage was replaced with a kind of pitiful indignation, and then only fear. I had to leave, for its eyes, as it lay broken in its last moments, turned more and more human, and the animal groans of misery twisted into what must have been a word, for it said this over and again, and it was what anyone would have said who had chanced upon such an awful fate.

"Whay...Whay...Whay!"

Why?

I washed at the first creek. So carefully I cleaned the weapon. Even the slightest nick with it dirty like that would be fatal. All the dark filth and blood washed away in the cold and gentle water. I was past terror, but shaking yet and did not feel glorious or relieved. I felt empty. I washed until the stench was gone. I tried to wash the memory away, but knew it was the curse of man never to forget such terrible things.

I marched as far from that valley as I could, but by late day the nauseous chills begin. By that night, I lay frozen with fever hardly able to move. I curled into a poorly made pile of grass I'd barely had the strength to cut. My temperature rose so quickly and so strongly that I did not expect to see the morning. Through my fevered brain ran stories of men infected by ogre turning to ogre themselves. I had the blade ready if that began to happen. I waited for my skin to turn pale green. It did not. It turned yellow.

The fever did not break for three days. I ate nothing in this time. I just laid up in the mound, leaving it only to crawl to the creek for water, and only then when the thirst had become unbearable. But on the fourth day the fever broke, and I emerged like a man recalled to life. With weak but steady dedication, I walked north again, to the escarpment.

The road of black sand led right to it then tapered until it almost disappeared, and I thought perhaps I'd missed a turn, for more and more the road turned to wet stones which eventually merged into the bed of a creek. By the time I walked in the shadow of the escarpment, there was no road. I followed the creek to the wall of the escarpment and then, just like before, the face of the looming cliff had a fissure running through it, but this one was much narrower than the gate of Hel. The creek spilled out like draining life. I had to stand a long time to think and calm myself. "It's not the same," I said. "Don't be a fool. Nothing is the same," I said.

I walked forward and listened and waited. The wind. The wind, the trickle of the creek. Nothing more. I entered the rift, the flowstone walls of the escarpment rising over as impediments to the very sky. They ran impossibly narrow. They bowed out so that only rarely one could see a patch of sky. The day was warm and lovely and blue. The path twisted. I could not see more than a few steps ahead or behind. The light fell in soft orange on the sandy ground and the creek ran right through the rift's center. Either bank was barely wide enough to keep your feet dry.

A steady wind moved through, and so it was not like the other. It held none of that unnatural dread. Only it had an unnatural narrowness and wound and turned so that you couldn't see more than a few paces ahead. I had the blade out and ready for whatever might come. Constantly, I felt that something followed close behind, an uncomfortable illusion of the curving walls, and yet I always imagined I caught a ducking shadow behind me. Sometimes I would retrace my steps to find nothing there. I walked on. Though the light fell in soft gold, and the trickling song of the creek trilled along the walls, after an hour I just dearly wanted out of the crevice.

The creek moved slowly. It tasted of minerals, slightly stagnant, but drinkable. The only other living things were small patches of green-black grass that grew in it. As I walked, I ran my fingers along the smooth courses of worn stone and wondered if this were not a route carved by the ancients who were said to have done things magnificent. As the day ran long, I began to dream what would be on the other side, but stopped those dreams, knowing I could run into a wall, a pit, or the jaw of a lion. I just had to keep on. That was the only rule.

He was a crude shock, a fantastic shock in the quiet of the rift where the only sound was the trickle of water. I yelped, jumped back. It was like stumbling on a corpse. He lay curled in a mix of sleep and pain and his abuse was evident. Almost naked, his skin flaked in patches, was bruised and cut and singed in various places. An arm draped into the water. The few oily rags he wore stuck to his skin. When I caught my breath and composure — and people have asked why I would be afraid of a ruined man, a foolish question — I said, "Hello?"

He moved his arm a little. He mumbled something and coughed and curled up a knee. "Hello?" I said again. He tried to stand now, and I could not see his face. A thin and gangly arm reached for the stony walls to pull up his weight, and I could not see his face. He began to pant, the drawn timbers of his ribs heaving in this effort. Burn marks ran along the inside of his arm, and I could not see his face. "Hello. Hello? What are you doing here?" His head began to bob severely, as if greatly drunk, as he tried to lift it. He wanted to look at me. "What are you doing here? Where does this go?" I asked breathlessly. Finally, he stood on both legs and swayed against the wall, and I still could not see his face for his head lolled forward so that he stared at his feet, and you could see where patches of hair had been ripped out and that he was missing his left ear. "Who are you? How did you get here? Where did you come from?" Surely, his ear too had been ripped off.

Summoning all his strength, he looked up. He was so young. His eyes were so young. A scar brutally bisected the right one at its center and continued halfway down the cheek. His lips were swollen and split. He was barefoot, his feet bleeding and scabbed and swollen, and he was so much younger than I, and obviously starving. I didn't know what to say. "What are you doing here?" I asked.

"Help."

A helpless voice. The voice almost of a child.

"I can't help you."

"Help me. I might be God."

"I can't help you. What are you doing here?"

"Do you have any food?"

"I don't."

"Do you have any gold?"

"I need to pass."

"I might be God. Please help me."

"Just let me pass. Just step aside."

Then he pushed off the wall and stood on both legs fully and breathed so hard I thought he would fall down again. He lowered his gaze and almost pointed at me, but then his hand dropped and swung at his side and he fell, leaning against the flowstone wall. "I have taken the bug and carried it for days to let it go in a new land, and this is written in the universe that I have changed all things forever! Is this not the work of God? Help me."

"I can't help you. I have nothing. Just let me pass."

"I have knocked on doors and hid in the dark and spied at the answerer who will not and never know the knocker or the guest who touched the door, but did not arrive."

"I just need to get through." His eyes were distant.

"Please give me something. Anything. A penny."

"I don't have it to give. I have a long way to go."

"I have stopped you. I am forever the author of your remaining life."

"You need to step aside. What are you doing here? How have you lived?"

"We have met in the wall. I have walked my whole life and you have walked yours and the earth has folded and folded again so that we meet here, each the shadow of the other's life, and I am dying, and I might be God, and I am dying. You cannot pass me for I am your shadow."

"I'm passing. Give me room. Just step aside a little. I don't want to hurt you."

"When I die, the whole universe, and you, will die with me."

"Please just move to the side. I don't want to hurt you."

"Give me something to eat. Our whole lives have come to this moment. Just give me something to eat."

"Please ..."

He began to weep. "They killed my mother."

"Please ..."

"They chopped off her limbs and raped me and I just ..." he fell to his knees as a dead weight then. The skin was so thin it immediately ripped open. He bled and showed no pain but only wept more. " ... I might be God!" he screamed into the ground. "Help me," he whispered.

I looked behind me again. "You can walk with me from here," I said to him, breathless myself, "but if this is a trap, I will kill you and the others."

"I do not walk with you," he cried. "I carry you! All things rest in me but I do not rest in them!"

"If you don't move, I'm stepping over you. If you attack me in any way, I'll kill you."

I tried to show him the blade but he wouldn't look up again. In a whimper he leaned his ruined body along the wall and there was just enough space to pass without touching him. I approached carefully and then leapt, in case he would try to bite me. When I looked back at him he slowly extended his body along the ground.

"Don't follow this," I urged. "There's dangerous land on the other side. Go back the way you came. Just go back."

He groaned and said nothing, looking more and more like a corpse.

"Listen to me. Listen! Go back. There's ogres and fires and demons ahead. Return the way you came, to whatever lies ahead." And then I asked to his heaving, ruined form, "Tell me this, please, what does lie ahead?"

Slowly, he began to laugh or maybe cry. This turned to the screaming of bizarre names or chants or simply babble. I couldn't know. I knew I would get no answer, so I left him then, just left him lying there with the creek curling about him. By late noon, walking quickly, I emerged from the rift into a field. Recalled again to life. My heart soared. In the distance, smoke rose as if from a chimney and I made for it. I thought of him constantly as I fingered the cold sliver of gold in my pocket, the last piece, all my wealth in the world. When the sun began to set on the far side of the escarpment, I turned and ran back. I had lived a long time without gold. I could live a little longer without it yet.

I ran all the way through the rift to our meeting place, but he was gone. I kept going, running fast to prevent him from going out the other side, but he was gone. I went almost to the other end, but he was gone. Just gone. It was long after dark before I emerged again into the fields. I have often wondered of it…how such a ruined man could have moved so quickly away.

It was not a chimney, but another grass fire that had caught up with some dried wood. There was no road. I just walked on and on by the sun and stars and shadow in a land that felt tamer somehow. The night fell cold, yet I did not make a fire. On the third day out of the rift, a monstrous pile stood in the distance: a fence of thorns that ran in a ring around structures which could hardly be seen through its density. Each thorn grew so large that it could pierce you right to the heart. I circled around the fence until I found the gate. A string hung there. I pulled it. Somewhere in the distance a bell sounded. I pulled the cord again. It was noon.

If a town waited within the thorny ring it waited in sleep. I pulled the string of the bell three times and it chimed in the distance, warm and lovely in its way, three times and I waited. I watched my back, rang the bell again and then again and then a frustrated voice from within said, "All right. I hear you. Let me unlatch this damned thing…damn it!" Suddenly, a door in the enormous curve of thorns lifted just enough for a man to crawl in. I peered at the low tunnel of teeth I was expected to crawl through. I hesitated until from within came a voice as hard as oak, "Well? You coming or what?"

"Who are you?" I called. "Where am I?"

"Eh? Hey! You comin 'in or dying out there?"

"But where is this?"

"Forget you then," and the mass began to lower.

"Wait!" It stopped. I crawled through, and if he had lowered it then I would be no more.

Inside waited a man with a countenance which somehow belied the sternness in his voice. He was older, but not old. He nodded without looking at me and lowered the gate behind us, securing an enormous latch with a complicated series of knots from rope as thick as an arm. An immense strength emanated from him although he was not overly large. You could feel his strength from some paces off, his energy, I suppose.

With the gate lowered and locked he turned and considered me with a look that said I had fallen from the stars. Then, for the first time, he smiled. "And what the fuck are you exactly?"

I had no idea what to say to that. Before I could answer he went on: "Just where in the Hell you coming from?"

"Selador."

"Sell-a-door?"

"Yes."

"And where might that be?"

"At the tip of the Southern Slope."

"Where?"

"At the tip of the Southern Slope."

He scratched his head. "The southern what?"

"Slope."

"Where in the fuck is that?"

"In the South. It's very far from here."

"No shit. Anyway, you got business here? Why you come here?"

"I'm going north, to find my father. I saw the gate and headed towards it."

"That's it?"

"Yes."

"Fuck what? You were wandering out there alone like that with nothing?"

"Suppose so."

"On the plains?"

"Yes."

"Fuck. How the Hell you alive?"

I shrugged. "I've learned how to live in the wilds. I came here from the rift."

"Rift?"

"In the escarpment."

"What?"

"In the escarpment. I came here through the rift in the escarpment." He scratched his head again, not bald, but shaved to a fine black stubble. He appeared confused. "There's a man lost in there. A boy. He may have gone through to the other side, but I don't know how. He was in bad shape. I went back for...."

"Who? What? What rift you talking about?"

"A boy, he's dying in the escarpment."

"Escar... you mean the long mountain, the plateau?"

"Yes."

"Rift?"

"Yes."

He shook his head. "No valley through the plateau, kid. I've no idea what you're saying now. You saying you went through Long Mountain to here?"

"I guess."

He shook his head again and grinned. "Long Mountain ain't got no hole in it, kid."

It weighed on me. "He may have been someone from here. It's a narrow valley and could easily be missed. There's a lot of vegetation on this side. A little ways out and I didn't see it anymore. It's hard to find but I can find it again. I went back once already."

"What for?"

"To give him some coin."

He sighed. "You look a little...haggard, kid. The sun can play tricks on you. Starts cookin' the brain."

"He's there. He is."

He lifted his enormous hand in placation. "Okay, all right then, so he is."

"The boy's in real bad shape."

He lowered his gaze. "People die every day, kiddo. Try and save 'em all is slamming your head against a wall."

"I thought maybe someone here would know him and want to look."

"Is that why you came?"

"No. I'm just passing through on my to the North, but I can lead you back. He must have gone out the other side."

He gestured to the blade even though it could hardly be seen from the front. "What's that hook you hiding back there?"

"Just a blade. A tool."

He smiled. "Fine, just don't try anything."

"No."

"You're safe here."

"All right."

"I mean it. You're safe here."

"I know."

"No, you don't. Stop leaning towards that knife."

"I… I'm not."

"On the inside you are. Stop thinking about it, about grabbing it."

"Oh."

"Okay?"

"All…all right," I said and I did.

"That's better. More balanced now." He looked me over slowly. "You been in the wilds long time, haven't you…on your own?"

"Yes."

"All right. A bit touched. You a little weirded out but it's fine. Is to be expected. Come on."

He began to walk away and waved for me to follow. I stood and called to him, "I can lead you back now if you want. It's three days from here."

"No thanks. I've more pressing business to attend to. And you won't get any from here to take an expedition led by you to Long Mountain. I can hardly believe you made it from there alone. And there ain't no rift."

"Why can't you believe I made it here?" I asked when at his side. He stopped short and gave me another look of pure confusion.

"Why? The fucking ogres, kid! They running all round those plains. More these days than ever."

We turned down a narrow and dusty street and the strange town had a quiet to it which lifted a chill in my heart. In Selador, a place as old as the sea, the maze of streets twisted and wound in such a way you could live there for years and still get lost among the ancient buildings of mortared stone. But this town had been made of wood: faceless structures of planks that lined broad streets of pressed dirt. Slits of gray windows peered out on us from houses and, though people may have been peeking from within, no voice rose but the moan of small whirlwinds, "dust-devils" they called them, spinning in the chill wind. After a time I had to ask, "Where is everybody?"

"They here. They inside, keeping quiet."

"But why?"

He stopped and gave me a hard look. "I already told you that."

"Ogres?"

"Yup."

"And so the fence. I've never seen a fence like that."

He nodded. "The fence too."

We came to a large and dry-planked building. An eave provided shade to what might be called a porch and on it benches of warped wood sat empty. Roland, as I would come to know him, pushed open a heavy door and waved for me to follow. Inside, it took some time for the eyes to adjust to the dark, but the familiar sour-sweet scent of a tavern hit me at once. A good amount of patrons occupied the place compared to the barren streets, and I half-expected them to all be like Roland, warriors of a sort, carved of iron and wood with spirits that never listened to fear; but they were nothing like him. But truth be told, no one was.

It took a long time for my eyes to adjust and I wondered why they did not let in more sun. My guide sat at a table with a waiting drink and a half-eaten plate of food. He picked up a spoon buried in a pile of brown mash and began to eat. "It was just this, kid," he said to them all, still chewing. "Says he's going north to…what was it … find your father?"

I nodded, still waiting at the door. Roland waved me over to the empty seat across from him. They all stared at me with a terrible, heavy silence. It all felt so incredibly unreal then, with their staring as if I were a wild animal lost from the forest. It took some time for me to understand the expression they wore…not hate exactly, but fear. It hung in the large hall like a black cloak.

"Relax!" he shouted to them all, slamming down his spoon. And then to me, "You're fine. Take a seat here with me. Don't worry. Wipe that look off your face." He spoke to an old man behind the serving table, master of the bottles and vials and platters, "Get him a plate and a cup of wine. Sit down, kid. Relax. All of you, just relax! While here you all remain under my protection."

I didn't move, and then the old innkeeper spoke, "Well, just what it is you brought me here, Roland?"

"He all right. Just a kid looking for his dad. Don't worry so much! He be right here with me."

The old man scratched his cheek covered with an enormous mat of hair. He made no move to get drink or food. I stood like a statue at the door. The silence was terrible. The staring was worse. No one spoke and no one smiled. At last the old innkeeper broke the silence. "I worry much," he said, "and with good reason. Maybe he one a them — jus' a different type."

A murmur of ascent rolled through the hall. Roland made a fist and punched the table lightly, yet the wood trembled and seemed ready to split. The reverberation carried through the planks of the floor and ran up the walls and dust fell from the ceiling. "An ogre! Really? You think he a fucking ogre? Listen, you old duck, I brought him in, so he's my responsibility. You — and him — are under my protection. Don't worry so fuckin' much, and get 'im a plate a food. For the love a God, he looks like he could use it!"

The old man grumbled and set about his chore. People lowered their glances. I made my way to Roland's table and sat down in the only other chair and rested my things beside me.

"Don't worry," he said to me, his mouth full of food. "You just a little dark for these parts."

"I can see that."

"They simple folk here. Most or none a them been around like I have. They never see anything but themselves. You all right. Just relax."

"All right."

"You're a bit of an oddity just for coming in alone like that."

"My father's dead."

He stopped eating. He sat back and looked at me and then took a second look at what I carried. "Is that right?"

"Yes."

"What you looking for then?"

"A sage"

"A what?"

"An immortal warrior."

He lowered his mouth to his plate and ate some more. "All right then," he said at last and shrugged.

"They're ancient ones of immense power. They can do anything," I said.

"Sounds great, kid. You're a weird one, aren't you?"

"I don't know."

"They weren't even going to open the gate. No one would be in the fields at this time. You rang too late in the day when no one should. You would've been left out there were it not for me. Ogres're tricky you know. And not all dumb like some think, but I ain't afraid." He took a large bite of food and chewed a mash of meat and potatoes. The innkeeper set my plate before me and beside it a cup of honey-wine. Steam rose from the food. The man said nothing, asked for no money. Roland nodded to him and the old man departed as silently as he had approached.

"There were always a few ogres," Roland continued, focusing more on getting the mash on his spoon, "but about a century back the great storm drove 'em up in hordes. It must have wreaked havoc on wherever they once called home. And so came the fetid beasts, more than could be handled, and in response grew the defenses of which you have already been acquainted. Ain't nothing getting through that fence without losing a good measure of flesh, but that doesn't mean they don't try, and doesn't mean it hasn't happened. But such structures are not quickly built. The smaller towns had to be abandoned outright, well, almost outright. Some tried to fight them back but…" Here he just shook his head and ate another spoonful in silence. "Anyway, in the long run them citizens, them refugees, were absorbed into the greater cities like this. Most live in the poorer quarters, on the outskirts, near the fence."

He began scraping the last of his gravy mash from the edges of his metal plate onto his spoon. "Meanwhile, the beasts smell us in here. Stick their rotted muzzles right against the thorns and drool at our kitchen smoke and human scent. The sound of a human voice falls to their ears like a dinner bell, they say. So, it's a quiet place for this, as quiet as can be. Much of the business happens underground." He swallowed and wiped his mouth. He had not yet drunk once from his cup.

"Of course the farming fields are too big to fence in, so they lay without and are worked in shifts: late morning and to something past noon. That's it and only on certain days. Today not being one of them. It's dangerous work and dangerous still. Archers stand at the perimeter as lookouts, but that doesn't mean they never come. They usually sleep in the days. Some say the sun falls on 'em like a curse. So on the dark days, the rainy ones, you gotta be careful. You never know. As for the rest — messengers, visitors, travelers returning home — they all know the rule, and it's the same for all the cities up here: three rings and wait three breaths. Three rings, three breaths. And don't go ringing it too much and making all that noise like you did. Got to give people time to arrive. The bells are within the town center, and none live near the gate. There's a reason for that too." He looked up at me, his meal almost done. "But you not from these parts at all so...."

"How did you know I wasn't an ogre?"

"I didn't," he said and smiled. "That's why I brought this: he hefted a pole of red oak, as long as he was tall, and stamped it on the floor. A rumble rolled through the all the tavern. Dust fell from the rafters.

"When they first got the gate built up they hung the bell right outside it. You swing the hammer and get in and it was the job of someone to wait an' listen for it and open the gate. But it happened once that the bell's ringing in an odd way, a sort of unnatural hesitation to it. The keeper starts lifting the gate anyway but the bell doesn't stop. Just keeps ringing over and over with that odd cadence. Ring, stop. Ring, stop. Ring ring, stop. Whoever it was were hittin' the clacker waited for the whole reverberation to quiet before striking again. Well, something tells him to stop lifting the gate, and so he ties it off with just enough space to crawl under. He does this and quietly so and when he gets to the far side peeks up and right there before him stands a fuckin' ogre as large as any that ever lived. Strangely, it doesn't even notice him or the lifted wall. It just standing and staring at that bell, tapping it with its finger, listening to its song. At first, the man feared to move. Said when the bell quieted the ogre would pet it in a kind of wonder, and then shove it sideways again and send it swinging and its eyes would go wide with the sound. The man said in this ogre he believed he saw a moment of what might be called natural delight."

He finished his last swallow of food and wiped his mouth.

"Was after that they used a line and a code. Ogres are smarter than beasts, but not so smart to know the cord would make the bell ring or ever know a code, a pattern."

He emptied his cup. "But they might figure that out yet," he said wiping froth from his mouth. "Anyway, I got some people to meet and business to attend to, but we will talk more tomorrow. There's rooms upstairs, and there will be music in the basement tonight if you're interested. Just feel free. No one will bother you. And me…I'm Roland," he said, standing. "Ho!" he cried to the whole tavern which mumbled in response. He gave me a nod and a wink and hefted up the pole of oak and left quickly.

Feeling awkward and alone in a crowd of people, I ate more quickly than I should have. When done, the keeper took my empty plate and cup and waved for me to follow. It neared dark and we hurried down a hall darkening like the day. He pushed open the last door and showed me my room. It was yellow. The wooden floor had an unclean mat sticking to it and the window was a slit covered in transparent oil-paper that just barely let in the view from outside. "Is not so dark," he grumbled and went to a corner table where stood a twisting sculpture of polished metal almost as bright as gold. He touched and turned it, coaxed and cursed it, brought from it a clanking sound and made it rasp and groan until, at last, a flame burned in steady fire! It reminded me of the candles I had seen in the villages near Karuna. "Don' waste the oil a the lamp," he said. "Is dear. When you go to sleep you turn this here all the way back." He pointed to a small wheel with outer ridges. "Don' was't nothin'. You wanna piss or shit, there a house out back. You'll see it. Bowl a water in the hall." Next to the lamp rested a cup. He tapped it once upon the table.

The slit in the wall ran the length of the room, but was hardly wide enough to fit an arm through. I looked out through the oil-paper to a translucent portrait of the wide, black sand road that ran through the town. "What is this?"

"Why, is a window. Don' touch it lest you tear it. If we gotta fix it, we charge you for that."

The room was small and stale. I wasn't tired and couldn't see the sky, heard nothing but the creak of the man's step on the floor as he turned to leave. The room grew smaller with every breath. "I'm going to take a walk before sleeping," I said to him. He shrugged without turning to look back.

"Do what all you wish, but don' go pickin' 'round that gate. An' if you hear that bell, don' answer. It don't toll for you."

"All right."

He went to the lamp and turned the wheel and the light went away. "If you not gonna be here, I not gonna waste it."

"All right."

He left. The late gold of the setting sun went away and away, and in the room darkness grew like a promise unkept. I lay down. The mat smelled of sweat and mildew, but was not uncomfortable. I unrolled the blanket over the mat and unwrapped the tooth of Kai-Tey, held it, thought of it, hefted the weight in my hand and then set it down on the hardwood floor. Beside it, I put the flint stone and strike and the unsheathed blade of the picarin and hid it all flat beneath the mat which I rumpled so they did not show so obviously. I stood back and considered it and the room. All my life's possessions hardly made a bump.

How had the world brought me there? I waited as the light faded from gold to gray just thinking and thinking, retracing my steps and adventures with a feeling of great unease. Why had he turned the lamp out? I could have. The smell of human sweat lifted through the blanket, and I knew I could have managed the lamp and it was getting very dark in the room and how had I come here and become this that I was? How long since I'd slept under a roof? Cracks in the ceiling ran like silent rivers. I counted them and named them and set wilderness and humanity on either side and he could have left the lamp on, and now I would have to get him again.

Dark falls so quickly indoors. The air does not move right. You do not hear birds beg the fleeing sun to stay. No chorus of cricket rises to greet the arc of Heaven.

I recalled the days before Gelidii, when first alone in the jungle, how I had almost died of fright from the looming shadows and howls and how each night would be my last but was not. It feels so unreal, this room. I thought of the time before, of my last day in Selador and how that fateful event had happened. How unfair was that? People can be so unreasonable. I did not kill him. He killed himself. No one asked them to come or to drink. My mind then travelled back and back, to before them when times were good. Everything was once so good. I thought of that time a lot and how quickly the world changes. The light faded further and he could have left the light burning, but did not. There was once a time when everything lived and he could have showed me how to light it again. Why did the world have to change so much? I got up and left the room. The mind is an endless stream of words.

The toilet reeked of human waste. Flies buzzed dryly around the fetid hole and I vomited into it. All that rich and salty-sweet food ejected itself out half-digested. There was nothing I could do about it. My stomach just couldn't take it yet, and eating quickly no less. I got water from the hall and washed my mouth and drank and then in the failing light walked the town alone.

How little this place was like a proper town. So quiet and ghostly. Sometimes a murmured voice rose from behind a wall. Sometimes a distant clank of metal broke the silence, but little else told of life and community in this place. Yellow-winged finches huddled for the night beneath the eaves of the silent structures; clusters of gray and brown sparrows warbled at the last rays of sun. I tried to listen to them. I had the gift, but had to be still to hear it clearly. In this place, the birds were easy to understand. Like most, they spoke in fragments: *human passing...human passing.* But most said the same thing over and over again, what birds always say at the end of day.

The sun is going away! The sun is going away! The sun is slipping from the sky! Why is the sun going away?

But they are quickly pulled into the bliss of sleep. Yet at times, in the heart of night, I have heard the cry of a bird awoken. And no matter the species, all but the owl speak the same lament: *The world is done. This world is done. It grows cold. It grows cold. The world is run.*

The streets lay in a simple crisscross of squares, making it easy to find one's way through. I tried to understand why such a small town would make such wide streets as I walked right up the middle of each, turning where I wished and just listening, waiting and watching too, but mostly listening in that universe of walls and dust, in that gallery of wood-planked buildings, each more faceless than the one before. The occasional set of eyes dared to glance through a slit of recessed oil-paper, and looked away if I caught them. They were watching me. I knew they must be. So, let them watch.

The street fed into what must have been the town center for to here it seemed all the roads led. There was a square, empty of people, and at the very heart of this rose an enormous statue made of metal that shone not unlike the lamp. An extraordinary piece of craftsmanship, too extraordinary to be for naught but the wind and sparrow and rain. It stood neglected in a coat of blackish dust. I ran my hand along the polished curves and lifted it away with dust. The metal beneath shone exquisitely bright, and from this metal a master had summoned blood.

It was a strange concept for a statue: a fierce and dying bull charged for a man with a sword who, leaning fast past the horns, sliced the bull's throat. Mouth open, not even knowing it had been cut, the gaze of the leaning beast fixed in fire as it readied to turn and charge again. Yet you could see the terror in the bull, and in the man, in both a defiance.

I rapped my hands against the belly of the bull and it rang out dully. The sound did not carry far, the metal being so thick, but it broke the sound of the empty wind. A dust devil crossed the square. Beneath the throat the astounding sword could be seen clearly. I had seen swords before, but nothing like this, so broad and cruel. I could just reach the cutting edge and it was actually live and rivaled even the blade of Gelidii in sharpness. It seemed such an engine could fell a whole army if wielded properly.

I had long known of swords. The soldiers had brought them in and even before them some few had come to Selador offered by traders as curiosities. We knew little of metal and nothing of this tool as a weapon. We were people of the lance and bow, and with these we hunted. And it was these we turned against the other in times of war.

Still, in the early days, when they first came to Selador, the soldiers of the king ordered all swords brought to them under punishment of death. I remember they gathered us in the town square where four old swords rested in a pile of bows and spears and other tools of hunting. It was the same captain who, in years to come, would swallow a fourth cup of dragon's brew poured by my hand that now simmered with a quiet rage as he paced a circle around the collected tools. "This it? Four? Really? Four swords. None more, huh?" No one moved. Everyone waited. The captain waited. We all hid our eyes. Do not be noticed. Do not be the victim of random hate. An elder, one who always wore a gentle smile, stepped forward and pressed his palms together in peace. "There are no more," he said. "We are not people of the sword." He smiled and opened his hands then as if to prove emptiness.

"Who are you?"

"One born and of Selador all his life."

"You expect me to believe this? Four? Am I a fool?"

"We don't know of them. These are collected ornaments. We no almost nothing of metal."

"Four?" The captain's anger rising now for he knew the elder didn't lie, and so by his arrogance he looked just slightly the fool. We knew this could lead to killing. "In all this shit-rotten town...only four damned swords?"

He kicked at the pile then and the metal flew with dull clanks. "Please understand," the elder went on, "we have no art to make them. We are only farmers. There simply are no more. Search our homes if you must."

"Four," the captain whispered to himself. He was thinking. The people of the crowd grew stiller and I saw the face of the captain and knew something terrible would happen. Because I was only a child, I began to cry.

"Understand," the elder almost pleaded, "it is not what we are."

The captain walked a slow circle around the strewn weapons. Ignoring the elder, he concentrated on the faces in the crowd. He then took up one of the surrendered swords and threw off the sheath to reveal a blade dull and pitted with rust. He caught the elder by the arm then and twisted it high behind his back. The elder groaned. The captain lifted the arm until there came a wet popping sound and the arm went limp, twisted to an impossible angle. The elder's face contorted in agony and he groaned until he screamed and all the children began to wail save for those stunned to silence.

The captain shoved the elder a step forward and then, without word or warning, hacked into his neck. We heard a wet chop and then the elder trying to speak but blood came instead of words. His head lolled to the side but had not been cut off. The sword was too dull. The elder kept trying to say something but his words all drowned in blood which so quickly cloaked his body below the neck. The captain let go and the arm fell limp and dead and the elder tried to lift it to the wound pointlessly. He pressed the other to the wound and blood raced through his fingers and he staggered but did not fall yet, and we watched stunned and he waved any away who would come near to help. There would be no helping him. The next strike took his fingers too and it took three more at least to sever the head. He stood almost to the end.

"All swords before the nightfall or ten more die!" cried the captain, breathless and pale. But no more swords joined the pile.

There were simply none to be had. Later, years later, Uncle spoke of it only once.

"Who would have thought an old man had so much blood?"

I shook off the memory and followed the road away from the statue through the evermore quiet maze of streets. The buildings became more neglected. I knew this must be the poorer quarters. The dwellings at the very edge stood empty and had that haunted feel of the abandoned things of man. No one stared out of oil paper here for there was none. Just the black slits of unseeing eyes. I thought of entering one of the dead buildings and shuddered.

By the light of an early-rising moon I came upon the fence much sooner than I had thought. On the inside it was even fiercer than without. It sloped downwards so that if something were to breach the top it would be impaled on a slide of thorns pointing up. I crept close to it and suddenly a shudder of wood knocked in the wind and my breath jumped and I looked back. Only the wind. I crept up to the barrier. I wanted to touch it. Metal! Vines of iron, thorns of brass, interwoven with natural ones. Here ran a thing impenetrable. And yet it had been breached before.

I followed it, testing the vine now and again with a careful tug, keeping a watchful eye on the houses empty of all life. On the outside of the fence there rose a faint scratching sound, a sniff or a cough of a dog or deer or rabbit that spoke. I walked on and so did it. Something followed, picked its way along feebly. It must be a dog hoping for food. I peered through the fence and saw nothing but, just faintly, could hear its breath and the soft settling of padded feet. Something followed. It had to be a dog. I realized then how the wind blew at my back and carried my scent out to the fields. I walked more quickly and then stopped and peered out again. Nothing. However, I heard its steps match with mine. The moon brightened and a faint play of silhouette could be seen just there, just across the thorns. Maybe a man. I crawled forward and saw perhaps the shadow of its step. It walked like a man. Such a long step. To be out there in the dark like that he would need help. I almost said hello.

Fate lifted the breeze at my back and then it groaned at my scent and I knew what I did not want to know. I backed away but my step landed too loud and it bellowed then, a soul-splitting groan of the agony of half-life and hunger, and I was running now and could hear the fence shake and snap in parts and knew it would never get through, knew the agony would stop it. And I was running and running and could hear it rage against the barrier but the agony would stop it and it howled louder and you could hear the fence being rent.

Voices rose from the town, and there came the faint peal of bells, but nothing could suffer through the fence. I told myself this as I wound through the streets until finding at last the tavern. Feeling my way through the lightless hall I locked myself in the room and lay down in the dark with blade in hand.

All night voices passed in the streets, frantic shouts of commands and questions and I did not move. I tried only for sleep. It must have worked, because I awoke to the stillness of the night with a terrific thirst. I went out into the hall. A faint ghost drifted through the corner. When it was gone I took water from the basin and slept again. Around dawn a knocking almost broke my door off its hinge.

"Get up!"

Roland.

"Okay. Wait!"

"No time. Time is all out. Let's go!"

I opened the door. Anger burned in his face. Behind him stood the innkeeper and a few other and they, all but Roland, had a look of common disgust. Roland spoke first: "You were fucking around the fence last night, weren't you?"

"What?"

"Don't bullshit me. Unless there's somebody else running around in a dress, you fucked up. Now you got to go."

I looked past him to the sea of stoic faces. I did not know what to say and so said nothing.

"Get your things, kid."

"I got them."

"Well, let's go then."

We walked down the hall to the grumble of curses. Roland just kept on at a steady pace, his pole knocking the floor with his stride. I followed with my eyes pressed before my feet. The main room of the tavern was filled with people and some pointed at me and shook their heads. A man whose impatience was evident approached Roland. "What is it?"

"Where you taking him now, Roland? Who gonna fix it? Who gonna pay?"

Roland breathed out a long sigh. He seemed tired. "As I told the mayor, he can't fix it. Look at him. You think he can forge? You think he's got money? Forget it. What's done is done. I'm taking him out and that's my business and his and not yours. As I have said, he is under my protection and that goes for you all as well. We stopped it, didn't we and, as I recall, this town owes me one, so why don't you all just step the fuck aside and leave us be. I'll need someone to close the gate behind us."

"Is early yet," said the man.

"Well, then I'll just leave it open."

Everyone was quiet. Roland slammed the wooden pole against the floor and the entire building shook. "You do not need to fear! Nothing, not a living thing on God's green earth will run past these hands and this pole. Now who the fuck is letting us out?"

"Aw, by all that lives, let's go." It was the innkeeper.

"Delightful," said Roland. "Let's take a walk."

As we left the tavern curses fell upon me as a general air of discord swelled among the throng. Roland just kept walking as if they were not there. "Ignore them," he whispered to me. "Just ignore them."

As we approached the gate, the innkeeper walked very quietly. Roland grew impatient. "Just get on with it old man. You tiptoeing like you gonna live forever."

"Hush you, Roland. We ain't all so brave."

"No, you are not."

"Hush, hush, hush you now!" came the tense whisper of the innkeeper as he crept closer to the gate. For a long time he pressed his eye to the fence to see what could be seen. I would learn he looked not for an ogre as much as fresh turned earth, for the beasts are known to bury themselves in a shallow pit and wait there for their prey. At last he untied the great latch and put his hands to the wheel. The gate rose slowly.

"Quick now," Roland said to me, "Lest he makes us wait another month!"

The teeth of the vines dove into the ground itself. When the lowest of them was a little ways along the ground the innkeeper waved us frantically through, but Roland stood straight and still. He stabbed a look at the innkeeper: "Do I appear to you some kind of dwarf or troll, a fox or a child? Am I a seeking beggar petitioning the pardon of your grace? Or does it seem to you that on this morning I am simply fit to bow low? Raise the fucking fence so I can walk through it like a man should."

The innkeeper, already sweating from his efforts, shook his head in frustration, seemed ready to tear at the demand. Nonetheless, he lifted the gate hurriedly until both Roland and I could walk upright through it. "Thank you," said Roland as we passed him. "See you next time, if we live." And with that we exited The City of Brass, to where I had no idea.

The world outside the city felt beautiful, open and free. "It's so peaceful," I said.

"Well, it's not. But maybe for you a safer place."

"They would have hurt me?"

He shrugged. "I don't know. They weren't too fond of you to begin with, and then you almost caused a breach. It took a lot of men to contain it. I know you didn't mean to, you were just a silly kid knowing nothing from nothing, poking around I suppose. But not everyone's as magnanimous as I in their forgiveness," he said, and smiled as if he had told a joke.

We walked through neat rows of crops and then to the outer fields, where attempts at a second fence had been abandoned. Then we followed a narrow road north to the wilderness.

"Where are we going?" I asked at last.

"To my camp. It's about two days walk from here."

"Oh."

"It's a nice place. Good crew I have."

"All right."

He stopped on a rise and blocked the sun from his eyes, scanning the horizon in all directions. He spoke calmly, but I knew he looked for something, for anything that might come. Gradually, as the hills rose and the trees thickened, the sleeping city and its fence could be seen no more.

He walked very quickly, almost as fast as Lyden, and I almost had to trot to keep up. As we walked he spoke of many things, except for those few times when he signaled for me to hold and hush. Sometimes he pressed a hand to the earth to listen. After the all-clear we would walk on and he would speak in a normal tone again. We did not hide in any way. He feared nothing, I thought, but would not be taken by surprise. "It's not too far to my place. Our place. You'll meet them."

"All right. Why am I here, Roland?"

He stopped and turned to me. "We'll talk about that later. For now, just keep your eyes wide open. Pay attention."

"Is there anything I should be looking for?"

"You don't have to whisper. If they come they come; that's what this is for." He hefted his staff. "I should start putting notches in this thing." He pointed to the blade hanging against my back. "You use that for anything besides picking your nose?"

"Yes."

"You don't have to whisper. I told you that twice now. Just talk normally. What will come will come. You can't spend your whole life hiding. That's what people don't get. They think they can sneak around forever and just creep through, day-in and day-out, but life doesn't work like that. Not well anyway. Just makes it all worse, such behavior. I ask again, what do you use that for?"

"I can kill with it."

"Ah, good. A fighter. Times like these are good for fighters."

"I'm just trying to get through."

He shook his head. "No, no, no. There's no in between in times like these, in a place like this. You got to pick a side."

"What?"

"You use that thing yet?"

"Yes. Once on dogs and then again on an ogre."

"An ogre? Is that so? That's a close weapon for an ogre. Their blood's poison you know."

"I do."

"You kill it?"

"I crippled it. It's dead by now."

He nodded his head agreeably, laughing. "Nice, nice. Very good. So I will assume you can handle that fairly well at least."

"I can."

"But what about your hands when empty? They good for anything?"

"It doesn't matter much when I have this."

"Oh yes it does. Draw your weapon."

I drew the blade of the picarin, the sacred hook of the drinking bird, and held it proudly between us. Before I could blink, before even the ache of the slap against the back of the hand could be felt, the blade flew spinning through the air in a whirling blur and stuck quivering high in the trunk of a tree. I cradled the hand in the other and nursed it, tried to stop the tears welling in my eyes.

"You see, sometimes, my young friend, you don't have a weapon. Therefore, your hands must be weapons too." From his coat he drew an amber vial of liquid and handed it to me. "Rub it in wherever it's sore. Rub it in well."

"What is it?"

"You worry too much. Don't. We'll get you ready. Rub that into both your hands in fact, but well into the one that hurts." I considered the vial and hesitated. "Be quick about it would you? These hills won't travel themselves. And stop crying."

"I'm not crying."

"Well, then stop making your eyes puffy with rain."

With the ointment the hand immediately felt better. Both hands seemed strengthened by the stuff. They seemed to tingle with energy.

"Let's go now, kid. Days like these we mustn't waste time." He turned and walked quickly off. When he passed the blade he knocked it loose with the tip of his pole and let it land safely on the ground. He picked it up and considered it, tested the edge with his thumb.

"Interesting piece. Damned sharp. Keep it well," he said, and then threw it spinning at my chest. I jumped to the side and let it slice into the grass. Roland walked swiftly off again, but shouted over his shoulder. "I can see you are not a master of it. I would like to see what a master of such a weapon is capable of. We have much work to do. But at least you were quick enough to not get cut."

Running, I caught up to Roland. I feared him now somewhat, this man whose story had already begun to weave into mine. It had been a dangerous test.

"You know there's a war going on?"

"I do not."

"Where you been exactly?"

"In the woods a lot."

"The woods? Doing what?"

"Trying to get here, to get to the North."

"Ah yes. North. To the great Sage!"

"Yes. And if you know of one, tell me. Tell me if they are real, Roland."

He spoke of other things. We walked until the afternoon when we stopped to eat. He rested on the ground and stretched out his legs with a long breath that sounded almost tired. "Why exactly do you look for this wise man? What you want to ask him? I mean, what question of life is so pressing you travel all this way to The City of Brass just in the hopes of finding some yahoo?"

"I want to ask him to free Selador, my home, from the rule of the king."

"And which king is this?"

I told him.

"That's him. That's one of them, anyway. And not the nicer one unfortunately for you and yours. A real prick in fact, and it's him we worry about most. The other is making in from the East now that the third is gone. So much for the peace of the three kings. The pacts are all broken now. Every treaty dissolved and they're grabbing for borders, weapons, soldiers." He gave me a sly smile. "Not too many good soldiers left, you know. A fighting man can earn good pay out here." Again he scanned all the horizon slowly, peering deep into the shadows and the taller grass and the caves of the forest. "Especially if you willing to march in ogre territory. They pay twice for that."

"Who does?"

"Either side. You pick."

"So you're a mercenary?"

He gave me a hard look. "If you want to eat hay, do the work of a horse, otherwise you do the work of a man."

"I didn't come all this way to be a mercenary."

"Oh, no. You came to hire one."

"No."

"No? How you want him to oust an army? With candy?"

"I don't know what he'll do. I don't even know if he's real. I've nothing against mercenaries. It's not that. And if he says to fight I'll go back with him, fight with him; but it's for my own cause I fight, my own land, my promise to keep."

He kicked the dry earth. It was red and swirled like a cloud of a million setting suns and rested again. "All right, then. I'm impressed. You know what?"

I waited.

"You know what?"

"What?"

"I trust you. I wasn't sure at first, but I am now."

"Thank you."

"No, no. Don't thank me. You probably going to wind up wishing I didn't, because when people are worth something, much is asked of them."

"Is this why you have me along, to ask something of me?"

"Maybe. I don't know really. The timing of your arrival was somehow uncanny. I've learned not to dismiss such things as mere coincidence. Look, you don't do anything you don't want to do. You can go back to The City of Brass if you want and I'll tell them to leave you be, and trust me they will. They know not to mess with me. And they owe me, besides. It's not like it got through the fence anyway. Almost, but not quite. But you're going north and my place is north, and I'm not so sure our goals are mutually exclusive." He kicked the earth again. "Like I said, these coincidences, they matter."

"And what is your goal exactly?"

He laughed and spun the pole above his head as if it were weightless. "That can be a long story. Let's leave that for later. For now I'm curious of something about you."

"What's that?"

"What kind of kid searches through this wild world not even knowing what he's looking for?"

I thought about that. "The kind who has nothing else to do."

Roland laughed. "I like you more and more. I'm gonna teach you how to use those hands. I trust you."

I nodded, unsure if I trusted him. I shrugged indifferently.

"No. Don't do that. It's important you know. And a secret too. These are the arts of my own family and our line, and they are devastating. When I am done training you, not a king in the world wouldn't pay you your weight in gold to serve his cause."

"Like I said, I'm just...."

"Yeah, yeah. The sage. I know. A sage." He stared into the gray distance with a soft smile. "If you want to get to a land where sages dwell, you had better know how to fight empty-handed."

I shrugged again and did not really know what to say, but I knew one thing about Roland: he had overwhelming courage. Fearlessness radiated from him. He peered into the forest with almost a smile of hope that something would rush upon us. "The crew's gonna think I'm crazy bringing you in, but it's my call, and I say you're in."

"In what?"

"The plan. The great plan!" He waved the pole mockingly like a wand. "The scheme to restore stability to the world, to at last bring the Medusa to ashes." He smiled.

"You said the Medusa?"

"That I did. Do not over-speak her name. It begets evil."

"I have heard of her."

His smile faded. He stood very still. "Well, everyone's heard of her, kid. That don't mean nothing."

"I have to urinate."

"Don't stray too far. You got an ogre once and should be proud of that, but they often run in packs here. I don't think you'll want to chance it with just that sickle of yours."

"I won't go far."

I went to a stand of bushes. When I returned he had unrolled a mat and was setting food on it. He spoke to me without looking up. "It's late noon already. Where does time go? Where do the days run?"

"I don't know."

"No, it's from a poem."

"Oh."

"You know poetry?"

"Yes. I can read and write. My Aunt had three books."

"Impressive."

"Yes. She was a teacher. And I read others too, that we borrowed."

"It's good you have an education. I have something of one. Not, I don't think, as expansive as yours in the academic arts, but an education all the same. I can read too, slowly, but I can."

"It doesn't matter."

"Don't say that. It matters. Two warriors of equal strength and training meet, which one wins?"

"The luckier one."

He shook his head. "No. There's no such thing as luck. A fleet of ships are tossed by a storm at sea, many vessels sink. Which captain has the greatest chance to return?"

"I don't know."

"The one with the most knowledge. There is no luck, only knowledge. After that there's work. It's good you have an education. Is probably much of what's kept you alive, though I'd wager you don't even know it. Is the more intelligent warrior who defeats the other. Let's eat."

We had stopped on a hill beneath the shade of a lone tree. Dense forest surrounded us below but we had clear line of sight on all sides. Nothing could surprise us. Roland had set out victuals upon a mat of palm: moist honey cakes of cooked grains, dried fruits, barley bread and fresh greens he had picked along the way now waited for us to begin. He gestured for me to eat as he stood with the pole resting on his shoulder. He scanned the land in all directions. "Don't wait for me. Eat up. You're too thin."

I began to devour the food. I had not realized my hunger which I had learned very well how to ignore. Eventually he sat with crossed legs and began to eat too. He broke a piece of bread and joked and spoke of the weather. As we ate, I realized with a sudden surprise how for the first time in a long time I was unafraid.

"Good?" he asked.

"Yes. Thank you."

"You're welcome." He looked behind him and paused at a particularly dense part of the forest below. "I don't know how much training you have had in the arts of war," he continued without diverting his stare, "but a place like this is very defensible. Higher ground's always more desirable." He took up a dried fig and chewed it slowly.

"But they can see us," I argued. "When I was alone I hid in the low places, or the dark places. I'd be down there in the thickest forest or hidden high in the dense canopy."

"Up a tree?"

"Yes."

"And what of tigers? And fucking ogs can climb, you know. You can't run. Trapped. Don't want no ogre treeing you."

"I'd beat them in any tree. You can be sure of that. I'd cut their hands clean off when they reached for me. I'd let them follow me up nice and high and then jump down behind them and cut their necks and knock them to the ground."

"Whoa, whoa! Easy, Killer. We're just having a nice meal," he said with a smile.

"I know. I lived for a year with a picarin. I am very good in trees."

A puzzled expression crossed his face. "A pic a what?"

"It's a tribe," I half-lied, "who live in trees. Sleep in them. Nest in them. When I had the time on the road, I'd make a nest of sorts and feel safe from what I heard passing below. But it's hard to find a suitable tree each night, and then harder still to build a good nest. You don't want to roll out."

"I wouldn't think so."

"Can I ask you something, Roland?"

"Ask away."

"What's in the oil-paper there?" I asked, pointing to the bundles that he had set beside the food.

"Curiosity is a symptom of the human condition," he said and took a wooden spoon from his shirt and scooped up some kind of grain. He slowly chewed a mouthful of this and did not speak again until finished. "Those people back there," he nodded to the direction of the city, "are shapers of metal. The best in the world they say. They've made engines so destructive they have uncrowned kings. They can pour iron like clay and make gold harder than stone. They are so accomplished in their art that some believe them to be wizards of a sort. They stay as neutral as they might, selling to any king for the right price, but sometimes that doesn't work. Your king...."

"He's not my king."

He nodded. "Of course, but the king who seized your home tried the same with The City of Brass. That's where I come in. My crew and I have made a solid reputation for removing the unwanted. This we did for that city. Thus, your lunch was free, and you survived enticing an ogre at the fence." He chuckled.

"Sorry."

"Ah, well. Is done and done. As said, there's a big nasty mother of a war brewing, and I needed some equipment. Fate had you show up while I waited for it to be forged. They were finishing them that day. These, here, were made in their secret forges hidden way beneath the ground, burning in what used to be mines. They pretend these have collapsed. They..." He quickly stood and focused very sharply on a shadow in the forest. I too thought I saw something recede from our sight. He took up the pole that had been leaning on the tree and waited and watched with a faint smile of expectation. "You not hungry anymore?" he asked over his shoulder.

"What's happening? Do you see something?"

"Don't worry. Eat."

"But what's happening?"

"You do worry a lot." He shrugged off the shadow and sat down again with folded legs. "Something's near, but I don't know what. You don't need to worry. It just won't help."

I stood and drew the blade.

"Relax. Finish your food. You're too thin. You'll know if I need you. Eat."

But who could eat at such a time? Perhaps sensing this Roland unwrapped the goods enclosed in oil-paper and continued. "Anyway, they are very much active, as you can see, and if you ask me, produce products more superb than ever."

I was mesmerized by the shining objects. The first was a magnificent sheath for a sword with an image of a phoenix emerging from flames. The intricacy of the work was hard to comprehend. These people could shape metal with the delicacy of the line of a quill. Roland lifted the sheath and smiled. "A gift for my Belladonna. Was her sheath already, but I had them repair its decorations."

"It's astounding."

"So it is. They do incredible work. This metal looks like brass, but it's not. Don't know what it is. Might not have a name, but it's harder than steel and near as bright as gold. And light too. Very light. Very quick. Will never rust, pit or tarnish. Amazing stuff. They say they use the blood of the dead in the mix. All are cremated there- don't want meat laying around- and all cremations are done underground. The master smith said the blood thing is just a myth started by this practice."

"If it's not, for my wares use only the blood from the heart. It's the strongest."

The smith master grinned. "How you know as that?"

"I just do. Blood has many uses. We felled three hundred at least freeing this place. Plenty of blood for your purposes. Three hundred silent hearts."

"If she ain't just a story Roland, we shall pour only the strongest blood in yours." He smiled with teeth of gold.

"Is Belladonna part of your crew."

"The best part."

"How many of you?"

"Five."

"Five?"

"Well, six with me. But for little jobs I don't bring them all. Was me and Bell who cleared The City of Brass."

I didn't know if I should believe him. "The two of you 'cleared' them?"

"Killed them. Yes. All of them. Some tried to run away but we had secured the fence. The ones stuck on the thorns begged to be killed. More nectar for the forge. Understand, these were killers we cleared, rapists and thieves, all acting under the orders of a despot who hired them for they cared not for the work of their hands. No ethics at all. The kind of men who slice infants like melons. Still, I would have let some go. Nothing's all evil, but there's no opening the gate at dusk and so, well, we had no choice really. Besides, it would have been too risky anyway to let word get back. We finished before dinner, was me and Bell, and I asked for these goods as payment. They asked for a year to finish the work. Have to 'grow' the metal they say. A year to the day I return for one night. Hear a bell ringing as I dine."

He smiled, wrapped the sheath carefully back, and lifted a second parcel bound with metal coil. He unwound the coil from what appeared to be a single block of brass with that striking hint of crimson to it. He tapped this block with his finger and what looked solid suddenly fell into clumps made of the slenderest pins, each as thin as a human hair yet surprisingly rigid. "These little gems are for the three Brothers of Iga. Not very talkative fellows. Mixed up in magic I think, and not all undark. I don't know, don't ask or really care. Have shadows of my own. They can throw a single one of these needles a great distance and have it land in such a way as to kill a man. A delicate art, impressive too, and one requiring exquisite understanding of the human body. They cannot kill with them too. Make you freeze save your mouth, and then you talk. Before us rest twenty thousand quills. These will bring more than twenty thousand deaths. I've seen it in practice. Truly a sight to behold. You seemed to have lost your appetite."

"I'm fine."

"Didn't say you weren't."

"I'm full."

"No you're not. I understand. I am too long a soldier. This talk comes common to me."

He carefully wrapped the needles again and took up the smallest parcel. "And this is for the last member of my troop, Dexter, as we call him. By the way, no one gives real names with us. Got it? No names. Names can be dangerous. Snakes follow names. Make something up."

"I will."

"Good," he said. Something pleasant, a name you always wanted.

I thought about this. Heroic or humble? Perhaps something funny?

Roland now held a magnificent dagger, shining with stunning beauty, exquisite in its light. A vine ran along the blade. "This is what you get for one who wants nothing. But I couldn't bring him nothing. He probably won't use it. Has his own special knives made by his own kind and these slice men like warm butter. Just turns them to ribbons. But this here is a damned good piece too. Almost too perfect to scar in war." He looked at his reflection in the blade. He smiled.

"It's the most magnificent knife I have ever seen," I said and did not lie.

Roland nodded. "They do good work. Real good work. Listen, about Dexter…he's perhaps our finest warrior. No, he is the finest — runs on the wind, can catch a deer by the tail. I've seen none like him. And he's a good sort, real good, always smiling and not in a crazy way, but with a genuine warmth that makes you like and trust him. I drew this troop together following rumors and trails of blood that led to the most lethal people on earth who yet had great integrity. I admire them all, am proud to stand with them. While warriors of such caliber do not come without mystery, it's always Dexter who amazes me most, so inexplicable are his abilities.

"We never ask the homes of the crew. When I told this to Dex he said he claims no home anyway, just the forest wild. Yet, with him I have bent the rules to know something more. I would like to know what tribe forges such a man. Perhaps even I could recruit more of his ilk. I long thought my own lineage about the best in the art of war, but truth be told, Dexter's abilities leave me breathless. And when I ask him to teach me something of his skills, something of those that defy comprehension, he grins and says it cannot be learned by me and the reason for this is a very silly one. Don't laugh."

"No."

"Please don't."

"Never."

He sighed and scratched his head. "He says he is elf, and I think he believes it."

I didn't laugh.

"And when you see him in action, you just might believe it too. In every other way he's entirely sane, but when I ask of his home he just looks up and smiles in that innocent way of his. 'Roland,' he says, 'I would not lie to you. As I said, I am an elf and from the land of elf, which man may never know.'"

"I see."

"And I say, 'Okay, Dexter. These elves must be a tough bunch to make the likes of you.' Then maybe he'll shrug his little shoulders and say in combat he is average, or less. Thing is, sometimes war breaks people to the world, and so they sometimes need to recreate it into an image of their own. Do you understand me? What war can do? How it crushed him?"

"Yes."

"You'll see it in his eyes -- the broken part, that sadness. And so again I ask that you do not laugh, for you do not know what brought him to that."

"I would never laugh at another's suffering."

He nodded. "Good. Very good. I saw something in you right away and now am hearing it. One more thing about Dex: He's small. Really small. Don't let it surprise you."

"I won't."

"And his skin…it's sort of red."

"Okay."

"So, try not to be shocked."

"I've seen many things."

"Yes, but nothing like him. Okay, I trust you. We need to keep some level of peace among the crew. We need mutual respect."

"Of course. Roland?"

"Yes?"

"Do you think maybe elves are real?"

He laughed, but only a little.

"Anyway, it's an interesting bunch. You should know that we do not take sides in the war to come. We are not for hire. We serve no state, no god, no king. Belladonna, is a daughter of the Sacred Wreath of the Phoenix, the god risen from ash. Their purpose and mine is the same: to destroy the medusa. Belladonna must be always a Phoenix, now and forever, but that allegiance in no way deters from our cause. Indeed, it is why I sought her out. We need her. Very much so."

"I understand."

"A third of the world died beneath her stare. That cannot happen again. And now the two great powers scramble for her. We think they may have unearthed the tools to find her. As we speak, they seek her out; for should either king get her, he will rule the earth, whatever life is left to rule."

"It seems the world has gone mad."

He nodded. "They know her danger. Will only threaten at first, but that never lasts. Things fall apart. If either get her her glance will fall and her glance must never fall again. And they believe she is here, in the Northern regions, and I believe they are right. Thus, to here their armies converge for war and it will not be a pleasant one. Not pretty at all, not even in a joke. They will fight to the last as they vie for her: ultimate rule or ultimate loss. But they will have us waiting for them, my humble crew with but one concern: that the Medusa rest only in those hands that would destroy her. For this, no one and no thing will be spared. For this, we would each in an instant die. As I have life, the Medusa will not rise again. You still don't eat."

"I'm listening, thinking."

"About what?"

"Nothing."

"What? We have no time for lies."

"What do you want with me?"

"Of course. Well, try and eat something. As said, there are no coincidences. You must be a survivor to have made it this far. If you had tried to go much farther north without preparation you would have died of cold, you know. But we can prepare you for that, teach you what you need to know." He took a few fast bites, chewed and swallowed. "What we're hoping to do is avoid the war by getting her first, and then destroying her. This the only the Phoenix can do. And this is where, perhaps, you come in. You see, I need all of us here. Only with the crew intact can we stand against the armies. Together, we are as close to invincible as mortals may become, but none can be spared at this time simply to deliver a message that may be of no consequence. It's a hunch that's all I have a hunch were she might be and the more I think about it the more sense it makes. But there is no time now for us to go, so, we need a runner. Someone, I don't want to say expendable, but someone we can spare and trust, and someone who has a good chance of making it." He smiled and pointed at me. "And that, I believe, is you."

"Where do you want me to go exactly?"

"Not so far. A few months is all if you don't get lost."

I laughed but did not mean to.

"What's so funny?"

"Nothing."

"Stop that. Just be honest. You don't have to hide anymore."

"I was thinking I've been lost for years."

Roland swatted my shoulder. It felt like being hit with a stone. "All the more proof that you are the one for this assignment. Listen, if you have a question, a concern, say it. Be comfortable with us. There will be enough trouble to come without creating it among ourselves. And do nothing against your will. You are free to go at any time."

"I understand," I said. "I have a question."

"Shoot."

"What is this hunch founded on?"

He smiled. "It came to me in a dream."

"I see."

"Listen, you don't have to do anything you don't want to. I mean that. Thing is, in the North, we believe Medusa to be in the hands of someone like you described: an old one in the mountains, an immortal warrior…a Sage, if you will."

And a chill ran through my blood. They just might be real. Roland began eating again. "So, you interested?" he said with food in mouth.

"Yes."

"Well, you don't have to answer right now."

"Yes. I want to go. I will find the medusa."

"No. Not your job. You just have to deliver a message. That's all. But this is quite serious. You have to be certain in your conviction. I believe he has her, but don't know for sure. He's a tricky old bastard and speaks in riddles. It's a dangerous journey too, and a cold one, real cold in the coming season, but we'll prepare you for all that. You have as good a chance as any, but you have to be certain you want to join this cause. Otherwise, you're welcome to go away."

"I want to join."

"All right."

Roland set down a fig he had just taken up and gave me a straight look. "Your mission is to find him and tell him this: tell him Roland said to stop fucking around. You just tell him that. Tell him Roland said time is up, that she burns now or never. You tell him if he doesn't bring her down, Roland will be coming up there to take her because there's sure to be others real soon. A real good chance of that. That's all. Whatever other business you have is all yours. Maybe it will work out well for all parties involved." He ate the fig. "But that doesn't happen often enough," he said without a smile. "One more thing. Tell him they found needles."

"Huh?"

"Just that. Just what I said. The less you know, the better."

We finished our lunch in silence and set out. In two days Roland pointed to a peak. "Our camp lies on the eastern side. It's an old place, elegant and quite beautiful. Open feel to the architecture. People abandoned it a long time ago for one reason or another. Who knows why? But the place suits us just fine." He pointed to the right. "Go more to the east and you hit the city of Scythia, to the west, Beheroh. But when you are ready, you will go north, across the water. Up there waits your Sage," he said and grinned. "No cities there. The waste land. But we have a boat waiting on the lake for you. At least we used to. It should be there. You'll skim over the worst of it. Don't look so worried."

"I'm not."

"Stop lying. If you don't want to tell the truth, just say nothing."

"It's just that we could go south from here, maybe a day from here, and we might find him."

"What? Who? What you talking about, kid?"

"Him, the one I left in the rift. It's not too far really. We could…"

"Whoa whoa. Hold it. You're talking about that kid you think you saw in a hole you think is real?"

"Yes."

"Just stop that. Enough of that. Forget it. There's no going back. We don't have time. Just let it go. Even if we tried, I promise, we'd find nothing: no kid, no rift. Nothing. Let it go. We've bigger concerns. Moving on."

I nodded and said no more about it.

"So, you want me to go all that way north just to give that message?"

"Yes."

"And what if he doesn't care what I say?"

"Just give the message, then your part is done. But don't soften it. He's got to know we mean business."

"I won't."

"Don't be afraid to curse."

"Okay."

"And don't forget about the needles."

"No."

"Good. You see that facing rock wall?"

"Yes."

"Extraordinary sight from our back kitchen."

"It must be very beautiful."

"Quite."

"Do you cook much?"

"Sometimes. It's pretty relaxed. We train hard so its catch-as-catch-can for food. But there's always enough to eat. You won't ever starve with us. Whoever lived there, once upon a time, tended orchards. They've gone wild but still yield apples, pear and peach. We dry the fall harvest and ready it for winter. Grow corn too. Some other grains. Then there's the fish and, of course, what we hunt."

"It sounds good."

"It is."

"You don't hunt people, do you?"

"What? No, no never."

"Good."

"I'd rather die before that." He paused in his step. "Look, I understand, but you need to relax a little. You can trust me not to harm you. I could do that in an instant at any time. It's not a trap, kid."

"I couldn't catch the little fish that nipped at my feet."

"What?"

"In the river of nymphs."

"What's this now?"

"I was just so hungry. I just don't want to ever be that hungry again."

"In that you are not alone. When we get there, you can have a fresh peach."

"Have you killed many people?"

"That's some question to ask a man."

"I'm sorry. I forgot my manners."

"It seems so."

"I've been a long time on my own."

"I understand." He stopped then and looked to the ground and set the pole into it with a scratch of dirt. "More than I can count," he answered at last. "It comes with the territory. But I don't kill for no reason. I am as I live, and live by the work I have done. All of us here have been in many battles. You should know that. You have a right to know just where you are and who you are among. And know that you can leave at any time. Provisions will be provided you to return at least to The City of Brass, should you wish to go. No one will fault you that. We only ask that once you commit to delivering the message you get word to us if you turn back before doing so. That's all. But you never have to finish what we ask of you. It gets cold up there, and though Dexter will give you a quick and safe trail, it is not without its dangers."

"But it's so important."

"Tis. Thus, we don't want anyone with half a heart going into it. You need to be firm in your resolve. And with him be definite in your words. Don't be rude, but don't be too soft. He can charm you to that, so don't fall for it. Gin needs to understand it's time. Make it very clear that it's time. Don't leave out the curses."

"No."

"I mean that."

"I understand."

"Good."

"Gin?"

He nodded. "For all I know it's his real name. At the very least he'll know was I who sent you. Just be real clear with him, clear and firm."

"I will."

"I believe you will."

"Good."

"But don't get lost. You must not get lost."

"No."

"You'll die if you get lost."

"Okay."

"I mean that. Pay attention up there."

"Okay."

"It's too bad you have to go alone, but you do. In some ways that makes your part the most trying, but there's nothing to be done for it."

"I understand. I'm used to it."

"Destiny at work perhaps. May it end soon."

"Yes."

Across a shallow river were the grounds proper. A lovely footbridge waited not far up at all, but Roland ignored it. Instead, we leapt from stone to stone to the other side.

"Impressive. You've good balance, real good."

"Live with a picarin you learn balance real fast. That or fall, and far."

"Severe, but effective."

Roland swept his arm towards the structure before us. "Here, for now, is your home. Welcome!"

The house rested between two mountains. Its impressive walls had been built of polished white stones and its roof was of shingles of red clay, some missing, but lovely all the same. Outside were open structures with floors of stone flagging and a simple roof. These they used for both shade and training.

We passed through the remains of a gate and then climbed the wide steps of the entrance. Above, hung small tubes of metal. Roland pet these and the air filled with delightful chimes. "They catch the wind," he said, "and so by this keep off evil spirits they say, negative energy, as we call it. These particular ones come from

The City of Brass. The finest in the world. Even that string is not fiber, but metal thread."

They chimed lovely and long. Roland pushed upon a heavy door but it did not move. "Barred," he said, confused. We went around back until we stood on the remains of an all-but-ruined slate floor. And I thought how the sun and wind and rain will turn all the things of man to nothing in time.

The land behind the house lowered to a meandering stream and then rose to a thin forest behind which rose the wall of rock we had seen, so high its crown could catch a cloud. From it jutted jagged shards upon which grew the occasional tuft of vegetation. Narrow waterfalls spilled down and made a soft hush as they splashed against the stone. (These would be heavy and plentiful after a rain.) In the shaded patches grew soft mats of moss. Long beards of bird droppings hung beneath barren clusters of sticks — the abandoned eyries of hawk or eagle, and among the rising crags clung centuries-old dwarf trees bent by the wind.

And in this hidden universe of stone yawned the dark mouths of caves. There could be anything at all in them, I thought. Anything. At the very top, the cliff turned inwards to join the mountain again, leading somewhere men may never have gone. But I wondered if they had, and if up there stood yet their relics; or was it simply wilderness over us, running away forever to the border of the sky?

"It's beautiful, isn't it?"

"Yes it is."

"It changes every day, one way or another."

A voice rose from the grass: "I heard you coming two days ago, Roland. Thought you would be here sooner."

"Dex? Where are you?" Roland looked in all directions.

"Right here."

"Stop messing around."

He stepped forward and waved his arms gently to distinguish himself from the background. Suddenly, the coloration that had made him all but invisible faded, and before us stood the tiniest man I had ever seen. He had pin-straight hair as black as night, reddish skin the color of a plum, and clothes of the finest woven fibers. His eyes reminded me of Lyden's: slender and gray, but his were warm, whereas hers were cold. They nourished no fire, those eyes, and when he smiled so did they, but sadly so. He stood not even up to my waist. The greatest warrior? He seemed a figure from a dream, and the dream spoke: "Welcome back, Roland. Glad you made it safely."

"I always do, Dex. Meet the runner."

He turned to me and bowed slowly. I bowed in turn. It became more difficult to believe him to be real. "Welcome," he said in that voice that pretended happiness.

"Thank you."

His eyes glittered as he widened his smile.

"So, are you on watch, Dex?"

"Yes."

"Anything I should know about?"

"There were a few younger ones not too far off, but they didn't come very close. They're gone now, or burrowed. I can't sense them anymore."

"All right. Anything else?" Roland set down his burden and began going through it.

"Belladonna took issue with one of the Iga over..." he touched his tiny chin, thinking. At that moment it all became a little too unreal for me. My heart raced and the world spun. "It's hard to remember with her," he continued in a soft and gentle voice, "and you know how the littlest matter can .... Your friend doesn't look well, Roland."

I felt a hand like a stone rest on my shoulder. "What's up, kid?"

"I...I'm fine."

"You're kind of pale ... in your own way."

"I'm just tired."

"We'll get you a room. Take a nap. Okay, Dex..." Roland held out the dagger wrapped in oil paper, "...for you."

The one called Dexter looked genuinely surprised, even shy to take the gift. "Roland, I asked you not to."

"I wanted to. Take it." The tiny red man bowed to Roland again and took the gift. When he unwrapped the dagger it glinted like a fire in the sun. Dexter smiled, and this smile was true. "It's magnificent, Roland." He spun it on the tip of his finger so quickly the weapon's form turned to a blur. "I will try to kill many people with it."

"Thank you," Roland said and chuckled.

"Is it of elven make?"

"You know it's not."

Dexter turned the gift carefully in his hand, tracing its form with his tiny finger. "It's so very, very fine, Roland, that I thought it might be. I wondered who brought you to our ancient smith."

"Yeah, yeah. I would have gotten a sheath, but I know you don't carry them like that." He turned to me. "He weaves them into his cloak."

Dexter smiled the smile of a doll and nodded and then swung his arm back and brought his hand forward now empty. The dagger was gone. Disappeared, and Roland laughed.

"And he draws them out even quicker," Roland said to me. "In combat, you don't even see them, and often not even Dexter, just blood. He's the fastest I ever knew…that ever will be."

"I am not, Roland. One day I may bring you to my home realm. Then you will see something."

"One day," Roland said.

"Are you faster than a picarin?" I asked, the suddenness of the question surprising even me. The one called Dexter looked at me as if for the first time.

"A picarin, did you say?"

"Yes."

"How is it you know of the Picarin?"

"I lived with one. I have the blade of one."

"Is that so?"

I held out the blade of the drinking bird. Dexter widened his tiny eyes and held his hand over his breath.

"Is…that…real?"

"Of course."

"May…may I hold it?"

"Of course."

In perfect wonder he received the blade, traced its lines with tiny fingers. He exhaled a breath towards the stone and watched the mist fade again and then held it by the handle. "The grip is not for a human hand."

"No."

"Wonderous. A blade of true Picarin make, of magic wrought." He then cut the air once with it, using, perhaps, the first arc of dawn. The blade sang beautifully. He then carefully returned it to me. "You must tell me, before you depart, about your encounters with this picarin."

"Certainly."

"Roland, I have to go."

"You all right?"

"Yes, but I have to go."

"Do whatever you need, Dex. I'll take watch."

"No. That does not matter. I will keep watch, but I have to go."

Roland nodded to him. "Then we'll see you when we do."

Dexter bowed once to Roland and once to me and then disappeared into the folds of the forest noiselessly. After a long while Roland spoke. "He can get a little emotional sometimes. Did you notice?"

"Yes."

"Don't know why that is, but everyone's different. Understand, we try not to ask too much concerning each other's past. It's easier that way, safer too. As said, Dex will mention that he's of the elves, and we let him his dream. It might be what keeps him together. Besides," he said with a laugh, "from the looks of him, he just might be. But we don't go prodding into what has shaped the heart, what's been lost, what's been left behind. We leave all that be. If they're here, they can slay gods and demons, and will if needed to bring her to the fire. Nothing else matters."

"I see."

"Don't speak of your home here. Don't tell anyone what you told me. They don't need to know and they won't ask."

"All right."

"You need a rest. Let's go find you a room. There's about twenty of them."

"It's an extraordinary place."

"Isn't it, though? Been here a long, long time. Just amazing what gets left behind."

Before we went in I considered once more the cliff. For whatever reason, it gave me comfort. It would survive the worst, even the medusa.

In the center of a large, vaulted room, Roland opened his arms wide and smiled. "Our humble camp!" His words echoed off the marble walls.

"Is this what a palace is?"

"This little place? No, no. Just a really, really nice house."

The windows did not even have oil paper. They were nothing but large, unbarred eyes staring into the world without. "Can't something come in?" I asked him.

"Sure, and they're welcome to try, but I wouldn't worry too much about that considering your company."

"What if we're sleeping?"

"There's always a watch. And we sleep light."

"What if it sneaks past the watch? What if it comes in on a different side of the house?"

"You worry a lot about open windows for a man who sleeps in trees."

"That's why I worry."

He laughed.

"Will my room have a window?"

"They all do, but you can sleep upstairs if that makes you feel any better."

"You mean higher up?"

"Yes."

"It would."

"Then, that's where we go. Follow me and remember: while here, you are under my protection."

The great hall boasted white stone with veins of green. Marble, they called it. The stairs, once broad and perfect, had been cut from this too. The remnants of a railing still stood. The upper hall, "the upstairs," had squares of black and white for the flooring and the magnificent blue of lapis lazuli lined each silent doorway. An eerie silence hung in all the house, and each room we past we past in silence, until a woman's sobbing broke it all apart. Roland went ahead, waved for me to wait, and ducked into a room. I waited until I did not. I peeked inside the room. A woman sat on a bed holding her face in her hands. She wept so hysterically her words came only in unfinished, halted syllables. He took her hand. She pulled it away. So gently he spoke: "Bell? Bell, what's wrong, my dove?"

She spoke at last, "Why? Why have you been gone so long, Roland? How could you have been gone so long?"

"But it was only five days, my love, just like I said."

She looked up with a tear-stained face, eyes puffy and wet. "Four!" she cried. "You said four! You said you would be back in four days, Roland! Four."

"Yes, I said probably four, Bell, but you know sometimes, in times like these, we have to make adjustments."

Her tone was tense, pleading: "But I was waiting for you yesterday. I took the watch from an Iga and he wasn't even grateful. I did that just to first see you walking home. I did that for us, Roland, because I wanted to see you and you to see me first, waiting here, knowing how deeply I love you. So I waited and waited, my arms open and ready, my heart longing for you who did not come. My heart a handful of dust. All that day I whispered the words I would say upon our embrace, imagined the ones you would say back, but the full day passed and then the night and still you did not come, though your love waited in the cold field under a starless night. But you did not come."

She broke into a fresh torrent of tears.

"And nobody cares! The Iga, they are so indifferent to me; and Dexter, I don't even think he's human. No one cared. No one came out to see me, to comfort me. They would not have cared if I died."

And Roland, with a conciliatory tone, rested gently his hand on her shoulder and said, "But my darling, darling Belladonna, a watch goes one day and a night. You know that. And if you don't signal for help, they won't come. They're not even supposed to. This you know."

She stamped her foot in the small puddle of tears that had pooled on the floor. "It's just…it's just…when you're gone they hardly speak to me. It's like I'm not a part of this, of anything!"

"You are a part of me, my darling, and always will be."

Her head collapsed into her hands. Her body shook with grief and Roland put his arms around her and held her tight and whispered words I could not hear. And then, from the cave of her hands her muffled voice cried, "Yesterday you should have been back, Roland, but you were not!"

Her tears fell like autumn leaves and so gently he spoke. "It's all right now, Belladonna. I am here, right beside you. I am so sorry to have kept you waiting. You know how I longed for you too. It was all I could think of on that long and terrible path I just…I had to be sure about the kid. He's going to be our runner, you know. We found a runner, Bell, but it was hardly worth it to miss a day with you."

"Oh, Roland!" she said and threw her arms around him. "Our time together, will it be long, Roland? You know what comes."

"No one knows how many days they are given, Bell, but I am thankful for every one with you."

"Oh, Roland, you do love me, don't you?"

"Of course, Belladonna, more than anything or anyone."

And she wept the more. He looked up from her shaking shoulder to me and spoke quickly. "Just go ahead and pick out whatever room is empty, kid. Don't worry about anything. We'll be along."

I followed the hall to the end, past closed and open doors, past quiet rooms in streaks of daylight lined in shadow, so many, such as I had never seen, each standing as an invitation to another world, a cavern of memory with passing light and dust collected through the ages. What voices had spoken in them once, what promises of love, what pronouncements of death had been uttered in the simplest of sentences in each? And where were they whose lives had passed here, whose hands had built it, whose spirits may visit yet with less touch than light or shade? This I wondered.

The door rested half open at the final room on the right. I pressed on it slowly, carefully. It creaked, as if calling to what dwelled within. A ghost had been caught in the corner, but it dispersed with the draft from the hall. The room stood almost empty but for a bowl of white glass resting below the only window. I took it up gently and turned it in my hands. Like the jezeth, it had been forged in profound and subtle beauty and yet was nearly weightless. A chain of unidentifiable flowers wove in blue about its belly and bragged a kind of humble glory. In quiet fascination, I tapped the side with my nail and it's ring disturbed the stillness of the room. I thought of Gelidii singing to the adamantine cave, and of Lyden, welcoming the dawn. Do they think of me still? Upon the bottom the maker had stamped his mark writ in a language forgotten. I tried to imagine his life: what courses it had followed to make a thing so beautiful, and if he dared to dream it would come to such a distant hand. Suddenly, the bowl became too precious to hold. I set it down.

The window had been cut almost as large as the wall. Only a maroon curtain separated it from the vastness of the wild. I pulled this to the side. Without, the towering cliff of rocks climbed up and up and again my mind wandered to where the body could never go. What lived upon that crown of wilderness? What mysteries stared down upon us with equal wonder? After it rained the falling water cascaded in silver strands. Lyden's hair. Below ran the stream whose warble could be heard in the still of night. This brings sleep.

This room felt safe. It was high enough. A fall from there could easily kill a man and the outer wall provided no holds to climb. Safe enough. Let any menace go first through the slumbering warriors below before getting to me. And yet, things have ways of getting in.

Indeed, more than once, an invader came. Yet, it only showed as I floated between the world of sleep and waking, so that I could not really know if it were real. Always the same: a thing cut from the darkness with a narrow skull and pointed ears, crouching on the window sill and staring at the man in semi-sleep. It had large orbs of eyes — red when catching the light of the moon. Thin and gangly arms held the window frame and moved the curtain aside just enough to show its form. Sensing it would pull me from the world of sleep, death's brother, breathless and paralyzed. I wanted to move, but was unable. I wanted to speak, but could not, except once, when my mind awoke just enough to whisper a question to the fading ether of the dream, the vision so dense it stopped the light. Upon my words it looked away, and climbed back into the darkness which bore it.

"Gelidii, is that you?"

Sometimes I awoke and could not sleep again. On such nights I kept a kind of vigil, watched the play of shadow in the forest below. On those nights I thought of home too much. On those nights, life felt piled upon itself. I did not want to leave.

In these nights sometimes I would take up the blade and gently recall the arcs of Gelidii, and they would sing softly in the stillness of the room. I would often do this until dawn surprised me.

It has always enchanted me, the dawn…how such rosy life could emerge from utter darkness, a promise that the world has not ended yet, that the enemy has not sneaked up on us and cut the cord of it all. In the worst of times, only dawn comforts me enough to let me slip into the oblivion of unguarded sleep.

In those first days I was weak and slept often. I was asleep when the door shook to its timbers with a sound like a mild earthquake. I shot up, heart racing in its cage, eyes wide and staring. I dared to say nothing. I listened.

"You in there?"

Roland.

"Yes."

I opened wide the door. She stood beside him, her hand in his, clutching it. Her shining black hair was pulled back from bangs cropped short. Severe, as if cut with a knife. Two long pins of gold held a knot at the back, and each of these terminated into a bird consumed in fire — the phoenix, demi-god sacred to Belladonna. "How you find the place so far?" Roland asked.

"It's just fine. I think I fell asleep."

"Good. Rest up. You need it. Rest all you can. You'll have to pardon my waking you, but I wanted you two to have a proper introduction." He gestured with his free hand towards her and smiled. "This is Lady Belladonna, ninth daughter of the Wreath of the Phoenix, Wielder of the Sword of Scars."

She placed her hands in prayer before her and bowed solemnly, and I did the same. She then held out her right hand, open between us. I only looked at it confused. Her expression hardened. The air became tense. Roland spoke quickly, "It's a custom for some to hold the other's right hand upon meeting. It is a gesture of peace," he continued quickly, awkwardly. "It shows you hold no weapon."

"Oh," I said, and quickly took her yet-proffered hand. When she held mine, she squeezed it hard, as if trying to crush the bones within. The muscles of her naked arm were like melted iron. She pumped my hand a few times fast and then threw it towards the ground.

"Bell."

"What, Roland?"

"He's one of the good ones, Bell."

"Why...don't you think I know that?" She turned back to me, "A pleasure to make your acquaintance," she said coldly.

"And yours."

"I must apologize for my earlier self. I get to crying sometimes. It can all be a little overwhelming, as you must imagine."

"Of course."

She stepped past me into the room and looked around. "Do you find it suitable?"

"It's fine."

"Good. That's important. Why did you pick this one?"

I shrugged. I didn't know.

"They are all empty up here. I come up here to be alone, or used to. So, why would you pick the last room?"

I didn't know.

"It says something about you," she said. "A man of extremes. Hardly a man, a boy, really." A smile beamed across her face. "Oh, he will make a lovely runner, Roland!"

"I thought so too, my Dear."

"We will send you to the end of known lands. We will send you to the great Northern Waste!"

"Don't scare him off it, Bell."

"Then it was meant to be as such, Roland!" she said venomously. "He should know all his part."

"He will, but you don't have to say it like that."

"Then let him not do it!"

She paced a half circle behind me. "You seem as a wild man, very much instilled with spirits of the wilderness and beasts. I sense them in you yet. More animal than man I should say. Comfortable in hearth and home you are not. These walls confine you. This roof hangs above as an omen and we…we oppress you." She stood right before me now. Her green eyes stared into mine. "This is good. This will serve you in what is to come. But, Roland, his hands are so soft!"

"I know, Bell. Leave that to me. I'll have them ready before he goes."

"You will need strong hands, Wanderer. My darling Roland has the strongest. He will teach you well, but know this: more than strong hands, you will need a strong heart. We don't want you if you don't want to be here. Do nothing you do not wish to do. We want none who would falter."

"I know."

"You can turn away at any time. Every step is but another choice."

"I understand."

"You do not. The lands will turn bitter before you arrive. Everything will have died. You will walk through the white waste and should you stray from the way, you surely will wander to the one death owed by all born. You must pass the Valley of Ice, where the white tiger will smell your blood. You must weave through the desolate fields of the heath monster, who, should it catch you, will devour you whole."

I said nothing. She smiled.

"Bell…"

"The monster will eat you if it catches you!" she promised, her eyes delirious with joy but her smile fading. "That is, if you do as you promise."

"I will."

"You say that now. You are safe now, but the way is long. There is much between here and there."

"I understand."

"No. You do not know what lies ahead. Before you find her, I assure you, you shall believe yourself to have wandered to the end of time."

Roland cleared his throat, his eyes tired and somehow distant. "Bell, don't worry. I got it. He hasn't been here a day."

She paced my room like a tiger. "We cannot suffer delay, Roland. The important parts must be known, lest we waste a day on one whom we should not."

"You must let me run the crew as I do, Bell. It's going just fine so far. I use a light touch."

She frowned and returned to him. He put an arm around her waist and suddenly she appeared almost childlike resting her head against his shoulder. I expected her to break again into tears. Roland sighed almost imperceptibly and then spoke to me, "What Belladonna rightly made clear is that the task before you will be a trying one, yet I believe you can and will do it, but there are very few of us. Everyone is incredibly important. We need soldiers ready to die for this without a second thought. I need to know that only death will stop you in your efforts. But you know this already."

They both stared at me as if awaiting an answer.

"I do," I said. "I understand," I said again, yet was not sure I did.

"It's not that we don't appreciate your own needs."

"I know."

Belladonna lifted her head from his shoulder. "And what are they?"

"He says he wants a sage to free his home from the king."

"A sage? You mean the old man?"

"I think so. It's him as much as anyone else by the sound of it."

"So is that why you have come to us?" she asked me. "To help you find the old man?"

"It's not like that, Bell. He knows nothing about it. I approached him."

She looked at me suspiciously and then back to Roland. A fresh tear ran down her cheek. "Why do you always think I am wrong? Why do you always think the things I think are wrong, Roland?" She folded her arms, hugging herself, and he went to embrace her again but she threw him off. She stepped away and would not look back. And so many tears, they fell like rain.

"Bell, my Belladonna. You are right to ask these questions. I would too. It's just that I've had the advantage of travelling with him and I've asked all this already."

She would not turn yet.

"Come, my love, without you we could never do this. You are the Mistress of the Sword of Scars. The only one. Your birth to it was writ in the course of the stars." Upon these words she softened, slowly, her emotions yielding like melting ice. "You are the finest part of us, the best part of us, but you do take too much to heart."

"It's so hard sometimes, Roland. It can be very, very hard sometimes. All this."

"I know, Bell. Wish I could change it, and it will change, but it has to be this way for now."

She nodded quickly as if she understood and then wiped her eyes and spoke to me. "How do you find everything so far? Comfort of a guest is of the utmost importance."

"It's a beautiful place," I replied. "Truly is. I've never seen anything like it."

"But you sleep on a stone floor. You mustn't. We will get you bedding."

"Of course we will," Roland added.

"We must. Do you know what I told Roland before he left? I told him to petition the stars for a messenger, to place one on this journey, for whatever plan he drew up fell short without one. We needed one more, one to set apart, so I said to Roland, 'Beseech the brightest stars, each a shining soul of a warrior departed, and beg their favor.' How could they not listen? No cause since the dawn of all humanity begs more importance than her destruction. So I taught him the prayers of the Phoenix: the summoning of the eye of fire, the stoking of the eternal ember. Did I not teach you these, Roland?"

"You did, Bell."

"And when the secret words were sung, did you not witness the rising light?"

"I did."

"And did I not say it then? Wasn't I truthful, my darling Roland?"

"You were, my Sweet. Everything you said was true."

"It was all true, Roland," she asserted. "All true."

"I know it was."

"But you didn't believe me then!"

"Now, Belladonna...." He opened his hands gently.

"You told me to say nothing. You said not to waste time, and I had to beg you to come out and sing the sacred petitions properly, but you didn't want to, Roland. I had to beg you, Roland!" She began to cry again. "The fate of the whole world...and I had to beg!"

"It wasn't like that."

"It was! Yes it was! And I had to lead you to the growing moon and there in the tall grass make your mouth know the secret words, the sacred names of the departed warriors who listen yet to the cares of humankind, and we sang them for the fate of the world, Roland. But it wasn't that. I am not crying because the world was almost lost. Only this: why would you not come just because I asked you?"

"My darling Belladonna, forgive me."

She paused for just a moment and then turned to his arms. Her muffled voice spoke from his shoulder. "'Ask the stars,' I said to you, and you said...do you remember what you said?"

"I said they're too far away to ever hear us."

She broke into fits of crying laughter. "Imagine that!" she said to me, "Imagine: the stars too far to hear the laments of men? But you are here, for they do listen to the just petition. You are here, your blurry dream connected to this most sacred cause to which we have thrice pledged our lives. The stars do heed the prayers of the brave, yet they must be humble enough to seek their aid. Your presence is a thin testament to the intercession of the divine, which has deigned to take part in this most deadly of games, upon whose outcome rests nothing less than the fate of the world. Yes, the stars have listened again."

Without a goodbye she left us and walked swiftly down the hall. At the head of the stairs she cried back, "And they always will!"

Her boots clomped on the stone, stamped through the lower chamber until we heard them kick open the front door and go out. He answered before I could ask: "Yes, she's always like that."

"Like what?"

"You don't have to pretend here. Belladonna had a strange childhood. She was raised as a Phoenix guardian, and so her first kill probably came about the age of ten. A just kill but, nonetheless, war shouldn't be a children's game." He sighed and rubbed the skin of his head, now gray-black with returning hair. "But, I understand. Phoenix training takes a long time. The joke is they cut their own cord." He smiled. "You look tired."

"I'm all right."

"I do love her, you know."

"I am sure you do."

"Well, some could argue that I'm just pretending to in order to secure her loyalties. I am not, yet I do not think it such a good thing for battle...to be in love...but I suppose people have been fighting besides their loved ones since just about forever."

"I suppose they have."

"Take a walk around the place if you wish but stay on the grounds. This is the wilderness, though it may not seem so from here."

"All right."

"You hungry?"

"No."

"There's food downstairs. All kinds. Just serve yourself. Take whatever you wish, only make sure you put everything away. We don't want little creatures or not so little creatures attracted to the aroma."

"All right."

"That's about it for now. You make waste out back, wash in the creek and the water running in it is sweet, so take that bowl there and fill it in the day."

"All right."

"Don't walk around outside the house at night, okay? That's what a second bowl is for. Don't leave the house at night."

"Okay."

"You're safe in here, but out there anything can happen."

"I know that."

"I am sure you do. Well, sleep or whatever you want. I have some matters to attend to. I will see you this evening."

"All right."

He stepped away and stopped again, his mind full of thoughts. "Listen, one more thing. Don't worry too much about what she said. She can get a little overdone, if you know what I mean."

"I understand."

"It's true, in a sense, what she said. You will be in a pretty harsh environment, but we will prepare you for that. You will be as safe as possible."

"I have not been safe for a long time. It doesn't matter."

His face tightened with concern. "Well, we want you to make it. We want you to have the best possible chance for success."

"Thank you."

"It's not really for you. It's the message."

"Yes. I know."

"Nothing personal, but it's not any one of us."

"I know."

"To be honest, I really don't know what he will do about your home."

I looked at the stone-cut patterns on the floor.

"Well, he might help. I don't really know. Again, this is your choice. You can leave now, or tomorrow, or whenever."

"I know that."

"We will give you a dove to carry to him. Once there, let it go. If you tie the green ribbon to its leg, we will know you have succeeded. Tie the red, and we will know things went poorly, or that you have abandoned the plan. If the dove does not come back, or comes back without any ribbon, we will assume you are dead and act accordingly."

"I can write a note."

He smiled again. "I like you. You're a good kid. Sure, a note would be fine. Use both. I had a feeling about you. Get some rest, some food, whatever. Enjoy these days, for those to come will not be so easy."

"I will. Thank you."

"Don't thank me. There's no reason for that."

He left and I lay down again, my whole life before me, my whole life behind me. I stared at the shadows growing longer in the room. I must have been far past exhaustion that day, for when I awoke the sky without was the color of ice. It took me sometime to realize this was not dusk, but dawn. I had slept right through the day and then the night. Thirsty, I pushed open the soft creaking door and walked down the hall now lit with torches. In the kitchen I found a bowl of fresh water and used the ladle to drink. I wanted open space and so stepped outside to the waking world, to the birds and the chorus of unbridled joy for the rising day. I listened very carefully. They said what they always did to the dawn:

"The sun comes again! The sun comes again!"

I found the creek and yes, its waters were as sweet as any. I drank again and again even after I had slaked my thirst, and then washed my hands and face feeling wholly renewed. I had to urinate. I crossed the creek and found a small path, an animal trail perhaps, and followed this away a bit so not to contaminate our water. For no reason, I went farther along the faint path until coming upon a clearing of tall grass swaying beneath the illumined rose of dawn. The trees about me hung heavy with fruit. The orchard. I picked an apple and ate it right there. Delicious. Above, a finch, bright yellow with black-striped wings, perched in a high bough of the apple tree.

"Hello," I said to it as best I could.

"Hello! Hello! Hello! Hello! Hello!" it said quickly and beautifully, and I could only smile because there is no greater joy than speaking to the little birds. The little birds are always so happy.

I should say here that I've heard others mention the language of the birds as a phenomenon that comes fully formed and with perfect clarity. It does not. As said, the mind should be quiet and open, the body at rest, the spirit calm. The heart should move peacefully in the chest. The blood should run its course softly. The breath nourish gently. And you have to truly listen, for the complexities of the language come but slowly to the human mind. The balance of your life could be spent in its study, and yet it is my belief that one could live to be a thousand and know but a small portion of this most ancient of tongues.

Yet, they are repetitive by nature, knowing the importance of beauty.

"Well you're a happy little thing, aren't you?" I whistled imperfectly.

"Hello! Hello! Hello! Hello! Hello!"

"So what's your name, little bird?"

"See Dee Nee! See Dee Nee! See Dee Nee!"

"Seedeenee? Seedeenee? Well, hello, Seedeenee."

"Hello! Hello! Hello! Hello! Hello!"

"And what are you doing on this fine morning, Seedeenee?"

She flapped from her perch and came lower to me. Facing me now, she spoke: "Oka Oka Oka!"

"Hmm."

"Oka oka oka!"

"What?" I asked.

"Oka!"

"What's that?"

"Oka! Oka! Oka!"

"That's a beautiful word, Seedeenee."

"Oka!"

"Okay!"

"Oka! Oka! Oka!"

"So nice meeting you, Seedeenee!"

"Oka!" She screeched and pointed her beak to the sky and readied to fly away.

"You have such pretty yellow feathers, Seedeenee."

"Oka! The sun has come."

"Yes, it has."

"The sun has come with oka!"

"Oh, you're going to fly, I see. So bye bye, Seedeenee."

"The sun has come with oka!" she sang again, and then shot from her bough to fly in a single morning what for me would be months of heavy walking.

As kids we would play a game. We would ask each other what kind of animal we would like to be. I always said a bird. Not so much to fly, but to be free of the chains of earth.

I watched happily until she was but a speck in the sky, and then I absently picked another apple, bright, red, and sweet. The juice ran like sugar down my cheek. The abundance unasked.

I chewed slowly and listened to the cicada. What a lovely morning. I threw the core spinning into the tall grass and watched it land for no reason but the grace of gods. Even so, I didn't see it right away. But, my heart did. Something dark had come. Where the core had landed the colors didn't seem quite right, and what was it, a pile of bones, moss? What was it in the grass there? Are those eyes? And then it blinked.

Thus, I had learned a new word of the ancient language of birds.

Oka!

Twice a fool I was.

Oka!

Fool of all fools, deaf to a hundred warnings.

Oka!

Fool. Be damned, fool. Toss your life on an apple.

Oka...

Oka...

Ogre

When it knew I knew, it lurched up and ran straight at me. A small specimen, a child ogre, if such things be, or just some lesser species of the accursed race. I don't know, but in the frantic momentary calculations of my mind, it looked no higher than my chin. Its speed matched that of a large one, for what its legs lost in stride they made up in frantic speed. It appeared driven by the same mute hunger as it stared wide and expressionless with small, dead eyes the color of ash. Its filaments of saliva awoke me. The gray strings of drool screamed a warning that it comes to feed.

I remember taking in air. Air would be everything. I would live or die by air. The ogre was so quick, so close, and they say they have hypnotized men with those eyes of a fish. It looked like a corpse by dark magic recalled from the lair of worms. It groaned and opened its mouth. Its dead legs stamped the earth. Air would be everything. And I had taken in air. I would live and die by air. When at last I ran I could hear the grating from its lungs, the rasping breath almost laughing. Could it be laughter? Did it know I knew not to where I was running?

But my legs knew. They headed towards the house, the creek and then the house. It was gaining. Its breath rasped louder now and then it mewled and I almost stopped so to end it now. All this fear, years of it. Its stench overcame like a wave. The new sun had just cleared the tree line and I glimpsed once to it, and then ran ahead into shadow again. The creek turned just ahead. Its grunts became orgiastic howls. It almost sang in a kind of low longing, like the moan of a dog.

Uhhhnnn, uhhhnnng...

The blade rested beside in the room, just beside the mat and I thought of it as my saliva tasted of copper and my lungs began to quit. It gained and was so close and the sickening stench almost made me vomit and if I did that I would slow and then I would die. A terrible death it would be. I said a quick prayer and had an idea. The best idea. The only hope, but it would cost a breath. It would slow me. It would cost half a breath, less of a step, one slower step, but there was no better plan. I would do it. I would pour all my heart and hope into a word.

It mewled constantly now so close, broken chants of perverse speech. Maybe they did have a language after all. But now I would speak. Now, my turn.

"Roland!"

My legs slowed just a little. It was just a little closer. The trees flew through that dying day and I measured the worth of a second call. The creek appeared before us now, running low and ebony dark. Oh, how could it end like this? Touch water again at least. I had lived so many lies I could never now correct. I never meant to run for the medusa. I never believed in a sage. I never loved Selador enough to die for it, to do all of what was to come.

Let me live and I will keep my promises.

Another breath. One more: "Roland...help!"

And there he was, balancing on the stepping stones of the creek, spinning the pole slowly around his torso as he tip-toed over the wet and slippery rocks with a gentle smile. When he upon the closer bank he casually waved me past him, still with an impossible smile. He must not see the ogre in chase. He would. I charged past him through the creek, up the incline on the far side and remember hearing a whoosh of air and then a dull thud, and then something tumbling through the grass and landing in the water.

I ran a ways more before daring to look back. Roland leaned on the pole with a pile of mossy bones at his feet. And then an odd thing happened: Dexter appeared from nowhere. He ran along on the creek, on stones or the water itself. I could not be sure. He and Roland had a good laugh. At their feet the ogre lay dead.

I returned to the site. Its arms and head lay sprawled in the water and I did not want to step in the creek.

"Why don't you finish it off, Dex?"

"You don't think it's done, Roland?"

"No, I am sure it is, but let's not take a chance of a scratch. Eh, I got it."

He lifted the pole and smashed the butt into the back of the thing's neck. There was a wet, cracking sound. The body writhed a little, but it was gone. The head had been struck so violently that the skull had lost its form.

Roland covered his mouth with his sleeve as a filter from the sickening odor. "You all right, kid?"

"I…I…."

"You're quick. Lucky for you you're quick. I told you not to stray too far, especially at dawn and dusk. Just the worst times."

"I…I…just wanted an apple."

"The small ones are just as filthy as the rest. One scratch and that's it. Yes, we have medicine, but you don't want to count on that. And you don't want to count on us, either. We can't be everywhere at every time. We got lucky this morning. Just understand that.

"I was in the next valley," said Dexter, "when I heard you call. Even at my best speed I wouldn't have made it here in time. I was running up the water right to you, but I would not have been able to save you. There are limits to all things, including the grace of elves. It had too much gain on you. Were it not for Roland we would have lost you. It would have gotten you between the creek and the house."

I looked at the pile of death and thought of all my life leading to that morning.

"All right," said Roland, "anyway, on the bright side, we got a dead ogre, and judging by its size I'd say it was burrowed somewhere, wouldn't you Dex?"

"Don't see how else I could have missed it being so close to us."

"They're trickier than they look," he said to me. "They hide. They wait. You can bet that, if this one came from a burrow he was not alone. Somewhere out there a whole nest of them is waiting for a breakfast which won't be coming. If we root 'em out now it's that much less we'll have to worry about later. We think your king's been feeding them his enemies. A way of training them, coaxing them to the fight. It could just be rumor, but it's possible. They've been partially trained before. You think you could backtrack it, Dex?"

"I am sure I can."

Roland looked at the level of the sun. "They should be fast asleep by the time we get there. Let's hunt." He turned to me: "You want to help us out?"

"I… I…."

"Just go back to the house and ask Belladonna for some blood of the sun. Tell her what it's for."

"I… all right, I…the blood of the sun?"

"That's it. You sure you all right? Would you rather wait here with it?"

I went to retrieve the blood of the sun, whatever it was: a strange poison sought from a strange woman. She opened wide the door to a room that reminded me of her: masculine and feminine, polished and rough, beautiful and deadly. The white walls hung thick with adornments curving into a ceiling recessed with intricate, patterned images. All of them carved of stone. There was a story there that I almost read, but could not as time would not allow. Pastel scarves of silk lifted in the stirring air and hints of jasmine and frankincense caught the morning light pouring in like gold. Over her windows hung translucent banners. Almost living statues of nudes and wrestling beasts glowed in marble. Plants that looked like miniature trees decorated a corner of her quarters. Yet, among all this delicate charm draped steely implements of death: swords of sundry types, half-hidden whips of metal chain tipped with spikes, whips of braided leather woven with razors, iron jaws waiting open, bizarre daggers of unfathomable make, so many daggers, and shields too. Upon the shield, a phoenix.

Her bed rested beneath a tent of white mesh which, like her once white blanket, was marred with crimson streaks of blood. "What is it?" she asked impatiently.

"You're bleeding," I said.

"What is it?" she asked again. She wore what she had earlier: a halter of leather and plated iron. Her boots ran in crisscrossed strips of leather up her calves and tied just over her knees. Each sheath showed the jutting handle of a silver dagger.

"What is it?"

"But you're bleeding."

"What is it, already!"

On each wrist a gold bracelet of a phoenix with a ruby eye. On her neck a silver collar, an opal at the center.

"Roland sent me for the blood of the sun."

"Oh, did he now?"

"Yes."

"And for what does he ask this?"

"What?"

"What does he want this for?"

"To burn an ogre's nest."

"You found an ogre's nest?"

"No. Not yet. One chased me and Roland killed it. We're going to track it back with Dexter to the nest, if there is one."

She gave me a look. "Hardly a day you've been here, and already an ogre chases you down?" I waited. "What's with you?" I saw no reason to respond.

She huffed and, not unlike Lyden, stamped off to the back corner of the room. The door waited open, so I stepped inside to the exquisite softness of a patterned rug. Her back was to me. She untied a chest of woven sticks of pale wood. Her fingers worked furiously on the intricate knots, and soon the chest lay open. In the heart of it, I spied three vials of clay, and she took one out and set it aside and spoke with her back to me, anger in her voice. "So you boys want to go off and have fun with my blood, my treasure. Yet no, not Belladonna! Belladonna must keep watch this afternoon. This day she sacrifices the gift of blood of fire, but she, no, Belladonna may not go! The house must be kept from evils too! Beg the blood of Belladonna, but she herself will stay behind!"

She began to drip a deep red liquid into a smaller vessel. She spoke but kept her attention upon her work. "The most precious of liquids I am to simply give out to pour on moss! I could ask the Iga to take my watch so that I might see my own proper fire, but of course they are God knows where! So you enjoy! Take! Take so that you, and not Belladonna, may witness the sacred fire poured into the pregnant nest!"

I said nothing. I waited. Her hands worked hurriedly pouring the liquid, sealing the lesser vessel with wax. She handed this to me. "Just take it: an elixir wrought from a thousand hearts, just take! Yours for the asking. So what if she can't come? How unfortunate for Belladonna, for poor Belladonna, to do naught but wait and keep house. Let Belladonna prepare the meal for everyone. Let Belladonna kill the first army. Belladonna will keep watch this day. She will get the flowers herself. Her swords shall on this morning dull as her soul sleeps in a room of dust! Belladonna will but await their return, evermore bereft of the sacred fire. Let her life count a wasted day."

She resealed her chest with its secret and nearly inextricable knots. "He knows I can't come today!" she cried, stamping her foot with all the fullness of a broken heart.

"Please don't cry," I said.

"And why not?"

"Because this couldn't be helped."

"I suppose he wants a sliver of her nest too? To hold the fire?"

"I don't know."

"I do. I know everything he wants."

With blinding speed she unsheathed a short sword and twirled her arm in an effortless blur. The slightest sliver of pale wood then winnowed in the air, freshly cut from her chest itself. She cast the quivering sword back into the sheath and caught the sliver of pale wood between the tips of her fingernails. She handed this to me and I put it carefully in my pocket.

"Do not drop the blood while you carry this nest."

"All right."

"Nothing will be left of you but a few teeth, if that."

"I see."

"Go then, Boy. Run along and play. Beg Belladonna's secret fire to pour on the deformed perversities so you may, on this day, find a story as Belladonna ages among the shadows!"

"You can go, Belladonna. I'll keep watch."

"Ugh! You? Please! You cannot even watch yourself. How is it you have lived so long, anyway?"

"I…thank you for this, Belladonna."

She looked down with quivering lips. In her wet, brown eyes ran a fresh flood of tears. She slammed the door behind me. In a half-muffled cry, her lament rang from behind the door.

"Boys have all the fun!"

I hardly believed how a few drops of crimson syrup could be anything but a poison, but there was much in the world I did not know, yet at least I knew that. I found them chatting by the ogre's corpse. Before I could step on the slippery rocks Roland held up his hand to stay me. "Dex, why don't you take it?"

"Of course, Roland."

He glided over the water and with his tiny hand lifted the blood from the cradle of my palms and hid it within the fold of his cloak. He then took the sliver of phoenix nest from my fingers. "Thank you," he said with a smile.

"You're welcome."

"You should come with us, kid. You have a lot to learn. What you think, Dex?"

"If it's between a nest of ogres or Belladonna, I suspect he might be safer with us."

They both laughed.

"First let's clean our mess," Roland said, and Dexter poured a small drop from the clay vessel onto the ogre's body and then with a dagger shaved a sliver of the pale wood and let this float down to it. We all stepped back, upwind. Dexter suddenly had a second dagger and drew the two together in a flash and by this shot a spark at the body. A ball of fire arose and then flames engulfed the corpse immediately. In a matter of moments it was reduced to ash.

Roland nodded. "All done. Nice and clean. Let's go."

We walked swiftly, almost running. Roland took long strides and Dexter hardly touched the ground, but rather skipped from flower tops to the tops of blades of grass, hardly bending either one, so much like Lyden he walked. Sometimes, he would leap and disappear in a low-hanging bough and, not entirely unlike Gelidii, follow it right to the thinnest terminus and jump slowly down again to the flower tops, to the grass-tips, and upon these he would run again. Sometimes he sang words I had never heard, not even from Lyden, bringing sounds neither human nor bird nor wind, but something of them all, and something else too. As we made our way he and Roland seemed amazingly calm. Perhaps this was but a show of courage. As for me, dread rose in the pit of my stomach. I did not want to find the nest of ogre.

Only occasionally would Dexter visibly focus on finding the trail. He would stop a moment, catching a scent too faint for us to perceive, or he would press his palm flat to the ground as he felt something we never could. Sometimes, he plucked a blade of grass and tasted it and spat it out. Sometimes he would straighten a bent flower petal and think. His expression revealed something of his discovery, for it would smile gently, or twist in revulsion, or simply remain, as it too often did, in a state of cold indifference. "It very clearly passed this way," he said lifting a crushed buttercup. Beside it ran the faintest depressions in knee-high grass. "Just look. The ogre is a clumsy creature. Its step falls even heavier than the humans'."

Roland squinted into the clearing ahead. "We have faith in you, my friend. Just lead the way."

When the day was half run, Dexter turned to us and pointed ahead. "We are very, very close! See how the dew did not evaporate here, but was brushed off by the legs of an upright creature?"

Roland and I looked at each other. "No, Dex."

"Well, that means it passed this way in early morning. That means the den is close. We would smell it if the wind were right."

In days to come, Roland would often say with unhidden pride how critical Dexter had proven to the crew. How the extravagant plan to contain the medusa would not be complete without him. He was the only one, Roland said, who could be counted on to do just a little more than was humanly possible.

"And we need that," he would say. "The task is beyond ordinary warriors, though they be cut from the finest cloth."

Suddenly Dexter ran ahead and leapt up to a boulder that rested in the center of a slow-moving creek. I felt it then: a gray pall that settled upon the forest. A sickening butterfly took flight in my gut. Rocks were strewn like bones. The sickly creek water moved like blood. Dexter pointed frantically to something in the muddy bank. "There! Just there! Surely you see that?"

Roland stepped gingerly on the stones, avoiding the mud. I stood beside him then and, yes, there it was, a print deep in the soft mud, the undoubted work of the ogre. "You see that don't you?" Dexter asked again, giddy, almost childish.

"We sure do, Dex," said Roland. "He ours?"

"It must be, Roland," Dexter said, and considered the sun. "They will be underground by now in this heat. They should be asleep too, but they will know he's missing. They share food, you know. People do not know that of ogre, but we do. They share food. They hunt for one another. They will be hungry. Their sleep will not be deep. They missed their meal," he said, and winked at me.

"Well," said Roland, "we gonna make their day a whole lot worse."

Dexter only leapt weightlessly from the boulder and floated to the ground on the far side of the creek to fade without a sound into the dense vegetation beyond.

We followed. The land got sicker with every step. Blighted land, he had said. Here it was. Even the sky was quiet of birds. The air hung pregnant with an odor of fetid disease. The very firmament seemed to shun the light it shed upon this little part of the earth. Dexter no longer strayed ahead. We found him waiting very still. Roland's shoulders hung round as if oppressed with rain, and no one joked and no one smiled.

With heavy steps we emerged from the dying wood to a low hill with all the beauty of a burial mound. Blackened trails traced upwards, deep and crossed like a profane curse writ in rotted blood. The trails all lead to the same place: the ogre door -a black maw just below the summit of the mound and into which must have been dragged the dead and the dying. The opening stared down at us like the blind eye of a giant. Over it, in crude covering, lay the dried ribs of tree limbs, some yet with desiccated leaves. I don't know why I think of them now, those leaves, how they ticked in the faint breeze, how they must have shielded the ogres from the sun.

We began to ascend the mound and passed the sun-whitened bones of human and beast, strewn and chewed, broken and twisted...all pocked with the punctures of fang. On some, rotted clumps of flesh still clung.

Soon, the atmosphere became infested with tiny flies that feasted on the marrow and blood-rot. They grew so thick that we had to cover our mouths with cloth. Except for Dexter, upon whom no flies landed, for he, like Lyden, could speak to all creatures.

Nearer to the entrance the stench became almost unbearable. I doubled my mouth rag. Roland did the same. Dexter had fitted flowers up his nostrils. We went upwards slowly, not just due to the steepness and the need for quiet, but something in the place held you back, pushed your soul away from it. And I thought perhaps, just perhaps, even they were afraid, if only a little.

We had no plan, and I did not ask. If I would trust them, I would trust them completely, and that was all. And so it was that when we came to the door I did not know what to do. It stared down upon us cold and dead and hungry and an unreal fear swelled in me. I began to fall out. Little fish curled before my eyes. I had not fallen out in a long, long time but the thought of being dragged into that pit, of what waited down there. As I swooned I began to draw the blade.

"Keep it. You won't need it," Roland whispered. "Anyway, you'll need your hands free for what you have to do. If you want to do it. You don't look so great."

"Why do you not order him to run off, Roland, so he can have no shame and no terror? He's obviously overcome."

"He can leave with no shame without my order, Dexter."

"I'm staying."

"Of we three, you are the only one who can die today."

"I'm staying, Dexter. I'm not dying today."

"You almost did this very morning," Dexter said, "and the day is young."

"Please don't scare him anymore than he already is, Dex."

"It's just the truth, Roland."

"That doesn't matter."

Dexter said no more and kneeled to pet the sick grass, which actually greened at his touch. "Forgive me, both of you," he said, his expression very distant.

"Forget it, Dex. We've no time for all this. Let's make this quick." Roland went ahead, gesturing for us to wait. He peeked into the black maw with pole at the ready and then gingerly tested the dry limbs. Eyelids of the cave. He crept back and whispered, "It goes pretty deep. They must've been here a good while. They dig in deeper all the time to hide more from the noon sun. Your job, kid, is to scoop as much of that dried timber as you can and heave it into the pit. The more we have to burn and smoke, the better. Work fast. Toss as much as possible before my signal and then run off... upwind, but not too far, in case there's a straggler. I'll heave in the blood and the sliver of nest and Dex will light them. It's far down there, Dex. You got to send it right down."

"That won't be a problem, Roland."

"Don't be anywhere near the mouth of the cave when it lights, kid. It's gonna scream flames. You need to be well away and upwind. Everyone clear?"

We nodded. Dexter bravely tried to smile, but could not.

It was hard to breathe. I felt dizzy and nauseous. They had brought me to see what my heart was made of but I was falling out. "It's gotta be quick," Roland emphasized. "They gonna wake as soon as the branches start to crumble down and they gonna be curious and not in the best of moods. Okay, I have to get the fuck out of here. It stinks. And these fucking flies! Now go," he said to me. I nodded. My teeth clacked.

"You cold?" he whispered.

"No."

"That was a joke, but you're not laughing. Know why not?"

"No."

"Because this no place for jokes. Go."

"You afraid, it's okay, Son."

"I'm all right, Uncle."

"Everyone gets afraid."

"I'm okay."

"Just don't listen to fear so that it rules you. You rule it. Use it like fire."

"Yes, Uncle."

"You get what I mean by fire?"

"I guess."

"It's strong. Can destroy, but it can create too. Same with fear."

"Yes, Uncle. I understand."

"Now let's kill some dogs."

"Yes, Uncle."

I heaved an armload of dried branches into the abyss. It fell much longer than I thought it would, down and down into the dark death below. Faintly, I heard the rustling of them tumbling down a steep incline and then the ominous quiet of them coming to rest on the cave floor. They must be sleeping just there. I listened, and yes, something began to stir from below. I grabbed more and more and dropped them in a fury and they snapped and crashed and then groggy, lifeless groans rose from the darkness of the pit. I broke away the last of the lid and dropped it in. The sun burned into the cave.

"Enough," Roland cried, running up and sending me away. He took aim at the deepest part of the pit and threw the clay vessel into the darkness with all his force. We heard it crack. He then threw in the sliver of nest which Dexter had woven to a stone and was already running back before it landed. "All right now, Dex! A light…please!"

The groans could be heard so clearly now. They were rising, closer. They were rising and my blood turned to ice and I staggered away and did not know my companions. At the edge of the mouth Dexter stood with two daggers drawn, but made no move to send a spark. Roland called to him. "Okay, Dex, old friend, just a spark if you would, and then we're done with this."

Dexter nodded but only stared down into the groaning pit. He showed no fear, only sadness. Now we could hear a scratching sound. They were climbing. They were climbing and they were close. Dexter crossed his daggers then, two of the slenderest knives I have ever seen, like the long twisting fangs of a great snake, almost like the tooth of Kai-Tey, but smaller. He held them as a natural part of his hand but pointed to the ground in a kind of dejection, like unwanted toys in the thin arms of a child, and I remember I could see half of Dexter's face as he stared into the abyss, and how the abyss stared right back. He did not flinch. He did not even raise the knives. The groans rose within and I knew what we all knew: Dexter did not want to do this. The creatures within had begun to howl.

"Light 'em up, Dex!" said Roland more urgently. I backed away and away on legs of water. "Go on, Dex, just a spark and we'll get breakfast."

But Dexter still did not move. The knives swayed in the gentle wind of the day as did his childlike arms. Roland kicked up a cloud of earth in frustration and the wind took it away. Dexter only stared absently down. He must see them now, and they his silhouette. "Good, Dexter!" Roland exclaimed, "Most nimble of all the elves, friend of man and earth alike to whom I three times owe my life…a spark if you would! A brief memory of the sun! Please, Dex. Time is short." Dexter lifted his head just a little and nodded, perhaps only to show that he had heard. "Dexter. Now, Dexter. The sooner the better. A spark."

"Sure Roland," he said, but still did not draw his daggers.

"Just a spark, Dex. Then it's done."

"Of course, Roland."

"You all right, my friend?"

And the groans rose and rose and howls turned hungry and feral and they yelped now and something was hissing and there so many and they were so close now and I backed away and away on legs of water, for we had opened the gate to the world of the dead, and the dead would claim us. Suddenly, I was screaming.

"I'm fine, Roland."

"Then a spark, if you would."

"A spark," Dexter repeated absently.

"Just a quick spark, good Dexter," Roland said and I was screaming. "It'll be quick and good and beautiful dear friend and noble warrior, Protector of the Earth."

"I am that, aren't I, Roland?"

"You certainly are."

"The protector of the living earth."

"You are the best, Dexter. She is yours to cradle and cherish, to nurture and grow. But these weeds we must uproot from the garden."

"Yes, Roland," he said absently, distantly, staring into the shadow and they must be so close and I was screaming because he would let them out. I was screaming. I did not want to be dragged in. "We'll just burn them all up in there, Roland, right?"

"That's the plan, Dexter," Roland said, and we could hear the gnashing of teeth and I was screaming, the same thing, over and over I screamed, but Dexter stood still as ever, was a statue made of leaves. Why had I put such faith in them?

Roland then heaved the pole on his shoulder and walked up to stand beside Dexter. He stared into the pit below. "I suppose I could do this the old fashioned way, Dex, but it would be a shame to waste Bell's precious elixir. And then the place would stay polluted. Be worse so even. And who knows if they'll all come out?"

Dexter smiled dryly. "She would not be happy to hear of her blood wasted, Roland."

Roland shook his head. "No, she would not."

And I screamed my petition again and again, the one wish I had, if ever I had a wish.

"Burn them! Burn them! Please, please burn them!"

"Either way, my friend, no ogre's running out of this pit."

"I understand that, Roland. We'll just give a spark then."

"Yes."

"We'll just burn them up in there and then there will be fewer ogres and the battle will be better for the king of the North and the men of the earth, for the ogre will be less."

Roland sighed, "Yes. I think so. It's too complicated for me to discuss right now, but we have awakened something and need to resolve it. That's what's most important right now. You know they can be trained. You know the Southern king has been feeding them human flesh, catching them and training them; so, if we let these go today we just might meet them again in battle."

"But you can't know that," said Dexter, "of these sleeping."

Roland nodded and his frustration showed, but not his anger. "It's true. Okay, Dexter. Don't concern yourself over this. I'll take care of it. You'd best give me a little room."

A claw emerged from the opening, yellow-green and enormous, far larger than the one we had killed that morning, larger even than the one I'd encountered on the fields of grass. Roland walked quickly towards it and I kept screaming, for I did not want to be pulled in.

"Please burn it, burn it, please, please burn them!"

"Wait," said Dexter to Roland. "I have not forgotten our oath. So, I will just burn them up in there. This will be done by Dexter, Protector of the Earth. I will burn these creatures alive."

"Please do," said Roland, waiting. Dexter's hands draped upwards and at that Roland ran back, towards me, into the wind. He waved me down the hill. "Shut up and run!"

But I only staggered backwards. I wanted to see it, to know it would be done. Yet, when a yellow arm the width of a tree trunk reached out of the cave, clawed into the ground and lifted out a face that cannot be described, I ran off with Roland. In a moment there came from behind us an enormous explosion, and then a blast of heat at our backs.

The whole sky burned red for a breath, and then the howls arose, not of hunger or rage, but of agony. Howls turned to shrieks.

At the bottom of the hill, we turned and watched. The ogres poured out like skeletons dancing in fire. They fell dying on the hillside with their skin falling away or all gone and in fire looked entirely human. A small one emerged with fire sticking to every part of it. I slammed its hands against its skull as if to beat the flames from its face. A grown one rose from near ashes and charged behind it. This crushed the younger's skull. An end of pain. I tried very hard to imagine a man holding to such intent and could not.

It was a clear blue and beautiful day. The only cloud was death's exhalation rising gently from the cave. It flowed like a river of perdition, moving in a toxic slick to the south.

Soon, nothing moved within and about the cave but glowing embers. A quick count had twenty-three and there was nothing more to do. "Let's go," he said. "You did good."

"But, where's Dexter?"

"Don't worry about him. Let's get out of here."

We hurried away. We did not speak. We washed in the first stream and continued without rest until we reached the orchard. Roland began to eat a peach and he looked somehow older. "The best," he said, his mouth full. "Try one."

"I'm not hungry at all."

He nodded, one eye on the forest without. He told me not to worry.

"About what?"

"About anything."

"I'll try."

"Do not try. Do." I brushed the dust from my clothes. "Sometimes," he went on, "I wonder who made this place. These trees stand in rows no more. Generations since their planting, but still they grow just fine. Times I wonder who first broke this soil, what manner of world they knew. I imagine it was a peaceful time, but who can know?"

"Where's Dexter? Why didn't he come back with us?"

"We eat the fruit of the seed of the seed of the seed," he said, taking another bite. "That is, until the peach trees won't be here anymore. Until the forest claims it all again, except maybe for one or two, which is all there would have been in the beginning." He considered the peach and the perimeter of the orchard. "What you think the first seed a man ever planted was? And who then took what he'd sown, lay his hand upon the fruit and first called it 'mine?'"

"But where is he?"

"That must have been the beginning of war."

"He should have come back with us."

"Practiced by only the human and the ant."

"I haven't seen him since the fire."

"He's fine. He'll be around."

"You don't even know he's alive!" I cried out.

He faced me with a heaviness I'd not seen before. "He's alive. He's not like us. He can outrun the wind, fade into the mist, walk atop the flowing water, make the dead grass grow. He lives and if not, something else will happen. Balance will come. It must." He waved a finger at me. "Something scared you. The sooner you let it go, the sooner you can be free."

He was right, of course, but the day had just been too ghastly. Anyway, my throat burned in talking. As Dexter was who knows where, the ashes of ogre lay a hundred paces ahead, and a plume of smoky death floated in the sky behind, and Belladonna left in tears and rage and anything, absolutely anything, could be waiting in the forest without. And I didn't know these people. Strangers. Now an arm draped lazily over his knee, pole resting invisible in the grass, and he was chewing, content in the day.

"Your mind dwells too much on the past, including the events of the morning, but nothing remains to be done. It's a trick old warriors learn: let it go. A fought battle is a simple thing, a thing done, won or lost, it's over. Why is it people got to make everything so fucking complicated?" He plucked another peach and continued with lunch. I scratched my name into the dirt and read it.

"Every day," I told him, "I think of Selador of which I can know nothing. Every day, I wonder where I'll sleep once I can no longer sleep where I am. Every day, I wonder what's going to get me, what the next fight will be."

He sighed. "Listen, life gives nothing to mortals without great effort. If you are to survive this quest of yours, you must be resolved. If you are to free Selador, well, it seems you must kill 'em all off, the invaders. No mercy, no remorse. All of them. For if even one gets word back that king will send enough forces to run you and yours off the earth."

"Selador's not that important to him."

"It will be if you do that. He doesn't like to lose ground. It'd be on principle. Perhaps the old man will have another plan. I don't know, but they're not going to leave because you give them candy. I don't know. We could do it after this, but I can't ask them to go all that way, not for a cause like that, not when you have no money."

"You might not all live anyway."

"Oh, we'll live. We can't lose."

"Are you so invincible?"

Roland chuckled. "We can't lose, Kid, because if we lose it's the end of the world." He then continued to turn the peach into a pit. I stared at the patterns scratched in the dry earth imagining them swirls in an endless sky, or caves to buried, secret worlds, and then thought of Selador.

"The woodsman were going on three days lost. He'd gone in too deep, got turned around, and in those lands unseen by most, hears a small groan like a squirrel in a snare. Maybe it's some dinner for him. But it's got a strange call, off somehow, unnatural even for a thing in pain. He'd never heard the likes of it for all his years. He follows it to thick bramble and waits, as the call were so strange. Sometimes great things have small voices. But then he prys apart the bramble with a stick, for on them grew thorns as long as your finger, and who knows what waits within?

"Well, he almost screams then, for in the heart of that bramble were a tiny man-like thing, wholly impaled upon them thorns. They ran through its back and poked out of its heaving chest. A gnome! He'd never thought them real, but there it were, life running out like falling water."

"Gosh!" said the boy.

"Yes," said the woman. "Wait," she said, rising from the couch. The cold of the room crept to his side in her absence. She crouched before the hearth and moved the black iron kettle in deeper, stoked the flames and the steam from the kettle rose out into the flue to the chill of the night. The tea would help them sleep. The room brightened with warmth. When she sat beside him again, she exhaled loudly. She was not young. "Well, he waits a time, for his heart could not believe his eyes, lets the bramble close around it and the groaning stops then, and he thinks maybe he were just dreaming, or he seen it wrong. Perhaps was a featherless chick from a fallen nest, a fetal ape mis-birthed. Anything it could'a' been. 'Then why you so afraid to glance again?' he asks himself, for he knew he'd listened to fear. So, he summons his courage and returns to the bush and with shaking hands draws the curtain a thorns apart, and there it were still, as real as the moon."

The boy stared into the lifting fire, his mind upon another world.

"Now, it's all quiet, not groaning not nothing. It lifts it's head and looks straight at the woodsman with eyes that were, but for their size, most human. And they were pleading with him, those eyes. 'Help' they say. And then this thing, this gnome, reaches out a blood-soaked hand no bigger than a doll's and the woodsman knows then it were no beast. Knows if he left it to die it'd rest on his mind forever, for sorry is the man who can't forgive himself."

"Using more courage than you might imagine, he presses into the spines of the bramble and with his heart ready to burst, lifts it free from its bed of agony with trembling fingers. Once free, the thing starts coughing up blood, too much, for a few drops would be half its life. A wet cry of pain escapes it, one as such turns the woodsman's blood cold, and he thinks it all done, for when a man coughs blood there nothing to be done for it. He would leave it there on a bed a leaves and let it pass in peace, but it starts speaking quick, with strange words in a voice that cannot be described: something like a human and something like a bird. It points then. It points the way to go."

"Gosh."

She nods. *"Indeed. Now, the woodsman looks but sees no path, nothing, but he follows the way it pointing. Soon, they come to a wood the likes a which the cutter never seen before. Strange flowers grew. Gray, quiet birds perched on low branches, warbling soft, ancient songs never heard by man. Trees start growing real close, so that the sun could scarce be seen. Soon, he has to walk bent, and then even crawl on knees and elbows, (for his hands held the little one). Every so often the gnome points the way, each time lifting its arm less. It's growing cold in his hand and he knows it almost done for. No small part of him wishing it were. And might be they have magic to heal it, or might be he bringing it but to die among its own."*

"They come to a kind of tunnel made of leaves and vine, and it's dark and darker in there, and quiet too. He wants to just drop it and leave, for from that tunnel one could never hope to see the sun, but he wants more to wash its blood away. The creature points onward down the shadow path."

"Is the gnome trying to trap him?"

"Let me tell the story."

"Okay."

"Are you cold?"

"No."

"Ready for tea?"

"After the story."

"Very well, Child. They come at last to a kind of wall, but is the bark of a great tree. The gnome cries out then, but it's voice were so weak now. Nothing happens. The woodsman counts his breaths, for night is falling fast. He wants to go very badly. There's something terrible about it all he can't understand but feels in his bones. He feels the tunnel pressing in around him as it just screams again and again, lifting its pale and crimson hand against the door, knocking. At last, the woodsman, he's done. Sets it right there gently down and turns away. It howls so terribly then, begins weeping by its fashion."

"Did he run off?"

"I'm going to tell you. Just as he were about to run off, a creaking sound comes from the tree, and a tiny door, once invisible, opens out of the bark. A yellow light floods the tunnel. The woodsman, too amazed to even run, sees shadows block the light within and suddenly they emerge from the tree: little people, just like the one who'd fallen. With one eye on the giant looming above, they retrieve their wounded and carry him in. When they close the door the tree is but a tree again, and the tunnel falls dark and natural. The woodsman runs his hand along the bark and feels no door, no seam."

With her right arm she held him tight, hoping life would be kind to him at last. *"Now, he were too amazed to run just then, and so were there when the door opens again and that yellow light burns from within, so bright like gold. But this time the door opens wider and wider, until the woodsman could pass his shoulders through. Silhouettes turn to little men and they emerge and gesture for him to enter the tree. They would grant him the privilege to see what had been forever hidden from human eyes: the secret world of the gnome."*

The boy stared into the fire with wonder: *"And what did he do then, Aunty? Did he go?"*

She smiled as warm as the hearth. *"Well, what would you have done?"*

"Do you think he will just go there and kill them?"

"I've no idea. He's a warrior, however, or was. I know that much. He might do nothing. I won't lie to you."

"But the dragon's tooth?"

"What of it?"

"I thought…" My words broke off and I wept.

"I really don't know what he'll do," Roland said gently. "The dragon thing is your story. I can only tell you what I know. I'm not even certain he's up there still, although I believe so. Are you all right?"

"Yes."

"He can fight like no other, however...you sure you're all right?"

"Yes."

"He could clear out your village single-handedly if he wished, if he would. Listen, don't assume so much. You have the sky upon your back it seems. You're not responsible for this all. Just take it as it comes and accept what happens."

"I promised I would try."

"And so you are! What's more, the end of your promise nears. Nothing lies beyond Gin. I tell you that. If he's not your sage then sages never were. You're tired."

"Very."

He watched clouds race across endless sky. "We'll give you a little training and off you go. There's not the time to train you properly."

"Is it true that they're invincible?"

"Gin? Sages? I've yet to meet the force that can bring him down, except maybe Dexter."

"You've been to battle with him?"

"Against him, my father mostly, but yes." A shadow ran across his face. I regretted the question too late. "They were strange times and they are gone. 'Do not burden your remembrance with a heaviness that is gone,' my father would say, and he's right. Gin's one of the good ones I think. Why are you still crying?"

"I don't know."

He took up the pole and scanned the whole of the orchard before leaving with those long strides of his. As he walked off, he spun the pole above him so it cut the air in a whoosh of blinding speed. "You can return here anytime now," he called back to me. "They're all gone and the peaches are delicious. They've no nest to hide in anymore and any stragglers Dexter will pick out."

"I don't want to come back here," I called.

"As you wish! It all is as you wish!"

Dexter returned in the evening. I saw his miniature shadow while staring out the window at the waterfalls of the cliff. "Hello," he said to me, his voice as if he stood in the room.

"How are you, Dexter?"

The moon was so bright I could see him shrug. "As I have been."

"I thought you might be dead."

"That was considerate of you."

"I didn't think you could outrun the fire."

"Roland told me you were worried about that."

He hopped atop the half collapsed stone railing about the court and balanced along its edge. He then unsheathed two knives as silver as the night, played with them. They danced like nothing, nothing I had ever seen. They became flecks of starlight which he could toss higher than the house. He would strike a thousand points in a breath, have their metal sing and chime, scratch a rainbow in the dark, disappear the weapons into his hand and cloak. He stilled then. His gaze went to the ground.

"It was a hard day for you!" I called down.

"They're only ogre," he said. "Their life is suffering. We did us all a kindness."

"You can come up here if you like."

Without a sound, he raced across the courtyard and up the wall. He stood on the sill. I laughed. "Please take a seat Dexter."

He bowed slightly and sat cross-legged on the sill. He pointed to my tunic.

"That's an interesting garment. Is it from a trader? These days, anything can be sold."

"It was gift."

He tilted his tiny head and scratched his little chin upon which grew just a hint of beard. "A gift? May I ask from whom?"

"A friend. She wove it for me."

He sat very still at my words. "Your, you say your friend wove this garment for you?"

"Yes."

"That cannot be."

"I don't lie unless I have to."

"Of course. I did not mean…But it cannot be. Your friend has told you a story I believe. How does it dry?"

"Instantly."

"Does it keep you cool in the heat and warm in the cold?"

"Yes."

"And its colors fade to what stands behind you when you wish to hide?"

"Yes."

"Humans cannot weave as this. Your friend could not have made it. It is of elven make. We put our love of the earth into every thread and these we draw from most all things that grow, and so the cloth can do and become almost anything. It is called weaving the harmony of chaos, an art both ancient and sacred. Humans cannot weave as such. Please speak truthfully, where did you get it? You are in no danger. You are not my enemy, so tell me, Brother, how did you obtain the cloak?"

"It was given me by my friend," I said again, "Lyden."

He gasped then, held his little stomach with his little hand. It seemed I could knock him off the sill with a feather. "Dexter, are you all right?"

"Lyden? Did you say Lyden?"

"Yes."

"How…how could you know this name?"

I told him.

"How do you know it was truly Lyden?"

"I don't. She said this. She was indescribably beautiful, and unlike you, very tall with white hair."

"White hair? You mean like an old woman's?"

"No," I said, "white like starlight."

"This is her. This is her. This is not possible, that Lyden would walk with a man. This cannot be. He held his tiny hand upon his panting chest and then curled up his knees and collapsed his face into their fold. "It… Lyden she…she walked with a man?"

"Yes. With me, yes."

He wept for a time and I let him. I understood. At last he lifted his gaze. "What…" he asked, broken in grief, "what, did, did she ever speak of me?"

"Oh. Well, she never told me much of the elves. She said I shouldn't know."

He nodded quickly. "I...of course. You are human. Of course, of course she would not speak of it with you because you are just a human. You should not know. You should not you have not the privilege."

He shook his head. His tears ran without check and his nose hung with blue snot. "No. My name. My true name. I will tell you and only you my true name and then we will know if she in all that time with you spoke it but once."

"Oh no you won't," said Roland, emerging from the hall. "You two are making a lot of noise for an elf and a man who lives by hiding. He said she never mentioned anyone Dex, so no need to break the rules now."

Dexter only panted in despair, closed his hands to fists of white granite and shook in unspoken rage. "How could she say nothing of me to one for whom she weaves a cloak!" he screamed, hysterical. Roland slowly stepped towards the window and lifted his hand in appeasement.

"Easy Dexter. Just go easy my friend. It'll be all right."

"No! No Roland, no! How could I not once be mentioned in all the days she shared with him? How could our life together go unsaid for so long?"

"It doesn't mean you weren't in her heart. It'll be fine."

"It's already ruined!"

"To say your true name now would be a terrible risk."

He stood upon the window sill a small fire of ferocity and rage and grief, his voice carried so loud now it could have shattered the stone walls of the house itself. "No Roland, No! As if elves ever have to worry for the direct assault of man! Tell me, Son of Man, Brother of the Covenant, did Lyden ever speak of....." and here he screamed a name which Roland made me swear never to repeat. In the devastating silence which followed, I could not tell him 'no,' so I shook my head.

It was like he'd been punched in the gut. The fire died in him. His hands went loose. He closed his eyes, and then let himself fall from the window. He landed with a thud on the stone flagging below.

"Fuck," said Roland. "Fuck Fuck Fuck!"

Looking down we saw him rise with the aid of his arms, and limp slowly away into the forest he so adored.

"Teach him so he can go."

"What's your rush?"

"He needs to leave. I don't like him here. He's not a true warrior anyway, just a wanderer with an unusual knife. What could he do against a fell army? Please," she huffed, *"Prepare his hands and set him off! One less man against me."*

"Do you think we're against you Bell?"

She folded her arms carved of wood and pouted. *"Sometimes I just don't know, Roland. I never know. Sometimes I fear you wanted only a daughter of the Phoenix."*

"No, Belladonna. That's not fair. Never. Yes, I needed a Phoenix, at least eventually, but it could have been any of them. And though none excel you in the wielding of a sword, I did not need to love you. Why would I do that?"

"To get me to surrender more. To fight more passionately. Men, you are so weak. You can never handle the truly difficult sacrifices. The lasting pain. Your crew would not be enough without Belladonna and you wanted her heart to make sure she stayed." She turned quickly away and cried at her vanity. She traced the curves of a jade dragon of jade she had found in the ruin of the house. She had cleaned it in creek water and moonlight, and wanted so badly to gift it to Roland, but knew it so dangerous for a woman to let a man know how much she truly loved him. *"What do you truly want me for more, Roland?"*

"What kind of question is that, Bell? Do you know what kind of question that is? How can I ever answer that but to say that I love you?"

"Get rid of him if you love me. Do you love me truly, Roland?"

"Belladonna, I tell you so every day."

She wiped her tears upon the sculpted dragon. *"But how can I ever know?"*

"Because I would die for you."

"You would die for many."

"But only happily for you."

She wept into her hands. *"Would you surrender the medusa for my life?"*

He waited. He knew not to lie. "No. It would be the same as killing you."

"Would you wish to live at all without me, Roland?"

He sighed, "Don't ask me so much, Belladonna. I'm only a man."

She heaved into cries then and pushed the dragon away from her table to the floor. It would have shattered had Roland not slid his foot under the fall. "Will you ever understand me Roland?" Her face collapsed into her hands, tears running between her fingers.

"I don't know," he said honestly.

"Why won't you try. Just try a little. Please Roland. Please try to understand a woman who holds your heart nearly as much as the medusa."

"That's not fair, Bell."

"When have I ever had fairness? How dare you speak of fairness to me."

"You understand the importance of our project."

"Is that all I am to you? A project?"

And he knew there was no winning this.

In a shaded room we rested our arms up to the elbow in what he called "punching wine."

"It soaks into the skin and acts as a kind of brace. It heals bruises and broken bones. We use it before training to protect ourselves and afterwards to heal. Now lift your arms out and rub it in until they feel smooth."

"What's in this stuff?"

"A lot of patience. It should be twenty years old at least. My father made this particular vat and I can't imagine a better one. There's a recipe of herbs and the alcohol, but the secret ingredient, the one in which the real magic lies, rests at the bottom of the vessel: the skull of the dragon...strong, strong stuff!"

I thought he was lying when my arms began to tingle. A definite energy coursed along the flesh. "And how did your father acquire a dragon skull, Roland?"

"He killed one."

I stopped rubbing in the wine. "Your father did?"

"Yes he did. Not alone, of course, but he was the leader of our clan and this he did. Was a dragon in the North, north of here."

"What was its name?"

"We never asked. Each leader should kill one during his reign," he said, looking forlorn at his reflection, broken in the dark and silent brew. "Not me, however. We'd disbanded before we had the time. Our little kingdom, scattered. There just wasn't time. It's a mistake to always think there will be enough. Tomorrow's not a promise. Anyway, my father killed this one and my grandfather one before him and so on. They say our great great grandfather got two in his reign, but dragons were more plentiful then. Anyway, now, the art of hunting them is lost. It doesn't matter anymore anyway. Rub it in more then dip and repeat."

"How many times?"

He didn't answer. "It's not just for this. Almost every bodily part has a purpose. Our warriors each eat some dust from the heart yielding fantastic vitality. Few drops of blood in your wine cures many things. The eye is said to bring prophecy. The meat of its leg, you can run like the deer. A bite of its tongue helps in speaking spells. A sheild made from its scales cannot be shattered. Arrow tip cut from its bone will pierce stone. Was the gifts of the dragon that made our clan so invincible That tooth you have," he shook his head, "that there is quite a thing. Never saw one quite like it. Can only imagine what can be done with that."

"Do you know the language of the birds?"

"What's that?"

"The language of the birds?" I repeated, feeling silly. He did not laugh.

"Can't say I do, Kid. That's enough. Now dip and work it in again. You're incredibly lucky to have found one, a dragon."

"I'm just going to give it away." A surge of raw energy ran from my elbows to finger tips. "Wow!" Roland grinned in that funny way of his and then gave a distant look.

"I'd be a rich man if went down there and plucked out the rest. Dragon parts are very, very rare these days. My family used to deal in exotics. Just a piece of dragon's worth ten white tigers, and not too many of them left either." He rubbed his arms more and more briskly and his face hardened into what could only be described as regret."But the times change and we are changed in them. The animals became more scarce and so did we. For reasons I cannot know, the fucking ogre multiplied and multiplied again, eating every damned thing that crossed their path. We'd find the carcass of a common dear half-eaten, rotted with some ghastly disease and you had to just leave it off. We'd find a gutted tiger and you couldn't even skin its fur. Contaminated. Sick. And then that damned war and…Ah well."

"I could never find it again."

Roland squinted at this. "You don't have to lie. I don't want to know. But if you did, you'd find him right where you left him. They can sleep for years, decades even. Although, some believe they awake and travel in secret caves that run beneath the world, swim in black and silent seas forever hidden from our sight. Don't you worry. I ply my trade as a soldier for hire, and the worst of battle is light compared to dragging the beast out its nest. You've never seen a woken dragon. I have. This very one." He nodded towards the vat. "It's a hell of a thing and real tricky work. First, the archers need to blind it. They can't miss. If they do, many more are lost. An awoken dragon flails its head like a tempest, screams like the falling sky. Some say the flyers spew fire, but not so. Myth. This was a flyer. We blinded it and then took a wing, severed the left straight off. It's critical to do this. You cannot let it fly. If it flies, you lose. You hold them down with these special hooks thrown along the spine I remember. Roll them sideways then and split the belly and wait."

"For what?"

"For it to die."

"So you have hunted one?"

"Not really. I was a kid in the back flank, lobbing useless arrows against scales of granite. Everyone said how brave I was, what a fine job I'd done. But my father was king of our little part of the world, and as such lead the hunt and would divide the spoils, which he did generously mind you, always giving extra to the widows of those lost." He shrugged. "I suppose there were better ways to act in this life. Some say the dragons are gods of a sort, and by slaying them my clan brought a curse upon itself. Who ever knows? But I, one nursed on the creature's blood, fed its meat and shielded in its scales, never wish to slay another. Let the few that remain sleep until the world ends." He looked into the ground, eyes filled with memory. "We ready?"

"Ready," I said.

"Let's get to punching."

"Yes!"

"I wish we had more time, but I don't wish for things anymore. I just make do. "

And so the training began that morning. We started softly. Roland taught that all of these practices were 'soft' by nature and to be careful. We began every morning by soaking our arms and hands in the vat of dragon brew and Roland said this would protect them from any damage, as would the gradual build up of the conditioning. "Don't go slamming your hand against a brick wall hoping it'll make you tough. You could ruin your reproductive organs. You could go blind or worse. Just do as I teach you."

"Right."

And so I would spend days crushing a bag of dried beans to powder, river stones to gravel, striking granules of iron. I stabbed my fingers into vats of fire-heated sand, into cold river gravel, into water and then at last into shredded brass. In this way I conditioned my hands so that the skin could not be cut, so that they could crush stone and bone and destroy the enemy.

"When your palm is conditioned enough, I will teach you to rupture any major organ of your enemy in a strike. When your fingers are conditioned, I will teach you to blind him in a strike. I will teach you how to cause a hemorrhage to the brain, split his skull, anything. You will be able to do most anything in a simple kind of way. There are numerous forms in my lineage, and a man could spend a lifetime perfecting just a part of one, but for you I will pick what might be the most useful of them, a fraction of a fraction of what we would impart to the least of our warriors. You need to survive to the North, to utter a message to an old man who might have something we need and they want. Hopefully, you won't need any of this. Hopefully, you will not need to fight. But even if you do not, this training will strengthen your body and sharpen your mind, and that alone may be its service."

I did not ask too many questions, but some I needed to know.

"Roland?"

"Yes?"

"How can I go blind just by hitting my hand, make a heart stop with a strike?"

"When you were very, very little, a parasite floating in your mama's tummy, everything, in its way, connected to everything else.

The connections are still there, whether you know how to find them or not."

"I see."

He scanned the land in all directions and then turned to the creek. He pointed to the clear pool from where we retrieved most of our water. "That pool is not fed from there, but by waters which begin way up in the mountains. It runs through rocky channels and valleys, even under the ground until it gets to us here. But, if you truly understood the water and its flow, you could pour a poison in way far away and have it kill us here if you knew when we would sip from this stream. But don't dwell on it. I won't teach this to you. It takes too much time. Let's train."

"This looks like a punch, and it is, but strike to the temple and it kills. A simple kick to the center of the sternum and it sends splinters into the heart. Hold your fingers like so and strike with the tip of the center knuckle to crack the rib. Then twist to separate the ribs. The tendons will sever. This strike, if delivered with enough force, punctures the lung with splinters of rib. Strike here with the elbow to rupture the kidney. This brings death. With this kick you separate the knee cap and the opponent collapses. Hit here, on the neck in back, here, and with properly conditioned palms the opponent suffers instant paralysis in all limbs. Remember that because sometimes opponents are in a drugged frenzy only death or paralysis stops. Remember that especially if it's an ogre."

"This removes both eyes at once. Extend the arm more...like so. Try again... No, not like that. Here," he pointed to his own face, "here, in this corner, drive the fingers in there and the eyes will pop right out. Too wide. Try again. Extend more and anchor the back leg. Good, much better. To stab just one eye make the hand into the claw of the dragon like I showed you. Keep the finger hooked. No. Like this. Good. The eye should dangle. Catch it by the corner and rip it out. Good. The eye will separate like a button hanging from a thread. Extend the arm more. Better. Hiss. Hiss and strike. Good. Arm, fingers, foot, hiss. Good. There you go. Careful not to hit the bones of the skull. Aim for the softness of the eye. Good.

The training went on almost every day. Sometimes Roland seemed rushed and frustrated and other times very calm. He would have long talks with Dexter or Belladonna over matters I did not know and often, while I sweated and trained, some of the crew watched lazily watched from the distance. Sometimes, Dexter would be there, and other times be gone for days. On a rare occasion I would catch a glimpse of one of the Iga, but almost never in the day.

I spoke very little to the others. The days raced away, some quick and some endless. Sometimes the training would be so painful I thought the sun stopped in the sky; but with it came a certain peace, and very soon, too soon, I felt quite invincible. Near the end, I could kill a man with a single strike at least a hundred different ways, or so I thought. My hands felt carved of oak, my forearms of iron. I felt invincible yet this was absurd.

"Don't use these fingers for ogre. You can't take a chance of even a scratch. Use your knife first, but if you are empty handed, a quick kick to the knee or throat, or if you have to, a hand strike to the throat - but then back off. Run. If it gets too close and extends its arm at you, side step and with that hardened palm deliver a nice upwards slap to the elbow to break it. The other arm would be useless then. Don't even worry about the other arm. Even an ogre wouldn't be able to hit you with the other when you crunch the first. The pain is immediate and hard to imagine. Only use strikes that do not draw blood with them. It can't bleed on you. Avoid its teeth like death. You slice your skin against them and show is over. Death in fevered madness."

One day Roland asked me to draw the blade. "Practice with it. You're stronger now, and though you can fight without it, it should still be your first line of defense. I don't want you to forget how to use it."

It did not sing as brightly as it once had. In truth, it sang a little less with every day of travel, and I could not say whether the stone had some attachment to the place which had bore it, or I was simply slipping in my skills without Gelidii's patient corrections. But even Roland was surprised at the songs when they came, and with a puzzled look admitted the strikes were like nothing he had ever seen before, yet he wondered why I spun in the same point.

"Because it is forbidden for Picarin to attack. They will only kill what can kill them, and so they wait until the enemy is within reach."

Roland shook his head and huffed. "What if the enemy hurls a spear at them?"

"They cut the spear."

"An arrow? Can this picarin cut an arrow, a cloud of arrows rushing through the air?"

"Yes it can," I said.

Roland squinted. "Can you?"

"No."

"Well then maybe you should take a couple of steps with that thing in hand. Try and combine those weird squirrely cuts you do with it with some of the footwork I showed you. Don't do anything too fancy. That thing will rip your gut out before you feel it. Keep it simple, but tricky. Simple, but fast. I like them. It looks good. I want you to spend each morning combining what I have taught you with that blade."

And this I did. For all I know, I am the first being to combine the strikes of the Picarin with footwork other than spinning in single point with an occasional kick from that same point. In a sense, I developed a style of combat the world had never known.

Roland said one day, "They look good. You look fine. You're almost ready."

"Great," I said. I didn't want to go. "So now what?"

"Now we fight."

He raised his hands and I mine. He fell upon like a storm of stones that pelted from every side. I let the storm rage in its course, blocked what I could, stood my ground. At last, I fought back. No strike landed. He swatted them off, blocked or parried, avoided them altogether. I lunged to grab his arms, to quiet him, steady him, stop him from punching me with fist of granite; but he drew me off balance by the elbow, and then leaned and hit me in the ribs with the heel of his palm. They did not break but almost broke. He followed this with a kick in the gut and I reeled back unbreathing and Belladonna had been watching from her balcony and now she reeled in the ecstasy of pure delight. "Make him more fierce Roland, my Love! You are doing wonderful Roland! The best instructor! Make his heart like fire! Hurt him my love! Ground him into the earth! Teach him so wonderfully well!" When he swept my ankles and knocked me down with a leopard's paw to the chest, Belladonna could not help but clap.

Roland waved her off and me towards him. I charged too quickly. Reckless. He stepped to the side and guided me into the dry, stony soil and it ground into my skin and ripped up a good part of my face and I was bleeding where my face and lips had crashed into the earth and Belladonna laughed deliriously and hopped as she applauded. Roland placed his hands on his hips and waited.

"Ready?"

I wouldn't answer. I had to trick him. How does one trick a warrior of a thousand battles, one who taught you all you knew save for a weapon forbidden?

"Use your sins."

I charged at him, right hand raised as if to strike. He stepped aside and threw me to the ground again. I knew he would do that, but not that he would also punch me in the fat of the leg muscle, making it go most dead. Breathing in the soil again, it occurred to me how long it had been since it rained. He leapt through the air then, arms churning like a tumbling hawk, and upon landing slammed an elbow into my gut. Having no breath at all is very bad for fighting. Even though I didn't need it just then, he decided to grab my windpipe and squeeze. Roland had the ability to connect his fingers on the other side and then pull. The proper execution of this technique, he said, immediately leads to cessation of hostilities, among other things.

"Roland! Crush his ribs! Break his throat! Oh bleed him out my Love, ruin him!"

"Bell! Stop that" Scolded, she huffed and folded her arms, pouting. He let me go.

"But how should he ever learn if you are but gentle?"

"Leave that to me, Bell."

"If our task truly needs the likes of him we are all in great peril, my dearest, dearest Prince Roland!"

"Listen Bell, we don't need him for…" and then, with his focus on her, from his blind side I swung my newly conditioned forearm into his jaw. He reeled back and staggered, threw a kick that did not connect as I did not follow, had even backed away. He nursed his jaw. Only after some time could he laugh. I waited for retaliation that never came.

"Good. Good hit. You're a sneaky one. Sneaky and vicious. That's good. Use that. Enough for today I think. Wash up and then rub the brew on your wounds. You're about as ready as we have for."

We bowed and parted as Belladonna cheered for the show, laughed deliriously at my wincing pain. She beseeched the departing

Roland to turn back and see me limping towards the creek. She had never seen a man so very beaten from "simple play!" Roland did not turn to see me walk away but I watched him go. No superlative warrior retired from that field, no iron tiger who swatted away legion like flies. Instead, an old man stood in Roland's clothes, his shoulders curved and covered, with a slow step and downward glance seeking how to lighten the burden of this world upon the back, how to free the remembrance from a heaviness that is gone.

As I applied the medicine to half my body, soothing aches that started in my core, I realized how much I did not want go.

And for whatever reason, after that day, Belladonna never mocked me again.

That night I thought of the roadless earth. I'd become accustomed to the company of others, to a house and home I did not want to leave although I must. Yet, as the day of departure neared, it became harder to sleep, for with each day closer my heart fanned an ember of fear.

It takes a long time for sleep to come to a mind full and body bruised. Some time before dawn my eyes opened for the thousandth time, turned to the eye of the window and it had come again, the visitor of spidery limbs, hunched and waiting, a hairless egg of narrow skull tilted and thinking, silent as shadow. It watched motionless and watched me and I did not move. I did not want to know if I were awake, but at last whispered a question to which I knew the answer.

"Gelidii ... is that you?"

I willed myself to consciousness. It was not fading as it should. Only when a groan rose from the struggle did it lean back and descend into the darkness which bore it. Eventually, I peeked out the window. The peaceful race of water cutting white below and nothing more. "Are you one of them?" I called to the nothingness. "Why do you come to me?"

And it took a long time to answer that question. Too much time. Even if a picarin were near why would it know of me? Perhaps they had in their kin a magic communion unknown to all else, a way of speaking messages through birds or winged creatures of the night? So many fantasies came and went that at last it had to be just a dream, until some years later a perfectly simple answer popped into my head.

It hears the knife

The drought began to kill everything. The stream ran low showing rock and plant, all its white swiftness gone. The waterfalls had dried on the cliff. The whole forest seemed to curl and die. Dexter commented on the drought only once: "People did this. They cut too much away. They have twisted things. People have put things where they do not belong. Droughts like this never used to happen." And I did not want to tell him they always did, and I did not want to tell him that even the most powerful magic of man cannot hold back the rain, and so I did not.

On a night shortly before departure the eldest of the Iga stepped beside me. He moved as silent as the moon. I had been training with the blade which sung differently according to the phase, now a waxing crescent, swift and sharp and one of my favorites.

The Iga wore only black and kept mostly their own company. If they spoke to anyone else it was usually to Roland, and this only when necessary. But now he had stepped out from the shadow and pointed to the blade and then to the moon. "They are sister and brother," he said, and I nodded and smiled. He made me uneasy. "I can hear them talking. You will do well to battle at night if you must go into battle. Your weapon prefers this."

"Oh?"

"So it seems," he said, and considered the eternal pattern of the stars. "The approaching armies have slowed from thirst and hunger. This is good for you. This sky blesses few, but it does good for you. Rivers will be more easily crossed. Your boat will run swifter. Stay near water when you go."

"I will see."

"But first do not get lost. He has much hope in you, more than you know. Do not get lost. You will perish if you do."

"I've been told."

"The heath monster will be very happy if you get lost. He is very hungry in the season of your crossing. It will smell you from very, very far on the waste of ice and hunt you and eat you. Make only small fires and hide the light. Bath in its ashes each morning."

"I will," I said, thinking of it.

"Hope I'm not interrupting?" asked Roland entering the courtyard.

"No," I said and the Iga said nothing.

"Good. We're going to have a nice dinner for you seeing how it's your last night and such. We have proper clothing for you, for the cold. Winter's coming and it gets cold and colder up there. Do not discard them, heavy as they are. You will need them dearly and soon, and when you do, you will be glad for them. Dexter will accompany you to the end of the second valley and there he will show you where we have our little craft hidden. The boat will carry you through most of the journey. You'll glide through terrain all but uncrossable on foot. We'll give you all the provisions you can carry, but take all you can from the land. Dexter will show you what he can as he walks you out."

"Okay. And when it's all done, can I come back here?"

"Listen, we won't be here long. When this last deed is done, when the medusa is slipped past the armies, we won't be coming back. We will part ways. This house will be empty."

"I see."

"After this, we go to what homes we have. I suggest you do the same."

"I understand."

On the last day all my possessions were secured. The entire crew waited at the table. Roland spoke to all but it seemed they had little to say to each other. The repast, a mixture of wild game, candies, a medley of vegetables and fruits, was laid out on ancient plates of shimmering white and blue glass. We had cups of silver and pitchers of water and wine, tea and nectar. I had never seen a fork before. In Selador we ate with our hands, save for soup, which we ate with a spoon. I still prefer to eat this way, and there is a method to it which is not important to explain, but it is a very neat and civil way to eat and not messy as some people think.

But Roland and the crew, save for Dexter, did not use the forks much, remnants of the house, but ate with two small sticks also made of silver. Roland held them like the beak of the bird. One of the younger Iga would show me multiple ways the silver stock could be utilized as a most lethal weapon for penetrating the softer parts of the flesh. I took two with me. It took me a long time to master the art of eating with them but I did, and now practice it still. Everyone ate except for Dexter who, throughout the entirety of the dinner, sipped only a small cup of milky blue tea of his own making.

No matter where I go or have been I note the custom of giving thanks to divinity before eating. In Selador they said the practice had always been there, but began in earnest after the third year of the great drought. They said at that time even the jungle below yellowed and hardly a birdsong could be heard in the leaves. Selador itself began to die away, first the sick and the very old and then the very young; but then even the strong began to die, not from thirst, but starvation. Water to drink is one thing but water for crops quite another. The air near the burial ground always hung sweet with incense. My aunt said it became so common the scent still makes her ill at ease. When the rains returned at last, many in Selador had abandoned the gods and I thought something similar had happened to the crew, for they simply began to devour the magnificent meal. But I would learn from Belladonna that Roland had forbidden all outward worship for any of the crew.

"Your hearts and minds belong wholly to you. This is my belief and yours to the extent I have come to know you, but let your prayers be spoken only in whispers, let your piety be hidden in the most inner folds of your heart. What divinity lacks ears to hear us wherever we may be? What deity is so jealous as to need such tangible gestures of smoke and sacred chant if they should distract us from the service of this most dire of missions? While you choose to remain among this crew, always recognize we are comprised of disparate entities to say the least. So much so, that what is holy to one may be profane to another, that the most sacred act of one may to another be a childish superstition. We cannot be blamed for not understanding that part of the other well. We are warriors, not philosophers. Our teaching has been in the art of combat, not the embrasure of paradox. I have already heard mockery among you and I will not hear it again. We cannot afford a loss of respect among us. This to the dissolution of our unity and that cannot happen."

He waited a moment. No one else had anything to say. "Our only true unity is the medusa, and I would not say she should be our god. Therefore, in any and all shared grounds, from this moment forward, let there be no practice of magic, no obeisance to the divine, no reading of auguries or tracing of signs in the stars, calculations of magical numbers nor bestowing of blessings or hurling of curses; no names of the holy shall be murmured in protection save beneath one's breath. We have thrown ourselves by our own free will to fight for the sake of those born in centuries not yet named, if such times ever come. We have surrendered ourselves this greatest act of love and piety. What god or gods would ever ask more? And if they should, would they be worth your devotion?"

He sighed. He was uncertain. He hated talking about what he could not hold in his hands. "And so I demand of you all that the her destruction be your only religion while counted in this number. I wish for you all to return safe to your homes, and once there you are free to dedicate the balance of your lives to the service of the divine if your heart so inclines, but for now we cannot risk division. We have agreed all that children not yet born deserve a world of breathing grass and soft seas, of skies that shed gentle rains, given by clouds that have not collapsed in stone. That is your only common prayer and promise."

He said no more about it.

I left with Dexter just before dawn. Roland gave me a simple goodbye. The Iga stood on the outskirts of the near forest and bowed as I departed. Belladonna's form blocked the candlelight of her window.

"It's going to rain at last ," Dexter said.

"But there are no clouds at all."

"You will. Be careful of cold rain as you go north and the season turns."

"I will."

He looked at me quizzically. Such an odd face, not unpleasant but strange. "Did you learn much with us?"

"Oh yes."

"What have you learned?"

"That I don't want to be alone again."

"Loneliness is a disease, especially for humans."

"And what of elves?"

"We are not like you. We can commune with all living things. Our lives are very long. In our service to her protecting this world sometimes requires us to bear great spans of time alone, but then I suppose we can speak to all and so are not really alone, though sometimes it feels that way."

"How long do you live?"

"This is our secret. Ah well, I can tell you that some, (but few, very few), have been killed. Some have lived already incredible ages. Some have decided to return to the dust. We arrows of the gods are made to last!" he exclaimed and grinned mischievously. "When I stop the northern army, they won't know what hit them. And they sure won't hit back."

"Why don't the elves destroy the medusa?"

He scratched his head. He had woven blue and red petals in his hair. He had coated his neck with flakes of metallic dust. Squirrels constantly followed him, and he could catch them, and make them come and run away.

"Our strength is not unlimited. Plus, she is ancient magic, very strong. Ancient humans set her loose and only humans understand her as much as it may be understood. And none but the Phoenix nurse the fire of her ruin. But I know that she cannot simply be smashed or burned or buried, not if you would have rid of it once and for all. And who can leave a thing like her undone? But I will play a part in her destruction." He smiled at me and winked. "It's nice to work together," he said, and reached up to pat me on the back.

We moved quickly, yet Dexter paused often to show plants that were edible or had some other use. I thought I would never know hunger again he showed so many. And there were more, he said, but they resembled so closely poisonous brothers he thought it best not to teach of them. We had not the chance to take. He said Roland would never forgive him if he let me die and laughed. I laughed too. And then: "Did Lyden respect you?"

"Towards the end, I think, in some ways. But she seemed to have a low opinion of humankind in general."

"Many do. And never did she mention me?"

"I'm sorry, but she did not. She did not like to speak except for what had to be spoken."

He smiled. "Yes. That is her."

"When last I saw her she was still in the elven realm. Couldn't you find her?"

We walked for a time in silence. He was looking down, lost in thought, uncommon for one whose active eyes normally darted everywhere, picking things out of the forest I could not see even when he pointed right at them. By the time he spoke again, all the lightness had left his step. "I've left that ancestral home," he said.

"I've done a terrible thing," he whispered. "But Roland frowns on us to ask too much of each other's past, even now."

"We've all done things were ashamed of, Dexter."

He shook his head quickly. "No. This is worse. A Sagittae of this earth, me, me, I've killed a holy thing. But I had to get away, you see. She knows why. I had to, but I can't ride the wind, so I killed it just to ferry my life across the terrible jaws of Eloen, the last river of Elf. Now I live among humans. I, a Sagittae, have cut the face of our mother. All trees are sacred to us but these have blood, and make no seed. We've never seen one born and only I have seen one die. How we have those we do remains a mystery even to the elf. Maybe they've been there since the beginning of the world, and we believe when the last one passes the world will end. So say some. Are you all right?"

"No."

"You look sick."

"I am."

"Do you want to rest?"

"Yes."

"What's wrong?"

"I'm so tired."

"There is a rich field of clover and mushrooms ahead. We should hold there for the day."

"I don't mean that kind of tired."

"I know. Let's stop anyway."

In two days we came to a river so broad it was almost a lake moving slow to the south. Dexter lowered a boat secured to an outcropping, and with it a two sided oar. This boat could be rowed against the current he said, and showed me how to handle it somewhat, helped me to secure my things and I was ready.

"Guard your clothing as your life. They're one and the same up here. You can drink from the river, but the forest creeks are better. Don't stray far from the river. But if you do get lost, follow water: the trickle to the stream and the steam to the river and out. If you stumble upon a bear or tiger, since you can't speak to them, kill them with your knife if they attack. Do not hesitate."

"I won't"

"I know. Again, the river branches at the mountain whose peak splits like the tail of a fish. You'll know it. You'll find it inside a month. Go to the right. Once the fishtail cannot be seen, what do you look for?"

"The white forest."

"Yes. Secure the boat there far far from the water and follow the map as we discussed."

"I understand."

"Ready?"

I sat in the boat. So narrow.

"And don't fall in."

"No."

"Ready?"

"Yes," I said, heart pounding. He pushed the craft which skimmed swiftly over the water, and then I pulled away.

"May the gods keep you!"

I nodded to him and he bowed from the river bank. Dexter stayed for a long time there. He remained until he became only a speck on the shore. Every so often I turned and he stood there yet and I waved again and again, and just barely a remote hint of arm waved in return and I could imagine his smile so clearly it could almost be seen. And the time came when I turned and at last the speck was gone and I heaved into a cry then, wept so deeply it surprised me, fought to stop it but could not, for destiny had so inexorably re-created me alone.

As the river wove north the forest hung increasingly still and cold and quiet, and the sky turned ever more gray, and this I knew to be the start of the season of cold which Roland said we had not the time to wait for to pass. At each camp I flattened out pine needle boughs and blankets along the floor of the boat, wide enough for one to lay flat and comfortable, and the wind didn't bite as you slept, and within you feel, in a sense, safe.

Of those days along the river there is little to speak of, but sure enough the days came when the heavy clothes that Roland promised would be needed were. Mornings covered in frost and then, for the first time upon my life, snow fell.

Soon, the mountains rose like gods, but the fishtail broke against the very sky. It loomed as from the landscape of a fairytale. Its peak seemed cleaved by a divine sword. I went to the right as the days fell colder in a way I did not understand. And one day I hauled the little craft and secured it in the white forest and then, with my life upon my back, said a quick prayer and again walked to the North.

I hated leaving the boat behind. The thought of sleeping without its protection made me shudder. And now the wilderness became ever more thin, the air frigid and fire difficult to make and the trees grew farther apart, and more and more the ground gave way to grass or barren stone and then, for vast expanses, nothing but ice and snow. I held up in strands of forest no matter how small or how little distance I'd covered for their protection and firewood. At night, in the cold unthinkable, when the very breath hurt the lungs, I thought perhaps they'd sent me to nowhere for reasons all their own, an elaborate trap. But I had too much time to think in those days, especially at night. Cold forbids sleep.

Howls rose to the thin air as I lay shivering in a wind-break of snow. Ahead, waited an enormous expanse of white waste, too much to cross that day. I couldn't make fire. Dead wood was scant and ice and wetness covered everything, so I lay on a bed of cut bough with all the cloth I owned piled upon me in a heap and in the heart of it I curled against the cold, and within thought of nothing but coldness, before sleep and in thin dreams, coldness, until the howls echoed from the ether of the moon, that crown of white fire upon a silver sky. Do not go to this place, to the true North, where the human animal is all but forbidden to tread; but if you do, the heavens are without compare.

I peeked out from the cloth, from the trees, from the shadows. It could be anything. Then, distant silhouettes of four-legged beasts ran across the frozen waste, yelping and barking and they snapped and leapt and these were wolves. Dexter had spoken of them: the white wolves of the North. The first few called to unseen pockets tucked in the wasteland and heath, and from these newcomers charged to the pack with passionate intensity to lend their throats to the infernal chorus -- a summoning of wolves. Thus, their numbers grew. Very soon a swarm of hundreds, at least, huddled and yelped and circled upon the frozen lake. And then, at a signal unseen, all fell quiet. Even from that distance I could see them listening for something, and then I heard it too: a low moan crying from the east, not wolf exactly. And in the next moment the pack ran off, moving as one and in perfect silence, answering to what waited in the land from which the moon had risen.

By morning they were gone. Nothing moved on the ice. Above, a blanket of cloud. A gray sky on a gray day and heavy snow. The map had been very accurate and replete with landmarks, but I could see nothing now, and had only my fading arrow drawn in the snow (a habit of the road I never abandoned) to tell which way to start. Soon, I could not see anything and should have traced my steps back but did not, and so became lost in a place one should never be.

Snow fell heavier and drove me to the first dark patch I found and in that stand of pine I made camp, and with great effort, a fire. I held up for two days and the snow did not stop. When it did, nothing was recognizable. Every horizon could be seen with crystal clarity, but nothing matched anything on the map. I set out, walking on top of the snow with special netting Dexter had made for my shoes. It is a terrible thing to not know the way.

The terrain became scarred with deep troughs of ice. And as I followed the basin of one of these a strange thing happened: a white tiger fell from the sky. It landed just ahead with a wet crack of the neck and I watched stunned as its limbs quivered and coiled and were still. It's yellow eyes remained open, staring, ferocious even in death. And there may have been some few, final moments when they still beheld the light.

When you live on the road you learn to quickly dispense with the luxury of being stunned. I immediately tried to react to this. Nothing behind. Nothing ahead. Nothing tracked from above, yet anything, just anything, could be on the other side of the wall. Everything has an answer and so did this. It must have been the unusual landscape of troughs. It had been tracking my scent and leapt from the height of the wall and slipped, and that had to be the answer, but it did not matter much. On the road you must be quick in thought and deed. Whenever tigers fall from the sky, you need to move on.

And I would have but just then another tiger flew overhead and landed dead beside its brother. Already dead. Something had crushed it. I drew the knife at last and then a grunt came from just outside the trough and there was a swift shadow and then an enormous gray bear crashed on the tigers. The knife seemed a silly toy in my hand. The bear was dead or dying and steam rose from the bodies, and that first tiger stared yet, and nothing made sense anymore. I recalled stories of raining frogs or snakes, but it was time to move on.

And yet, here was meat. With a few quick cuts I'd have a week's worth of warming food. I had to be quick. I raised the blade to the flesh of the bear when the earth shook. And then shook again. It were as if a giant stamped its feet just outside the trough. And then a roar rose and my heart shook and I gripped tighter the blade for something big was just outside the wall, and it walked away for a time but then neared. It had entered the trough and would see me there, and I knew then with terrible clarity how lost I was, for here was the realm of the heath monster. I knew that as surely as I knew anything and I had to think.

The belly of the bear had been ruptured. The beast so much closer, such enormous strides and I had to think, and considered the crimson of the blood against the snow and how the belly had split and how there would be no outrunning this and no fighting it. I sliced the belly open wide and crawled in. A moment later the heath monster stood over its catch. It had a strange, rasping breath, like distant thunder.

It plopped down, sitting by the pile. I felt the bear shift as one of the tigers was dragged into the air. I heard the first bite, a wet sound of ripping flesh and ground bone and as it chewed you could feel its teeth turning the tiger to mash, almost see the drool spill from its enormous mouth until, half way through its meal, it belched and then bellowed a roar that rolled over the frozen plains. And my heart turned to ice, and know I knew how little I knew of the world. Very faintly then, from far and far, another roar called back.

I had no plan. I waited in the pool of viscera and the reeking guts and at least it was warm. My only plan was hope. Let it not eat the bear today. Let it eat tiger and fall to sleep. Strangely, part of me wanted to show myself and confess to it and beg its pardon. And then it roared and the other roared again. Silly thoughts.

It was amazing how much and quick it could eat. I heard the carcass of the tiger drop and then bones being ripped free and cracked and marrow being licked and sucked from the hollow. It roared again into the abyss - the roar of a thousand lions, the howl of ten thousand wolves - and I curled deeper into the bear and waited. The other called again, so much closer now. How swiftly they walk. Perhaps it was saving the bear for "her," but then its hands gripped the gray back and heaved us into the air. Selfish beast.

The ribs compressed around me and I let go of the blade, watched it drop through the slit of the belly and land flat in a growing pool of blood. I could see something of the monster now: part of its legs and it's black, humanish feet. Its jaws bit into the back of the kill and tore a hunk of meat away and when it wrenched the meat free the bear shook and I fell to the pool of snow and blood and knew not to move. It sensed something, but in stillness is invisibility.

It began to chew again and I can only assume the bear hid me from its view, or that it thought I was a piece of gut. I'd landed right on top of the blade and took it. When it roared again it was not a good time to move, but it was the best time to move, and I crept under a raised knee and quietly and quickly turned towards its back, and so became a speck of red wandering on an endless sea of frozen white.

The blood quickly froze. Dusk approached. All of me and my clothes had soaked through. They say you go numb and grow tired. Numbness crept from my hands and then up my arms, and for a frighteningly long time I had not felt my toes and soon could not feel my feet. My face ached from the cold. My limbs grew slow and heavy and I tried not to think of the growing dark.

The stars came out too beautiful, even for that place. I was dying. Ahead, shone the gate of the world to come, a blue light glowing like a dome over the ice. I looked behind for my body lying lifeless in the path, but it was not there. The celestial blue rose in spires, in spiraling arches and arcs in forms not to be imagined and not to be written. So much light. Closer, tubes encircled the spires and blue water ran through them, racing from beneath the earth to the highest points of the architecture. A temple of the stars. From the entrance you could hear within the sound of rushing water and through it all an exquisite music not of this earth, like nothing I'd ever heard, ever. The light so penetrating you could touch it.

Like a dream, I walked through the portal to the warmth within, and in there saw her. She rested on a crystal throne, and with limbs as elegant and mysterious as the temple itself, drew the water through its courses with but a gesture of the hand. Her hair hung in filets of gold. Her eyes like shining sapphires. When she saw me she wept tears of diamonds. She was the most beautiful creature I have ever seen, ever.

She smiled with a sadness and beauty that cannot be written. I was filthy, of course, reeking of carrion and dripping gore and staggering in sick and exhausted. She spoke with words unlike any I have ever heard and her voice cannot be described. I said something I do not recall. She answered in my language.

"You…You are human?"

"Yes. I am ready now."

"For what are you ready?"

"To be judged. To have the deeds of my life put on the scale."

She smiled again and pointed her finger straight up and spun it in circles and a chorus of glory spun above us and the spires turned and formed a new temple and the swirling blue rose to the stars and lowered again and the blue liquor ran everywhere.

"You are human?" she asked again.

"Yes. Please let me die."

Her smile went away and diamonds fell again. "What bitterness speaks those words?"

"I've done so many terrible things," I cried. "I killed a man. I knew the drink would kill him and I gave it to him anyway, poured it heavy and wanted him to die. I've forsaken my home, let them pay for my running. And I never kept my promise. I never found the Sage and now the world could end because of me. I want to leave now!"

And then I fell to my knees and hid my face in my hands. My fingers hung swollen and blackening already and I could not move them. They would have to be removed. My feet too. "Am I alive or not? Where am I?"

"What do you wish?" she asked in that voice of soft magic.

"To go through the gate. Not to die a hungry ghost."

"What do you seek?"

"To be let through."

"What else do you seek, beside the gate of death? What has brought you here?"

I mumbled the answer.

"This," she said, gesturing to the miracle about her, "is not a gate, but a vessel. It waits between worlds, for there are many beside this one."

I shook my head in confusion.

"It flies," she said, "between the stars." She pointed to the last star of the seven sisters. "There, beyond there, lies my home." Her face fell to sudden sadness then. Diamonds littered the ground. "I have been here for ten thousand circuits of the sun to await him. This vessel, wounded in war, crashed on this little world of lovely blue so long ago and I await him now, call to him with these songs and wait and will wait. I cannot leave or all is lost for us. I send my voice to the deserts of darkness between the stars just to reach him, to hear of his living and the fate of our children and race. Ten thousand circuits I have called from this shattered ship, and I too tire from this destiny's demands; but I do keep on, alone in wreckage calling, striving to get word to almost infinite points of light, lest all be forsaken."

She wiped a diamond away. She had seven fingers on each hand.

"The frost has poisoned your flesh." She waved her hand before her and the ground softened beneath my feet until I lowered and then floated in a pool of blue liquor. All the coldness melted away, all ache and frostbite gone. I sipped from the pool and was suddenly enormously restored, no thirst, no hunger, giddy even. And then the ground formed again and lifted me out and the blue water dried to dust with the scent of spring flowers and before I could thank her a door opened to the left and a line of bright blue led out of the temple and away into the abyss. "That will take you to the warm valley. In there, I should think, you shall find your Sage."

And the crystal pillars closed behind me, and for a time the ground itself sped me away, and as it did the music faded, she faded, the glow receded into the horizon past, and after each step the line of bright blue receded into the snow, yet while upon it the cold did not touch me.

The path had no perils then, and soon came the day when the peaks to the west matched those writ on Dexter's map. Yes, this is it. Perseverance. I felt like half my life had been spent in searching for this place. Indeed, it almost had. Yes, this was it. It was here or nowhere. Perseverance is everything.

"If he's still alive he's in there. We think so. Just seek him out and you'll find him. He could be anywhere in that valley, but look for an oak tree, an old one. He lives nearby it they say. 'The Sage of the Oak' some call him."

I entered the valley where the earth bloomed warm and green and water ran sweet and the air turned redolent with the scent of lavender and apple flower, hibiscus and magnolia, just a hint of woodsmoke. But now in the valley proper I had, at last, abandoned all hope. There of all places, so close to the end, my heart had given up. It all felt so empty. I walked on anyway. What else to do? Cross this one last passage and no matter what you do or do not find this is the end of it. After this, you leave it be. After this, go back to carve some kind of life out of the balance of your time.

The sky hung in a vault of formless gray. It would rain soon, or snow, or whatever it did here. I lifted out the jezeth, a gray opal, hollow and magicless. Just what was it after all? Nothing. And no sage could lift the hardness now settled upon my heart. And nothing could ever restore an instant of time, nor recall life to where it had fled, and no act of justice could undo an injustice, and nothing had meaning anymore, and no matter what the valley held or did not, nothing could be worth the cost. In short, I was afraid.

A foot path led to a pond. Beside the pond grew a tree with white flowers. Beneath the tree a man who was old but not old squatted on his haunches. He was fishing, staring intently at where his line broke the water. I blinked and rubbed my eyes but he was still there. He toyed with the reed to give life to the line and I rubbed my eyes again but he was still there, gazing into where his line broke the water the way some gaze at the stars. And I shook my head and he did not disappear.

"Are you … are you… are you…"

"Hush!"

And just then the stick became alive, bending towards the water by the unmistakable tugging of a fish. He heaved and a trout lifted into the air and he swiftly dipped his right hand to the water and then caught the fish by its belly. It wriggled in his hand and the man who was old and not old faced me and smiled.

"Want it?"

I was speechless.

"Well?"

Speechless, but the fish struggled ever to be free. The man then shrugged his shoulders and tossed it back and with a plop it was gone. Without another word he stood, and with a flick of the wrist, whirled the line around the tip of the reed, pressed the hook gently into the line itself and then turned and walked away, whistling extraordinarily well. He walked so quickly I had to run.

"Wait!"

"Oh, so you can talk after all?" he called over his shoulder. "And just what should I wait for?"

"For me!" I ran faster now. "Wait for me!"

"Well, just who are you? And why worth waiting for?"

"Please go slower. Please wait. I'm lost."

"I can see that," he said, without slowing or turning around. "What do you want?"

"I'm looking for someone. Please slow down."

He did not.

"You've come a long way to look for an anything."

"I'm from Selador, from the Southern Slope."

To my surprise, this made him stop. He looked at me a second time. "You've come a truly *long* way."

Years pass like water. My name writ in water.

"I have. I truly have. Please help me. I need to find someone."

"You said that."

"Please be him. You have to be him. I can't go on." I hated that I'd begun to cry. I did not know what to do and then remembered it. I drew out the great tooth, a weight carried so long and so far, and tossed it on the ground before him. It exploded into the ground where it hit then rolled long-ways until stopping at his feet. I pointed to it. "That! Please, please take that! It's from a dragon. They say you... that a sage ... is anyone else here?" He did not answer. "They say The Dragon Sage will help someone in great need if they gift a token of a dragon. I give that to you freely, but help me!"

It sounded so silly now, so childish and hopeless and futile and I, more than anything, wished the tears would stop. This was not at all how I envisioned it. He looked puzzled. "Just me," he said.

"What? What are you saying?"

"You asked if any others were here. Just me, and, of course, now there's you, but you knew that already." He took up the great tooth of Kai-Tey. For just a moment he could not hide a silent awe. He hefted its weight in his hands, traced his finger along its spiral, tapped the tip. "This is, well, this here is quite a thing."

"Please. I just can't carry it anymore. It's so heavy. I don't want it anymore. I need to give it away. I needed to bring it here. Just take it. It doesn't matter who you are."

"So, who's gone and told you about sages and dragons and all this nonsense?"

"It's meaningless. I knew this. A stupid thing. Just burn it. Such a stupid thing to do!"

He scratched his head. "It's hard to burn dragon tooth I imagine. Some say they breathe fire," he joked. "You look tired kid, and hungry, and quite lost. Come on. I think you're all done in for today. You've come far, too far maybe. I'll take this tooth and you carry the fishing rod okay? Let's start there." And he did not look very strong, and did not seem magical at all. He seemed a hermit who spent his days perfecting the art of catching trout, this man who was old and not.

We reached a precipice and rested. In the grasslands below deer grazed. White cranes crossed the sky above. He smiled at the expanse, pointed at the clouds with the tooth and explained the coming weather. It was, I saw at last, a lovely place.

"Are you Gin?"

"Damn it!" he cursed, and struck the earth with the tip of the tooth and rock and soil scattered like dust. "Damn it, damn it, damn it!" he repeated, and then stood abruptly and began to walk away.

"Where are we going?" I called, running after him. "Please wait! Please be Gin. You have to be."

"And why is that?"

"Because I can't go on anymore."

He didn't answer.

"Where are you going?" I asked.

"I'm going home. I've no idea where you're going."

"You said with you. You said to come with you."

"So I did." Orphans. "So, who told you that name?"

"Roland."

He stopped. "Well, well. Full of surprises aren't you young one?" He laughed with anger. "I should have figured he'd be behind this somehow. He still some kind of tough guy?"

"Yes."

"Good. So, what's he want with me?"

"The medusa."

He stood very still then. "What's that got to do with me?"

"He sent me to tell you it's time. It's very, very important you know that you can't wait anymore. The needles…"

"Yes yes. I know all about it." He began to walk away again.

"Listen. He said you really can't wait anymore. You really can't fucking fucking wait!"

"Oh, this sounds serious now. Swear words and everything."

"They're coming for it. They can find it and you and you can't wait much longer."

"Heard you the first time." He then mumbled something and cut the air with the tooth as if it were a sword. "And that's what this is for I suppose? My cooperation?"

"No. That's another story."

He sighed. "Ah God. This is gonna be a long day. Let's go."

We came to a cliff wall overlooking much of the valley. Fairly high up, partly concealed behind the foliage of a tree, the mouth of a cave opened into the cliff. The trunk of the tree grew alongside the wall and had within it divots and footholds so that one could climb it almost as stairs. The man who was old but not old climbed the tree almost as swiftly as he walked. He did not use his hands. At the top, he disappeared into the shadow of the cave and was gone. I waited. So this was the oak. And then I climbed after him.

A branch too wide for its height acted as a bridge into the cave proper. You had to balance to enter. Inside, he sat cross-legged on a finely-woven carpet. "May I?" I asked, crouching on the branch.

"Of course. You've good manners I see. Welcome."

"Thank you."

"You walk on branches well."

"I've had practice."

"So it would seem."

"You have to help me."

"No, I don't."

"Please help me."

"Let's eat, have tea, relax. It's a wonderful home. You haven't even yet taken in the view."

I turned and gave the valley below a quick scan. "I need help."

"You're starting with this already?" He sighed. "So what exactly you want me to do kid?"

"Free Selador, and bring the medusa to Roland, please."

He laughed. "Oh that's it, eh? Travel half the world for a tooth? And while Im at it, deliver the most loathsome weapon ever wrought by human hands to the trust of a mercenary?"

"Yes."

"You can keep your ivory."

"I don't want it ever again."

"You look hungry."

"I don't care about that."

"Well, you should. Look, I'm not anybody. I'm a hermit, a fisherman, a retired soldier at best."

"Please help them."

"Who? Roland or, what was it? Sell a door?"

"Yes."

"Well?"

"Selador."

"Stop crying."

"Please...They raped children before their parents, murdered them, made them eat their flesh..." He lifted his hand.

"Okay, that's enough of that. I've heard enough of that. I know how it goes. Take a bath. It'll be dark soon. You don't want to be out there in the dark."

"Please. It has to be you. They speak of you still, of the things you can do and they said you live in a cave near the top of an oak tree. You are him, just like the elders said. The Sage of the Oak."

He sighed. "Actually, it's an ash, but this particular species looks similar enough from a distance so ... a highly forgivable mistake."

"I crossed the world...the tooth..."

"Just how exactly... never mind. Take a bath and let me think. There's a hot spring not far to the left. All this talk wearies me."

I nodded and climbed to the branch, looked closely at the leaves. "How could they get this wrong?"

"The species? I don't know really. Maybe someone hoped I'm something I'm not. A long time ago a fine people lived who believed trees to be sacred things holding all the mysteries of the universe. They learned the spirit of each type, and the oak was the protector, the shelter, the strength. Maybe it's the tree they wanted to see. So tell me this, why are your tears blue?"

When I returned to the cave the man stood on one leg bent at the knee with the other crossed over it. At first I thought he sat on a stool but there was no stool. Despite the incredible strain of this feat, his face showed no sign of fatigue or strain. In fact, he sipped a cup of tea in this position and rested it on a saucer balanced on the folded leg.

"Much better. All clean."

"I feel better."

"That's good, real good. You have a lot of heart making it all this way from the Southern Slope. I remember it clearly now, just how far it is. Was there once. Have some tea. Help yourself," he said and gestured to a kettle half set in the ash and coal of a low fire.

I sat cross-legged on the exquisite rug and sipped my tea from a metal cup. It tasted of tree bark and cinnamon and a hint of berry. It warmed the body and calmed the mind almost immediately. The place had comfort. The ash leaves blocked wind and rain and the most glaring rays of sun, yet blocked none of them completely. For a time we sat in silence as the last rays of sun entered from the Southwest in the glorious fire of dusk. For some few moments the cave glowed illumine.

"It is called 'Tranquility Tea,'" he said.

"It's wonderful."

"It comforts the spirit without being an intoxicant. Dispels unnecessary fear."

"I needed it."

He nodded. "You've come a long way. It's understandable."

When twilight came he shifted to the other leg. "So," he whispered, "why did you ever think you would find a sage? I mean, before Roland?"

"From stories told to me as a child."

He nodded. "All things have humble beginnings. But you believed in them?"

"No, but I had nothing else to believe in. So, you are him after all?"

He ran his hand through his scalp and sighed. "I knew eventually someone would ruin it all."

"Ruin what?"

"My peace. My hiding. You can't hide forever. Eventually, things get back to you. Sometimes in the form of a scrawny kid who cries blue."

"Are you immortal?"

"No. Just very long-lived. It's simply a question of diet and exercise, and not very difficult exercise: click the teeth, soften the lower back, clean the blood, wash the marrow, stoke the first fire, beat the heavenly drum. Fairly simple really once you know them. Would you like to learn?"

"Me? You would teach immortality to me?"

"Of course. Why not? You seem like a good sort. But you should do them every day, or most every day. That's the trick. And repeat the system as many times as you have time for."

"Yes, I would like to learn."

"Good. I will teach you tomorrow."

"Are you going to help me?"

He lifted a hand for me to stop. "Please don't ask again. I heard you. I may be old but am not deaf. Let me think. I need time to think."

"I'm sorry."

"Forget it."

How warm and comfortable this cave. Walls clean and dry and like most caves in which people lived, it did not run to deep into the mountain. A second chamber, dark for being out of reach of the fire, lay behind the main, but that was all. He had things stored back there. What, I could only guess. Why he would ever bring so many possessions to such a remote location confounded me, but maybe he had been up there a long, long time.

He eyed his humble home. "It's a good place this," he said. "I laugh when I think how we have returned to the caves, and how fine they are. I suppose some kind of lesson rests in there, but I couldn't tell you what. I love when it rains. In this valley it almost never snows, but we get chilly nights, and I do so love the rain on a chilly night with the fire burning low. I will never tire of that. Sometimes it rains for days. And from up here you can see birds fly low over the valley floor and watch them from above. I will never tire of that either."

"It's beautiful, but lonely. And boredom. Living so long."

He shrugged and scratched the back of his head in that unique way of his. "We all get bored from time to time-the price of our humanity-but I never met a man so bored he didn't wish to live another day." He sipped his tea again and set the cup down. "But tell me your story now. It must have been quite an adventure."

I did not know where to begin, and so began at the beginning, or what I thought was the beginning. It amazed me how quickly years could be summed up in sentences. He listened well, and sometimes smiled, sometimes laughed, and often, for no reason I could understand, he appeared terribly saddened in moments where the story seemed quite plain. Soon, the parts that needed telling were told. Our tea had not even gotten cool. The fire still needed no more wood than when I had begun. Half a life summed up.

He then lowered down and rested his legs. Sitting normally, he fed the fire. He stared within the dance of light and I knew his thoughts were not with us. Then, from the back of the cave, he retrieved cushions and a red blanket and set these fairly close to the fire's warmth and wrapped his long body in the blanket and reclined against the curves of the flowstone wall. As he stretched out his legs for a moment the color faded from his face and he appeared as a ghost. For the first time, the man looked very tired and very old and still his thoughts were not with us. He pursed his lips and blew a silent exhalation into the coals. The flames rose as if ushered by magic. A ghostly glow engulfed the fresh log and we watched it burn for a time and I remembered Uncle telling me three things a man can look at forever are the stars, the sea, and a fire.

"That's quite a story you have," he said at last, his voice distant. "Almost hard to believe in parts."

"It's all true. It is."

"Oh, I know that. I trust your witness. Only, don't be surprised if people doubt you, and don't be too upset when they think you are lying, or perhaps insane."

"I don't care what people think."

He smiled. "Yes you do. You wouldn't want to meet the one who doesn't, although, perhaps you already have."

"I just won't tell it then."

"As you wish. Can you hear the waterfall?"

Very faint and far, the rush of falling water touched my ears. "Ah yes!"

"Tomorrow I will show it to you, but don't go there after dark."

"Why not?"

"It's a water source, best avoided at night. In fact, don't wander around the valley at all in night. There's no need to."

"I won't"

"The cold drives a lot of things to this valley."

"I understand."

"You think I'm being too cautious."

"No, not at all."

"Fine then. Good you understand. At my age you don't need surprises."

He burned incense then and it reminded me of Karuna. Sage or not, I liked it there. Just wonderful. So much life. In the branches of the ash lived gray-green birds and when he called them they came and even perched on his finger. "I raised a young pair so many years ago. These are their children."

"They're beautiful."

"Indeed."

As he spoke to them I thought of Lyden and realized how I had not for a very long time. "They are the best guards a person could ask for," he said. "They see everything. Everything, and scream when a scream is needed. Can't tell you how many times they alone scared something or other off."

"Strange creatures," I said, pointing to the paintings of fantastic animals running along the walls of the cave.

"Yes, but all gone now. Not a single one left. Make a pretty picture though."

"What's gone?"

"Those animals. Every one of them. All wiped clean from the earth. Few are they who knew they ever even existed. About as gone as you can get."

The world was too vast, held creatures beyond number, beyond reckoning. I did not believe them to ever be real.

"What happened to them?"

He shrugged. "Oh lots of different things, but, in short, the world just moved on. They did not belong on her anymore save as the life of nourishing soil, and the proof of that is that they are not here anymore. It did not matter their beauty, their strength, their purpose, and all and any divine favor they may have earned did not matter, because they are not here anymore, not at all and not one, and I see the doubt in your eyes…"

"Oh no, no no …"

"You do not lie very well. It's fine. You shouldn't believe me. What reason have you? And yet, despite your doubt, and having never even known of them before, you lament their demise."

"They're very beautiful. You paint well."

"Oh I didn't paint these. These were here before I was born. These were old when I was young."

"Sage, tell me this, what was the world like when you were young?"

The faint smile he had ran away. "You would not believe it, not even in your dreams. You'd think me cracked, but be too polite to say it."

"I can understand the past."

He laughed dryly and rubbed his hands briskly. "Mayhap I should tell of it once more. It's a long, long night tonight, the longest of the year in fact, and I assure you I am one of the very few who know that anymore." He sighed and the fire rose. "It fades," he said, "and yet some parts are so fresh. Well, so … so when Gin was a young fool and not an old one, he lived in the height of what might be called the 'Epoch of Man.' At that time this whole earth, all of her: water and dirt, sea and sky, all of it, were ours. We'd cut and hewn our way out of the wild until at last every part had a human name and print and we feared no creature save ourselves. Indeed, not a woods left standing could get us lost, and maybe that's why we lost hold of it. Maybe we just didn't want it anymore - with the mystery gone. We took it all. Many had an abundance rare now even to kings." He shook his head and stared absently into the fire. "I was born in the midst of that, and you could try to imagine it but never will. You may as well hear of a world ruled of dragons."

"I have heard of the age of dragons."

"Yes, well, yes that's fine. Understand, I was a child of the abundance. But you are a child of the fading. The human family has become a shadow of the shadow of itself. Each generation running thinner than the one before, clinging to life in scattered packs; poisons, sterility, disease, and then there's war, even when there's so little left to fight over, and fighting costs so much. I suppose it's just our nature. I would not be surprised if the second to last man dies by the sword."

He laughed then without joy.

"And we were so brilliant all along, but now we are dying, with a little patience." He poured more and sipped his tea and set the cup down again and folded his hands. "It amazes me too how peacefully it all goes away," he continued as he stared wistfully into the vault of the cave. A long, low mewl rose from the distance. He raised his head and listened. Another followed. "It could be anything. Mountain ogre. Anything. But don't worry. Nothing will come up here. Anyway, when I was young, and even when I was first old, in the first lifetime, a single congregation held more human hearts than you have met in all your travels, even in all your life up until this day and add on those to come. You could not believe how many of us there once were, you who have walked for years and seen but a few men. And nature too, how she has faded. Once, herds of animals ran so thick it took three days for them to pass. Once, you could hop across a valley jumping from back to back of one beast or another and never touch the ground. Once, flew flocks of birds so thick they shadowed the sky."

He laughed again without joy and stared into the fading fire. "There was once such abundance and yet now you, in all your travels, through the wilderness and paths of humanity, what have you seen? A few animals here and there, some pockets of people here and there, a monster or two and there's a reason for that. I bet you don't have a brother or sister?"

"No."

"Sterility. The poisons of the past that will not so easily go away. Yet, in the time of my birth we still flourished. And though we knew the earth was dying we pretended that it was not. People hate the truth. Although, we always imagined that she would fix it somehow and she is. She's fixing it all right. She's shaking us off. Getting rid of the problem. And for all of our genius we can do nothing to stop it. We have not the resilience of a simple cockroach for all of our astounding brilliance. Do you know what people used to be able to do?"

"No."

"In the Epoch of Man they could pick up a shell and speak into it and talk to one another no matter how far the other person was. They could be on the other side of the earth, just as far, farther, than all of your journey ten times, and even see them too, in perfect clarity and color they could from a shell see them and hear them as if they stood right before them."

"From a shell?"

He shook his head. "Of course not a real shell. One made by people. I'm just trying to give you an idea."

"We have writing too, and pictures so finely drawn you would think the person stood on the wall."

He shook his head. "Not like that. Not writing. You would hear my voice, see my face moving. And do you know what?"

"What?"

"We could once fly above the clouds, and even into the cold reaches of space. We could even plunge the depths of the great oceans, drop from the air in the heart of the deepest wild and be flown out again. Indeed, and we had such weapons we could end all the world a thousand times over."

The infant sets his hand upon the father's gun.

I thought of what he said and it did not astound me.

"Lyden can ride the wind, and Karuna's people went to the depths of the sea."

He smiled gently but shook his head. "Not like that. I don't mean acrobatics or pearl divers. You can't understand what I say because it's too far removed. I know you think I'm telling stories, but I'm not. Don't deny it. I see it in your face."

I did not deny it. From a pile of neatly cut wood he took a log and fed the fire, removed the kettle, poured, and sat down again.

"Help yourself."

I did.

"At the end, when I lived in what I would call my second life, for I was about a hundred and fifty or so, the 'Epoch of Man' reached its height. We gave to ourselves then the powers of the old gods. We rode horses with wings, made objects appear out of thin air, could fly in a ship like glass to the far side of the moon and return to a field of the earth for lunch. Oh, there were injustices, as there always will be. We had our poor, our removed and trammeled upon. They will always be among us, but if one had the means, miracles abounded for the asking. And I won't pretend to know why, (although some say God spits on such blasphemous pride), but at the apex of our achievement, when we had wrought every dream and pleasure this little world could yield, God glanced upon the earth he had forgotten and whispered to it a word, and with this word He sent us back to our childhood. In a single moment, all at once, every serkit failed and never worked again. In a breath, the whole world wide, all the lights went out! No power but the sun. No engine but the beating heart."

He waved his left hand over the fire with a flourish and the flames extinguished. For a moment the cave fell to dark save for the red glow of the coals. In the next moment the flames returned. Gin smiled.

"They gave all kinds of theories while this luxury could be afforded: an unprecedented flare from the sun, a new weapon over-triggered by mistake, an act of deliberate undoing by those who had suffered from injustice, or by those who had gone mad. Some said, those few who still believed in such things, that at the moment of first dark they heard the voice of God. And the voice was angry.

The infant sets his hand upon the father's gun.

"But we don't know, not now and not then how every serkit failed. It doesn't matter anymore anyway. But, well, it was amazing how fast it fell apart. We could do nothing without our energy. We could not move water nor grow food, at least not at the same level we needed. Thus, so suddenly, an earth of nine billion souls could only support one." A pall fell over his face and he stared deeply into the fire and whispered. "Just amazing how fast it fell apart."

He then went to the mouth of the cave and watched for something in the moon-washed valley below. He spoke with his back to me. "It bothered me more than a little the dead and dying, trapped in rooms that could never be opened, the drowned under the sea, the fliers tumbling from the sky, the suffocated colonies of the moon: twelve thousand souls laying yet in her carious grin and I can never look at it and not think of them. Unrotted, desiccated masks dying so very far from home."

"I would have certainly died too, but I had many tricks by then, secrets too. Still, I barely made it. I went to the place I and others like me know and we tucked ourselves away and waited for the world to settle again, which it always does. But then, I don't know exactly how or when, but some few years later they launched her- God knows why- but they did and for too long a time the world fell to gray. A third of the earth gone for what purpose we could never know but we know this: she was the last of the great weapons, for she ran on a different kind of energy, one unlike any that had ever been tapped before."

"The medusa you mean?"

"Yes. Her. She needed no serkits, no elektrisity. The medusa ran on a brand new kind of power: she feeds on the essence of life itself. Inverts it to ghastly effect. I don't know how exactly, but she flies off the ground until she reaches the stratosphere, opens and exhales death itself from her maw. And all that fall beneath her breath turn to stone. She only flew once, and it took a third of the world, turned it all to stone and it still is. No recovery. Who would do such a thing, have both the knowledge and malice I can only guess but don't know. I don't know. I just don't know. But damn the results are ghastly."

He returned and sat and rubbed his eyes looking tired now and old.

"The medusa's charm is to reconstruct the process of life begetting life to the process of unbecoming. A clarion of death in perpetuity. No recovery. Not even the land recovers. Forever to the unbecoming. At least as far as humankind may know. I don't know who or why … maybe they just wanted it all done. Maybe she launched herself. I don't know. They call it now, that third of the blighted earth, the land of the staring dead. Don't ever go there. It haunts the mind. You see the expression in the faces it happens so quickly. A brief agony and then … don't go there. There's nothing there. Don't go there ever."

"I won't."

"Good. Odd thing is, she did not get the name 'Medusa' because she turns things to stone, as does the lady from a myth no one knows anymore. It was the shape of the weapon that gave her that name, a shape that could not be avoided. She's about the size of a human skull and when the science was done the crown kept appearing as a nest of serpents. They redesigned her again and again to get rid of it, but no matter what they did serpents draped from her crown like hair. Thus, they called her the "Medusa." The turning to stone was just coincidence. Her original function was simply to stop life, not to kill, but to stop life. It's different. I doubt anyone knew just how the science would fall out."

"You know a lot of history Sage."

"I've had a lot of life."

"You don't look so old."

"Well, thank you. And how old does this old kook look?"

I knew that if people were healthy they appeared younger than they were. And I knew it was always best to under-guess age.

"Fifty?"

"Sail on."

"Sixty?"

"Sail on."

"Sixty-five?"

"Sail on."

"Ninety?"

"Sail on."

And it went like this until it became ridiculous.

"Nine hundred?"

"Sail on."

"Seven thousand?"

"Sail on."

"Just those exercises keep you alive that long?"

"Well, it's a lot of things. You need to know something about herbs and places to be. You should know how to fight, because if you live to be my age you will have to fight sooner or later. But there's another secret to living long, and those old kooks who live in the mountains I spoke of, the first home of my teacher, they taught this to me. The earth holds some secrets: caves with water that runs from the beginning, along this lie beds of giant crystal, crystals larger than that ash outside. If you know how to prepare yourself, you can quiet down your whole body and sleep in there for a very, very long time. I don't know why it works, just how to do it. Your heart will beat once an hour, so after ten years you have aged a day, maybe two. You emerge from the cave to an entirely new world if you've the courage to step outside again. Not everyone does. This way, when even the exercises and the herbs don't hold you up so well, you can take a nap, as they say, and leap frog through time." He smiled. "You don't believe me."

"No, no. I do. It seems possible. I just don't understand why you would want to keep living so long. Sometimes it's hard for me to get through a day."

He laughed.

"Well, when I sleep in the crystal caves it's like that time doesn't count. You don't even dream. The only sensation is the pulse."

"Pulse?"

"The heartbeat of the earth. You feel it every decade or so coming from way below and yet at the same time from the lacing between the stars. Then it feels like your crystal bed scatters, turns to nothing, to atoms and then a tingling wakefulness takes over and if you're not careful it will wake you up all together and spoil the hibernation. It's very difficult to achieve the state of hibernation.

Sometimes it takes months. You don't want to be woken before your time."

"No, of course not," I said as a dread sank in, for I had given the tooth to a madman with mad stories. And I knew then there never was a sage but only the story of one. Suddenly, he laughed gently again.

"I see the fear on your face, the doubt. That's good. You shouldn't believe in such ridiculous things without proof."

"Oh no! It's not…"

He raised his hand. "Listen. Here's a better story. Once upon a time, in the Epoch of Man, people made stone vaults in which they would place artifacts of their era. And so, when a weapon or a solar pulse or God or something all together different sent us back to our childhood, those who could find the time and the energy and the sanity began to preserve what was being lost in such vaults. They called them 'Time Capsules,' because they were a portrait of that moment. And since they knew it was all collapsing they made many more and put a map in each capsule pointing to the others. This way, the children of the children of the children might find them and not have to start all over again. And they put in these vaults the good so it may be repeated, and the evil so it may be avoided. And they had much to teach, for the human animal did quite remarkable things, wonderful things."

He rose and put another log on the tiring fire and sat again and exhaled in his way which carried his breath across the room so the flames could more quickly consume it. I realized only then how chill the night fell in the otherwise temperate valley.

"So, ten thousand years or so go by and a scholar of sorts finds his own life torn to ribbons by the savagery of man or natural calamity or both, perhaps even just a madness living in his mind; it doesn't matter. The thing is, he has nothing at all and so, this scholar of sorts, sets out and unearths one of these capsules and begins to read, to decipher. He learns all kinds of things. Not just about ships that could fly to the stars, but all kinds of things. How to meditate, how to fight with a sword, the ten thousand paths of worship. He learns medicine and advice for keeping a mind together, a spirit strong. And for all of its shadows and faults, that old world that was gone shone more brightly than his ever could again; and so he adopts the legend of the immortals, and thus becomes one himself. You like that story better?"

I could say nothing. He smiled.

"You know, your own story is not so strange. These things you talk about: elves and dragons, fairies and ogres, these were old when I was young. I believe you you know, every word you said. You're not lying. Just, what I can't figure out is if these things have always been there and were, when humanity had its go, simply sleeping, hiding, waiting for things to quiet down again; or if what you saw and met and knew are the spillage of our science, the shadow of which could make every manner of abomination and fantasy. At one point some of the less scrupulous nations had 'The Circus of The Bizarre' where a visitor could see the monsters and the angels once relegated only to dreams. And who knows, maybe that is why God, if God be, sent us back to our childhood. And then, of course, you were drinking from uncertain sources. All kinds of things can be in the water these days, and you were eating unknown flowers that can have strange effects on the mind."

"No. I know what I saw."

"Okay. I know. All right. I believe you. I just wanted you to know all the possibilities. I believe every word of your account. I truly do."

"Not even the ancients could have made the things I've seen."

"Fine."

"Not even them. They couldn't have. I know they couldn't have."

"Fine. That's fine. The question now is, what exactly do you want from me, besides the medusa? What do you want me to do exactly about this Selador?"

I hung my head in my hands for I had no answer. "I hoped you would know."

"How convenient. Well, I've no idea. Surely you don't expect me to walk half way across the earth and slaughter a bunch of tired and ill-lead soldiers?"

"I don't know. I don't know."

"Let's forget it for now. Tomorrow I'll show you some of the valley. We'll catch some fish for dinner. You look hungry even though you ate."

"All right."

I asked no more concerning it. He was right. I'd done my part. Now, for Selador. As the days went by he taught me the exercises as promised, and they were not very difficult and I do them still when I have time. It was comfortable enough up there in that warm valley and the cave so safely off the ground. The only thing that bothered me was when he spoke of the past, which was always a thing unbelievable.

He told of people flying to other planets, sending machines hurling among the stars. He said the sun was a star only closer, and smaller too than most. He said that time pet every beast and plant into another form even so that men once were apes, and before apes, fish, for according to Gin all life came from the sea. He said wingless dragons once ruled the world, and how the world existed long before people or dragons. He said the earth flew around the sun, and that there were more stars than sands in the sea. He spoke again of the metal eyes that could see anywhere on earth. He said he once had a tube which could fit in my palm, yet flood the cave with light like sunlight.

"It's all true, but you don't believe me at all."

"I do."

"And you with stories of elves. Want your tooth back?"

"And then we have it. It. The horrible genius behind her making is that any part of her remains as lethal as the whole. We cannot bury her so deep that the earth would not spew her out again in fragments, each a thousand thousand little deaths to guarantee our eventual extinction. To burn her by ordinary fire would lead to a cloud of perennial destruction. To drown her would promise a sea of waste once the waves wore away her shell. And if opened, her stare soon turns the most fortified cell to stony dust. Only her shell keeps her, made from the same stuff. And only the Phoenix hold the fire which can truly kill it. At least they once did. May they still. Them needles are cut from her shell. There's two they say, and if treated just right will point back to their source. I did hope this was forgotten. Roland spoiled that. Okay then. Okay. I'll do what I can to get her to Roland and his little bird. I'll do what I can for Selador too. I can promise no more."

"Thank you. Thank you."

"Roland's a good man," he said late one night. It would surprise you how we first met, but it doesn't matter anymore. What kind of woman is this Belladonna?"

In a bed of gold colored silk they lay.

"Oh Roland. Take me tonight."

"All right Bell."

"Oh Roland, Kiss me." He caresses her all but naked body searching with the tips of his fingers for a place not lifted with scar. He finds one and kisses her there.

"Oh Rol, oh yes Baby Rol. There. Yes, there."

He kisses her again. "But don't cut it."

"No no no. Not there. That's your spot, Love. Never there. Swords are forbidden there, forever."

"All right Bell."

He kisses her more and more gently and firmly and she writhes her hips against him until secretly lifting the hidden sword from under the bedding. She smiles mischievously and runs it flat against her breasts and then tilts it to draw a thin red line of blood above each of her aureole and she groans in passion then and he waits, and she pulls him close and the cold steel rests between them until the fresh trickle of blood spreads between them. It's warm and she kisses him again and again and again and whispers secrets to him never before told to anyone. He runs his hands through her short hair. "It's fine Bell," he whispers. "It's all fine and wonderful my darling Belladonna."

Then, her passion rising, she lowers the blade and draws it lengthwise and deep across the lips of her vagina and the blood gushes to the sheets and her tears wet the pillow and she is smiling. Tears flood her eyes the more and she is smiling and groans in ecstasy and the blood pools under the cleft of her groin and he curses himself for not catching her in time and his thighs catch wetness and its warm and she lowers her hand and soaks it and lifts the wet palm to his face and paints his cheeks in crimson and draws swirls in the mask of her blood.

"Oh sweet Roland, do you love me?"

"Of course, Bell."

" Do you see how wet I am?" She slides her hand wet along his jaw.

"Yeah, Bell."

"I'm so wet for you, Baby.'

"Yes my love."

"Only for you, my Roland."

"And I am only yours."

"Do you love me so much, Roland?"

"Yes."

"Fuck me now, Roland. Please, fuck me now. Right now... I need it now."

"Of course Bell."

"You do want to, don't you?"

"Of course. Please don't ask that again."

"Roland, you are my last and only love."

"All right, Bell."

"Now. Hurry. I'm gushing."

"Listen, there's a better land. You've come a long way and to try and make it back to Selador, well, what's there? Even if the soldiers left by now, what's there for you? An elderly aunt and uncle who may not even be with us by the time you return? If you return? Friends of your youth who by now will have married, left or died? You are past the age when friendship is everything. You are young, but not so young. You would have been married now too had you lived a normal life. Do what you will of course, but in exchange I ask your word to leave this place."

I nodded, but my heart agreed to nothing.

"There's a good land across the sea. Not as wild as this, nor as old or ruined. Did you see the forked mountain, the fishtails?"

"Yes."

"Its river has a tributary not far from here. I'll draw you a map to get you to it quickly, but the way is clear. You just got lost getting here. Don't go back to Roland's camp. I'll take care of things. Stay in the center of the river during the day. It's wiser this way. It's not that it's so dangerous, but be safe. Before a month passes from my lintel you should come to a village at the mouth of the river, perched right where it spills into the great sea. Seek out the black ships - it's the pitch between the timbers that, well, it doesn't matter – ask for them and find a captain you trust. He should ask only the price of your work to take you over, but you might get a little extra if you work well. Put all of this behind you and go to the new world. Trust me in this. It will be a better life for you ... so says the Sage," he said and laughed.

I thought about what I would leave, and realized I had left it already. "All right," I said to him, "I'll give it a go," and I meant it.

"Good," he said, "Good." But then a shadow fell over his face. "I want you to leave soon. And be careful with that gem. It gives me a great deal of comfort knowing one exists."

"What you keep in that rag under your neck?"

"The jezeth."

"Let's have a look at it."

Like so many others even he could not speak at first sight of it. He peered into the heart of light for a long time and his thoughts ran far and away. "My oh my," he whispered at last. "It's been a long time since I've seen one of those. My, my, my."

"It's a star of the first creation," said the younger.

The older man gazed in stunned silence. When he spoke, he whispered.

"It's what we used to call a Christmas ball. Amazing one has survived so long. Just amazing. And in truth, it's the loveliest I've ever seen. The sea must of polished it just so."

"What do you call it? What does it mean to you?"

"It celebrated a man some people thought a god. My teacher, who was very old when I was young, said he met one of those who learned under him. The only thing he told my teacher that has not been written elsewhere was that this god thought children should be especially protected. Nothing new in that. But he felt that extended to our every deed. 'Wherever you go remember there are children near,' he said to the friend of my teacher, 'and act accordingly.' And then they called him 'Father,' and then 'Lord.'"

"That's it?"

"Yes, but I don't suppose it matters much in times like these, but maybe it matters more than ever. Be careful with it. It's a very delicate thing, and it may be the last one."

The younger tucked the jezeth beneath his shirt.

In the last days spent with him he refined my exercises, letting me make my mistakes and learn by degrees. He often stood in the meadow and slowly draped his hands back and forth, pulling and pushing nothing but the wind and when he did this he himself moved like wind-bent grass. An amazing phenomenon occurred in this:

colored illumination played between his hands. This practice he called 'tossing light,' and when Gin tossed light, well, that was something to see.

When he finished he sat by me and smiled. "I would show you how to do that and more had we time. I would trust you with all my secrets had we the time."

"But we don't. That's what Roland said. He said there's not enough time."

"No. Just keep on, and maybe one day, on the other side of this story, we can meet again. But for now, you have to move on. Something's coming. It's far away yet, but it's been awoken and I need to prepare."

"Is it a good thing?"

"No. It is not."

Towards the end of my stay Gin told me of his first language, and even showed me how to write my name in it, something I delight to do even still, and will here. The language sounded strange, alien, yet beautiful too. When he first heard my name he chuckled.

"Why do you laugh at it?"

"It's nothing. Just has a funny ring in my first language. Don't worry. No one on this earth will ever tease you for it."

I believed at last that this was the Sage, and knew why he had told me what he had of the past: it was a test, a test of manners, of patience, to see if I would be so rude as to call him on his lies, be so cruel as to deny an old man his dreams.

On my last day he took a metal disk from his pocket and opened it like the shells of a clam. Inside, a needle slowly spun, steadied, and then stopped.

"I know this. It points to wherever the heart desires. A trader once offered it for the jezeth, but his also had a magic pool in the upper shell that showed the perfect image of the soul."

Gin rubbed his chin in thought. "I think you mean a mirror. Not a magic pool. Don't think there's too many of those left either. Not to the heart's desire, but to north this points. Always north. Use it with the map to help get you back. It took me a long time to get it to work right, but I don't need it really. Be careful with it is all and always trust it. It will be there when the clouds obscure the sun, when the sun hides the stars."

He gingerly pointed to the patterns on the face of the tool. "This," he said, "the lightning bolt, means north. Across it, this here, the snake, is south. The twin valleys are west, and the flying eagle, here, means east. It's older than you can imagine, and I don't think there are too many left on this earth. I don't see us making such things ever again." He closed it and put it into my hand. "Go now."

I bowed to him.

"I need to tell you something, Sage."

He held his hand up. "Just go," he said, and I did.

Not too much more to tell. I paddled the Sage's narrow boat to my own and found the knot to mine had not slipped. I left Gin's boat in its place. I had no reason for this other than I felt I should. In the small town that survived as a port to the great sea I secured a position on a black ship as a "Skinner." The ship would sail in seven days. Much of that time we spent loading all manner of goods to the hold. One day, we hauled barrel after barrel of liquid.

"What's this?" I asked my companion, sweating and tired and unhappy already.

"Is water."

"Water? Why we need to haul so much water?"

"You wanna go three months no water?"

"To drink?"

"Aye, and cook."

"Can't we drink the water from the sea?"

Work paused.

"A bit salty ain't it?"

"Salt?" I asked, and this became a great joke among the crew.

They laughed as we trudged half the earth into the hold, as we set keel to breakers, and forth on the godly seas. They laughed through the uncounted hardships to come, through storms plunging us into the maw of the abyss, split by an imperfect prow cut by imperfect men; they laughed as we coasted the wild and raging ocean on timbers three fingers thick, dove through mountains made of water, and in splintered buckets ever bailed that which called us always down. With no promise of touching another side, let them laugh.

A little more of things only I can say. In the days at the town on the port the children played a game where they kicked a ragged ball across a field of dirt and patches of grass. A girl, young, but not too young, with bright and brilliant eyes and a swift kick, a daughter at the house where I boarded, who smiled with the other children but not too often, whose countenance showed a poet's sadness when she thought no one saw her, who never jeered at the other when the ball rolled past their flag, who never frowned when they rolled it past hers, who kept her dress well sewn and clean, who kept herself clean and was careful with herself, this girl sat beside me in the shade beside the ball field the day before I left the land of my birth forever.

She stared at her feet, smiling lightly. She folded her dress neatly and her hands were clean and her hair brushed and she was so careful and in some ways older than I would ever be. I nodded to the port, to the ship that would be mine, smaller than the rest but a good one I was told. "They can sink," I said to her. "It happens."

She nodded.

"I have something I would not want lost in the sea. I would like to give it to you to keep as long as you wish. When you do not want it you can give it away, but it must never be sold or traded, and it cannot be stolen. That's part of its magic. To be honest, I don't really know anymore what it is, but I know it's a very special and I believe it would be terrible if it were lost at sea."

I unwrapped the jezeth and held it out before her. Her eyes grew wide. "Take it. Use it when the world is over gray, when you cannot find the light in the darkness. Please take it."

I lowered it into her hands and she closed them around its light. She said nothing. And then she said thank you. In the morning I sailed on.

I cannot write much about the sea. I do not have the skill, for a story of the sea is one of the human heart confined by narrow timbers, and I do not have the pen or the spirit to write of something so deep. But I can tell a little.

The black ships made their livelihood by harvesting the rarities of the remotest waters. We fanned a metal net in the wake of the stern and attached to it hooks hid beneath the surface, waiting metal teeth slicing through the deep blue. Some few ran especially deep, and I wondered what ever could we harvest that lived so far below the sun.

There were seven of us skinners, and hardship forged a kind of brotherhood among us. Our job was to slice creatures of unspeakable magnificence, and if they were of a type too common or unwanted, to simply cut them dead away and free the net for more. It was serious work, and so we joked all the time.

Our tool, the skinning knife, was a kind of rectangular short sword. The metal preserved in oil drawn from the skull of a whale, but the skinner was not so easily protected. As we had to lean out and hack at the kill, many a skinner in past crossings had either been stricken by a watery beast or, more likely, caught in the net and dragged too long under water. Usually, I heard, since the ship never stilled and the hooks always held, the death of a skinner was to drown in a slick of his own blood. But we strained with our knives to haul the bounty, reached far over the stern to our job with life in hands. Every day something else died. Almost always, we had no fear.

The process was simple enough: when the net became heavy with catch we slowly winched it in and lanced the beasts loose, or by one method or another, harvested whatever portion of it the human prized. Rarely did we take anything for its meat. We once caught the giant squid. The captain howled with delight: "Cut thick behind her eyes! Each one holds a pearl! And so, while we cut any tentacle that could wrap us by the neck and pull us in, we cut a hunk of meat behind each of the eye, dropped this wet upon the deck and the captain picked it up and with delight pulled shining orbs like mother of pearl from behind each one. "Now try and get the beak."

We did so, and cut the rest free to the endless blue.

As the captain peeled the orbs clean from the meat of the eye he smiled, lifted each to the fading light. "These as fine as any I've yet to haul." And they were truly beautiful, each almost as lovely as the jezeth, and I wondered what the world looks like through eyes like that. I thought then of Karuna, so far and past, she felt as a dream within a dream. And in my exhaustion, in the rocking sea, in the strange alien faces around me, it was so hard now to remember hers.

"Worry not boys," cried the captain as the white and pink meat floated down. "The sea wastes nothing. Nothing."

One day we caught a school of fish whose scales held the color of gold even in death and these were valued on land as coins. We strung them on lines and the captain counted them each day. We often caught gray fish with ridges of viscous teeth, some so large they could devour a man whole; the others told me this had actually happened. From them we mostly took only the fins and threw the rest to death. We killed so many of these toothed beast that we filled three enormous salted troughs with nothing but fin. By the time we finished our crossing, I wondered if there could be any but a few left in the sea, and though I knew it to be a sin, was secretly glad we had taken such violent creatures out of the water.

We took all parts cherished for whatever reason people cherish things. The captain wished our wake to be always red, and it almost always was. The killing bothered me some at first, not for meat, but to slay leviathan for a bauble, well…But soon it bothered me less. If not done by us, this would be done by another.

The only exception, the only catch which disturbs me still, is that of the "sugarfish," as Captain called it. These are prized beyond all other species for the simple delicacy of the meat. It was noon when, from a sea as quiet as the stars, the net pulled heavy and then heavier, so that the ship heaved in its course. The captain came to the transom and considered the churning water. Sometimes it was better to let the mesh tow for a while to catch more ahead, but draw too long and the hooks could cut right out of the meat. "Hold sails!" he called to the liners. "Draw 'em in!" he said to the winchmen.

I could see his anticipation. He knew: a joyful suspicion that this catch had something special. When the first of the great tails broke the water the captain first became breathless, as if all his life poised on this moment, but then threw his hat to the deck and howled in savage joy. As the net came in and we saw the size of the catch, he surged in primeval joy, in madness.

"Sugars! We got sugarfish! We hit Sugars! In! In! Haul 'em up! Break your backs why don't you? Look! They lifting off the hooks as we speak! Easy now. Easy now. Go easy now and now break your backs why don't you? In a hundred crossings one sugar is rare, and we got here a pod! Whole damned pod!"

The winchmen pulled until they could not. Others took over. They were close and we readied our blades over the stern. The captain waved them down. "No skinnin'. We bring 'em up whole. Waste nothing!"

The first to hit the deck struck us dumb. The only sound was the screaming of the creature. A terrible sound, horrific and not entirely inhuman. With long and nimble side fins this fish beat the deck and grabbed at the mesh as if to lift itself off the hook. It tore its flesh against the awful barbs but would never get free. The captain, delirious to catch just one, had us work the stern to secure the haul. "Ready with hooks! Back of the skull! Let not one get away! If not one get's free and extra vial of dust for all you!"

We took up the hooks but no one gaffed at the haul. We pretended to not have a clear draw. Yet, the winchmen hauled in more as other sugarfish writhed on the deck in howling agony. They would not stop screaming. The captain beheld them with a kind of ecstasy. "Pull! Winchmen! Pull them all in! It's a haul once in a thousand crossings! Pull until your spines split!" He now cried in childish glee. "Turn her harder now! Turn for your life's worth, for God has graced us with a pod of sleeping sugars!"

The sugarfish worked in coordination, pulling not in a confused frenzy but at times all at once strained against the mesh as if to break it, and they almost did. Other times they would in unison pull downwards when the ship's transom sank in the valley of a large swell and I swore they did this to sink us. But they never quite did. But soon they began to tire, having bled out so much. Soon, all resistance stopped and all were pulled aboard. Now, twelve sugars writhed and flapped on the deck and the captain paced and rung his hands and had been crying with joy. He gave orders, but it was very hard to hear him over the screaming.

"They slippery," he said, "and can strike you with them pec fins. No meat is worth that of the sugars. Is the sweetest most precious meat on earth or sea, for they feed on the finest delicacies of the deep. Skinners! Cut em here," with the side of his hand he gestured a chop at his own collar. "Just there cut 'em. Take 'em off where it looks like a neck."

We hesitated at this. The screaming.

"The sooner you do your work the sooner we get peace!" the captain cried, but still none of us moved. It was the upper part of the sugars that bothered us. It looked so damned human.

The captain paced and shouted menacingly. "At the necks! Just cut 'em all at the necks and take their damned heads!"

But no one of us would go first. Without another word, the cruel captain shook his head in disgust and took a knife from the hand of the skinner nearest him and went to the largest of the catch, raised the blade beneath the late-day sun and cried, "Is just a fish! Even God don't weep at its killing!" And then with one blow he chopped its head half off. The rest of the pod howled in unison, in grief no fish should ever know. One by one the captain took the heads of each sugar, until all the deck rocked in silence, until there remained only the voice of the eternal sea. "Waste nothing!" he howled to us, returning the knife. "Skin clean every piece of meat and salt it and store it cool."

This we did, for the deed had already been done. We talked about it after, what struck us so terribly about this haul. For some it was the screaming that seemed to have a kind of garbled language mingled to it; for others, it was the humanity of the eyes; but for me, the image which haunts me still, is that of the last two to be killed, a male and female, (you could tell the females for they had the suggestions of breasts), who lay side by side at the end of the captain's murder line. It was just how they ceased to struggle with the shadow of the knife over them, but instead reached their fins to each other, fins whose tips had the suggestion too much like fingers, and held them together when the knife fell to neck. They did not let go even in death. We had to pull them apart to harvest the meat.

We did not leave that area for three days in the hopes of finding others, but never did. My fellow skinners and I had not given all the meat to the captains precious barrels, but would secretly drop slivers into the sea. A warning. We caught no more sugarfish on that crossing.

And one morning I was called awake at the break of dawn and knew, with utter certainty I knew, with an ever-breaking heart I knew that the peris had been freed.

And like all things, that crossing came to an end. We landed here and were given some gold dust and I wandered from the port an orphan. By the end of the voyage I swore to never sail again, but now I wonder. The years rush by quicker, and this life, which I once thought very long, grows shorter. Maybe, when my concerns here are few, I will return to the wild continent and see if Roland still resides with his crew somewhere, or even, knowing now the quicker way, find old Gin in his cave, with that smile of his which might outlast the sun. And perhaps even there will come the day when I summon my heart back to Selador, to at last know the whole of my own story, the destiny of the home I abandoned so long ago.

But for now I live, as you know, with a wife more beautiful than twilight, and a daughter, the blossom of our heart - and I could begin to write of the miracle of these but think the world would first dry of ink, and anyway it's a common occurrence, and not for what people are wont to read.

Dearest friend, first to welcome me to this temperate land of gentle hills and sweet water, so long have you stayed with me, I beg now, stay a little longer. There is a reason I end it now: I have told what this land, thrice blessed, could never know. Let these leaves be my apology for wearing the face of a stranger in the crowd, for pausing even now at the edges of the fields at dusk, and for those days when a sickness unknown here overcomes me, and I shiver under a blazing sun, lie in quiet darkness, and mutter words to none: All these are but symptoms of my travels, the grazing kiss of straying too long on the road alone. Soften your heart to the distance you say rests within my eyes, to my forgetting at times to laugh at the delightful and absurd. And for those moments when I forget the astounding beauty of it all, forgive me. I am only a man.

May this labor scatter all the shadows of my past. Let them be spoken of no more. I have left nothing worth saying unsaid. I pray this finds you in the grace of gods, that the bitter wind rises only to your back, that fortune keeps your every step until we meet again, with joy, after the passing of the season of rain.

Faithfully yours,

Snorri

He stood with uncertain legs on the hayrick, all the world about him enormous and clear. And she was so far down, so far away.

"Do not be afraid! Jump, Snorri, jump!"

He believed her but she was so far away. Then, with a breath of hope, with all the courage of his life he leapt into the openness, into the weightless clarity of flight and falling, and among the astounding beauty that could only live for moments he too became the infinite, a breathless cascade of light and love falling or flying until she caught him, with love and the joy of perfect laughter she caught him, holding him tight in the nurture of her embrace, in that time never to be again, in that moment when everything lived.

BOOK V

Gin

J. A. Scheffer

Gin

Christ, these wars. They coming on for how long now? So few left and they coming again to me, and for what? So, I have her. So, I do. They won't let her sleep. This is not even real anymore. Why won't they just let her sleep? He rubbed his eyes, tired. "What you gonna do, old Gin?" he asked himself. "Dragged again into the fray," he said to no one.

"So what am I going to do?" he asked now to the sky but the sky did not respond. Staring towards the sun he imagined the origin of all earthly light, millions of miles away, floating in incomprehensible proportions through void and waste and crystals of ice and dust and how did all this knowledge die? And now, by Christ, again to war.

"That kid. How many times will he come to me? Do I in every life have to see his begging face?" He's been thin of late. He's fading, I think. Maybe this be the last one. Christ, those eyes. They never change. That's how you know. What have I done to him? What do I owe him? Your hands are not clean, old man. So, after it, if I should live, I will go to his king. Why have they come at the same time?

There are no coincidences

"Please, Sage, Gin, Sage, please help them…"

Emaciated he was. Never so thin before. His face fell to his hands and he rubbed his eyes. He climbed to his home and struck a small fire. Walking to the back of the cave he pulled back the aged rugs an uncovered the medusa, tapped the shell absently with his knuckle listening to the hollow within.

"She is weightless, almost without matter."

He could see his mutated reflection dully in its shell like tarnished silver. "Maybe you are magic, after all…," he whispered to it, "…the absolute darkest magic that could ever be, and maybe therein lies the final threshold of science."

He had opened it only once, out of necessity. The ribbed shell-lips cracked just enough to let forth a breath of ancient air from a world that would never be again. Inside, lay a thing unthinkable. He closed it with shaking hands, sealing it perhaps forever with a word all his own. Many nights he wished he had just not looked. He could have done it without looking. "You won't fool me," he said to the medusa. "Nothing fools me anymore," he said, but knew this to be untrue.

He fell asleep and awoke to the dark. For some reason it frightened him. He stepped out to the plain below. The full moon hung shining like a blessing above. He knew now what bothered him: it still had not been resolved. In the last life, with so much asked and given, it had not been resolved.

Christ!

In the cave again he relit the fire with a breath and made the tea which brings tranquility. He sipped it with shaking hands. "Why are you so nervous, old fool? Just take her to Roland. If he is truly with a Phoenix there's no better time. Then to it."

We are the empty men.

She has to die.

We are the stuffed men.

She has to, has to die.

Leaning together, headpieces filled with straw.

It will be her or everything else.

Next morning, the man who was old and not old could barely do his exercises. No peace came to his mind. A bad start to a fresh journey. He touched the ground and felt it solid. "This is not a dream," he said to himself. He touched the ground again. "You are not dreaming." He had to do this from time to time.

"In sleep our spirits lift to the ether and there meet others both dark and bright!"

In the stricken land, the blighted continent, in the Valley of the Fallen, all those months with no cricket chirp, no birdsong. Christ. Only those miserable worms nesting in the eyes of the dead, nesting everywhere. Did they eat stone? And the water stuffed with dead grains. The rain, I remember, fell as sand.

"She requires an altitude in the upper stratosphere. All water vapor must float only in particles of ice for her to open. Upon her exhalation there has been the observance of a kind of worm, small, yellow-brown, species unknown. We don't know why this is."

"'Selador,' he says this time."

Selador

You have to move on. There comes a time when you have to move on.

He could be mistaken for a ghost or a shade slipped up from the world beneath the world. A mirage that had no reason. A thought formed in the air and blown away by the wind. An observer on those plains of frozen waste would see a figure which did not walk on the ground or fly, but glided soundlessly in a cloak of gray. When it paused, it became stone. When it sped, the ground did not disturb in its passing. The only certainty for the observer would be that the figure went inexorably south, unwavering in its course, unfaltering in its purpose.

A day out from Roland's base a tiny man with red skin appeared before the figure. "You are the elder one, are you not? The boy found you?" asked the tiny, red man.

The figure nodded, stunned. He'd never seen a full-grown person so small with such perfect proportions. He had to ask, "Where are you from, little one?"

"The elven realm."

Gin smiled. "I see. So then, I suppose you are an elf?"

Dexter nodded. "The Northern Army has landed and already marches south. They will vie on the field of Gidon against the army of the Southern King. This is for her. You have her I know. I felt her two days ago. They can find her now with their mechanisms, those needles. They wait for their every twitch, are learning more and more how to read them. They will vie for her to the end. Each runs to kill the other for her. Had you stayed, they would have found you."

"Perhaps."

"They would have. It does not matter how far north she was hid. The King of Nede alone has two needles and in the moments they can be awoken they...We don't know who or how...."

Gin held his hand up. "I know. They must have searched long and hard as those needles are tiny things. They were cut from her shell once upon a time and with the right preparation-can't imagine who would know how- are drawn back to the source. But this is no easy trick. Yet, tell me this: with no such tool, how did you know I had her?"

"I am sick."

"I see. Does she sicken all the elves?"

"Yes."

Gin squinted into the flashing eyes, black and wet and animalistic. Crescent moons of gray iris. "He told me you were very quick."

Dexter nodded, nauseous. "That I am." Dexter had never encountered a human with so much energy, yet he had to lean against a tree, for the illness she caused. "We do have a common purpose, yes?"

"You don't look well."

"I will be fine when she goes. We do work together, yes?"

"Sure, I suppose, but I've other matters to attend to."

"She must...must be destroyed."

Gin shrugged. "It's been tried before," he said and smiled. "You look worried."

"I'm only sick."

He tried to recall if he had ever in all his years seen anything like Dexter, but could not; yet he had forgotten much and tried always to remember that. Sometimes it surprised him, the things he had forgotten. And sometimes, too, what he remembered. This Dexter leapt from the pages of a fairytale: sprites and unicorns, nymphs and peris, anthropophagi, jinn, mara...elf – the guardian of the forest and earth. This one reminded him of elf. Yet, skin could be dyed with toxins and paint stone, and for a man so small to survive in a world so ruthless, he would have to be fantastically quick, unspeakably lethal. And as people are born for ages uncounted, eventually, well, anything could happen.

"It's okay to be worried," Gin said. "The elven realm must be charming."

"Please, Elder of Man," Dexter was breathless now, "we have little time for little talk. You have to take her to Roland now. He is with Belladonna of the Phoenix, they who nurse the fire of her destruction."

The sage leaned against his great spear. He felt sorry for the tiny man being so ill. He squinted at him, thinking. "Would you like me to carry you to the camp?"

"No, please, you need only take her away."

It took all his strength for Dexter to lift his head to look in the elder's eyes. Such energy! A red cobra coiled up his back. Golden fire encircled his hands. He smiled brightly and yet, in the pool of his eyes, a well of darkness hid. Silence settled between them. He had to ask again, "You *are* with us, yes?"

"Of course, Little One. Why wouldn't I be?"

"I don't know. But it would be terrible if you were not."

"I'm not the enemy. So, how's Roland been?"

"Fine."

"Good to hear. He still some kind of tough guy?"

"Yes."

"Good. They'll be looking for him, those kings. He's not the only one with spies."

"He knows this." Every word was a labor. His vision blurred. Had he been able to eat anything of late he would have thrown it up.

"I hear he's sleeping with this Belladonna?"

"Do you ask if they perform coitus?"

"Yes."

"Yes."

"Good for him, Bearer of the Seven Knives."

Stunned, for a moment Dexter forgot his illness. No one had ever seen even one of the hidden knives. "You've sharp eyes, Elder," he said, voice shaking.

Gin grinned. "So, do you trust her?"

"I do."

"Good. Sooner or later one must take a leap of faith."

"I don't know," he mumbled sick and pale. How humans did not feel it astounded him.

"Do you think they're truly in love?"

"How would I know?" Dexter spoke as loudly as he could. "Humankind remains a mystery to me, even as I dwell among them."

Gin did not laugh. "Sometimes I feel much the same way."

"It has awakened again, hasn't it?"

He had not wanted to speak of it.

"And that is the true reason you've finally come?"

"Sometimes things have more than one reason, Dexter. Does it matter?"

"You could have stopped all this sooner, but choose to sleep. Only the shadow of man has spurred you awake, but now the day runs late."

"Says you. None know the darkness which dwells in the hearts of men. This," he said, hefting the medusa, "is not safe in any time in any hands. Leave me to my decisions, and I will you to yours."

"It has grown stronger, Elder."

"Yes it has," said Gin, "but I've many tricks. Anyway, I think I should get some space between you two. We could talk all day otherwise."

"Another day on this trail, less if you hurry." Dexter tried to point behind him, but his arm collapsed half-risen.

"I know the way. Please be well."

"Be careful, Elder of Man."

He bowed to the tiny man who could only nod back. As he walked away, life returned to Dexter by degrees.

Just before dusk he stood at the ruins of a gate. He attempted to read the remnants of a weather-worn name etched in a plate of stone on the gatepost. He laughed without joy realizing he must be the only person on earth who could read the fragments which survived the ravages of time. Roland and Belladonna waited on the portico of the mansion. "Why does he squint at the ruins, Roland?" whispered Belladonna.

"I don't know, Bell. He's strange like that."

She folded her arms and fixed her face in disdain. She hated the Sage almost immediately. He reminded her of pretend magicians who fleece the ignorant for money, or fools who felt age alone merited wisdom. "Is he daring to ignore us," she muttered fiercely. "And now he touches the stone again."

"Bell, I've not seen him in many years, and under very different circumstances."

"Did you win?"

"No one won, but we are not enemies anymore. Weren't even then exactly. They were strange times, not unlike these."

"Do you think he has her?"

"Why else would he have come?"

"He looks like a ghost."

"He might be. Ho, Gin!" Roland called at last.

For a moment he just kept staring at the etched ruins, tracing his finger in a lost letter and thinking of the letter and all it had once meant. He looked up to them, bowed and smiled. "Roland," he responded, "It's good to see you again. You look well. May I come in?"

"Yes."

Gin entered the gate. Belladonna stood as rigid as steel, staring at the guest with eyes of fire. Gin smiled at her. "This must be your daughter," he said to Roland, and she immediately wanted to kill him.

"Uh…no, Gin. No. This is Belladonna of the Phoenix. Belladonna, Gin."

"Pardon me. How nice to meet you, Belladonna of the Phoenix," he said with a low bow which she did not return. He feigned ignorance and looked to Roland, "Can she speak?"

"Yes."

"Then it must be me. Ah, well. You are looking much healthier than when last we met, more well fed. She must be a good cook."

She would leap from the step and cut off his head.

"Gin, please."

"Since when is proficiency in the culinary arts an insult?"

Her hand lowered to the sword.

"Bell," said Roland, "We spoke of this. Please."

"In fact," said Gin, "I tire of sustaining this old carcass by naught but the dew of morn and the breath of the four sacred winds. A good meal with bright company would be delightful. Hospitality too has not fallen away completely, has it?"

Roland sighed. "Listen, Gin, are you really hungry? Do you suggest we stay and catch up on old times? Does this sound like a pleasant evening?"

"Was you who asked me to come, remember? Would you have an old man cross a vast and dangerous wild to simply drop a package and be gone? Hm? And then send him off unfed into the wild, at night and alone?"

Roland sighed again. "Fine. If you would like to come in, we can prepare a meal for you, and you can stay the night."

"Roland, no!"

"Easy, Bell. It's my crew. Please remember that. He would be my guest, and I would expect you at least to respect that."

"Thank you, Roland, but I am afraid I've another matter to attend to." Roland looked confused. "I just wanted to be asked. I remember a time when it would be unthinkable to have an elder, to have anyone, travel so far on a mission in so remote a country and not offer him a rest and meal upon his arrival. I just wanted to know that things have not changed so dreadfully."

Roland could not believe this peculiar person had made him feel a pang of guilt for not offering dinner. Yet, he had. "Again, you can stay. Feel free."

"No, no. It's too late now, and you have made it clear I would be an imposition."

"Well then, there's not much left to do, Gin. Do you have her?"

"I do."

"May we have her?"

Belladonna became motionless. All her life had been sacrificed for the obtainment of the medusa, and now it might be here. It felt unreal to her. Could it really be this unpleasant old man had her life's purpose hidden beneath his cloak? Gin waited. His smile went away. He read both their eyes, especially Belladonna's.

"You ask a lot, you know."

"I do. May we have her, Gin?"

"Do you know the rock of the world rests on the wing of an angel?"

"Enough of this, Roland" cried Belladonna, and she drew the Sword of Scars and pointed it at the old man's throat. "Give us the medusa or your head."

"Bell!"

"It's all right, Roland. The impatience of youth is part of its charm."

With a flash of fire she cut the air and the air cried. Roland groaned. Gin smiled. "What a magnificent sword, Belladonna. Breathtaking."

"Bell…."

"One skull stays or two! Give her, or I cut off your head!"

She tensed every muscle in an arm as strong as the iron it held. She wanted all blood, all power summoned to it. She might play the game where you see how many times you can sever a person in half before all the pieces fall to the ground. She pointed the sword at him again and he could feel the energy flying from the tip. With his finger, he turned circles in the air between them. "I've not seen such as it for a long long time, if ever."

"Sheathe it, Bell. Please."

"Roland, no! No, Roland, no! He has insulted me, you, even the Phoenix and now, if he truly has her, he hides it from us under filthy cloak of gray which mercifully covers his weak and bent body!" She shook the sword at Gin and the steel rang. "I should kill not just you but the entirety of your bloodline, the whole of your village for such an insult!"

"Good luck with that, young lady. My village has been gone for a long time, and as for my bloodline, well, anyway." He spoke to Roland then, "She's rather rash and irritable. Is she always like this, or perhaps the crescent moon wanes?"

Roland held Belladonna by the shoulder. Even through her armor he could feel her boiling rage. "Gin, please! Belladonna!"

"Do not say 'please' to this thing, Roland!"

"Belladonna, please…"

"How could you ever, ever say…"

The sage leaned the great spear against the remnant of the gate and held out his hand. "May I hold that magnificent weapon, young lady?"

She almost laughed in disbelief.

"She doesn't even let me touch it, Gin."

"Well, she lets you touch other things, Roland. As for me, I would just like to see the etching on such a rare and exquisite weapon…feel its weight."

Roland tightened his grip on her shoulder. He did not want it to go like this. It did not have to go like this, but her eyes had become vacant. She had slipped past his control.

"Roland," she said much too calmly, "remove your beloved hand from my shoulder."

"Bell, no. Please, no."

"Do not call me that. Don't call me anything. Remove the hand from the shoulder of Belladonna. I love you too much to cut it off."

"Oh, just let her go, Roland. She wants to show me that pretty sword of hers. Just don't run with it, young lady. You shouldn't run with sharp objects."

"Promise me you won't hurt her."

Belladonna could not believe what she heard. "Roland! I am a daughter of the Phoenix!"

"Yes, but this is different. He's tougher than he looks, Bell. None of this is necessary. The both of you, please listen. We just need to get on with things. This is insanity."

She did not listen. Instead, her eyes traced to where the tendons of his old neck connected to the shoulder, noted carefully the outline of his trachea, the movement of his throat as he swallowed. She must only sever some tendons, cut only part of his windpipe. She wanted his head to loll, but not fall off, wanted him to breathe, but with great effort. He must have a pronounced rasp in his breath, but be unable to speak. He mustn't ever be able to speak again. This was most important. One must be so careful when operating on the throat: a hair too deep and they bleed out, just a glance on the wrong spot and their own blood chokes them. She needed to be so careful now. She could do it all in three cuts, about the time it took to blink, but she had to be so careful in this. How feeble he looked. Yet, Roland's estimation was not to be taken lightly. Perhaps he had some fight after all, and perhaps armor hid beneath that ragged cloak, perhaps even other weapons, ones which might be dangerous, something beside that crude and over-sized and all but useless spear. She dearly hoped he had some fight. With a sadistic pleasure, Belladonna imagined removing any limb which dared lift a weapon against her. May he draw double daggers! May both hands grasp the spear! After, she would keep him in the basement, in a cold and dim-lit corner where she alone would tend to him. She would be happy to be his nurse. Oh Gin, may you live forever! For the first time in as many days, Belladonna felt deliciously happy.

Then Gin spoke: "Roland, I think she really just wants to show me her pretty sword. Let her go. I won't kill her. Either way, you are out-voted."

And before the shadow of his hand had left her shoulder, Belladonna leapt with the screaming sword towards the Sage. She stepped only once on the ground between the steps and the distant gate before lifting into the air again. On her second descent, the Sword of Scars, spinning in blinding speed, aimed at the upper part of his neck. Gin winked at her, and then placed his hand over his mouth to cover a yawn. She was beyond him in all ways, and Roland saw her rage for what it was: temporary insanity. She might just kill Gin after all, he thought, and surprisingly, this distressed him. But then, without noise or contest, with hardly any movement at all,

Belladonna plopped on the ground facing the portico, legs crossed and arms folded, her hands cupped one in the other as if in meditation. Gin stepped slowly back, admiring in the late-day light the exquisite etchings on the Sword of Scars. He smiled waved it softly before him and smiled. "Lovely," said Gin as he paced behind her. He eyed her bare neck and said, "Truly magnificent."

Belladonna was a little dizzy, greatly stunned, entirely confused. She did not yet know what had happened. It would be a moment before she even uncupped her hands.

"Don't do it, Gin."

"Do what, Roland?"

"Behead her."

"Do not beg for me, Roland!" Belladonna screamed. She had not even felt him touch her. "Let me die now!"

"Never ever cease to fight if you can fight. As you have life, as you have breath, fight. Fight against the impossible. Fight until there is nothingness."

A tear ran down her cheek. "Let me die now, please!" The tear dropped to her lap.

"Kill her? Why would I kill such a vivacious young lady as this?"

She drew two hidden daggers from her belt. Impossible, but she would try. She had to try. It was the law. Gin walked away keeping his back to her. How dare he? She stood with daggers at the ready, but he only cared about the sword in his hands and waved it so as to summon the wind. The trees nearby swayed. Belladonna knew then she had underestimated him, but that didn't mean he could not be killed. "Most beautifully wrought," he went on. "Shining work. And in it the Phoenix and the Seven Great Stars. And here, the Dragon and the Tiger. Powerful. Divine. A fine tradition. Such a weapon begs one to believe in magic." Its energy was ancient and tried. He could almost count the number of souls it had freed from their mortal coil. "The people who made this weapon are long gone. How the Phoenix found and preserved it, I shall never know."

"No, you shall *not*, demon! Is *not* yours to hold!"

He turned to her. "No, it isn't but, well, you attacked me with it, so I took it from you. If you throw those daggers, I will split them with this. And if you charge, I will take them from your hands. I am not your enemy, Child of the Phoenix. Please put the daggers away. If you could not defeat me with a sword like this you have no chance with little knives."

She trembled in rage and grief and shame. If she put the daggers away it meant…she could hardly think it…but it meant, for the first time in all her life since consecration, it meant she had been defeated.

"Leave the medusa and I will spare you," she demanded, but her words were broken.

"Dear Child, it is I who hold the great sword. Yet, I'll tell you what: hit me just once and I will give you the medusa without hesitation. And to make it fair, since you've only those little, lovely, knives, I shall lend you a weapon most powerful. The stuff legends are made of!"

Gin lifted the resting spear from the gate, unwrapped the tip and revealed the great spiral of the tooth of Kai-Tey.

"Gin," asked Roland, "You, you made it into a spear?"

"Yes I did. And it took no small amount of labor. For a meet shaft I had to venture to the heart of the Mountain of Adamantine … and let me tell you, there are more pleasant strolls. Then, of course, there was the hollowing to be done. Have you any idea how hard a dragon's tooth is?" He then spoke to the distraught Belladonna: "Cheer up, Young One. You shall be the second person ever to hold it. He then hurled the awesome engine lengthwise at her gut.

Ooof!

Her arms flew forward, but she did not lose the daggers. She flew all the way back to the portico, her back crashing into it, yet held the daggers still. Were it not for her halter of iron and leather, her ribs would have cracked. She writhed for a moment on the steps. Roland bent to help her, but she pushed his hands away. She rolled the great spear off and stood. She wanted very badly to hold her stomach, but would not give Gin the satisfaction. She could not help her coughing.

He waved the Sword of Scars back and forth playfully. "Young lady, do not attack a master with unequal arms. Take my weapon. I assure you, none other like exists in all the world." She sheathed the daggers and bent to the spear. So damned heavy. First it slipped, and then she grabbed it again and just barely could she lift it. Gin did not laugh. "A hefty thing, yes, but strong. One hit, you win forever."

With all her strength she pointed the spear at Gin. "This weapon is slow and clumsy." She complained in straining breaths.

"Says you," said Gin. "Like anything else, you get used to it."

"Ugh!" She charged on wobbly legs. When she thought she might be close enough, she threw it. It did not even reach halfway to him, yet when it hit the ground, the dirt scattered widely in a kind of explosion. Then it lay cold and still.

"Let's stop this, everyone."

"Sure, Roland," said Gin.

"No!"

"Bell, please."

"No! He has disgraced me!"

"That's debatable, young lady. Here, take back your lovely sword. You should never throw a spear. You've just lost your weapon." He sent the sword whirling through the air blindingly quick. Roland thought she would not dare to catch it, but she leapt up like a cat and had the grip in her hand perfectly. With a fierce flourish, she charged at him again. She stopped when the tip of the spear rested against her throat. It had pushed in just a little. A trickle of blood ran down and she coughed again. Somehow, with one hand, he could hold it out perfectly straight. It rested in her jugular notch. A simple push and she would be done, and she knew this and he knew this, and she had not even seen him retrieve the weapon. Roland's voice came as if from another world.

"He's not like us, Bell. Just leave it alone."

"Oh shut up Roland! You don't understand this! You never understood me!"

She clashed the Sword of Scars against the belly of the tooth and sparks flew and the sword shook, but the spear had not deflected at all. She could feel the tip cut another layer of skin. She held her arms out: "Kill me!" she demanded. Laws were meant to be broken.

"Oh, come now. Why would I kill you?"

"I have disgraced the Phoenix. Kill me."

"No, you haven't. You just needed to learn some humility. Pride and bravery are fine, but without humility they are very dangerous and often distasteful. I have come only to give what you have for so long sought, what you have been trained your whole life to acquire."

She rested her chin on the tip of the spear and her tears ran down onto the weapon. She had thought herself almost as a goddess once.

He had taken that from her. "Then give us the medusa, Old One, and go."

"Say 'please.'"

Her tears fell like rain. "Kill me. Please."

"Just say 'please,' and I will give you the medusa and go. I carried it a long way. I hid her for decades. At least you can extend a simple courtesy, a word."

She looked back at Roland for whom they were both a mystery. "Gin, what's the point of all this?"

"As I said, pride without humility is dangerous, Roland, for her and everyone else. If she is too proud, she cannot be trusted with it, and so I won't give it to her. It's my device to end all life and earth itself and whoever wants it must say 'please.' It's not a lot to ask considering."

Then, he looked to Belladonna. "Did you not swear to do whatever it took to get the medusa, young one?"

Red, wet eyes, numb past hatred, looked into his. "Please," she whispered, and then immediately drew the Sword of Scars crossways through her lips, opening them right to the gums. Sweet, cleansing, purifying blood carried all her soul's poison away, flowed freely from her mouth and coated the great tooth upon which Belladonna rested her chin and smiled. Gin understood the required madness for her lot, but feared she might be just a little too insane for the task at hand.

"Well, that was not so hard, was it, young lady?"

She relished how she had turned the great ivory crimson, said nothing, but began licking swirls in the blood upon the tooth. He drew the spear away. She missed it now, almost went to chase it, but he flicked it clean and then spun it once, as quickly as one would a sword, and with the tip launched the medusa he had rest upon the ground high above the head of the warrior from the god of ashes. She had never seen it, yet knew it instantly. She ran back, leapt, and caught her life's fate in the air above the portico. She landed beside Roland, cradling the end of all things in her arms as an infant.

And it was true: the medusa had almost no weight. And it was true: that of all the generations of the Phoenix, God had seen fit to place it in her hands. Hers. She would set it upon the sacred fire. Her hand would redeem the world. She would set it to burn, and to the flames eternal, be first to rest her sword within that pyre to which all the Phoenix would at last rest theirs. Overcome, she turned to Gin and smiled a ghastly smile.

"Tha... thank you!" she cried.

He folded both hands over his heart and bowed to her. "You are welcome, Young One. May you find your destiny."

She nodded quickly, covered her lips with her hands, and leaned in close to whisper to the shell a word taught to her when she was but a youth. Nothing. She repeated the word louder. Nothing. Gin cleared his throat. "That's not going to work. I changed that a long time ago."

In the voice of a frightened child: "But how? Why? Why would the word be changed?"

"The old word was known by more than the Wreath of the Phoenix. Rather unsavory types with not the best intentions had it, and who knows who else? Only I know it now, and only I will."

She panicked and stood, a sick feeling rising in her gut. "And I... I too will know it. You must tell it to me. Please. Tell us the word. Please."

Gin smiled calmly. "You say 'please' without my having to ask. I'm proud of you, Belladonna. Honestly. You learn quickly and are genuine. I have faith in you and your abilities, as much as I may in any living person." He sighed and scratched his head and had to look away, "But to tell you or anyone the word runs too much risk. You will have to destroy her and her shell. That's all."

"No, no, no, please, no. You must. Without it, she may not be ruined. For centuries we have nursed the sacred altar of the fire. Understand, please understand, when the Age of Confusion yielded to the Age of Loss, the first Wreath of the Phoenix followed riddles and myth, portents in the sky to find the fiery throne of the god. Into this the medusa would be tossed. And it was there, beneath the world tree they found it, but much had already burned. We have nursed remnants of the nest, but it is much exhausted, never to be lit again save by the phoenix itself. But the stuff is almost gone. We may not pierce even the shell with what little we have. So, please, she needs to burn directly. She must be opened. Please, give us the word."

"No. The fire's fuel is not my concern."

"It is everyone's concern!"

"You will just have to do your best. If they should wrest her from your hands..."

"Belladonna cannot be defeated on the field of battle!"

"I defeated you."

"You are not human."

"Yes, I am. Just practiced."

"I would die before revealing the word."

"I know you would, but they have ways of making you talk, just in case you cannot cut your throat first."

"No torture would…"

He raised a finger. "I am not speaking of torture, by and large a useless tool. They have ways of coaxing the word from you in your sleep. Drugs that would make your mouth ramble. And even once, devices were that could read the words right from your mind…even after death, if you were not too far gone. Who knows if one lies around yet, powered by some new source in this world which God saw fit to return to its childhood? No. It's too risky. The word stays with me."

She wanted to scream but felt only empty then. In the theater of her mind the last of the precious fire licks a hole in the shell and is then exhausted. She sees the stare break out upon the earth forever.

"There is no God," she whispers, and collapses over the shell. Her forehead rests on its silver ribs and for a moment she floats high above the house and trees and clouds and higher still until the earth becomes a bright and blue ball against the cold stare of space. How lovely it looks. A gem against the desolation of the void. Clouds stretch like the fleece of lambs above the great waters lit with tips of light and then. But then, it trembles. A shadow grows from the East and everything folds under it. Everything goes silent and gray and is gone. Just gone. She hears the groan of the world, sees the earth die on its axis.

"And now the sun has nothing to do,
And now the moon rises blue,
For no flower gives the sun his grace,
And no sea shows the moon her face."

Roland kneeling beside her, "Bell, Sweet Bell, are you all right?"

"You will be denied many things other children have, but sacrifice fosters great reward. Blood will become a nectar for you. A

sword will be not an extension of the arm but the house of the spirit. You will know the voice of the land. You will know the song of the wind. Pain will be a dear friend in whom you take comfort. Your mind will be emptied of all resentment and hope and despair and past love. We will fill it with the secrets of the Phoenix. It is we who will recall the earth. This has been ordained by God. It has to be. You are no longer an orphan child. Take my hand. You are hungry today, but will not be tomorrow. Today you will be cut. Rejoice in this, for it illuminates the path to divinity. Delight in blood, for it connects the spirit to the soil. Today, you are born as an instrument of salvation. Today, you become the mother of all that will ever be. Do not be afraid."

She could not answer. She absently stood and lifted the medusa like an infant born still and with it went inside.

"Well, Roland, I suppose I should be going. Enjoy your war. They will be here before too long, you know."

"I don't enjoy war, Gin. I never have."

"That's why we can trust you. Do your best to protect her."

"Of course."

He waved goodbye to the hidden Iga and faded into the trees.

He came to a low rise ahead of a darkening sky. He felt it so strongly now: cold and ancient and not entirely inhuman. It approached without cease.

"Is not man or beast or god that comes"

He unwrapped the spear and threw the cloth away. Hung on his neck by a red string, an ancient jade carved long before his birth he lifted and kissed and let fall again beneath his shirt. He muttered a prayer he thought he had forgotten, trying in that moment to recall the entirety of his life, but could not. His hands shook and this too surprised him. He could not recall the last time he had truly felt terror.

"Look to the sky when there is nothing else. The stars will guide you if not obscured by clouds and, once you learn to truly pay attention to them, they will assert the permanence of things."

The air, long stuck in an unnatural stillness, now began to turn in a slow and cold gyre. The grass and wildflowers bent to it. He pressed his palms against his ears to warm them and close out sound.

He closed his eyes and tapped the base of his skull and counted to forty-eight. This done, he felt calmer. The wind grew stronger. A signature of its presence.

"Master your own emotions. You alone rule your mind."

She stands on the porch, her blue dress lifting in the rising wind. The pressure of the atmosphere drops like a stone in a lake. "Get in. A twister's comin'!"

He runs to the cellar, confused.

"Where's your little brother now? He was with you! Where's the little one at?"

He didn't know.

"Where'd you leave him last?"

He didn't know.

"Where's he? Where'd you leave 'im last? Oh, get in, by God's love, and pray. She shuts the door and latches it and goes out into the maelstrom. In minutes the wind grows to a train overhead and he is only a boy and he is screaming trying to open the door she had latched against the wind. And the train roared above and the sky broke things against the cellar-door and she had been gone too long and he knows this and screams. After the storm, they are gone, both of them lifted into the sky, and the reverend saying how God had taken them into his embrace. This God leaving him an orphan. Nothing even to bury.

The ground murmurs in a low rumble. Like a blanket tossed by a careless god, a horde of winged creatures swarmed the sky blotting out the last of the late-day light.

What's this now?

He looks up. Birds? Bats, locusts, birds, whatever could take to wing flee in a screaming cloud and here was something he had never seen before. "Nature has learned your name," he whispers to the sky, "and so begins the numbering of your days."

Crouching, he set his back against a broad trunk and tented the shaft of adamantine over him. The head of the great spear stabbed into the earth. He held it tightly, knowing what must be coming next.

A sickness in his gut. And then the leaves began to tick. Rain? No. He pulled a squirming cricket from the fibers of his sleeve, and then a spider. A moment later both died. He dropped them gently into the cup of his hand and exhaled on them slowly, willed energy to them, he wanted them to live. For some reason it seemed very important and for a moment they did and they crept on uncertain legs to the edge of his hand, but the wave of sickness rose in his gut again and it was then they fell away lifeless and he lowered them for good to the wilting grass and more and more of the bugs fell dead from the leaves and sky.

He pulled his hood tightly over him. Smaller birds and bats began to tumble through the canopy, would beat dead or dying wings against the ground until their hearts just stopped.

A low earthquake comes. And then the coughs and grunts and baying and the yelps and the mewling of the charging and trampled beasts. First came horses, weaving in stricken terror and some crashed into the trees and he could hear the dull crack of skulls, the splitting of legs. The slower creatures followed. Every manner that lived therein. He crouched and waited, held the spear and waited. The earth fell quiet again, and the grace of light descended from the firmament again, and the last of the howls faded over the distant hills. He stood.

"Is not man or beast or god what comes."

The dead and dying were littered everywhere. Creatures all but ruined tried yet to stand and run and this amazed him how life never surrenders. The awful groans of the beasts. He swept his hand across the expanse of forest. All went quiet. "Requiescatis in pace" he whispered, and then walked to the shadow in the East.

It grew unnaturally cold. He kept his eyes before his feet. He crested a low rise. Below, raged a storm of dust and shadow and darkness and turning flesh and it paused at the Sage cloaked in gray, spoke to him from its mind, from a heart reptilian and cold, ancient and pitiless. Gin lowered his hood and smiled. "There you are, you rascal!" he said.

"Gin, slippy slippy Gin slip in Gin," it thought and crawled towards him.

He would not speak back to its mind. He spoke aloud: "You still not dead, eh? You don't look so good. You look like Hell. You are Hell."

It had the eyes of a giant crab. "Slippy tippy slippy Ginny Gin Gin. Go go go goog gone Ginny Gin Gin. Human tip and slip in blood. Go Gin go. My turn. You go."

He scratched his head and smiled. "It is nice of you to remember my name. Some people have difficulties with names. I confess I've been known to do this myself. I would recall yours, but you don't have one, do you? Seeing as you fused with an ape. Apes don't have names, do they?

"I'll just call you 'Fuzzy.' Have you been feeding again, Fuzzy? I smell blood. Please, don't speak to my mind. It's unbecoming, but it seems you may have lost your throat. Is that it? Oh that's it. You have not recovered yet, have you? I may not have killed you, but at least I shut you up."

He spun the great spear in the air and it howled against the falling dark and the turning demon mewled and groaned but could not speak. "Listen, I know what you want. I do not have her, and you know that and you will not go to where she is. You will not go past this hill even. From here you go back to the abyss."

It began to uncoil and rise until it towered above him. Beside it, the man appeared no bigger than a doll. It slithered up the hill. It gurgled at the spear. "A toy Ginny Gin has a toy of sticks and bones? A toy it brings to strive with a god?"

Its scaled belly jutted out swollen red, and then it vomited a torrent of blood and bile out towards the man who spun the spear above his head so quickly it splattered the deluge away and fanned a spray of crimson on the ground before him. "I don't mean to be overly critical, but you are vulgar. You lack all grace. To you everything is just there to be eaten. Kill and eat. That's it for you. And no, this is no stick, no toy I hold." Here he lifted the spear well into the air and almost shouted. "This is a gift brought to me. This I hold is the toothpick of God!"

And he leapt in such a way that it may be he flew. And he spun the great spear so furiously the air scorched red, and he smashed the great tooth into the neck of the beast, which howled with new agony.

He readied to fight more when he landed on the ground but did not need to. It had already begun to slink away. He had opened another hole in its throat, and the stench of graves exuded from it. It groaned and squealed. Its head lolled but was still attached. If he did not remove the head it would live. It receded between the hills and he followed it. He would kill it this time. Maybe then things would get better. He followed in the path of its blood. The thing hurried away and away to ever lower ground until it churned into a river. It buried itself in this and sunk lower and lower, took the ravines to the sea and this to the abyss which runs beneath the bones of the earth. There, it hid.

Gin left off the chase at the river's shore. He would never catch it in water. The forest on each shore sickened as it passed. At least from that place it was gone. Then, he turned towards the castle. He owed the boy that much.

The pale castle blotted out the better part of the night sky. Built on the top of a table mountain, it ran so high that the loftiest towers broke the running clouds and needles pierced the light of stars. The low moon folded under it. The night of his approach rose clear and cold and if he listened, (as he could hear things both distant and faint), he picked up the flapping of the white flags beaten by the wind on even the highest turrets. A rapid pounding, like the march of war. Below, beneath walls of broken stone teeth, a natural gorge encircled the entirety of the mountain. And below and below again, a torrent of white water flooded the gorge, fed through a maw that opened to the sea. Before the laying of a single brick, the pale castle numbered among the most impregnable, most fortified places on earth.

Three bridges led in. One shone bright and clean, was replete with guards in dress uniform ready to protect and salute dignitaries, all royalty, the elite, those who came and went in an air of polished refinement and privilege almost unknown. This bridge never lacked a perfumed smoke to adorn the air, nor candles to float in glass orbs of cobalt blue, nor exquisite mosaics of sylvan scenes to delight the eye of the crosser. Above, a cover plated in gold repelled the rain and deflected the harsh sun, astounded all who saw it by the majesty of its illumination.

Far below, almost out of sight, hung a utilitarian bridge for the workers, guards, soldiers, anyone else who did not merit passage on the finely veined marble above. Although far more difficult to descend to and ascend from, this lower bridge of unadorned gray stone was critical in its function. Over it, wagons daily carted food, wine, cloth and tools, adornments and messages, weapons and oil, anything that could be needed, anything. As the land surrounding the castle proper was scant and the soil weak, all sustenance had to be brought in, and so most all day and into the night the rumble of wagon wheels could be heard on the bridge of gray.

Few knew of the third bridge. But the sage had heard many things over the years, and at some point someone had poured a whisper of it into his ear: The Bridge of Skulls, suspended at the terminus of a crooked trail which wound The Forest of Curses. Originally built to terrify those who would be led across it -- prisoners of war, all the sundry enemies of the king -- this bridge acquired a metaphysical meaning for the royal family, so much so that each would cross it at least once as they had life. For it had been built with the remnants of the dead, and spanned the most tumultuous part of the gorge, and so the royal family believed that when noble blood tread upon its bones there came a certain power over the kingdom of death. But what interested Gin about the bridge was the simple fact it was left unguarded. Anyone who wished could walk right over, for a guardian waited on the other side. Perched upon a narrow ledge, hidden in the folds of the castle walls, the lone and vicious parvus, pet of the king, would meet any trespass. And Gin knew this too.

The Bridge of Skulls had a distinct odor to it, and looked to him rickety and frail. An obscene structure, he did not wholly trust it to hold his weight. The entirety of the deck had been made of cut human femur, the railing a mixture of arms and ribs. Finger bones hung on strings and knocked in the perpetual wind that rose from the gorge. Above, an assortment of human skulls hung from a roof of bone. Exhausted torches stood in macabre holders, and he could smell the fuel yet. Human fat. He wanted to joke, but such a place did not allow for jokes. "We have a king with a taste for the dramatic," he said, this the best he could do. He tapped the bridge with the spear. It groaned and swayed in the lifting wind. He sighed and looked back to the curtain of twisted forest, then forward again. "All right, then. You didn't come this far to turn back, old man."

He stepped on the bridge. He did not want to touch the railings. The river ran so far below it could hardly be heard. The walls of the gorge were impossibly steep and jagged, like a giant's teeth running down and down into the abyss. He thought of the victims that had crossed here, of what must have befallen them in the hands of the king. "Thank God for death," he whispered to himself, and then the wind lifted so fiercely he stumbled sideways. For a moment, when he held the rail tied with tendon and dried flesh, his hand felt dirty. He wiped it on his cloak before gripping the spear again. He held the spear at the ready. He knew the thing could not go on the bridge, but he held the spear at the ready anyway.

He noticed that the bones had been cut into designs, each more intricate and ghastly than the one before. He wanted very much to leave the place. Not just the bridge but the castle and the whole damned kingdom. He thought of tomorrow and how it would all be done. He advanced with his eyes pressed before his feet. Just before stepping on the land of the castle proper, he kneeled and waited, squinting into the darkness. It hid. It always hid from its victims. He listened and touched a hand to the ground. There it is. There. A heartbeat. Do not be afraid

Peering into the deepest shadows of the folds of the castle wall, he saw them, slits of black cat eyes cut in pools of yellow. They stared at him. They too were waiting. "All right, you son of a bitch. I'll go first." He leapt out and jumped and the spear screamed in the air. "If you are going to fight, fight."

The parvus lunged from its den and stood as tall as a tree with neck raised, ready to devour Gin as it had so many others, but Gin had a trick. He jumped, but he did not land. He held "suspended in the breath of God," and when the neck loomed long before him, he severed the head from it with a single, vicious strike. The body crumbled and the head made a wet thud when it hit the stone. The heart pumped fiercely out the last of the blood, and the headless neck flayed wildly about, trying to bite something perhaps, trying to grab something with teeth it no longer had. Gin flew slowly back and landed far enough away that the dying spasms of the slashing tail and the clawed limbs could not reach him.

He paced and watched it die. He felt immediately tired. It had been a long journey, and to walk in the breath of God has its price. The eyes in the severed head followed him, frightened and searching in wild confusion, for what had happened. For a disturbingly long time the mouth opened and closed as if trying to speak or scream. He wished it had landed facing the other way. How long would it take to die? By God, he was tired. The world had changed so much since he had last ventured out. The land more empty, more violent. People had almost no center now. The larger towns had become so dangerous, the villages unfriendly and charging high prices. How long will the parvus take to die? And all the land dying in gently by degrees, and so little food now. It really must be time for the good earth to move on. Try again with something else. How is it still alive?

We who were living are now dying with a little patience.

He waited as the body writhed, and the dark blood exhausted from the thrashing neck, pooled on the black stone and ran off to the cliffs and down into the river. Still the parvus moved a little, and so he waited yet, sitting with folded legs with the spear resting across his lap. Feeling disturbed, he tried to quiet his mind.

"Just breathe. Think only of your breath and dismiss any other thoughts."

When Gin opened his eyes again, all was still. The spirit of the parvus had left the flesh. He stood and climbed its ruins. Along its swollen center there must have been fifty ribs on each side. Part snake, part lizard, its scales over-lapped as plates of armor and covered all of it, even the throated neck whose length reminded Gin of a giraffe, and he smiled at the memories of giraffes. "Foolish king, to have so much castle guarded by a thing with so much throat to cut," he said to none. With the tip of the spear he lifted the dead weight of an absurdly long claw. "What a thing," he said and leapt down softly to the stone landing. Kneeling before the severed head, he pried open an eye. It seemed alive yet and gave him chills. "What made you, foul parvus?" he whispered to it. "Are you of nature born or the work of the ancients?" Inside the beakish mouth, rows of teeth hooked backwards so they could viciously grip prey. Deep purple gums held them in place, so dark they were almost black. The ears grew in long flaps with wiry hair hanging from the tips, and atop its head two horns grew in small, ebony curls.

He knew they had captured the parvus almost a century earlier. He wondered just how long the species lived. The thought of it trapped on that dismal precipice for so long sickened him. In a rank corner stood a fetid mound of flesh and bone, half-eaten and rotted, and he could see human parts among the meat. They ran them over the bridge. And when that would not suffice, above the pile, in a slit in the castle wall, was a murder hole. Its appetite had to be enormous. A century at this miserable table! And they would just throw meat down to you. There could be no other way. "You would have thrown yourself from the cliff had you known. But we are not allowed to know how hard life is going to be or we'd never want to wake up each day." He let the eye fall closed again.

He turned towards the ancient door, triple-locked for so long that no one had the keys anymore. The rails were as thick as man's forearm and the wood the hardest kind and triple layered, so it seemed more wall than door. Surely this wood and iron stood as impenetrable as stone. Webs stretched in every corner, and he thought again how much he hated places like this, yet he laid his left hand on the door and pushed. It groaned and then split with a shot like thunder.

Shards and dust clogged the air, so he covered his mouth with his sleeve and closed his eyes for a moment. When the air cleared, he stepped inside to a world more lavish than any he had seen in very long time.

Decadent furs as deep as a man's wrist adorned the floor. Exquisite tapestries warmed the cold stone of the walls, and wherever the eye would rest, a sculpture or painting delighted its vision. Lamps burning spermaceti drained from the skulls of leviathans hung in fixtures of gold so delicate they appeared to float in mid air. The entirety of the arched ceiling had been painted in magnificent tinctures so bright they shone almost as luminescent as true day. And the story they told was the story of the kings: the passionate vanquishing of rivals, the slaying of behemoths of the forests, the ripping of sea serpents from the waves. Political enemies of the kingdom, now forgotten save for their faces depicted in sharp recognition, hung delimbed or decapitated before the stern countenance of a righteous executioner — and behind every part of the painted ceiling, lending strength and approval to every deed, shone the vivid light of divine blessing. Gin spent a moment taking it all in, breathing a mild perfume floating in the air, which he found rather enchanting. "A bit overdone," he commented dryly to himself. When he went forward, his feet disappeared into the rug of lush white fur. With every step, he stained it with the blood and grime his feet had collected. He took a childish delight in this.

The windows did not allow one to see out, but the stained glass held the most exquisite patterns of color. Yet the most interesting thing about the hall were the translucent orbs fixed in seemingly random places. Gin could not know this, but they had a very particular purpose. On one day each year, the winter solstice, the orbs caught and magnified the last light of day and directed it to a particular spot. The throne of the monarch would be set there, and on this day alone the peasants could enter the pale castle and behold their king. Some underwent an apostasy as he inexplicably became bathed in the light of God.

For any of the inner chamber to reveal the science of the orbs meant death.

The lavish hall gave way to a passage narrower than the hall and simpler, but magnificent in a way all its own: the entirety of the passage had been cut from the rich blue of lapis lazuli. The sage could not quite believe so much of it had been gathered in one place, but he ran his hand along the stone and it was true. "You've nothing better to spend your money on, do you, King? By God, you must be bored."

Halfway along the hall of blue, he stopped. He felt something, something he could not place, but it was there and it was important somehow, but he did not know what it was or how it mattered but it did. And then something occurred to him: where were all the guards? Where was anybody? The king almost never left the safety of the castle, so he must be here, surrounded by rings of protectors and servants. But where were they all? Obviously, he had walked into an ambush. That was fine. What concerned him was that icy feeling in the pit of his gut.

He proceeded through the empty halls and chambers with luxuries uncounted until coming to the first of seven doors. He opened each one in turn. None were locked. Upon opening the final door, he beheld a circle of armed guards, bows, spears, lances and swords all pointed at him. Behind them stood a magnificent throne of gold. On the throne sat the king. He looked young and very foolish. The king pointed to Gin and said with a slur, "They say ya be comin'."

Gin leaned on his spear. He sighed and tried to smile, but could not. "Did they now?"

"Yeah, they did."

"You know, it's rude to point."

The king shook his head, laughed and lowered his hand slowly. He wore ten rings and these clacked against the golden arm of the throne sculpted into the form of a lion. His thoughts seemed somewhat scattered.

The king pointed again, his arm swaying. "Ya killed my parvus, didn't ya?"

"You don't see me pointing at you, do you? Anyway, it attacked me first."

"Its job wuz to attack any entering my house without askin'."

Gin shrugged. "Well, it's over now and I have a small request before I leave."

The king did not seem to hear him. "No man ever walked that bridge over and lived."

"Apparently, I have broken the tradition."

"Is gonna be real hard finding 'nother parvus. They rare."

"I'm sure you'll find a way. Listen, I don't want waste you time, and I really must be going. I just have one request."

The king laughed and turned to his guards on all sides who did not laugh, but kept their eyes and weapons fixed only on Gin.

"Request? You don' walk in here requesting. Is a demand right?"

Gin nodded. "It concerns the village of Selador, on the Southern Slope."

"The where? What's that?"

"Selador, part of a small district in the southern part of the empire. It rests at the termination of what's called the Southern Slope. Your generals could direct you there eventually. I ask only that your armies, or whoever occupies it in your service, leave. We will draft this as a formal treaty and send it today. These parts, Selador and her neighbors, are meaningless to you. They contribute nothing. They have nothing. They are not even part of a viable route resting at the terminus of the land. They were the last discovered."

The king glanced at the guards, who did not return his look, but kept their eyes and weapons fixed on the sage. He rubbed his chin and squinted. "So, why...why would someone like you care about a little nothing of a place like this...this sell-a-door?"

"Yes. Because I had a friend from there and I'm keeping a promise. That's all. When you get to be my age, you realize the importance of keeping promises."

The king laughed loosely and, feeling some elation from the drug, slapped the shoulder of the guard who knelt the armrest of the throne. The guard almost loosed his arrow at the heart of the sage.

"Oh, I keep my promises. I told this place once that they all better pay their taxes in full or I'd cut off all their hands. Well, they didn't really believe me. We used their hands to fertilize the royal garden. You should see the roses! Roses love bone. There's something in it they love. I think it's 'cause the hands do the work and roses work so hard to keep beauty in the world."

"It's the calcium and the phosphorous."

"Wha's that?"

"The minerals in the hand bones of your mutilated subjects. That's what helps your roses grow."

"You wise like they say. They call you 'Sage,' right?"

He sighed and scratched his head. "I've been called that. It matters not. Now, I don't mean to be rude, but if you could summon your secretary and your swiftest courier...."

"You should see the garden."

"Another time."

"Ain't no one grow roses like me."

"I am sure no one does."

The king nodded, "And I tend to them myself. Prune and trim them and everything, and no matter how dry it gets, no matter the drought, I make sure they've got water."

"Lovely. If only you could do the same for the people."

The king continued as if not hearing him: "But, you know what the most important thing is that you need to do for 'em?"

"What's that?"

"Talk to 'em. And not just anything. You got to talk with love and say good words."

"This is true. I don't mean to seem impatient, but...."

"They grow so beautiful for me when I talk to 'em right. It's like they love me. They do love me. Nothing in all my kingdom is as beautiful as a rose is."

"I'm glad you enjoy your garden. I have a small garden."

"Where's that?"

"That's funny."

The king wagged a finger at the Sage. "You know I think this world would be a whole lot better if everyone took the time to grow roses and speak to 'em with good words."

"Surely, but these are difficult times for hobbies."

The king rubbed his hands angrily on the giant pearls set in the grip of the lion's arm. His rings clacked against the golden limbs. "If

I knew a person who could love half as true as a rose I…," He shook his head, "…I don't know what I'd do."

"Listen," said Gin, "It's been a long walk."

The king stood on the base of the throne. The pedestal had the appearance of polished eggs set in gold, but it was really the crowns of polished skulls set in gold. He was not tall or very strong and so his armor had been made extra light so he could move quickly and without struggle. The armor did not have to be effective. Kings had long ceased placing themselves in the perils of war. The guards repositioned themselves to cover the king.

The king waited.

The Sage waited.

"You can send them out if you wish. I'm not here to kill you. That would do no good."

The king laughed, "Listen, I've had more men say that and then try to kill me than I care to think."

"Prudence is the better part of valor."

"Wha's that mean?"

"It means you can't be too careful."

The king looked at the Sage with a distant gaze. "You are a wise one like they say. Can you read?"

"Yes, I can."

The king shook a finger at the Sage with a knowing smile. "I thought so. They tried teaching me, but it hurt my head. All the letters come out backwards and all kinds of stupid stuff."

"Had I the time, I would teach you."

"They said I couldn't be taught. That I were meant for higher callings."

"People say a lot of things. I could teach you. It would make you a better man."

The king looked at the ceiling, encrusted with jewels and fine paintings. The crown slipped from his head to rest on the gilded crowns of skulls. He grinned and picked it up and handed it to the guard kneeling to his left.

"Better than a king? I hang men for sayin' less."

"Better than you already are."

"Secure that in the vault," he said to the guard who took the crown. And then, to the Sage, he said, "It never did fit me right. Too big for my head. I hate wearing it, you know? Hell, I never asked to be king ... never even asked to be born."

"None of us do," said Gin.

"Is like we all here by some kind a blind mistake. I mean, I like you, Sage. You seem all right and you not afraid a me. Get so tired a everyone bein' afraid a me. If we could choose who we become before being brought in, maybe it would all be better. But no, they leave it up to chance. You ever see a baby happy it's born? No. They come screamin' into this cold and dusty world, thrust naked and helpless into the arms a strangers." The king met the eyes of the Sage with an infinite sadness. "We could'a been friends if we'd a chosen what we were gonna be. In different times. Different places."

Gin sighed again. He had a terribly uneasy feeling. The king asked him almost in tears, "Don't you got somethin' to help me? Some wisdom to impart?"

"Not really. I don't do that too much. Maybe you should try learning to read again. There's a lot to learn by reading."

The king collapsed into the throne and slammed both hands on the claws of the lion. He almost said something, but did not.

"All right," Gin said peacefully, raising a hand in a placating manner. "Again, as I've taken too much of your time already, I need you to call your quickest horseman and secretary."

"I don't do what others tell me."

Gin rubbed his temple as if he had a headache. Why must everything be so difficult? Without taking his hand from his temple, he opened the palm towards the king. The guards, with all eyes on Gin, did not notice when the king's face began to pale, when he suddenly became unable to catch his breath. He leaned forward in a kind of suffocation, but it was not that. He could breathe. However, fingers of ice clutched his heart. The blood just would not move through it. He felt his life running away. He felt himself drawn towards a lightless abyss, and as his eyes welled in tears, he looked to Gin, "Please," he whispered to him, "my father...."

Gin lowered his hand then, and life flowed through the heart of the king once more. "Again, I ask you...please summon your quickest courier and your secretary to carry a royal order. This will be our treaty. You can tell them I will dictate the conditions of it. Have your secretary bring the royal seal."

His breath barely caught, the king rapped the nearest guard on the helmet. "Do it," he said barely above whisper.

While they waited, no one spoke. Periodically the king heaved into outbreaks of tears. The guards did not react much. They had seen his moods before. Gin walked slowly to a window that had lost a piece of the stained glass. He stared out through the small opening to the sky and almost smiled. "You can see the ocean from here," he said to no one in particular. "How lovely. It's been a long time since I've seen the ocean." And then he felt it again and glanced behind him to nothing there. He wanted only to finish this business and leave. Soon, a thin, bald man entered the chamber. He did not knock, as all the doors stood open. Beside him was a young man of slight frame, the rider.

The king swayed a drugged glance at both and pointed to Gin, "Do what he say."

Gin turned. He spoke first to the rider: "Prepare the three quickest horses of the royal stable. You are going a long way. Take all three and ride a different one each day so as not to wear out any one horse. Do not bother with supplies now except the barest essentials. The secretary will give you the gold you need, and much more, a very generous amount of gold to both compensate you well and obtain the supplies you will need en route. Make this journey with the utmost speed, your swiftest message. Become the wind. You leave for the Southern Slope in minutes, as soon as the horses are saddled. You go there to deliver a peace treaty of the highest importance to the ranking general. As you get closer, they will direct you to him. The secretary will meet you in the stables in moments. From this window we expect the dust of your hooves in minutes, not hours. Go."

The young rider bowed to the king and left. He would abandon his whole life by this simple order. The empire was so expansive that a courier crossed it only once, and lived the rest of his days on the other side.

The secretary copied the correspondence as Gin dictated. The conclusion of the treaty stated that any message ceasing to nullify this one should be considered an act of treason and the messengers are to be immediately executed. Gin read the final treaty and gave it to the secretary who gave it to the king who closed it with the royal seal. In a little while, the rider with two riderless horses tethered to the first could be seen racing south. Gin smiled. "They are very good, your staff. They do go quickly when they need to."

"It's my leadership," said the king. He had taken more drugged powder and was beginning to feel calm again, even a little confident.

And then Gin felt it so clearly. His gut went cold. "I don't think you've been completely honest with me, King, have you?"

"They told me you'd be coming," he said, and Gin winced. He should have figured that statement out sooner, but it did not matter. It would not have mattered anyway. "I know these guards can't stop you. They nothin' to you, I know that. They tol' me wha' you can do."

"And who is that?" he asked, but already knew. He looked out to the sea. He did not want to turn around.

The king nodded drunkenly and smiled, "You know who, don't ya?"

When the last dust of the rider settled to the south, his mind wandered over the great expanse of his life then, all of it, and knew at last the one moment that meant the most and he smiled. So long ago. He did not want to turn around.

"They like you, right?" the king went on in slurred words. "They thed you'd be coming. These fellas, there. They told you'd be coming."

"Did they now?" asked the Sage in an absent whisper. He considered the distant play of water lit with tips of light.

"Yup, and they here now. You don' wanna turn around, doth yah?"

"It is a lovely view from here."

"Uh, yup. 'Tis…'tis," said the king.

Then a voice as cold as winter's river spoke. "Come Gin, too long has passed since our good embrace."

"Evurlak, you lousy creep. Are you as ugly as I remember?" he replied without turning around.

"Stay, my little birds. Silly names, Gin? To this you resort?"

"Why not? Should I be polite with you, you freak?"

He turned at last. It would not be good to keep his back too long to them. Around the throne stood twelve shadowy figures, all very tall and thin and pale in robes of black. The better part of their faces were concealed under a hood. "You hide your eyes, Evurlak. Something wrong with them?" Gin asked, and the one called

Evurlak growled. "Why don't you tell your friends what I did to your face?"

Evurlak outstretched his long, gangly arms and held those beside him back. "Stay, my Thieves of Light"

It was then a crouched and bent man in a purple robe crept from between the figures in black. With a cackle, he threw a string of tied bones across the chamber and they brushed against Gin's gray cloth and rattled against the floor. The Sage slid them away with his spear. The bent figure cackled again and limped towards the throne. Gin sighed, "Your wizard, I suppose?" he asked the king.

"That he is."

"How quaint."

"And he smart, too. He can read the flies of birds. The tossing a signs. Saw a hawk catch a sparrow and said it meant I'm gonna have a victory an' a real good one and soon. I the hawk."

"Good for you. That's lovely. Sounds like he instills confidence in you. But those other friends of yours, well, they aren't the best sort to be associated with. You should be careful with them."

"They can do them things you can, right?"

"Somewhat. How did you find them exactly?"

"They found me. Came in here about a month back, marched right into this castle and didn't have to kill my parvus neither, saying they 'heard' you about ten days back, and that you was coming here."

Gin huffed and kicked the ground. "I knew I went too hot on that damned worm. You freed it, didn't you, Evurlak? With the help of your little crew here, right? That's the only thing that makes sense."

The hooded horde began to titter and hiss and make the tiniest steps closer to Gin. Evurlak lifted his hands in the air as if a bird slowly flying, and the others of his crew followed suit. He spoke from beneath his hood: "The sins of man freed him. I but broke the bars of wrongful confinement."

"You know how many died to get that thing in…oh, never mind. That's a cute dance. Tell me, Evurlak, you still fuck dead kids?"

At these words, the fluttering stopped, the hissing stopped, the laughter stopped. Gin stared at the hood where the eyes would be and awaited an answer. He knew he could see through the hood. Then the followers of Evurlak began to groan. "Stay, my Lids of Dawn," Evurlak spoke. "Be patient, my beloved gods."

Gin shook his head and laughed without joy. "I remember you would dress them in lovely gowns, especially the boys, and paint their faces up to look alive again before you defiled their corpses. I remember you once had a little orgy: seven dead children all painted and pretty and you had strings to their wrists and jaws and moved them like puppets and then you dragged their bodies to the …."

"Cease!" screamed Evurlak.

Gin smiled, "Oh, am I embarrassing you? You called it 'flower picking' I remember, when you harvested their fresh corpses from the spoils of war."

"Stay, my Sweet Crows, my promises of shadow."

"Damn," said Gin shaking his head and slamming the spear against the floor which, without quite meaning to, he struck with such force the flagstones shook so as to cause three archers to slip and release their arrows. Gin brushed two of the arrows aside with the flick of his hand and did not bother with the third, for it missed all together and shattered against the wall.

The king's guard now knew what they faced. Gin scratched his head in frustration, "I didn't sense you at all. Hardly at all."

The king began to snicker. "They told me about that. How if you was close enough you'd know they here. But this castle got deep, deep secret chambers. They been waiting in them. They like it down there, I think. Been sort of sleeping in a weird kind of way down there. Sort of floating like between sleep and awake. Said that way you wouldn't know they was here. When I tipped my crown, that were the signal for them to be gotten. It takes time to wake them from that almost-sleep."

"Very clever. But it wouldn't have mattered. I would have come anyway."

The king rubbed his chin and the light beard he could barely grow there. "I ain't so sure of that. But they juth like you, right? They can do the things you do, can't they?"

"You keep asking that."

"'Cause you look scared. I might not read letters, but can read a man's face well enough. You thought I was stupid, didn't you?"

Gin lowered his eyes to the king. "No, just ordinary."

The king pretended not to hear the comment. "They said you were dangerous, real dangerous, and comin' to kill me."

"Had I wished to kill you, you would be dead."

The king nodded. "I believe that. I don't understand then why you're here at all."

"I told you. It's already done."

"It can't be just that. They told me you have her."

"I don't."

"You hid her somewhere? That's no good. That's not safe. She safest with me."

"I delivered her to destruction. That's all. She is already gone."

The king shifted in his throne, a tremble of terror running yet through his heart. "They can't do nothing."

"Who?"

"No one. No one can't do nothing with her. Nothing can kill her. She needs to be kept locked up. That's all I want to do. Tell me where she is and I will tell 'em not to hurt you."

"I don't think they will listen to you. I think they will try and kill me anyway. But you can rest your mind, King, I do not know where she is. I got rid of her."

"Do you know who I listen to, my friend, when I don' know what do to or what the answers is?"

"Who's that?"

"To God."

"Oh."

"This throne here is occupied not by a king but God. Thus, my victories are great."

"How do you know it's God who's talking, and not just your imagination?"

The king laughed and shook his finger at the Sage. "You a very honest man. Most wouldn't talk to me like that. You wouldn't understand the voice of God because he don't speak to you, but if he did you would know 'cause there ain't no doubting it."

"And what does he say?"

The king smiled. "All kinds of things. Sometimes he tells me to spare someone or some place, and I do. Other times, he tells me to destroy them, and I do. All kinds of things. He come to me a lot, especially at night when I dream. Sometime he a pillar of light. Other time he a shadow."

"Good for you. It must be nice to have God as your advisor."

The king pointed to the Sage. "You laughing at me, but you don't know."

"I'm not laughing at you."

"You laughing at me in your heart."

"I'm not laughing at all. There is nothing to laugh at here."

"She with the Northern Army?"

"Perhaps. I don't know."

"Wait," said the king to the Sage. He folded his hands in his lap and leaned his head back. He stared at the painted ceiling and muttered a chant before closing his eyes. The crows then began to advance slowly. They floated over the floor. Gin fixed his eyes on Evurlak. He truly wanted to kill Evurlak. Even if he died, it would almost be worth it just to kill him. Evurlak smiled, and then all of them smiled and their teeth were like those of wolves. The king, in a voice wistful and distant, spoke from his trance: "Wait," he said, "wait," he said again. They had bizarre weapons hidden under their robes, and Gin counted them and waited. The king awoke from his trance, "Ah," he said absently, "I see now. I understand. God has answered my concerns. He say you don't have her. He say you don't know where she is. Thank you for being honest with me, Sage."

Gin nodded to the king. "Your god is quite correct."

"He always is," the king replied and smiled contentedly. He then noticed the advancement of the crows. "Them dark ones are coming for ya, Sage."

"Yes they are."

"Tell us where you saw her last."

"I can't do that. She wouldn't be there anymore anyway. It wouldn't matter."

"Then tell us."

"I cannot."

"They gonna kill us all with her!"

"Unless they destroy her. That's all they want to do."

The king shook his head violently. "I say it already. It can't be broke! It can't!"

"Let's hope you're wrong. Your friend wants you."

Evurlak rested a silent hand on the shoulder of the king. "Be still, Child of the Sun. She will be found. Know that. Half the world in darkness dwells, and of what is lit rests half in shadow."

"Wha..what does that mean?" asked the king. "What you saying?"

"It means she will be brought to you, to us," he said, smiling with wolven teeth. His thin lips seemed made of blood.

"So…so if this Sage don't have it, what you gonna do? Do we let 'im go?"

"Be still," said Evurlak, "Here, good King, drink." He poured a heavy dose of the drug into the king's cup and brought it to his lips. With the cup emptied, the king soon began to fall away. He gazed lazily at this room filled with such a strange air of amber. He slumped in the throne and a string of thick drool ran from his mouth. The wizard wiped the drool away and leaned a whisper into the king's ear. The king opened his arms and the wizard crawled into his lap, curled his palsied legs up and held the king at the waist.

"We goth to go now," the king slurred, "We goz to go," the king mumbled. He began to pull blindly at the lion's golden paw. "We…we hath to goes thou," he said, fumbling with the right arm of the throne until the third claw lifted with a loud click and the throne fell through the floor and was gone. The king and wizard slid down and down through the depths of the castle to a room sealed and deep and hidden and safe. The podium of skulls closed behind it. Evurlak laughed and stood where the throne had been and laughed at Gin. Gin stared back.

"Ushers of the Shade," he said, bursting with joy and pride, "the moment is upon us."

"How poetic," Gin said bitterly and lowered the spear towards Evurlak.

"Hold!" cried the captain of the guards and raised his sword. Gin spoke very calmly to him: "You should all leave. You and your guards."

"Hold!"

"I tell you to leave. The king is gone. You have no stake here. Just go."

"Be still!" the captain ordered, and Gin said no more to him. He could not waste words now. He could not waste breath. As the crows floated through the guards silently in a vulgar display of power, the guards leaned away from them.

"A toy," said Evurlak in derision, nodding to the spear.

"That's what your friend said, until I split him in half with it."

"It cannot be killed. Unlike you, it is bound to the very life of earth. It cannot be killed, dearest Gin, soon to fall to the sunless vault."

"That's what you say."

With a countenance of brief regret Evurlack gestured to the narrow window.

"My, the sun is low in the sky.
Another day is dying;
Look how red the warm sun sets.
Hear the sea, her crying."

"I would let you see it once more, Brother."

"We are not brothers. We never were. Get on with it."

"Look once more upon the gentle star, and the blue world which blossoms beneath it."

"If you think I'd turn my back on you you're crazier than you seem. If you're not going to fight, I'm leaving."

Evurlak ran his fingers through his long ashen hair, tugging at the dry strands. He stared absently into the floor, and his face could not be read with any certainty. The lesser crows who adored and followed Evurlak in all things tugged their own strands of dry hair and lowered their gazes. After a time, as if stumbling upon a grand revelation, Evurlak lifted a long, black nail and pointed it at Gin. He smiled and then he spoke in breathless ecstasy: "He will not be counted," he said. "Sweet Doves of the Waning Moon, he shall fall from the sacred number!"

The crows clasped their hands between their knees and bent in rapture and delight. They began to echo what the leader had said. They laughed and pointed at Gin and slowly wove towards him through the throng of guards, looking always back towards Evurlak for his approval. When a kneeling archer blocked the path of Evurlak, he rested his right hand on his iron helmet and whispered to him: "move." A red glow emanated from the hand of Evurlak and for a moment the helmet too glowed red, but then collapsed in molten iron dripping down the skull of the guard. He howled and dropped the bow, tried to rip the molten helmet from his head but could not, and Evurlak smiled when the sockets of his eyes filled with liquid metal.

The captain and all guards were stunned into silence. Then the captain cried an order: "Kill them all!" The guards, having forgotten

Gin, set upon the crows and were quickly slaughtered. Evurlak did not join the fray but, as each guard fell dead, he collected the eyes and put these in his pocket. When the last guard was killed, the crows, mouths smeared with blood, began to dance and hiss and flap their arms like wings among the bodies of the dead. Some kissed the cold lips of the fallen, others took large neck-bites into their throats.

Gin sighed and scratched his head. "Very charming, Evurlak," said the Sage. "You were always such a piece of shit."

When the last of the eyes had been collected he turned and pointed at the eyes of Gin. "Now, my gentle demons, set upon him. His number will be lost."

They began to spit blood at him and he flicked it away with the spear in disgust. "How vulgar," he said. "How tasteless."

"Sad Elder of the Waning Moon, to die among the stones cut by the hands of your enemy."

"Just shut up. He should never have taught you. I don't know why he did that."

He took a deep breath. He tightened his grip. They were upon him with the fullest passion of the heart, desperate to kill or to be killed in the ecstasy of devoted service.

"My child, we take this journey with joined hands. I have chosen you to be counted among the number of the magnificent. With this comes the promise of immortality, eternal bliss, and the possession of powers so astounding you could never have imagined them, not even in your dreams. As a god, I can impart all of this to you in a wink, but you must be tested. This is the way. You must be battered past pain, defiled into abject loyalty; you must embrace the agony that leads to perfect strength. Yet the disease of doubt dwells in you still. The specter of fear lurks in the corners of your soul. I see this as I do everything. From me nothing may be hidden. As your Lord and Father, I shall re-create you to a perfect being, but the process will be long until at last you are healed.

" If you perish in the course of your becoming, I will fly to that world to which your spirit goes and grant you there eternal bliss. But if you falter in the battle against the enemies of God, know that there exists a dark and terrible place into which are cast souls stained yet with fear, selfishness and dishonor. From that place these broken souls are never born again. Even I could not reach you in that place. Nothing would grieve me more. You were dying when I

found you, my child. There is much healing to be done. Let us begin today with an embrace."

With every manner of attack they set upon him. With teeth and nails of poisoned claws and a cache of weapons as varied as they were bizarre. They exhaled evil energy upon the Sage at every moment, and he could feel the shredding of his aura and the constant pull to drain his essence. They hurled such smoking venoms and blinding acids that centuries of portraits, dating right back to the first king of the first line, melted from the walls. The flesh fell from the corpses of the guards.

A mesh of elven hair (seven years it took to find and kill an elf) protected the breath of the crows, and they had coated their skin in a balm made from the fat of a dragon. Gin coughed. He rubbed his eyes. He kept his breathing shallow.

They were so quick, almost as quick as he, and at times a little quicker. They attacked incessantly, working both together and apart. As the battle dragged on, he thought often he had gotten too old for this kind of thing. From the pale cave of his hands Evurlak hurled destructive energy towards the Sage, but this done from a safe distance, the outskirts of the fray. He stood on the corpses and shouted for the others to follow.

The first Gin would kill, a woman-crow called Viageta, had always believed herself to be among the finest of the crows, although her skills were the most immature and least perfected. To Evurlak, she held no promise at all, and he would have killed her himself, in secret, a long time ago, but felt the disposing of her life could be put to some use. At last it had. The wizard had given Evurlak an enchanted net which he swore could not be broken by any force. Evurlak did not believe nor disbelieve the wizard, who warned him not to test the net save in battle, for the net only loosened for the dead.

"It is a sweet and sacred delicate delicious art, the net of the soul. Take it and with it kill the one who comes."

"Give it here then, Wizard of the Realm."

Evurlak held the net out and cried to his followers: "Who among us would dare approach the enemy so as to bind him within this tool?"

He spoke this directly to Viageta, whom he well knew always wanted to prove herself. She kneeled before Evurlak and begged for the net. Evurlak smiled to her: "As you wish, Child of The Golden Heart." He placed the net in her hands.

"I so love you, my lord and savior!" she said weeping.

"Rise now, Midnight's Rainbow."

With net in hands, Viageta floated over the heads of the battlers towards the Sage. She went closer than any yet had dared and cast the net towards him. With a simple lifting of the hand he threw it back upon her and wrapped her within it by twirling his finger. She fell to the floor immediately, writhing in agony, for the more she struggled the tighter the net became. Every intersection of mesh held a venomous thorn. Indeed, it appeared unbreakable as the wizard had promised. She twisted in convulsions of terror and howled in pain until she became quiet shreds. The net loosened.

Before he knew she was actually dead, her lover came to free her, unmindful of the Sage's spear. When he touched her lifeless body his arms became entangled, and Gin smashed them apart at the elbow. The stricken warrior stared in disbelief at his bleeding stumps, but before he could scream Gin split his throat and sent both lifeless bodies flying towards Evurlak. No fewer than three crows dove to protect him.

"That's two, you filthy creep," he said. Evurlak made no response.

The third kill was a crow to whom Evurlak had entrusted a blinding potion. Over-confident, he ran too close to Gin, who removed his lower jaw with a swing of the spear. He dropped the poison on the floor and the glass vial cracked. He staggered closer, unable to think clearly, and Gin punched him with such force that his heart exploded. Darts of his own ribs shot out of his back and cut the crows behind him.

"I do hope he had some kind of miserable disease. That's three down, Evurlak!" he cried.

Evurlak smiled. All the fallen were entirely expendable. But Gin knew his breath was failing. It was becoming impossible to keep up. It would be only a matter of time. He tried to think of some little-used trick, but nothing came to him.

He killed one more, a crow who had overleapt his stance and, avoiding the spear, came within reach of his hands.

"Let me give you a bit of light," Gin said to him and touched him with the tip of his finger. The crow became consumed in an intense white flame and ran in circles screaming until he fell, a small mound of ash.

Once, Gin almost killed Evurlak, almost split apart his pale and fetid neck, but his adherents acted, one and all, for his protection. It took too much energy and attention to kill him now. And it was not worth the effort, because the crows were getting to him now. He had to be honest about that. Half of his left hand had been bitten off, and an eyelid had been torn away. For a moment, he wondered how quickly he would heal, until he realized he would likely not have the chance to. They had caught him with darts which broke through to his lungs, and Gin could feel them slowly filling with blood. His great spear, for all its magnificence, had but limited use in the chamber. It was too large, and he kept smashing it against walls and pillars. It was not the right weapon for the space. He noticed with a decided dread that while he fought them back with all he could, one or two of the remaining crows could rest in turn. They would wear him out like this. And so they would get him. It was only a matter of time, and a little patience.

Do you know how wolves catch a deer when the deer is faster?
No.
They don't all run at it in a pack. The deer would outrun them every time. They line a valley rise, each wolf a half a mile down from the other, and when the deer follows the valley center (for prey will always take the easy course, the low path) the first wolf runs out and the deer goes. But when the first wolf is run out, the second wolf is waiting and it comes down the valley wall and takes over the chase. And where can the deer go? It can't run back. It can't run out the valley. It runs from the second wolf and when it's exhausted, the third is waiting. By the fifth wolf, the deer is done, its breath all gone.

The battle shook the castle. Faint rumblings could be heard, even in the most distant rooms. No one dared enter the chamber of the throne, and all the guards were dead. Gin wondered what he could have done here with the sword of Belladonna, but then stopped thinking like that because it did not matter. They would not take the spear, however. The time had come to insure they did not take the spear.

He kept missing his shots, and they began to strike with more force and accuracy. He would not get Evurlak, standing back there too far away. But he would do what they would never expect: he would throw the spear from his hands. The crow who had bitten his hand off soon would come close again. When he did, Gin summoned all of his energy, a lifetime of strength, and spun the spear once. This crow mocked him, laughed at how the arc of the strike missed, but then Gin spun it a second time and the crow almost laughed again until Gin loosed his grip and hurled the spear at the knees of the crow, and cut its legs off their.

The great spear kept going. It crashed down and down through the floor, through endless rooms and corridors. The castle stones exploded.

Gin had hoped to send his spear into the heart of the mountain itself. Let them find it there, if they can. But the castle ran deeper than even he knew, and the weapon came to rest in the hidden bowels of the cellar.

For a moment no one moved, save for the crow wailing on the ground holding the stumps where his leg had been. Gin's weapon gone, he stood before them nearly defenseless.

As prophesied, he will not be counted.

They set upon him, and for a time he fought with his one good hand and both feet. Maybe he could kill one more. But his chest filled so rapidly with blood now.

An odd fact about the castle that the Sage had heard once long ago almost stunned him. How important it would be. When they built the chamber of the throne, a natural pit had been discovered. Rather than fill it in, the early kings used this as a tool of execution. No one knew how deep it went, but when people were dropped in, they fell past the reach of their screams. When they did hit at last, there was no sound, no thud or splash. It was as if the void devoured them. If you had at least two prisoners, it worked very well to get confessions. Why had he always remembered it? It rested just behind him now, marked off by a low wall. There were reasons for all things. He came to believe that long ago. He understood now. He understood everything now. As he fought, Gin stepped closer to the pit. He had a plan...easy to execute. The setting sun made the stained glass windows glow with ethereal beauty. They would not drink his blood. Evurlak would not collect his eyes. Gin folded his arms and stepped onto the low wall. He could hear the howls of Evurlak as he slipped away, down into the endless pit.

After some time, in a tomb of rotted bone and jagged rock, body broken and cut off from wind and light, the ancient life of the Sage ebbed away at last.

The crows entered the hidden chamber of the king. The king rolled on his satin covering in a stupor. He could not see clearly. Evurlak sat beside him in the royal bed and lifted the king's gentle hand. "This Sage has butchered the royal guard and a third of my number. We stopped him at great cost. He is gone."

"Yuh ... yuh killed 'im?"

"Yes, good king. The deed is done." Evurlak licked the blood from his fingers and wrists. "Now, for our price."

"You said he had thuh medusa."

Evurlak raised a long black nail. "And he did. I said not that he would bring her here."

"I thought that was the deal."

"Do not be foolish, king. Be patient. Where is the wizard?"

"Gone."

"Hiding, as wizards do. Come over to me king."

The king shook very badly, "You ain't gonna take too much, right?"

Evurlak smiled. "You will not die. I promise you that."

The crows climbed onto the bed of the king and marred the satin silver and golden beddings with streaks of blood. They circled the king closely. The king cried as they bit into his skin. Evurlak licked his tears away.

As a matter of trivial spite, the wizard had sent three assassins by a shortcut known to but a few to catch and kill the first rider and burn the treaty ordering liberty and peace to the inconsequential land of Selador. But on their tenth night out, in land so dense their bodies could not be found by ought but beasts, they set their blanket over a nest of baby cobras, and before dawn each man had been bitten to death. And so the rider, after a long time, arrived at the small village with an order sealed with the insignia of the king himself. All the soldiers vacated their posts and left Selador and her neighbors alone forever, and thus it was that peace came to this land for a very long time.

The construction of the castle never really stopped. Its walls and towers expanded with the empire, and so the current form had been centuries in the making. The Mountain of the Table, upon which it stood, was made mostly of limestone and had scant earth or vegetation. It was from this rock that the first builders cut the stone for the fortress's walls. The castle shone pale under a bright moon, having almost a magical glow. Thus, it was known as The Pale Castle.

No one knew exactly how many rooms it had. Some estimated over a thousand, but older sections had been sealed off for one reason or another and new sections added with the expansion of the empire, so it became impossible to know the true number. Oftentimes, a builder would break down a wall and discover an abandoned hall replete with rooms not entered for centuries. As with any castle, secret passages ran through its walls and in those walls were hidden chambers, built for the safety of the royal family. This structure became so vast that many passages, as well as the triggers to their doors, had been forgotten. It was not unheard of for someone to press the tail of a statue only to have a room appear behind a turning wall.

Rumor held that the castle even had secret tunnels which bore into the mountain itself. The old stories told how the first kings discovered pools of gold and diamond in the depths of the Mountain of the Table, and from this built their initial wealth. Darker stories tell of caverns running so deep into the mountain that they touched the gate of the dead. From this eerie acquaintance, the royal line is believed to have obtained the power of prophecy.

The deepest known level of the castle housed the dungeon. The kingdom kept prisoners there not just to separate them from the sun and hope and dreams of escape, but to keep the screams and the smell of decay far from any guests and occupants above. The dungeon was a low, dank, fetid chamber. Dripstone deposits hung in stalactites between the smoke-blackened vaults of the high ceiling. The stones of the floor were among the oldest in the castle, and from them one had to climb many stairs before reaching a wall high enough to allow a window. What made this dungeon unique was the presence of six inescapable pits bored into the mountain. They were cylindrical, but no one could say when or by whom or for what purpose they had been built. The earliest annals of the castle make no mention of the pits. For all anyone knew, they were there before construction began.

Their purpose became being a dungeon within the dungeon. The slick stone walls were entirely unclimbable, and the floor of each pit barely allowed for a captive to lie flat. Each prisoner lived in perfect isolation from the others and, if there were enough light, which often there was not, only had a narrow view of the soot-stained ceiling above. The foulest of food was thrown in sometimes. Water trickled along the floors and they drank that or nothing. Sometimes a bucket was lowered to collect their waste. Sometimes it was not. No one condemned to a pit had ever left it alive.

These pits were not for the common criminal. The laws of the land had to be upheld by the subordinate villages. If the king's guard or army had to intervene, the lawbreaker was summarily executed. But the dungeon was reserved for particular prisoners, namely for those and their families who threatened the rule of the king. It had always been like this.

The dungeon-keeper, a man called Creber, by a defect of birth had no hair on any part of his body. By perhaps the same disease his flesh hung the color of ash. He had an enormous gut, a pronounced limp when walking, and a posture so crooked as to be deformed. He did not wash and rarely left the area of the dungeon, thus his body smelled like a corpse. He wore rags, if he wore anything. The general population of the castle shunned him, and so his appearance and dress mattered little.

Shortly before his father's mysterious death, he struck Creber in the skull with a club. This gave the boy his slow and slurred speech, making it difficult for him to shape even the simplest of words. An obscenely fat, protruding lower lip, the result of a series of beatings, made this condition even worse. As a child, he often slept outside with the dogs; as dungeon-master he slept on a greasy mat in a windowless cell. He wore an absence of expression, a distinct emptiness in his eyes, and he never felt remorse for the functions he performed, no matter how egregious, for he often entertained the notion that no one else was real, and so could not actually feel pain or terror.

It was a cat who got Creber his job. A member of the Royal Guard, on return from a long and bloody campaign, spied the young

Creber de-limbing a writhing cat that was tethered very tightly to a tree. He cut the leg in sloppy chops with a dull a knife and then skinned it and placed the meat on the fire for food. The other limbs had already been removed, and Creber had enough mind to cauterize the stumps so the cat would stay fresh. By this age, Creber was a beggar and eater of garbage.

The guard knew of the vacancy and asked Creber if he would like to live in the castle of the king. Creber smiled. He had few teeth left. His eyes hung crooked and his mouth filled with drool. As he tried to answer, the guard knew he would be perfect to keep the dungeon, for the sight of the man should instill fear in the incarcerated. And it was so. When the chained victims were dragged pleading into the darkness of the dungeon, upon the sight of Creber, with his vague and absent smile, they would cry like children. Indeed, some of them were children, and to Creber their hysterics were an act, or an illusion, and he would point to which the pit the guards should throw them in. He was the perfect dungeon-master.

Creber had little to do. He fed the prisoners rotted scraps of food. He dragged them out when they died. Sometimes he had to kill them. Sometimes he had to trickle fire over them. Sometimes he had to pour acid over them, but often he just left them to die. It was amazing how soon inhabitants of the pits became diseased.

"Tell me, Dungeon-Keep, how is it you kill the condemned?"

"Wethe pur wethe pur burlin oils on un un on em. Theys die righaway or a thuh festers soon enough. Then wethe drags, weh weh wethe drags 'em out with thuh hook."

Having no one else to speak with, Creber often leaned over a hole and spoke to the naked and squirming soul down below. He would tell of the many trials of his life, what difficulties he had undergone, how much he had suffered, more than they could ever know. He would make to them all confessions, knowing they would tell no one.

Sometimes Creber made the victims break the law of silence and sing a chorus of him as if he were a god. He would ask if they truly understood his suffering.

"Yes, yes, yes, you poor, poor man. We love you. I love you!"

Sometimes he made them weep for him. If they did not weep loudly enough, or sing well enough, he covered them with coals, or covered the opening of their pit and shut them in total darkness.

Children were always the most difficult to contain. They were always crying, always screaming for their mothers. He often had to punish them the most. At least they died quickly.

The king visited the pits only once. His father had recently passed and, as he was still a young man and lacking confidence, the peasants who had suffered a particularly harsh winter were hungry and angry and so they perceived the king as weak. It was time for revolution, but the uprising failed and the young king ordered the immediate execution of all partakers and their families.

However, the three high leaders, two of whom ranked as generals in the Royal Guard, he ordered thrown into the pits. Creber was to make their stay as uncomfortable as possible. The king had to cover his nose with a perfumed rag of delicate silk when he entered the main dungeon. Creber limped before him, giddy to show the creativity of his work.

The king had come to his dungeon! The king!

Into the first pit Creber pointed with a crooked finger to a man twitching near death. He lay there, surrounded by human bones and flesh, his head matted with clots of blood. The man's five children were poised over the rim of his pit, swords their throats. The oldest was brought first. The guard cut his throat and threw the limbs into the pit like meat.

"Eat that or we kill the next."

This was done from oldest to youngest, and when the baby's gentle face, pale with terror and confusion, stared at his mad father in a pit slipping among the skulls of his siblings, the baby fell mute. She could say nothing. When her head was cut off and tossed in, the prisoner slammed his head against the stone wall in the hope of death, but due to his weakness, he could not quite hit it hard enough.

Creber smiled at how smart this torture had been. His king would appreciate him. The king would invite him upstairs. Giddy with joy, Creber almost hopped to the next pit, into which he pointed and laughed, slapping his knee. The king, summoning all of his energy to not faint before his guards, hesitantly leaned to look into the pit. At first he did not understand. All he could see was a swarm of crawling brown fur, but when the victim heaved in a spasm of agony, he saw the mass of fur to be rats and under it a man in chains being devoured. Too much of his throat had been eaten for him to scream. Creber tried to apologize for this. "Yuh..yuh..yuhz shoods a herds 'im 'ester… 'erster… 'erterdays. Ersterday. Yuh…yuh…yuhsterday. He's a screams a scre..scre …yuhsterdays he's a lot screms."

The king almost vomited. But he had requested to see the three leaders punished and, since he had never been to war, he had to prove that he feared no blood or pain, that he had hardened his heart. Creber loped over to the third pit and in a crooked, childish way danced a ring around it. He kept stabbing his enormous fat arm and pointing within. This had been the top leader, and the king requested the worst punishment for him. But the king did not want to look. The accompanying guards did not want to look. The room began to spin. Creber danced and clapped and mewled a strange little song around the rim of the pit. "ook in ther. Ook! Luh..luhh luuk. Look!"

The king just glanced in. At first, he thought it was empty, but then the floor of the pit moved. A gutteral cry of primal agony rose out of the pit and only then could he discern the vague outlines of a man. Creber was so excited he could hardly speak: "ithe! E E E eten in ithe!"

The king did not understand. He looked to the guard, who answered stoically: "He is being eaten by lice."

The king almost fell away. He left the dungeon and managed to make it to his private chamber before vomiting. He sniffed a heavy dose of sedative powder and, before collapsing into a dreamless sleep, ordered all three prisoners immediately put to death.

In the years since, the king never again visited the dungeon, nor did he ever invite Creber to the main floor of the castle. Creber waited for many years to dine in the king's shining company and a long time passed before he abandoned the dream of a formal invitation. He often felt deeply sad until he realized at last that the king, like all others beside himself, had never been real. And so, when he was told to look for a spear that could be in the lower parts of the castle, he did not tell them of the one which crashed through the wall of his cell.

He opened the greasy latch, some blood staining his fingers yet, and what was this lovely lovely thing from above? It ran at an angle out of the utmost part of the wall and stabbed the heart of the room. He ran his fingers along the length. He smiled with glee at such an instrument, perhaps dropped by God. He had to get it free. He pulled and pulled, but it wouldn't come out. He pulled and shook and grunted and groaned, but it hardly moved. Yet it moved a little. Just a little each day. Sometimes, he chiseled away the rock around it. Sometimes he pulled so hard that he howled in frustrated rage at how it stuck fast. But one day, at last., the final hold gave and the spear came free. There it lay on the floor, along the length of his room. Creber danced in joy. He needed both hands to lift it and stabbed imaginary foes in the air. The spear belonged to Creber now. The spear came to Creber from the dream of the king, from the dream of the God. It was his thank you. No one would take his thank you away. He hid it, rolled in his greasy sleeping mat.

At night, he curled next to it and licked the tip of the magical spiral and whispered to it as a lover. The only lover he had ever known. Creber wanted to love and be loved. Sometimes he masturbated against the spear, and only once did he touch the tip of the spiral, which shredded the tip of his finger. He cried and howled but no one could hear. When his sobbing slowed, he felt scared of the weapon, afraid that a tool of the gods had slipped and fallen to the earth. No man should possess this, he now knew, for it had hurt him like everything else. But he could not get caught with it. He knew the punishment for lying to the royal order. He did not want it anymore, but would not throw it away. He wanted to sell it. With the money he would buy a prostitute. That's what he would do. He would buy love from a world which had so little.

Creber left the castle about once a month to drag the dead to the graves. Onto a simple cart he loaded the mutilated bodies, half-eaten with disease and burns, their faces showing anguish even in death. Under a stained tarp he dragged them across the lower bridge and through the nearest village and to its outskirts and then to the grave mound for the anonymous. He knew he would need at least two corpses to cover the spear, but none in the pits was ready to die yet. Starving would take too long, so he heated oil and scalded two to death. He dragged them out and laid them on the cart over the spear. They smelled of rotted, roasted meat, and their faces were frozen in torment. He covered it all with a tarp and made for the hall that led to the lower bridge.

He didn't need to wave to the guards, for they didn't wave to him, so he rolled the cart and spear and horses right out of the castle on the dirt road to a vendor in the town who knew Creber. Sometimes there was gold to be taken from the teeth. Sometimes the vendor had a request for a female corpse if it were not too rotten or deformed. Creber asked for him outside the tavern gate. A man with a black pointed beard and sharpened eyebrows came to the road. Everyone in town knew Creber carried the dead from the castle. They stayed clear of him as if a bad omen. None knew that he was the torturer. Even the trader did not know Creber to be anymore than a mule for the dead.

"Is later than usual. Whatcha got for me from the dead, my Creber?"

Creber shook his head and slurred: "Nuh, nuh nuh ook unda it. Ook! Ook!" He lifted the tarp and the trader covered his mouth at the stench.

"There's nothing there I think I want."

Creber grabbed the wet flesh of the corpse and slid the spear out from beneath it. It slipped from his hands and fell with a clank to the cobblestone road. The trader squinted. He still didn't know what it was.

"Ook! Is a spears! A special spears! Spear a kings! Spear a gods!"

Using all his strength, Creber lifted it for the vendor to see. Creber's enthusiasm fell. The vendor had a very practiced way of looking unimpressed.

"What use it? What would I do with it? Who would want it? It's too big."

Creber let the bottom drop against the stone and swung the tip to his face. "Ook at uh tip! Is tooth! Is magic tooth! Is tooth 'ike a dragon!"

The trader had never seen such a spear, but the mastery of the craftsmanship was obvious. "Well, I don't know. What do you want for it Creber?"

He wanted a prostitute. He knew that, but now he wanted a pretty one.

"Ifty seceres"

"Fifty! You had a wonderful dream last night didn't you? I wish I could dream like you, Creber."

"Fuhrty"

The vendor scratched his thin black beard. "Forty for this? It's so heavy, and cumbersome. Who would want it? As a favor I will give you twenty."

Creber's heart sank. Twenty sesternes wouldn't buy the filthiest harlot the town could produce. He wanted a pretty one who would wash and paint her face like a flower."

"Irthy. Pluz. Irthy."

"Thirty is just too much for it. It's just too useless. I'm sorry I offered twenty. Good night, Creber."

He wanted to cry. Nowhere else to go. "Unty! Iv Creber unty esterns."

The vendor sighed as if unsure. All right then, but you unload and clean the foulness of the corpses off. Why do they smell so terrible?

"Ey in the pits a lon' ime."

"Well, clean it well. It could have disease. Bring it around back, and I will have them carry you out some water."

Later, with the help of two others, the man carried the spear away after giving the dungeon-keeper four copper coins. Creber went to the whore house but none of the women would sleep with him for only twenty sesternes. He was just too filthy and foul. He cried and they let him cry and then told him to leave. He buried the bodies in the mound for the nameless dead and returned to the castle and to his greasy mat. He told his story to the captives still in the pits and they pleaded with him for death, as they always did, but he said another spear would have to fall from the sky before he would set free. He saved the twenty sesternes a long time in the hopes of the gods dropping more of their wares.

The vendor sold the spear for five hundred sesternes to a merchant in a whaling town. It took three men to launch it and its chain lanyard from the pulpit, but the weapon paid for itself ten times over in the first season. When the great tooth of Kai-Tey pierced the broad back of the leviathan, the whales did not have to be chased long. Their hearts simply exploded. The ship holding that spear killed more whales than a whole fleet. It made the whaler who bought it so wealthy he bought the finest ship to be had and set to sea to fill it to the gills with oil. He hung the lance over the cabin door until it would be time to use it, for they would sail to the southern horn where the sperm whale flocked in the greatest number.

And it was believed by some that the lance had magical properties, and so would keep away all storms and protect those sailors who lived under its shadow. But this, alas, did not prove true.

In their first crossing of the southern horn, where the sea could rise like mountains, a storm split the ship and all were lost. Spear, captain and sailors all went to the depths of the mysterious sea.

It would be the last time members of the crew would see each other together. Dexter would go north alone to hold back the Northern army.

"Kill as few as possible Dex, but stop them. Bell has to get through. That's all."

Dexter nodded. "I will Roland," he said, and bowed once and departed.

"Iga. You go this night and get ahead of us. Thin the Southern army as much as you can. Kill as very many and we may make it through. They are too close for mercy."

"We will do so, Roland," said the eldest of them. With no more words, the three departed.

Alone together, Roland turned to Belladonna. She was crying. "Why do you cry, my lily of the morning?"

She stood as if terribly cold, hugging herself in the warm night. Roland threw his arms around her, tried to kiss her, but she would not let him. "We could wait until morning, Bell. Let's wait until morning." She pressed her face, running with tears, into his shoulder. She could not speak. "Or do you want to leave now? Tell me what to do." And for a very long time he only held her as she wept, and then carried her to their bed where, for several hours before dawn, they slept.

They left at the break of noon. She took all which the Phoenix had given her and tied a fillet in her hair. Roland had wrapped the medusa with eight cords and held it over his shoulder. Belladonna had become a different person. Her eyes brimmed with fire and hate. Roland was much the same. "We don't have to rush, Belladonna. The Iga will slow them a lot. I am confident of that. We may not even have to fight at all."

"Let us go," she said icily. "The sooner we leave, the more I can kill."

Roland took a last look at their home for so long.

"Do we let it stand?"

"It could give comfort to the enemy."

"All right then."

Belladonna placed a stick of the sacred nest just within the main entrance and carefully wet it with a drop of the blood of the Phoenix. At the ruins of the gate she left the dragon of jade. She paused, and then drew a metal rod against the Sword of Scars shooting a flash within. Instantly, flames engulfed the house. He held her hand as they watched it burn. He knew she wanted to cry. At last she did. They waited until the ancient roof fell with a groan. She had tied her hair that morning so fiercely tight, but yet a strand had fallen loose and traced her outer eye and cheek. Roland would tell her. Her hair could not be in her face, but it looked so beautiful there for now. An ash landed on this strand, and she felt its weight and lifted it off with her nail and considered the ash for a moment and then blew it away. She re-tied her hair. All tears had dried. "Let us go," she said without regret. She would not cry anymore. It was time to go to war.

The Iga attack in the shield of darkness. As the stars dim their stillness turns to invisibility. As the sun hides their souls rise in the mist of unfathomable blackness, and thus they are known as the Children of Shadow, the Army of Shades. Some believe the Iga can summon ghosts, and read the future in the mountains of the moon. But to the armies of the Southern king, in their long procession north, the Iga would be known as "the demons who kill in dreams," for each morning rose to another horde of dead soldiers, some with eyes open yet, some boasting sliced throats or pierced hearts while others had wounds invisible. The only evidence of death, besides the absence of life, was their eyes glazed in a peculiar gray. This began to wear away at the reasoning of the soldiers, who feared ever more that the enemy could kill with a curse.

"They've not even been touched with nuthin'. They doin' words to the undergods. How we spare us from this?"

And so it was that the vast army of the empire of Nede had been culled by a third as they marched to the field of Gidon without ever once drawing sword or arrow...without ever once seeing the face of the enemy. They became quite desperate.

The commander paced among his troops, reading their exhausted and terrified faces. He called them to a circle on a morning especially thick with the dead that were laid in a row with their wounds covered. Coins set on the eyes. Too many to bury each day. He paced at their feet, many bare and cut, as the names of the fallen were read aloud. When a name was not known the crier called out the town or province the soldier hailed from. At the end of the reading of the names, almost four hundred of them, the captain spoke: "This is not the seal of gods! Gods do not side in wars. Gods do not bother with the daily affairs of men." He waited for them to understand this. "Nor is this the work of lesser gods, demons of the earth who also are loath to bother with the daily affairs of men. The superstition of your minds will crush you faster than any onslaught of the enemy. How many times have you pleaded to your God and received silence as the answer? And is prayer nothing more than an appeal to magic, to an intervention above what nature and man can do by the work of their hands? How many times have you yourselves called upon magic to help you in your hour of desperation and loss? In your time of terror? Has it ever stopped the cold procession of death? Has it ever made suffering cease anymore than nature would do in her course? And yet you cower as if the eye of God rests on your every step. As if, at last, he finally cares for man anymore than the chaff that falls from its fruit. The gods are absent and blind. They may well have forgotten this earth and all who walk upon it. These men, cold beneath the noon sun, prayed often for their salvation. Where are they now? What has come of their prayers? Nothing. Pray in your hour of need. Nothing will come of it. Starve over an empty plate, as I have, and ask God to fill it, as I have. He will not. The plate will stay empty until you lift your hand to hunt or sow or kill, or curl it into the cup of a beggar. Whatever you choose, it will not come easily, for life gives nothing to mortals without great labor."

The eyes of the men fixed on the iron presence of the commander, he who had seen more war and ruin than he could tell of. "Listen, know and hear this well: whatever kills us is not blind nor absent, but very present and very sharp." He kneeled at a corpse and pulled back its head. He showed the weary soldiers the gash in its throat. "This…this is the work of assassins. Do you really believe the gods sink from the stars to strike with an ax? And as for those who died of wounds invisible, I have heard of this before, of men who could make your heart stop or your brain hemorrhage with a single touch. This is nothing new. No, these are not gods or demons, but assassins of the highest degree, and this tells me we are near our goal."

The commander squinted against the setting sun and let the corpse's throat close again. He then touched the forehead of the unknown soldier and whispered briefly something no one else could hear. He then stood and continued walking the line of the dead. He then took a brass needle from his shirt pocket and held it gleaming in the late-day light. "We pulled this from the heart of a dead brother. The gods do not leave weapons behind." He threw the needle to the ground.

He scanned the outer hills. A thin smile crossed his lips. "I've no doubt they watch us now and do not care. The attacks began with these hills and in them they hide. I assure you that. And they plan to have us done before we reach the plains to the north. I assure you that too. This has to be their plan. And if you do not believe they are men, they will succeed in it. But if you are brave, and hold to the truth, they will be killed, however many or, as I think, few there are. We will have victory. Know that it will not come without a cost.

"Find your courage again. Be not afraid of fate. Seek your destiny. I ask for volunteers to sleep this night on the outer foothills. You will dig trenches set with spikes as traps, but this will be a trick. This will not be how we kill them. Assassins of this degree would never step into a pit which hardly tricks a beast. I need volunteers of the bravest, the finest, the unafraid. You few will sleep this night on an eastern and western flank. Almost half, I fear, will perish. Know that. But know this too: if nothing is done, all of you will. And myself. I say no more. I need twice one hundred volunteers. The willing must show up before my tent at the thirteenth hour. To you alone I will reveal my plan."

The commander retired to his tent and waited as his words were sent through all the soldiers. Before dark, a mob of nearly three hundred crowded outside his tent. He swept his hand to quiet them. He held up a single crystal vial. "It had another purpose, but, alas, we have it as we need it. A very exquisite poison called Angel's Tear is this. It cannot be detected by anyone. No known antidote exists. You men, boldest and bravest of all our crew, you shall go into the shadow of dawn with poisoned rations. A pitiful feast for a final meal. They will strike the East or the West flank, but I think not both. They must be hungry. This land is barren. They will take some food from the dead. All of it will be poisoned."

He had the name of each soldier-volunteer committed to a list. When done, he held the scroll high in his right fist.

"The names of the brave and the martyrs from whom the cowardly assassins will pluck their death shall be passed down for generations. I promise you that. You already will never be forgotten. May God keep you all."

He turned and entered his tent.

"I have less than a thousand needles left," said the youngest of the Iga. "We must try to kill more than one with each needle."

"It is difficult," said the oldest. "And you risk killing none."

"But we can do it. The kidneys are soft enough. We can pierce through two men if we throw true."

"Thrown too hard they become inaccurate. The heart and head are still best. No other shot can be trusted. The sleeping sun scarcely protects us now as their terror has so augmented the night guard. Please be careful," said the eldest.

"We will, Father," said the oldest son.

"You are the hands of the earth. You are her knives and sword, her arrows and her breath. The son must now become the father. Fight your best, so that you may not just kill but live, and perhaps even I shall too. But if we do not..." The eldest Iga stared at the ground a moment, finding it hard to continue. "...If we do not live to see the mother night again, know this: no warrior has ever risen to the stars for a more noble cause."

He stared into the eyes of his sons. His expression changed. "But, it will be better if you go. Two crows flew across the rising moon. A bad omen. The preservation of your lives is equal to the preservation of my own...so run now. Go home. Please. I will love you as deeply as ever...even more, knowing you both are safe. And my fight will not be heavy."

"We will never run," said one son.

"Please go."

"We will never leave this cause or our father," said the other son, and they did not.

At dusk they observed members of the army lighting fires in flanks far from the main body of troops. They then dug crude traps of grass-covered ditches with spikes at the bottom. So obvious. The Iga counted them and then the needles. Everyone on the western flank would die in perfect silence, and with hardly a groan. Half the eastern flank lay dead just before first light. Many of a cut throat as needles were precious. Only as the darkness dimmed did the Iga creep back to the safety of the hills, and with them food taken from the side of still-trembling corpses.

By morning the youngest had already died. The father tried to crawl to the older but it felt like razors slicing in his stomach. His sons screams were drowned in the blood that frothed from his mouth. With the last of his strength the father lay beside his sons dead and dying. All was beyond words. They folded their hands over their hearts and found the names of their ancestors written in the stars. The army had freed itself of the demons who walk in the night.

The horizon teemed with life. A gathering swarm of tired and terrified soldiers encircled Roland and Belladonna. They bore all manner of sword and spear, arrow and sling. They had torches, pointed stones, clubs and bizarre weapons too: tubes that ejected a cloud of darts; metal sleeves of shooting fire; chain-tethered blades that whirled through the air to separate head from neck, leg from waist, arm from shoulder, or it could slice off a face.

And they had dragged from so far enormous catapults of onerous weight to hurl boulders to crush the other. These engines could, with a certain matrix, launch a barrage of arcing daggers so as to darken the sky like a storm-ridden night. And also to the field of Gidon they brought exploding orbs of poison whose breath blinded the enemy, whose breath closed the lungs in noxious gas, melted skin from bone in shrieking agony until the life closed out with lungs swelled in blood.

And to the field of Gidon, glass eyes they brought, which could harness the smallest hint of sun to set the vestments of the enemy afire. And they brought shattering spheres of metal, whose splinters would usher in the most fantastic mutilations of the flesh. And they had in their number necromancers who spoke to fire that could leap from sleeping bottles to envelop the enemy in burning suffocation.

Every form and petition of death, too many to mention, they had borne from the farthest reaches of the earth, all from the work of hands and days conceived in the shadow of the heart. These they brought to the field of Gidon, the land to which the needles always turned.

Belladonna and Roland stood side-by-side on a low rise before the field. Their shoulders touched gently together in a kind of calming caress. And not one of the gathering enemy, for all their weapons, dared approach too close to the pair — the man and the woman many feared were immortals, perhaps even gods.

With so many killed on the road the army was not what it had been. To the degree it could be replenished, it now marched as a mixture of mercenaries, freed criminals, the insane and children, all bought, coerced or forced to serve among the number of the army of the Kingdom of Nede. And so it was a weak army, as armies go, but not less than a swarm of ten thousand souls. In that alone was strength.

Belladonna was angry. "Why has it taken them so damned long?"

They had been waiting for days at the pass of the White Mountains to cross to the south where the Wreath of the Phoenix waited, but could not risk going through first lest they be ambushed in the single, narrow path, or fall prey to a rain of boulders from the high cliffs. They needed them to come first, to follow the needle to the open plains where waited the medusa. Belladonna had taken it form Roland and secured it to her waist. She said it was to better protect the invention, but in truth, she did not want Roland to die.

Roland squinted at the first torches. "I'm guessing the Iga slowed them, but it's them, see that banner?" he said pointing to it.

"I do," she said, still angry.

The rising light revealed an army hunched in fear. The Iga must have slaughtered them, but would have signaled Roland if they were here, and so they were not. That meant the two of them would have to stand alone against an army, with a pole of oak, a sword, and a few daggers. This while they held the deadliest weapon their world had ever known which.

Roland scanned the horizons in the rising light, counting and surmising the uses of the various weaponry. He had never seen so many people gathered in a single place. They poured more and more out of the mountain pass. The sun broke the line of the horizon. He turned to Belladonna and smiled. He held her hand and she his. She was crying.

"We will not die," she said. "Never from the likes of these. Ugh! Look at them. Clumsy and terrified. Eyes dim. Ears deaf. Their limbs do not speak to one another. Their weapons crude and brutish. Even from here the creak of their joints offends my ears, their stink assails me. And look, Roland, look! The rising day has such hope! Look! Oh Roland, some of them are but children! This will be easy, my love!"

"No battle is easy, Bell. You don't have to talk like that. We might have a victory, but we won't until we do. Try not to kill the children."

She stabbed him a glare of ice. "Oh, no, my beloved, not even as they toss their toy arrows at my heart, or play innocent iron against my limbs?"

He sighed. She was right, of course. "Just try not to. They often run. Let's hope so. If you can afford to, throw guts on them. That often works."

She did not answer him, but whipped the Sword of Scars from its sheath and cut the air with blinding speed. When her anger subsided she touched his hand. "You would have been a good father my Roland."

He smiled.

Suddenly, a mewl of pain rose from the approaching horde. Belladonna pointed with the sword. "Look, Roland! Look what they have done now!"

He stared at the origin of the piteous groans. "Ogre. They have them trained after all. I feared this. They gorge them with corpses and the ogre are theirs. In their minds, they know now a feast is coming."

The ogre were in chains. A ring of men with torches and lances surrounded them. They pointed to Roland and Belladonna and were saying something. The ogre turned their yellow eyes upwards in mute acknowledgement. Belladonna crossed her arms defiantly. "I fear neither man nor army, nor any damned horde of ogre."

"I neither, Bell, but I want you to know that I love you very much. I want you to know you are the only woman I have ever loved, and I would trade the medusa just to spare your life if I thought the world could in any way survive it."

She shook in tears, and immediately wished to run the enemy lines and begin killing. She hated that she could not stop crying. It did not become a warrior of the Phoenix to cry before a battle. She hated that they assumed she cried because she feared for her life. One of them arrogantly smirked and she vowed to kill him first with as much cruelty and agony as possible. She turned her eyes to Roland: "But you will not die today, my love," she promised. "An augur once told me I would never die on the field of battle, and so neither will you, for if you die today, I will throw myself upon the Sword of Scars to be so betrayed by fate."

Roland watched the ranks carefully for any premature attack. They, like him, were waiting for full light. "Oh no you won't," he said. "If I fall you cut your way clear and get her back to the Phoenix. That's all. I cannot go into this thinking you are not dedicated in full to our function. Is that clear, Belladonna?"

She pouted and more tears fell to the grass of Gidon. Her breath was quick and panting.

"Bell? Please be with me on this. I don't mind dying if I know the mission is carried through. Please."

She wiped her eyes and looked up. The armies through the pass now began to thicken around them. So many. Where could they all have come from? She bravely lifted her chin and sniffed. "But there's no one ever like you again, Roland. Why would I go on in a life where there are none like you?"

Roland sighed. "We just have to. Fate has put the medusa in our hands because we can do what others cannot. We alone must destroy it, even with, well, even with…"

"…Our hearts a handful of dust?"

"Yes, even then."

The vast army now encircled the low rise. They were as an ocean around the two warriors. "Let us kill these fools now. I am hungry for their blood."

"The sun is almost above the horizon, Bell. Let's watch it together. I hope they let us watch the rising sun in peace. I want to watch the sunrise with you. That's all."

"And I with you, my Roland." She unfolded her arms and wiped her tears away. She then took his hand and rested it against her cheek. She would have kissed them if they could not see.

"Are you glad to be a warrior, Bell?"

"I suppose," she said absently. "Are you?"

"I don't know. I used to be, but I never really had a choice. Often, I thought it must be nice to be a fisherman. A small boat on a gentle sea, a cast net, a wife like you...children. It would have been kind of the stars to let me be that."

And Belladonna began to cry again. "You know they cut us?"

"I know."

"They make sure of that for the girls: no children, ever."

"I know. I don't care. I love you."

"In the next life, you will be a fisherman and I your wife, and we will have lovely children and never worry about the affairs of kings and death's seduction. There will be no swords by then and no medusa."

"I'd like that very much. Oh, Bell, just look at it!"

In the east, the first arc of the sun broke like a ball of crumbling fire. Every soldier, every one, watched it with the same question, and for a moment, all fell still.

"It is a blood-sky, Roland."

"It is."

"The gods are watching."

"They are."

"We must not shame ourselves."

"Never."

"I will not go on if you fall."

"Don't say that."

"I will never go on if you fall."

"Don't look right at it."

"Do not die."

"Look away from it."

"Promise me you will not die."

"It will give you a blind spot."

"Promise."

"I promise. Please stop crying."

"We were not supposed to happen."

"Nothing happens that is not meant to be. You are so beautiful this morning."

She smiled.

"We need to separate."

"No, Roland!"

"We have to. There are too many. If we stay close, it's a waste. You take the west, but don't descend. They'll have the sun in their eyes."

"I don't need that!"

"I'll go east. We'll find each other by sundown. We will. I'll pretend my gourd is the medusa. Hide her as best you can."

"You are not going to die today, Roland!"

"I can't help fate if it…"

"You will not!"

"I won't. I'm sorry."

"Oh Roland, I am. Let us not argue. Let us never argue again. The Phoenix could teach me how to kill and kill but only you have taught me to care to live."

"That's the finest thing anyone has ever said to me. Please stop crying."

She wanted to scream. They carried off the ruse masterfully. They quickly kissed once, but not goodbye. Belladonna set off with the medusa tethered by a strip of leather beneath her gown and Roland tied the gourd under his robe. The first song of morning birds. The sky calls back the dew. The first arc of sun breaks the horizon and shunted away the darkness. With no signal given, the first arrow arced into the sky. It sticks in the grass just where they had stood. Neither deigned to look back. The sound of the army thickening, the weapons readied calls Belladonna to speak a secret word as she draws the Sword of Scars across her arm. And Roland to take a knee and touch his forehead in whispering prayer to the ancestors. After, they turn to each other, and for the first time he realizes how young her face, too young for this, and even from that distance he sees a new kind of grief.

She turns her eyes away and ran like a deer to the first of the battle. Roland walks to the heart of the sun, a man of shadow and silhouette. When he turns to see her once more she is gone.

A barrage of arrows so thick that it blotted out the sun came to Roland. He spun the pole and some he broke to splinters and some he sent back to the horde. These arrows, many dipped in poison, stuck into the chests and throats of the front line. Three times, the archers launched and three times lines of soldiers fell until the commanders understood and called the archers off.

Belldonna fought gloriously, as only a child of The Wreath could. Of everything launched, arrows and fire, anything, she sent back upon them with invisible speed. Of the first soldiers within her reach she preferred to delimb, often both hands or both feet, rather than killing outright. Many she castrated threw their genitals to their screaming faces. She laughed. She felt wonderful now. If a moment allowed she licked their blood, and from the first close kill dipped her finger in this blood and with it drew stripes of war upon her face and thickened this until it became a mask. She wished she had more time to strike terror—so wonderfully this halts the attack, weakens the resolve—but with so many coming the mistress of the sword sliced throats like a scythe through grass, punctured hearts as a sower divots the soil.

But the army seemed to sprout two men for every one fallen. At last, she misted the circle closest her with the blood of The Phoenix, and to this she set a spark. The fire would give her time to rest, hone the edge of the sword. Only now she notices how lovely the dawn.

The army retreated, though a commander would howl at how could nothing but a lone woman drive them all back. Yet, those closest to Belladonna were fortunate. The ones slightly farther away took far too long to die. Their skin melted off but they wouldn't die. Some would have even lived out the day as the blood of the Phoenix, (which could never be extinguished, but only exhaust itself), ate through to their very bones. The army of Nede needed a better plan. Belladonna went east to find Roland. The army of Nede now reduced its number in bringing peace to the mortally wounded.

The northern army did not understand. The grass cut them. Every weapon raised was shattered. Every bowl broken, rations burned and the whole army stopped cold in every advance. And yet, not one killed.

"This land is cursed, Captain," said a division leader. "We cannot cross it. Is cursed."

"All lands are cursed in their way."

The captain liked nothing about the campaign: the objective, the scope, the result of victory. But he absolutely dreaded defeat. The king of Nede was mad.

"But this one...the men bleed as they set foot on the field, Captain. Our hands split open. Our weapons are broken. We see no enemy, but dust flies into our eyes as if thrown."

"What do you suggest we do, then?"

"Go back."

"And let Nede run the western earth?"

"Yes, for now."

The Captain sighed. How could he explain this to his king? How could he let anything but utter defeat deliver the medusa to Nede? He could not, and so the army tried once more, an aggressive advance, but they were cut even more deeply. They were fighting angels. One man howled in a berserk rage and rushed to the field. Hands unseen pulled him into the grass and then beat him unconscious. But the beaten soldier had drawn the threat to an exact spot. Unconcerned for the loss of one, archers were ordered to draw a thousand bows, only to have the lines all snap, almost at once, as if cut. The army retreated.

Dexter would go south again to find the crew, but first he must speak to his own.

"Good Dexter, so long since you have been with us, Brother."

"I know."

"You smell of human."

"Yes."

"The Sagittae have decided to eliminate them."

"You cannot. That is forbidden!"

"We have decided this. They cannot be trusted."

"I have lived with them. Some are fighting just now to make it better."

"Dearest Brother, lost from us for too long, this lies beyond their powers."

"Just give them a little time."

"This will not return her to you."

He lowered his head. "I know this. That is not it. Just give them a little time."

The elder sat back in his throne of blue stone. "Since we are not unanimous, they have a little time at your request, but should they move again to her destruction we will finish what should have been done in the age of the silver cup."

Dexter bowed to the elders and went south.

Roland fought the army of Nede well. He crushed heads and limbs, sparing children as much as he could. His simple pole, wielded with a lifetime of practice, held back an entire army. They set the horde of ogre on him, each one twice the size of a large man, but he had no fear. He broke their knees and necks, split their jaws with the deadly pole. At last, it was a bird that would be his undoing. Of all things, a bird. It swooped from the sky in silence and plucked the pole from his unseeing hands as he spun it overhead, never expecting an enemy from the sky. It lifted the weapon away, away and away. The pole receded into the infinite sky. He watched it go and clenched his hands of iron into fists and blades.

He struck they who approached with such incredible force it could not be comprehended. Their hearts split. Their ribs shattered. Their faces caved into their skulls. When the ogre came again, he paused. He knew he must not break the skin. At last, as they fell upon him again and again in the thickness of the battle, he could not help ripping their flesh. He punched into their stomachs, split them apart and broke their ribs. Tiny cuts managed to break the shield of the flesh of his hands. He would wash later, but for now he had to make sure he was not eaten. He fought until they fought no more. He fought until the living went away.

Belladonna followed the mounds of the dead to where they lay thickest. She stared at the faces of the dead, but he was not there. Her heart swelled. Something called her to the forest on the border of the field. She found Roland beside the sweet-flowing stream. She laughed.

When she found him he was already dead. His flesh was bloated and had turned a rotted green from all the poisons. She did not cry. She would never cry again. Tears had no meaning in a world like this. She rolled him on his back and a stench already rose from the corpse. She laughed again because he had been so clean in life. She then split his chest open and removed his heart, balancing it on the edge of the sword. The poisons had turned it black, and what a ridiculous color for the heart of such a noble man.

And she laughed in the tall grass that swayed softly beneath the bright sun as she bore his heart to the field. She needed to speak with him now so dearly, and what kind of world could live without his voice? She smiled at how nothing would ever be the same again. She made a small pyre of the nest of the phoenix and wet this with the last of the god's blood. With her sword, she placed Roland's heart atop the pyre and walked upwind. It looked like a swollen piece of charred meat. How strangely the poison worked and how dearly did she need to…please…speak with him once more…please…and could his voice really be gone from this world

She drew the sword and the metal rod. "Oh, how could his voice be gone?" she asked to nothing. The spark flew. She kneeled and folded her hands in silence. The heart of Roland exploded into ashes, and when she arose, nothing remained but a ring of black.

She laughed derisively as she walked among the dead and dying. She would sometimes slash at corpses, removing half-hanging heads from necks, or fingers curled yet about the grip of a silent sword. In the field, the blood had collected in pools, ran in rivulets, was of such a quantity that the very air smelled of copper. At times, Belladonna stopped and knelt by a slashed-open corpse and dipped her sword in the viscera to shine its metal. She smiled then and licked swirls from the dripping blade to redden her lips. She then decorated her face with blood and wove blood into the locks of her hair. She threw the fillet away, and buried the ancient emerald — a token of the Order. The only adornment she wished for was death and blood. She made a necklace of severed fingers and, with a tendon as string, wore this proudly around her neck.

She found a living enemy curled up and dying on the ground. She knelt beside him and smiled. She caressed his young cheek and he wanted to scream for he thought her a demon from the world below. Then, with the tips of her fingers, she popped each eye out from its socket and lifted them by the thin strings of nerves which connected them to the brain, and she then turned them in all directions to show the defeated man how expansive her victory had been: a whole legion felled by two. The dying soldier, trying desperately not to beg for death, began to weep, and the tears pooled red in the hollows of his sockets. Belladonna let his eyes drop to stare unblinking at the ground as she held his shaking body and spoke to him as a gentle mother-nurse. "You were so handsome once, when you had your lovely, brown eyes. Did they enchant fair maidens once? Did your mother kiss them? So, so sad now," said

Belladonna in soft, demonic mockery. "Belladonna promises to make all well."

She kissed him and lifted one eye so it could see her clearly…how when she smiled, flakes of dried blood broke from her skin. With her as its last sight, she then crushed the eye in her hand and let the gray gelatinous matter run between her fingers, plunging the young, dying soldier half into darkness. It was then the young man screamed, and Belladonna whispered for him to be calm, that all would be well if he just stayed calm.

She then lifted the other eye and saw fear in it somehow, and she kissed the eye and then, leaning close into his ear, whispered, "Remember the light, my love." Belladonna forcefully broke the orb free from its cord and the young soldier screamed anew as he was plunged full into darkness. Belladonna stood and cut his throat so deeply that his screaming stopped.

She staggered away among the litter of the dead when she found another soldier who had been hit in the leg by Roland. When he saw her, he stood and tried to run staggeringly away. Belladonna smiled as she grabbed his narrow shoulder, but he was so small. She spun him around. He cried like a child. Yes, he was a child. Only a boy. Belladonna lifted the Sword of Scars, and he looked into her eyes, this little, little boy. She lowered the sword. "You shouldn't be here," she said, and took him by the hand. Over the next rise the second army of the realm of Nede swarmed like the sea. "You should never have been here," she said to the boy again, who thought her death incarnate. She lifted his chin and kissed his forehead.

They set upon her. Ten thousand strong launched all they had upon her. And for a time she kept them back. For a time she deflected every arrow and dart, hurled their poisons and smoke back upon them. She once sheltered the boy from a rain of arrows by spinning the sword up and down her leg. It had taken her ten years to perfect that, and she had and he was safe, and she had told the boy to stay within reach of the sword. She could protect him if he stayed, but another rain followed and, overrun with terror, ran out from its protection. He was cut down by a hundred arrows. Belladonna yelled the name of her son, who perhaps heard it once in his passing.

Roland!

She would not cry. She had been raised to fight, with an idea of saving the world, but now rose the question she had never dared to ask: did such a world deserve saving? And she feared the answer her heart spoke. But she would not cry and would never cry again. A wasted life. She whipped a deluge of arrows away again, for she would not yet sleep in stone, even though maybe it were best she did. She would not cry as her eyes rested on the blood of the young Roland, soaking fresh through his tattered rags, and he was so thin. Why hadn't they fed him? Who sends a child to war with no food?

She knelt to the battered body and rested her hand in his crudely chopped hair, and it amazed her how tired her arm had become, and she turned his white face up and his eyes were open yet, but no life played in them. She would never cry again, for she knew at last with perfect clarity what so few ever learned: that life had no meaning at all.

An army of endless soldiers, an army of like hearts beating for the shadow to rise again, marched to quell the ever-rising hunger in their guts. Fear and madness and death heaped upon death surrounded this army like the sea, and the army surrounded her like the sea and she rested his head gently down in the hold of her hands. How could this not be the will of God? They are part of his creation too. Are they not part of his creation too? And the boy, a flicker of a son, is this not a message from God that His will shall be done? And she was so tired now. It amazed her to be so tired. It amazed her so that she stood again.

And the sky went dark again, and she did not quite know that the Sword of Scars spun above her — the reflexes of a lifetime of pain and training, such that she could again send the sword spinning to the tip of her outstretched foot and call it back again. The arrows fell and fell and fell, and they must be nearly exhausted. When the sun shone on her again, she began to leave the field of Gidon.

The dead lay everywhere. She stepped over and over them, hardly believing it the work of her hands. Why did her legs tire so much? Why had God taken her husband and son in a single day?

An old soldier, sick of war and death, slipping in the carnage that surrounded him, nocked his final arrow in the bowstring and drew until the tendon nearly shredded. He cursed the name of God and let arrow fly to the heart of the sun. He then turned away, dropped the bow to the ground, and left the fields of war forever.

Belladonna readied to face another legion when the unwatched arrow lowered through its arc and plunged into her neck. It shocked her for just a moment to see the arrowhead protruding from her throat, her viscera dangling wet from the jagged edge of stone, cords that would no longer produce any words that she would ever try to speak…and yet, she tried to laugh, but could not.

And she now knew she would never cry again, for in a few moments she would drown in her own blood and how she longed to see Roland and her son in the world to come, there where the medusa could never be made, where even swords were unknown. Her great burden had been lifted. With a smile she played with the dangling viscera upon the arrowhead.

She wiped the Sword of Scars and sheathed it. Suddenly, she wasn't tired at all anymore. Alas, one more thing to do. She staggered to the shadow she had seen and rolled the medusa to the bottom of a hidden ravine put just there by God in the beginning of the world. Then, with the last of her breath, she returned to her boy and lay beside him, taking his hand in hers. It surprised her how quickly it had turned cold. Belladonna lay beside him and turned her eyes to where she heard the most magnificent music that ever was, from just beyond the arc of the firmament. How wonderful it would be to go there. All she had left to do was close her eyes forever. This she did and was gone.

With the king much indisposed of late, the surviving army delivered the medusa to the crows. The tall one, the leader whose name they did not know, set her in a secret hold deep in the castle walls. About it, he summoned every manner of poet and priest, prophet and sage, the mad and the sane alike, to speak, under the gaze of a crow, a multitude of sounds until they should, by the darkest of chance, utter at last the secret word of her opening. Days and nights without end they petitioned the shell, on and on with passionate intensity, a ring of endless babble.

Epilogue

And in the decades to follow, the sun would bless the day for him to bury his wife, once more beautiful than twilight…and in decades more, his daughter, the blossom of their heart.

And he knew it to be a good thing, an inevitable and natural thing, but that did nothing to stay the waves of fantastic grief that weakened his legs as he stood beside the grave of an elderly woman. The keeper of the obsequies spoke to the man he thought was young, for in all this time his hair had gained but a splash of gray.

"Are you her son? Her grandson?"

He didn't reveal that it was his daughter.

"Yes."

"Well, Sir…we should know for the proper rites."

"Just bury her. Here. Put this in with her."

And they did. And he had heard once that every day is a good day, but he could not believe that just now. He had implored her, as he had her mother, to do the exercises of the Sage, but neither had lived an easy life — no one does — and they could not do what they would not. And suddenly, when the last mound of earth covered her in darkness, he knew he had also buried a home.

He arrived again at the port where he had landed so long ago and departed from that world upon a jet black ship. The latest vessels were cut with different lines and ran faster now. They promised to sink less, too. Again upon the great salt sea, which always changed yet remained the same, he stared at every dusk and dawn and came to understand that life lived in between and was forever both.

And still they harvested whatever the sea would yield, but now it was different: the mesh, made of finer stuff, ran longer and slowed the ship less; kites flew hooks wide of the transom; lines of toothed metal sliced through the dark and brooding silence of the depths.

It was one of the deep-set lines which tensed in the very midst of the sea, held so fast the ship heaved in its course so that those standing fell forward. The line stretched in white heat and, for a precarious moment, all the timbers of the hull strained as a decision was being made. Something had to give. And then the line went slack, and the bow lurched into the sea again. A bounty had been plucked from its floor. They hauled it in.

"Is a stone, a reef. Something. Not a fish, shelled or otherwise."

"Keep a-pullin'."

He watched. He had paid his way in gold and did not work. So he watched as they drew up and up the mystery from the lightless world. All crowded near the stern. "Give 'em room to haul!" the captain howled. "Give 'em room now, all yeh! Back...before you sink us in!"

They dispersed but a little as the haulers coiled on deck the line shining with splashes of crimson. It bit into their palms as they hauled. They cursed and swore until at last an unnatural form appeared below the waters. The image now clear extinguished an unspoken fear like breath to the candle flame. For the haulers all knew the stories of creatures rudely awoken from that immense and lightless world of hunger, beings incomprehensible that dwelled in the kingdom of the blind. But here was a simple thing, perhaps even of human hands.

"What's it? A stick? What's it now?"

"I dunno. Is nothin'. Bring'er on deck."

They lowered it and freed it from the strangle of line, which for all its fierce teeth had not bitten into the object at all. Nor to it had any barnacle stuck, nor had rot eaten through, and yet it seemed like a thing from another age, like it had been down in the Deep almost forever.

"It a spear? Wha's that tip curling like so? A lost harpoon?"

"She too heavy for that. A beam a some kind. A relic from a drowned one."

"It's mine," he said to all on board.

They parted as he approached, said nothing as he lifted the great spear of Kai-Tey with one hand and twirled it against the sky. He smiled imagining how only Gin could have fashioned such a weapon, and for the first time allowed himself to dream that Selador might actually be free.

He retired to his quarters with the prize and no one ever questioned him, not even the captain. They say that ships die of two things at sea: too much movement and too much stillness. When this ship had sat for twelve days with "not enough wind to curl smoke," the mysterious passenger stood in the stern and draped his hands against the arc of the dawn horizon. From this act he called down a breeze, and then a wind which grew ever stronger, filling the sails and roiling the sea. The wind bore the ship to a place where the skies did not refuse to turn unasked. And so no one questioned him about the spear, nor about anything.

They landed in the old port, which but for the stone cliffs had changed much in more than a lifetime of building and tearing down. He disembarked and walked away without a look back. He did not want to look back. He did not want to think about what he had experienced once in the land of the sleeping sun.

He searched for a time for the house of the girl to whom he had given the jezeth. It was gone. It had just been a shack after all. He asked some of the locals about the family, but they had not heard of them. Gone… to who knows where. They asked where he was from and to where he wished to go, warned him that war filled the outer lands. He was cautious but unafraid. All was destiny, and fear would not play into his.

He came to the intersection of the Old King's Road and looked north, wondering about those of his past travels: if they might still be there, and about the balance of their lives. And for a moment considered tracing his former path to the cold steppes to find Gin, or even Lyden. But he would be enshrouded in the land of ice, and she hidden in the dense forest tucked among biting rivers and mountains impassable. Anyway, he would likely never find them, even if they could be found. And so he turned south, and with the great spear cloaked on his shoulder, walked through lands littered with the smoke and ruin of war in too many places. At night, beside a fire, he would unwrap it and wonder by what processes sea water could so darken ivory impermeably.

"Nothing stains so well as blood."

Eventually, after being lost more than once, after going up roads and paths and places with stories all their own, the smoke of war lessened as he neared Selador. Eventually, the signs of war were altogether gone. Eventually, he walked in an oasis of peace. Even the neighboring lands lived in calm.

He wanted to know if this was his work. It had to be. It did not matter, but he wanted to know. And so he inquired anywhere he could. Some thought it part of an ancient pact, while others attributed the peace to divine superstition. Others believed it to be something of both. It did not matter, but he wanted to know why none of the kingdoms would tread on the Southern Slope.

"Have you heard of Gin?"

"Who?"

"A Sage?"

"A what?"

"Nevermind."

His spirit lifted when he saw the familiar outlines of the low hills he never thought to see again. But in the town proper, much had changed. Even the ancient tavern was gone, and he did not ask why or when. In time, he met the descendants of people he once knew and even, he supposed, distant relatives of his own; but he would never tell them that. He did not want to know what may have happened after he fled so long ago.

He said he was a refugee and took up fishing on the clear lakes. Life began to fill again as he made something of a home. But when too much time had passed, he retreated more and more, for he had not aged appropriately. And he remained for a long time on the outskirts of the town, living in a cabin made by his own hands on the far side of the waters.

And the occasional visitor would go there to petition him for help or guidance of some sort they believed only he could provide. He did what he could and did not promise to do what he could not. Yet they were amazed by what he could do, and some called him a wise man and others a sorcerer. But there were those who still believed in the old ways.

He lived in a grove of oak tree, and had smiled when they first called him "Sage," but truly wondered at the cycle which made him "The Sage of the Oak."

Yet, like all things, it would begin to recede at its crest. Like all things, it would succumb to the promise of change. Too soon the sun would make the day for him to move on.

Again, he went to the North.

www.ingramcontent.com/pod-product-compliance
Lightning Source LLC
Chambersburg PA
CBHW031050260626
47172CB00001B/11